She took the all-too-familiar canopied path to the tomb.

Sweat clung to her back, her lips were chapped, and a headache hammered her. She ignored the discomfort as she rushed toward the caved-in opening of the tomb. Until now, she'd avoided returning out of cowardice. But this was where she needed to be to better understand the aftermath and why tinieblas were drawn to the islands. She knew she needed to swallow her own anxiety, if she truly believed herself a protector of this community.

Dense greenery encroached on the dirt path. The air smelled sweet and bitter from the rotting sea grapes hanging off surrounding bushes. Reina hacked an opening through the leaves. She met the lagoon facing the tomb's mouth, with its crystalline waters reflecting prisms over her skin and clothes. A man sat on the largest boulder flanking the lagoon. He rose, as if awaiting her. He had dark brown skin and long, straight white hair crowned by two magnificent antlers, thick, like those of a pure-blooded valco.

Reina froze. The clearing quieted. Her heartbeats thrummed in her ears.

Then a name rolled out of her mouth, and Reina wasn't sure if she'd been the one to put it there.

"Ches?"

Praise for

The Sun and the Void

"A sweeping fantasy that is evocative and captivating! I loved the beautiful world and intricate characters woven into an enthralling tale of ancient gods, dangerous magic, family, and love."

—Sue Lynn Tan, *Sunday Times* bestselling author of *Daughter of the Moon Goddess*

"Capricious gods, dangerous magic, and ancient vows straining under the weight of her characters' desperate humanity, Gabriela Romero Lacruz has gifted us a classic epic fantasy with an original, inventive setting. A rich, enchanting read and an impressive debut."

—Ava Reid, *New York Times* bestselling author of *Juniper & Thorn*

"A gorgeous epic of family and power, gods and magic, longing and betrayal, *The Sun and the Void* pulls you in with a fascinating world and keeps you turning pages with richly drawn characters, unfolding mysteries, and plenty of action. A compelling, heart-twisting read!"

—Melissa Caruso, author of *The Last Hour Between Worlds*

"*The Sun and the Void* is a powerful and enthralling tale of struggle and hope, gods and mortals, in a lavish fantasy world. I absolutely loved it. A fantastic debut."

—H. M. Long, author of *Hall of Smoke*

"A delightfully tangled web of magic and curses, gods and monsters, love and betrayal. This read is perfect for readers who like their fantasy served with a healthy dose of anguish. Prepare to be thinking about this one long after you turn the last page."

—M. J. Kuhn, author of *Among Thieves*

"A spellbinding sapphic epic fantasy.... The lush worldbuilding and delightful blend of love, betrayal, and curses set the stage for a powerful and promising new series. This is a gem."

—*Publishers Weekly* (starred review)

"Romero Lacruz excels in her enchanting world building, with lush descriptions of beautiful landscapes and vivid depictions of folklore and traditions with a hint of realism.... Fans of N. K. Jemisin, Tomi Adeyemi, and Nisi Shawl will appreciate this fresh voice in fiction, especially when it comes to its commentary on colonialism, strong female characters, and the intricacies of magic used for good and evil."

—*Booklist*

"An enthralling new world of gods and monsters.... This ambitious, thrilling series opener pulses with vitality and imagination."

—*Shelf Awareness* (starred review)

"The lush and varied landscape as well as the clear effects of colonialism and revolution are all inspired by Venezuela, creating a rich, complex world.... An ambitious new fantasy with a unique setting and broad cast of characters."

—*Kirkus*

THE
RIVER
AND THE
STAR

By Gabriela Romero Lacruz

THE RIVER AND THE STAR

The Warring Gods: Book Two

GABRIELA ROMERO LACRUZ

orbit

orbitbooks.net

Copyright © 2025 by Gabriela Romero Lacruz

Cover design by Lisa Marie Pompilio
Cover images by Shutterstock
Cover copyright © 2025 by Hachette Book Group, Inc.
Map by Gabriela Romero Lacruz
Illustrations by Gabriela Romero Lacruz
Author photograph by Jaxon Gluck

Orbit
Hachette Book Group
1290 Avenue of the Americas
New York, NY 10104
orbitbooks.net

First Edition: October 2025

Orbit is an imprint of Hachette Book Group.
The Orbit name and logo are registered trademarks of Little, Brown Book Group Limited.

The publisher is not responsible for websites (or their content) that are not owned by the publisher.

The Hachette Speakers Bureau provides a wide range of authors for speaking events. To find out more, go to hachettespeakersbureau.com or email HachetteSpeakers@hbgusa.com.

Orbit books may be purchased in bulk for business, educational, or promotional use. For information, please contact your local bookseller or the Hachette Book Group Special Markets Department at special.markets@hbgusa.com.

Library of Congress Cataloging-in-Publication Data
Names: Romero Lacruz, Gabriela, author.
Title: The river and the star / Gabriela Romero Lacruz.
Description: New York : Orbit, 2025. | Series: The warring gods ; book 2
Identifiers: LCCN 2025001400 | ISBN 9780316337175 (trade paperback) |
    ISBN 9780316337359 (ebook)
Subjects: LCGFT: Fantasy fiction. | Novels.
Classification: LCC PS3618.O64 R58 2025 | DDC 813/.6—dc23/eng/20250221
LC record available at https://lccn.loc.gov/2025001400

ISBNs: 9780316337175 (trade paperback), 9780316337359 (ebook)

Printed in the United States of America

LSC-C

Printing 1, 2025

For Hassan

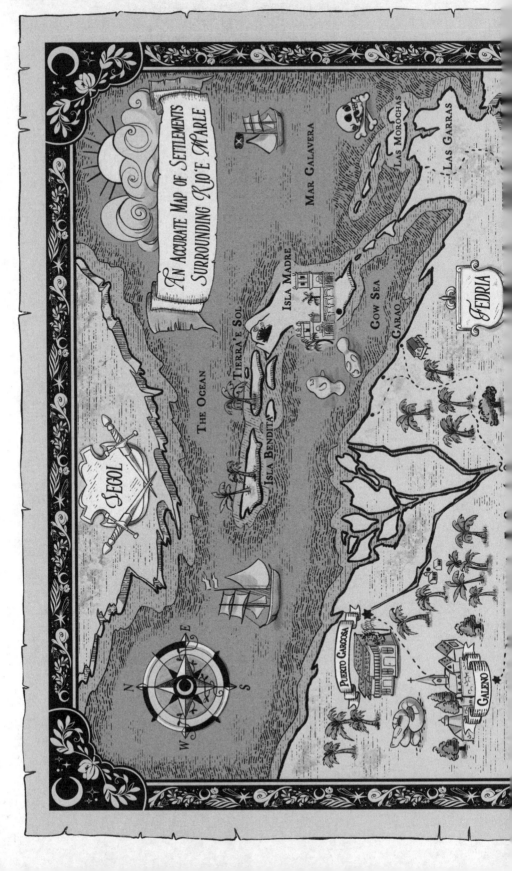

Timeline

THE KING'S DISCOVERY (KD)

1 KD: Segol's voyagers first arrive in the lands that later become the Viceroyalty of Venazia, colony of Segol

326 KD: Rahmagut's Claw becomes visible to the naked eye

344 KD: Samón's and Feleva's declaration of independence

344 KD: Establishment of the sovereign countries of Venazia and Fedria

348 KD: Fall of the Viceroyalty of Venazia and Segol's defeat

368 KD: Rahmagut's Claw becomes visible to the naked eye

Major Families

Silva

Seat: Puerto Carcosa, the coast of the Cow Sea
Banner: an onyx crocodile on scarlet fabric, for the red
blood of felled armadas over a crocodile coast
Notable Members:
- Don Rodrigo Agustín Silva Zamorano, king of Venazia,
  appointed by La Junta de Puerto Carcosa
- Doña Orsalide Belén Zamorano de Silva, queen mother
- Marcelino Carlos Silva Pérez
- Francisco Miguel Silva Carranza

Águila

Seat: outskirts of Sadul Fuerte, the Páramo
Banner: a soaring golden eagle on ivory fabric, for the
riches amassed beneath the Páramo peaks
Notable Members:
- Doña Feleva Lucero Águila Cárdenas, full-blooded valco,
  deceased caudilla of Sadul Fuerte
- Don Enrique Gavriel Águila de Herrón, half human, half
  valco, born in the year 328 KD, caudillo of Sadul Fuerte
- Doña Laurel Divina Herrón de Águila, born in the year
  328 KD

- Celeste Valentina Águila Herrón, three-quarters human, one-quarter valco, born in the year 346 KD
- Javier Armando Águila de Bravo, half human, half valco, born in the year 344 KD

Serrano

Seat: Galeno, the Llanos
Banner: three stripes—brown, blue, and yellow—for the rich soil of Galeno, the plentiful rivers, and the nourishing sun
Notable Members:
- Don Mateo Luis Serrano de Monteverde, governor of Galeno
- Doña Antonia Josefa Monteverde de Serrano
- Doña Dulce Concepción Serrano de Jáuregui, born in the year 326 KD
- Doña Pura Maria Jáuregui de Valderrama
- Décima Lucia Serrano Montilla
- Eva Kesaré Bravo de Águila, three-quarters human, one-quarter valco, born in the year 348 KD
- Néstor Alfonso Serrano Monteverde

Duvianos

Seat: Sadul Fuerte, the Páramo
Banner: an orange flower with a red sun rising over mauve fabric, for the fields of flowers under Páramo dawns
Notable Members:
- Doña Ursulina Salma Duvianos Palacios, born in the year 305 KD
- Don Juan Vicente Duvianos, born in the year 328 KD
- Reina Alejandra Duvianos Torondoy, half human, half nozariel, born in the year 347 KD

Contador

Seat: Galeno, the Llanos
Banner: a diagonal partition of black and white, crossed by a golden key, for the establishment of order in the colonies
Notable Members:
- Don Jerónimo Rangel Contador Miarmal
- Doña Rosa de El Carmín

Villarreal

Seat: Galeno, the Llanos
Notable Members:
- Don Alberto Ferrán Villarreal Pescador

Castañeda

Seat: Los Morichales, the Llanos

Bravo

Seat: Tierra'e Sol, the coast of the Cow Sea
Banner: two mirrored laurels on a diagonal partition of navy and yellow, for the abundance of Fedria and its sea
Notable Members:
- Don Samón Antonio Bravo Días, half human, half valco, born in the year 326 KD, former chancellor of Fedria, the Liberator
- Ludivina Gracia Bravo Céspedes, three-quarters human, one-quarter valco
- Doña Maria Elena Céspedes de Bravo
- Don Vicente German Días Trujillo

A note on names—

Persons are given a first name, a middle name, and a single family name by each parent. Upon marriage, persons can attach their partner's family name to their own and drop one of their last names. A single parent only bestows a single family name to their offspring. When neither parent is able to bestow a family name upon birth, persons are given the name of the city or settlement where they were born. Full names are seldom mentioned in everyday speech. *Don* and *Doña* are honorifics to express respect. Married persons, heirs, landowners, and elders are addressed by their honorific. When neglected, it is a sign of disrespect.

THE
RIVER
AND THE
STAR

Part 1

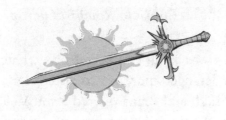

1

Doña Ursulina's Miracle

Moonlight showered Maior. She was radiant in a gossamer gown, like a beauty plucked out of an oil painting. Reina took her in so deeply, half listening to her chatter, too distracted as she considered her good luck. How she could take Maior's hand in hers anytime she longed for the contact, unhesitant and unafraid. Oblivious, Maior tucked her raven hair behind her ear, revealing the dotted constellation of moles on her neck, the sign that had sent them on a colliding path.

Soft breezes enveloped them as they headed for the docks. Reina squeezed Maior's hand and delighted in her blushing smile. Two soldiers trailed behind them, following Reina's lead.

Together, they had spent the day scouring Isla Bendita, the smallest inhabited island of Tierra'e Sol's cay formation. Reina had organized the expedition after rumors of demons had reached the Liberator's manse in Isla Madre, of animals found with their chests carved open and emptied of hearts. The gossip sounded like the dangerous first sighting of a tiniebla or two. So she'd enlisted the soldiers to aid with their swords, and Maior to serve as their healer. But their search had come up empty. They'd failed to find any tinieblas. Reina was worn out and ready to return home, though a bit disappointed.

"So you had a bucket of moras," Reina said absentmindedly, following Maior's recounting of her past.

"Oh, yes, I was about eight years or so. I ate so many I think I looked like a deranged murderer to Sister Maria—she was a young nun," Maior said, and Reina offered a soft laugh, imagining it. "I gave her a fright. My whole face was smeared with red goo—"

"A man-eater," Reina noted.

"And it gave me the worst stomachache—" A sudden agonized scream cut through Maior's words.

Reina turned in the direction of the sound: the jungle they had just emerged from to reach the docks. With a flick of her fingers and wrist, Reina quickly summoned the enhanced sight and strength of bismuto from her geomancia rings. The spell opened her eyes to the unseen, in case a tiniebla lurked about.

Maior blanched, her beauty interrupted. "Is that..."

"What we've been looking for," Reina finished for her as apprehension tightened her chest. The scream could only mean the tiniebla had found a new victim. They needed to move fast.

Reina ordered one soldier to stay with Maior and the other to follow her into the jungle so they could cover twice as much area. Then they rushed after the screams, which shortly quieted. In the jungle, they split.

With Reina's senses on high alert, every shadow took on an alarming shape. Vines looped over thick trunks, twisting, becoming vipers. Slick leaves the size of banners tugged her clothes like the faint grip of phantoms. Anthills gave under her boots. As the knotted greenery impeded her path, Reina hacked her way through with Ches's Blade. *Her* golden blade.

A void emptied the sounds of the jungle. The amphibians and nocturnal critters hushed, as did Reina, pausing. For the first time in a month, since she had emerged from the rubble of Rahmagut's tomb, Reina's instincts prickled her skin with a warning. She felt a familiar yet uncomfortable constricting in her chest from the pumping of her iridio heart.

But warmth from Ches's Blade flooded her with reassurance, even as she was still brittle from the last time she'd fought tinieblas. The thought of encountering the heart-ravenous demons again, how their bodies were amalgamated from parts of random animals, reminded Reina of her grandmother, who'd commanded tinieblas in Rahmagut's tomb. Doña Ursulina had used them to sacrifice innocent women in the name of Rahmagut.

Reina would never be same after her grandmother's betrayal. She was changed, fragmented, taking people's words and turning them around and around in her head, evaluating the true intention beneath them. No longer was she desperate to achieve unimpeachable acceptance—now she knew such a thing was a fantasy. She was not a broken girl begging for love anymore. She was a woman rebuilding from nothing, without a family or home.

Her handle on the golden pommel of Ches's Blade grew warmer. Despite her grandmother's plots and lies, Reina had survived. She still had a future, and she was alight with strength and the drive to find atonement by serving her new community.

Maybe it was this actualization, or maybe something else. But since emerging from the tomb, her skin vibrated anytime she wielded Ches's Blade. She had done the unimaginable for her grandmother, yet her heart blazed with her belief in Ches. If the tinieblas were Rahmagut's creations seeding chaos into the world, then Reina would be Ches's agent, vanquishing them. Tierra'e Sol and its people had welcomed her with open arms. In return, she would gladly keep them safe.

She shoved vines away from her face as she entered a swampy clearing. Twigs snapped ahead. Reina plunged forward, circling the pond and continuing down a path that could not have been carved by an animal. She slid down a steep incline and arrived on two shaky feet beside an outcrop where a hunter's cabin stood.

She crossed a cloud of gnats and glanced around the cabin's back door. Upon inspecting the hinges, Reina found it had been forced open. She announced her entry, but no one answered.

With her boots tracking in mud, Reina stepped into a small kitchen. As she passed a corridor, her nose wrinkled from the sharp smell of recently spilled blood, intensified by her bismuto spell.

She shoved open a door and found a middle-aged man lying on a bed soaked in an overflow of red. His eyes stared blankly at the ceiling, mouth agape. His fingernails were lifted and bloodstained from a struggle. His robe was torn open in the middle, the fabric mopping up the blood leaking from his chest. His ribs had been snapped, his chest carved empty.

Reina covered her mouth with her fist, swallowing the nausea. She didn't bother inspecting him further. This was the work of a tiniebla.

Fuming, she whirled on her heels to search for it—to give the tiniebla an end befitting its actions.

The house was silent, save for the gentle twinkle of wind chimes coming from the porch. Reina tore into every room, finding each one empty. A door squeaked from the back patio, followed by the clatter of hooves on tiles. She rushed out and immediately met the bipedal fiend.

The moon lit a creature with the upper body of a man and the legs of a goat. The head was in the twisted amalgamation of a jaguar and a capuchin, with flared nostrils and a spotted forehead. The dead man's blood was still smeared across the tiniebla's sneering mouth, with tendrils of red sticking to the edges of its lips.

The tiniebla swung a pustulated arm at her, entering Reina's reach. Time slowed to a crawl, as if her bismuto-dilated pupils and swollen muscles could react to movements far faster than these.

Reina's blade severed the arm with ease. The monster let out a deserving howl. She swerved back for a finishing blow and nearly threw her body with a strength she didn't know she had. Surprised, she found her balance and cut a life-rending gash through the tiniebla's middle. The monster faded into nothing. As a creature of shadow, it left no physical remains.

The lack of challenge was . . . disappointing. If not for the need to see the tiniebla, the use of bismuto enhancement felt unnecessary.

After sheathing her blade, she slipped out of her leather gloves. She lifted a hand before her, inspecting her bismuto-ringed fingers under the moonlight. This strangeness in her body unnerved her. The strength—could this be the result of training with Don Samón's soldiers? Had she truly not challenged herself completely since entering the Liberator's service?

She scowled. Ever since the night at the tomb, Reina had wistfully nurtured the idea that its destruction would bring the end of tinieblas. She had worked under Ches's guidance, smiting her grandmother and causing the sanctum to collapse. She'd hoped this had been enough to counter Rahmagut, the god of the Void whom Doña Ursulina had nearly sacrificed Celeste and Maior for. True, it was a naïve wish, but she'd reasoned that if Rahmagut had no altar to be worshipped, then surely his manipulations of the physical world from the Void would end. But a tiniebla in Isla Bendita turned this theory on its head.

Just as Reina was wondering how it had made it to the island, and if it was alone, another scream pierced through the night and right into her heart. Reina sprinted back into the house. She drew her blade and followed the cries, finding she had missed a door to an underground cellar, which was slightly ajar. She kicked it open and was assaulted by a metallic scent she knew all too well.

The cellar thundered from the toppling of furniture. Reina descended and found another feral tiniebla towering over an adolescent nozariel boy. The room was in disarray, as if from a mad chase ending with the boy using a small crate as the only barrier between him and the canine mandibles snapping for him. He used the crate as a shield, terrified and blind to the threat, for without bismuto he was unable to see the tiniebla that had already bitten a large chunk of his arm.

Reina tackled the tiniebla off him, shoving the boy away as the creature swiped at her. She swung, decapitating it in a single strike.

Afterward, she knelt by the boy, who heaved as he held his bleeding arm. "Something—I couldn't see—*something bit me*," he said.

Reina's breath caught upon seeing the large bite. Her own healed arm itched with the memory of the tiniebla attack she had endured a lifetime ago. "Who else lives in this house?" she asked.

He was too horrified to answer, so she moved closer, shushing him while gently wiping tears away. His cheeks and pointed nozariel ears were splattered with blood. "It's all right," she said. "The tiniebla is gone. Another one will not get past me." Which raised the question: How many had made it here? "Does anyone else live with you?" she asked.

He nodded and sobbed, "My father."

Reina held her breath. "What is your name?"

"Juan Pablo."

Gently, she inspected his wounded arm. The ring on her middle finger carried a solution of galio with enough potency to allow her to cast simple first aid spells. But Reina didn't have the expertise to mend such a bite, with its concave emptiness revealing tendons and bone. Suddenly, Juan Pablo curled on the ground, as if struck by a pain more immense than just his injured arm.

Reina cursed. Her hands trembled as she moved him to get a better look. Moaning, he shut his eyes in agony. He gripped her wrist, seeking reassurance, but Reina's chest fissured even more.

"And my father? Is he all right?" His big, teary eyes bore into Reina. "Please—he is all I have."

Before Reina could answer, he screamed in anguish.

Reina knew exactly what that felt like. She had nearly died from a tiniebla bite when she crossed the Páramo Mountains in search of a better life. She knew the tiniebla's corruption was going to take his heart.

The devilish whispers in her iridio heart rejoiced, awakened after a monthlong slumber, mocking her.

Reina hauled Juan Pablo over her shoulders and sprinted back through the jungle, enraged. Despite her search, the tinieblas had still taken a life. What if there were more? How were they supposed to scour every cay of Tierra'e Sol? And where were the wards guarding against them? Had Reina's arrival or the events in Rahmagut's tomb triggered attacks never seen in these parts before?

She returned to Maior's and the soldier's shocked faces.

"I found tinieblas," Reina said, gently lowering Juan Pablo so he could sit on the docks' briny steps.

He watched her with big, confused eyes. She understood his bewilderment better than anyone. She tried calming him with whispers of hope that sounded like lies to her, for she knew no words would be enough.

Maior grabbed her bag of supplies from the canoe. She brought bandages and several vials sloshing with different galio solutions. The soldier lit a torch while Maior's galio healing made quick work of stitching whatever she could of the wound. Then she yanked Juan Pablo's shirt off to inspect the source of his pain. Stunned, they stared at the varicose black stains crawling from his arm to his heart, as darkness claimed the healthy tissue and replaced it with necrosis.

"Reina?" Maior looked to her for reassurance.

"One of the tinieblas got to him," Reina said with gritted teeth. She hated admitting it aloud, while the poor boy was still conscious and desperate for some reprieve. "I was too late. Maior... the darkness—it's going to corrupt his heart. It's what tinieblas do. It's what they did to me."

Scowling, as if refusing this fate, Maior summoned a different galio spell to her hands. Reina's bismuto high lingered, allowing her to view the manifestation of Maior's geomancia—a soft lavender hue—as it twirled around her fingers like satin laces and curled within her palms before she pressed them against Juan Pablo's chest. There, the galio spell tried to take root, digging. But as Juan Pablo groaned, it was rejected. The darkness only spread farther.

"We should go back to Isla Madre," Reina said as the second soldier returned from the jungle. She felt a panic rising in her throat. She'd lived because Doña Ursulina had acted quickly after her tiniebla attack.

Maior ignored her. She tried a different vial of galio. And another. Splotches of red spread about her neck. She switched through several pairs of rings from her bag to fight the rot. And Reina watched with a hollow growing in her belly as she realized Maior's geomancia couldn't hold a candle to the roaring firestorm of Doña Ursulina's dark magic. Her beating iridio heart was a miracle bestowed from darkness.

They were wasting time.

"We have to go to Dr. Baltasar! This is *not enough*," Reina snapped, wrenching Maior's hands away from the boy.

Immediately Reina realized she'd overreacted from the reflection in Maior's wounded eyes.

Juan Pablo howled in pain, and there was no time to apologize. They ushered him into the canoe and rowed back to Isla Madre at full speed. Maior faced away on the ride, her wavy hair surfing the air. When Reina placed a tentative hand on Maior's lower back, aching for her attention, Maior flinched and didn't meet her eyes.

Dawn arrived in Isla Madre. Reina paced the halls as Juan Pablo's screams echoed through the infirmary. There was no escaping them. She could be a coward and leave. She could pretend she wasn't affected, but her very bones understood the pain ravaging him. And his likely fate.

Dr. Baltasar, Maior's employer, had sequestered her and a few other nurses to aid him with Juan Pablo. The boy's cries seemingly went on for hours. Until they suddenly stopped.

When a hush quieted the infirmary, Reina stormed out, the need to retaliate blazing through her veins. But how would she? How could she stop these creatures that seemed innumerable and unstoppable? The moment she slayed one, or a dozen, another came back. She'd thought the blood she spilled in Rahmagut's tomb would be the end of her violent path, yet the bodies kept piling up.

She walked without thinking and took a detour behind the infirmary. She stopped beside a window, drawn by the familiar voices coming out of its halfway-open shutters. Dr. Baltasar said, "You must learn to let go, Maior. The mercy was to stop his heart."

Reina gripped the handle of her blade as the adrenaline from her earlier fight resurged.

Around her, Isla Madre's bustle came alive with the arriving morning, unaware of the lost life. Music flowed from one of the houses sitting on cobbled roads. The wind lifted wayward sand around Reina's legs and brought the smell of baked bread. A trader passed by her, guiding a donkey and his cart of freshly harvested mangoes. When he offered *good morning*s and waved, Reina had no choice but to let go of her anger. She offered him a meek wave back.

This was her community now. In the short, first month of her stay, the people of Tierra'e Sol had welcomed her with the same openness Don Samón afforded her. Reina wore a pained smile as she considered how innocent they seemed, isolated from the mainland's conflicts. If Reina, Maior, and Eva were going to make this town their new home, they needed to shield it from the darkness they brought due to their involvement with the god of the Void.

Desperate for answers, she took the all-too-familiar canopied path to the tomb. Sweat clung to her back, her lips were chapped, and a headache hammered her. She ignored the discomfort as she rushed toward the caved-in opening of the tomb. Until now, she'd avoided returning out of cowardice. But this was where she needed to be to better understand the aftermath and why tinieblas were drawn to the islands. She knew she needed to swallow her own anxiety, if she truly believed herself a protector of this community.

Dense greenery encroached on the dirt path. The air smelled sweet and bitter from the rotting sea grapes hanging off surrounding bushes. Reina hacked an opening through the leaves. She met the lagoon facing the tomb's mouth, with its crystalline waters reflecting prisms over her skin and clothes. A man sat on the largest boulder flanking the lagoon. He rose, as if awaiting her. He had dark brown skin and long, straight white hair crowned by two magnificent antlers, thick, like those of a pure-blooded valco.

Reina froze. The clearing quieted. Her heartbeats thrummed in her ears.

Then a name rolled out of her mouth, and Reina wasn't sure if she'd been the one to put it there.

"Ches?"

2

Ches

As soon as she said it, it felt right. But it was a shock to see that her god of the sun was a valco—entirely unlike the way she'd imagined him.

He was dressed simply, in a white cotton shirt and ankle-length fishing pants. His unmoving smile confirmed it all. "*Reina*," he said.

His voice sent chills through her.

She did the first thing that crossed her mind. She collapsed to her knees for a deep bow, her forehead grazing the packed dirt beneath. How else was she supposed to revere he who gave light to this world?

A soft hand on her chin lifted her head. She hadn't even heard his approach, as if his steps were made of sunlight. But it made sense that he had the power to be everywhere all at once.

"There is no need for that. And it is much too late for reverence. I have been with you for some time now." His words filled the clearing, coming from all angles.

Reina rose, meeting his red eyes, which were curiously devoid of pupils. It unnerved her for a moment.

His smile widened. She shuddered from being perceived by him, rocked by a surge of emotion she didn't know she'd been bottling up.

He looked at her the way her father, Juan Vicente, did—filled with love and empty of the judgment everyone else held for her half-breed nozariel existence. It was like a homecoming. Reina shrunk to the size of a child and pressed her grimy palms against her eyes as tears rushed out of her. The ache for her grandmother, whose life she had brutally ended, crawled out of her heart. Guilt constricted her throat, preventing her from breathing. Reina shook as she recognized how vulnerable she was once again, starting from scratch, without the family and home she'd once thought guaranteed with Doña Ursulina and the Águilas. How could she, the fragmented creature she was, be worthy to face a god?

Ches squeezed her shoulder until she had no more tears to give. When her breath returned, it was clean, free of the weight she'd carried all month. Reina wiped her face. She couldn't even muster embarrassment for breaking down before him. Perhaps he had planned this.

"It takes courage to pick yourself up," Ches said. He motioned her to join him on the same slippery boulder where he'd sat.

"Thank you," she said, and he nodded. "I am confused—*surprised*," she said, quickly correcting herself, "that you are valco." Though she wondered if she was being shallow, for being disappointed that he wasn't of her kind.

His upper lip twitched. "Everywhere, mortals depict me in their likeness. With antlers and without antlers. With tails and without. Those who built the tomb where you saw my statue were fallible. Do not take their portrayal as the ultimate truth. How I appear is not what is important, but rather that I am able to appear at all."

Reina frowned, not understanding.

"I hope by now you are comfortable with me," he said.

"I've always been."

He raised his bushy brows. He wielded otherworldly beauty, with his high cheekbones and smooth, thick lips. "No. You renounced me. You claimed Rahmagut as your patron."

Reina's cheeks warmed. Indeed, soon after Doña Laurel's death and darkness had descended over Águila Manor, Reina had convinced herself that Rahmagut would be the god to solve her suffering. But like any cheap remedy, it was never true.

She shook her head. "I was wrong." She almost bowed again, but Ches's gaze arrested her in place. "You were always my patron."

"I am more than that now. I am inside you."

Reina squeezed her shirt, breathless. She froze and searched his eyes, finding nothing but unwavering truth.

"I am presenting myself so there is no doubt. I was gone, but I have returned. All the power my banishment denied this world is here, in your body."

Reina cleared her throat, remembering to breathe. "You were gone, and now you've returned, through me?"

"I can take over your mind, bring you here or anywhere, whenever I wish. I am back, Reina, imprisoned in you, as you are chained to me."

Her chest faltered. The elation she'd felt after crying crumbled into confusion. "I'm your vessel?"

He nodded. "This is not an invasion. But that is a capability I wield."

Reina's stomach turned as she remembered how Doña Ursulina had controlled her. The moments that weren't her own. The terror of being trapped in her own body, performing someone else's actions. She hated what Ches was implying. But what was she to do against a god?

He leaned in closer. "Now listen to me. You are my host for as long as you live. I chose you. But you are not unique. There have been others before you. Do not squander your life. I command it."

"I won't," she replied. "I'm ready to fight." She'd lost everything, except her strength, which was as sharp as the golden blade hanging from her hip. She knew she had to protect the people of Tierra'e Sol, and Maior. She'd promised, after all.

Ches nodded, satisfied. "The events resulting in my sealing destroyed my physical body. Thus, I am forced to exist in the bodies of mortals, like yours. But it is important that you never doubt or forget: Your death does not mean the end of me. I will simply find a different host, and our bond will have been a waste of my time. This holds true even for the person that charlatan chose."

"Rahmagut returned, just like you?"

A strong gust lifted the leaves strewn about the clearing. Ches's anger was answer enough.

"And he took someone else?" Reina guessed. By mere process of elimination, she supposed it had to be someone who was in the tomb with her. Reina's stomach clenched, hoping Maior's possession by Doña Laurel had barred her from also hosting the god of the Void.

"He chose the person best suited to wield the power of iridio."

Reina sucked in a deep breath as she immediately knew the answer.

"Eva?" She grimaced. "But how could this happen? I thought my grandmother meant only to commune with Rahmagut. She couldn't have known she would be unsealing him." She didn't add *or you* at the end, but as scorn flashed through his eyes, it was clear he knew her thoughts.

"After our sealing, I slumbered in the Void." Ches's voice echoed in the clearing. Gusts whipped at Reina's braid. "But that man—that viper—instead of admitting defeat and slumbering with me, continued to intrude into the physical world." Ches rose, giving Reina his back, as if he wanted to avoid showing the ugly hatred on his face. "He continued making tinieblas, knowing their devastation undermines the faith mortals place in gods. He planted dreams in people, fabricating stories of our strife, pretending his power matched mine. From the Void, he behaved as a patron to practitioners of Void geomancia and seeded tales of his Claw. Soon enough his legend gained validity, and it served as a motivation to offer him sacrifices every forty-two years."

Ches faced her, and she knew he was challenging her to see if she understood the ties that fundamentally brought him and mortals closer together. "Gods gain power from sacrifices," she said.

"The damas your grandmother butchered in the tomb, both during your time and when she assisted her lover forty-two years prior. The babes you abandoned in the mountains."

Reina's cheeks blazed with shame. She would never be able to erase the dark stain of what she had done. Even to this day, she carried those deaths with her.

"Eventually, I grew strong enough to break free from the seal."

Reina knew she would be blasphemous for pushing back, but she couldn't stop herself. "How did you gain power from those sacrifices?"

Ches's lip curled in dissatisfaction, and a chill of fear stirred through Reina. "Rahmagut survived the Void because he bound himself to me. Every sacrifice made to him also fed me. Now listen, I am not here to bring you fame, riches, or conquest. I am not your tool. I may not share the ambitions of a mortal, nor the desire to reign over your life, but I will not be undermined."

Reina shook her head. "I wouldn't—"

"You couldn't," he barked, and the words were a tremor that shook the clearing. Moist leaves collapsed from the canopy. The lagoon shuddered. "Let this moment be an introduction. Remember my likeness. You will need to grow strong with me. Rahmagut cannot be left unchecked. He threatened this world once, and I fear he may do so again."

Reina's pulse quickened as she stared at her hands. More questions threatened to bubble out of her. But to a god, every question could be a challenge. "But why now? If you came into my body after I destroyed this tomb, why are you appearing to me now?"

Her heartbeats were loud in his silence. Had she angered him again, in daring to demand answers?

She stared down at her boots, and he replied, "Because it is now that you chose to return to the tomb. It took you all this time to muster your courage to face me. You were not ready, so I gave you time."

In that moment, Reina's heart filled with love for him. Ches was a god. He didn't owe her anything. He behaved in ways she couldn't comprehend, and it was nonsensical to assume she could. But he understood her. This was enough.

She glanced up, offering a smile of gratitude, but he was gone.

The lagoon was once again silent without him. Feeble rays of sunlight filtered through the canopy. She extended her arms to feel the sun on her brown skin and realized that since emerging from the tomb, she indeed had been experiencing the world differently.

She wielded heightened senses. It was why she ran twice as fast, even without bismuto. Why she'd nearly cut herself from the fierce swings of her own sword. Breezes rustled around her, tickling trees that appeared brighter and more saturated to her eyes. The lagoon's surface shone, more crystalline than ever. The jungle smelled wetter.

She was bound to Ches forever.

Reina searched within herself, prodding for him, wondering if she would feel it. She only sensed his company, like an unseen presence in a room where she wasn't alone, and it was how she knew she hadn't made this up. She knew Ches would be silent unless he chose to show himself, which was fine with her.

Bound, until death.

She wished she could ask him how he felt about this. How would he feel about going through her life by her side? Living as she lived?

Perhaps he had chosen her out of convenience, but that didn't diminish how special he made her feel. Hosting him was an honor, and now, her greatest challenge. She was not going to disappoint him.

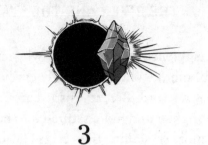

3

Daughter to Father

Every afternoon, the sun left Tierra'e Sol in a salty haze. Eva reveled in the idleness as she approached Isla Madre's plaza with her hair salt-wild and her espadrilles muddy from the day's gathering of geomancia reagents. The townsfolk were silent, retreating to their homes to prepare supper. Babies cried distantly, as did seagulls. Even on the cobbled path from the plaza to Don Samón's manse, one could hear the waves. They carried a healing rhythm. A coming and going, its predictability bringing the comfort Eva so desperately needed after the chaos she had encountered when she left Galeno.

The path to the manse hugged Isla Madre's burial grounds, a resting place for the island's inhabitants long before Don Samón moved in. Every time Eva passed the grounds after sunset, curiosity and apprehension would fill her, raising the hairs on her arm. The grounds weren't empty.

Sometimes, from the corner of her eye, Eva thought she could see the ghosts. They clung to the land, hiding behind the mango trees planted by the island's first settlers. She saw them in the gardens surrounding the Pentimiento chapel as well, shooting furtive glances before disappearing around a corner. Men with mustaches, espadrilles, and jipijapa hats. Children and grandmothers. Just as the Benevolent Lady Laurel Águila still haunted Maior with her perfectly healthy countenance—save for her ghostly, see-through pallor.

These were people who had died yet were not truly gone. Eva wondered if the same was true for gods, who supposedly left remnants of themselves as traces of power for people to fear or exploit. It was how Rahmagut could dip his influence into the world to create his tinieblas, even before he had the good luck of residing in her body. Eva shivered at that and pretended not to notice the strange sense of amusement stirring within her. She did that a lot these days, since Javier had attested that she had emerged from the tomb with something clinging to her shoulders. (Again, she shuddered at the thought.) She hated never being alone. She hated toying with the possibility that the shivers running up her spine and the heat flushing her ears weren't innate reactions of her body, but rather proof of the Void god's return. She'd rather believe she was ill, stuck with an ever-recurring fever, than accept any other truth.

Eva wasn't afraid, not exactly. Rahmagut's icon in Doña Rosa's house signaled he was misunderstood and not at all how the Penitents painted him. But why would someone so powerful choose *her*?

The cobbled path forked near the construction site of a new house, which was cluttered with half-laid bricks and a wheelbarrow. It was the lot Don Samón had granted Reina. Every time Eva passed by, she caught a glimpse of something new: Reina's helpers hacking down the tall grass, shoveling clay from the foundation, or wheeling imported materials from the docks, Reina hard at work alongside them in sweat-drenched clothes. A month had passed since their arrival to the island and it already felt like they were living entirely different lives. Reina hadn't wasted a second carrying on. In comparison, Eva felt lazy and aimless, spending her days chasing reagents to tug and expand her knowledge of geomancia. A spoiled, comfortable woman.

As she arrived at the jasmine-entwined gates of Don Samón's property, she took a deep breath of that sweet air, accepting that this was now her new life.

If she had ever started off as a guest, the staff had quickly adjusted their routines to make her feel at home. Her plate was always served beside her father, Don Samón, at the dining table, across from her half sister, Ludivina. The cooks noted when she requested her arepa be made extra toasty and repeated the favor for every breakfast. In the courtyard with the caged parrots, where she took to withdrawing with one of Don Samón's many manuals on geomancia, the cooks snuck her small plates of guava bocadillos wrapped in dried bijao leaves and replenished goblets of the day's juice, a small wildflower of matching color plopped in as garnish.

A breeze caressed the palms flanking her, then lifted her curls. Distantly, dark clouds ferried closer to the island. It had stormed the night before, but perhaps the skies weren't through with the nightly rain.

In that moment, Eva tasted freedom. She was on top of the world. And she was rotten, for enjoying it alone. Javier was prisoner and she was free. Four stone walls were his everyday companions, while she could enjoy the paradise that was Tierra'e Sol, even though they had both caused Celeste's near death in Rahmagut's tomb.

The inside of her right forearm itched. Eva raked her fingernails along the rash. The skin was red and tender where yesterday it had not been. She ought to leave it alone and let it heal, but part of her believed she deserved it. For her inaction. For having this perfect life, mostly out of luck, and avoiding broaching the topic of Javier's release with her father, while Celeste was still recovering.

Eva had idled long enough. She was ready to open her heart to her father, as she had promised she would. It was time she sought justice for Javier.

Eva met with Don Samón as he emerged from a path leading to the surrounding jungle. His gloved hands carried a heavy rock. Likely extracted near the tomb's entrance, the slab was carved with a depiction of a solar eclipse. Don Samón smiled upon Eva's approach, and together they walked toward his outdoor workshop.

"Is that a solar eclipse?" Eva asked conversationally.

"Oh, yes, the tomb is filled with them."

"I've always wondered why that's his symbol," Eva said.

Don Samón looked delighted to be the one to teach her. He said, "Well, some folklorists say the god of the Void performed his darkest deeds under the veil of an eclipse. When the moon completely blocked the sun, he felt he was shielded from Ches's scornful eye. You can only imagine what darkness Rahmagut had been dabbling in, to want to hide."

The back of Eva's neck pinched, as if bitten by a mosquito. She massaged the spot, feeling indignant. "If he was so concerned about Ches's opinions, couldn't he just do his work at night?"

Don Samón offered her a warm smile. Eva liked seeing it. "Even at night, the sun still shines elsewhere. Physicists, voyagers, and cartographers have confirmed it. It just so happens at night, we are merely facing away from the sun."

Eva nodded. "An eclipse would block the sun's rays completely."

"And Ches's power, if such a thing exists." As if struck by the thought, he added, "I was sent a missive by an astronomer in Segolita. He believes there will be another eclipse. You might be able to see it with your own eyes."

It sounded fascinating. "I would love that." She motioned at the slab, chuckling. "So what are you doing with that? Preparing for it?"

He scratched his beard. "No. I'm keeping myself busy. I'm trying not to think about that boy in the infirmary, Juan Pablo. The one who died from the tiniebla attack."

Eva had heard. She'd consoled Maior, who had succumbed to tears after her shift with Dr. Baltasar. The presence of tinieblas made Eva equally uncomfortable. "I'm surprised a tiniebla made it to Isla Bendita. Does that mean they could come here, too?"

Don Samón sighed. "I'm sending Dr. Baltasar to set up wards on all the islands. This one is already protected by the chapel and by my soldiers. We just have to remind folk not to go deep into the woods. I know you've been tinkering with new geomancia reagents, but I don't want you straying far either."

What would he say if he knew Eva had had a personal encounter with a tiniebla nest? Would he be impressed? "If there's a way to hunt them, I could probably do it. I can help," she said.

He shook his head. "Please, Eva, I need peace of mind, especially this week. I have some lingering anxieties about Enrique."

"You must meet with him?"

"I cannot send his daughter without even bothering to escort her. In fact, it has been discourteous not to offer him passage to the island this whole time."

Eva frowned. She didn't need an explanation. Having the caudillo and his battalion on the island, where they easily outnumbered Don Samón and his soldiers, filled her with unease.

"We can only be glad for the sea," she said.

"Indeed. But I will not let Enrique take me for a coward. I will meet with him."

Eva followed him along the sandy path, her ankles brushing the palm trees felled by a storm just the night before. Violent rainfalls were expected in the islands. As if answering her, the skies thundered.

"Is there history between you?" she asked.

Don Samón's eyes creased in a small smile. "Yes, but of the good kind, I suppose. We campaigned together when we were your age. More than once, we saved each other's lives."

Excitement swirled within her as she imagined what it must have been like, when more valcos still roamed the continent. Before the war had decimated their numbers and when geomancia was still practiced without shame, reservation, or scorn from Penitents.

A fat drop of rain landed on Eva's nose. She wriggled it away but was rewarded with a half dozen more.

They scurried to the workshop as rain showered the grounds. Eva exchanged a glance with her father. They were trapped together.

Don Samón deposited the slab on a worktable, slightly out of the rain's reach. They stood under the awning's shade, tucked beside a redbrick turret housing his smithy. Other pieces of the tomb were arranged like a collection. There were slabs with antique writings and hieroglyphs of valcos, nozariels, and the extinct yares. A cracked skull and rusted swords. Pieces of clay decanters and broken stalactites that Don Samón's men had dug up from the collapse. This extraction from the tomb was part of his obsession with Rahmagut and his suspicion that the Void god was no longer sealed within its depths. He cataloged his findings quietly, without Eva's input, as she avoided broaching the subject.

"You have good memories of the caudillo?" Eva inquired to fill the silence.

Don Samón let out a chuckle that could be confused for a scoff. "You could say that. He certainly has a reputation. Some people meet Enrique and incorrectly take him for a cold man, but he has strong opinions and passions. He followed my cause not just because Doña Feleva expected it of him. He was also hungry for legacy."

"And were you?"

He shot her a long, shrewd look dampened by his smile. "I expected some kind of recognition for all the trouble I went through," he said, acquiescent. "But only because I knew I risked losing everything. My family's fortune—I pillaged the coffers to pay for the cause. Your inheritance...it's nearly all gone now."

Eva looked down, in case he caught the blush in her cheeks.

"My life was fractured. My feelings were not spared. People I thought I could trust turned on me. I lost a best friend, and the love of my life."

Eva didn't fail to notice his breath hitching. Her own chest constricted, bracing her for the overdue conversation.

He pointed at a nearby lopsided palm tree pelted by the rain. One of its branches had been snapped in half by last night's storm. He said, "After the papers were signed and Segol agreed to permanently withdraw, I was like that tree. There was barely anything left of me. And yet the work was not done. I had to take the position of chancellor immediately after, to make sure our young government didn't fall to Segol's lingering influences still encroaching on our new borders. They tried to blockade us, and they tried to plant spies. There was so much internal bickering between the major families of Fedria and Venazia—infighting between those who believed governing should be an inherited family affair and those, like me, who'd had enough of kings and monarchs. So many debates and disagreements about our stance as freed nations. Families like the Serranos who were not happy to lose the economic advantage of the institutionalized slavery of nozariels."

Eva nodded gravely. She was glad she had left the Serranos behind.

"I don't tell you this to admonish you, Eva. I just want you to understand that I worked myself to the bone, until we rewrote the constitution and the first president was elected. Enrique and I do not control the way we were lionized. We didn't seek fame. It was just a natural consequence of our very visible contributions to these nations. And now, I'm just tired...and ashamed I never reached out to you."

She understood—she could sympathize. But that didn't stop the bitterness from clawing up her throat. The part of her that refused to forget how miserable it was to spend her life unwanted, when all along she had a place where she could belong. Her heart was still broken from pretending to be someone she was not. She had grown up with the Serranos' privilege, but that didn't make her ache hurt any less.

"I wish you had come for me. I really do," she said.

Don Samón startled. For a moment, in the brightening of his carmine eyes, Eva thought she saw an unwillingness to apologize.

"I admit that after I married Maria Elena I couldn't bring you into my life anymore. Doing so would have been improper. I married her soon after the war ended—it was a political move, so that the society of Segolita would be more willing to accept a valco as their leader. And despite my failure at having a successful marriage with her, I really did try at first." He glanced down, wounded. "But I guess the heart doesn't care for politics, does it? She could tell mine belonged to someone else."

It was Eva's turn to glance away.

"Even if I had come for you, Eva, Doña Antonia would have stood in the way."

"She made everyone believe you had bewitched my mother. That you put a baby in her without her consent."

A flash of anger overtook his face, but it was gone in an instant. "And you believed it?"

"When spun the right way, the story is credible," Eva said with a cocked brow, aware of the lack of compassion in her answer. "For as long as I knew my mother, she lived with melancholy." The memories angered her. She felt cheated of a childhood with a happy mother and father. "The way I saw her, it made sense to believe that it was because you put a dark spell on her."

Don Samón squared up, antlers and shoulders facing her evenly. "I abhor the implications."

She knew she was being a disrespectful creature. But with everything she'd been through, she allowed herself to impart some of that pain to someone else. "I wouldn't be telling you this if I believed it anymore."

Surprise returned to his eyes.

The raindrops filled the silence, growing louder as they hit the puddles on an island already saturated by yesterday's rainfall. Eva's heartbeats were riotous. "Obviously, I didn't know her before you," she said. "But when I did know her, she was smart, and loving, and there was clarity in her eyes. She was only befuddled in the stories the gossipers made up about her. She raised me as best as she could, despite my grandmother's disapproval." The corners of her eyes stung. "Can you tell me how someone can be so loving, yet so sad?"

"We are complicated creatures."

Eva squeezed her eyes shut and shook her head. "No. She was trapped. She was suffocated. I know that must be it because I also lived in that cage. But unlike me, she had daughters anchoring her to Galeno. I'm sure she couldn't just leave, like I did." This was a conclusion Eva had arrived at in her days in Tierra'e Sol, when all she had were empty moments to ruminate on the things she regretted. When she thought back to her mother, her uncle Néstor, and her half sister Pura. Even her grandmother and the aunts and cousins—despite their mistreatment. How she missed them.

Eva didn't divulge that the only reason she'd had the courage to flee Galeno was because Javier had been there with her, guaranteeing a future with the Águilas. The opportunity for a new life. She would never have undergone such a journey if she'd had children to think about.

Don Samón said, "If I had come back for her—"

"She might still be alive."

He wiped his face with his hand and turned away, perhaps to shield Eva from the hurt in his eyes.

"I get it: It was a person for a country." The back of her neck burned as she let the words escape her. She was being awful. And she was going to lose everything if she let her emotions push him away.

"That is unfair."

Eva swallowed down the sudden desire to hurt. She hugged her arms, fending off the idea of prodding him more, seeing how far she could go. "I know. I'm sorry," she said, sighing. "But if we're going to start afresh, have a proper daughter-and-father relationship, we shouldn't have resentments between us."

"You resent me?"

"I resent not having you in my life sooner." She waved at the manse behind the large flowering gardens, with its brightly painted walls and mosaics. It was true she was even jealous of her own little sister, Ludivina.

His cheeks and neck flushed. "I'm sorry I abandoned you and your mother."

The apology left her feeling empty. She didn't need him to apologize, not anymore. She just wanted an honest relationship, unlike the twisted love she'd experienced with her maternal family. The Serranos loved her but disliked her, and she hated that.

Eva held his gaze, but this time she was disarmed. She hoped he saw her ache and, hopefully, her desire for more.

"Will you take me as your father?" he asked. "Will you allow me to guide you, to make up for the years my politicking and cowardice robbed us of?"

Eva took a deep breath, softening. "You are not a coward."

"There are so many things I would do to make it up to you. I will write to the president, or we will go to Segolita, and I will make sure you are written in the books of my family."

Eva waited, her jaw tightening.

"I will give you my name. You will be recognized as my firstborn."

The corners of her eyes began to burn. She nodded, fighting to hold herself together.

"You are to be acknowledged as the heir that you are. Everyone wants to give me accolades, to send me gifts and thank me for how I've stripped myself into a skeleton of a man. But the war is over. Everyone else is rebuilding. And you and Ludivina are the legacy that matters to me now. I want that."

He stepped closer, then took her hands in his big, warm pair. She never imagined that taking the reins of her life would lead her to a clashing path with this man. Her father, whom Doña Antonia had slandered until even Eva had believed he was a monster.

There were little habits about him that reminded her of herself. How he held his quill in his right hand and penned extravagant calligraphy just like hers. How his forearms were covered in a quilt of hairs, and Eva's own forearms were hairy, unlike those of the Serrano brood. How the shape of his antlers angled outward like her stunted pair, unlike Celeste's and Javier's forward shapes, confirming they hailed from different valco lineages. Even a few nights ago, while she and Maior whispered secrets to each other under blankets, Maior had told her how she'd noticed that Eva and Don Samón walked with the same gait. Eva couldn't deny that Don Samón was her father.

"I want to stay with you. I want to be treated as your daughter. I want to act as such. Back home, my education only went as far as what was needed to become some useless, docile wife."

He laughed, and Eva's smile broke free.

"But I see Celeste, and she's been raised like someone who's meant to succeed the great Feleva Águila," she added.

He cocked a brow.

"I want Tierra'e Sol to know me as your daughter, and to become an expert at geomancia. I want to use iridio like valcos are meant to."

At this, something in her stirred awake. Her eyes became hyperaware of everything around her. She knew that if she looked up at the sky, it would take no effort to observe the gulls flying away in the far distances, in great detail. Or to count and catalog the raindrops splashing on a nearby puddle, as useless as that was. Eva knew why, but she hated to admit it to herself.

Don Samón's gaze flicked to her antlers, which Eva now tried to keep out of view to avoid his seeing how they'd permanently turned black. He said, "Iridio is destructive—"

"Are you going to condemn Reina to her death, then? You know she needs it to live." Eva wasn't sure of the words, but she needed to make a case while keeping the attention away from her own cravings for it. "Half of the instruments you have in your workshop— they need some iridio to work properly."

"They're not necessary—"

"Do you refuse to use geomancia? You said it yourself: It was part of our culture before Penitents turned it into a bad thing."

"I don't denounce geomancia," Don Samón said. "But I have already told you what would happen if that *god* returned—if he can even be truly called a god."

Heat lanced through Eva.

"Rahmagut left a dark legacy. You crave the education of an heir? I will show you what I know of him. After supper, I will run you through the history that's been archived through generations. He lusted after iridio like you now, but his ending was not a happy one."

Eva raked the rash on her forearm, indulging in the pain. She had him in the palm of her hand. She knew he longed to become the perfect father, to make up for years of separation and heartache. But how would he react once he discovered the truth? That she was the corrupted one—that Rahmagut wasn't safely tucked away beneath some godly seal anymore . . .

Don Samón pushed back his ash-gray hair, which was frizzed by the rain. He stared at the arriving night as crickets chirped around them. "This land was nearly destroyed by his ambition. I would never let that happen again."

Eva followed his gaze toward the blackened jungle. "You would give everything of yourself again to stop that? Let someone else worry."

"Who, Eva? Who will realign a world without balance?"

"Not you. Your new focus is us. Family, remember?"

He smiled in agreement and opened his arms. Eva only hesitated for a split second before entering his embrace. Her chest warmed. It felt right.

As he held her, Eva wondered if maybe she ought to confess outright. Offer it as her part in this new bond they wanted to cultivate. Something burned up her belly, like the indigestion of a particularly flavorful meal. Eva scratched the rash on her arm again, feeling something within her. She reminded herself that she could admit the truth to her father if she wanted to. She was in control, and her nonadmission was her choice.

But first, she wanted time to accept what it truly meant to share a body with the god of the Void.

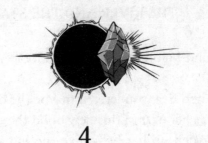

4

The Galio Rebel

Visiting Javier had become Eva's habit, and their secret. When the moon was high and the manse residents were safely tucked beneath their covers, Eva planned to do it again tonight.

She supped with Don Samón, Ludivina, and even Celeste, who had regained the strength to leave her room every now and again. After time together in his workshop, Don Samón had forgotten to tell her about Rahmagut's dark deeds. He instead reveled with his daughters over food and drinks. Eva snuck more than her fill of the toasty pork-stuffed arepas and bundled them in a napkin beneath the table, waiting. When the servers passed a platter of amapolas, she grabbed one and tucked it into the napkin as well. She listened in silence as Celeste retold a memory from her child-hood to the attentive Don Samón and Ludivina. All the while, Eva counted the moments until she could sneak out for another rendezvous.

Later, she placed the bundle in a small basket as her peace offer-ing for Javier. A gift that could ease her guilt.

Eva meant to petition for Javier's release. If she cared for him, and for justice, then she should admit his actions hadn't been with-out cause. But how could she broach the subject as Celeste still roamed the halls, her bandaged belly a reminder of what had hap-pened in Rahmagut's tomb? When it was Javier's sword that had impaled her? Eva was a cowardly wife for waiting so long to speak the truth: how her foolish attempt at controlling the tiniebla's darkness had been the catalyst of his mutation.

The rain let up later, after supper. The tide rose, filling the path to the prison fortress with warm shallows. But that didn't stop Eva from lifting her evening gown and wading to visit her husband.

Javier was no longer captive on the first floor. The rains made keeping him there inhumane. He had been switched to a higher cell, where he had a window with a view of the sea's horizon, a bed, a table for his plain bread meals, and a mounting pile of books that Eva would bring as contraband.

Eva ascended the winding stone staircase, her nose wriggling from the smell of brine, when she heard voices beyond the landing.

"I used to feel confused as to why you would want my death . . . as if the bond we had growing up didn't matter."

Apprehension filled Eva. From the low tone of admonishment, she knew it was Celeste. She froze, debating whether to continue her ascent.

Javier's response was too soft to hear.

Celeste rejected it with a scoff. "I don't need your excuses. I will never forgive you. Now I just pity you. Your actions were that of a desperate animal."

Eva decided she didn't care if Celeste learned of her secret visits. She couldn't listen idly to this any longer. She hurried up the stairs.

"You are not a person anymore," Celeste said, flinching as Javier slammed his hands against the cell bars in reply. He bared his teeth, drawing short of snarling like a caged beast.

Making her retreat, Celeste nearly bumped into Eva. And Eva hated herself when an apology left her lips.

Celeste's scowling eyes noticed Eva's basket. "Treats for your husband?" Her voice was heavy with condescension. "So you *do* care," she said before disappearing down the steps faster than Eva could retort, leaving Eva fuming.

The heady silence was shattered by the slamming of the iron bars. Eva was reminded that whatever she felt paled in comparison to how Javier must have felt swallowing Celeste's insults.

His eyes were inundated with black. "How sweet of you to visit me, wife."

Eva loathed craving his company and meeting his darkness instead. "Please, don't let Celeste get to you. She's understandably angry, but…you must snap out of it." She tried not to string the words like a command. The last time she did so it hadn't ended well.

He licked his bared canines in an animal motion, just like the tiniebla he housed. "When are you planning to get me out?" He slammed the bars again, imprinting salt and rust on his palms.

Eva ached to reassure him, but uncertainty reeled her back. The mark on her lip itched, reminding her how the tiniebla had forced his hand in the past.

As he refused to settle down, she moved closer. "Enough of this, Javier. If you don't change back, I will leave," she barked, and he paused.

He couldn't hurt her. Even though she could stop him now, the tiniebla wouldn't dare raise a hand to its lord and master.

With her basket of food in one hand and iron key in the other, Eva allowed herself into the cell. "I need Don Samón to trust me more first. I'm waiting for Celeste to be returned to her father," she explained.

"You both want to punish me." His voice sounded as though it were coated in char.

Eva searched his eyes, noting the way his darkness moved back and forth as if in a tug-of-war for control. "Who honestly believes this? The tiniebla or you? I'll leave if you let it control you. I can't speak for Celeste, but if I wanted to punish you, I wouldn't be here."

She hated threatening him. She wanted to stay, to sit beside him and watch him wolf down the arepas, which had grown cold, the pork congealed. She liked the quiet moments when she could sit in his company, seeing him find entertainment in her recounting her mostly uneventful days, because that was all he had: her.

"Even if it wasn't my idea, I'm starting to believe it, too," he replied in a guttural, superimposed voice. The veins around his eyes and temples had blackened, stark against the paleness of his skin. His face twisted. "I wouldn't be thought of as some kin slayer if it weren't for you."

She pursed her lips, grinding her teeth to abate the guilt. He was right.

His clenched fist trembled. He pounded the iron bars beside her and Eva's heart jolted. Ceiling dust landed on her lashes. Eva shoved the basket into his hands so she could wipe her eyes clean.

Was she a fool for placing herself close to him, acting as if he could find redemption? How long would these bars hold? And was Javier strong enough to stop the tiniebla version of himself from bringing death and terror to Isla Madre? It had already happened once, in Rahmagut's tomb.

"I'm losing my sanity here," he whispered.

Eva gently pushed him back, creating distance between them. His forearms were clammy. "Don't you want to eat?" she offered. "The cook made arepas with pernil."

The darkness retreated, revealing his tired, crimson eyes. He sat on the bed, which creaked as Eva joined his side.

"I'm sorry for taking so long. My reputation matters here. Don Samón—*my father*—" she emphasized, reminding herself that she needed to get used to it already, "he wants to do away with iridio and Rahmagut forever. If he sees you like this, he will not trust me. He will be devastated."

Javier looked away, his shoulders shaking. Then the corrupted voice said, "Pretending to be the good, proper daughter. How slick of you."

Eva clenched her jaw. She wasn't pretending. Don Samón was everything she'd dreamed of in a family.

She grew tired of this back-and-forth. "Face me."

Tiniebla Javier did as commanded.

"I want to speak to Javier. You will let him be."

His lip raised in a sneer. Then the darkness vanished.

Javier sucked in a breath. He squeezed his temple and pushed his hair behind his ears. "Thank you—for stopping it—for coming."

"I thought you could keep it under control," she said. "How

can I trust that you won't lose your mind to it, after I vouch for your release?"

His gaze was wounded. "There are good days and there are bad days."

Eva hated this. She knew she couldn't argue with him. There was a distance between them, and she found herself craving the touches they sometimes shared. His fleeting adoration.

Then she remembered that it was the tiniebla who worshipped her, not Javier.

The idea was foreign, an intrusion placed in her mind by the Void god.

"Can you control it?" she said.

"If that's what you need from me, I will fight it," he said. "If you promise to get me out. Here, alone, I have nothing. My mind decays."

"I will. I said I will."

She still wanted to save him, to own up to her mistakes. And besides, she liked Javier as a husband. Not just for his valco blood and Águila name, but because he recognized her as a worthy equal. She might have been his ticket to wealth once, in his scheme to have a future in proximity to Don Samón, but Eva had proved herself to be more than that. Javier knew this. His respect for her didn't just stem from the tiniebla's adoration for its god.

He unbundled the food basket and paused. "You brought me an amapola."

"Yes. You should eat more fruits and vegetables. It's not good to survive on just arepas, you know."

He lifted the fruit between them. "Are you trying to imply something?"

"What would I be implying?" Eva said, exasperated. "That you need to eat better? I mean, yes, I don't know where the instinct to care for you came from, but there you have it." This was a lie. She cared because she'd caused this.

He smiled. "You have no idea what this is? Don't you have them in Galeno?"

"Do you not want it?" She rolled her eyes and made to snatch it, but he moved it out of reach before taking a large bite. The fruit gushed with red juice.

"I love how innocent you are sometimes," he said, taking a second bite.

Her cheeks heated. "Rude! Explain."

"People say there's magic in the amapola. If you share the same fruit with someone, your fates will be tied forever."

A breath caught in her throat. "I had no idea. They—they have them everywhere here." With her heart deflating, Eva watched him lick his lips after he finished every last bit.

"Not that I wouldn't share one with you," he said, reading her, his smile roguish.

"That's what it sounds like."

"I'd just prefer to share one if it's something you truly mean to do. Not because you didn't know."

Eva stared at her hands to avoid his gaze. She squeezed her cheeks, embarrassed, and he laughed.

He devoured the arepas next. With his mouth full, he asked, "Next time, if it's not the jailer himself releasing me, can you at least bring me a solution of galio?"

"Why?"

"I was thinking—maybe I could try to revert some of the tiniebla turning with a healing spell."

Eva picked at her skirt, still blushing from the unshared amapola. "No."

He glowered. "Why?"

"Maior told me how she freed herself from Águila Manor."

"Oh?" He sounded genuinely curious.

"Reina gave her litio rings—to reassure her, I guess. Maior didn't know anything beyond a few galio spells, and she still managed to break herself out with the litio. I know you're capable of just as much ingenuity."

Javier laughed. "Reina's always been a fool."

A fool in love, Eva thought. What would it be like to feel that way? To be so enamored it evaporated her senses? She found a loose thread on her skirt and unraveled it.

She lay beside him, expecting him to follow her lead. When he didn't, she asked, "What's the matter? Did I thoroughly predict your plan to escape?"

He clicked his tongue. "That's not it—"

She giggled.

Annoyed, he said, "If you will listen—you can bring the galio solution and I can show you how I use it. Then you can take it back."

She giggled again, tugging him to lie down beside her. They stared at the cracks in the ceiling, as they did nearly every night.

After a while, his silence sparked her curiosity. "Maior learned galio because of her Penitent order, Las Hermanas de Piedra, who use geomancia and prayer to heal. But why did you? It's so . . . unlike you."

He chortled. "It's so unlike me to be useful and nurturing?"

"Precisely."

He stretched and yawned by her side. His hand rested over his belly, contentedly filled with arepas. "Growing up, I studied all geomancias. That's how I could teach you. Enrique expected it of me, as part of my education. Until I grew older, and he realized the threat I could become."

Eva frowned, trying to imagine a childhood in Águila Manor. The absence of the Serranos' Penitent way of life sounded refreshing. "What do you mean? A threat to him?"

"There was one time when I was returning from my swordsmanship lessons," he replied. "I was thirteen or fourteen, and I was aglow with litio and bismuto. I'd gotten into the habit of using them while training. I couldn't get enough of how powerful they made me feel. You know, the overconfidence of youth."

Eva turned to him, resting on her side to listen to his tale.

"Enrique and I got into an argument. I couldn't tell you what about. It doesn't matter, really. Those were tough years between us. All I remember is that he slapped me across the ear so hard it dizzied me." He grimaced from the memory.

Eva's hand twitched with the urge to comfort him.

"To this day, I can't be sure if he hit me so hard because he

thought I could endure it with the geomancia. Or because he
wanted to break me." He glanced at her as he said, "I had a ringing
in my ear for the rest of the day. And that's when I decided galio
would be my rebellion. He'd never be able to break me, because I'd
always patch myself up."

Eva looked away, painfully aware of her heated cheeks. "I'm
sorry. He sounds horrible. How could you live in a home like that?"

"It was all I knew, and I normalized it as the valco way. We're not
supposed to be fragile, like humans. We're creatures of strength."

"I . . . disagree. Violence is not the way of a valco. We are greater
than that." This she was learning from the most honorable valco
she'd ever met. The Liberator. *Her father.* How lucky she was, to
have the privilege to call him so. "*You* should believe yourself better than that," she said. "We are the last of valcos. We have the
power to change how the world remembers us from now on."

His gaze widened, taking her in so deeply, as if she were a gem
he was beholding for the first time. Eva was almost sure this scrutiny didn't come from the tiniebla's adoration. She couldn't shake
the feeling he was seeing her in a new light. Her chest fluttered
when he nodded and smiled.

MAIOR DE APARTADEROS

5

Deer Skull Piper

A chilly mountain breeze bit Maior's skin. Goose bumps rose along her arms. A sensation long forgotten, missing from her new life.

She hugged herself, and her finger snagged on the soft satin of her dress. The material was richer than anything she'd ever be able to afford. With dismay and a sinking heart, she realized she was once again in a body that was not her own.

The Páramo Mountains rose in layers of blue beyond the bedroom window. Doña Laurel Águila's bedroom. Familiar pieces of dark wood furniture surrounded her. The bedposts and dresser were engraved in floral imagery. The bookcases were bordered by rococo whorls. With a deep breath, Laurel settled into her routine, and Maior couldn't even protest. She witnessed it all, trapped behind the windows of Laurel's eyes in a memory, or whatever punishing nightmare this was.

Laurel draped a hand over her round belly. Her babe greeted her with a soft nudge from within. Laurel's chest fluttered as she anticipated meeting him, caressing his velvety soft cheeks, embracing him with warmth as she gazed into his eyes. Blue or red colored, it didn't matter; she would be content. Her heart swelled, filled with purpose. How her body so graciously carried their greatest source of joy.

Maior followed Laurel's motions as if she'd never departed Águila Manor. From a drawer Laurel withdrew a sapphire her mother had left as inheritance. It rested on her bosom as she latched the necklace around her neck. She settled in front of the vanity mirror to appraise it, but the woman reflected was blurred around the edges, abstract and faded. There was creamy pale skin, a black bob of hair, and freckles here and there, but Maior couldn't tell herself apart from Laurel. None of this made sense, just as dreams seldom did.

Pensive, Laurel reached into her drawer and ran her fingers along the smooth side of a blade gifted to her by her adoring husband. The hilt was solid gold, ornately sculpted into the shape of twirling orchids and laurels. "A dangerous knife for my capable wife," Enrique had said the day he'd gifted it. Laurel pressed her index finger against the knife's tip, pricking it, seeking pain. The body they shared winced. Satisfied, she went about her day, with one unmemorable moment blurring into the next.

All the while, Maior wished she had the power to scream herself into waking up. She had the inclination to kick and fight—anything to free herself from reliving Laurel's life. Maior was stuck in a loop where everything existed exactly as she'd witnessed it during her captivity in Águila Manor, yet nothing could be truly defined. The edges were faded, the details blurred, but the emotions stung so very poignantly.

Once afternoon fell, Laurel came out into the gardens of the manor in a flurry of blue skirts as Enrique appeared from the conifer paths lining the property. The witch, Doña Ursulina, tailed him.

Enrique greeted Laurel with a wet kiss, and disgust roiled through Maior. How she hated being trapped against his lips. She shivered as his big hand cupped Laurel's belly, feeling for their babe.

In a warning tone, Doña Ursulina said, "Perhaps it's better you wait inside, my Benevolent Lady, so that you do not see what we bring."

"Enrique and I do not keep secrets from each other," Laurel said like a lash.

"Then you will want to use your bismuto, mi amor," Enrique said, close to her ear. Like a songbird without voice trapped in a cage, Maior despaired.

Laurel summoned her bismuto and gasped at the half dozen tinieblas shadowing Doña Ursulina's every step. She cradled her belly protectively and said, "You brought tinieblas to our home?"

Doña Ursulina waited for her commander to reply.

"Controlling tinieblas with Void magic is forbidden, we know," Enrique said, shifting his eyes to the fir trees, ashamed but unrelenting. "But there are other ways it can be done."

"We want to... How shall I put this? We pioneered the use of iridio; thus we must know all that is within the realm of possibility," Doña Ursulina said, leading the way to the smithy. The tinieblas followed her like dolls under a puppeteer's thrall. Under her control, they lacked any interest in Laurel or Enrique.

Laurel almost hesitated to follow, but her curiosity won.

"If I am capable of doing this, it is only a matter of time before others can do the same, so I must get ahead of it." Doña Ursulina said the line she'd probably sold to the caudillo to get him to agree to such blasphemy. Laurel crossed herself. Later, she would pray for their souls to be forgiven. She knew her Pentimiento Virgin was merciful.

"Aren't you the greatest geomancer to ever live?" Laurel said. "You inspired fear in every curandero, bureaucrat, and commander during the war. The *king of Segol* knows your name. Your residence alone keeps this home safe from any bandit or monster who might be lured by our iridio. Of course you can do this."

Doña Ursulina raised an eyebrow as she stopped in the center of the smithy, where a table was cluttered with artifacts and notes from her underground study. "I know you never throw compliments without merit, so I am flattered," she said. "But I do not lie to myself with the idea that I am unique. I am who I am because I have dedicated countless years to the pursuit of the arcane. I was not born this way. The tinieblas are under my grip thanks to Void magic."

Laurel crossed herself again. Maior, too, feared the impertinent way Doña Ursulina had admitted to her own damnation.

"And yes, my soul pays a hefty fine. I wouldn't ask this from anyone else bearing the Águila standard. *I* understand the risks."

Then she offered Enrique a toothless smile while adding, "However, my studies have led me to an interesting artifact."

Doña Ursulina's fingers traced the crown of the deer skull atop the worktable. The skull was coated in black clay, with two medium-sized antlers branching outward. She lifted the skull to her lips and blew on a small opening in the clay. A deep whistle filled the smithy, just as shivers shot through Laurel's body. It stirred the tinieblas. They shook their heads, coming off the stupor Doña Ursulina had placed them in. They regarded Enrique, Laurel, and Doña Ursulina with crazed hunger in their eyes. Even in a dream, Maior wasn't immune to the prickle of fear running along her neck.

Doña Ursulina blew the flute a second time, reeling in the monsters to focus solely on her.

"This was how ancient practitioners of geomancia used to control tinieblas," Doña Ursulina said, handing it to Enrique. "It was how your valco ancestors regained some control over the chaos in their lives. The clay is mixed with a delicate spellwork of iridio. Some say Rahmagut himself taught his followers the technique, so that he could grow his influence, sharing his abilities with the generals who led his armies."

"Mi amor!" Laurel exclaimed to Enrique. "This is a sin."

"It will not be Void magic if I play an instrument," he replied, bringing his lips to the opening. Laurel could tell the black clay sealed every orifice of the skull, save for the blowing and whistling holes.

Enrique's song came out as broken, dissonant jabs of air. It was erratic and nonsensical. Laurel realized it didn't need to make sense. The tinieblas focused on Enrique, enthralled by the flute.

"You have them in the palm of your hand," Doña Ursulina said. "Tell them to withdraw."

Enrique waved a hand in dismissal. The tinieblas obeyed, backing away through the smithy doorway.

Laurel gripped Enrique's arm, digging her nails into his long-sleeved tunic. "That is enough, Enrique."

Her husband only chuckled.

Heat seared her cheeks at Enrique and Doña Ursulina's contempt for her fears. Deep in her bones, Laurel knew she was right to oppose this madness. "Just because you can do something doesn't mean you should," she hissed. "We are civilized. We set the example. What will your daughter think, if she sees you commanding demons?"

"That is Ursulina's role," Enrique said, shaking her grip off.

"Then let it be hers. You don't need to play piper to tinieblas. You are the protector of this realm. It is your duty to banish these monsters, not to be their master."

"*All right*," Enrique growled. "Destroy one another," he commanded. Immediately, the tinieblas pounced on each other. They fought until they died, vanishing into thin air.

Finally, as Enrique abandoned the flute on the worktable and Doña Ursulina left them both, Laurel felt like she could breathe soundly.

The afternoon flew into evening in the blink of an eye. Enrique, Celeste, and Laurel played memorization games by candlelight, giggling, fingers sticky from the sweet syrup of their quesillo dessert. Once, Maior would have noted Javier's absence as odd. But by now she knew he excused himself from their family time, scorned.

Later, Laurel surrendered to her impulses and snuck out to the smithy. The grounds were empty. The song of crickets masked her footsteps, and moonlight guided her path.

In the smithy, with trembling fingers, she reached for the clay-covered skull left abandoned on the worktable. The instrument's iridio spell stung to touch. Laurel wasn't foolish enough to grab it without first protecting herself with a prayer, litio, and bismuto.

Enrique would be annoyed, not angered, once Doña Ursulina conveyed the truth about Laurel's interference. Or maybe Laurel could simply deny she had had a hand in breaking it. Regardless, she knew Enrique would always believe his wife.

She lifted the skull to smash it against the floor but was stopped by approaching footsteps and a merry whistling.

Javier crossed the open doorway and saw her. Immediately, the whistling ended.

"Isn't it a little late for you to be prowling the grounds?" he said, his eyes narrowing.

Laurel lowered her arm. "I could be saying the same thing to you. Where have you been all evening?"

"I've been following a tiniebla."

The deer skull flute burned in Laurel's grip. She was sick of their dark magic. "You, too, are bringing tinieblas into my home?"

He winced. "What? No. I've been tracking it. I'm sure I spoke clearly, or are you slow of understanding? *Following it*. So I can slay it before it devours your spoiled little heart, especially as you're skulking about at night. What are you doing here, exactly? Shouldn't you be—I don't know—spreading your legs for Enrique?"

"You miserable little imp!" Laurel howled, storming toward him. "You will speak to me with respect!" Moonlight streamed through the door, showering them as Laurel slammed the deer skull flute down on him.

He grabbed her forearm, stopping the skull from clattering against his antlers. "Respect is earned," he said with gritted teeth.

How had things gotten to this point between them? Somehow, the lonely child who had shared a manor with Enrique had grown up to become this envious, viperous creature, coveting the happiness she'd built for their lives. But she'd had enough of overlooking his petulance.

"And you have lost every ounce of it from me—from all of us," Laurel said. "You call me spoiled, yet it is *you* whom Enrique spoiled rotten, letting you believe you could get away with your ungrateful attitude and filthy words."

Laurel shook her arm with all her strength, but it did nothing against his steellike grip. She wrangled and wrestled, and in the struggle the flute flung out of her hand. It shattered against the cobbles.

"And that burns you, doesn't it?" Javier said. "It burns you that I can do what I please and your words mean absolutely nothing to me. It burns you that by betrothing me to Celeste, Enrique effectively made me his heir. Once he's gone, there'll be no one to protect you, and I'll be free to command Celeste as I wish. She will be the one spreading her legs—"

Laurel slapped him hard with her other hand. In his shock, she broke free from his grip.

Suddenly a loud snarl ripped through the night.

A lizard-like monstrosity on hind legs entered the smithy, its talons clicking the cobbles and its long bull's tail swaying in ecstatic anticipation. The tiniebla paused, delighting in the enmity radiating between Laurel and Javier. Foaming with spittle, the tiniebla's wolflike snout snapped at Laurel, too fast for her to evade it.

Javier shoved Laurel away from the attack, his hand dangerously close to her belly. She crashed against the floor as his fist sent the tiniebla reeling in the opposite direction.

Hatred filled her. She saw red, from his blatant disregard for her constitution and the health of her babe. She didn't care about his intentions—whether he'd thrown her on purpose or accidentally overreached. He jeopardized the life she had worked so hard to create. The baby he'd never shown excitement about. Nor could she forgive his words, or the distressing scene they painted in her mind: the idea of him forcing himself on her precious Celeste. He was a threat to her children.

Laurel twisted her hands in an elaborate motion to conjure an advanced spell of litio that seized Javier, rooting him to the spot.

And it wasn't hard.

In her youth, she'd been just as ambitious as Enrique. One didn't charm the son of Feleva Águila without the cunning to sabotage, intimidate, and thoroughly best every other paramour prowling on the fringes. Laurel didn't earn Enrique's heart from good looks and luck alone. She'd survived a revolution as the daughter of a broke loyalist. She'd endured Feleva's disdain for not being the valco bride Feleva had wanted for the blood purity of her descendants. She'd cemented her reputation in Sadul Fuerte and earned a new moniker: the Benevolent Lady. Laurel accomplished all of it because she was educated, charming, *and* a capable geomancer.

She rose to her feet as Javier gagged, his face turning purple as she denied him the freedom to breathe. The hatred in his eyes turned to terror as the tiniebla skulked toward him. And Laurel smirked.

As long as Laurel lived, she would never allow a union between Javier and Celeste. It didn't matter if Enrique tried to sweeten her up with talk of what his mother wanted. Feleva's wishes had always been irrelevant to her. And the only way to change Enrique's mind was with real-life consequences. How it would destroy the family's good name if his wealth and reputation were inherited by a monster.

Laurel's hidden locket of iridio blazed as she conjured a deconstruction spell, breaking down the tiniebla into its most basic, shadowy essence.

Tears pooled in Javier's eyes as he stood there paralyzed. Laurel granted him a second or two to despair of his future before hurling the black plume of tiniebla into his mouth. A curse, which he had given her no other choice but to put on him.

A million whispers roused around them, called by Laurel's Void magic. They chattered and hemmed like an army of gleeful demons running in circles. Then came a man's laughter, smoky and confident. The approval of the god of the Void.

Laurel clenched her fists and prayed to protect herself, thinking about her Virgin.

The tiniebla's putrid smoke assaulted Javier's nostrils, ears, and mouth. His body gave a wild convulsion, fighting to reject it, but Laurel steadied her hold on him. For a second, she wondered if he was going to die.

Unfortunately, he endured.

Mouth agape in a silent scream, Javier was freed from Laurel's magical vise grip only when she willed it so. He fell to his knees, gasping for air. His palms shot up to his ears as if fending off a deafening noise.

"You threaten my children for the last time," Laurel said.

He grasped at her blue skirt. "What did you do?"

"You know very well. And if you remain in denial, time will show."

"*Undo this!*" He refused to let go, begging, so she yanked her skirt free.

"I suggest you let go of your fantasies of becoming heir to this house." She smiled.

Laurel didn't care about his reply or anguish. She left the smithy with Maior reeling from the truth, speechless.

The power of geomancia running through Laurel's arms electrified her. She was inebriated with it, realizing that despite the years of unuse and avoidance her capabilities continued to pulse within her as strongly as ever.

She ascended the stone steps to Enrique's chamber, drunk on her display of power and the simple solution to *the problem of Javier*. Enrique awoke, confused but tender, as she climbed her naked body over his. But in the darkness, his eyes read her.

Maior protested, voicelessly, as indeed Laurel spread her legs to straddle Enrique. She took his big, meaty hand and placed it around her neck, where he squeezed. "Ravage me," she ordered.

And Maior thrashed and cried, but it was all for nothing. She could scream until her vocal cords ruptured, but it wouldn't wake her from this nightmare. She had no control of the scene playing out before her. Of the pain and pleasure. Of his thickness tearing her open as Laurel arched her back and begged for more.

A hand grabbed her by the shoulder. Maior was yanked awake. She found herself sweating beneath her own sheets, in the humid evening of Tierra'e Sol. Her vision struggled to adjust, but she recognized the mass of curls towering over her.

"*Oh, Eva.*"

"You were yelling."

Tears welled in Maior's eyes. She twisted around, turning away from Eva, for she was too ashamed of her dream. Her tongue tasted sour. She felt violated. She dug her face into the pillow, shuddering.

Eva massaged Maior's neck. She gave her a gentle squeeze. "Another dream?"

Muffled by the pillow, Maior yelled, "I'm trapped in her horrible memories!"

Eva slipped under the covers. She embraced Maior from behind, shushing her. "It's all right. It's only a dream. She can't hurt you while you're awake."

"You don't understand," Maior said. "The memories make me sick—how would you feel if you were dreaming about sleeping with the caudillo?" She twisted around to face her friend.

Eva made an exaggerated gag, successfully coaxing a small smile from Maior.

This wasn't the first time they'd talked about it. Yet no amount of bemoaning could make Eva understand how unbearable the situation was becoming. Maior faced the ceiling, then pulled at her hair. "And this dream...was by far the worst..."

Eva gently pried Maior's hands away.

"What happened in it?" Eva squeezed Maior's hand. "You don't have to say, of course."

Maior looked away. She wasn't prepared to give breath to the words. To change the subject, she instead asked, "Where were you?" Eva smelled of salt and jungle humidity. "Were you with Javier?"

Eva's brief silence was admission enough.

Despite Maior's dislike of Javier, she couldn't help but pity him. After witnessing what the Águilas' family life was like, Maior's hatred had turned toward Laurel instead. "I saw how he was cursed," Maior said.

Eva sat up. Maior had her complete attention.

"Was it Celeste's mother?" Eva asked.

Maior also sat up to clear her head. Her hair shaded her eyes as she recounted, with as little detail as possible, the way Laurel had used Void magic to curse Javier. Laurel's hypocrisy was not lost on Maior. Laurel had admonished Doña Ursulina for her interest in Void magic, only to turn around and use it on Javier for her own machinations.

Eva draped a hand over her lips. "Oh no... *Javier.* I feel terrible for him."

Maior clicked her tongue. "Why? He's still a bastard. The tiniebla didn't force him to steal me away from my home."

As Eva brought her into a hug, Maior couldn't help but look past those horrible moments in Águila Manor, both from her dream and while she'd been prisoner. Someone else would have kidnapped her, if not for Javier. He wasn't the architect of Enrique's and Ursulina's plots. But she wasn't ready to let go of her apprehension. Especially as certain words or smells still triggered her memories of what had occurred at Rahmagut's tomb, and she remembered the moment when Javier had lunged for her with his sword raised, the murderous intent in his eyes, and Celeste's blood, which had stained the sharp metal of the blade as he swung at her.

"Then we would have never met," Eva said softly.

It was fruitless to linger on the what-ifs. Now Maior had a problem she needed to solve before she could close that chapter of her life forever. Pensive, she said, "Laurel used Void magic on Javier, and Doña Ursulina used Void magic to bind Laurel to me. What if there's something that works for both of us…a curse breaker?"

Eva pulled away. "Like they used the same spell or are related somehow?" She pursed her lips, shifting her gaze as she said, "You couldn't save that boy from the tiniebla attack."

"Juan Pablo?" Maior whispered. She wouldn't allow herself to forget his name. Her cheeks heated. "What does he have to do with this?"

"Yet Reina lived through it when she was attacked—at a high cost, sure, but *because of* Doña Ursulina. That's how strong and knowledgeable she was. Her spells were powerful."

Maior frowned as she said, "Don't you believe you can surpass her as geomancer? At the tomb, you looked like you could match her. And what of Javier? You visit him because you care about him, don't you?"

Eva winced. "Is it obvious?"

"Why else would you visit him every night?" Maior was happy for anything that brought Eva joy, but she simply couldn't understand how that could be him. "What do you do with him, anyway?"

Eva pinched Maior's cheeks. "It's nothing like that! We just talk. I never imagined you'd have such a filthy imagination."

Maior pulled away with a lopsided smile. "I don't. I just want to understand."

"Javier is my husband," Eva said in a serious tone. "I chose this path, and now I must accept where it goes. It's my fault he did what he did."

Maior paused, shocked. "What do you mean?"

Eva sighed and raked her fingers through her hair. "I was horrible: The moment he told me about his curse, I tried to control him—through the tiniebla. He trusted me, and I immediately took advantage of him." Eva worried her lower lip, and Maior gave her the time she needed. Finally Eva said, "I did it because I was so fed up with him, and the way he treated me—"

"So you admit he is a bastard," Maior muttered, drawing a small chuckle from Eva.

"I suppose—yes. But it doesn't excuse what I did."

Eva paused, as if wary of Maior's reaction.

And Maior's heart skipped a beat as she swallowed the truth with difficulty. She remembered the moment Javier's blade had almost impaled her. She'd survived only because Eva had arrived at the right moment. Maior could have just as easily died, like all the other damas.

Eva inched forward, grasping for Maior's hand. With a deep exhale, Maior accepted the gesture, and they squeezed each other's hands. She almost drilled Eva with more questions, but what would getting to the bottom of it change? Their friendship could not be tarnished. Besides Reina, it was the one sure thing Maior had.

So Maior said, "It was a mistake. You didn't know that would happen. What matters is that you fought for me, and for Reina."

Eva nodded feverishly. "And I'm determined to make it up to you. I'm going to help him, *and you*. If there's anyone who can do it, it's going to be me."

6

Magic in the Water

Reina rose with the dawn, invigorated. She sparred with Don Samón's soldiers in the yard. As she overreached and tripped, making a fool of herself in front of the seasoned warriors, she laughed everything off with them. They could think whatever they wanted, for Reina knew she was blessed.

The rest of her day slipped through her fingers in a blur. After sparring, she took it upon herself to scour the jungle for tracks or clues hinting that a tiniebla might be lurking in Isla Madre, and then planned to take a canoe to the other islands for a similar search in the following days. Even though she hadn't known Juan Pablo personally, his death still stung. And with Ches within her, the responsibility weighed on her shoulders now more than ever. By the time nightfall arrived, she was too spent to seek Maior—to properly apologize for the way she'd spoken to her in Isla Bendita.

The next day, before she headed for the docks, Don Samón cornered her in the foyer. He commanded her to accompany him in taking Celeste back to her father.

"We shall leave tomorrow after breaking fast. She says she's ready to go, and Enrique's restless," Don Samón said. "I'd like you to be there, for my peace of mind. Enrique and I are old friends, but he brought a large army with him. It seems unnecessary and calculated. I would be more comfortable if you were there."

She hesitated but then nodded solemnly. "I am your sword."

Reina grew jittery as she understood what needed to happen next. She'd avoided saying goodbye all this time, but she couldn't dodge Celeste forever.

She now wanted to see Maior, too. Reina needed to be fair and honest. Maior deserved to hear the news directly from her. Besides, this could be Maior's chance to return home to Apartaderos, if she'd changed her mind about staying in Tierra'e Sol.

Reina found Eva and Maior getting ready to leave Eva's room. Eva wore fishing pants and a cross-body knapsack, and Maior was unfastening her nurse's apron as they giggled about an inside joke Reina didn't understand.

She paused, jealousy blazing through her to see them so content in each other's company. Maior still slept in Eva's bed. And Reina was a fool for allowing it, especially after what Ches had said about Rahmagut possessing Eva. But how could she sway Maior away from Eva without telling her about Ches? How could she even prove Ches's existence to a Penitent as devout as Maior? It would only paint her as a jealous, controlling lover.

Maior spotted her first and beamed. "Reina! Are you joining us?" she asked. Eva also smiled in greeting.

They had no idea how much their closeness affected her.

"No. I just need to speak with you," Reina said from outside the door.

Maior dug out several amapolas from her apron and plopped them into her dress pocket. "Now? Eva and I are about to visit a . . . cenote?" she hesitated, her eyes begging for Eva's help.

"It's like an underground pool. I just don't want to go alone," Eva offered. "I wouldn't call myself a coward—"

"Only a chicken needs *me* to come with. What am I supposed to do? Cuddle a monster to death?" Maior said, her cheeky gaze turning to Reina, as if fishing for the small laugh that inevitably burst out of her. "Reina would probably be a better protector."

Eva pouted. "I tried going once! It's not that simple."

Reina observed Eva, and she couldn't sense anything out of the ordinary. Eva's demeanor was unchanged from when they'd met at the Plume. This was the same woman who'd fought Doña Ursulina alongside Reina, to save Maior's life. Their trust had taken a hit after Eva vouched for Javier, but with time, Reina had learned to let go of her grudge. Eva couldn't be held accountable for her despicable husband's actions forever.

Reina supposed their conversation could wait. "All right. I'll kill monsters for you. No need to cuddle anything."

"Only cuddle you, right?" Maior giggled.

Reina blushed, and Eva clamped a hand over her mouth, bursting with snickers. She led the way out, and Reina and Maior followed, their hands grazing as if aching to hold one another.

They crossed the courtyard path to the beach, and Reina's mirth faded when Eva scratched the crown of her head, exposing her antlers. The antlers hadn't been black when she first got to know Eva in Gegania. Somehow, without anyone else noticing, they had darkened after emerging from the tomb. The first sign had always been there. She'd just been too ignorant to notice it.

She uncomfortably considered what Ches had said about Eva. Was Eva keeping Rahmagut secret?

"So, why are we going to a cenote?" Reina asked.

"I've been doing a bit of research on geomancia lately," Eva said.

Reina's suspicion spiked. *"Why?"*

Eva faced her in bewilderment. "Because I like it, and I want to be good at it. You know this."

"Eva might be able to free me from Laurel," Maior added.

"We'll see. It's just a bit of research, all right?" Eva clarified, flustered. "I have some manuals on geomancia, and my father says I can find the reagent I need there. But I also don't know what to expect."

The answer was enough, for now.

Maior peeled one of her amapolas open as they entered the jungle's shade. "I brought us a snack, in case we get hungry," she said. Juice dribbled down her wrist, the red streaking her pale skin like blood. She lifted the fruit for Reina.

Reina winced.

The magic of a shared amapola was supposed to tie fates forever. Every child believed it. Every romantic believed it, as Reina had once upon a time. But Doña Laurel had died the very same day she'd shared one with her beloved caudillo. And Celeste had twisted a knife in Reina's heart the day they'd shared one before entering Rahmagut's tomb—the same day Celeste nearly lost her life. Reina refused to try again. She couldn't risk her future with Maior in such a way. She couldn't accept it.

Before Reina could even decline, Maior read the displeasure written across Reina's face. The light faded from her eyes, but she quickly said, "It's all right if you're not hungry."

Eva took one of the fruits without a second thought. The juices exploded at the corners of her lips as she took a sizable bite. Once again, Reina was stung by the barbs of jealousy.

They lost themselves in the jungle surrounding Isla Madre, on a canopied trail like the one that used to haunt Reina's dreams. They trekked beneath the leaf coverage of Tierra'e Sol's abundant greenery. This time, Eva led the way, guided by a stained and rumpled map. Monkeys hooted as their footsteps disrupted the otherwise solitary thicket. Parrots flapped overhead. Maior hummed the familiar tune of an aguinaldo, recalling the folklore of her chilly homeland, which sounded out of place in such a tropical setting. And it filled Reina with belly-twisting apprehension. Perhaps she might want to return home after all...

Soon enough, they reached a clearing. Eva lifted the map and pointed at a crooked sign propped next to a big crevasse in the ground. "We're here!" she announced, rushing to the wide opening and unlatching her cross-body knapsack clattering with empty bottles.

Plants crawled toward a limestone pit, concealing the last edges of stable ground before a steep drop into a glistening crystal-blue cenote. Vines dangled above the water, brushing the surface and highlighting the vast height of the fall.

Maior stopped near the edge and gasped. "It's gorgeous."

Eva leaned over as well. "My father was smart to make this place his home. Everything here is beautiful."

Reina squinted at Eva, as if staring had the power to reveal the god inside her. Could it be that Eva didn't know about Rahmagut?

"What's the matter?" Eva asked, catching Reina's glare. "Don't tell me you can't swim."

Reina scoffed. "We have canals in Segolita. Every street kid learns how to swim or drowns."

Eva hummed, impressed, and smirked. "Father said this cenote here is connected to other underground pools. There should be a cavern farther down that we can access." Inching forward, she pointed at the hooded cave opening accessible from the water.

"You're going in there?" Maior asked, alarmed.

Eva took a deep breath and faced the cliff. "I'm jumping. It's the only way down."

"Why?"

"Come on, Maior. Don't be a chicken."

"How will you get back up?" Reina asked.

Eva pointed at the braided vines hanging from one side of the pit. "He told me to bring bismuto, to make the climb up easier."

It didn't look horribly difficult, in Reina's opinion.

Eva began undressing to her smallclothes, then she relatched the knapsack across her chest. She had a wild look about her as she faced the elevation.

"Are you sure? It's too high," Maior muttered. Reina sensed panic in her voice.

"It's completely safe. Father said so." Eva glanced back at Reina, as if seeking reassurance, which Reina gave her with a nod. Eva grinned, then ran off the cliff to jump feet first for the pool.

A loud splash resonated throughout the canopy. A flock of parakeets took off. Anoles scuttled away, offended by the ruckus.

Maior leaned over the drop as Eva emerged from the water with a hoot. "You must come in! It's divine!"

Indeed, Eva had made the plunge look enticing. Reina shook off her linen shirt, too, relying on her wraps to maintain her modesty. "I'm going in," she announced.

Maior flushed, backing away. Reina couldn't help smiling. "You won't drown. I'll carry you." Nothing would ever harm Maior, not if Reina had a say in it.

"I know how to swim," Maior replied. "Eva has been teaching me, at the beach."

Reina clenched her jaw. She should have done that. But part of her appreciated that Maior also had Eva to rely on. As much as Reina wanted to, she simply couldn't be everything for Maior.

Maior leaned over for a better look and her face turned redder as Eva called her name, encouraging her to jump. As she moved away, her cheeks caught a beam of sunlight filtering through the canopy. Near her collarbone, her skin was beginning to peel once again from pink sunburns—a consequence of life in the islands. But she was beautiful, nonetheless. Every time Reina looked at her, she discovered something new to admire.

Reina extended a hand. "Let's jump together."

Maior's eyes revealed the hurt she still wielded from the rejected amapola.

Reina regretted it. But she also couldn't shake the fear of making pledges with magic neither of them understood. Maior didn't know everything about her—not really. Reina wore a façade of being strong and capable when in reality she was all holes and fissures on the inside, filled only thanks to Ches's existence within her. And how would Maior see her if she ever learned this truth? Would they even get that far?

Maior's hand was hot as their fingers intertwined. Reina's heart fluttered, and she indulged in a smile that Maior matched.

She felt like a fool for getting lost in Maior's eyes. She never wanted to look away.

Hand in hand, they sprinted for the drop.

Reina's belly rose to her throat as they plummeted. She was swept by a thrill. Water rushed through her hair, undoing her braid as their feet broke the water. A coolness engulfed her body. The cenote tasted sweet. She plunged deep, becoming completely submerged with Maior beside her. And it felt like a reset. As she kicked upward and broke the surface with a grateful lug of air, she was cleansed of all worries. Nothing but Maior's eyes mattered as the island sun filtered through the trees, creating diamonds over the water.

Reina dove for a glimpse underwater, drawn by the clams glittering on the pool's floor. How they would make pretty necklaces. A school of coral-pink fish glided around her legs. As she resurfaced, a small turtle dodged them. Eva tried grabbing it but laughed when it swam away, too quick for her.

Maior kicked like a puppy to stay afloat. But as Reina and Eva were adept swimmers, they didn't have to worry about the pool's depths.

Eva smugly demanded thanks for discovering the spot, then guided them to the cave opening. There, a small pocket of air allowed them to safely paddle through the tunnel toward another section of the cenote, where the leaves overhead were so dense only a few rays of light spilled through.

"Father said it'll be in the third cave. That's where I want to go," Eva said.

A tall, mossy boulder served as a natural bank to the water, where they rested for a few moments before carrying on. Then they swam through a second tunnel with a slimmer air pocket. Reina's chest fluttered in anticipation as the light behind them grew dimmer the deeper they went.

Darkness engulfed them in moments. Maior's grip on Reina's hand tightened. "I won't let you go," Reina whispered close to her.

"Eva?" Reina called, noticing how her voice echoed against the low tunnel ceiling. If the water rose, they would have no choice but to dive to get out. Reina could manage it, but she wasn't sure about Maior. Then there was the matter of swimming in the dark...

She took a deep breath, reminding herself of Ches's presence within her. This couldn't be a trap. Either way, his strength would keep her safe.

"Just a little farther," Eva said. Her voice echoed more widely this time, as if the tunnel had opened to the third cave.

"It would help if you told us what—" Reina said, but the words melted in her mouth as she glanced at her hand, which was now aglow with a blue shimmer.

Eva laughed. She kicked and splashed the water between them.

A million glittering dots came alive with their movements, fading after a few seconds.

Giggles bubbled out of Maior as she, too, splashed the water. "It's like I'm casting iridio!"

"What is this?" Reina asked into the darkness.

Eva twirled her hands like a dancer, igniting more light. "These cenote pits exist all over the island, but this one is the most accessible. The water glows because this cave, where the sunlight doesn't reach, is home to miniature bugs that produce light when they're moved, like this."

"*Bugs?*" Maior exclaimed shrilly. She flapped on the water, as if trying to get away, but the agitation surrounded her in even more glimmering blue.

"You can't escape them." Eva laughed. "Not here. The bugs are all over the water, and they're too tiny to be seen. The manual in Don Samón's study calls them *plankton*."

Eva added, "Thanks for accompanying me. I don't think I'd have the nerve to reach this place on my own, with how dark it is."

Reina regretted doubting her. "It's no problem," she said, even though she probably wouldn't be able to do anything if a tiniebla attacked them while they were half naked in the water.

She swam farther into the cave and found that the shimmering brightened the deeper she went. It produced enough light that she could spot Maior's and Eva's silhouettes. She scanned the empty cave, seeing as if she'd used a spell of bismuto on herself, but it was thanks to Ches.

"This makes me think of how in the holy book, the Virgin emerged from gold-glimmering waters," Maior said.

Eva and Reina laughed at her. "I think this is a bit different," Eva said. "This is real."

"You don't know the Virgin isn't real. You believe Rahmagut and Ches are, don't you? So what makes those gods more real than mine?"

Reina looked away. How would she ever tell Maior about Ches? And how would Maior swallow this truth, after being taught to believe the Virgin was the one true goddess?

She said nothing. It was Eva who broke the silence. "*Well.* I wanted to come here and collect the water to test out some new solutions for geomancia." Her bottles clattered as she struggled to open her soaked knapsack in the darkness. With Maior's help, she uncapped the first one.

"So that's why you're always in that study?" Maior asked cheekily. "I thought you were just making up lost time with the Liberator."

Eva chuckled. "I need to do that, too. Anyway, I found some manuals on ways of mixing natural substances with geomancia solutions to guide or alter the effect of a cast spell."

"You're harvesting light," Reina said at once.

"Nice! And here I thought you were all brawn."

Reina rolled her eyes, not that Eva could see it.

Maior laughed. "Definitely lots of muscle."

Reina was glad the darkness shrouded her burning-hot face. She suddenly wished she could have more of Maior's validation.

"Father said he will teach me how to mix some solutions, so I've been collecting different things lately."

"I've seen Dr. Baltasar put spiderwebs in galio," Maior noted. "He said you have to think of it like a rope, guiding the bone to realign itself. It makes for quick mending work."

"Exactly," Eva said as she filled her bottles one by one. "Light-emitting plankton, spiderwebs, grass fibers...I feel like there are so many possibilities and so many things waiting to be discovered."

"And you'll be the one to do it?" Maior's voice echoed in the darkness. Reina approached her in case she was growing tired of her dog-paddling.

"I want to discover it all."

Once Eva's five bottles were filled with water, they swam back through the tunnel.

Reina's fingers and toes had shriveled like prunes, so she climbed on the boulder of the middle chamber for a break. Maior followed.

"You know what? Why don't you stay here awhile? Clear your minds and all, after what happened with Juan Pablo. I'll go on ahead." Eva didn't wait for an objection before swimming away.

Not that Reina had any. She watched Eva go, wondering if she had planned to give them this privacy all along.

Reina lay down, allowing her muscles to relax over the boulder while she listened to the distant, soft drips of water trickling along the crevice's limestone walls. Maior lay beside her, the waves of their black hair overlapping.

Reina knew the quickening of her heart while they were alone was silly. She could slay tinieblas and whistlers with a single strike. The granter of light shared her body. Yet, now faced with the tough conversations she needed to have with Maior, she cowered.

"I like your hair when it's down. Why don't you do it more often?" Maior said.

"I don't know what to do with it. And it gets in the way." Maior said nothing, and Reina figured she ought to clarify. "I was raised by my father, and he never knew what to do with my hair besides keeping it braided." Reina smiled as the memories returned. "He was a good father, but he was terrible at doing hair."

"Let me style it one day. We can put flowers in it."

They burst into laughter, imagining the absurdity.

Maior moved closer, and Reina faced her. Water clung to Maior's long lashes, forming droplets like gemstones. Reina decided this was the moment to apologize—to open up her heart.

"I'm sorry for yelling at you in Isla Bendita," Reina said as a pounding started in her chest. "For saying you weren't enough. I panicked and I acted like a complete fool."

"But you were right. I wasn't enough. I couldn't save him." Maior frowned.

Reina tried reaching for Maior's hand, but she pulled away. "A tiniebla can cut you or break your bones, but its bite is what corrupts the heart. It's what they're after, since they don't have one." She sighed. "He was bitten. You wouldn't have been able to save him. I was rash and inconsiderate to put that on you."

"We are supposed to save lives. How can you say that? Ursulina saved you from your tiniebla attack."

Reina's cheeks blazed. She sat up, assaulted by the memories of terrible pain in her chest, like mountains colliding. Doña Ursulina's method of saving her had been brutal. After the procedure, Reina woke up a new woman. Saved, but forever changed.

Maior also sat up. Her face softened.

"You are not Doña Ursulina, and you do not want to be," Reina said.

Maior shrugged, eyes downcast. "I've never had anyone die under my care. We had to stop his heart."

Reina slowly brought Maior closer, draping her arms around her in an embrace. She gave her plenty of time to move away if this was not what she wanted. But Maior squeezed her so tightly. Pressed against Reina's chest, she said, "And I wish I hadn't gone through that alone. I looked for you afterward. Where did you go?"

Reina knew Maior could feel her stiffening. She wasn't ready to share her truth, but she also hadn't thought of an excuse. So she said the first foolish words that crossed her mind, regretting them immediately: "I figured you would want Eva there, not me."

"What?"

They pulled away.

Jealousy speared Reina. "Every night, you sleep in her bed."

Maior's lack of a reply dragged on so painfully, Reina had to meet her eyes. Was there something else going on between them? Was Reina a fool for assuming they were just friends?

"I don't want to be alone at night," Maior muttered.

Reina winced. "But you choose *her.*" Her chest constricted as the whispers of her iridio heart resurfaced. They chanted gleefully as she remembered how Celeste had told her she'd never be good enough. She couldn't have possibly fallen into the same situation again.

Maior noticed Reina's wounded face and reached forward to squeeze her forearm. "No—Reina." Maior covered her face with her hands. "I wish I was with you, but I'm scared and ashamed—"

Reina's voice broke. "Why?"

"I keep dreaming of Laurel."

"Doña Laurel?"

"Every time I fall asleep, I'm reminded she's still inside me—that my body isn't *just* mine anymore. I wake up feeling invaded. I don't want it to affect the way I feel about you. I just found it easier to deal with it with Eva."

Reina realized she'd been clenching her jaw. She took a deep breath to clear the heat blazing through her veins. "You can confide in me. You know that, right? I *want* you to."

Maior covered her face again. "I feel awful every night with Laurel. She suffocates me."

"How could she suffocate you?" Reina asked. Every happy moment in Águila Manor had been because of Doña Laurel. "She saved your life several times." Reina also found it curious that despite the enhanced way she now experienced the world, she still couldn't see Laurel's ghost, as valcos could.

Maior scratched the scars on her arm, where Doña Ursulina had bound her to Laurel's soul. "I wish I could be cleansed."

"That's nonsense. You're not *dirty*."

Maior went silent in her frustration.

Reina hated seeing Maior like this. Slowly, she moved closer and placed a hand on Maior's lower back. When Maior didn't flinch, Reina snaked her arms around Maior's middle to hug her from behind. She rested her chin on Maior's shoulder.

"We will find a solution in due time," Reina said. It felt useless, but it was all she had.

Maior hugged Reina's arms, leaning back into the embrace.

With the water drying off Reina's skin, she was left cold and shivering, yearning for Maior's warmth. She wished she had the courage to squeeze her. She craved it. But she feared Maior's repulsion upon feeling the raggedness of the device in her chest. If Maior indeed was going to return to Apartaderos, maybe it was best that Reina be cautious. Maybe it was for the best to enjoy the simplicity of what they had, without complications.

So she mustered the courage to address what she needed to from the very beginning: "Celeste is being returned to Don Enrique tomorrow morning." In her arms, Maior stiffened.

They pulled away. Reina picked at her calluses. "I wanted to let you know in case you want to return home. This—this could be your last chance."

"You want me to leave?" Maior said.

"*No*—I want you to have the choice. It's up to you this time."

Reina's cheeks heated. "You ended up here due to less-than-ideal circumstances and you deserve to choose—"

"And I told you: I choose Tierra'e Sol." Maior straightened.

Reina let go of the breath lodged in her throat. She smiled.

"I want to stay. Yes, it's definitely been an adjustment. It's beautiful here, but you can't run away from the sun. I miss the morning breeze of the mountains and eating smoked goat cheese, *and almojábanas*. I hate not being able to find some dark corner where I can just pray," Maior said, in good spirits.

They laughed.

But Maior's mirth didn't last. "I wasn't sure at first. Every time I think about Celeste, and you, I feel like such a fool for staying. Sometimes, when you're distant, I can't help comparing myself."

How could Reina admit that her trepidation stemmed from being afraid? She couldn't let her desperation for companionship ruin this fragile thing they had.

"I have a lot on my mind, after all that happened," Reina said, hoping to skirt the issue. "And with Celeste still on the island, it's just strange. I don't want you to be someone I use to get over her."

Maior smiled tenderly, like Reina's answer was good enough.

"I'm still learning, you know? This is new to me," Reina said.

Maior nodded.

"Am I also your first?" Reina asked.

"I didn't have many choices in Apartaderos. It's a very small town. Straying from the norm was frowned upon."

"Straying from Pentimiento?" Reina asked, with a smugly arched brow.

"I know how you feel about it. But I grew up orphaned, Reina. I had Las Hermanas de Piedra and my chapel. That's it."

"I know what that's like," Reina said, turning away. "But your Virgin didn't give *me* any comfort."

"You never embraced Her! When I was lonely and lost, the Virgin helped me."

Reina grew restless from the accusation. There was a tremor in her chest, but whether from her transplanted heart or from Ches, Reina couldn't be sure. What she did know, though, was that

Maior's Virgin probably disapproved of both. She knew she had to keep the truth about Ches to herself.

"You say that, yet everyone used your religion as a reason to exclude me. I don't think you'll ever understand."

"Try me."

Reina shook her head. "When the world is built for you, you don't have to worry about changing yourself to fit within it. Your existence is correct by default. It wasn't hard for you to embrace Her."

Maior's nostrils flared. "You're making a lot of assumptions about me."

Reina picked at the rock's moss. "You're right. I'm sorry. But I want you to see that the things I believe in or don't are for a reason." It was difficult to admit. She hated looking back at the person she used to be, at the choices she made, and seeing a desperate, broken girl. "When I was young and fed up with the way the other kids treated me, I used to ask my father: Why did you have me with Beatriz? I resented him because I was born nozariel. And that is such a sad thing for a child to feel. But it wasn't my fault. Everyone around me treated me like I was lesser than, and at some point... I believed it, too."

Maior's hands pried Reina's away from the moss. She lifted Reina's knuckles to her lips and kissed them. "Then it's our responsibility to make a future where no other child feels that way."

Reina's stomach fluttered. She was just a woman trying to find her place in a broken world—though, with Ches's blessing, maybe this would be her job. "What are we supposed to do? We are just..." She trailed off, then smirked as she added meaningfully, "Two women."

"That we are." Maior smiled and inched closer. "But being here on this island with you, Eva, the Liberator, and his people... I feel like a new person. Empowered. Don't you?"

Reina licked her lips, and the motion drew Maior's gaze. The attention felt good. Reina remembered to nod.

"I like this new me," Maior added. "And I like that I like you."

Reina was dizzy on the words. "I like you, too." She paused, hoping Maior could see the sincerity in her eyes. "I will do better. I promise."

They drew closer. Reina's heart was afloat when Maior kissed her, more intensely than ever before. And Reina shivered, from the drying water and from Maior's blazing touch. She craved peeling the layers of their wet smallclothes—to feel Maior's bared skin— but never mustered the courage to do it.

Sunlight passed over them, and darkness began creeping into the cenote, so they decided to head back. Reina dove to the pool floor and harvested a shiny clam, secretly pocketing it before they climbed the vines and dressed.

Later, once she had changed for supper and Don Samón's cuatro-playing melody flitted through the rooms of the manse, Reina carved the shape of the Virgin on the clam's mother-of-pearl. Dexterous and precise with a knife, she drilled a hole above the Virgin's head and ran a thin twine through it.

Maior beamed the moment Reina gifted her the necklace as an apology for all her presumptions. She tied it around Maior's neck, letting the Virgin rest above her bosom. And, in return, Maior plucked a hibiscus from the Liberator's garden and stuck it in Reina's hair.

7

A Roomful of Antlers

Reina stepped into the manicured gardens outside the manse and found Celeste already awaiting departure. A blue sky carried a breeze that swayed Celeste's airy dress. A party of servants loaded all the treasures Don Samón meant to gift Enrique onto a cart. The goods were supposed to be a gesture of goodwill and farewell, but they were undeserved, in Reina's opinion. With all his wealth, Enrique would merely shove the crates into one of his many vaults, forevermore fated to gather dust instead of benefiting anybody.

"I'm happy you had the nerve to see me off," Celeste said as Reina helped her climb onto the cart.

"Don't be unfair. No one is happy about this." This was a lie, but Celeste didn't need the truth now.

Their moment to speak passed when Don Samón joined them. He climbed into the cart with them and gave the order to depart. Some small talk was exchanged between Celeste and Don Samón while a donkey lugged them through the path to the docks, where a galleon was ready and waiting.

Upon arriving, Reina glanced about. "Where is Javier? Won't he be given back to his brother?"

Don Samón steeled himself. "Javier's crime is not without nuance. I do not intend to turn him over today."

Reina had to hide a flash of anger from showing on her face.

Javier's monthlong imprisonment wasn't enough. Celeste had nearly died because of him. Maior, too. If anyone had the capability to dole out a meaningful punishment, it was his brother.

The galleon took off, embraced by the breezes of Tierra'e Sol. Reina circled the deck until she found Celeste standing against the railing, her gaze fixed on the dolphins swimming alongside the ship. Celeste had a bulge in her midsection from the thick layering of bandages protecting her healing wound. Her bangs were buffeted this way and that, carried by the riotous wind.

"I wouldn't have minded staying a bit longer," Celeste said the moment she noticed Reina's approach. "But I can't stand how quickly you've moved on. Excellent job there."

Reina's underarms grew hot. "You really have no other instinct but to inflict pain?"

"I can't help if my words reflect how I feel. *I* am honest," Celeste said in a low breath, as if implying Reina was not.

"I just want the best for you."

Celeste snorted. "Leaving is what's best for me?"

"We must put Doña Ursulina and Rahmagut's legend behind us. Águila Manor is your home."

"How easily you wash your hands."

This time, Reina let her anger show. "You know my grandmother planned everything. I don't have to repeat it every time. Or are you simply making a sport out of making me look like a fool?"

Celeste smirked bitterly. "Yes—maybe my instinct *is* to see you hurt a bit. You know I was raised under the principle of an eye for an eye. Don't you remember the story of the rancher and the bounty hunter? Last I checked, I was the one with a hole through my belly."

Reina squeezed the bridge of her nose and swallowed the sourness. She understood Celeste's frustration, but the one thing Celeste wanted to make it all up—Reina's unwavering loyalty—she couldn't grant.

Celeste snaked her arm into Reina's elbow. The gesture spoke of friendship and of reconciliation, and Reina surrendered to the ache tugging her ribs apart even more.

"What can I do to get you to come with me?" Celeste asked

softly. "Águila Manor is going to be so lonely. I won't even have Doña Ursulina to loathe."

Reina chilled. Indeed, she had wondered about Celeste's life. The manor was already a cold place without Doña Laurel.

"Are you going to make me get on my knees and beg?"

"No, Celeste."

Celeste shrugged. "If you can give me up this easily, maybe your affections weren't as deep as you said they were."

"I already explained myself. I'm tired of having to fight so much for you."

In that moment, Reina thought of Maior, and of how easy things were with her.

"You wouldn't be fighting."

"Your father will not allow me back. Please, Celeste. Remember how he banished me with a spell of iridio?" Reina grabbed her shirt with a fist. Beneath were the ragged edges of the contraption keeping her alive. "He only meant for me to return with his wife brought back to life."

Celeste laughed, and Reina wanted to shove her.

"But we'd be returning together. You've fulfilled the requirements mi papá imposed on you. Stop relying on worthless excuses." Celeste's hand reached forward, and Reina was overtaken by the instinct to flinch. But she remained stoic as Celeste tucked loose hairs behind her ear.

"We are cousins," Reina reminded her. Reina had revealed this to her days ago, on a sunny morning not unlike this one, but Celeste had swallowed the truth with a straight face and indifference.

"All the more reason to stick together as family." Celeste's eyelids lowered as she cupped Reina's cheek. "But to me, that wouldn't change anything."

Celeste's eyes held a treacherous spark of hope. Reina drowned in their brightness, wondering if perhaps her future could be just as bright. Perhaps her decision, made during a moment of darkness, didn't have to be final. Here was Celeste, inviting her back. Reina draped Celeste's hand in hers and leaned her cheek into the caress.

But...all this time, she'd nurtured some grand idea of what her relationship with Celeste would look like if realized, only to now see that it was a fiction. She'd deified her, turned her into something else. But the real Celeste lacked the ability to heal Reina's wounds, or to see her as an equal.

Reina knew she would always live in Celeste's shadow. She would be only a handkerchief for Celeste's woes. She would be following the footsteps of her grandmother, letting the Águilas' fame veil every milestone and accomplishment, never daring to reach for something beyond them. She remembered Doña Ursulina's bitterness and how Juan Vicente had run away from it. In her final words, Doña Ursulina had made it clear how she'd wasted so many years in the Águilas' shadow, and her regret for it. There was no guarantee Reina could break free of their generational marks. And even now, while begging for her, Celeste didn't hide the truth of their imbalance. Reina had a place in Águila Manor for as long as Celeste allowed it.

She was the last of the Duvianos, but that didn't mean she was fated to suffer through her family's pain.

No, what Reina wanted was a fresh start. She wanted a home that couldn't be wrenched from her hands. She wanted a family she could nurture without hurt, who couldn't be ripped away from her. A bond between equals.

Tierra'e Sol offered her that. And Celeste's words were lies through smiling lips. Being cousins did change everything.

Reina closed her eyes, her smile softening.

Finally, she opened her eyes and found Celeste even closer, her bangs swaying in the refreshing salty breeze. Reina's eyes stung when she said, "I didn't think of you as a cousin."

"I know," Celeste purred.

Hollers filled the air as the galleon finally settled by the mainland docks. Sailors rushed to anchor the ship. The deck shook beneath their feet. Reina used the instability to move Celeste's hand away and take her whole body in an embrace. Celeste tensed, startled, but melted into Reina. Celeste's silky hair tickled Reina's nose. The deck bustled around them, with attendants hauling the crates and gifted chests, disembarking. Seagulls cawed overhead, disgruntled at being displaced by the arrivals. The world was chaos but all Reina could hear were the thunderous thrums of her heart as words waited on the tip of her tongue.

She steeled herself and said them: "You called me a duskling. You led me on. You broke my heart. And you never once apologized."

Celeste shoved herself away, her face red. "What?"

"You still believe you're right to treat me this way." Reina shook her head. "I loved you. You know this. But it is best that we part ways. Goodbye, Celeste."

Celeste's face hardened. Reina was sure she would spew a barrage of insults. But in the end, Celeste accepted it with grace.

"Fine." She turned away, disembarking first.

A man wearing a blue jacket with padded shoulders greeted them on the docks. He pushed up his slim spectacles, and Reina immediately recognized him. He was a mining accountant, a man of Segolean breeding who helped Enrique manage his fortune. Was he here as Doña Ursulina's replacement?

He exchanged a few pleasantries with Don Samón, glancing inquisitively at Celeste. He guided them through the cobbled roads of Carao, a fishing village named after the pink-flowering fruit trees that grew along its streets. People in military jackets with the Águila insignia littered the corners and alleyways of the village. They watched with bored expressions, temples dripping sweat, and hands lazily resting on the hilts of their swords. Apprehension filled Reina as she counted every soldier in a tally. They were easily outnumbered. What was Don Samón doing, entering the mainland without proper backup against the caudillo of Sadul Fuerte?

Reina glanced at Don Samón leading the way, but he seemed unbothered. Then she noticed all the eyes observing them. Townspeople stood on balconies. Waving grandmothers who sat in rickety rattan rocking chairs pointed at their Liberator with a smile. Children followed them in bright-eyed adoration.

Don Samón felt safe because the community made him safe.

Once, he'd explained to Reina how Carao was technically part of Tierra'e Sol because it touched the Cow Sea, and thus he was its protector. To them, Don Samón was like a caudillo, not only a symbol of the revolution but also their reassurance of protection. An attack against him was an attack against them. Maybe he was right not to feel threatened.

Finally, they arrived at a large town square bordered by sea grape bushes, where a copper statue of the Liberator on a horse stood at the center. It was a surreal sight, to see him immortalized while he walked right beside her. "That's where the local priest places tiniebla repellents," Don Samón told Reina, pointing at the statue. "But I see the ward is weak—about to run out." As only valcos could see geomancia with the naked eye, Reina trusted his word. "We'll need more iridio from Enrique to replenish all our wards," he added.

La Cantimplora, the inn across the square, was their destination. They entered the sea blue–painted brick building and followed the accountant through shadowed halls smelling of pork and salt water, until emerging into an inner courtyard.

A tall man with sturdy antlers awaited with his back to the door. He sat at one of the many tables, finishing an abundant breakfast. At the center of his table was a curious artifact, lying haphazardly and so out of place it piqued Reina's interest. Pieces of fragmented black clay surrounded a deer skull with the antlers still attached. There were also pliers, brushes, and an assortment of potion vials.

One of his subordinates said his name, and he turned, confidently leaving his seat. The caudillo of Sadul Fuerte rose to meet them with an authority that stilled the air. His attire was casual: a white linen shirt that was tight around large biceps, and light brown pants, hemmed above the ankle.

Enrique's dead-blood valco gaze surfed Reina and Don Samón before settling on Celeste.

"*Papi*," Celeste said. She sounded younger, playing the act of an adoring daughter. She crossed the courtyard and fit into the embrace of his much bigger frame, squeezing with relief.

Enrique rested his chin on her crown, his expression hardening. "You're unharmed," he muttered, though the words were loud enough for the whole courtyard.

"If I could help it, she would never be in harm's way," Don Samón said.

"And yet she nearly died," Enrique countered, pulling himself from Celeste. "Where is Javier?" he said.

A pause hung between the two valcos. "He is in my custody."

Enrique moved Celeste aside, behind him. "He should be in mine."

"Enrique—as I said in our letters, we will not be discussing Javier's fate at this time."

The caudillo's blood-red eyes moved to Reina. "I see you are still in one piece. Unlike your grandmother."

Reina was too busy reeling her trembling heart in to formulate a reply. As valco, he could see the iridio magic keeping Reina alive, and any display of fear or weakness would only fuel his disdain.

"You slaughtered your own blood," he added. "I ought to be asking you if you are in cahoots with the rat that is my brother."

"I would never hurt Celeste," Reina said automatically. If only he knew how she had almost snuffed the life out of Javier.

Enrique scoffed.

"Would *you*?" Reina asked as blood rushed to her ears, her pulse nearly deafening. "We almost sacrificed the nine damas. Celeste is one, so she had to die. Did you know that?"

"Reina," Don Samón warned as Enrique's lips drew back in a sneer. "We're not here to discuss that."

"What Ursulina made me believe is none of your concern. I don't have to justify anything to the likes of you." The caudillo turned to the Liberator and said, "The insolence of this duskling is astounding. This is the company you keep now?"

Don Samón shook his head. "We don't speak that way here."

Enrique laughed. "You're trying to control how I speak now? With what authority?"

"I am merely asking for some decency from you. As caudillo, you set the example."

Enrique took a step forward, his condescending amusement evident.

Don Samón remained stoic, unfazed. "And Reina is free to choose who she works for. She is not yours anymore—"

"Not that I would want her."

Reina held her breath as her gaze met Celeste's, seeing nothing but ice worthy of the peaks she hailed from. She clenched her jaw, forcing herself to believe the words hadn't stung.

"I never wanted her. She was Ursulina's pet. You can keep her," Enrique replied.

Don Samón didn't have an answer, and Reina was grateful. But Celeste's reunion with her father was finished, and their time at the inn was dangerously short.

Reina glanced about her, seeing that Enrique's soldiers now surrounded the doorways and windows. If the caudillo had a sudden change of mind, or a hunger for bloodshed, he could end their lives with a mere command. Reina placed a hand on the hilt of her blade. For the listening presence of Ches within her, she asked, *You wouldn't abandon me now, would you?*

He gave her no answer. But he was a god. He didn't owe her anything.

The Liberator gestured at the chests under the courtyard's doorway. "I brought you some gifts to carry you through your journey. Amapolas, for you to keep or sell once you arrive at the Páramo."

Enrique shrugged. "They'll be spoiled by the time we get back."

Reina didn't miss Celeste's smirk. "We may return sooner than you expect, Papi," Celeste said, and it sounded like she finally intended to share with him the powers of Gegania. Doña Laurel's family home, which created portals across the land.

Don Samón was oblivious to her meaning, so he said, "Let your men have them, then."

A darkness sparked in Enrique's eyes. It was fleeting, like the flicker of a lonesome firefly in a dark jungle. Reina knew what the caudillo was recalling. The memory stung her just as much. The day he and his wife had shared the amapola was the day Doña Laurel died.

"Very well." Enrique raised his chin, inspecting the inn. He was unsatisfied. "And the woman from Apartaderos?"

Reina's heart jolted.

"What?" Don Samón asked, surprised.

"The eighth dama. The one Reina stole from my manor," Enrique said.

The urge to defend herself surged through Reina, but dread held her back. There could be only one reason why Enrique would be interested in Maior, and it was a terrible one.

"Maior de Apartaderos," Enrique clarified for Don Samón.

Realization dawned on the Liberator, and he raised his brows. "Why are you asking me about her?"

"You are returning what belongs in my purview, no?" Enrique placed a hand on Celeste's shoulder in an uncharacteristic display of affection. "I'm allowing you to keep the duskling, who had an education and is useful only thanks to my resources." He bared his canines like the predator he was. "You should have seen her when she arrived at my manor. A sniveling creature—barely clinging to life."

Reina inhaled to steady herself. She was sure her iridio heart throbbed with the colors of its magic, divulging just how much she hated him.

"I'm wondering why you're harboring my treacherous brother— wondering what kind of deal he offered you—"

"There is no deal."

"And I'm supposed to trust that we are friends? On the same side? Yet you deny me the people with whom I have a score to settle? So, I repeat: Where is the eighth dama, who was my property?"

"Maior doesn't belong to anybody," Reina blurted out, earning her Don Samón's concerned glance.

Celeste snorted. "Well, she still has mi mamá in her. Are we supposed to just accept that?"

Red fire flashed in Enrique's eyes, just as the fire of betrayal burned in Reina's chest. Celeste was alive *thanks to Maior*, and Celeste still had the nerve to kindle the flames of Enrique's demands?

"You deny my wife eternal rest?"

"No," Don Samón said quickly.

"She was denied eternal peace. Hand over the woman. I will not leave without her."

Don Samón's throat bobbed. He looked like was on the verge of conceding. So Reina quickly said, "No. Leave Maior out of this."

Enrique glared like he was seconds away from taking Reina's neck in his hands and snapping it in two.

Don Samón lifted a hand as the caudillo marched forward. "Wait. Enrique, let me go back. Reina and I will discuss."

"There's nothing to discuss," Reina said. She could feel the smirks of the spectators. She could imagine their glee that the tailed nozariel, Doña Ursulina's spawn, was prepared to writhe and beg for a human's life. Her grip on the handle of her golden blade hardened. She knew if she hesitated to draw it, Enrique could outpace her. Her heart raced, adrenaline pumping in anticipation.

Enrique stopped an arm's length away from the Liberator. For a second, his mask faltered, revealing a sunken weariness. His perpetual hurt from losing Doña Laurel. "Samón," he said, his voice softer, younger, appealing to the version of Don Samón he'd known and fought side by side with against a common enemy. "You call yourself my friend—a hero to everyone—and you allow this dark magic within your own walls? You knew Laurel, yet you ignore her, trapped in Maior? If you truly are my friend, then you will return the woman to me before the week's end."

Don Samón pressed his lips together. "What will you do if I hand her over?"

"*No*," Reina exhaled, anguished.

"I will give my wife eternal peace," Enrique said slowly.

"Just like Ursulina did with the other damas," Celeste added, her gaze boring into Reina, filled with scorn. "By taking a knife to their throats."

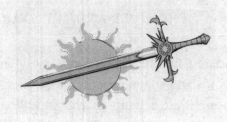

8

Nightcleaver

Reina and Don Samón returned to Isla Madre in silence. Gazes were averted. The injustice of their meeting in Carao blazed in her chest. They'd left after Enrique and Don Samón grew tired of arguments that led nowhere. Enrique's shrewd eyes and vulpine words never wavered. And Don Samón deflected and parried him, but he never effectively said no, as if Maior were merely a hostage to be bartered for a heavier coffer. During the journey back, Reina had gripped the galleon deck railing until her knuckles drained of blood. Even the salty wind slapping her face hadn't been enough to quell the heat bubbling her blood. She couldn't swallow Enrique's audacity of claiming a person as an object, and how no one had the guts to deny him.

Not even the hero of the republic.

Soon enough, their cart reached the jasmine-draped gates of the manse. Reina waited for Don Samón to jump down from the cart's rackety wooden step before turning to him.

"He was out of line," she said in a low voice, such that the servants wouldn't hear them as they walked back to their daily posts.

Don Samón's brows twisted in disagreement. "Reina, you were out of line."

"*Me?*"

Don Samón squeezed his temples. "Yes, you. How could you even think to challenge him?"

Her lips opened and closed as she fished for words, though none could accurately convey her disillusionment. That hadn't been her intention. Rather, she would have preferred to deny Enrique entirely.

"And yes, I mean challenge him in the literal sense." He stepped around her, passing the gates. She followed him. "He can misinterpret any word whichever way he wants, and he can very easily claim that what you were saying was nothing but a challenge, to be resolved with a duel."

Don Samón was right: Her adrenaline hadn't missed a beat in coursing through her, preparing her for violence at the inn. It was luck it hadn't come to that. "Maior is not an object for bartering—"

"I understand that." Don Samón's voice warmed.

"If he wanted to right wrongs, why didn't you just turn over Javier? He wanted to kill Celeste. *He almost did.* That could have appeased the caudillo."

Don Samón's jaw sharpened. He stopped in the foyer. "I will decide how I negotiate with Enrique."

Reina wrinkled her nose. Was the Liberator playing favorites with his daughter's husband? Javier wasn't someone worth defending.

Don Samón went on. "I fully expected to walk out of there without trading anybody. People are not sacks of escudos to be bartered or exchanged. But you speaking up—all it achieved was to show him Maior matters to us."

"She does!"

"We don't want Enrique to know that. He will want to take what we want most. His favorite way of negotiating is by screwing you out of a deal." Don Samón threw a hand in the air. "I know how to handle him, and I wasn't planning on using Javier and Maior as bargaining chips at all."

"Why didn't you just hand over Javier?" she repeated wearily. She couldn't let it go. This whole month, Reina had slept soundly with the reassurance that one day Javier would be away from this island, and she wouldn't have to worry about him threatening Maior's life again.

Don Samón paused before ascending to his bedroom on the second floor. He watched Reina sternly, letting the silence unravel the layers of her own lack of foresight. "Let me make something very clear, Reina," he said in a low voice. "I am the one who will make the strategic decisions henceforth. It is inappropriate for you to take this role of advisor, when you have proved that you cannot successfully negotiate the peaceful surrender of a single person."

Reina ground her teeth but did not look away.

"Anger and swords are not the way to resolve differences. Not anymore. I want you to be reassured that I will defend Maior, as you are advocating so fiercely for her."

Reina's worries were unabated. How could she convey how much Maior mattered to her to someone who didn't understand how bare and empty Reina had been prior to coming here? To the Liberator, who didn't grow up alone and cast aside by the world's antipathy?

"I am your caudillo now. You are duty bound to serve me, as I am duty bound to protect you. But I don't want this repeated. Your hotheadedness stripped me of all bargaining power. What would you have done if Enrique had challenged you to a duel?"

Reina opened her mouth, but he interrupted her.

"Nothing, because it would have been my duty to step in. But do not drag me into an unnecessary fight."

Reina's chest pounded with both uncertainty for this path and fierceness for the oath she'd made to protect Maior. When she was younger and foolish, she had obeyed Enrique and her grandmother despite the objections she'd held deep in her gut. But that had been a costly mistake. She had soiled her hands and her honor, done things she now had to carry with her. Her bones, her skin, and even her feelings could be patched, but her scars would forevermore be etched on her. "I am capable of defending myself," Reina said.

"Against Enrique?"

"I would try. I can prove it." She knew she could put up a for-midable fight. Perhaps she could persevere with wits or luck or a miracle. Her life since arriving at Águila Manor had taught her anything was possible. Maybe...even her god would intervene.

A sharp pain in her side came as a reply. Reina pretended it was nothing.

"I will duel you," Reina said, clasping a hand on the hilt of her blade, where the sunlight had warmed the metal during the ride back, stinging her palm. "Your strength is equal to his, no? Let's see how I would fare."

Don Samón chuckled, but his eyes grew fierce.

Reina smiled. "You'll be at an advantage, since I hate Enrique with all my being. I can't bring that energy against you."

"And are you the kind of fighter who needs hate to become worthy of your immortal blade?"

Reina shrugged shamelessly, even as she was surprised to discover he was aware of the blade's origins. But he was the Liberator, and she was the fool for thinking he wouldn't know.

"Well, if I refuse, you'll think I'm craven. I have no other option but to accept."

They went separate ways to arm themselves before meeting again in the large training yard behind the manse. Chaguaramos growing on sand bordered the area. The sound of waves came from the nearby shore. It was high noon by then, and the smell of roasted meats wafted down from the kitchen, attracting a flock of circling gulls.

Reina arrived first, sweating in anticipation, wearing the navy military uniform of the Bravos. Epaulettes crested her shoulders, and shiny golden buttons fastened the jacket in place. The material was thick, concealing any indentation from the tubes sticking out of her chest. A scabbard held her golden sword, attached to the belt around her waist.

When Don Samón descended into the yard, in simple trousers and a linen shirt and without any armor to protect him, Reina blushed, embarrassed of being overdressed. He wore a complete set of geomancia rings—thick bands of antique gold finish, holding litio, galio, and bismuto solutions for his index, middle, and ring fingers, respectively. Litio for protection, galio for healing, and bismuto for enhancement. A saber in an ornately crafted scabbard hung from his waist, the leather holster cut and imprinted with looping iconography of orchids, araguaney flowers, and the laurels of his family's banner. His silky hair hung from a high ponytail.

The fighters who had lingered after sparring hollered as Don Samón and Reina circled the yard. Their cheers attracted passersby.

"What's that? Reina's going to duel the Liberator?" one of the sparring men called out. "I can tell you how it's going to end," he said, calling his comrades over to watch.

Others whooped for Reina.

Don Samón chuckled, waving them down. "At least she has the nerve to duel me. Unlike some of you."

Reina drew her golden blade slowly, reveling in the whistling sound it made as it slid out of the scabbard. She angled it so the sun's glare reflected on its shiny surface.

Don Samón blocked the gleam with his palm. "Ah. Well done, Reina. A fair amount of theatrics is always good when you demand a duel."

Reina laughed. "I don't think I'd have time to show off with the caudillo."

"If it's a valco duel, you would," Don Samón said.

"A valco duel?"

One of the fighters watching rolled a drum out of the shed's shadows. With an open palm he slapped the leather top to a rhythmic pace. Reina cocked half a smile. She'd heard the drums before. It was how the Liberator's soldiers hyped each other up during a fight. And now they were doing it for her.

"If you ever fight Enrique, at least request one," Don Samón said above the beat. "So that it will not be to the death, as humans do."

In a low, uncertain voice Reina said, "But I'm not valco. He'd never accept that from me. How is it different?"

"A valco duel is a showmanship of skill, and magic. You set your terms at the beginning, and you use all the geomancia you are proficient in. Of course, not all at the same time. Surprising your opponent is still part of a duel's strategy."

To prove it, he extinguished the distance between them in a flash. He swiped his saber down at her. Reina skipped back, the air leaving her lungs in a shock. He swung again in the opposite direction, the blade singing as it nearly sliced her belly.

Reina jumped back. She almost tripped from overreaching, and she cursed, betrayed by her body. Ches's presence made her stronger, but clumsier.

Reina tossed her golden blade aside to summon a last-minute bismuto spell. It was a gamble she had to take as Don Samón pursued her relentlessly, barely missing her. Hands freed of her blade, she slapped them together, flicking her wrist, thumbs, and fingers in a bismuto incantation to swell her muscles and sharpen her sight.

Immediately, her nose took in a waft of sour adrenaline coming from Don Samón, and her own sweat. She squinted, her vision dazzled by the punishing high-noon sun overhead. The humid air surrounded her, clogging her nostrils with its unwelcome heat. Yet despite the distractions, Reina could feel her muscles growing. Every bone in her straightened, tightened by reinforced tendons. The sensation was exhilarating. The thrill of battle made her skin hum. Reina smirked.

Don Samón paused, as if unsure of her actions. "Out of everyone in this land, you are the only one capable of wielding Ches's Blade. And you throw it aside, just like that?"

Reina's answer was reaching for the sword, rolling forward as Don Samón's saber swiped at her. Hair from the tip of her braid was severed in a clean cut.

She jumped to her feet and parried with a slash of her own. Don Samón didn't even lift his blade to block or counter. He dodged with ease. But as she went for him a second time, her unsure limbs missed him again.

Grunting in frustration, Reina swung, but he sidestepped her. He elbowed her side, digging right where it would hurt the most. Reina sucked in a breath.

"I thought you were going to be a match for Enrique," Don Samón said, tucking stray hairs behind his ear. His clothes were free of sweat and wrinkles.

Reina marched forward. She feigned a strike. When he moved to dodge, she hooked him on the jaw with her left fist.

He scoffed, stepping away. Without her dominant hand, the punch had hardly grazed him. "Is this the best you can do, Reina?"

She charged again. She predicted where he would move, and their blades clashed together.

Don Samón reinforced the block by taking his hilt with both hands. He shoved her with the brunt of his weight. Reina's boots slid back on the packed ground. A sharp ache stung her ankles from the opposing force.

She freed herself from the parry, ducking, but it proved to be a mistake. Quick handed, Don Samón grabbed her by her braid. Fire licked her scalp as he tugged her toward him, raising his saber to her neck, pinning her against the blade's edge. Reina thrashed but only succeeded in cutting her tender skin.

He whispered in her ear, "It's over."

"Release me and we'll go at it again," she said.

"The outcome would be the same. I didn't even get to show off what I can really do."

"Neither did I," Reina growled.

He freed her and shoved her to the ground.

But Reina faced him with a wide stance.

"I didn't even use geomancia," Don Samón said, lowering a palm beneath the length of his saber, imbuing it with a crackle of lightning. It reminded Reina of Eva's collected plankton from the cenote. "You're still too slow."

The words were a needle in her side, enough to shoot her with a fresh dose of adrenaline.

He smirked at her silence. "Enrique wouldn't have hesitated to buff himself with geomancia. He would have thrown everything he could at you, just to make quick work of it, and to turn it into a proper performance."

"I know how the caudillo fights," Reina said, charging again. She poured all her strength into the swing.

Instead of dodging, as she expected, the Liberator swung back. Their blades met with an earth-shattering clang. A shock wave erupted, shaking the chaguaramos and lifting a cloud of sand. Seagulls cawed and flew away. The drummer paused in shock.

The impact rattled Reina to the core. Sparks of her bismuto popped over her cheeks, ignited by the opposing force. She held on for a second, fire raging through her grip and shoulders, her teeth clattering, but her legs gave. She was shoved back, and she tripped, falling on her own ass.

Before she could even get up, Don Samón pushed the tip of his saber beneath her chin, lifting her gaze to meet his. Towering over her, he said, "You are not ready."

Her nostrils flared. The defeat was humiliating.

"Train, grow, and *don't challenge Enrique ever again*," he said slowly, his carmine eyes glowing. "It's my command."

She moved her chin away from the blade brusquely, uncaring of the new nick it opened. "Sí, señor."

He smiled broadly and sheathed his blade back into the ornate holster. He offered her a hand and, when she accepted it, pulled her to her feet. "I defeated you, but not as quickly as I expected," he said.

A flush returned to Reina's face.

"And believe me when I say: I can now see why that blade appeared before you, and why you're able to wield it. It is no wonder, with your fierce sense of justice and loyalty."

Reina lifted Ches's Blade between them, smug. Don Samón ran a hand along the sharp edge and said, "It doesn't materialize for just anyone. You do realize how special that is, don't you?"

Reina had no words. She'd been too caught up in reminding herself of all the ways Doña Ursulina had played her and all the injustices she'd endured to properly appraise what it meant to hold such a weapon. Dozens traveled to the Plume in search of it. *Celeste* had slayed the watchbeast guarding it. But Reina had been the only one capable of wielding it. Ches himself chose her.

"A cleaver of night," Don Samón said. "That's what you should name it."

Reina bit her lip. "You know the legend."

"Of course I do. I remembered it when that comet came."

Reina wondered if his opinion of Ches was as sour as his of Rahmagut. Would she ever muster the courage to admit she hosted the god of the sun? Ches never specified that it needed to be a secret, but Reina wasn't ready to open up to her commander yet. Just as Don Samón was testing her, Reina wanted to know him better first.

"How about Nightcleaver?" she asked cheekily.

"A fitting title. You know, naming something makes it yours."

Reina pretended to be unbothered and said, "Well, it doesn't respond to anyone else. *I've* earned it."

She glanced at the expectant audience. They regarded her with wonder and admiration, entirely different from the treatment she'd received from Enrique's soldiers, who used to besmirch her name and acted as if her employment was merely the result of nepotism.

Don Samón chuckled. "Indeed. I was right to hire you." He glanced fondly at the paths leading to town. "It's my mission to serve this nation, to protect the meek and disenfranchised, and to lead people who also share that same mission." He gave her a coy look. "For that, you already fit right in."

The back of Reina's neck blazed. Those were the words Reina had always craved from Doña Ursulina and Enrique. Perhaps it was her good luck that they never said them. "Thank you," she replied.

He beamed. "Very well! I think it's time for lunch. Shall we eat?"

The witnessing soldiers caught up to them as the Liberator led the way to the manse. They ruffled her braided hair and told her she'd done a splendid job. Reina accepted the compliments, but deep down she was unsatisfied. Don Samón's words were earnest, but Reina wondered if they also meant to distract her from why they'd dueled in the first place.

Enrique's threat loomed in the back of her mind. She needed to be ready, even if she wasn't planning on challenging him any-time soon. If Don Samón and Enrique were equally matched, then Reina had a mountain ahead of her to climb. They were valco and she was nozariel, but she had room to grow. Reina ran a hand down her shining blade, her fingers stinging from the hot metal. What if Ches's Blade—no, *her* Nightcleaver—was only the beginning? Reina didn't know Ches's reasons for returning in her body, but his presence felt like a new, open door.

One day, when—not if—Enrique came knocking to claim the woman housing the spirit of his late wife, Reina needed to be ready to reply in kind.

9

A Temporary Salve

Maior was hypnotized by the afternoon song of cicadas drifting through the open infirmary windows. She yawned, wishing she could withdraw for a nap. But even her siestas weren't spared from nightmares. Laurel trapped her in exhaustion. Maior ached for a long, undistracted sleep, but unless she accepted Laurel's memories, she would never get the rest she desired.

Maior folded the clinic's freshly washed towels and bandages into a neat pile. Eva sat across her, at Dr. Baltasar's desk, deeply engrossed in one of his many books about healing. Eva pulled at her curly hair as she read, yanking in frustration.

Maior perfectly understood Eva's mood as the hours dragged and they weren't any closer to finding answers for their curses. She couldn't even help Eva with the research. Maior's reading was still so primary and underdeveloped, despite Reina's help. Maior had dedicated many late afternoons to studying the most basic books, but her literacy was a long work in progress.

"*Hey*," Eva said, startling Maior from her aggressive folding. "Is everything all right? The towels don't deserve your wrath."

Maior pouted. She didn't want to admit why she was angry. It was too embarrassing, and she'd rather remain composed until the end of her shift. She had a house visit later in the day, to treat a child who had mal de ojo, and she wanted a clear mind before seeing him.

The truth was that, soon after grabbing lunch with the staff, Maior had learned of the gossip keeping Don Samón's manse abuzz. The servants had wasted no time in extracting tales from those who'd accompanied Don Samón to deliver Celeste, and blushed and giggled in delight as they told Maior how the caudillo of Sadul Fuerte had asked specifically for her. They were overjoyed that such a powerful man would have an interest in her. "Look at our Maior. She has him completely obsessed!" the girls teased with feathery pats to their chests. Maior gave them a fake smile and fled to the infirmary as soon as she could. If only they knew the truth.

"I've had a long day," Maior muttered, hoping the gossip hadn't reached Eva. But as Eva hardly fraternized with the criadas, not out of malice but due to her highborn habit, it was unlikely she'd heard already. "And speak for yourself."

"Well, I found something," Eva said.

"Oh?" Maior circled the desk, even though she could not read the text Eva pointed at.

"Nothing on exorcising. Maybe you're better off talking to the priest." Eva wrinkled her nose in displeasure.

Maior blushed, stung. Lately, she'd avoided confession precisely because of Laurel. She'd broached the subject with the priest who helmed Isla Madre's chapel—but more as a hypothetical, to avoid suspicion. She was glad for her covert strategy, for the priest had cast shame on the very prospect of anyone serving as a tool for a resurrection Void spell. According to him, Maior's hypothetical woman was already damned.

Eva continued to point at the page and Maior asked, "What does it say?"

Eva cleared her throat, understanding. "You know how I'm gathering ingredients to mix with geomancia? Like the plankton?"

Maior hmmed in agreement.

"It turns out you can also mix iridio with the other geomancia metals to reverse their effects."

"What?" Maior felt out of her depth. "How is this helpful?"

"Let me explain." Eva seemed elated at the opportunity to teach geomancia. "Iridio is used broadly, yes, but its innate property is that of achieving order. You see, 'order' is against the nature of the world—thermodynamically, everything naturally wants to head in the direction of chaos. This causes iridio to have properties like negative pressure, heat drain, and cancellation. It perfectly explains why it feels like I'm sucking energy out of the sky whenever I summon a fireball. The release of that stolen energy manifests as fire exploding in my hands. It's why tinieblas, creatures of iridio and the Void, make the air turn cold." Eva pointed at the text in front of them. "This concept of cancellation can be applied to the other geomancias. This book has recipes for mixing iridio into galio to drain health or to addle the mind. There is one for achieving a deep sleep. It places a weight so heavy on the mind, you won't be able to recall any dreams."

Maior couldn't understand Eva's excitement. "Or you'll be trapped in them."

"Unlikely and irrelevant," Dr. Baltasar said from the doorway, approaching his desk as Eva slid out of his chair. "The body will simply be unable to form any memories while asleep under such a spell."

Dr. Baltasar had peppery-black hair and always wore the old army uniform of the revolution: a navy jacket with a crimson bodice, white pants, and black knee-high boots. Once, Maior had asked him about his insistence on that attire, and he gently told her it was a self-imposed soldier's uniform. A reminder of his mission to serve their new republic.

"It is a delicate tonic. Titrate the wrong concentration by mere milliliters and you will not wake up at all." He twirled his pampered mustache disapprovingly. "Don't dabble in advanced medicines you don't understand, Eva. I have dedicated decades to my practice for a reason."

Eva cocked a brow in displeasure. "Then you can fix the tonic for her."

Maior squeezed Eva's arm, hoping to reel back Eva's tone. The last thing Maior wanted was to cause trouble for anyone.

Dr. Baltasar was unfazed. "Whatever mi señorita wishes is my command."

Eva was speechless.

"I shall have the tonic ready on the morrow." Upon noting her surprise, he added, "As long as Don Samón continues to supply the clinic, my services and our stores are yours. Now, is there anything else I can help with?"

Eva quickly grabbed the book she'd left open on his desk. "I shall borrow this. Thanks."

Maior watched Eva head for the door. She was partly amused at the flippant way Eva had taken the tome, and partly nervous at having to answer to her superior. Maior wished for some of her confidence. If Eva were possessed by Laurel, perhaps she would have found a solution by now.

Once Eva was gone, Dr. Baltasar gave Maior a long look. He plopped onto his chair, weary. "Doña Eva is intelligent, but I do not recommend such a potion. The risks far outweigh whatever you wish to avoid. Why is Doña Eva so adamant I make it for you? Is there something I need to know about?"

Maior wrung her hands. She lowered her head so her hair would shield the shame in her eyes.

"Is it because of that ghost clinging to you?" Dr. Baltasar said.

Maior sucked in a breath. "I don't want to dream anymore," she admitted softly.

His pause revealed his surprise. Dr. Baltasar knew there were peculiarities to Maior. He saw the ghost of Laurel whenever he used bismuto on himself for medical purposes, and Maior liked that he never prodded her about it. Around him and the other nurses, she could pretend she wasn't cursed. Maior was fine with pretending, until she fell asleep.

"To dream, one must sleep," he said, stroking his mustache. "Perhaps I can teach you how to use a mixture of galio and bismuto instead. Something so basic that the risks are minimal. It will keep you awake through the night while leaving you energized. You won't need to sleep at all."

Maior smiled. "That sounds powerful…and perfect."

The rain clouds that visited the islands every late afternoon returned like clockwork. They snuck up from the horizon, blocking the descending sun behind a mantle of gray. The rain caught up to Maior as she left the last home in her round of house calls.

Dress and espadrilles soaking, Maior ran to the Pentimiento chapel to escape the rain and finish her day's work by tallying the supplies she needed from the market. Her soles squeaked on the tiles as she pushed the heavy door open, her nose wringing from the burning incense. She crossed herself upon entering.

The chapel was big enough for the small population of Isla Madre. The roof and piping groaned as the rain-heavy clouds thundered outside, raindrops pelting the stained-glass windows, drowning the chapel in the sounds of a downpour. Yet Maior felt perfectly safe. This was her sanctuary, the flickering candles and the towering icons of saints and the Virgin grounding her in the belief that no matter where she was in the world, she would always be at home here.

Maior wondered what it would be like to visit the cross's holy site in Segol. The great crag where, after miraculously revealing Herself to all Her believers, the Virgin jumped over the edge to return to Her heavenly realm. The crag collapsed on itself, the mountain reshaped by Her power, leaving nothing but a cross fissured on the rock. It happened too long ago to quantify, but the priest of Apartaderos had assured Maior that a mark remained on that mountain as the earthly proof of their goddess, and many made pilgrimages to visit it. The cross of Her vanishing confirmed that the events written in the holy book were true. Maior didn't need to see the proof to believe, but the idea of such a visit sparked her imagination.

Suddenly a shadow emerged from the door to the garden, and Maior jolted. "Reina," Maior breathed as the figure stepped into the soft candlelight, holding wildflowers and a package. Her chest calmed, and she smiled.

Reina cleared her throat. "Hey. I was looking for you."

She adverted her gaze, scratching her temple, and it took Maior a second to realize why. The white fabric of Maior's soaked dress was doing a terrible job of concealing her curves. It clung to her sides and breasts, and perhaps had lost all its opacity. Maior had the instinct to cross her arms, for they stood before the Virgin's altar, but she also didn't want to give Reina the wrong idea.

Maior grabbed Reina's free wrist and guided her out through the back door.

Behind the chapel was a garden of orange-blooming birds-of-paradise and a tall bush of hibiscus, modestly manicured by the chapel's volunteers. The hibiscus plant was as tall as Maior. Today, five magenta hibiscuses bloomed, shuddering from the weight of the water pooling in their centers. There was a bench next to the back door, under the shade of a balcony large enough to keep them dry. Maior gestured for Reina to join her on the bench.

A red-streaked bandage was tied around Reina's neck. Maior forgot all about her transparent dress and instead lifted Reina's chin for a better look. "You have cuts. Why?"

Reina freed her chin, wincing. "I dueled Don Samón." She leaned back and gave her arm a good stretch. Her rain-damp sleeve tightened around her flexed bicep, her shoulder muscles rippling.

Maior's breath caught as her gaze lingered.

"I didn't do too bad," Reina added, smirking, well aware of the effect she had on Maior.

"Why did you duel him?"

"I wanted to show him what I'm capable of."

"I thought you already did that at the tomb. That's why he hired you," Maior said, wringing the water from her short hair. Reina's eyes flickered to her chest. Maior glanced away to the blooming hibiscuses, biting her lower lip as she realized she loved Reina's attention. That she wanted more.

"There was another matter to be resolved," Reina said stiffly.

"What matter?"

Dodging the answer, Reina gave her the wildflowers and the bundle she had somehow managed to keep dry. The package unraveled to reveal three freshly baked almojábanas.

Maior gasped. "How did you find these here?"

"The baker told me he learned how to make them when he visited Sadul Fuerte with Don Samón some years ago. And he owed me a favor . . . so I asked him to make them for you."

Maior beamed and immediately took a big bite. She moaned at the cheesy flakiness melting on her tongue.

"They're probably not as good as what you can get in Apartaderos," Reina muttered.

With her mouth full and her cheeks reddening, Maior said, "It is better than nothing."

She inched closer, aching for Reina's warmth as the rain dried off her body.

"Would you like some?" Maior lifted one to Reina's lips before Reina could reply.

Reina took a gigantic bite.

Dismayed, Maior gasped, "*Hey!* Leave some for me!"

Reina had a smug look as she grabbed Maior's wrist to stop her from moving the flaky bread away. She finished the rest of the almojábana in another large bite and licked the cheesy flavor from Maior's fingertips.

Maior held her gaze, arrested in place, her chest so fluttery she didn't dare move.

"And the flowers?" she asked once she had gathered her breath.

"For your hair, so I can return the favor."

Maior smiled. Nevertheless, she moved away in suspicion. She loved Reina's gifts, but she also knew Reina wasn't someone who picked flowers for no reason.

She gave Reina a questioning look. Don Samón had taken Reina to Carao with him to deliver Celeste. She *had* to know about the caudillo. But as Reina let the silence drag on, as if nothing was amiss, Maior grew fed up with waiting. She said, "I heard the most delicious gossip in the kitchens today."

Reina groaned.

"About how the Liberator is handing me over to the caudillo of Sadul Fuerte."

"*What?* No."

Reina's denial reminded Maior of the time Reina had deceived her while pursuing Rahmagut's legend. A small panic settled. What if she was being kept in the dark again? "I know I'm being used to negotiate with Enrique Águila," Maior said in the bluntest way possible.

Reina tried grabbing Maior's hand, but she slid out of reach. "He's not negotiating. Don Enrique demanded that you be handed over."

Maior's cheeks burned.

"But Don Samón wouldn't let that happen," Reina said. She scowled. "*I* wouldn't let that happen."

Shivers shot through Maior as Reina cupped her face. With her thumbs, Reina caressed Maior's cheekbones. Reina knew she had the power to enthrall Maior, to make her forget everything—to drown her in the tamarind shade of her eyes. "Remember what I promised you in Gegania?" Reina said, her gaze surfing over Maior's lips. "I'll protect you."

Maior felt like she was under a spell. She had many reasons to be frustrated, yet she couldn't help but lean into the gesture, aching for the intimacy. Her body hummed with sensation, missing something she never truly had before. She was in the palm of Reina's hand, and she knew Reina knew this. She had to. Maior was purposely being lulled into forgetting the difficult conversations. But the stability of her life simply couldn't hinge on fairy-tale promises of love and protection. Not every problem could be solved with Reina's sword.

Maior pulled away. "If the caudillo snatches me in the middle of the night, just like he did the first time, there'll be nothing you can do to stop him."

Reina's eyes burned in disagreement. "You're making it easy for him when you spend your nights with Eva."

Maior rose to her feet. "If you want me to sleep in your bed, just say so!"

Reina also stood with ruddy cheeks. "Maior—"

Maior cut her off, because she wasn't finished. "Just be honest about what you want. I told you I'm afraid to sleep alone—*I am cursed*. I sought Eva because I wanted to give you space while Celeste was still on the island. I understand why you wanted to take things slow and keep your distance, but deep down, I haven't shaken the fear that I'm just a consolation prize—I'll never be as perfect as—"

The words were snuffed out of her mouth as Reina pulled her to her chest. She curved around Maior, over her shorter stature. Reina tucked her nose into the crook of Maior's neck. "You are not a consolation prize," Reina said, her words tickling Maior's skin. Sparks went off inside her. "You are *perfect*. You are who I like, and who I choose."

Maior hugged Reina tightly. She buried her nose in Reina's chest, feeling the raggedness of the iridio contraption beneath Reina's shirt. She found safety there, an ease. Like a child longing for validation, she asked, "Really?"

Reina pulled herself away. "Yes, really! I was ready to fight the caudillo to the death for you."

"I don't want that," Maior grumbled. "I just want to be cleansed."

Reina cupped Maior's cheeks again. She brought Maior closer, like she was moments away from stealing a kiss. And Maior desperately wanted her to.

Reina's devotion was a lovely tune, but Maior couldn't help her stomach from turning. She couldn't endure Laurel and Enrique for one more night. She glanced away to the hibiscuses. "I am so tired of seeing her memories."

"The dreams can't hurt you, can they?"

Maior shook her head. It was a nice thought, that her safety was always Reina's number one priority. "What, are you going to bust into my dreams with your golden sword?"

Reina grinned. She tapped the hilt on her hip. "I have this blade to protect what's good and true, and you are good and true. If I allow Enrique to take you away, then I am nothing but a failure."

Maior wanted to roll her eyes. "Reina, you're more than someone who swings a sword around."

"This is what gives me worth—"

"*No!* You don't need to serve anyone to have value. You don't have to constantly prove yourself." She grabbed Reina's hand and pressed it against her bosom so Reina could feel how hard Maior's heart beat for her.

Reina didn't answer right away, like she disagreed.

The rain had stopped without their noticing. The rain clouds were replaced by the dusk, which shaped long shadows around the chapel's gardens.

Reina tucked Maior's hair behind her ears. She lifted her chin, taking her in so deeply. In their closeness, Maior could observe the nozariel scutes along Reina's nose bridge. How rare and special they were.

"Maybe tonight, you can come to my room instead," Reina said softly.

Maior sucked in a breath. She could see hope in Reina's expression, and the desire to be trusted. The invitation was equal parts thrilling and reassuring. Maior found she had no other answer but a yes.

They agreed to walk back to the manse before the sky changed its mind and unleashed a second torrent.

"What happens in your dreams?" Reina asked as she took Maior's hand in hers.

Maior stared at the muddy path to avoid revealing her shame. She swallowed. If Reina was jealous about Eva, her mood would most certainly spoil once Maior told her about Enrique and Laurel. "I saw how Laurel cursed Javier," Maior mumbled.

Reina scowled as Maior recounted some of it. Not because she cared for Javier. Rather, Maior knew, because Reina loathed him.

"So Eva was telling the truth," Reina said as Maior finished her tale.

Maior nodded. She didn't mention Eva's hand in Javier's loss of control. That was a secret Eva had shared for Maior's ears only.

"And you say they had a flute made out of a deer skull?" Reina asked.

"It gave them the power to control tinieblas. But Laurel broke it when she confronted Javier," Maior said. Reina was silent. Maior found her staring at the horizon, where the wind buffeted the palm trees. "Why?" Maior asked, squeezing Reina's hand to snap her out of it.

"Enrique had something like that with him at Carao's inn. It looked like he was trying to repair it."

10

Rahmagut

Eva returned to the jailer's tower for her nightly visit. She slipped out of her espadrilles and crossed the risen shallows barefoot. As soon as she arrived, she heard voices from the second floor once again. She rushed up, curious, only to find Javier alone, balancing on the headboard of his bed to reach the metal bars of the window. One of the bars was loose in his hand.

It looked like a useless exercise. The window was still too small for his frame. How she pitied him, and she wished she could comfort him. She rattled the jail key to announce her arrival, and Javier jumped down like a child caught in the act.

"I brought you supper," Eva said. She opened the door to hand him the platter, then tucked the key in her dress pocket. He accepted the food with a red face.

Today's peace offering was a golfeado, a cinnamon roll topped with sugarcane syrup and cheese, and a dinner of manta ray minced with a red pepper sauce. He wolfed down both, in that order. The hollows in his cheeks were a testament to how much he needed it. Don Samón's jailer wasn't starving him—his imprisonment was comfortable and humane—but it was clear his diet of bread and dried meats wasn't enough to maintain his looks and strength. For someone as lean as Javier, his weight loss was starkly noticeable.

"No amapolas this time?" he joked, fishing for a reaction.

"Your brother asked for you," she told him, unfazed, watching him scoop up the last of the oily sauce. He stuck his finger in his mouth, sucking it.

"He wanted me back? Why?"

"I think it's to punish you. But don't worry. My father doesn't want to budge. He says it's a sign of weakness."

"Absolutely. Give Enrique a hand and he'll take the whole arm."

Happiness fluttered in her. She was glad his mood hadn't spoiled despite her failures to negotiate his release. It was a delicate matter. They needed to let time heal some wounds. Eva knew anything she asked of Don Samón he would probably grant her—with the correct handling, of course.

"He asked for Maior, too."

Javier's eyes hardened with the ancient weight that often preceded the tiniebla taking over. "I presume the Liberator denied that?"

"Of course he denied him," Eva said. "But your brother's not backing down."

Javier was silent, and Eva wondered if he had any guilt for how he'd treated Maior. Eva's heart chilled as she considered that perhaps his silence came from a place of strategy. He knew she was close to Maior.

"So if the Liberator's not turning me in, what does he plan to do with me?"

"Nothing. He knows you belong to me," she said.

He gave her the smile she'd wanted. "You condemn Enrique for treating Maior like an object, yet you speak of me the same way."

Eva grinned. "And you don't like that?"

"I'd like to get out. Then you can do whatever you want with me."

She laughed. She couldn't get herself worked up over such things. Javier seldom meant what he said. "I will ask for you next. I promise."

"You promised this last night, and the night before."

Eva pouted. She didn't want to hear the list of all the wrongs she hadn't righted yet, even if she did deserve it. She just wanted to sit with him and exchange banter to be carried away by the wind.

Javier stepped under the torchlight. "There's something you need to see."

Eva swallowed the lump in her throat as he unfastened his shirt. He took his time, one button at a time, teasing her patience. But once the fabric uncovered his body, Eva understood his hesitation.

Javier did not reveal the smooth, sculpted skin Eva remembered from the night they signed their marriage papers. Leathery patches covered his body, sprouting from the belly button, crawling up to his chest, and traveling farther down to the areas concealed by his pants. Eva blushed. She recognized this rough texture. She'd seen it in other tinieblas.

The rhythmic waves and stormy wind outside were drowned out as Javier stepped forward to be within her reach. Eva was afraid to breathe and disrupt this silence.

Pity for him welled, now more than ever, after Maior had confirmed he'd told her the truth. With one callous action, she'd cost him a month of his life. He was losing himself to the tiniebla because of her.

"I don't know if this is meant to happen at this point—or if it's because I'm trapped here."

He gently took her hand and ferried it to his heart, where the corruption manifested like a burn scab. It was rough beneath her touch and hot, like an infection.

Slowly, she gave in to the instinct of tracing down to his belly, feeling the rough texture, letting reality sink in. She met his eyes, fearful, but there was no discomfort in his expression.

"If I don't find a way to free myself, I'm going to turn permanently. I'll be lost to it, Eva," he said, his tone chastising. "If you don't—"

"Tomorrow, you'll be a free man." She cut him off. "You don't have to try to escape through the window. I don't think you even fit."

He blushed and refastened the shirt in place. "You want me to trust your promises when you know I never like leaving my fate in the hands of others. I have waited—"

"You wouldn't be here if it weren't for me," Eva admitted.

His eyes rounded in surprise.

"I accept responsibility for what happened in Rahmagut's tomb."

Javier grew bold, gently tracing her jaw with his knuckles. Eva's heart thrummed. She steeled herself to stop her shoulders from quaking. The last thing she wanted was to bloat his ego with the knowledge that he had such an effect on her.

"This jail cell is no place for your husband," he muttered.

"That you are." She shook her head, remembering her wits. She backed away against the bars and finally had the space to breathe freely. "Will you please trust me?"

"I'm *trying* to trust you, but I'm restless. I'm lonely."

She sucked in a breath. "My company isn't enough?"

"No. *You're* the reason I haven't lost my mind yet. Every day I sit here wondering, *ruminating, Is today the day she grows tired of me?* Because what else will I have? I don't want to be this pathetic. But you're the only one I can count on."

It was her turn to hold his face. "You're no such thing." She couldn't muster the courage to admit how much she looked forward to returning to him every night. How with every visit, she discovered something new that she liked.

He leaned into her hand. "I'm not used to relying on others. I'm often disappointed."

"And you believe I will disappoint you?"

He shook his head, moving closer, letting her touch glide over his neck. He was warm.

"I'll set you free. But afterward, you cannot let anyone see what happened to your skin. Not my father. Not Reina. This stays between you and me."

"I'll be whatever you want me to be."

She scurried out before the rains returned. Lightning streaked the sky as she emerged from the prison. When lightning struck a second time, she had the distinct impression it formed the shape of a wicked grin in the sky.

Cold air enveloped her as she met the cobbled path to the manse.

The skies grumbled again. Eva swung the wrought iron gate open, wincing as it sang with a rusty creak.

The third time lightning struck, closer, thunder upheaving the manse's nightly peace, Eva saw something on the beach. At first, she thought it was a trick of the light. But the shadows crawling up the shore grew larger, some bipedal, feline, monstrous. They emerged from the shallows in a march. A handful turned to a dozen. Perhaps even a hundred.

Eva cast a simple orb of light with her iridio pendant, taking a deep breath as the pleasure of summoning iridio raised goose bumps on her arms. It was a bridled version of her fireballs, strong enough to light the perimeter but not flaming enough to ignite the island. Her veins hummed in anticipation. How could Don Samón seek to end something as amazing as iridio?

With a wave, she shot it down to the beach, spinning the fireball to avoid the palm trees clustering around the path. It crashed against the shadows, revealing the sickly, amalgamated bodies of tinieblas. Some squirmed and hissed as her fire consumed them.

The sight made her stomach sink.

Eva sprinted inside, hollering for Reina, for Don Samón, for anyone who would listen.

By the time she reached her father's bedchamber, he was groggily peeking out of his door. She panicked. What if it took them too long to get ready for battle? Should she have stayed outside, repelling the tinieblas for as long as possible?

"Eva? What's happening?"

She pointed behind her, doubling over to catch her breath. "Tinieblas. Storming the beach."

"Tinieblas?"

"Yes! Hundreds of them!" Suddenly a scream pierced the night.

Don Samón bolted back inside his room and Eva sprinted downstairs to hers. Relief flooded her as she saw Reina and Maior stepping out of Reina's room. Reina was tying her curls in a high ponytail, and Maior's hair was tussled from sleep. As Eva explained, Reina's face darkened.

"More tinieblas?" Maior asked, hugging herself.

Instead of answering, Reina merely commanded her to hide in her room.

Another scream ripped through the night. More voices erupted from the manse. They came from the servants and the soldiers as they divided themselves into those hiding and those charged with defending.

"I need to grab my gear. You go on ahead," Reina told Eva. Then she insisted that Maior stay sequestered inside.

Eva didn't linger to watch them argue, even if she thought Reina was being unfair. But maybe stifling Maior was Reina's way of showing love.

She ran out the back path. Hands spinning, she placed a ward over the gates: a barrier of glittering gold that wrapped around the garden perimeter, as tall as the chaguaramos. The ward tugged at her concentration, but she maintained it to protect the most vulnerable sheltering inside the manse.

Finally, raindrops pelted down on Eva as she reached the town square. The statue there should have been pulsing with a repellant iridio spell. But it had run out.

Lightning streaked the sky again, stripping the darkness for a split instant, revealing a horde of amalgamated shadows storming toward the village. Eva pumped bismuto into her legs, even as she knew she wouldn't be fast enough to save those houses closest to the shore. She reached one home just as a woman ran out, her infant pressed to her chest, both screaming in terror.

Eva summoned a blazing ball of iridio that ignited and banished the tiniebla pursuing them. Then the woman crumpled to her knees in thanks.

"*No*. Get up!" Eva begged, but a snarl wrenched her attention away. She turned, heart in her throat, to find a tiniebla with the body of a monkey and the snarling face of a fox sprinting for them. It was flanked by a second one, draped in shadow. Fire burst out of Eva's palms, uncontrolled. She shoved the striking tinieblas back before they could shred the woman and her babe. The woman screeched, the sound a dizzying keening enhanced by Eva's bismuto. Eva's fire evaporated the tinieblas, catching the house in the process.

Eva said to the woman, "You must go into Don Samón's manse. It's the only place that'll be safe."

Wiping her tears, she took off as Eva commanded.

Eva allowed her barrier to waver for the woman, her child, and a few other townsfolk.

Lightning struck a nearby palm tree, splitting it in two and setting it aflame. Eva covered her ears with her hands, but it wasn't enough to block out the resounding thunder, her senses magnified from her bismuto high. She surrendered to her knees, her ears ringing.

A flaming chaguaramo became a beacon in the night. Despite the pelting rain, it allowed Eva to see tinieblas rushing into homes and swiping at unsuspecting inhabitants. Unless the townsfolk burned their own bismuto to see the tinieblas, they would have no inkling of the terror stampeding into their homes. The woman was lucky she'd heard the tiniebla's stomps and had fled right into Eva's path before she and her babe were devoured.

A horn erupted in the distance, joining the sounds of rain and thunder. When the horn went off a second time, several doors swung open, and families streamed to the streets, running for Don Samón's manse.

Eva rose, even as she was weighed down by her soaked dress. These tinieblas were storming the island for a reason. The horde easily outnumbered all the island's capable fighters. Darkness was coming, whether they were ready for it or not.

She followed her instincts and ran for the town square. Reina appeared by her side, glowing blue with the swell of her bismuto spell, along with Don Samón and a handful of guards.

To his soldiers, Don Samón shouted the command of rounding up as many villagers as possible and escorting them back up to the manse, which had been made an impenetrable fortress by Eva's ward.

Reina sprinted ahead, meeting two tinieblas, her blade slicing the rain and their shadowed bodies in half.

Eva followed the screams coming from her left. A group of tinieblas scampered over barrels, water-filled buckets, and strewn patio furniture in pursuit of a family who'd heeded the call of Don Samón's horn. She crossed them as the tinieblas leapt into the air, their claws outstretched. She summoned a barrier that depleted the last of her litio. The tinieblas collided with the barrier and ricocheted off the barrels, which gave the family ample time to move on.

Electricity streaked the sky, lighting the dark street. Eva saw the silhouette of antlers. But when she blinked, it was gone. Perhaps it was another tiniebla down the street. With the rain blurring her eyes, she couldn't be sure.

Eva went from house to house, checking indoors for anyone who had not yet heeded the horn's warning. She entered one house and crashed into a man who was fleeing a tiniebla. The impact sent her flying against a door, and she smacked her shoulder on the wood, which splintered. Eva howled. When she touched the spot, her fingers came back moist with blood.

Throwing panicked apologies, the man tried lifting her to her feet. "No! Run to the manse!" Eva commanded him, squinting back her tears.

The tiniebla stood victorious, standing upright with the hind legs of a bull and its face veiled in darkness. The creature lunged for the man, even though Eva was closer.

The terrified man circled the drawing room, and Eva found herself in between him and the tiniebla. Then another appeared at the door.

With a sick apprehension, Eva wondered if she should control them. All the books on geomancia warned that controlling tinieblas was a sin—an act from which there was no return. She'd done it before, with terrible consequences.

But maybe she could use her iridio differently. Theoretically, she could. For soon after returning from the cenote, she'd spiked her pendant with an extract of glowing plankton water. It was supposed to give light.

She'd never tested this before. If she tried it and failed, she could end up with her arm bitten, or worse. But as more tinieblas teamed up to pounce at the cowering man behind her, Eva threw her hand forward in her mad gamble. Time halted. Their rabid mandibles were a split second away from lacerating his arm.

Bolts of cyan light burst from her fingertips. The thunderous whips struck the tinieblas across the chest. The creatures splattered against the brick wall, the lightning charring them into nothingness.

Eva clamped a hand over her mouth, shocked. Her stomach tingled and her blood raced from the delicious high. She'd wielded lightning!

A string of satisfaction wound in her chest. It was a foreign sensation, possibly the signature of her invader, filling her with doubt about her own capabilities—taking credit for what she'd achieved. Stubbornly, Eva swallowed it down.

The man she'd saved sang a hundred useless words of apology and gratitude as she shoved him out of the house. Then she commanded him to seek shelter in her father's home.

Screams and thunder shook the night again. She used a simple mending galio spell to stitch her ripped shoulder back together, then replenished her bismuto enhancement before running outside.

Don Samón and Reina had taken positions in a narrow alleyway serving as a chokepoint. The tinieblas ascended, keeping Reina and her golden sword busy. She howled with every swing, her shoulders heaving from exhaustion.

Eva yelled her name, and Reina whirled around. Eva sent her last thread of galio, depleting her rings to douse Reina in temporary vigor and to numb her wounds. Reina's thanks came in the form of a nod. Then she turned back and hacked a sprinting tiniebla in half.

Don Samón emerged from one of the alleyway's back doors as he escorted a young family out. Three toddlers and parents who couldn't be older than Eva. Would they survive? They had to.

He swiped the slick hair out of his eyes. "Head back into the manse!" he commanded Eva, his words ringing with authority—and an edge of panic.

"No. You need help!"

To prove so, Eva threw her hand at the chokepoint. Lightning crackled from her fingers, shooting directly at Reina, who predictably dodged out of the way.

The lightning struck the ascending tinieblas right on their chests, banishing them upon impact. The exertion left Eva breathing heavily. Nonetheless, she smirked, satisfied.

Still, several dozen more rushed up the cobbled path. They seemed endless, while the iridio in Eva's pendant was not.

Eva scrambled to a ladder propped against the wall. She tested its strength.

"What are you doing?" Don Samón called behind her.

"I want to see them all," Eva said, and used the ladder to climb up to a balcony, through which she could reach the roof of another house. Her espadrilles nearly slipped, but she stood high, where she had a view of the hundred tinieblas rushing in their direction.

Eva's heart plummeted in a panic. She had mastered iridio spells. She could throw fireballs and produce lightning, yet she knew the little iridio droplets sloshing inside her pendant wouldn't be enough to banish them all. Her father, Reina, and the other soldiers were growing wearier by the second. Their forces weren't enough, and the sheer number of tinieblas practically guaranteed Isla Madre's fall.

She sucked in a breath to clear her mind. There was only one thing she could do to save them. She had to dig deep into the dark regions of the Void and expend the last bit of her iridio to take control of them all.

Anxiety rattled her again.

Her first attempt at controlling tinieblas in Gegania had ended horribly. Controlling tinieblas on a small scale was unpleasant but doable—this, she had proved in Rahmagut's tomb. But stepping into realms she didn't understand, like trying control Javier, had yielded terrible results.

Except...her options were to live a lifetime with the consequences of her daring, or to have the guaranteed destruction of Isla Madre.

If Eva walked this new path, where she considered herself courageous, where her life would be dictated by her own actions, to be worthy as Don Samón's heir, then she had to do it. She had to disregard every warning logged in the geomancia books about controlling tinieblas, and her father's admonishment. She wielded the power of the Void, and if she didn't use it now, against the real threat of her people dying, she would be nothing but a coward.

She would succeed only if she opened herself up fully to *him*. If she shattered the door separating her consciousness from the darkness lurking within her and gazed into what waited inside.

Eva took a deep breath as the iridio in her pendant simmered. She closed her eyes and saw four pupils gazing back at her.

She gasped.

"*They're coming for you*," said a man, with a deep voice like cinder and smoke.

Eva couldn't let her terror take over. She'd sought this out. She opened her eyes again and curled her fingers like talons in the tinieblas' direction. "*Tiempo que pasa no vuelve!*" she howled at the top of her lungs.

The stampede ceased immediately. Nausea roiled through Eva as she held the tinieblas in place. The iridio in her pendant sizzled, burning her chest. Her stomach turned, as if gravity were pulling her endlessly into the deepest depths of the Void. The air emptied out of her lungs. Eva was hollowed out by the spell, and by the welcoming of Rahmagut's presence, which filled her up until she felt like she was going to vomit the piece of her identity that belonged to her. His strength pulsed in her arms. Her skin prickled and hummed. Her hair swayed despite the rain, magnetized. She swelled with the emergence of his power.

With a flick of her wrists, she severed all tinieblas in half. Sickening cracks reverberated all through the island. A hiss of putrid blood erupted as necks and limbs split from their torsos, and as they were creatures of the Void, they dispersed into emptiness.

A hush fell. The rain slowed, resembling every other unremarkable evening downpour. The fires died down with the rain.

Eva glanced down below her, where Reina and her father stood with their mouths agape.

A smile crawled across her face. She was filled with Rahmagut's purring satisfaction. "*What a display*," he told her. "*Not that it was necessary. Tinieblas belong to us. We are their masters.*"

Exhaustion pummeled her. She collapsed, and she had no recollection of ever landing.

11

The Perfect Daughter (Who Lies)

When Eva came to, the morning smelled sweet. Her balcony doors were open, letting in a breeze not yet warmed by the island's sun. She was enveloped by the soft sheets of her bed. Maior made a big fuss when she noticed Eva's eyes flutter open, checking her pupils, squeezing her cheeks, and patting her antlers. Eva pulled away, overwhelmed and annoyed. Dr. Baltasar watched his nurse from a distance, pleased, his gaze shrewd as he said some words about using galio to refresh Eva's spirit—and something about Eva's fatigue being caused by using too much geomancia at once.

Satisfied with her prognosis, Dr. Baltasar left.

"How long have I been out for?" Eva asked Maior, who helped her sit up against her big pillows.

"Just for the night."

"And the tiniebla attack?"

Maior frowned. "Don't you remember what happened?"

Eva swallowed. She did remember, and even when she tried to suppress it, a second presence stirred on the edges of her mind. Rahmagut. He slithered in the corners of her memory, igniting every moment of it, reminding her that she had willingly shattered the barrier keeping him repressed in exchange for the power to end the attack. The sick sound of the tinieblas ripping apart reverberated in her mind. She shivered. Rahmagut using her body like a den made Eva want to vomit. She pressed a fist to her lips.

"I remember I destroyed them," she said in a weak voice.

Maior exhaled in relief. She threw her arms around Eva and squeezed, her nose pressing against Eva's curls. She pulled away and said, "I didn't see it, but there's so much buzz about what you did—that it was a miracle."

Eva's cheeks warmed. The news troubled her. She didn't want accolades. She wanted space to process what she'd done. It was a relief that her gamble had paid off and the island was saved—that her sacrificing the integrity of her identity hadn't been for naught.

Eva bit her fist, the corners of her eyes building with tears. She glanced away from Maior's expectant gaze, terror simmering inside her. Despite Maior's obvious concern and love, how could Eva share what had truly happened with her? Eva ached for the reassurance from someone who could understand. Someone who already housed a demonic entity against their will. Someone like Javier...

Before Eva could reply, her bedroom door swung open. Reina entered, her eyes narrowed, but she paused at the sight of Maior.

Maior noticed the aggressive entrance. "What's the matter, Reina? Eva's just woken up."

Reina cleared her throat. She held her hands behind her back. "Great. I'm happy to see it."

"Then why are you barging in like this?" Maior asked.

"I passed Dr. Baltasar on the way here. He seems overwhelmed," Reina said, arching a brow with an unspoken accusation.

Maior rose from the bed. "Yes, I shall go. I just wanted to make sure my friend was all right." She passed Reina stiffly. "Do you need any kind of healing?"

Reina's jaw clenched. "I'm all right. Please go help the poor man."

Unhappily, Maior offered Eva a quick goodbye and left.

Silence descended on Eva's bedroom as Reina closed the door behind her, pressing on the handle to make sure it shut. Birdsong flowed into the room, along with the happy chatter of gardeners tending to the courtyard beyond Eva's balcony. Reina waited until Maior's footsteps were long gone.

"You dealt with the tinieblas all at once," Reina said in a flat tone. "You had help."

"*She knows*," Rahmagut said. "*Capable Reina.*" Eva watched Reina's slow approach, noting how she didn't react to Rahmagut's words. "*I speak only to you*," the Void god purred.

Eva sucked in a breath. Reina started ranting, her words loaded with accusations, her hand firm over the hilt of her golden sword. But Eva couldn't breathe. She felt trapped in a nightmare. If she closed her eyes, would she see Rahmagut's four pupils gazing back at her? The eyes of a monster who now shared her body.

"*And I do it gladly*," the male voice said, clearly capable of understanding her deepest worries and desires.

"Eva? Hello? Are you listening to me?" Reina said, leaning forward with her fists pressed against the bed for a better look at Eva. "You killed all the tinieblas like that because you are host to the god of the Void. To Rahmagut," Reina growled. "Are you aware of this?"

"*I was wondering when she was going to ruin your fun*," Rahmagut muttered. "*She is just like you.*"

Eva thought she understood, but she couldn't be sure. Her world was spinning, and she couldn't tell up from down. She covered her face with her hands in shame. At least, in the darkness of her closed lids, she couldn't see those pupils gazing back at her again.

"*Just like you have me, she has Ches*," Rahmagut said. "*That's why she's accusing you. Use that.*"

In her mind, Eva dared to ask, "*How is that possible?*"

"*Our seal was shattered.*" His answer snapped the last shred of deniability. She could speak directly to him, and they were caged with each other.

"*But it was* your *tomb.*" What was Ches doing in Rahmagut's tomb?

"Eva?" Reina repeated, expectant.

"*Trust my words, niña*," Rahmagut said.

Eva swiped at the air near her ear as if swatting away a pesky fly. She sat up, challenging Reina's cold tamarind eyes. "I can hear you!" she said. "You don't have to yell in my face."

Reina drew back, her hand returning to her blade's pommel. "How did you kill the tinieblas? Tell me right now!"

"You know how!" Eva snapped. "That's why you stormed in here. What, are you going to cut me in half like a tiniebla? We managed to make it through because of me—because of *him*," she said, her voice breaking as she avoided his name.

Reina stared, stunned.

Eva flung her covers off and crept toward the edge of the bed to get up. She wavered as a dizziness took over. In the end, she wasn't sure she could manage to stand up straight, so she remained on the bed. "Admit it! You know only because you also have Ches within you! You are as sick as I am."

Ire blazed in Reina's eyes. Rahmagut had spoken the truth. Reina snarled, "I am *not* sick. There is nothing wrong with me." She drew dangerously close, as if she didn't fear Eva at all.

"You're harboring an ancient entity. I beg to differ."

Reina sneered. "Ches gave life to this world. His light is the reason you and I live. Everything that exists is because of him. But *Rahmagut*"—she spat his name—"only brings chaos and discord. His own blood-damned creations slaughtered a dozen families and destroyed the homes of a dozen more—"

"I don't have to answer for that," Eva said quickly. "I stopped them! Maior said it herself: I saved everyone!"

"If tinieblas didn't exist, no one would need saving. Have you no compassion for the dead?"

The accusation burned Eva's neck and ears. Tears welled in the corners of her eyes, and she gripped her sheets until her knuckles turned white. As she took a deep breath, it dawned on her just how unnecessarily unjust Reina was being, and how callous Eva's own words had been. Now was a time for mourning the lost lives, yes, but Eva also deserved some grace.

Then she realized: The anger broiling her was not entirely her own. She was playing right into the animosities of the god of the Void. Perhaps Reina was, too.

Eva took another deep breath and wiped her face. "Of course I feel horrible about the lives we lost, Reina. You're forgetting I was there with you, *fighting*. I gave it my all."

Reina still scowled.

"But the tinieblas didn't attack because of me. Rahmagut has been within me since we emerged from the tomb." Her downcast eyes avoided Reina's. Her heart thrummed from her admission. "I've known about this all along. I was just...in denial." She found herself aching for Javier's company once again. He'd known from the very beginning. He would probably understand more than anyone...

Reina was silent.

"Ches has been inside you since that night, right?" Eva prodded in a small voice. She prayed it would soften Reina's sharp edges.

Reina nodded.

"So you know I speak the truth." Eva sighed deeply. "I'm sorry, but I think you're being unfair. I managed to stop them *because of* Rahmagut. My geomancia alone wasn't enough. Trust me, I tried. Without him, we'd all be dead."

Reina let go of her sword. She crossed her arms and took a deep breath. "I'm glad you stopped them," she muttered, as if it pained her to do so. "So...he didn't cause the attack?"

Eva searched within herself. She poked at his presence, demanding an answer.

"Why would I give you the power to destroy them if I were the one behind the attack?" he said after a while.

"They're your creatures."

"Indeed, they are. My imagination conceived them, and their creations require my power. But after they spawn, I don't control them unless I make concerted efforts to do so. You know the spell. Tinieblas behave according to their heart-starved natures. But, Eva, darling, I have been locked inside you. You opened the door for me."

"Are you controlling them right now?"

"I am trapped in your body. I would have to use your hands and spells."

Finally, Eva met Reina's expectant gaze. "It wasn't him. I would know."

Reina took another deep breath. Eva's bed creaked as Reina sat on the edge to stare at the sunny balcony.

A pair of butterflies twirled in the air and paused to inspect a wrought iron chair. The air hummed with the rhythmic sound of the waves. Peace had returned to their sunny paradise. Eva continued to have this life thanks to the sacrifices she'd made. She was trapped with Rahmagut, but at least the people who mattered most were safe.

"Where do we go from here?" Reina asked. She offered a pained smile, which Eva matched.

The words unspoken were clear: What did it mean to be chosen by the gods of the sun and the Void?

"*We didn't have much choice*," Rahmagut said flippantly.

Eva ignored him. "We were able to save everyone because of the gods. I don't think they are the problem." With genuine curiosity, she asked, "Have you told anyone? About Ches?"

"No," Reina said.

"Not even Maior?"

"Not even Maior."

Eva crawled under her covers and propped her head back on her pillow as her exhaustion returned in full force. "Maybe we should keep this between us until we figure out what brought the tinieblas."

"The truth won't be easy to swallow," Reina said in agreement.

"Who knows how everyone will react." And besides, Eva still needed to petition for Javier's release. She desperately wanted it.

"I think...we need to be careful," Eva added. "People react in strange ways when it comes to what they believe in." Treacherously, her mind took her back to the moment the people of Galeno turned against Doña Rosa. Now Eva perfectly understood that Doña Rosa had been innocent. Eva was the one who ought to be prosecuted for Void magic. With Rahmagut, she was the guiltiest geomancer of all.

Reina rose. "I'll keep your secret, if you promise to keep mine."

"Yes—of course."

"And I'm sorry for the way I spoke," Reina said, surprising Eva. "I let my emotions get out of hand. I don't think it was Rahmagut either." She headed for the door.

"Then who?" Eva said.

Before Reina could answer, Don Samón entered the room. His

surprise at seeing Reina was short-lived. He rushed to Eva's bedside and draped his warm hand over Eva's. "I am so glad to see you awake," he said.

Eva's chest fluttered with both apprehension and joy. Worry streaked his face. "I'm all right. There's no need to worry."

"Yes, there is—you didn't see what I saw. You fainted and fell from the roof. If it weren't for Reina's quick thinking...I don't even want to imagine what would have happened."

Eva blushed and Reina scratched her cheek, avoiding her gaze.

Eva couldn't believe that despite her suspicions, Reina still made consistent efforts to keep her safe.

"It was my duty," Reina reminded him. "But...I'll leave you to it."

"Eva, how did you do that?" Don Samón asked as Reina stepped out of the room. "Is this truly what you can do—what I failed to witness the night the tomb was destroyed?"

Pride shone in those carmine eyes. Eva liked seeing it, but she couldn't properly enjoy it. The real answer would only lead to his disappointment. This pride would rot before her eyes if he ever learned the truth. Amusement stirred within Eva, like the satisfaction of a dog rolling in a field of grass. "*You're enjoying this, aren't you?*" she thought, making a point to purse her lips, lest she speak out loud.

"*It is your shame that makes it all the more delicious, niña.*"

"*Stay out of this.*"

His smugness traveled through her again, until she felt his presence fade away.

To her expectant father, Eva deflected with "You know I have an interest in iridio—I've been trying to tell you all these days. I have a talent for it."

"There were at least a hundred tinieblas out there. I thought surely this would be our demise. Normal casters don't do what you do with iridio."

"I just did what I had to. I couldn't let the tinieblas get to us." Eva looked away, her chest tightening from the lies. She realized she'd been scratching the rash on her forearm when her fingernails lifted a scab, stinging.

"My daughter, it breaks me that you had to resort to Void magic to save us. I am disappointed in myself that it came to this."

Eva winced. And how would it pain him if he knew the real truth? "I am all right. We lived, and that's what matters to me."

"It is not that simple," Don Samón pressed on. "Void magic has real consequences. It damages the heart and soul. Geomancers are taught to believe that controlling tinieblas is a sin, because the consequences are not properly understood. Maior told me what happened at the tomb—how you had to seize their control from Doña Ursulina. Your antlers turned black after you emerged, and I understood; I knew you had suffered from this before—"

So he'd already noticed... "What? That's not— Just because we don't understand something doesn't mean we have to automatically fear it," Eva said, fluffing her curly bangs, hoping to hide her black-tainted antlers.

Don Samón was robbed of words, like he was seeing her for the first time as the fool that she was. But being fearful of something they didn't understand was exactly how the Serranos had controlled and repressed her life. Eva had changes she had to reckon with, and being afraid would only get in the way.

He leaned back. "I suppose you are right. You don't deserve to be chastised."

Eva appreciated his willingness to listen and consider her. He didn't dismiss her desires for their differences in age and status, as Doña Antonia would have. "I don't *want* to control tinieblas," she said. "If we'd had a choice, I wouldn't have. But we were out of options last night." Finally, a truth she could stand by. If given the choice, Eva would gladly go back, at least to keep the door separating her and Rahmagut shut. But what was done was done.

"Actually, Father..." Addressing him as such for the first time made Eva's heart skip a beat—how right and overdue it felt. "There is something I must tell you." Cold sweat dampened her palms.

She was surprised when his hand held hers. "You can tell me anything," he said as his eyes searched hers, devoid of any judgment, holding only gentle anticipation.

Eva looked away to the balcony, watching the few gulls who

circled the skies. Their cries filled the silence in her room. "I must ask that Javier be released from imprisonment."

"You told me he is cursed to turn into a tiniebla."

"Yes, but he was keeping it under control. He's been fighting it." Eva sighed deeply before admitting, "He had some control, until I broke it."

"What do you mean?"

She chewed the inside of her cheek. "He kept his curse in check, but that night, before we went into Rahmagut's tomb—I attempted the spell to control tinieblas on him."

Don Samón's expression darkened.

"I tried to take away his free will." Eva recounted the events leading to the destruction of the tomb. Javier losing his mind. Celeste's near death. The destruction of the tomb. She knew she had crossed a line she'd never be able to take back. If Javier deserved to be locked up for what happened in the tomb, then so did she.

She turned away from her father, her face aflame with shame and regret. "Everything that happened that night was my fault. I forced everyone's hands. If you will imprison him, then you must imprison me as well."

"Javier drove his sword through his niece's belly. His crimes are different from yours."

But how could he punish someone who had no control? Shuddering, Eva covered her face with her hands. What was the appropriate way to address Javier's crime?

Eva flinched as her father squeezed her shoulder. Gently, he told her, "This is why I insist iridio and Void magic are dangerous. Look at this pain you're carrying."

Eva shook her head. "I *know*. But I'm not naïve and foolish anymore. I want all of us to be safe and happy, and I want to be fair, like you."

Don Samón pulled away. She watched him, curious of his reaction, wondering if her bait had been evident. His eyes were hard, his lips a thin line. "Javier is cursed to turn into a tiniebla," he repeated. "How can you request his release after our lives were threatened by them last night?"

In her chest, Eva's heart twisted and turned. He was going to deny her. She opened her mouth and realized her first impulse was to give a contradictory answer: *I can control him.* She was a wretched creature.

She tried a different route. "But nothing is guaranteed. What if there is a way to break his curse and save him? Being alone is hastening his turning—"

"Have you gone to see him?"

Eva felt herself blushing. It was a silly question. There was no way not a single servant had seen Eva crossing the path to the fortress. That no one had caught a glimpse of her white nightgown smearing an otherwise inky-black night. "He is my husband. You were delighted when you found out he'd married me. The son of your old friend, Doña Feleva. How can you expect me to give up on him so easily? You told me we are the last of valcos, and that we must protect each other."

Don Samón smiled and nodded. "I wasn't planning on keeping him imprisoned forever. But I needed to gauge Enrique's reaction first. I thought he would care more about his brother attempting to murder his daughter, but he seemed aloof—consumed by other desires." He scratched his beard. "And you're right: He is your husband, the future father of my grandchildren."

Heat speared through Eva. She cleared her throat, shocked.

Don Samón went on. "But I have this nagging sense in the back of my mind that we are not safe. The tiniebla attack ended, but until we determine its cause, it could happen again. Our lives were threatened, even though Javier had nothing to do with it. So if you ache for his companionship, and you promise you will help him, and he can take up arms if the need arises..."

Eva nodded fervently.

"...then I shall trust you." Don Samón held Eva's hand again. "We will free him. But perhaps we should wait until there is less sorrow in Isla Madre. I want to focus on my people first."

Eva pressed her lips together. It wasn't ideal, but she'd gotten what she wanted.

Don Samón rose. He walked toward the balcony doorway, pensive.

"I went back to the tomb this morning. The magical signature that used to ebb and flow from it is completely gone. The cave is nothing but stone and rubble." He shoved his hair out of his face in frustration. "I spin it around and around in my head and I cannot make sense of it. I wonder if the tinieblas, the tomb's destruction, and the gods' unsealing are all tied together somehow."

His side glance met Eva's. Expectation weighed the air as he waited for her answer. In the end, Eva admitted, "I don't know where the tinieblas came from." She clenched her jaw as the presence within her stirred.

"*You know why he's asking. He's suspicious,*" Rahmagut said, skulking in the darkness. "*Aren't you trying to be the perfect daughter?*"

Eva ignored him. She'd made Reina a promise. And she couldn't shatter her father's heart today. "I'm sorry I can't help more," she muttered.

Don Samón dismissively waved a hand as he headed for the door. "Don't be. You've done enough. Rest now. You deserve it."

12

Tugging the Ribbon Undone

The morning after, Reina woke with a headache and a bad feeling in her gut, which had only worsened after she'd wrangled the truth from Eva's lips. Either Eva was a tremendous liar, or Rahmagut had had nothing to do with the tinieblas. Reina also considered the possibility that Eva was so far gone under Rahmagut's influence she couldn't answer truthfully at all. If Rahmagut was like Ches—Reina's belly twisted painfully as punishment for such a thought—then he had the ability to seize Eva's voice, controlling her reply much like Eva had controlled the tinieblas.

Such thoughts left Reina feeling sour. So far, Eva had done nothing but protect Isla Madre. Eva cared deeply about the Liberator, Maior, and the people they served. Reina struggled with finding her suspicions justified.

All morning, she burned with an impotence as hot as the sunlight on her shoulders. For someone housing a god, she was failing terribly at protecting her people. First, she couldn't save Juan Pablo, and now the people of Tierra'e Sol couldn't rest believing they were safe from darkness anymore. Reina would be exceedingly obtuse to remain oblivious to how her arrival on the island, with all her connections to the Águilas, Ches, and the god of the Void, had marked the beginning of the tinieblas' reign of oppression in Tierra'e Sol. The recent attacks had to be more than a coincidence, and no one else was better positioned than her to find and squash their source.

Without answers in sight, Reina's day was swallowed up by a pointless search through the jungle. Don Samón had assembled small parties to destroy any tinieblas lingering in the islands. Reina's group scoured Isla Madre—even the remains of Rahmagut's tomb—but found it devoid of any tinieblas. They didn't even find footsteps or traces of the horde's disruptions. It was as if, before emerging from the beach, the tinieblas had marched underwater from the mainland. It made Reina consider a worse suspect: the caudillo of Sadul Fuerte, who was still in Carao, awaiting Don Samón's answer for Maior.

The afternoon was humid and hot when Reina caught up to the Liberator in an open corridor leading to the courtyard. He was heading to the dining hall with purpose, after speaking with a general about his searches on another island. Reina joined Don Samón to give her own report.

"Are you telling me they can walk underwater now?" he said with a snort.

Reina shrugged. "They don't need food. Why should we assume they need air?" All tinieblas wanted were hearts.

Don Samón clicked his tongue, unconvinced.

"You haven't told me what you plan to do about Enrique's demands." The words fell out of Reina, but she couldn't bite down the nagging question any longer.

Don Samón stopped by the doorway to the dining hall. He faced her with a frown. "Reina. One problem at a time."

"He gave us a week to hand over Maior," Reina said, as calmly as she could. "What if the tinieblas were sent by him?" Don Samón's brows shot up when Reina added, "What if he's testing you?"

He regarded her in disbelief. "You're accusing him of intending to slaughter an entire island population just because I didn't give him what he wanted. If Doña Ursulina were still around, I would toy with such a possibility. But to control that many tinieblas? I cannot think about Enrique at this moment," he said in dismissal.

Reina didn't shy away. "I can go to the mainland and ask around—"

"You will stay here and support our restoration efforts," Don Samón snapped. "Enrique will not take kindly to you sniffing around. When the time comes, I *will* visit. You can rest easy."

Reina clenched her jaw. The answer wasn't enough. She couldn't trust he wouldn't continue his game of diplomacy. What if the next time the valco commanders met, Enrique offered to exchange Maior for the safety of Don Samón's people?

The pang of iridio draining from her heart hit her before she could press more. Fuming, Reina circled back to her room and found her iridio vial running low. She titrated the last few droplets into her heart and headed to the infirmary, where Maior had been stationed for most of the day, for a refill.

Inside, the building stank of blood. Reina sweet-talked a nurse for Maior's whereabouts and was allowed into the back storage, where she found her. Maior sat on a stool, overlooking a counter covered with ledgers and other medical supplies. She rested her head on her fist, nodding off. Her hair was up in pigtails held by yellow ribbons, with three wildflowers from the bunch Reina had gifted her tucked behind her ears. Reina had no personal inclination for accessories or flowers, but she found Maior's femininity so irresistible. How she would love to make those ribbons undone...

Biting her lower lip to stop a smile, Reina crept behind Maior and poked her side. Maior jumped and yelped. Her face turned as red as a poppy.

"*Reina!*" She smacked Reina on the arm, and Reina pretended to be wounded.

Like almost everyone on the island, Maior hadn't gotten a good night's rest. Nevertheless, Reina teased, "If you sleep on the job, it'll only be a matter of time before Dr. Baltasar sacks you for negligence."

Maior rubbed her face to shake the sleep off, making her lips extra thick and plump.

Dr. Baltasar entered the room, chuckling. "Maior, tired? Good thing I found a moment to make you the tonic you wanted," he said, extending a small vial that Maior immediately snatched and pocketed. She avoided Reina's questioning gaze as she thanked the doctor.

"What is Maior taking?" Reina said.

Dr. Baltasar opened his mouth but then thought better of it. "I suppose that's her concern, and not yours."

It only further piqued Reina's curiosity.

Chuckling nervously, Maior took a vial containing a black liquid from the counter, grabbed Reina by the wrist, and dragged her out of the room. Reina followed obediently until arriving at a room near the back of the clinic. The dusty room was weatherworn, its curtains the only barrier to the outside world after the windows had been smashed and left without repair for months.

"What are you taking?" Reina wouldn't drop it. She was already dependent on one geomancia reagent. The last thing she needed was to discover the same for Maior.

Maior worried her lower lip and handed Reina the iridio solution. "I assume you came for this."

"Please don't dodge my question."

Maior rolled her eyes.

"What's wrong? Don't like it when someone fusses over you?"

"It's different," Maior said, waving a hand. "I won't die, but *you* will. You have your iridio now. Fill up your heart or I'll do it for you." Her fingers found the scars along her forearms as she crossed her arms. Sometimes Reina caught her picking at them.

Reina held Maior's arms as they sat on the dusty bed. "What are you taking?"

Maior sighed and twisted her lips, avoiding Reina's eyes. In the silence, doubts crept into Reina's mind, reminding her about all the concessions Maior had made to live here with her.

Staring at the floor, Maior said, "It's a galio potion Dr. Baltasar offered me. It makes it so I don't need to sleep."

"That's absurd. You're a nurse, aren't you? You realize that's absurd."

"It's just temporary."

"Because of Laurel?" Reina asked.

In response to her silence, Reina leaned forward and squeezed Maior's cheeks, forcing her to face her. "Whatever concerns you, concerns me," Reina said softly.

Maior pried Reina's hands away. She moved closer so their shoulders were side by side and they could both stare at the bright outside world beyond the fluttering curtain.

"I already told you, I don't want to sleep. In my dreams, I relive Laurel's life. I loathe it. I am tired of it. The caudillo is often in my dreams," Maior said pointedly. "And even there, he is a bastard, but his wife adored him. I . . . relive their intimate moments together—"

"*You what?*" Reina said.

Maior winced, wounded.

Reina realized she'd overreacted. A thing she had promised not to do anymore. "I'm sorry."

"It's not that I want to!" Maior said. "That's why I'm going to take the tonic, and Dr. Baltasar promised to teach me how to mix it myself. I'll never have to sleep again."

Reina groaned. She tried to embrace Maior, but Maior resisted her. Reina said, "Please—you'll harm yourself. Not sleeping is like not eating, or like me not taking iridio. It will only end in disaster." She lifted Maior's chin and offered her a tender smile. When that didn't work, Reina pulled back and allowed her jealousy toward Enrique to fester into something else. No matter how hard she worked, there was always an obstacle waiting to topple her happiness. Maior was a light in her life. Their moments together gave Reina immense joy and meaning, because they led to a road where she could finally find the home and belonging she'd been denied all her life. But Maior's torment and the tiniebla attack still stood in her way. Both seemed to have a common root cause.

"You said that in your dreams Laurel had an artifact to control tinieblas," Reina said bitterly, recalling a similar curiosity in Enrique's possession when they met in Carao's inn. "Coated in a black tar?"

"Black clay," Maior corrected.

The similarities couldn't be a coincidence. Reina shot to her feet. "Don Samón thinks he can trust Enrique." She glowered at Maior, incensed from her sudden realization. "But it's obvious the caudillo wanted to weaken us. *He* sent those tinieblas. It makes sense why he took a whole month to do it: He needed time to gather such a large number of them. He's still obsessed with the idea of resurrecting his wife. He demanded you because you're all that's holding Laurel to this life. But I'm not going to sit back and let him do what he pleases. I don't care what Don Samón commands. I took orders from my grandmother once, against my instincts, and look where that took me."

"Reina—?"

"Enrique thinks he can threaten us? He thinks he can demand you without consequences? No. I'm going to listen to my instincts for once. And the only thing they tell me is that for this to end I must go to the mainland and kill Enrique myself."

Reina nodded to herself as Maior gaped. "For you. For me. For all of us." The words felt right, and overdue. She would never rest easy while he lusted for Maior.

Maior rose to meet Reina. "No. You're mad! That doesn't solve anything." Maior pressed her hands to her heart. "I will still have Laurel within me! No one is asking for that."

Reina looked away. She lacked the courage to shatter Maior's hopes by speaking plainly about her own possession by Ches. Their separation could be achieved only with her death. Once, Javier had attested the same about the spell Doña Ursulina had used to bind Doña Laurel to Maior. Even if Maior had been too stricken to remember, Reina hadn't forgotten. Javier had no reason to lie about this. Maior's pursuit of "cleansing herself" could very easily be a fool's gamble. What was solvable, however, was the threat of Enrique. "If the caudillo isn't around, then it won't matter."

"It matters to me! It matters to his daughter, who *you* have feelings for." Maior pointed at Reina. "Do you think Celeste will still like you if you kill her father?"

"*What?*" Reina said. "I told you—Celeste and I are cousins. We are history. We were best friends, and I ruined that. I don't want anything else between us. And I know killing Enrique doesn't fix your dreams, but I feel it in my bones: He deserves to die at my hands. No one wants to say it, but it makes sense that the tinieblas attacked us because of him. How can you have compassion for someone like him?"

"So you're admitting you're a killer?" Maior said with narrowed eyes.

"I've never pretended otherwise. *I murdered my own grand-mother.* You saw it." Reina crossed her arms as her heart raced and consumed what little iridio remained. "I have done far worse things than killing Enrique. But he must go. He will not threaten you anymore. He will not threaten the Liberator. He will not use tinieblas against us."

Maior's gaze withered.

Reina sighed and wiped her face. "I'm sorry. I *know* sometimes fighting for our survival is brutal and messy, but you don't have to concern yourself with it. I'll do everything to keep you safe, even if it turns me into a bad person. I don't care about dirtying my hands as long as you don't have to suffer. Please, trust me."

Maior squeezed Reina's arm. "You're not a bad person. I wouldn't like you if you were."

Reina held her breath, just as she held on to Maior's words. She'd never grow tired of hearing them. *Maior liked her.* Their stolen kisses made this obvious. But it was one thing to surrender to the pull of attraction, to admire the shape of Maior's curves and long for what hid underneath her clothes, and another to hear it from her lips. To know these feelings were reciprocated and true.

Reina wrapped Maior in her arms. She gently tilted her chin up and made Maior's lips hers.

In her arms and between their lips, Maior whispered, "If you think my not sleeping is a foolish solution, I agree—but I don't want to be in Águila Manor every time I close my eyes. But you conspiring to kill the caudillo of Sadul Fuerte, Reina, it is mad."

Reina pressed her thumb to Maior's lower lip, indulging in its softness. "He wants you, and I will not let him take you."

"Here's an idea: How about we find a way to free me? Why don't you help me get rid of Laurel?"

"If there's a way, I will help you," Reina said without thinking, though she had no expectation that such a solution existed. But perhaps it was what she needed to say so Maior would calm down and Reina's instincts could take over, guiding her to trail her lips down Maior's neck as Maior whimpered but welcomed them.

"I'm not weak. I'll find my own way," Maior said softly while Reina pushed her down onto the creaky bed. Maior's pulse quickened beneath Reina's lips. "I can't be like this forever."

Reina didn't care either way. She liked Maior exactly as she was. If Laurel was a permanent part of Maior's life, Reina would simply learn to look the other way.

She laid down Maior, whose pigtails were now lopsided. Reina took her time tugging the ribbons, marveling as she undid Maior's hair. She was so beautiful, with her flowers still above her ears. "You don't have to change anything. You are perfect," Reina said. Maior had already accepted Reina and her heart of iridio. Reina owed her the same.

"I don't need your approval or protection," Maior muttered stubbornly.

"How can you deny me that?" Reina whispered as her hand traveled under Maior's skirt, tracing her stockings until her touch glided over her bare thigh. There was no rejection in Maior's eyes, so Reina dared to venture farther up, meeting the soft folds of her belly. Reina didn't know where she was going. All she knew was her ache for more—and an instinct to discover places she hadn't been to before. How her stomach clenched, and her heart raced, greedy for Maior. "You said I was your protector," Reina said.

Maior smiled coyly. Her hand joined Reina's under her skirt, and Reina feared she was going to be expelled, a boundary crossed. Instead, Maior's fingers guided her toward her middle. And Reina obeyed, docile, as Maior nudged her down, where Reina's fingertips discovered a carpet of hair and a wetness below.

A silence enveloped them. Reina held her breath, her own lower belly pulsing. Did Maior share her curiosity? Was this the invitation to explore more?

As Reina's fingers reached for the first fold, discovering a mound, Maior exhaled a moan. She sat up immediately, and Reina withdrew, scared.

"No," Maior breathed, one hand bringing Reina's fingers back to that wet center while the other held Reina's neck, preventing her from retreating.

Hesitation held them prisoner. But finally, Maior admitted, "That felt good."

"Do you want more?" Reina asked. She was under a spell. She was flying over the fluffy clouds of Tierra'e Sol. She was engulfed in the warmth of Maior's center.

The moment Maior breathed "Yes," Reina's emboldened fingers reached for more—two, then three exploring her and stroking exactly as she wished Maior would one day stroke her.

Maior whimpered and moaned. She squirmed on the bed, making Reina wish she could reach closer—deeper. Suddenly, Maior grabbed Reina's wrist to stop her. "*But* I must get back to work." Her face split into a smile. "We're still in the infirmary."

Reina glanced at the dilapidated room, at the rotting wood of the storage chest and the dust accumulated in the corners. At how filthy the bed beneath them was.

"Fine," Reina said, easing back sticky fingers, her chest twisting in disappointment. But she felt safe that Maior was hers. No one was going to take her away. There would be time for more.

As if knowing the power she had, Maior reached forward and tenderly kissed Reina, teasing her with the promise of what was to come.

13

Discord in the Ranks

Upon Dr. Baltasar's insistence, Eva spent the whole day after the tiniebla attack bedbound. She had bruises and cuts she hadn't realized she'd amassed. Secretly, she had hoped Maior would be the one to treat her. Instead, she got an unpleasant woman who gushed about "the miracle" Eva had granted Isla Madre. Once Eva emerged from her room the following day, she found the island a somber place, as its inhabitants mourned the people they'd lost.

Dressed in a gray gown, Eva accompanied Don Samón and Ludivina to the village chapel after lunch, where a few volunteers, including Maior, had hastily organized a memorial service. The day was cloudy. The usual hum of life that accompanied early afternoons on the island was gone: There were no drums played by resting laborers, no calls of exasperated mothers summoning their children for a bath and lunch, no braying from the donkeys returning from the jungle paths heavy with the harvest of plantains. Carnation bouquets had been hastily propped against some of the houses, in memory of the dead.

A heady energy weighed the island. Eva prodded Ludivina and her father, wondering if their valco blood hummed like hers, but found they were oblivious to the discomfort. Eva's arm hair rose as she glimpsed the island's destruction and saw shadows where there ought not to be. She caught movements in the trees or in the hanging laundry when there was no wind. Could these be an omen of the tinieblas' returning? Rahmagut's disagreement filled her, but he gave her no answers.

She hesitated outside the chapel doors.

"*Are you afraid?*" Rahmagut purred in her ear. "*We won't catch fire. This is nothing but a regular building filled with false idols.*" Then he concluded, as if in addendum, "*Pretty art.*"

More sweat trickled down behind her ears. She wished there was a breeze to lift the heat. "*False idols? Because you are so true? Besides, it's just that it's stifling in there,*" she explained. In Galeno churches, she'd never burst into flames either, but there were times when she had grown faint and nauseated, when she had to grip the pews in front of her to remain standing. As the afterthought struck her, she asked him, "*How do you know about that superstition?*" Pentimiento had arrived with the Segoleans, as far as she knew.

"*I may have been sealed away for years, but I heard the whispers of your world. I listened to the fear. I planted discord. It is very boring, otherwise.*"

"Eva?" Don Samón asked as he noticed her lagging behind.

She took a deep breath. She knew she was expected to practice Pentimiento with her father and Ludivina. Until now, Eva had dodged all their invitations to Mass, for she had abandoned the religion since leaving Galeno. But today's service was too important for her to miss.

Squeezing her hands tighter, Eva stepped within the stifling shade of the small building. Vaulted ceilings with the amateur frescoes of angels and saints decorated the apse, faces of despair and rapture juxtaposed within the painting. Eva's mouth opened at the sight of a tailed nozariel woman with long black hair pacing the altar behind the priest. She wore a loose dress with an overabundance of goldenrod and crimson in the pattern. The service was moments away from beginning, and no one seemed to acknowledge the casually dressed woman stepping out of bounds. She met Eva's gaze, impassive, then left through the chapel's back door.

Eva sat next to her father, who didn't notice anything amiss despite his valco blood allowing him to perceive geomancia. Perhaps the woman was yet another ghost, like the many spirits Eva saw roaming Isla Madre.

Rahmagut's laugh reverberated in her inner ear as the service began.

"Who was that?"

"Why, your Virgin," Rahmagut said in that mocking tone she'd begun to despise.

Her nose wrinkled. A nozariel? She looked nothing like the brown-haired, blue-eyed woman in Pentimiento depictions. And why should Eva take his word for it?

"You shouldn't. Just like you shouldn't trust them either."

"Who is them?" Annoyance overflowed within her, but his reply never came as he retreated, and Eva was stuck with following the motions of the service in silence. Thankfully, it passed in a forgettable blur.

Though the music didn't return to the island, everyday work bustle did. Don Samón and his head matron devised a reconstruction plan and assigned workers to rebuild the affected areas.

Still in her stuffy gray dress, Eva chewed the inside of her cheek as she surveyed the endless stream of petitioners who lined up in the dining hall. Campesinos waited for a word with their Liberator, begging for support to rebuild their lives. Eva sat next to her father on Ludivina's former chair, which Ludivina had gladly relinquished upon his revised succession plan. Now that Eva had to be the one trained in matters of Tierra'e Sol governance, Ludivina had the freedom to enjoy her childhood.

Each campesino followed the same mannerisms as the person before them: They offered their undying gratitude for Eva's miracle, crowing about how her arrival to the island was a boon. Eva accepted the reverence with a tight smile and wondered if they would say the same things if they knew it was thanks to the god of the Void. Then they extended invitations for her to visit their homes and eat their dinners or take from their family heirlooms, before finally addressing Don Samón, requesting compensation for their damaged homes or livestock.

The long line neared its end, with the sky turning a deep red beyond the windows, when Reina burst into the dining hall like a hurricane. She passed the campesinos and approached Don Samón with a scorn that made Eva's stomach turn. Reina pointed behind her, saying, "What happened to keeping him locked up?"

Eva pushed out of her seat. She held her breath.

Don Samón's surprised gaze traveled from Reina to Eva, disappointment settling as Reina's meaning sank in.

Reina stepped closer, her voice shaking as she said, "I thought you understood. He needs to be restrained, but he's just—"

"I didn't—we haven't—" Eva muttered, doing her best to ignore the soft chuckles ringing in her ears. She knew Reina was talking about Javier, but Eva and her father had agreed to release him *later*.

Don Samón followed Reina, who led the way out to the descending beach path, the one Eva had taken many times when the moon was highest. Walking the same sand-covered cobbles and with the setting sun gilding his antlers, Javier entered the gardens, his face in shadow. *How?* was all Eva could ask herself. Her chest fluttered, and she was uncertain if the light would reveal the twisted expression of his tiniebla taking full rein. If they would all see her as his conspirator, vouching for his innocence when he was too far gone.

"Halt, this instant," Don Samón said.

Javier listened, which showered Eva with relief.

"What is the meaning of this?"

His face still shrouded in shadow, Javier lifted an iron key on its chain—the one Eva had used time and time again to cross the bars separating them.

Eva's hand automatically shot to her skirt. The last time she'd handled that key, she'd stored it in her dress pocket. Her eyes narrowed. She'd forgotten to hang it in place because *he* had taken it from her. She let out a huff of disbelief. All this time, she'd assumed his proximity during her last visit had been born out of his desire for her . . . not so that he could steal the key!

"Eva Kesaré gave me the key. You needed my sword during

the attack and you didn't have it. You can't expect to keep your son-in-law locked up forever."

There was a flicker of hurt in the glance Don Samón directed at Eva.

With a clenched fist, Reina stomped down the path. She was unarmed and her clothes were sweat stained from volunteering to rebuild Isla Madre.

"Reina, please," Don Samón said.

She halted. "You cannot release him. He can't control himself—he almost killed Celeste *and* Maior."

"Yes, I can."

Don Samón and Eva also approached. Whatever sunset light remained allowed her to take in the details of Javier's face, how his eyes remained mocking, but valco.

Reina's disbelief and betrayal twisted her face as she watched Eva. But Eva was also unwilling to back down. Maybe Javier's release hadn't occurred in the most optimal way, but his place wasn't behind those iron bars.

Relief and Rahmagut's approval washed over her.

"Reina, he was possessed," Eva said softly. "It was not his hand."

"Tinieblas killed our people two nights ago. He's *turning* into one!" The words grew big and loaded with the possibilities awaiting Eva and Javier's future life. "You call yourself Maior's best friend, but don't you care that he tried to kill her? How can you let him loose?"

Eva's temples throbbed from the accusation. She measured her reply carefully and said, "The tiniebla inside Javier wanted to sacrifice Maior for a particular purpose." Her brows shot up, and she hoped that Reina would read her silent plea to drop it. Couldn't Reina see that the tiniebla wouldn't be inclined to harm Maior now that Rahmagut had been freed from his seal? But the more Eva explained now to appease Reina, the more questions Don Samón would have.

Within her, Rahmagut chuckled knowingly. It sparked Eva's fears that she was missing something. Were Javier's tiniebla and Rahmagut communicating somehow? And was Eva just foolishly stepping into a trap? On the matter, Rahmagut was smug but unresponsive, so she pushed the thought aside.

"The tiniebla doesn't want that anymore," Eva added, though unsure. "Right, Javier?"

Don Samón grew suspicious. "What was the purpose? What does it want now?"

Eva's heart skipped a beat. A confrontation would only unravel their truths. Was Reina so oblivious? Didn't she want to keep their gods a secret?

"I'm in control now. I promise," Javier said, stepping forward. Eva saw that Reina was tempted to lunge for him, but Javier raised his hands, pleading. "I know you refuse to believe anything I say, but I still want to let you know that I never meant to hurt Celeste. What happened that night—it was not in my control."

"I will never trust any word you say. You taught me that the first day I met you," Reina said.

"I don't have a reason to antagonize you anymore—"

"Because you had a reason before?"

"I'm practically banished from my family now—stripped of everything I grew up expecting. You're not interested in my side of the story, so I won't waste your time. But my allegiance now is to Eva, and thus to the Liberator. Enrique...I have always loathed. Let us find common ground there."

Reina was unappeased, and Eva feared an escalation. She held her fists to her sides and, in the softest of words, whispered, "Hold your tongue." Javier's eye twitched almost imperceptibly, signaling that her command had worked. Eva hated doing it. But she was walking a very fine line, and she needed Don Samón and Reina to calm down. She couldn't risk Javier ruining it with his signature contempt.

"If neither of you is willing to see eye to eye, we must agree to be civil," Don Samón said in a level tone. "I had already made the decision to release him."

Behind them, a small crowd of witnesses had gathered, including soldiers who were organizing the island repairs and nosey maids hesitating before taking the gossip up to the kitchens.

"How can I trust you won't lose control? What's to stop you from murdering someone?" Reina asked.

"*Me*," Eva said. She loathed admitting the dark power she

wielded, especially after promising Don Samón that she would be cautious. As if he were watching the most entertaining performance, she heard Rahmagut laugh.

"Reina, I need you to be obedient," Don Samón said. "You don't need to agree with everything I do, but trust that I have the wisdom to command, and that I have a reason for the decisions I make. We already went over this."

Reina stepped back and lowered her eyes to the ground. In soft, insolent words, she added, "You say that you are different—"

"From Enrique? I am. But Eva is my daughter, and she saved us all. I believe she at least deserves the benefit of the doubt in this regard."

It was bitter seeing Reina's wounded eyes. Once, Eva and Reina had bonded over their shared dislike for Javier. How easily Eva had changed her tune. She felt like a traitor, corrupt for smearing Reina's hope in Don Samón's leadership. She felt trapped and tugged in all the wrong directions. His release was what she'd wanted, but Javier had gone about it all wrong...

"Keep away from Maior," Reina growled at Javier.

"I have no intention of even saying a word to her."

"Don't forget that I can break you," Reina said, before storming away, her shoulders tense.

"All right. Enough of this spectacle," Don Samón announced, and his staff quickly scattered. He told Eva, "We discussed this, but not once did I say you could take matters into your own hands."

"I told Javier about the attack. I'm afraid there'll be another one. I freed him now because we need all the help we can get," Eva lied. "I apologize, Father."

The word was magic, disarming him. Somewhere deep in the depths of her consciousness, the Void god offered his compliments.

Don Samón crossed his arms, still displeased. "Make peace with Reina, if you can. I cannot have this discord within my own ranks." He pointed at Javier and added, "And you—if you step out of line even once—"

"I understand my place. I am not a child."

"Indeed, you are not."

As soon as her bedroom door shut behind her, Eva shoved Javier against a wall.

"Easy there—I didn't know you were so desperate for me," he said, his hands rising in the small distance between them.

"You need a bath," Eva said with bared teeth, angered by his nonchalance.

"Is this meant to be…an aggressive offer?"

She pushed off him, both to thwart his joke and because she genuinely could not stand the smell of his grime. "I can't believe you stole the key!"

"Should I have waited until you took your sweet time to feel sorry for me? Maybe by then I would have gnawed my hands off, or sprouted a tail and become even more hideous than Reina. If that's even possible."

"I was working on it! But now you've made my father think he can't trust me."

"Well, he can't," Javier said, and Eva wished she could punch his arm.

"I had to lie for you!"

"Because it's better to have an ambitious daughter than a possessed son-in-law you can't control?" he asked, stepping closer, as if he could still use his usual charms. Alas, with his stained clothes, the effect was entirely lost.

Unfazed, Eva said, "Don't make me turn you into a puppet."

Javier raised his palms in the air and retorted, "I quiver at your threats." He met her glare in earnest as he added, "And you didn't lie to him. Not really. I'm more useful to you free than imprisoned. Have you forgotten what I'm capable of?"

"It is precisely because we remember what you're capable of that no one wants to see you free!"

His cheeks reddened. She couldn't handle the contradiction it inspired in her. How could he be so pitiful, yet so unbelievably infuriating at the same time? And why did she care about his feelings at all?

She stormed to the balcony doorway. It was better to stare at the smear of the moon's reflection on the water than to see the hurt in his eyes.

She flinched as he placed a gentle hand on her shoulder. He pulled away from her rejection.

"I'm sorry for acting alone. I wasn't lying when I said I couldn't wait any longer," he said.

"I know," she said softly.

"I don't intend to keep you in the dark anymore. I know it wasn't easy to vouch for me, but you still did it."

His words sparked a fluttering in her. It made her afraid to face him.

"No one told you to visit me and keep me company every night after what I did at the tomb. I owe you for that, and I intend to pay it back. I owe you for many things, actually."

Eva braced herself as she turned around. There was no deception in his eyes. "Promise me you'll be by my side?"

Her heart jolted as he said, "That's the only side I'm on."

"You'll keep my secret."

Like an oath, he repeated, "I'll keep your secret, even if you already told everyone about mine."

Eva smirked. "Honestly? The tiniebla was your alibi." She yanked his pinky finger. "And you absolutely cannot tell anyone about Rahmagut."

His tilted his head. His words were soft when he said, "If you command it, I physically can't."

Eva chewed on the inside of her cheek. She knew she didn't need to command him into silence. Even if he had complicated things with her father, perhaps Javier was deserving of some grace and forgiveness.

"I'm not going to order you around," Eva told him, pretending she wasn't affected by his rare, crimson eyes. "Just don't do it." She let go of his finger. "And why are you so...grimy? I don't remember you being this gross when I last saw you." She chuckled and he rolled his eyes.

"I didn't free myself just now," he said as her eyes doubled in size. "I was out there killing tinieblas."

Eva had to remember to close her mouth. She glanced at his antlers. "Those were *your* antlers?"

"You saw me?"

"Yes! But I figured it had to be another tiniebla. It was too dark and rainy to be sure." Suddenly, she wished she could throw herself on him in an embrace. "You were helping us against the tinieblas...Why didn't you reveal yourself sooner?"

"Because it would have cost me my life. Reina would have used the opportunity to cut me in half. You would have assumed the worst—that I had lost myself—"

"*No*—"

"*Yes.*" He shook his head, adamant. "Just like you commanded me into silence a moment ago. You don't trust that I can contain myself." His jaw tightened. But how could he expect her to trust him so suddenly, when his actions had always been so unpredictable in the past?

"I worried about you. And the fate of this island," he added after a second. "No one could have imagined that you were going to kill them all."

Eva nodded, her heart swelling.

"I didn't intend to free myself immediately when I took the key from you." He turned away in anger. "I was willing to wait one more day, as you repeatedly asked me to. But part of me...struggles to trust people. I feel no comfort in leaving my fate in someone else's hands." His eyes were soft when Eva reached for his arm. "So, yes"—he sighed—"I freed myself when I heard the attack, and I went back to the jail after. But you didn't visit me last night. I had no idea what was happening out here. Were you injured? Were you done with me?"

She tugged him closer and rested her head on his shoulder, wrapping her arms around his arm. They faced opposite directions, but their closeness was new and exciting. She wanted to embrace him in thanks. "I wish you would have just said that from the beginning."

"You know I like to have my fun with you."

"*Too* much fun."

Was this what being on the same team felt like? Her cheeks warmed from the realization. The trust of a spouse was something she hadn't felt until now. Eva had viewed their marriage as a transaction, but now, it felt different. No one else understood her as intimately as he did. No one else could give her the safety she sometimes needed, now that she had Rahmagut. Reina was possessed by a god, but she'd never give Eva the camaraderie she craved. Reina worshipped Ches; she probably didn't have any problem accepting him within her. But Javier understood. He was also trapped against his will.

Rahmagut's amusement was like a showering of dirty water. *"And you don't worship me?"* His tone was full of mockery, so Eva ignored him.

She left to call for a servant who could ready Javier's bathwater and to put some distance between them. She didn't return until hours later. To her immense relief, Javier was tucked in bed, awake but silent, observant but keeping to the close edge of his side. By his nightstand were empty bowls and his dinner utensils. She almost smiled but stopped herself. It would only reveal that she cared.

It took some willpower to resume her usual routine of slipping into a nightgown behind the wooden changing screen in the corner, after enjoying Maior's company for so many nights. She slipped under the bedsheets in the darkness but clutched her freshly refilled iridio pendant in her hand, her fingers still weighted with her geomancia rings. Without meaning to, her mind took her to the moment when Tiniebla Javier had pinned her beneath him, proving just how powerless she had once been. But that was in the past. Now a single word was enough to rein him into obedience.

The thought lulled her to a comfortable sleep.

She awoke later, by Rahmagut's tomb.

She found herself sitting by the lagoon flanking the tomb's entrance. Near her, on a boulder, sat a man with a long face, light brown skin, wavy black hair cut close to his jaw, and eyes with two pupils each that watched her as if they knew her deepest, darkest desires.

Because they did.

14

The Void Gem

Bronze pauldrons and gauntlets were all that covered his muscled upper body, aside from the black ink crawling from his neck down to his built arms and his lower belly. A fine belt engraved with intricate patterns held up rudimentary pants, shielding the path of the tattoo from view. His boots were worn and muddied from the jungle. A tail like Reina's switched behind him, restless, the tip extending with long ringlets of black hair.

The moon was full and high, painting the clearing in shades of gray. Eva hugged herself. She still wore her sleeping gown, the airy linen fabric providing little protection against his monstrous, piercing gaze. She had to look away from his all-seeing eyes. Shivers ran down her back.

"I have been inside you," he said, as if in response to her shyness. There was a mildness in his tone, and a comfortable strength. He had the upper hand here.

"This has to be a dream," Eva said, wishing for clarity. But the jungle buzzed with crickets. A mosquito flew near her cheek and she swatted it away. It didn't feel like a dream.

"Rahmagut?" she whispered, terrified.

He did not reply. His smile only widened.

There was a rustle behind him. As Eva's sight adjusted to the darkness, she saw eyes in the shadows flanking the Void god. An audience of tinieblas. She sucked in a breath. In her rib cage, her heart pounded.

"You worry about your modesty and how you appear to me, but I have been in your mind, and in your heart." He rose, sidestepping the glistening lagoon and threatening to approach her.

Eva stood as well.

"I know you crave power and recognition, for someone who has accomplished so little."

"Not for a lack of trying." The words escaped her before she knew she was saying them. Eva raised her chin. She thought of the night at the inn in El Carmín. Only here, Javier wasn't around to safeguard her from the consequences of her foolish words.

"I know you crave companionship. Even if it comes in inadequate forms, like that husband of yours."

Fear froze her—how he knew so much about her while she knew so little of him. Eva found herself forcing each breath.

"I know you enjoy the power you hold over me."

"No," she lied, her gaze flicking to the shadows behind him. She instinctively reached for the pendant hanging around her neck, to check if it was still there. Its weight pressed against her collarbone. She'd imagined that this god had brought her here disarmed, but as her hands felt for each other, she found she still had her geomancia rings.

Eva found some measure of strength. "It's my body. You have no right to be here."

He waved a hand in the air. "We would both benefit immensely if you weren't so afraid."

"How?"

"Eva, sit. Relax. This is all in your head." He dipped his fingers into the lagoon, swirling them as if enjoying the cool water. Each one of his fingers was adorned with geomancia rings, too. Some even had rings sitting on the middle knuckle.

She sat, more not to contradict him than because she wanted to. "You're in my body because I am powerful," she said callously.

He nodded. "You were the better choice." When she squinted in confusion, he added, "For once, Ches and I were in agreement. We went where we desired and the outcome is that I am now here, with you. I'm about to make you the most powerful woman to ever walk this land." He smiled. It was a look that enthralled Eva, not just for what it meant, but because of the way he said it. Flippant. Assured.

She shook her head, snapping out of it. "I'm not falling for this again," she said, thinking of Javier.

"Again? How often do you converse with gods?"

"You've been in my head," she said with nostrils flared. "You know how I got here."

"Yes, but don't act as if you're powerless," he said sharply. Leaves shuddered, as if stirred by his displeasure.

Eva glanced away, her cheeks heating. She was reminded that, once again, she was foolish and overconfident.

Rahmagut said, "You can tell me to leave, as you have. You can summon me, as you have done as well. All I ask in return is that you do not attempt to get rid of me. It's a fair thing to ask, no? Life is a beautiful thing worth preserving, yes?" When Eva didn't immediately answer, he added, "Please, Eva, enough with your fearful act. I don't wish to harm you. I would have done so already if I wanted to." His smile warmed, like he was regarding a long-lost friend.

"You wish to live through me?"

He nodded.

"Haven't you lived for thousands of years?"

Laughter barked out of him. He massaged his temples, amused but woeful, as if she couldn't be more wrong.

Eva relaxed against the boulder. She supposed she could get used to this—his presence and attention. The truth was undeniable: She shared a body with a god who *chose her.*

"I spent too many years sealed away," he said. "Even trapped in your body, it is like a breath of fresh air."

"Maybe you should find your own body," she said, mimicking his lighthearted tone.

He tilted his head. "In due time, I hope we can strive for that." Eva couldn't ignore the sharp longing weighing his gaze. "Eva, with me, you are a changed woman. And the world will no longer view you the same way."

She crossed her arms, wishing to contradict him. But she couldn't.

"Our secret will not be kept forever. The name Rahmagut is one that inspires fear and ambition in many. There will be those who seek to undo us."

Her father came to the forefront of her mind.

"Ches walks this land."

Reina's disappointed scowl came to her like an admonishment.

"We must vanquish him."

Eva frowned. Was her bond with Reina strong enough to withstand the gods' animosity? When they'd fought over Javier's release, she could already see their tenuous relationship fraying and unraveling. It felt as if every time she ran into Reina, there was something to argue about.

Eva shut her eyes. All she wanted was to be a Bravo heiress. She was supposed to finally come into the person she was born to be— an educated, confident valco who was neither afraid nor weak. Yet she had everyone around her—from Rahmagut to Reina—pecking at her constantly, placing their expectations on her.

Perhaps...this would be her challenge. Perhaps she *was* fated to become the strongest geomancer in all of Fedria, and Rahmagut's return was just a stepping stone. With an ally as powerful as him, she would have no one to fear or bow down to.

"You were sealed away in the Void all those years," Eva muttered. "What was it like?" She had so many questions. If he wanted her trust, he needed to give answers.

His gaze shifted to the caved-in tomb. "I don't remember."

"Why were you sealed?"

"I don't remember."

"How did you end up sealed there?"

He stayed silent.

"Do you remember anything?"

His irritation became obvious as he glanced down to his hands and toyed with the gold ring on his middle finger. "After so many years trapped in the Void, a veil fogs my memories. The reasons for why I do things feel unclear. All I have in me is a purpose to live, and a hatred for the person who took my life from me. My mind would have faded, too, in due time. But I held on. Slowly, it returns."

"Who took your life?"

Fear stung her when he glared at her. "Need you ask?" he barked, and the trees trembled again from his echoing words. "Do not insult me. I live inside your mind. You know I speak of Ches."

"I'm sorry," she said, meaning it. "You live inside my mind, but you don't tell me everything."

Rahmagut rose. Eva was frozen while he towered over her with his masculine strength. "I am your friend, but not without conditions. Do not confuse me for your minion. You are mortal, and I am a god. I do not owe you answers. I give you what I wish to give, at my leisure."

He gently lifted her chin. His touch was hot, bordering on scalding. "Eva. Breathe."

She obeyed. It calmed her. Nevertheless, she was arrested by his eyes.

"Now, I brought you here because I do wish to give you something. It is something you must retrieve. A gem."

He extended a hand like he expected Eva to take it. She hesitated. His palm was warm when she complied, and large, the single folding of his fingers surrounding all of hers. Eva was not a small woman. She'd never been a small child. But Rahmagut had a build unlike anyone she had seen before. Vitality exuded from his very skin. He gave her the leverage to descend from the boulder and guided her toward the collapsed cave opening.

"What is it for?" Eva said.

"It is a concentration of my power—something I crafted before I was sealed away."

More questions blazed through her, and Eva bit the inside of her cheek to keep her silence. He'd just attested to not remembering the events leading to his sealing, yet he remembered this? It was obvious he was spinning her into a web of lies. But how was she supposed to carve a way out?

"If you retrieve it, it will be yours," Rahmagut said, like a lover, his hand squeezing hers.

She nodded. In their silence, it became hard to ignore the desire blooming in her belly. It was an ache that reminded her of her lonely days in Galeno, when she wished her life was something more. When she longed to have the courage to break free. She was struck by a need to descend into the tomb. It didn't make sense why she would want this, unless she was feeling Rahmagut's yearning.

"I promise you it will be worth your while," he continued. "It will give you everything you want."

What *did* she want?

She wanted to bring pride to her father. She wanted to save Javier from his demon and have a proper marriage. She wanted to be fair, but also to take her own pleasures. "I want to be undeniable." The words fell out of her lips before she could stop them. They felt true, and revealing.

"Do you think anyone denied me, in my time?"

"I know nothing about your time. Only tales and superstitions."

"How will you learn the truth if you fear what's ahead?"

They spoke with the impenetrable cave before them, side by side.

"The tomb was destroyed," Eva said, feeling foolish at having to state the obvious.

"It is in there. I feel it in my bones. Don't you feel it in yours?"

She was suddenly filled with ambition, and curiosity.

"Retrieve it now, before it is too late."

She twisted her fingers for an incantation of bismuto. As the spell kicked in, Rahmagut rushed to the cave entrance. That broad torso of his swelled as he displaced one boulder after another. Eva watched with her mouth agape. The cave groaned as he unearthed as much as he could from his tomb, the surrounding jungle trembling.

"More!" he bellowed, and Eva understood her task.

She summoned the inflaming strength of bismuto again, watching in awe as it surrounded them both in a golden sheen.

Rather than standing idly while he dug deeper into the opening, Eva summoned an explosive energy of iridio to her hands and pushed it forward to help him.

Rahmagut shoved silky black waves out of his eyes and granted her a smirk of approval. As the cave swallowed them in dust and darkness, their golden iridio illuminated the tunnel's rocky walls. They descended.

The journey to the tomb's sanctum was inconsequential. There were no tinieblas, no words with the Void god who seemed more like a phantom conjured by her own imagination than a real entity.

As the tomb's sanctum bridge had been destroyed, and the caving of the previous tunnel had opened an underground stream, Eva and Rahmagut waded through the water to reach the elevated center. A rancid smell filled her nose as she ascended to where the collapsed statues of Ches and Rahmagut lay. The smell made her stop. She recalled that night. Reina's grandmother had murdered seven women on this very altar. Their bodies likely remained beneath the rubble.

Eva glanced up at Rahmagut. The realization of where she stood washed over her like a cold bath, freezing her muscles and sending tremors through her core. What was she doing here?

His hand draped over her shoulder. "Do not waver," he said. "You've made it too far to back out."

She gulped and immediately regretted it. It was like she was swallowing the very rot in the air. "I'm not a bad person," she said. Was this for him? Or to remind herself?

"Should I be responsible for the actions of others? Should you?"

Impatient, he grabbed her wrist and yanked her forward, to where his statue's face had been smashed upon collapsing. The smell grew stronger. Eva tried fighting the tug, but his grip was unbendable.

As they stood before the ruptured statue, Eva found the source of his desires. A glow of geomancia bounced off a stone set in Rahmagut's eye—the statue's eye. Eva distinctly remembered this statue had sat with its eyes closed. Perhaps when it collapsed the layer of stone or clay meant to depict his left eyelid had cracked, revealing the glimmering stone beneath. She nearly chipped a fingernail trying to pry it out.

"*Niña*," the god growled beside her, "use your tools."

Indeed, she popped it off easily with a boost of bismuto.

Her skin prickled in fear as the gem clattered to the ground, released from its hold. But this anxiety wasn't hers. Rahmagut was worried about the gem shattering, unleashing what it held inside.

Eva retrieved it, feeling it icy to the touch, leeching her warmth and strength. It reminded her of iridio's innate negative-pressure properties. She inspected its smooth midnight-blue surface, marveling at the way it caught the glow of her geomancia, the reflected glimmering like a million tiny stars.

Beaming, Eva presented it to Rahmagut, only to find herself alone in the sanctum.

She took in a heavy breath, calming herself, even if it came with its faint note of rot. She considered calling his name, then decided that would only turn her into a scared child. No, that Eva was no more. She clutched the Void gem close to her heart. The gem tugged at her, sucking. Her fingers tingled. In her palm, she now held all Rahmagut's immense power.

When she returned to her room, she had no recollection of how she'd made the journey from the tomb. But the tangible proof was in her hands, the gem leeching her heat, as was the mud and grime clinging to her espadrilles and nightgown.

"Where have you been?" A voice startled her as she approached the changing screen. Javier's red eyes glowed in the darkness. He sat up on the bed, his tiniebla-scarred torso uncovered by the bedsheets.

"That's none of your concern," Eva whispered. Slipping out of her muddied gown, she added, "Did you forget how many times I snuck out to see you? I made it into a habit. Now I can't sleep right." She smiled at her lie.

15

Duality

Boots, clothes, and braid drenched in salt water, Reina found herself on the sandy bank of a river mouth. The night grew meek as the sky welcomed the rising sun in the far horizon. She squinted at the palms by the bank of the river, wiping the moisture from her eyes. Behind her, the serene waters of the Cow Sea lapped an otherwise undisturbed beach. She was confused.

Her boots sank in the unstable sand as she turned, finding herself in the company of a tall man. Antlers. Smooth dark brown skin. Warm eyes, red, like the sky right before dusk. Her god.

She nearly threw her forehead to the sand in reverence, but he lifted a hand between them, keeping her in place. "We're not in Isla Madre," she said. The differences between the beaches were minuscule, but she knew the island well by now. This looked like the beach she had crossed shortly after traveling from Gegania. "Is this a dream?"

"Don't treat it like it is, or you will get hurt." He paced the sand, and she followed obediently.

"Why are we here?" she said.

"The power of my opposer grows, and tinieblas are coming. You must stop them."

Her hand automatically traveled to her belt. Nightcleaver hung from it. She had no recollection of ever dressing or arming herself. She had spent her day in casual clothes, volunteering about

Isla Madre. She cleared her throat, also remembering how she had fallen asleep tangled in Maior's arms.

"I couldn't stop them last time," she said, swallowing the shame threatening to bubble out of her. A handful of tinieblas was a terrifying challenge for most people, but she could handle it. A horde, however, was impossible for her alone. "Rahmagut gave Eva the ability to destroy all tinieblas at once," she said.

Ches faced her with nostrils flared. "You will compare me to that man?"

Reina's neck blazed. She realized her blasphemous mistake. "No, I mean—"

"Did Rahmagut create the sun? Did he grant this world the nourishment needed for your species to exist? *No!*" he said, his voice a resounding echo. "He couldn't because he is not a real god. He exists within your friend thanks to the part of me that he stole...without which I am unable to predict and prevent his scheming. Otherwise, he would be as useless as that ghost inhabiting the body of your lover."

Reina frowned. So Ches did know of Reina's affections and experiences. He knew what stirred her blood and made her chest twist and flutter.

Ches watched her, unflinching, his expression free of disapproval or reprimand, like he accepted her exactly as she was.

"I was wrong to compare you. Please forgive me," Reina said.

"It is done," he said impassively.

"Everyone believes him to be a god."

"Tales that evolved from lies."

Reina exhaled, relieved. She was comforted by the admission, not just from overcoming the embarrassment of knowing Ches was privy to her relationship with Maior, but because of Eva. Ever since she'd wrangled the truth out of Eva, Reina hadn't been able to shake the concern. It'd weighed on her shoulders. The stress had killed her appetite, as she worried that Eva was up against a god all on her lonesome—that Reina, thanks to Ches's possession, was the only one capable of managing Rahmagut's return in Eva. But Ches comparing Rahmagut to Laurel sparked hope.

"What's Rahmagut scheming? Is he behind the tinieblas?" Reina asked.

"I said I can't know."

She glanced down at her boots, ashamed her questions only inspired disappointment in him. It wasn't her intention to displease him. She just wanted answers, and the peace to live free of the Void's darkness. "Is there something I can do to stop him?"

"I prefer he be vanquished altogether."

"Tell me how and I will do it," Reina said earnestly.

"You will have to end all those who host him," Ches said without hesitation. "Including Eva."

Reina's mouth dropped. She stared down at her scarred and calloused hands and was deeply ashamed to consider them the hands of a killer. Her neck blazed. She was incapable of accepting such an order. In fact, it transported her to a previous time, when she was trapped in an equally abhorrent disposition—in a murder plot designed by her grandmother. But these were Ches's words... How could he ask that of her?

She opened and closed her mouth several times, unable to muster the right words. But he was inside her, she reminded herself. He *knew* what lurked in her heart. "I can't do that." Reina's heart thrummed as she spoke honestly. "Eva's a part of my life."

Ches was indifferent. "Maybe you can, maybe you can't. It is impossible for us to speculate on it at this time. If I need to act, I shall. Your only role is to be my host."

She locked her jaw, disturbed.

"Do not agonize over it. If you're the one fated to do it, then you will find yourself capable."

His words gave her no reassurance. What kind of path lay ahead that Eva's end would be necessary? Reina grew sick toying with the idea. It would dismantle her life. Don Samón, Reina's commander, cared deeply for Eva. *Maior* loved Eva.

"Your feelings about Rahmagut and his host are not what's important here," Ches said.

Reina couldn't be stung by his words. They were not new. She had grown up being reminded of how little her opinion mattered.

Of course he would feel this way as well. He was great and she was merely lucky to have the privilege of serving him.

"I want you to consider yourself like a house to me—a dwelling," Ches said. "Your body serves to shield me, to give me a physical form so I can walk this land."

"Forgive my insolence, but do I have some of your powers?" She extended her sunburned forearm for him to see. "I feel stronger, but my skin still peels."

"Enough with the apologies. I am angry, not unreasonable. And to answer your question: I am divine, but your body is mortal."

Behind her the sun began to rise, revealing the smoothness of his eyes, rubies under the sunlight, unmarred and infinite. The dawn gilded his antlers. He was here with her, but there was nothing real about his appearance. Would her hand go through him if she extended it beyond his torso? Was he made of air? Of sunlight?

"But yes, your strength is multiplied. To wield a fraction of my power is a simple and just trade for the privilege of holding my existence. However..." He paused, gazing at the lapping sea. He stepped closer to Reina, cupping his palm over the crown of her head as if she were a child. To him, perhaps she was. "We coexist in a battle of wills. Yours against mine."

"I don't wish to battle you," Reina said automatically. She was giving herself willingly.

He smiled. "That's because I don't try to overcome you. I prefer to be your guest."

She nodded and he moved his hand away.

"I could take over if I wanted to, using my own strength until your body could handle no more. Until your bones shatter and your skin dissolves. That would be the price of utilizing my strength."

"So...I'm powerless—"

"*Or* you can wield it alongside me. You can open your soul so that it coexists with mine when my divinity exudes from your mortal shell. You can see when it dazzles your eyes or feel when it burns your skin, and guide me to pull back when necessary. It will be a dance of our consciousnesses. A state of duality where we exist as equals within the bounds of your body."

Reina's eyes rounded in concern. How could she pretend to be an equal to a god? How could he expect her to have the same measure of mental strength as him? "A duality?"

He gave a small laugh. "You can call it that, I suppose."

Reina was reminded of Don Samón and the blade that was no longer Ches's, but hers.

"It is something I have done in the past," Ches said.

"With who?"

His smile warmed. "Don't concern yourself with it. My intention is to underscore that it is possible. I need you to master this. I need a body I can wield so I can vanquish Rahmagut."

Reina swallowed his words with a wavering ego. Maybe she wasn't unique, but his power would be a boon. It would help her forge a new path where she could solve all her problems without having to hurt Eva. Reina was willing to do everything within her reach to protect her new life. She thought of Maior, and a passion ignited in her chest. Her happiness was within reach.

"All right. Then let us do it," she said.

"You are hungry for more?"

Reina thought of her newfound purpose, of the words she had blurted out to Maior. She thought of that moment when Don Samón had overcome her best efforts at a level-headed duel. Her real enemy wasn't Rahmagut, but Enrique, for twisting people's lives in the pursuit of his desires. As long as Doña Laurel haunted Maior's body, Reina knew everything she cared about was at risk of being taken away. Unless...she became powerful enough to best him. Unless she was successful in her gambit to end his life.

"Let me reach Duality with you," Reina said, hoping he wouldn't inquire about her reasons. Maybe he already knew.

"We shall start slowly," Ches said. "We shall attempt the simplest step of existing simultaneously. The first taste."

Reina nodded eagerly.

He placed his hand over Reina's, superimposing his body over hers. A flash of colors ripped through Reina's mind at that instant. Fugues of blood and fire, conquest and rebirth. Scenes rushing past her eyes as if she were seeing every life lived before her. Faces she knew and people she'd never met. Juan Vicente teaching her "Heart of the Llanos." The beat of drummers reveling to Saint Jon the Shepherd. Celeste handing her the machete with the iridio-enhanced tip. The familiar smear of Rahmagut's Claw in the night sky. A church in Segolita crumbling as fire raged out of its arches and spires. A slimy, bloody newborn with thick black hair nestling into her sweaty arms. Two pairs of eyes, not her own, giving Ches the ability to see. The burial of the last living valco.

It was too much, as if an axe had split her head in two. The ache was incomparable to when her heart had been replaced. Reina howled and fell to her knees on the sand. Tears streaked her cheeks. She wiped them away and discovered a trail of blood from her nose.

Standing before her, Ches said, "It will get easier every time, but not without stretching your tolerance to the pain."

She breathed deeply, her body shuddering. He waited in silence as she sat back and cleaned the bloody snot and tears from her face. Her head throbbed. She squinted away from the rising dawn.

"Was it too much?"

Reina smiled. Her god cared. "I am too weak, is all."

"It is not weakness. It is your body telling you something is wrong. You were born to wield a mortal mind. You are not yet equipped to support a god."

Reina pushed herself up to her feet. She wavered, ignoring the headache. Pain wasn't something she hadn't experienced before. Her existence was one of suffering. From the loss of Juan Vicente to the loss of her heart, of her family. And she was tired of losing. She was tired of being pushed around for everyone else's agenda. Reina was building a brand-new life. She had a future to look forward to. Her heart pulsed for Maior. The years they had ahead, the good times that would come, if the caudillo of Sadul Fuerte didn't take it all away.

"Can we do it again?"

Ches didn't hesitate in fulfilling her request. His hand graced hers, entering her body, and images consumed her mind again. New scenes of soldiers slaughtering each other in battle; people giving birth to new generations; her own memories of holding hands with her father, and of the nun who took pity on her when she became orphaned. The migraine in her head lessened, though, enough that Reina was conscious of every nerve along her skin. It was as if she were being scorched by flames.

When Ches let go, Reina retched onto the sand.

The moments passed in silence, along with the pain, and Reina asked for it again.

She withstood the agony several more times as dawn draped the crystalline waters of the Cow Sea. As it unveiled the fluttering spindle palms behind her, the scuttling lizards licking moisture off leaves, and the gulls who circled above her.

Reina endured it while Ches was a conscious entity sharing her body. Duality burned through her, but the pain was bearable enough not to overwhelm her senses. Taking a step forward was a dizzying battle of pain and wills. She did it slowly, gritting her teeth, curling her palms into tight fists. They walked for a few minutes—it was all she could handle—before Reina was reminded of Ches's earlier words.

Tinieblas were coming.

She saw the shadowed creatures trailing out of the jungle behind her, the sight enabled by Ches's valco eyes. At first they were a handful, snarling and hooting, amalgamated and amorphous. Until Reina saw the endless procession, like the horde that had attacked Isla Madre. She stood mere paces away, but they ignored her, as if she were not there at all. They deviated west, toward the edges of Carao, where Don Samón and Enrique had met for parley. But Enrique's banners were gone. The village was completely devoid of protection.

With a stiff arm, she reached for Nightcleaver, but her mobility was impeded in Duality. She couldn't do anything as the first few tinieblas ransacked the house at the edge of Carao. In the beautiful dawn light, a husband and a wife fled their home in terror, only to have their hearts wrenched out of their chests.

Reina wanted to scream and couldn't even do it.

She retched again as Ches let go. He stood beside her, immobile and unfazed by the ensuing massacre.

"Awaken, Reina." His words echoed in her ears. They carried a dizzying, ethereal quality.

She gulped down air, the muscles and bones she'd abused in her hunger for Duality rejecting her command to move.

"Rise, Reina. Tinieblas are coming, and you must stop them."

16

Call to Arms

Reina rose with a gasp. Maior rose, too, her hair tangled and her squinting eyes a testament to the fact that she had forgone the sleepless galio tonic. Her hand tried to seduce Reina back under the bedsheets, but Reina resisted her.

Premature dawning still draped the outside world. Reina was back in her bedchamber, her body in one piece and intact, missing any ache from Duality's aftermath. What she had experienced had been a warning.

She didn't know how to explain it. She just knew her meeting with Ches had been a premonition. Carao was moments away from being razed by tinieblas.

"What's wrong?" Maior said, rubbing the sleep from her eyes.

"Tinieblas," Reina muttered as she flung the covers off and rushed to dress. "There's going to be another attack."

There was no time to explain. If her dream was true, then the attack would happen shortly after dawn. Judging by the sliver of light peeking from the watery horizon, they had an hour, if they were lucky, before tragedy arrived on the shores of Carao. She commanded Maior to dress, and to prepare for the worst.

Within moments Reina was banging on Eva's door to wake her, then on Don Samón's. He answered, and maybe it was the familiarity of the scene and not just her conviction that swayed him to prepare his units to cross the Cow Sea.

"Ready your troops. I'm going ahead," Reina announced before taking off toward the docks. She couldn't wait until Don Samón's galleon was loaded and ready. Every moment they wasted would be a life lost.

A bismuto spell renewed Reina's strength as she took a canoe for the short distance between Tierra'e Sol and the mainland. She rowed ferociously. Then she glimpsed a fire on the horizon. The attack was starting.

Reina docked and rushed to a village resonating with cries of pain. Nightcleaver whistled out just in time to sever a tiniebla in two. She leapt from one to the next, her lungs burning as she slayed them one at a time. At the center of the town square, where Don Samón's copper statue stood, the repellent spell exuded weak, glittering threads. The spell petered out after banishing two or three tinieblas, leaving the village defenseless against the incoming horde.

The sun rose, its low point on the horizon dazzling Reina. She stopped a tiniebla from climbing through the shattered window of a home, yanking it back by the hooves. The demon's claws slashed at her. Reina ducked and severed its hawklike head in one clean swing.

The screams of a woman drew her into another home. Its door hung from broken hinges. A rattan cross lay strewn across the drawing room, useless in its promised protection against demons. Reina rushed in and was met with a tiniebla headbutting her with its sharp horns. The impact knocked the air out of her. A sharp pain flared as her side bled. Reina swung mercilessly at the tiniebla, banishing it from existence.

The sun rose higher, just as the screams of terror and agony climbed in dissonance around her. People ran out of homes, children and valuables in hand, only to be struck down by creatures they couldn't see. They ran into alleyways unsuccessfully, meeting gruesome ends in the claws of monsters that never hesitated in going for the heart.

Reina's attempts were like trying to cover the sun with a thumb.

It was a repeat of the night in Isla Madre. By herself, she simply wasn't enough, and Don Samón's reinforcements weren't arriving. Ches was in her, but he remained quiet. So she forced him out with Duality.

She thrust his spirit forward, forcing his strength to rush through every vessel in her body. Ches entered her thoughts. Her nerves flared, and a resounding headache addled her. Burns ate her skin. Her bones vibrated, throbbing, but she was flushed with strength. She was able to leap twice as far and strike thrice as fast. Night-cleaver raised, Reina zipped through the horde like the godly vessel she was. Her every cell imploded, agonizing her, but she endured, ending the horde.

Don Samón's party arrived too late, once it was done. Once the newly orphaned children sat huddled in the town square under the statue's shade, crying for the loss of their families. Once bodies littered the ground, their chests carved open, blood and entrails spilling out with no heart in sight. Reina watched them as she stood beside the inn, where the able-bodied tended to the injured. A terrorized girl clutched her arm tightly, and Reina didn't have the heart to let her go.

Sweat drenched her clothes and bangs. Blood coated her forearms. Tears streaked down her cheeks. Her shoulders and elbows bubbled in blisters from the strain of Duality, which she had gratefully relinquished after slaying the final tiniebla.

It was a victory tasting thoroughly of defeat.

Upon meeting Maior's rounded eyes of concern, Reina collapsed to her knees. Immediately Maior took her in a soft embrace. Reina shuddered for the lives she had failed to save.

Don Samón strode from one shattered dwelling to another, his brows furrowing as he took stock of the damage. The wounded and scared huddled inside the inn. The village elders accepted whatever provisions Don Samón's soldiers could spare, and the appointment of a few men equipped with bismuto as protection from further attacks.

The inn overflowed with people, so the innkeeper could grant Reina a only small, dingy room filled with grain crates, barrels of beer, and a tiny bed. There, Reina found a moment alone to catch her breath. She closed the shutters, expunging the meek, slanted daylight, and began wiping herself clean with a washcloth. She gave the door her back as it creaked open, allowing Maior in.

"How did you burn yourself?" Maior muttered as her hand hovered over the painful blisters on Reina's shoulders.

"I don't know," Reina lied. "I've been sunburned for days." It wasn't much of a stretch. Such was the life in Tierra'e Sol.

The first blister cracked as Reina turned to look. Pus trickled down her back. Maior wiped it up with a moist, prickly cloth, and Reina sucked in a breath. Her forearms were covered in burns. She was too afraid to look at her thighs. Judging from the chafing of her pants, her legs hadn't been spared.

Her body hadn't reacted well to the prolonged exposure to Duality. Ches had warned her that her skin would melt off, that her bones would crumble, as her body wasn't yet ready to endure his divinity. Reina had played a risky game, but she also couldn't stomach not doing everything within her power to save as many lives as possible.

"It's all over your arms," Maior said.

"If you can't spare the galio to heal it, just numb me," Reina said, aware that Maior had to care for the other injured people.

Maior gave her an incredulous squint. "I saw the fire, but your clothes are not burned. They don't smell like smoke either. What's going on?" She leaned forward, tipping Reina's chin upward as if she were trying to seduce the answer out of Reina with a pout.

Reina held her breath, and her words. She couldn't tell Maior about Ches or Duality. Each admission would only unravel one truth after another. She didn't want to imagine how Maior would react to Ches's return and the danger of Rahmagut in Eva's body. One day Reina would muster the courage to tell her, but today she was tired.

"*I'm fine,*" Reina muttered. Her hand squeezed Maior's side, bringing her closer, hoping the proximity would make Maior give up her inspection.

Maior stepped back. "Your injuries disagree."

"I can't kill tinieblas if I'm concerned about being pretty. It's my job."

Maior scowled and swallowed her retort. She soothed Reina's pain with galio, then dressed the cut on Reina's abdomen and bandaged her blisters. She did it in tender silence, her fingers leaving a burning trail along Reina's belly. Perhaps she understood Reina had no interest in recounting the brutal event. Then she exited to continue her nursing duties, but not without first planting a kiss on Reina's lips, leaving her aching for more.

Don Samón's soldiers patted Reina on the shoulder once she rejoined the common area. They thanked her earnestly. Reina blushed as some of them even bowed their heads when she passed them by. The survivors had recounted the event to all curious ears: Their lives had been upended with the arrival of dawn, but they lived thanks to the nozariel woman who had cut down tinieblas faster than the eye could blink.

Reina ate her rationed bowl of mondongo silently, her ears burning as the children scrutinized her without shame. A small crowd sat at the dining table she'd chosen, as if proximity to her gave them safety and reassurance. One boy even asked her to teach him how to fight like her. She nodded, muttering, "One day," and the boy beamed.

Soon enough, the Liberator returned from assessing the damage. Reina followed him to the courtyard housing an outdoor wood-fire oven, where the innkeeper promised they would have privacy to talk. Several banana trees grew in the yard, providing shade to tables covered in flour dust. Two romping kittens followed Reina's heels in curiosity. Past the clay roof opening and the hanging potted plants, the sun showered them with light.

Don Samón sat on a creaky bench, wiping the sweat from his face. Reina lingered near the closed door, awaiting his interrogation with apprehension.

"How did you know Carao would be attacked?" he asked.

Reina knew the question was coming and had a lie at the ready. "I was at the docks, coming back from Isla Bendita. A fisherman came from Carao asking for help. He told me the village was being attacked, so I decided to warn you before rushing ahead."

Don Samón paused, his brows curving. "You were searching for tinieblas in Isla Bendita?"

Reina gave a brisk nod.

"Do you not rest, Reina?"

"I had a bad feeling," she muttered, and this wasn't a lie. The uncertainty of the tiniebla attacks, Rahmagut's presence, Enrique's threat, and Javier's release had been weighing on her mind relentlessly.

Don Samón wiped his face again. His jaw was taut, and Reina feared he would interrogate further. It seemed his exhaustion won, for he let it go. "Very well. Thank the Virgin I have you. There were deaths, sure, but at least there are survivors. I'm grateful for that, and for you. Thank you."

Reina stared at her boots as warmth filled her. Her smile was bittersweet. She'd rather prove herself in less devastating ways. "It is my duty."

"I don't know what to do about these attacks—I haven't felt this powerless in years—"

"Enrique is sending the tinieblas, and we have to confront him," she said without thinking. She was simply tired of waiting with her arms crossed.

Don Samón winced. "How can you suggest that?"

"The first attack happened immediately after you met with him and denied him what he wanted."

He gave her an unconvinced frown.

"Enrique has an artifact to control tinieblas. That deer skull thing—you saw it when we met him, right? He was trying to repair it when we delivered Celeste."

Don Samón groaned.

Reina went on, ignited by her belief. "Doña Ursulina gave it to him so he could control tinieblas without Void magic. Maior told me so."

"Maior?"

"She relives Doña Laurel's memories in her dreams."

Don Samón groaned again. He rose and turned to the unused oven. "That is absurd. Your proof is a dream?"

Reina paced the yard. "You know her possession is real. You can see Doña Laurel in her. Those aren't just dreams. The caudillo never had a need to use or repair the flute because Doña Ursulina did his dirty work. But... I killed her," Reina said with a tight chest. She gulped down the shame. "So he repaired the flute to control tinieblas himself. And yes, I believe Maior's account because I used to serve his household. It was my job to observe everything, and I know he doesn't see you the way you see him."

Don Samón shot her a side glance. "How does he see me?"

"As a rival and as a threat."

"I have nothing to threaten him with. And why would he let me see this flute if he's using it as a weapon?"

Reina smiled bitterly. "Of course he would be blatant about it. He was sending a clear message. And if you didn't know what the deer skull was, then he had no reason to hide it."

Don Samón's neck reddened.

"He sent the tinieblas to undermine you. It forces you to use up the iridio in your stores for the tiniebla repellents, and your coffers end up fattening his. He's weakening you so the next time you meet with him you have no option but to hand over Maior. He is winning in every way."

With a broken scoff, Don Samón said, "That is quite the elaborate plot just to get her."

"Then why wasn't he here to protect Carao? We met with him recently and he's already gone without a trace?" Reina decided to ignore Celeste's threat of giving him access to Gegania, which would explain the sudden vanishing; however... "He departed so conveniently—I thought he intended to wait for Maior." Her palms grew slick. Her tail switched behind her restlessly.

"Enrique has the most powerful army in Venazia. He doesn't need to hide behind dark magic to get what he wants," Don Samón said.

Even if her proof was questionable, Reina felt so sure of the caudillo's animosity. Had Don Samón never seen the wicked, disdainful side of Enrique? Had Reina been such a successful fly on the wall in Águila Manor that only she understood how little the caudillo regarded the lives of others? If he cared so little for the lives of those who served him—something he had proved when he banished Reina from his lands—why would he care for the people impacted by his stratagem of weakening the Liberator? Her blood boiled as her anger sparked anew. She remembered the cries that had echoed in Carao amid the attack. She remembered the cavalier way he had demanded Maior's handover.

Don Samón crossed his arms. "We cannot be equipped with ignorance. Would you have me storm Águila Manor while I have these tinieblas to contend with, or without even making sure Enrique is the source?"

"Let me do it," Reina said. "You've seen what I can do."

"What?" he blurted out.

Irritation speared her. Don Samón wasn't oblivious to her strength. Now his soldiers understood her worth and the townsfolk recognized her name. Not as the granddaughter of the infamous Ursulina Duvianos, but as Reina Duvianos, the wielder of a god-granted blade.

"Let me find the source of the tinieblas. We can't just wait for Enrique to attack us again."

"No," Don Samon said, his voice as firm as his visage. "I do not want you to go looking for him."

"We can't sit here and wait for his next move!"

Don Samón approached, towering over her. Fear rippled along the back of Reina's neck. She hated the reaction. She hated how he could probably see the iridio shuddering in her heart, revealing her discomfort.

"You may have your opinions on Enrique," he said. "You are entitled to them. But you are not considering the true implications should I endorse this. It would be an act of war against one of my oldest allies."

"And sending tinieblas isn't?"

"Easy, Reina. We don't have real proof. You are asking me

to swallow too many ludicrous tales. I have made my decision on the matter. You may have saved these people from tinieblas, but you are still no match for Enrique and his resources. I will not lose you to your bullheadedness. I will not instigate a war on a hunch we can't prove. Perhaps it is your own bias creating this conspiracy. You need to let go of this hatred and—"

Before he could finish, a great hubbub rose from the common area beyond the door. Reina stiffened, apprehensive of another attack. She swallowed her objections and, imagining the worst, led the way back inside.

A local boy had come into the common area, yelling about sighting military men. Reina rushed to the nearest window and saw people dismounting in the stables. A party of seven, commanded by a man dressed in a navy jacket with epaulettes and embroidered golden laurels. They swiftly entered the inn.

"Don Libertador!" The commander waved a hand in the air, completely disarming the nervous eyes watching him. He had brown skin with even darker sun spots peppering his cheeks and nose. Coils of gray hair peeked out from under his navy cap.

Recognition washed over Don Samón. He met the man halfway with a handshake, then a hug. "Don Rigoberto, my friend!"

The man took stock of the inn's common area, of the wounded lying in cots and of the uneasy soldiers standing guard. He grimaced and said, "I am going to assume this was caused by tinieblas?"

Don Samón nodded.

Don Rigoberto pressed his cap to his chest and bowed his head. "It fills me with sorrow to see it."

"How did you know?" Don Samón said.

He handed Don Samón a rolled parchment, the crimson wax sealing it engraved with the laurel-and-stallion emblem of the Republic of Fedria. The inn's bustle quieted down as Don Samón unrolled the message.

"A summons from the president," Don Rigoberto said before Don Samón could finish reading it through. "We need you, Libertador."

This was when Reina noticed the tired bags under the man's

eyes; the windswept hair; the wear and lack of shine on his rich leather boots. His entourage also looked worn and weary.

"This is a call to arms," Don Samón said, turning to face the inn, his gaze traveling from Reina to the other soldiers under his command.

"Indeed." Don Rigoberto added, "What happened here isn't unique."

Reina's mouth slackened as her theories against Enrique weakened before her eyes.

"There have been other attacks elsewhere? Where? How many more towns?" Don Samón growled.

"A hacienda and a settlement west of Segolita suffered an attack two nights in a row," Don Rigoberto said. "The cabildo sent reinforcements, and the tinieblas were held off, but not without experiencing significant losses. Before I left the city, I got word that La Cochinilla had been completely decimated."

"*Decimated?*" Don Samón said, rousing whispers of distress within the inn.

"Our archbishop of Segolita, Monseñor Sebastian, and the archbishop of Galeno, Monseñor Lorenzo, both agree: We are entering a new era of demons."

Reina didn't say a word, but maybe her scowl was loud enough to draw Don Rigoberto's attention. He eyed her, his gaze traveling to her swishing tail, noting how she stood in proximity to the Liberator.

"Why would they say that?" Don Samón said.

"When you sent us word of the ancient spirits unsealed from your island, our Monseñor Lorenzo communed with the Virgin and confirmed it."

"*Ancient spirits?*" Reina exclaimed.

She knew she was speaking out of turn. The Liberator probably expected her to simply watch from the fringes. But she couldn't withhold her irritation for any slander toward Ches.

Don Rigoberto waved a flippant hand. "Spirits. Demons. Names that come up only in folklore: Ches and Rahmagut. Those gods the nozariels worship."

Anger blazed through Reina.

Oblivious, Don Rigoberto told the Liberator, "While they were sealed in that tomb, all was well. But as you said in your letters: They're not sealed anymore. They roam the land freely, insulting the Virgin, and She will not protect us if the pagans and disbelievers continue to worship them. Their influence is what stirred the tinieblas."

The innkeeper, who was handing out coffees, gasped and clutched the cross hanging from her neck. Murmurs replaced the inn's silence.

Reina watched Don Samón with disbelief. She knew he practiced Pentimiento, but she never imagined he would have such an opinion of Ches. So her hunch to withhold the truth from him had been right. He'd never understand Ches like she did.

She ground her teeth at their ignorance and audacity. The people of Isla Madre and Carao lived *because* of Ches and Rahmagut. Prayer didn't protect people—geomancia and the gods did.

"We need your leadership, Libertador," Don Rigoberto said.

Don Samón nodded solemnly before seeking a table where they could talk more privately.

Reina followed him, whispering heatedly at his heel, "You will leave Tierra'e Sol undefended if you heed the call to arms."

"If the president needs me in Segolita, then we must make haste," Don Samón told her wearily. "Not doing so is treason. The archbishops are correct. We have entered an age of magic, and these attacks are just the beginning. I cannot stay cloistered on my islands with my arms crossed any longer."

Reina wished she could howl at him to let her pursue Enrique. At least she would be doing something!

"Whatever the source of tinieblas may be," Don Samón said, "it will become apparent to us soon enough."

Lips pursed, Reina nodded stiffly before withdrawing from the inn's watchful eyes. She grew incensed by the leash Don Samón had placed on her. She wouldn't fight it, because she cared for him as a commander, but she also wouldn't abstain if the opportunity to end Enrique's life presented itself. Tinieblas attacking other towns had dismantled her theory, but Reina wasn't prepared to let go of her enmity. Maybe that made her a fool. Maybe she was lying to herself, spinning webs to justify violence against Enrique. But if he made one more move to take Maior away from her...

No—Reina would never again obey a command blindly. Doña Ursulina had taught her that lesson the hard way.

Part 2

17

The Future of Valcos

Sitting between Segolita and Carao were stretches of the Llanos called the morichales, named so for the overabundance of moriche palm trees flooding the countryside. To pass the time on the long journey to Segolita, Eva made small talk with the man leading their caravan. She was astride a stubborn donkey that didn't obey her, but rather followed the guide's steps, as if walking by inertia. The guide kept her entertained with tales of trickery and conquest, of scorned lovers, and even of a llanero in a jipijapa hat who was able to defeat a fire-spitting ghost with a mere contrapunteo duel.

Presently, the morichales were flooded. It was normal for these parts, the guide attested when the caravan stopped by a small settlement consisting of a brewery, a banana plantation, and a fruit stand bursting with said bananas. The rainy season flooded the Río'e Marle basin. The overflow settled on the morichales, creating a natural habitat for the caimans, the rodent-like lapas, and the chigüires that submerged as Don Samón's entourage disrupted their peace.

As they didn't have enough horses, donkeys, and mules for the entire party, and their carts would inevitably end up stuck in the flood, they had to take the long way to Segolita, doubling their travel time.

Eva was hot and irritable when Don Samón and his stallion caught up to her stubborn donkey. Beaming, he pointed at the wooden fences in the far distance. She squinted in the direction, dazzled by the setting sun, until a building came into view.

"I recognize that place!" he said. "Cheer up, Eva. It's Hato de los Lobos. You will sleep in a soft bed with a full belly tonight."

A leaning araguaney tree shaded the arched gates of the large hato, a vast pasture for raising cattle that was commanded from a central hacienda.

Eva gave him a smile, even as she was aching and sore from the ride.

Their caravan was met fondly by a middle-aged caporal riding a sorrel horse with a mane more blond than red. The head cattle handler was probably a good decade older than Don Samón, judging by the wrinkles and white whiskers in his mustache. He was another former ally from the war, and Don Samón hugged him after dismounting. As Don Samón proudly introduced her as his daughter and the caporal beamed at Eva's stunted antlers, she instead noted how his horse's mane was covered in braids and silk ribbons. It struck her with a pang of homesickness. The Serranos had many horses. Braiding their manes was how she and Néstor used to pass the time. With a deep twist in her belly, Eva hoped that wherever he was, Néstor got to live the life he'd always dreamed of.

The dirt road into the hacienda was flanked by a conuco of yucca, plantain, and sugarcane on one side and a fenced pasture of snoozing cattle on the other. The hato's land was vast and never-ending, the pastures disappearing beyond a horizon line bordered by moriche palms. The constant hum of cicadas blanketed the air, along with a heat that created rippling mirages. The hacienda was composed of several white stucco and red clay–roofed buildings, bustling with people. Women in aprons hauled rattan baskets while men shouldered machetes or sacks of freshly harvested sugarcane. A flock of hens grazed freely near the entrance. Their half dozen chicks were chased by ruddy-cheeked nozariel children.

"How is your father, the old man Don Gerardo?" Don Samón said as they neared the stables.

"Still kicking. Still staying alive to spite the reaper. Still speaking fondly of you, and wondering when you will visit," said the caporal.

"Then it's his lucky day!" Don Samón said, and the men laughed.

Don Samón's and Don Rigoberto's parties dispersed, the carts and carriages disappearing beyond the stables while the animals were herded inside.

In the messy coming and going of people, Reina approached Eva and whispered, "A word?"

Eva shot a glance at her father, Javier, and Ludivina. A dark-skinned elderly woman, Don Gerardo Lobos's wife—and the caporal's mother—fussed over them. She kept the men busy by handing them cups of a sugarcane guarapo drink. It gave Eva the peace of mind to skulk behind the stables with Reina.

Eva couldn't shake the feeling that she'd done something wrong as Reina scratched her cheek, waiting for a gofer to walk out of earshot before speaking. "I need you to be honest with me," Reina said.

Eva stomped her foot in annoyance. "Reina, we are on the same side here. I haven't lied to you, and you've barely spoken to me since we left Carao."

"I needed to ride in the back. I thought I saw a stranger following the caravan. My job is to protect your family."

Eva rolled her eyes. "What can I say to put you at ease?"

Reina stepped closer to look deeply into Eva's eyes, as if through them she could see into Eva's heart. In close proximity, Eva noticed the darkened circles under Reina's eyes. The freckles on her nose and cheeks had doubled from the spicy sun. She was as weary from the travels as Eva.

"Is Rahmagut the one causing the tinieblas?" Reina asked in a low voice.

As if summoned by the mention of his name, Rahmagut chuckled, appraising the scene.

"I already told you no. He can't do anything without using my body. I'd have to be the one controlling them," Eva said.

Reina chewed her chapped lip, then sighed. She stepped back, wiping the perspiration from her temples. "How can you trust he can't control you or force you to do things you're not aware of? Have you ever blacked out?"

Eva's neck warmed. The Void gem weighed her pocket, cooling her riding pants with its perpetual heat leech. "*No*," Eva said, hoping her exasperation hid the lie. She grabbed Reina's arm and pulled her closer to the building's shade, whispering, "Maybe, just maybe, your unease comes from a place of bias after hearing everyone speak of Rahmagut as if he's some kind of demon."

Most people hadn't seen him like Eva had, with the longing to live so sharp in his eyes. She wasn't conflicted about his foreign presence any longer. Seeing him in the flesh had made her realize he wasn't monstrous. Their encounter had unnerved her, sure, but it also helped her accept their circumstances. She was trapped with him, and vice versa. She'd drive herself crazy if she didn't move past it. For now, the tinieblas and helping Javier and Maior were her priority.

"That's what Doña Ursulina used to say," Reina said, wincing.

"His name has been slandered by the Penitents forever."

"But my grandmother was also a murderous witch, so maybe we shouldn't believe the things she said," Reina said, cocking a brow.

Eva huffed. "Reina! It is thanks to *them* that we stood a chance. Are you really going to agree with my father and denounce the best tool we have to fight tinieblas?"

"I don't intend to denounce Ches," Reina said dangerously.

"Then?"

Reina's gaze was heavy with meaning Eva couldn't understand. Eva waited for Reina to say her piece. When she didn't, Eva said, "I refuse to live in fear and shame."

"And you have no intention of telling your father, correct? You saw how he agrees with Rigoberto and those archbishops."

Eva sneered. The name Monseñor Lorenzo was one that ignited a magma deep in her core.

"Well, I'm glad to hear you're not stricken by it..." Reina said, glancing to the field behind them, her gaze settling on Maior, who was introducing herself to the criadas on the property—always with her ears on the ground. "Has he spoken to you yet?" Reina muttered. "You do know you'll be bound to him until death? Doesn't that scare you?"

Eva's mouth hung open.

Reina groaned at Eva's obvious surprise. "You didn't know?"

"*Why didn't you tell me?*" Eva barked at the entity within her.

"*You never asked.*"

"*I didn't ask because you pick and choose the things you say—and you leave me in the dark.*"

"*Eva,*" he said in a warning tone.

She ground her teeth.

"*Why don't you think instead of the power in your pocket?*" Rahmagut said, like he was aware of his own overreaction. "*Your desire to become the greatest geomancer in the land. With me, you've effectively achieved it.*"

"*I'll believe it when I see it. And what is* your *desire?*"

"*The destruction of the tomb and my unsealing is my second chance at life. I told you: I simply wish to live. You give me this possibility, and I give you my power. We both benefit immensely.*"

Reina snapped her fingers in front of Eva's face. "Eva? Hello? What is wrong with you?"

"I was speaking to him," Eva explained, blushing.

A shocked scowl twisted Reina's face. "You're speaking to Rahmagut? *Right now?*"

Eva shrugged. "Yes. Don't you?"

"No!" Reina tugged her shirt collar as if she were burning from the realization.

Eva rubbed her temples. What caused this difference? "*Did I open myself up too much that night?*" she wondered, foolishly perhaps, for Rahmagut gave her no answer.

"Do you hear his voice in your head?" Reina asked. When Eva nodded, Reina dug her fingers into her scalp like she couldn't accept the implications. She grimaced, stepping back to create distance between them. "What is he saying?"

Eva almost grabbed Reina's arm to tug her closer. What was she stepping back for? "Nothing bad. Don't you speak to Ches?" Eva asked.

"No. Not like that," Reina grumbled. "I have no need to. I give my body to him fully. He can take control of it whenever he needs it. That is why I worry for you."

"Well, *he* can't do that," Eva said, hesitating to say Rahmagut's name.

"Because he is not like Ches at all," Reina muttered with an arched brow, stepping farther away and leaving as Javier emerged from around the corner looking for them.

Eva had no opportunity to retort. A boiling anger crawled up her throat at allowing Reina to have the last word. If it weren't for Javier, she'd have yanked on Reina's braid.

"Eva? Is everything all right?" Javier tugged Eva's elbow. "Why are you looking at Reina like that?"

Eva took a deep breath to loosen up her face. Indeed, her rage had been irrational, and perhaps not her own. "It's nothing."

"They'll show us to our room now," he said, beckoning her to follow him to the patio, where the servants awaited them.

The hacienda had many buildings vacant as the family's progeny had moved to Segolita seeking better political appointments. Eva freshened up in the one assigned to her and Javier. The lodge was perched on a hill, and the window had a stunning view of the morichales surrounding the hato's eastern side. Inside, her room had a rosary nailed to a wall, a cross made of dried grass hanging above the doorframe, and a clay icon of the Virgin standing on the wooden storage seibó across the bed, as if to supervise or deter the nightly activities performed therein. Rahmagut hemmed in distaste upon seeing it.

A drizzle descended on the property as Eva slipped out of her sweaty riding pants and into a ruffled shirt, skirt, and belt. She stepped out onto the porch, her espadrilles slapping on a puddle from a hole on the roof. There were potted ferns hanging from the awning, and a hammock, which Reina and Maior had already claimed. They sat side by side, swinging idly, Reina with her freshly washed hair freed from her braid and Maior finger-twirling the curly ends of Reina's tail.

"I was told each eagle created a peak so that shrines to the

Virgin could be placed at the highest point," Maior murmured as she glanced at the woven rattan tapestry that hung against the patio wall, behind the hammock.

Reina coughed in disagreement. "That has nothing to do with the Virgin."

"The shrines are there," Maior said, as if proving a point.

Reina sighed deeply.

Eva took in the elaborate art, noting how the different shades of rattan created contrast to depict eagles turning into mountains. There were five of them. Going from left to right, each eagle looked more like a snowcapped mountain than the last.

"What does it mean?" Eva asked.

"It's an old tale," Reina said, watching the children playing with each other in the yard facing the lodge. "When Ches created the world, he was lonely. He's a deity, and like all deities he craves worship. So he seeded his will in people, asking for sacrifices in exchange for blessings and boons."

Eva noticed Maior's pout of disagreement.

Oblivious, Reina continued. "But it was difficult to reach him because he was the sun. So the eagles perched on the Páramo with the intention of creating a path to him. One by one, they became one with the soil. Their bodies solidified and their plumage became the snowy paths you can take to the peaks."

Reina stretched and leaned back on the hammock. "But their sacrifice was futile, because the closer the land is to the sky, the more treacherous it becomes. The peaks became glaciers, and there's no safe pathway to reach the sun." She chuckled with an ease and familiarity, as if she were recounting an event she'd experienced for herself.

Was that Ches speaking through her?

Rahmagut's discomfort came like a scratch in Eva's throat, like he agreed with her query.

Maior oohed.

Reina playfully tapped Maior on the nose. "I'm surprised you don't know the tale, Parameña."

Blushing, Maior stuck her tongue out. "They don't teach us

nozariel things," she said, and they were the wrong words, as Reina was visibly annoyed.

"I didn't say it was a nozariel tale."

"It's of Ches," Maior said.

Reina looked away to the morichales, like she was letting Maior have the last word in a disagreement that would never be resolved. In a way, Eva felt as ignorant as Maior. There were so many things she didn't truly understand, as if the real truth had been forcibly rewritten and it was thanks to Javier, her father, and Reina that she could finally see a different point of view. Eva grew annoyed at her grandmother for allowing her to live her life oblivious. How could ignorance benefit anybody? Why not just state the truth?

Rahmagut laughed at her. *"Ignorant and docile. That's how I like my followers."*

Eva blushed in shame. She almost told him to shut up.

Instead, she just watched the children chase each other despite the drizzle and mud. A dog and a piglet chased them as well, as if attempting to emulate the children's game. The children giggled and grabbed each other, making circles as they sang, "¡San Isidro Labrador, quita el agua y pon el sol!"

Almost as if in answer to their game, the clouds parted for a rainbow. Maior saw it first and pointed. The yard burst in oohs and aahs and giggles.

"These people are just trying to live their lives in peace," Reina muttered, shaking her head. "And we're bringing the shadows right to their doorstep."

"How did you know tinieblas were going to attack Carao?" Eva asked.

Instead of answering, Reina said, "How did *you* know the tinieblas would attack Isla Madre?"

Eva squinted at the morichales in displeasure, but Reina's lack of reply was answer enough: Reina hadn't yet told Maior about Ches, and *he* had warned her. Eva supposed she understood Reina's lack of honesty, for how devoutly Penitent Maior was. "I saw the tinieblas emerge from the beach," Eva said after a while.

"You just happened to be there?" Reina asked.

"I was seeing Javier. Happy?"

Reina grimaced. "You told me you disliked him, and how quickly your tune has changed."

"Javier is my husband. Am I supposed to hate him forever?" Eva looked away, hoping Reina would drop it.

She wasn't ashamed of marrying him anymore. She was glad for it, actually. Her life had changed for the better because of him.

Javier had promised her: Once he was free and safe from the tiniebla, he would be a true husband. Someone to cherish Eva, just as Reina and Maior had each other to cherish. And Eva very much craved that in her life. Even to herself, she hated admitting she was jealous.

Maybe thanks to the children's singing, the rain clouds departed, and the sky turned pink right as the sun disappeared beyond the horizon. As dinnertime approached, Eva headed to the dining hall, encountering silent, antlered people crossing the open corridors of the hacienda. They wore old-fashioned clothes and shot her disgruntled expressions before vanishing around corners. She stopped in her tracks, stunned. Then, as Rahmagut confirmed her suspicions, chills ran through her. She was seeing the unseen—spirits lingering from lifetimes past. And it filled her with sadness, for they were a reminder of her dying kind.

"*Focus on the positives: You have the eyes of a god*," Rahmagut told her, as if she cared about such things.

Inside the dining hall, benches screeched against the tiled floor as criadas arranged as many tables as would fit. The center of the hall was left noticeably empty, for what Eva could only assume would be the evening's dances. The wrought iron chandeliers were lit, flooding the hall in a warm glow, and supper was served early. A proper pabellón of rice, black beans, and well-seasoned pulled beef from one of the hato's many cows. Eva, Javier, and Ludivina sat near Don Samón at the end of a large oak table, beside the head of the table, where a beautifully carved chair remained vacant.

It wasn't until the dessert of mango jalea was being scooped into Eva's bowl that an elderly man with a cane entered the hall. Eva's eyes doubled in size at the height of the man's antlers. They were chipped in places, and brown, but they were thick and large, like Don Samón's.

The patriarch hobbled to his empty seat at the head of the table. He had dark brown skin like the bark of an araguaney, and pin-straight white hair that streamed down behind him. His liqui liqui was embroidered with troupials and laurels. Eva licked the jalea from her lips as her eyes searched for her father, surprised. Don Gerardo Lobos, the head of the house, was half valco.

"I see you still surround yourself with mulatos," he told Don Samón by way of greeting, his voice gruff and spent.

Eva had been called that sometimes in Galeno, a term of endearment hiding an insult beneath. Humans sometimes referred to half-breeds that way, comparing their lack of blood purity to that of a mule.

"Cachicamo calling the morrocoy *conchudo*," Don Samón replied, smiling and rising to greet the elderly patriarch. The two pairs of antlers nearly clanged as the men hugged.

Javier slithered closer to Eva's ear and whispered, "You saw his son earlier, the caporal, without the antlers. It's a curiosity, isn't it? To have a valco for a father and not even grow shitty ones like yours."

Eva grabbed Javier's pinky and twisted it upward, not stopping until his mouth opened in unvoiced pain. She immediately regretted it as she caught a glimpse of the leathery tiniebla rot creeping out from under the long sleeves of his liqui liqui, reaching his finger.

"*Hey*—I'm just telling you," he said. "He's had an army of sons, and not a single one grew antlers. What a shame the wife had to be such an adulteress. Couldn't she at least have bothered to make a few more of us?"

"You're making a lot of assumptions."

"It's what everyone says behind closed doors."

"Just because they don't have antlers, does that make them not valco?" Eva said. "What about being able to see geomancia with the naked eye? What of their strength?" Javier's silence piqued her curiosity. She glanced at him and discovered him leaning so close. "There are other tests," she whispered after regaining composure. "You cannot be sure they are not his children."

"If they don't look like valcos, then they are not valcos," Javier muttered darkly. "If they can blend in with the humans and not have to deal with their groveling, or if they can go through life without fear that a conniving human might slaughter them in their sleep, then they are not valcos."

Eva's first instinct had been to protest the unfairness of his prejudice. Then she considered how easy her life would have been if she hadn't been born with the antlers, or if she weren't so sensitive to the unseen magic in the air. If she could pass as human. Doña Antonia would certainly have been a different grandmother to her.

"Javier?" she said, scooping the last of her jalea.

"Hmm?"

"Is it a coincidence that their last name is Lobos and yours is Águila?" she asked.

"Taking names after great creatures. Not a coincidence at all. We are a strong, prideful kind."

The answer satisfied her. Indeed, she was proud of being valco. "And what about Bravo?"

Javier shrugged. "How would I know?"

Eva stewed, wondering if the name came from Segol.

Javier surprised her when he slid his untouched jalea to her side. "Do you want mine? You know I'm not a lover of sweets."

A flutter of wings awoke in her chest. Was this a peace offering, after he insulted her antlers? She accepted it wordlessly, finding his gaze on her smile, but missed her chance to thank him as Don Samón announced them to Don Gerardo: his daughter, progeny of the lovely Dulce Serrano, and her husband, son of the great Feleva Águila. Javier rose from his seat with a bright, fake smile, and Eva and Ludivina followed.

"And here I thought we were the last to grow antlers," Don Gerardo noted, lightly petting Ludivina's ivory antlers. He smelled sour and ill as he drew closer to kiss Eva on the knuckles. "But I applaud you for a most successful matchmaking—uniting Feleva's bloodline with yours. I suspect an army of little valcos will be terrorizing your island soon enough."

"That is the hope!" Don Samón asserted.

"We won't have to wait for too long, I hope? The first valco is on the way?"

Eva burned, and Ludivina offered her a covert smirk.

"I don't think Eva will take too kindly to you prying into the details of her marital life," Don Samón said, saving her.

And Don Gerardo laughed. "Please, Samón, let this old man have his amusement."

Hot-cheeked, Eva stared at the ground as her father and Don Gerardo chuckled. She could feel everyone's eyes on the crowns of their heads. It was a rare sight, to see valcos from three different bloodlines in the same room.

She was glad when Javier's hand pressed against her lower back, gently guiding them back to their seats.

They sat again, and the small smile he offered her wasn't fake. It was filled with hope. She wondered...Perhaps he dreamed of a similar future as Don Samón. And for the first time, the thought didn't sound so bad.

18

Nozariel Strength

Eva abandoned Javier in the dining hall for some fresh air after the distribution of anise liquor started to make her head spin. She denied a fourth refill, but not without realizing it was Don Gerardo himself who had encouraged his servers to keep her goblet topped. To what end? Her drinking confirmed there were no little valcos on the way, so Eva could only imagine he was hoping to expedite matters. Her heated chest was a sign that even Rahmagut agreed.

Outside, a star-blotched sky lit the night. A mad joropo followed Eva out as she left the hacienda, the rapid rhythm of the harp, cuatro, and maracas threatening to take over her espadrilles. Other giggling people trickled out of the building as well, loudly sharing jokes or finding pockets of darkness to veil their alcohol-inspired passions. A twinkle of fireflies followed her down the path back to the lodge. She smiled at their light, and their company.

Part of her also hated the way Don Gerardo's questions had highlighted the inadequacies of her unconsummated marriage. Even if Javier had never bothered to broach the subject. Nevertheless, his lack of desire stung her. Back home, her cousins used to joke about men not having self-control. And Eva had wholeheartedly believed this when, in a burst of rebellion, she'd ruined her own purity by rushing into the bed of a stranger. She'd met eagerness instead of resistance from the man, a traveling trader who promptly left her in shame the next morning. But Eva had never seen this eagerness in Javier. (And there were many moments when they had been forced to share a bed.) If consummation was their duty, what was stopping him? She blushed. Perhaps she wouldn't deny him if he tried.

"*Your marriage was signed with iridio,*" Rahmagut noted with a yawn. "*It cannot be so easily annulled.*"

Eva clicked her tongue. Had Javier anticipated this and used the iridio contract as a workaround? The thought made her feel uglier.

No—she was foolish for letting her insecurities weigh her down. Their coupling was an inevitability, even if he had no true interest in her and found her repulsive. Indeed, eventually they had a duty to fulfill, a dying species to help repopulate. But this future would never be realized if he turned into a tiniebla.

Sighing, Eva prodded within herself, telling Rahmagut, "*You say that with you I'm the strongest geomancer. But I have no idea how to break Javier's curse. Or Maior's.*"

A rumbling filled her chest.

She scoffed. "*That was your cue to tell me how.*"

"*You are demanding. Is this really the tone you wish to take with me?*"

"*I'm sorry, that was the anise speaking. But please? You . . . discovered tinieblas. Surely you know how to fix him?*"

In his silence, Eva imagined him pensive.

"*There are binding spells that change the properties of the objects being bound,*" Rahmagut said. "*Similarly to how you cannot separate a solution after two substances have been mixed. If the process was reactive and the result is homogenous, then the change is permanent.*"

Eva pressed a palm to heart, breathless. Just like Javier was also changing. Could she have been thinking about this problem incorrectly? "*So teach me how to stop it from progressing, until I figure out a curse breaker.*"

Rahmagut gave a grunt. "*Learn to coax. You cannot demand things from me.*"

Rolling her eyes, she said, "*Do you have the ability to break his spell at all?*"

His lack of answer infuriated her.

"What if I gave you control of my body to do it?"

His amusement coursed through her, as did his irritation. *"Then you'd be a fool. You would sacrifice yourself for the chance to save your apathetic husband?"*

Her cheeks heated. The answer was a resounding no.

"Ah—you were testing me."

Instead of replying, Eva reached into her pocket and pulled out the Void gem. She held it up to the light of a faraway lantern. It was icy between her fingers. *"Is this supposed to amplify my geomancia?"*

"No."

"What does it do? Teach me how to use it." She tossed it in the air like a marble before catching it in her hand.

"Do not play with things you do not understand, Eva Kesaré," he said quickly. Despite her anise-addled imagination, Eva reckoned she heard panic.

She tucked the gem back into her dress pocket. *"Would you look at that: He knows my name."* She smiled.

"You will mock me?"

"I want to understand what you know. Please! There should be some advantage to sharing my mind with you."

"Your geomancia is already enhanced," he said.

"But what about practical spells? Things you experimented with when you had your own body—when you created tinieblas? Tell me how to cleanse the tiniebla oppressing Javier."

"I told you," Rahmagut barked, *"I don't remember."*

The words echoed loudly in her inner ear. Her belly twisted, like he had the capability to squeeze her bowels and inflict pain. Eva doubled over, struck with the urge to retch.

The crunch of dead leaves came from behind her. Eva swung around, fully expecting drunken lovers looking for privacy. She saw nothing but darkness. Even the fireflies had abandoned her.

She took a deep breath and thought, *"I'm sorry."* But it was as if her words dropped into a bottomless, dark well, for he had withdrawn once again.

The joropo changed rhythm to a quieter, slower melody. It

underscored the silence of the night, unnerving Eva. She hadn't realized it until now, but Rahmagut's presence had kept her company. She couldn't believe she was missing it…

Nevertheless, the air felt different, like the darkness had grown sentience. Eva rushed toward the lodge, squinting behind her, hyperaware of any sounds. She wasn't useless anymore—a tiniebla couldn't sneak up on her if she kept her wits about her. She called for Rahmagut again and was met with silence. Was he punishing her?

More footsteps followed. Eva whirled. A built man stood in front of the faraway lantern light, his face shrouded in shadow. "Rahmagut?" she murmured, stepping closer. Maybe this was another apparition, and it was why she couldn't feel his presence within her anymore. Instead of better seeing his face, she caught a glimpse of a tail swaying behind him.

He'd materialized for her.

She approached, saying, "I'm sorry for the way I spoke—I was out of line."

In close proximity, Eva realized she was staring at a face she didn't recognize. A long, hooked nose, bushy eyebrows, and thin lips that twisted with the wicked intention to hurt.

Eva gasped. Immediately she twirled her hands, using iridio to summon fire. But the man yanked the pendant hanging from her neck, her skin burning as the chain snapped. The spell fizzled in her palms and was violently sucked out of existence as the iridio pendant left her body. Without it, she was disarmed.

She ran. And like a demon, he pursued her.

She sprinted up to the lodge. From the sounds of his stomps, he was going to outpace her. Eva pressed her hands together, weaving and unweaving her fingers to summon bismuto. The magic zipped through her body, electrifying her soles with an extra push.

Her lead lasted mere seconds. The pursuer's footsteps doubled in speed as well. He expunged the distance and yanked her curls. Eva yelled as he ripped out her hair. She jumped onto the porch. Fear showered her as she noted, from the lack of candlelight, that the lodge was probably empty. She was alone.

Purple threads of iridio geomancia hurled past her, unhooking the hammock from the ceiling. The spell took control of the hammock, winding it around her body to bind her. Her cheek slammed against the floor as she fell. Blood bloomed in her mouth.

The man flipped her over.

She cried, "No!"

He was built like a bull, his treated leather armor tight against a muscled chest. A machete hung in the scabbard around his waist. His nozariel tail swayed behind him, the tip armored to wield a knife. He was aglow with geomancia, the purple hue in utter contradiction to his vicious assault. "Eva Kesaré de Galeno, correct?" he said, his tone amused.

"Who are you?" she yelled, kicking him on the shin.

He stepped back, groaning. "Don't take it personally."

A pressure built in her temples as Eva spread her arms, her bismuto spell giving her the strength to rip herself free from the hammock. She twisted and squirmed, unraveling the fibers, and kicked him again before scrambling into the lodge. She slammed the door shut behind her, pressing her body against it.

The door thundered as he rammed against it. "The more you fight me, the more you'll get hurt!"

Heart thrumming, Eva slapped her hands together to coat her body in the protection of litio. It turned out to be the right move, as his fist opened a splintery hole through the door, impacting Eva's lower back. She crashed to her knees.

The door exploded behind her as the man rammed it a second time. He broke through and unsheathed his machete. "Your grandmother misses you. She very much would like you back."

The air left Eva's throat. Doña Antonia had sent him? The world froze in that moment—as she imagined him violently ripping her away from her new life and thrusting her back into the Serranos' prison.

She couldn't let that happen.

She scampered down the hall, panicked tears streaming down her cheeks. She yelled Javier's name, tugging on the invisible strings between them with the command to save her. And how pitiful it made her feel! How it highlighted that she was just a meek woman without the power of iridio.

"Stop running already—you're making my life difficult," the man called, his boots echoing in hot pursuit.

She burst into her bedroom and slammed the door behind her. There was no way out, so she punched through the window shutters, her litio coating sparing her fist as she managed an opening big enough for her body. With no time to think, Eva dove into the darkness.

Rocks and grasses scraped and banged her as she rolled down the hill adjacent to the lodge. The impacts depleted the last of her litio protection. Eva nursed her left temple where blood trickled down. She glanced up at the window, half expecting the man to jump out as he had burst through the other doors. Clatters and yells erupted from within the lodge, purple light flashing in the darkness.

Eva scrambled up and turned for the hacienda, running blindly in the darkness. She didn't get far, crashing against a rock-solid chest. She yelped as bulging biceps squeezed her in place. The man's chest rumbled with laughter. Her heart traveled to her throat as she realized she was caught.

"Now I see why Doña Antonia insisted on me. You're not an easy mark at all," he said, lifting her with ease.

"Let me go!"

He clamped a gloved hand over her mouth and sprinted toward the chapel. Eva squirmed, but her best efforts were minuscule compared with his strength. She was a doll in his viselike grip. A black mare awaited them behind the white stucco building, under a pocket of torchlight. The man bound her mouth and body. He then tossed her over the mare's back.

Just as her panic was leaving her breathless, as she imagined her horrific fate, Reina emerged from the shadows like a specter. Her golden blade dazzled Eva, reflecting the torchlight. Reina's lip and temple were bleeding. She'd been the one who'd fought him at the lodge.

"Get your hands off her!" Reina howled.

The man groaned upon seeing her reemerge. "Listen—I spared you once. I'm not in the business of killing nozariels, but if you get in my way I won't hesitate to use lethal force."

Reina swung at him, undeterred.

"Really? You stubborn creature!" He blocked her, parrying with such force that Reina's shoulders shook.

Javier, too, rounded the chapel, calling, "Who's there?" He was without his sword, his steps swaying as if he were drunk.

Eva screamed his name, but her voice came out muffled and unintelligible.

"You give me no choice here!" the kidnapper said, charging at Reina so fast Eva barely caught a blur of his tail. Reina blocked, but her knees yielded from the force. He shoved her to the ground with ease, the knife on his tail slicing Reina's cheek.

He gave Reina no reprieve. With a brutal howl, he swung a second time and would have cut Reina's head clean off were it not for Javier, who tackled him to the ground.

Dust coated their sides as they skidded on the packed dirt. Quick footed, the kidnapper sprang to his feet. Javier rolled in similar fashion, but he swayed, his inebriation addling his speed. The man kicked him on the lower back and raised his machete. The blade cut the air with the intention to impale him. Eva screeched in her gag.

Reina scampered to them and struck the man's machete, deviating its angle. It sliced Javier's side, unleashing red rivulets. Javier yelled, stepping back while putting pressure on the cut. Annoyed, the man kicked Reina in the gut, knocking the air out of her and making her fall to her knees.

"Enough with the meddling," the kidnapper said, kicking Reina's blade far away. He grabbed her by the braid. "Good on you for keeping your tail," he said as Reina held her belly, breathless, his own armored tail switching behind him. "But you're giving me no choice here." He pressed the sharp end of his machete to Reina's neck.

Eva whimpered in her gag, feeling useless. "*Where are you?*" she growled to herself, scraping the furthest edges of her consciousness for a sign of Rahmagut. "*Give me the strength. Help me. You promised.*"

"Get your grimy hands off her!" Javier snarled, kicking the kidnapper on the shin and toppling his balance. As the man fell to his knees, his tail slashed at Javier like a viper. And this time Javier evaded him fluidly, a leaf swirling between boulders in a turbulent river.

Freed from the man's grip, Reina rose, kneeing the man's wrist to disarm him. He roared from the crack. His machete clanged to the ground, where Javier took it and pressed the sharp tip to the man's neck.

"All right—you got me," the man said with a chuckle. "I have been defeated."

"This wasn't a joke a moment ago when you were ready to take my life," Reina said.

He shrugged. "You should be used to it, no? Occupational hazards? Who are you, anyway? The girl's bodyguards?"

Eva snarled that she wasn't a girl, but with her gag, it came out as a muffled cry.

Reina and Javier exchanged a look. They read each other, and Reina nodded. Javier stepped back, allowing Reina to knee the man in the face. He groaned. Blood streamed down his nose, pooling in thick clumps on the ground.

Reina fetched her fallen sword before rushing to free Eva.

Tears of relief streaked Eva's cheeks.

"Are you hurt?" Reina said, lifting Eva's chin for a better look. Eva shook her head, wiping the tears from her face, ashamed of her uselessness.

From the ground the man coughed and laughed. "Of course she's not harmed. I must deliver her in one piece."

"But you are," Eva told Reina, summoning a thread of galio to close the crimson line on Reina's cheek.

Reina shook her head, muttering pointedly, *"Javier."* She hurried to swap places with him as Javier stepped away, sucking in a breath at the horrible cut in his side. The exhaustion or blood loss drove him to his knees. Eva rushed to him. She pressed her hands to the bleeding gash, panicked, as the gush was undeterred.

"Don't get in my way," he muttered, his lips and cheeks pale.

She leaned away so he could perform an elaborate crisscrossing of his thumbs and fingers. His galio spell stitched the gaping muscle and flesh back together, but it resurfaced the darkness in him. A black tar coated his palms and fingers. He rubbed his fingers together, then gave a look of disbelief when the darkness didn't fade.

Eva threw her arms around him, squeezing. The tremors in her body eased as he gently hugged her back. Into her neck, he whispered, "I'm all right, but I must assist Reina. She cannot restrain him alone."

He was right. She was foolish to let her emotions distract her. They pulled apart. Javier forced the kidnapper to his feet with the kidnapper's own machete, then yanked the knife from his armored tail, disarming him.

Weapons pointed at his back, Reina and Javier ordered him into the dining hall.

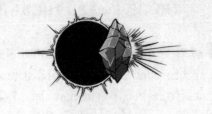

19

Las Orquídeas Blancas

The lively joropo ended abruptly as Reina and Javier shoved the battered man into the room.

Don Samón abandoned his cuatro, shocked, as he took in their bloody states. "My daughter," he said. He opened his arms, almost automatically. Eva didn't miss the doubt in his eyes. His fear that she would reject this gesture. But she diminished the distance, entering his embrace. Her fear was renewed afresh as she buried her face in his liqui liqui. This was her father, and they'd been so close to being ripped apart.

His hand lingered on her shoulder as they parted. "Explain yourself." Don Samón's thunderous voice hushed the whispers of the remaining partygoers. "What is the meaning of this?"

When the man dallied, Reina kicked him in the back, forcing his knees to hit the flagstones. "Easy now—" he grumbled.

"What's your name?" Reina said.

"Pucho de Las Garras," he said, shrugging. "What does my name do for you, exactly?"

"He said he meant to take me away," Eva said. "My grandmother hired him."

Pucho raised his palms in the air. "I am a hired sword, not a spy. You can get all the answers you want out of me. Just promise my life will be spared."

Javier scoffed. "So you can try again later?" He gestured at the blood staining the length of his abdomen. "He nearly took my life, and Reina's. Let me repay him in kind."

"Then I'll take my information to the grave!" Pucho howled.

"Do you know who I am?" Don Samón said.

Pucho smirked. He studied Don Samón's antlers, and Javier's, and even Don Gerardo's. "Never thought I'd see so many valcos in one place. This must be the last of my days indeed."

Reina pushed her blade until blood bloomed on his shirt. "Answer our questions."

The mercenary hissed, shooting Reina a side glare. "The Liberator. I'm taking the Serrano girl away from the Liberator. Those were my instructions."

"Why?" Eva squeezed herself, surprised that her grandmother would miss her. She supposed she also missed the Serranos. They had clothed her, fed her, and given her an education, even if a sheltered one. There were many bad times, but there had also been good ones. Though...if Doña Antonia had truly meant the best for her, she wouldn't have hired such a beast to steal her away in the night.

Pucho spat blood to the ground. "The bitter woman fears for your life."

Eva struggled to swallow the answer. Fear rocked her shoulders again. The thought of returning to Galeno like a prisoner made her feel like puking. All this time, Eva had simply assumed her family was unbothered by her running away.

"Funny she would hire a nozariel," Javier noted, gesturing at the tail. "Doesn't seem like something a Serrano would do, unless..."

"She recognized the difficulty in extracting the girl. Give the old hag some credit, no? She was right," Pucho said, chortling.

How Eva burned to stop him from calling her a girl. But it would only highlight how utterly useless she'd been.

"He followed us from Carao," Reina told Don Samón, startling the watching crowd. "I saw a man wearing a jipijapa hat on the same black mare waiting outside the chapel."

Pucho chuckled.

"I thought it was just my mind playing tricks, after that guide bored us to death with his tale of the fire-spitting ghost when we stopped at the plantation," Reina said. An older woman in the crowd made the cross on herself. Noticing, Reina scowled. "But there are no ghosts," she growled, digging the tip of her sword deeper, "just sneaky bastards willing to kill. And for what?"

Pucho shook her off. "Indeed, you saw me, like I saw you. I was glad your lot saved me the trouble of having to get a boat to Tierra'e Sol."

Eva grew green from this back and forth. "What does Doña Antonia want with me? Why does she fear for my life?" she said, stepping closer to better look into his eyes. In the dim light, they were two black, remorseless orbs. His scutes were like chipped armor over his nose.

He gave her a smug look. Everyone waited in anticipation. He knew he had their attention, and he was enjoying every moment of it. "Doña Antonia didn't tell me her reasons—"

Reina pushed on the blade, making him suck in another breath of pain.

"But I'm no fool," Pucho said. "I investigate before I take on a job. She's one of the principal financers of Las Orquídeas Blancas—"

"*Who?*" Eva and Don Samón croaked at the same time.

At their surprise, Pucho laughed. "Did I catch the Liberator himself unawares?"

"Speak already!" Eva howled.

Pucho raised a forefinger in the air, side-eyeing Reina and saying, "If you poke me one more time, it'll be the last word I say."

"He thinks he won't talk," Javier said, and for an instant Eva thought she saw a fleeting shadow worming in and out of his cheek. "We'll see how he feels after I've lifted all his fingernails and cut off all his toes."

"Ah, yes, a torturer like your brother," Pucho said, scoffing. "And yes—I know who you are. How many people with antlers do you think are left? The anemic younger brother of the caudillo of Sadul Fuerte, who, by the way, I passed on the way to Carao. He also took his host to Segolita."

Eva didn't miss the tightening of Javier's fist.

"Enrique's in Segolita?" Don Samón shot Reina a furtive glance.

"Enrique Águila is another caudillo backing Las Orquídeas Blancas," Pucho said.

"And when do you intend to tell us who Las Orquídeas Blancas are?" Don Samón said.

"Who are they? Penitent fanatics, I tell you," Pucho said after glancing about the room, perhaps to discern how freely he could speak. "An order helmed by the archbishop of Galeno and his most adoring follower, the mighty Doña Antonia." He smirked at Eva, like he could look into her soul and see the heartache she'd already endured from such a pair. "They've roped the archbishop of Segolita and a whole lot of caudillos into an alliance between the military and the Pentimiento Church. Somehow, they have this idea that the gods of the Void and sun have been unleashed—that they are walking the land, bringing about the tiniebla attacks."

Quick like an afterthought, Eva and Reina exchanged a look.

"Las Orquídeas Blancas are after the source of tinieblas?" Don Samón muttered.

"What does that have to do with me?" Eva said softly, unsure. Was her question the one to open the box of truths she'd kept lidded all this time? But she desperately needed to know.

Pucho smiled as his gaze surfed Eva's black antlers. Her chest thrummed in anticipation. Maybe she was a fool, for pursuing this interrogation with everyone at Hato de los Lobos as witness.

"Las Orquídeas Blancas believe the gods can exist only while possessing the bodies of mortals, and geomancers are the first suspects. There's an inquisition, and a fervor. People suspected of using geomancia are being tried. Some have been killed..." Pucho gave her a mocking, tender look. "And Doña Antonia knows her granddaughter dabbles in the dark arts. She wants to make sure you don't get snatched and killed for it. Better to see you safe in her clutches than dead. Such love—I'm touched."

"That's absurd," Don Gerardo said, emerging from the obscurity of his table. "You bring these slanderous tales to the property of a valco. Geomancia is in our blood."

"Do I look like a Penitent to you?" Pucho snarled. "I also use geomancia, or did old age melt those valco eyes of yours? I'm giving you the answers you want." His tail swayed from side to side, feline-like.

"You're guaranteeing no sympathies with it," Don Samón said.

"I don't expect the comforts of a guest, with the way your son-in-law is looking at me."

"You cannot expect to be freed after you assaulted my daughter."

"I would if you had any honor. I was just performing a job."

"Our catching you doesn't stop you from trying again," Eva said as ice ran through her veins. Pucho's failure mattered little against Doña Antonia's desires.

"I intend to walk away from this business altogether," Pucho said. "Or not—I'll gladly take the free, comfortable ride back to Segolita if you insist on keeping me. I shan't be prisoner for long either way."

Don Samón shook his head, disappointment weighing his brows. "A shame to see such a capable man waste his talents working outside the law."

"Easy for a valco to say," Pucho snarled, and his tail slammed the flagstones.

"Take him away," Don Samón told his soldiers.

Eva watched Pucho be escorted out as uncertainty stormed within her. Doña Antonia and Las Orquídeas Blancas were right. The gods had returned, and they resided in the bodies of two geomancers. Never mind how they came to this conclusion, if it rallied every commander and religious leader under the same banner. Las Orquídeas Blancas. Even the name was sanctimonious. Eva couldn't stop the memory of Doña Rosa from resurfacing—the injustice of her death. Now, thanks to this call to arms, it was Eva and Reina who were heading directly into the inquisitor's path.

"Are you injured?"

Eva flinched as her father pressed a hand to her back.

"No." She was, but they were minor things. Small bruises

incomparable to the trauma of seeing Javier and Reina almost lose their lives for her.

Don Samón herded Eva out of the hall and through the open corridors, following the natural flow of people leaving the dismantled celebration.

"He almost took me away," Eva said in a small voice, unable to hide her fright.

"And if he had, I would have depleted all my resources in bringing you home."

Home. Where was that for Eva now? The thought of returning to Galeno iced her veins, but Tierra'e Sol also felt like a dream—something ephemeral. It didn't have the permanence of a home, not yet. As she glanced up, finding ease in his eyes, a realization struck her. Home was with her father, wherever he was.

"And I would do anything to return," she said.

He cleared his throat, blushing. Somehow, he'd guided her to a quiet courtyard. In the distance, Javier searched for her within the thinning crowd, but seemed assuaged upon spotting her with her father. He carried on alone.

Don Samón waited until the closest person had walked beyond earshot before saying, "Eva."

"Yes, Father?"

"In light of these events, I'm afraid I cannot delay my questions any longer. Ches and Rahmagut were unsealed the night you and Reina destroyed the tomb. The archbishops have confirmed this now."

Eva painted on a most neutral face, steeling herself.

"Did you see anything out of the ordinary? Did you experience anything that hints at where they might have gone? Was there a light of geomancia pointing in any particular direction? A coldness to the air? A tremor?"

"No," Eva said quickly. "The tomb collapsed over us."

He sighed. "I hesitate to trust anything these Orquídeas may claim. On the surface they present one cause, but I won't know for sure until I insert myself in their politicking. There could be other motives, especially with Enrique involved."

"Right."

"But if they suspect the gods chose geomancers—"

"And you wonder about us, because we use geomancia?" Eva asked shrilly, hoping her fabricated tone would reveal the outrage at his insinuation.

He winced. "I shall trust your word."

"Thank you."

"But others may raise similar questions."

She grabbed his hands, sighing deeply from the sin of her lies. But what would she achieve by confiding in him now? The tinieblas and the gods were not linked, and as far as everyone was concerned, the real problem was the tinieblas. "I would hope the people you command are loyal to you, and they keep what they know about the events of the tomb to themselves. We endured a horrific night because of Ursulina. That's all there is to it. I don't want to keep recalling it."

He nodded gravely. "This is the last I will speak of it."

Finally, Eva could breathe.

"We're lucky we have Reina and Javier. Let us cherish that. And I hope, from the looks of it, that they have made peace." He chuckled. "All right, you go on ahead. I must say our farewells to Don Gerardo. We shall depart at first light."

Freed, Eva scampered up the path to the lodge. She hated walking again in the darkness. Thankfully, she found Javier trailing behind Reina and Maior.

She caught up to him and said, "I called you many times. Didn't you feel it?"

Javier avoided her gaze as they walked together. "Yes."

"Why didn't you come?" She had strung her plea for help as a command. How could it have failed?

"I didn't understand the urgency. I thought you were trying to control me by calling me back. And I enjoyed feeling like a normal person again, surrounded by people who know neither what I did at the tomb nor what I am. They just treat me like the son of Feleva Águila. It was like I was back in my old life."

"All right, and what about the fact that my command didn't work?"

He sighed. "It did work. I just resisted it."

Her mouth opened, stunned.

"I'm not your dog," he said dangerously, pausing before they reached the lamplight illuminating Reina and Maior as they picked up the mess on the porch.

Was he so oblivious to the reason for her outrage? If he could resist her commands, what kind of assurances could she have of keeping the tiniebla on a tight leash?

He shrugged. "I did come, eventually."

"No one is going to break your curse if I get taken away!" Eva said, her voice cracking. "I was the one who advocated for you to be freed."

Finally, he faced her. He placed both hands on her shoulders and said, "Eva, I don't want anything to happen to you. You're my only ally *and* my wife. I apologize for resisting your summons, but maybe don't act like I'm nothing more than a pawn to you. Stop correcting when and how I say things. Don't use your control over me unless it's against the tiniebla. How would you like it if someone took away your free will?"

A pressure built in her chest. Eva realized she'd been holding her breath.

"How would you like it if the words were taken out of your mouth?"

She ground her teeth.

"You would hate it! You would throw a fit," he said lightly, bringing humor to diminish her tension.

"I was completely useless," she said, lifting a hand to her neck, feeling the absence of her pendant. "Pucho took my iridio. Without it, I was nothing."

He stepped back. "No—you saw how he bested me. I wouldn't have been able to handle him alone." He glanced up at the lodge, where Reina cleaned up the hammock fibers. "Eva, you're the most impressive caster I have ever met. You're not nothing."

She blushed.

"He's not just anybody. He's a seasoned warrior," Javier said.

"Did you hear what he said? The alliance of caudillos and the archbishop are after me?" Eva wrung her hands. Thinking of Monseñor Lorenzo filled her with loathing. She was never going to forget the fervor he'd inspired in Galeno, and his blatant ignorance. A darkness wound in her. Rahmagut's presence returned from the depths of her mind, where he had conveniently secluded himself all this time. He agreed with her hatred. And it annoyed her. He'd abandoned her when she needed him most.

"What did your father tell you?" Javier said.

The cricket song was loud in Eva's hesitation. Her chest constricted. "He wanted to know what I knew about the tomb. I had to lie to him."

Javier scoffed. The lamplight revealed his disdainful smile. "He swallowed it up, didn't he? You have a father who cares. And to think you were so ready to reject him. I still remember the look you gave me when I told you the truth." He shook his head. "I can't believe it."

Eva crossed her arms. "I was fed lies."

"The fact that he's already accepted me speaks mountains of his commitment to you. He's going to protect you. Whatever the Orquídeas do, you'll always have him by your side. It's amazing to me how you don't realize how lucky you are. It must be nice."

"Must be nice? Your mother was Feleva Águila, the most famous valco in the history books. You had *everything I wanted* growing up."

An owl hooted in the distance. She felt the tiniebla in him resurfacing. It was like a hush in the night, the crickets quieting.

His eyes narrowed. He stepped closer. "Mother died when I was still in diapers. I grew up passed around from one nanny to another. The only constant in my life was my brother, and his fist." His words came out low and muddied, the tiniebla feeding him with darkness.

Eva could tell he had not yet lost control, but he teetered on the line. She steeled herself in place. The last thing she wanted was to cower before him. Part of their agreement was that of being equals, but how could they achieve that with the threat of violence always hovering over their relationship? If Javier was going to raise a hand against her again, then they might as well get it over with. Let him reveal his true self while she still had the power to remove him from her life forever.

"No one cared about me. You wouldn't have liked my life growing up," he muttered.

"You didn't make it sound that way in our letters," she said softly. Even if he had grown up motherless, he'd still been showered in wealth. He'd had the best education. Her assumptions weren't without basis.

As if realizing the creep of corruption, Javier took a deep breath and stepped back. He rubbed his eyes, like he could wipe the darkness away. It worked.

"Because I didn't want you to see me as I am. Would you have followed me, someone cursed to become a tiniebla?" He shook his head. "You saw how that mercenary spoke about me: the loathed youngest son of a famous house. Would you have come with me if you knew how Enrique made sure I'd never be taken seriously by the society of Sadul Fuerte?"

The questions disarmed her. *Would* she have married him under different circumstances, if she had known of his stained reputation and the truth of his family? If the Serranos hadn't driven her to self-banishment with their ignorance? Even if they were the last of valcos, as Don Gerardo had pointed out, would that have been enough for her to overlook everything else? In a small voice, she said, "I don't know. But at least my decision would have been informed."

"You don't know," he parroted. "That alone gives me reason to believe you wouldn't have. And I couldn't afford that kind of uncertainty—not when losing my mind is the only sure outcome."

"Lovely. Thanks for admitting your deception." Now if only he could apologize for the wrongs against her pride...

He tried grabbing her elbow, but she moved her arm away. "You used me to get out of Galeno," he said, as if somehow that held equal weight to all he'd done.

"You used me to get close to the Liberator," she said, mimicking his tone.

"Correction: I'm using you to get this tiniebla out of me."

She grimaced, crossing her arms. "Well, good luck breaking your curse when the Orquídeas take me."

"I will never let that happen," he said softly.

The way he said it, so automatically his earnestness was undeniable, inspired a fluttering in her chest. How could he have the power to do that?

"And I'm joking, I'm not using you at all—not anymore," he said, as if the honesty came with difficulty. "I'm only *hoping* that you can help me. Trusting you, like you said."

Somehow, things between them had changed. Sure, he had hit her, and she had violated his agency. The two wrongs didn't make a right, yet it felt as if they were treading the right path, putting those things behind them. She trusted him now—she couldn't deny that. She didn't imagine he'd hurt her again, even if the power to control him gave her the upper hand. His saving her went beyond the necessity of breaking his curse, right?

"It's getting late. Let's get some rest before we head out tomorrow." He gently brushed her curly bangs aside, drawing nearer for a better look as he said, "And let me mend that cut on your temple."

Don Gerardo's insinuations resurfaced, making Eva feel like a blushing little girl.

They were more than just tools for each other. They were friends—partners...

"It's just a minor thing," she murmured, moving aside to give herself some space, and to clear her mind.

He hesitated in following her to the lodge, looking rejected, so she grabbed his hand. There was a spark when their fingertips touched. Their magic.

"How are you feeling, by the way? You lost a lot of blood," she said.

Maybe it was her imagination making her feel his hand squeezing hers.

"I could use some sleep, definitely. But I don't think any more assassins or tinieblas will be sneaking up on us tonight."

He helped her up the porch—not that she needed the steadiness.

Eva paused. "Javier, wait."

He did, his brows bunching.

"I don't want to need you, or Reina, or my father against the Orquídeas."

He nodded, understanding.

She gestured behind her, to the lighted chapel down the hill. "If I'm ever in that situation again, I want to know how to defend myself."

His hand did squeeze hers this time. "Then I shall teach you how."

She smiled. She was about to make a quip about the first time he taught her geomancia, to lighten the mood, but Reina emerged from the lodge.

When she saw them, Javier quickly let go of Eva's hand and called Reina's name.

"Yes?" Reina said stiffly.

For a moment Eva had the panicked instinct to reel Javier back, to take the words from his mouth, even if he'd just begged her not to. She couldn't handle any more discord tonight.

"Thank you," he said, surprising them both. "Thank you for stopping that bastard from taking Eva, and for saving my life." He extended a hand between them, amiable. In the porch's lamplight it was impossible to miss how the tips of his fingers were still stained by his curse. He noticed it at the same time as Eva and Reina, but by then it was too late to pull back.

Reina hesitated, frozen by the gesture and the state of his fingers. When she didn't take it soon enough, he withdrew the hand, embarrassed.

"I shall thank you as well," Reina said, her tone softening. "You also saved mine."

"You and I may not see things eye to eye—"

"You made sure of that since the day I joined your family."

He nodded, chastised. "But we can at least agree on our shared hatred for tinieblas and Enrique?"

Reina gave a nod. She went inside and entered the drawing room, where Maior stood behind the window, watching.

A lightness took over Eva's chest as she followed Javier into the lodge. Until now, Eva hadn't realized how much she cared for Reina's approval. How in that moment, it felt as if a balance had been restored.

Within her, Rahmagut paced the bounds of her consciousness, his disagreement nearly palpable.

SAMÓN ANTONIO BRAVO DÍAS

20

The Return to Segolita

Reina's belly was in knots as they neared Segolita. Her anxiety had started when, on the fifth day since leaving Hato de los Lobos, they'd come upon a crossroads with a nailed wooden sign marking their proximity. The moment of reentering the city gates she'd once fled was upon her. Her heart twisted in her chest, the iridio whispers awakening and stretching in delight at her discomfort. She tried not to think of the city streets and alleyways, how they had been both a refuge and a torture while she navigated a life alone. How she had to work from dawn to dusk to survive.

In the flat savanna of the Llanos, there was no hill or mountain impeding the view of the looming city walls blurring from heat mirages. The cathedral was the tallest building, peeking over the protective stone fortress. The road was muddy and busy, littered with the steps of hundreds, along with their waste. A throng of travelers herded into the city, their wagons heavy from hastily packed clothes, valuables, and food.

Reina passed haggard faces. People in ragged clothes and bloody bandages. Looks of pain, surprise, and then idolization met the antlers of the Liberator as he rode his steed in the vanguard. There was music in the air as musicians joined the hubbub with treses and cuatros, a maraca here and there. They played woeful tonadas, slow folk songs telling the story of lovers separated by shadowed creatures who came in the darkness of night.

A sea of tents covered the fields outside the city gates. Banners flapped over every other one: the scarlet sea and onyx crocodile banner of the royal Silvas; a diagonal partition of black and white crossed by the golden key of the Contadors; banners using the tricolor of the Republic of Fedria in new arrangements, with stars and laurel-flanked emblems. The flags of smaller families, too many to catalog. Her breath caught as she even spotted the golden eagle soaring over the ivory fabric of the Águilas. Reina knew Enrique was in Segolita, but that didn't make the sight sting any less.

Soon enough, at the city's studded double doors, Reina found a new banner: a white orchid against black, the flower outline stitched in red thread. With the color arrangement reminding her of a priest's habit, she knew it was Las Orquídeas Blancas.

Reina avoided eye contact with their soldiers, though their attention wasn't on the caravan itself, but on the antlered Liberator leading the convoy. The people of Segolita knew their war hero was returning. It didn't take long for a crowd to form along the cobbled streets. People leaned over balcony railings. Children ran up behind the onlookers. A musician serenaded them with "Heart of the Llanos" to the melody of his cuatro.

Nearly every house had a flag of Las Orquídeas Blancas perched on a windowsill. Their black banners flapped oppressively as Reina's party rode to a vast town square overrun by pigeons. At its center were the green-rusted statues of Samón Bravo the Liberator and Feleva Águila. There were other players immortalized in statues, people who undoubtedly now worked within the walls of the cabildo, the seat of Segolita politics.

A palace built for the viceroyalty during Segol's rule, the cabildo itself stood across the impressive baroque cathedral in an identical arrangement to the governor's palace and the cathedral of Sadul Fuerte. This town square layout was a standard established by the colonial powers of Segol. A church, the government building, and the townhomes of those clerical and political officials surrounding a town square made for a most efficient layout of every settlement established during the former Viceroyalty of Venazia.

Gold-blooming araguaney trees shielded the cabildo's grounds from curious eyes, just as its wrought iron gates and posted guards protected it from unwanted visitors. Those same guards welcomed the Liberator's party without question. In fact, they lowered their hats to their chests and tipped their heads as the Liberator and his entourage entered.

Her first time inside the cabildo, Reina took in the beautiful wall panels, all polished wood carved with quotes from the early thinkers who had inspired the revolution. The floors were of brown and beige tiles arranged in elaborate patterns, and portraits of present and former officials lined the walls. Don Samón deftly navigated its corridors, not stopping until reaching a waiting area with floor-to-ceiling bookcases. The wait was short, as soon enough a man of medium build and olive skin the same shade as Don Samón's emerged. They met halfway for a tight embrace.

"Samón."

"Vicente."

"You've arrived!"

The man was dressed in tight pants and high black boots, his vest threaded with designs of storks in flight. His wavy black hair was cut short around the sides, allowing for a pompous tuft on the crown of his head. He wore a curled mustache. It took a moment for Reina to recognize him, for she'd glimpsed him only once or twice during her time in Segolita. But her mouth opened once she did.

This was Don Vicente Días, president of the Republic of Fedria.

Don Vicente invited them into his office. He and Don Samón exchanged jokes, noting how their peace had made them fat and content, while time had thinned their manes a bit. They laughed with a familiarity that sparked Reina's memory. Of course they acted as if they'd grown up together, because they had. It was a well-known fact that Fedria's current president was none other than the Liberator's first cousin on his mother's side.

Don Samón didn't waste a beat in introducing Eva. Don Vicente beamed and lifted Eva's knuckles to his lips. "I remember your mother," he said with a coy smirk. "The sweetest thing, like her name."

Don Vicente beamed again as Don Samón gestured for Javier, who approached with his hands behind his back.

Javier wore gloves, despite the afternoon's warmth. In fact, his outfit of a jacket and knee-high boots revealed no skin. Seeing him concealing his true self despite the heat of Segolita brought Reina great satisfaction.

"So *you* were that child Feleva was carrying when we signed the declaration of independence in this very room," Don Vicente said. "You take after your mother, did you know that?"

Javier startled.

"I see you and I see Feleva," Don Vicente added, amazed. "She was a secretive woman. I would love to inquire about your father, but…"

"She took that information to the grave," Javier said.

The president shrugged. "I figured as much. As long as he wasn't a loyalist, does it matter? Not that you were raised as one. Enrique was your conservator, correct?" He smiled at Don Samón, who seemed pleased with his son-in-law.

Javier's gaze fell. "I have her name, which is what matters."

"Indeed." Don Vicente added, "Your elder brother is in Segolita, as is his father, Esteban. Now, that's someone Feleva couldn't keep secret."

Don Samón and Don Vicente discussed Enrique's arrival, but the words went in one ear and exited through the other. Reina was too stunned—stuck on a single detail: This "Esteban," Enrique's father, was in Segolita. The man who had given his seed for both Enrique *and* Juan Vicente. Reina's grandfather.

Her chest constricted uncomfortably, her breathing coming out broken. The whispering of her iridio heart awoke from her agitation. For a moment Reina was transported to the sanctum of Rahmagut's tomb, when Doña Ursulina had admitted the ties she shared with the Águilas.

Warm fingers entwined with her own, taking hold of her hand.

Reina looked down and met Maior's concerned expression, snapping her out of the chokehold her thoughts had on her. Maior pressed closer, grounding her back in reality.

Don Vicente took a deep sigh as he circled the long table at the center of his office. "I didn't foresee the formation of this order of Las Orquídeas Blancas when I requested the help of the caudillos. Monseñor Lorenzo did this on his own, without my leave. He came to Segolita and took advantage of having all the commanders in one place to sway them to his cause. They pretend to be a force against tinieblas, but I know they're using the alliance as a license to persecute innocent people."

"The flags are all over the city," Don Samón said.

The president nodded, defeated. He moved the wooden pieces arranged on the table's wood-burned map of Fedria and Venazia. An eagle sat firmly over Segolita. "The caudillos have spread their armies from Puerto Carcosa all the way to Lake Catatumbo, where the tinieblas are most active."

"Our country occupied. How could you allow this?" Don Samón's voice echoed in the room.

"I don't have a choice," Don Vicente said, and it was obvious he lacked Don Samón's strength in leadership. "They say their only purpose is to eradicate tinieblas. I met with Enrique when he arrived. He attested the same."

"A cheap excuse to flex their powers against ours! Enrique will always have a secret agenda. *Vicente.*"

Reina had to agree, and her blood boiled at yet another one of Enrique's transgressions. She wasn't naïve enough to believe Enrique acted from the kindness of his heart. Quelling the source of tinieblas would ultimately harm his coffers.

The devilish whispers in her heart intensified as she imagined killing him with her own hands—the way it would feel to avenge all the injustices he'd put her through. Grinding her teeth, she pictured a covert assassination.

"What would you have me do?" Don Vicente told his cousin. "Misuse the military to antagonize them and weaken the country so that tinieblas can annihilate us all? We don't have the forces to stand up against Venazia face-to-face. Enrique alone could devastate us and I need him as a friend."

"I'm aware," Don Samón said.

"For now, I'm using our forces to protect what we can, the cities key to our economy—those that remain standing, of course." Don Vicente wiped his face woefully. "We've always operated under the assumption that we're sister nations, united in our freedom, but separate—"

Don Samón cut him off: "Your excuses mean little to me. I'm disappointed that you didn't foresee this." He paced the small office, his gaze avoiding those who watched him, as if he couldn't allow them to see his rage. "They've bound your hands. Now Fedria's weakness is blatant. Even if we survive the tinieblas, the caudillos are taking notice. Once the last man who fought in the revolution dies, their descendants who have never seen a war—those spoiled kids raised during peacetime—they will set their eyes on this republic. That is the only way monarchs justify their existence, through chaos and discord. I already hear that tune with the Orquídeas."

A thick silence settled between the cousins. This time the smiles and shared past couldn't stop the festering disagreement. Don Vicente wielded only half of Don Samón's charisma, and when he stood chastised in front of a crowd of the Liberator's party, he became smaller still.

"I will allow it for as long as they keep my people safe."

"Then why did you summon me?"

Don Vicente sighed. "I called you as a guarantee and a deterrent." He glanced about the room, as if steeling himself to voice an undeniable truth. As if it pained him to admit it, but it would be foolish to pretend otherwise. "You are the only person Enrique fears."

The president and the Liberator dismissed them shortly after. There were private plots to concoct, and conversations to be had.

Surprisingly, it was Don Rigoberto who guided them to their

lodging in the city: Don Samón's family house, now home to his estranged wife and Ludivina's mother. At first, Don Rigoberto tried dismissing Reina to one of the many run-down inns of Segolita's older neighborhoods—which was all she could afford either way. But Eva fought him, demanding Reina's and Maior's company.

Don Samón's natal residence was just a few streets from the cabildo, in a neighborhood characterized by the block-long, single-story residences of Segolita's richest families, called La Parroquia. The house took up an entire block, with its many open corridors, courtyards, open kitchen, vegetable garden, and stables forming a labyrinth around its abundance of rooms. The façade was of well-maintained brick, blanketed by crawling vines. A head matron named Doña Tomasa greeted them beneath Casa Bravo's marble doorframe. A slender woman with ginger hair met them in the foyer.

"Mamá!" Ludivina cried, running to her arms.

The woman's plucked eyebrows rose at the newcomers as she held Ludivina in an embrace.

Maria Elena Céspedes de Bravo wore a gown without ruffles or volume, the silver tones washing out her already pale skin. She had freckles all over her face and shoulders.

Maria Elena had expected them, Reina soon learned, but that didn't stop her from lifting her nose unpleasantly as Eva introduced herself. She pursed her lips, insulted perhaps that Don Samón had brought his daughter by another woman to her domain.

"Reina's staying with us," Eva declared to Maria Elena.

Maria Elena appraised Reina's rudimentary clothes, then her tail. "The guards stay with the servants."

"She'll have a guest bedroom, like myself," Eva emphasized, her left eyelid developing a twitch. Reina watched it with a concealed smile. This was the reason why she'd felt so othered when she lived here. The revolution had freed nozariels, but the old expectations lingered.

After a bath and a change of clothes, Eva and Maior invited Reina for a stroll through La Parroquia, to acquaint themselves with the neighborhood. Reina declined, for she had something else in mind. She headed to the cabildo while the sun descended beyond the araguaneys. She sat on a nondescript bench hidden within the hedges. She waited in silence, her tail curled firmly behind her to avoid suspicious looks, until Don Samón finally emerged from the cabildo's studded double doors.

He was perpetually accosted by people who recognized him. At some point Reina had to push past a crowd to reach him. He saw her and said her name in relief.

Reina glared at a priest who wanted to sidestep her for an audience with Don Samón.

"Yes, let us go for a stroll," Don Samón said, his eyes conveying gratitude for saving him from the crowd.

The hedges and topiaries swallowed them, allowing a short reprieve.

"Now you know why I dislike coming to the city."

"I dislike it as well," Reina said. After a while she added, "For different reasons." He waited patiently, and Reina sighed. "My kind is hated here. There's no denying or avoiding it." She wasn't oblivious to how the humans' acceptance of her within these new circles came thanks to her proximity to the Liberator and Eva. Otherwise, she'd be sneered at and excluded as she'd always been while living here.

He gave her a nod of validation. "Segol's legacy weighs heavily on Segolita. It is the problem with old cities. They cling to the past."

"You've done a great job with Tierra'e Sol," Reina said, finding herself missing its lack of decorum in day-to-day life. The absence of boxes separating people by their species and gender roles.

He glanced away, his cheeks red. "That is the highest compliment, coming from you."

They turned deeper into the maze, the shadows of dusk elongating. "I met your wife," she said, killing the time until she found the moment to say her piece.

"A bitter woman, isn't she?"

Reina withheld an opinion, for it wasn't her place.

"Thank the Virgin Ludivina is nothing like her."

"She couldn't be. You raised her."

He beamed at her. "You are just full of compliments for me today, aren't you?"

Reina scratched her cheek, looking away. She took in a big breath, finding the courage she needed, now that there were no walls between them. "Don Vicente mentioned that Enrique's father is in Segolita."

Don Samón frowned. "You are to stay away from Enrique. You know that, right?"

"This isn't about that," Reina said, dodging the long strands of bearded moss hanging from the tree overhead. Some ogling faces recognized the Liberator from beyond the outer gates, and Reina led the way farther into the hedge maze.

"Then?"

"I would like to meet Don Enrique's father."

A weight lifted off her shoulders as she said the words. She sighed deeply. She was bared and disarmed when speaking truthfully, especially with her commander, to whom she wanted to present a cool and composed façade. It terrified her to let him see the hollowed-out person she was. But she hadn't been able to shake the thought. Her grandfather was in the city. This was her chance to patch up the holes of her family history. An opportunity to solidify her own identity.

She expected his surprise, just as she expected the discomfort of having to explain the technicalities making her Enrique's niece. "We're blood, not family," she corrected as Don Samón gaped.

What she didn't expect was for him to so easily agree. Immediately, Don Samón guided her back to the president's office, where Don Vicente gave her instructions to ask for a man named Esteban the Cat in the Old Quarter. He painted a picture of who to look for: a man in his sixth decade, pompous like a peacock, with the green eyes of a cat. Overflowing with anxiety, Reina left to look for him.

21

Esteban the Cat

The Old Quarter was a decent neighborhood to find work or to pick up gossip in. As the name implied, it was one of the oldest boroughs, established some two hundred years prior. Its age became its downfall, for as the city expanded with more neighborhoods and new constructions became more attractive to families growing generational wealth, the Old Quarter turned into a hub of shadier enterprises. Now it was overrun with underground combat dens, the occasional gambling house, and, if you knew exactly where to look, two "competing" brothels owned by the same family.

Not much had changed since Reina last visited. The cobbles were still buried in mud and other questionable brown mounds. Men still loitered on the steps of crooked buildings, whistling and catcalling. The city guard still peeked from the alleyways, more interested in exchanging escudos as hush coins with thugs and business owners alike than in keeping the peace.

Reina entered the first inn along the long line of row houses and was promptly told to look in the establishment next door. In the second inn, the server gave her a scowl and said if she was in association with Esteban the Cat, she ought to pay up for all the escudos he owed.

Reina was forced to trade some coins for directions at the inn where he'd been seen staying for a whole fortnight. The lead took her to a dilapidated building crawling with cockroaches and the occasional scurrying rat, which turned out to be a scam. Most people would have lost their resolve by now, but Reina knew this was the Old Quarter way.

She entered another inn near the canals. The ambiance was livelier than in the previous inns, overflowing with people drawn by the contrapunteo duel on the center stage. Someone brushed by her, asking if she wanted to place a bet on either singer: one middle-aged man wearing an old uniform from the revolution, and an older man of salt-and-pepper hair with a cuatro in hand. Reina shooed the solicitor away, wary of more scammers.

She fought for access to the bar, to ask the keeper for another lead. Behind her, the crowd was aflame with the deft lyricism employed by both duelers. Reina was nearly tempted to pause and enjoy the contrapunteo.

Reaching the bartender, she repeated herself four times to be heard above the lyrics and hollers, which exploded as one of the singers emerged victorious. "Esteban the Cat!" she said. "Does he come by here often? Have you seen him?"

The bartender looked at her, miffed. "What do you mean, 'have I seen him'?"

"I'm looking for him!"

"What is someone who doesn't know what Esteban looks like doing looking for him?"

Reina winced. "What does that mean?"

"Take your quarrel elsewhere!"

Annoyed, she withdrew another escudo and slapped it on the nicked countertop. "Where can I find him?"

The bartender gave her a suspicious look, pocketed the escudo, then pointed at the stage where the winning singer was asking for more challengers.

"What?" Reina said, fearing another scam.

"He was just there—the one who lost."

Reina tried whirling around, but she was compressed between shoulders. The crowd's density made it impossible to bolt after the older singer. She got on tiptoes and managed to get a glimpse of his gray hair as he exited the inn.

"*Shit.*" She was so close. She found it hard to breathe from both the crowd and her own anxiety.

Reina slithered and shoved her way out, until someone yanked her by the tail as some sick joke. Blood rushing to her ears, Reina swerved to meet her assailant. She shoved him in retaliation, then dodged his drunken swing. The man's fist connected with someone else, stirring a chain reaction of yells and fists. As Reina caught sight of a guitar being thrown in the air, the entire inn broke out in a brawl. Somehow, she managed to rush to the door. The evening's dark swallowed her, and she accidentally stepped in a vile-smelling puddle as the inn's bedlam spilled into the street.

The situation wasn't much better outside. Three men had Esteban the Cat trapped between them and the building. Esteban raised his cuatro and hand in the air. From what Reina could piece together, he had joined the contrapunteo duel with borrowed money.

Her blade whistled out of her scabbard as one of the attackers lunged at Esteban with a drawn knife. Whatever was happening between them wasn't her problem, and she lacked context, but she wasn't going to watch idly as three much fitter men ganged up on her potbellied grandfather.

She yelled at them to stop, inserting her blade into the group to parry the attack. Esteban waved his hip like a dancer, dodging the subsequent strikes of the other two assailants. As Reina parried, she and Esteban met gazes. "The eyes of a cat" was an overstatement. Esteban had a perfectly normal human face, and surprisingly white teeth beneath an impish grin.

Their backs pressed against each other as they faced the attacking men. "Well, thank you señorita, not that I needed the rescue. Are you sure you should be in these parts at this hour?"

"Do I look like a young lady to you?" Reina growled, watching the assailant ditching his knife to unsheathe a machete.

"Fair point. Now, who sent you?"

"If you stay alive, I can explain everything later."

There was no time to argue. The machete man swung to

disembowel Reina and she blocked. The contacting metals let out an earsplitting keening. An electrifying jolt shot up from her wrists to her elbows. She was nearly shoved to her knees from his weight. Thankfully, Esteban gave Reina space to thrust with the full force of her shoulders. She didn't give the man a second to recover, kicking him in the shins. He howled, awkwardly swinging at her a second time. His attack was sloppy. As she parried, his machete went flying in the air. The man gaped at the swerving blade, then his fearful eyes found her, as if he believed her to be cold-blooded enough to end his life.

Esteban had already incapacitated one of the men and was swinging his cuatro at the other one's head. The man raised his weapon and blocked the swing, the sword catching on the cuatro's base.

"Oh well—I can get another one," Esteban said, shoving the cuatro against his assailant, further notching the sword within the instrument. Then he took off running down an alley, abandoning his guitar.

"Wait!" Reina yelled, sprinting after him.

The defeated men pursued. They hurled insults, calling Esteban a cheat and Reina a duskling.

Esteban shot her a grin. "Run, girl, run. The people here aren't too forgiving."

Reina cast bismuto on herself, electrifying her feet, and realized Esteban was already glowing in the golden sheen of his own geomancia.

They turned a corner, then scurried down an alleyway impeded by lines of drying bedsheets. Reina slapped them away, afraid to lose sight of Esteban. Something told her she wouldn't be seeing him again if she did.

Esteban slipped into a workshop through a broken back door. Reina followed, dodging the startled hound who guarded the area. She leapt, preventing the hound from biting her tail, and caught up to Esteban.

"How are you so agile?" she huffed. "Aren't you...elderly?"

Esteban laughed. "Anything can be faked with magic. So, why're you still following me?"

They kicked open the workshop's front door and slid down a street of slippery cobbles. The hound turned its attentions to their pursuers, buying Reina and Esteban time to cross the bridge over the stinky canal and disappear down another block. Sweat drenched and panting, they plunged into a crowd of even more refugees coming into the city. There, the throngs swallowed them, and Reina and Esteban lost their pursuers.

Reina wiped her temples, brushing back sweaty bangs. She glanced up at Esteban, who was taller than her just as Doña Ursulina had been. Esteban found a railing to lean on. As the gold of his bismuto spell wore off, his breathing became agitated.

"Don't give me that look. I will live," he said in a weak breath. "I always do."

Reina couldn't help herself from smiling. "I suppose you don't reach your age by not living."

Her joke was silly, but it sparked a laugh in him.

"Why did you intervene?"

"I was afraid you'd be killed. Or that you'd run away."

He frowned, backing away as if indeed he was considering doing exactly that. "Who are you?"

Reina reached for the badge affixed to her vest and angled it so that nearby torchlight could reflect the mirrored laurels engraved on the gold. She wished she was wearing Doña Ursulina's badge, the sigil of the Duvianos. Alas, she'd replaced it for one symbolizing that she now served the Bravo family.

He made a grimace. "What does Samón want with me?" He turned to leave. "Tell him I'm still retired."

She followed, afraid he would start thinking about disappearing. "I'm only showing it because I want you to see I'm not part of any other association."

"Mm-hmm? Then?"

"I'm Juan Vicente's daughter, Ursulina's granddaughter."

Esteban paused. His bushy brows quivered as he watched the canoes swaying on the canal. "Juan Vicente? That's a name I don't hear often."

"Juan Vicente Duvianos." Reina circled him so he had no choice but to face her. She patted her chest, feeling the raggedness of her transplant heart beneath her clothes. "My name is Reina Duvianos. I'm your granddaughter."

"Yes. It would seem so."

The joviality he'd worn because of her help vanished. Reina's heart drilled into her chest as she waited. She held her breath, afraid to speak or swallow. Reina was flooded with the memory of Doña Ursulina's disdain upon meeting her.

"A nozariel, are you?"

The corners of her eyes stung as she anticipated his rejection. Reina nodded.

His narrowed green eyes indeed reminded her of a cat. He glimpsed at her tail, then took her in.

"You take after Juan Vicente *and* Ursulina. Niña, what are you doing here?"

As his demeanor changed and he guarded himself, Reina realized he had concealed his strength well. He'd never been in true danger against those men.

"I'm not a niña."

"To me you are."

In his appraising silence, every doubt and insecurity crept around her, squeezing her. He had had many years to find her. His never doing so spoke mountains to his indifference. She should have considered this sooner.

Unclenching her jaw, Reina said, "Doña Ursulina is dead." This shocked him, as she had expected it would.

"The old hag's gone?"

"May we walk?" she said. "I wish to speak to you. If you have no interest in me at all, or if this brings you great discomfort, just say the word and you'll never see me again."

He smiled. "You sound like Juan Vicente's daughter indeed. Now, where do you think he got *that* from?"

Reina glanced down at her grimy boots. "Not Doña Ursulina."

He laughed. "I do have an interest in you, and in this meeting. I am surprised, is all," he said, joining her on the nighttime stroll.

The canal was rank with the smells of human waste and the

polluted waters. They detoured back toward the crooked town-homes, down quieter streets where people loitered by doorsteps with half-empty bottles of rum at their feet.

Reina's heart thrummed in an anxious frenzy. Cold perspiration slicked her palms as her grandfather walked in silence beside her, waiting for her initiative. She had a million things to say, but no words seemed adequate. "I guess...my first question is, Where have you been? I am twenty-one years old and never once did my father speak of you."

"How about you treat me to a drink? Aguardiente helps in airing out the family's dirty laundry. I know a quiet place right around the corner."

Reina followed him down an alley where a back door opened onto a dingy bar of tables crammed together in too-close proximity. The establishment was mostly empty, yet Reina immediately saw a certain bull-built nozariel taking up one of the tables. Pucho de Las Garras's sharp canines glinted beneath his grin as he recognized her in return. He rose, his armored tail swaying in anticipation.

"If it isn't Pucho," Esteban hollered with open arms, approaching him. "I see you're still in one piece."

"You know him?" Reina said, bewildered. "When were you released? *And why?*" she asked Pucho.

Pucho's hand rested against the hilt of his machete as he appraised the situation. "I told you the Liberator wouldn't be able to keep me for long. It wasn't hard to free myself, in the mess of this city."

Esteban watched them with delight. "You know my grand-daughter?"

Pucho whistled.

"He nearly killed me," Reina said, her hand gravitating toward her sword. Adrenaline pumped through her from the memory. She'd never seen a fighter more proficient. Perhaps Don Samón or Enrique. A cold bead of sweat trickled down her temple as she remembered his angled machete flying for her neck.

Esteban placed his fists on his hips. "And do you plan to try again?" he asked Pucho.

Pucho chuckled and shook his head. "My job hinged on secrecy. I've been fired."

"Why do you know this mercenary?" Reina asked her grandfather.

"He trained me. Taught me everything I know," Pucho supplied, reaching for his flagon. He took a sip, then raised it in the air for Esteban. "His talent with the sword—few have it."

Reina couldn't close her mouth. The pieces were falling together, making sense, yet she'd never imagined this was the circle her grandfather navigated in. He couldn't be more different from Feleva and Ursulina.

"And that granddaughter of yours put up a formidable fight." Pucho chuckled with a smirk. "The apple doesn't fall far from the tree, as they say."

Esteban looked impressed. "I got to witness some of that myself. Can't say I don't like to see it."

Reina crossed her arms. His compliments relieved some of her apprehension. "So you're both mercenaries?"

"Indeed. Wouldn't be alive if it weren't for Esteban the Cat— and the streets that raised me, of course," Pucho said, giving Reina a pointed nod. "And I recognize my kin when I see it."

Reina pursed her lips. Unlike him, she'd found no pride or joy in it. The Águilas, not the streets, had taught her how to wield a sword. "There's nothing unique about the streets raising us," she said. Little had changed in Segolita since she'd left. The strata of society remained untouched, and nozariels continued inhabiting its lowest rung.

"Did you come looking for me?" Pucho said.

"I came to talk to my grandfather, in private," Reina replied.

Pucho settled back on his chair, raising his flagon in acquiescence.

"We'll catch up later," Esteban said as they passed him, heading for a table in the farthest corner.

A plump nozariel brought them a bottle of aguardiente as they sat on uneven stools. Esteban took two hearty shots. "So you're a warrior. I see you wield a fancy sword."

Reina took a deep breath while she watched Pucho across the

room completely lose all interest in them. Her cheeks heated. "I call it Nightcleaver."

Esteban laughed. He offered Reina a shot as well, and she wriggled her nose before taking it. The clear, bitter alcohol burned her throat on the way down. She grimaced.

The subsequent tingling gave her the courage to say, "My father never spoke of you. Why?"

"Juan Vicente was an intelligent man, and a proud one. He likely understood nothing good would come from you asking about me. How much do you know?"

Someone near the bar picked up a cuatro and started playing a sorrowful melody that kept them company. It permitted Reina to speak without worrying about being overheard. "I know Juan Vicente is not your only son."

A grin found Esteban. "I don't consider either of them my son. Yes, I sired them, and they might have my height, or my teeth, or whatever other trait you'd like to assign to me, but that was my only use in that relationship."

"Why?"

He chuckled. "Why did Feleva and Ursulina use me to bear their children?"

"Well—I understand Feleva wanted to have an heir or whatever. But what about my grandmother? And why *you*?"

She meant no offense. She just couldn't help herself from observing his shaggy and ephemeral demeanor, as if he were apt to forever disappear into an alleyway if she blinked for too long.

She also couldn't deny the size of his shoulders, nor the steadiness of his big, calloused hands. The way his gait had a slight skip, as if from an old injury that had never healed quite right—from the revolution, perhaps? He wasn't a person to be trifled with.

"Why me..." he muttered.

To clarify, Reina quickly added, "I would have imagined Feleva and my grandmother to have preferred someone from a wealthy family. Coffers of wealth. Estates. Prestige. An inheritance."

"Then you didn't know them well enough."

Reina just frowned, dumbfounded.

"Feleva hated men from a young age. Her first love was killed by two jealous men. It was an event that colored her view of the world," Esteban said.

Reina was reminded of Celeste's tale of the rancher and the bounty hunter.

"She did not want a man in her life. She did not want to be ruled or reeled in. She wanted to build a life on her own terms. I was younger than you are now when I first met her and Ursulina."

Reina reminded herself to breathe. "What about Doña Ursulina? How was she back then?"

Esteban's chest rumbled in low laughter. "The Ursulina you knew was probably a lot different from the Ursulina I met. In our youth, she was a proper young girl, the only daughter of aristocrats from Segol. Her relatives fled to their motherland after the revolution. They were neither revolutionaries nor interested in the colonies. Loyalists."

"A proper young girl..." Reina parroted, struggling to paint a picture in her head. With time and distance, she was realizing her grandmother had been truly evil, to concoct such plans and see them to fruition. And this made Reina evil as well, for participating in the kidnappings and the tests. She didn't lie to herself anymore. Her heart was a crude amalgamation of iridio and she was a desperate, monstrous creature. She failed to see a past where Doña Ursulina wasn't the conniving, oppressive force Reina had known her to be.

"Well-mannered, soft-spoken, apprehensive of the expectation that it was her duty to marry a man. Feleva was her exact opposite in this regard. I believe this dazzled Ursulina. And me? I come from a family of soldiers. It's how my father made his coin, and how my grandfather did as well. Bleeding for princes and caudillos."

"Were you their friend?"

"We were very close, for a time, before they used me as breeding stock." He stared at the clear aguardiente bottle, lost in faraway memories. "I met them in Sadul Fuerte after Feleva's father hired me. The man was paranoid he'd be assassinated for being valco when the humans were fruitful and multiplying. He had a small army of mercenaries. It was my first proper job."

"How did Ursulina meet Feleva?"

Esteban scratched his scruffy jaw, squinting as if scraping his mind for the memory. "The Duvianos held political appointments in Sadul Fuerte. But Ursulina and Feleva were already thick as thieves when I met them. Already sneaking away to broom cupboards and holding hands when no one was looking. It's why I liked them, to be honest." He grinned at Reina as he said, "I may not look it now, but I was quite the heartbreaker back in my day."

Reina offered him a friendly smile.

"Their indifference was refreshing. And besides, I wanted to buddy up with the heiress of the house. It was what my father recommended. So...that's how it all started."

The silence crept between them. Mainly because Reina still had so many questions and not an inkling of how to tactfully navigate them.

She stared at her scarred hands—her fingernails, which she'd painstakingly cleaned during her bath. She wondered how her life would have been with Esteban in it. Even Pucho had had that privilege. She wondered what it would have been like to be raised in a normal household, with both parents present and the history of her lineage cleanly cataloged in family trees. To be confident of her identity.

Her silence piqued his curiosity. "You want to know why me? Feleva chose me because she saw me for the man with no ambition that I am."

Reina was stunned he would speak about himself in such a way.

"I don't care for pedigrees or family fortunes. It's all fleeting in this life anyway. How many families have risen and fallen since the revolution? Feleva had to kick and bite her way to fame. She did... unspeakable things for the iridio."

"I know about Rahmagut," Reina said. She didn't want him to spare any details for her sake.

He sized her up, his thick eyebrow arching. "Then you know the quality of her ambition and cruelty. My fathering Enrique—it was no grand plan. She wanted to be a mother and we were enabled by rum. Can't say I was entirely on board with it but..." He took another shot of aguardiente. His pupils drifted apart in his ine-briation. "I didn't imagine anything would happen." He winced. "Valcos are not easily conceived."

"What about my grandmother?" Reina asked, already bracing herself.

"Ursulina? She worshipped Feleva. In her eyes, the sun rose and set for Feleva. The stars shone for Feleva. Ursulina's entire orbit revolved around Feleva."

Reina glanced away. She hated the similarity to her own obses-sion with Celeste.

"They were happy for a time, until Ursulina had the great idea of asking me to father her child. I wasn't the brightest, back in my day, and I thought I was doing them a favor—helping them build the nucleus of their future family. I didn't predict the mistake of crossing a woman capable of pursuing Rahmagut's legend."

"Why would that be crossing Feleva?" Reina asked, her cheeks warming in the anger it sparked.

A glass shattered somewhere. Someone else shouted a curse. Pucho rose from his table, waving Esteban goodbye before swaying for the door.

"Feleva always wanted more. It's like she had an emptiness in her heart. Nothing satiated her. Nothing stopped her. And her being the last of her kind? It wasn't a burden. She wore this fact like a crown. Then the iridio gold came pouring in and she became a nar-cissist. A woman like her never saw Ursulina as her equal. Naturally, she was enraged that Ursulina and I acted without her approval."

Reina ground her teeth. Enrique was the same.

"Ursulina's attempts to impress her always came up short. I know their relationship was never the same afterward. I was ousted—and thank the Virgin for that."

"I understand keeping a distance from Enrique, but what about Juan Vicente? Didn't you care about him?" she asked hotly.

He'd mentored Pucho yet hadn't bothered with his own blood?

Esteban faced her evenly. "Is this why you sought me out? To demand things from me? I'm a musician. I'm retired. I go where the tide takes me. I have no interest in the politics of your family."

He took another drink, then moved as if he meant to leave the table.

"Wait—that's not what I meant. There are no politics," Reina blurted to stop him from disappearing into the night. Just because she'd found him once, when he didn't know she'd been looking for him, didn't mean that she'd be successful a second time.

"With the Águilas, there are always politics. Feleva was murderous. Ursulina was obsessed. And I have outlived them because I kept my distance. You know what Feleva did with her second child?"

"Javier?"

"Shortly after she gave birth, she murdered the father like some blood-damned black widow. She made everyone believe it was a freak accident, but I saw right through her lies. It got me thinking—maybe she was enraged he didn't give her the daughter she wanted. But now I've come to realize she simply didn't want anyone challenging the authority of her doted-upon heir. Do you think it was safe for me to try to be around those boys? No—I got as far away from her as I could. I'm sorry you being alone was the consequence."

"Well, she's dead now," Reina muttered miserably. "And Doña Ursulina."

"What about Enrique?"

"He has a daughter."

"So you're not alone—"

His smile dropped as Reina glared at him.

He raised his hands in the air. "Listen—I gave you answers. I'm sorry they are disappointing. Do as I did and stay away from that family. And . . . just let me live the rest of my days in peace. I want neither glory nor a legacy."

He emptied the last of the aguardiente into his glass, then chugged it. Reina didn't even have to tell him she had no coins for another drink. He got up and left with a drunken wave. She watched him go as her heart twisted itself. As heat built in the corners of her eyes and a pressure built in her nose. She had to squint to stop any tears.

She'd gotten her answers, yet she was still empty. Feleva had a void in her heart. In a way, so did Reina. She had holes all over her body and no idea of how to fill them up. She was supposed to be a vessel for a god and use his boon for good. Yet she felt so exhausted. So empty and wrung out.

Maybe she was the fool, for imagining meeting Esteban would go any other way but this.

She gave the last of her escudos to the bar owner. With her pockets empty, Reina exited to the streets.

22

The Acceptance of Family

The streets of the Old Quarter were somber this late at night. The alleyways were riddled with people like her, ending their days with sadness, a bottle of aguardiente in hand. The people on the streets weren't old—the backbreaking labor imposed on them never allowed for long lives anyway—but they looked it. Reina saw the hardened and cracked faces of coughing miners from the silver mines just west of Segolita. They extracted so many riches for their patrones, yet lived clawing for pittances. Reina used to be part of that workforce, until she left for the promises her grandmother offered. Her life had hardly improved in leaving—instead of being enslaved to Segolita's class economy, she'd enslaved herself to iridio. She had committed horrible acts, and still her hands remained empty of the one thing she ached for the most: a family.

Reina returned to Casa Bravo, telling herself if the house guard denied her entry, she'd just sleep on their doorstep in protest. The guard surprised her by welcoming her inside. The Liberator and his estranged wife sat in the drawing room, deep in a hushed conversation; Reina dodged out before they could notice her. She scurried through the corridors quietly, avoiding the creak of doors.

When she entered her guest room, she found Maior waiting for her, awake.

Maior shut the book she used to practice her reading. She left it on the side table. "Reina, where were you?"

Reina took off her vest and sat on the bed with her back to Maior. She wiped her face. The walk back from the bar had done nothing to clear the sadness from her throat.

Maior gingerly reduced the distance between them. She held Reina from behind. "I missed you. I was waiting for you."

Reina's nose grew stuffy. She wanted to hold on. She hated to be caught in tears over this again. How could she be so pathetic?

Maior squeezed her tighter.

"I went to see my grandfather," she said after a long while. Once the passing seconds had patched the frayed fabric of her sense of self. Once the holes in her chest had been mended and she could muster the air in her lungs to speak.

"Your grandfather is in Segolita? He is alive?"

"And I'm a fool, you know? A complete idiot!" She wrangled herself free from Maior's hug, facing her in anger.

"Reina—"

"Clearly I don't learn from my mistakes! I went looking for my grandfather in the same way I searched for Doña Ursulina two years ago. Did you know that I crossed the mountains blindly, thinking my life would change?"

"Stop," Maior grumbled, grabbing Reina's wildly gesticulating hands.

"And I did it again—I went to him so desperate for a family— when I should have learned the lesson the first time, because we know how disastrously that turned out."

Maior gave Reina's hands a jerk, forcing her to snap out of it. Their gazes swam together, the weak light of Maior's candle illuminating one side of her face, leaving the other in shadow. The motion forced Reina to focus on Maior's lips. It forced her to acknowledge how close they were.

Maior's hand cupped Reina's jaw. Reina found it impossible not to lean into it.

"You're not a fool for wanting a family, Reina." Maior smiled, her eyes growing shinier. She licked her lips and drew Reina into an embrace, where Reina surrendered. Her voice muffled by Reina's braid, Maior continued. "It is natural to want it. We see people who have stability, who have a house and someone to care for them. Who share blood and histories with a community. It's something we never had."

Reina's hand slithered to Maior's lower back, pressing her closer. To extinguish the air and so that there was nothing but clothes between them. They did have this in common. This sense of being utterly alone, if not for one another.

Maior undid Reina's braid and dove her fingers into the roots of her hair. A glitter of bliss surged as Maior gently massaged her there.

The tightness in Reina's chest lessened. She couldn't focus on it any longer, not as her lower belly fluttered, awakened and hungry. She burrowed her nose deeper in the soft waves of Maior's hair. The smell of it was so familiar by now. It made Reina feel at home.

She gave in. It was easy. Not just because every night together there was a new discovery coupled with a delight to be had. But Maior also gave in to the allure of falling asleep in Reina's arms, forgoing her questionable galio tincture.

Maior pulled away, unbuttoning Reina's shirt. "You're not a fool at all for seeking it out," she said as Reina lifted Maior's skirt in turn. "It's my favorite thing about you, actually."

The words gave Reina pause. "What do you mean?"

Maior's cheeks were so rosy and plump from the heat in the room. "You think you're not brave, but that's not true. You have so much courage. You crossed the mountains for a better life." She gestured at the door, as if she could point to the towns they had passed on the journey to Segolita. "You risk your life for strangers all the time. You saved Eva *and* Javier."

Reina liked seeing Maior's grimace at the uttering of his name.

"You're my protector." Maior pursed her lips in a pretty smile, then she moved Reina, laying her on the bed.

Reina obliged as her heart drilled against her ribs. Gently, Maior fluffed a pillow behind Reina's head.

"So what? You took a chance with your grandfather and it didn't work out. At least you did something. You weren't frozen by the what-ifs," Maior added, unfastening the binds around Reina's chest.

Reina held her breath as Maior freed her breasts from the layers of clothes. There had been utter darkness the last time she had been this exposed to Maior, with nothing but the stars twinkling beyond the window of their cabin in Hato de los Lobos. This time, the flicker of candlelight unveiled all the scar tissue affixed to the crystal contraption of Reina's new heart.

Reina's hand twitched with the fearful impulse to stop Maior. But another part of her waited in delighted anticipation, at what the night could lead to. Maior took her in a kiss. Her hands traveled down Reina's sides, squeezing, thumbs pressing against her breasts, leaving a trail of electricity in their wake. Reina found it hard to breathe.

"If you'd never followed your heart to Sadul Fuerte, we never would have met. I'd be alone in that shitty town, thinking I was broken, never learning how good you feel. Can you imagine?"

Reina smiled and Maior giggled.

Maior pecked Reina's nose playfully, then her jaw, then her collarbone. And Reina couldn't stop her trembling as Maior's lips explored her skin.

Maior stopped near the atrophied flesh covering the tubes and crystal in Reina's chest. For an instant Reina almost panicked, imagining Maior's hesitation was born out of disgust. Her insecurities screamed at her to squirm away. But Maior's small smile was a reassuring balm.

Maior's thumb ran along the scars, as if feeling for every ripple and mound in detail, memorizing them. Her forefinger circled the tube Reina often had to unscrew to refill herself with iridio. "You've endured so much," Maior whispered, "and it's changed you—*for the better*, no matter what you say. I'm sorry meeting him was disappointing, but family is who accepts you. Not who shares your blood." Then she lowered herself and placed soft kisses everywhere her thumb had been. Reina closed her eyes, arching into her lips without meaning to. She couldn't help it—it felt as if Maior were worshipping the part of her that made her odd. Maior's every kiss was a prayer. It made Reina's skin vibrate. She hungered for more.

She pulled Maior up close to her face. "You're right about that. Meeting you changed my life."

Pressed in a kiss, Maior muttered, "For the best?"

Reina knew Maior craved validation, and she gave it gladly. "You've showed me what real happiness feels like." The sincerity of their feelings—how uncomplicated being together was. How it gave her a purpose and excitement for the future. Reina treasured it fiercely.

"You're happy?" Maior knew the power of her fingers as they ran the length of Reina's tail, which coiled in delight. She traced Reina's thighs, circling every cut and scar as if her touch were a salve.

"More than ever." Reina tugged the overabundance of laces and fabric from Maior, delighting once her breasts came free. She loved seeing them. They were full, the nipples enlarged in the softest shade of pink. "Let me be the one keeping you awake tonight."

Reina took her pleasure in tracing every inch of Maior's soft skin, squeezing her sides, and taking Maior's breasts in her mouth. She wanted Maior to feel revered as well. She wanted to fill her up with a happiness that displaced all the obstacles threatening their future.

Reina's heart soared as Maior whimpered her name—as she arched herself and pressed closer to Reina. With her sharp nozariel hearing, she relished in Maior's heartbeats, noticing their wildly thrumming quality. It encouraged Reina's hand as she reached between Maior's legs, seeking her warm center. Reina forgot how to breathe as her fingers encountered Maior's wet folds. They were drenched. It made her want to kiss Maior even harder. She marveled at the slickness of Maior's sex, unable to comprehend how something so warm and moist could exist here. The sensation made Reina incredibly wet—if she wasn't soaked already.

Ravenous, Reina slipped two fingers in, her eyes searching Maior's for the slightest sign of discomfort or regret.

Maior's eyes rounded, her cheeks flushed red. She was so beautiful with her button nose dotted in freckles.

"Is this okay?" Reina whispered.

Maior's reply came as a kiss. Against Reina's lips, she said, "I want to be filled with you."

The words were a fuse, and Reina's heart was ready to explode.

Reina thrust a third finger in. She was immediately surrounded by warm ridges and undulations, Maior's muscles clenching, squeezing Reina's fingers and drowning them as if they were a glove made precisely for her. Outside, Reina's thumb trailed upward to press against the center of Maior's pleasure, a spot she circled and rubbed. Her fingers thrust as Maior ground into them.

"Good. Because I want to live inside you," Reina said before she realized the meaning of the words—how they revealed an unexplainable desire. "I want to be so close there is no end to what is you and me."

Maior's cheeks flushed red. Her rounded eyes glimmered. "I would love that. I want it all," she said, and kissed Reina passionately. She gripped Reina's back, her fingers digging in as if she were falling. As if Reina were the only stable ground amid an endless abyss.

Electricity shot from Reina's belly to her spine. She loved how pleasing Maior made her aflame. Somehow their bodies were in perfect synchronicity. They burned in a shared fire, starved, no kiss being enough to replenish their lungs.

Maior clung to Reina's shoulders. She screwed her eyes shut and cried Reina's name. Maior's thighs convulsed as she threw her head back, gasping for air. The wet folds of her center squeezed and shuddered like they meant to create a void, and Reina had no choice but to be sucked in.

Reina knew exactly what she'd done. She could feel the tremors in her hand, which was drenched to the wrist. Her other arm cradled Maior, who whimpered and hugged her back. She knew she needed to hold perfectly still, for Maior's sake. Finally, when Maior had the strength to open her eyes, Reina found them glossy.

"You're okay. You survived," Reina said softly, if a bit cheekily. "My whimpery girl."

"That was..." Maior trailed off, unable to conjure the words.

"Amazing?" Reina finished for her, smiling. "How did I get so lucky?"

Maior giggled and pressed her nose against Reina's nose scutes. "Do you want to·feel it, too?"

Sending Maior over the edge had already brought Reina so close. It would take barely anything at all for Reina to unravel. Still, Reina hesitated. Her heart did a silly little pirouette. She was moonstruck, but was she deserving of this devotion?

Maior dug into Reina's shoulders even harder. "Please, let me."

And who was Reina to deny her?

When she smiled her consent, Maior dove into Reina as if the thrusting had done nothing to satiate her hunger.

Their bodies tangled and entwined. Maior drove Reina to see stars several times that night. Vaguely, Reina wondered if this was what real love was supposed to feel like.

23

The Bravo Legacy

As the rising sun warmed the morning, the cicadas' song dominated the Bravo training yard. Eva listened to them with heavy huffs, as she and Javier had been training together since before the break of dawn. Her trousers and shirt clung to her body, drenched. Her nose and cheeks stung from a sunburn. And her curls were beginning to break free from the topknot where she'd fastened them shortly after waking up.

Already Eva was drained, which had been foolish of her, for she was supposed to attend a luncheon at the cabildo. Don Samón meant to introduce his treasured firstborn to all his friends, allies, and rivals.

"Ten more swings," Javier barked from where he stood under the shade of a bougainvillea.

Eva's arms were like buttery noodles. She'd been swinging the same sideways motion with the wooden practice sword so many times she'd already lost count. She sagged, moaning. "C'mon, I've been at it all morning. Enough with the swinging and teach me an actual move. Let me try a real sword, at least."

Javier picked at his nails, indifferent. "Being a fighter isn't meant to be a stroll through the gardens. I am training you as I was trained."

Eva rolled her eyes. "I don't need to be as good as you. You have *years* on me. Show me something in self-defense. This must be our rule: You can put me through all these stupid motions, but I have to at least learn one thing every day."

He kicked off from the tree and unsheathed his blade. "Do you want to learn things the wrong way?" he drawled.

"What? No."

"The motions are so that your body memorizes them. So that every strike is perfect. Do you see me swinging my blade around like a clown? Do you think I move without precision?"

Eva shook her head. On the contrary, Javier resembled a dancer born of air.

"Strike me. I want to see it."

Eva hesitated, watching as his left hand angled his sword downward in expectation. She was already at a disadvantage with her practice sword. Eva marched at him with the wide-leg stance he'd taught her to use in a previous session. She swung down at his neck in a two-handed grip.

Javier blocked with a simple flick of his wrist. The reacting force threw her to the ground. Eva grumbled.

"Too slow." He offered her a hand up.

Eva slapped it away and got up on her own.

"Again," he commanded.

Eva swung and was repelled in a similar fashion.

"Don't you want to at least surprise me?"

Angry and hot, Eva pushed to her feet and thrust for his belly.

It immediately became clear the move was the wrong one. Javier sidestepped her strike, then yanked her by the wrist and pressed the cool blunt end of his blade against her neck.

"You're dead now," he said.

They were so close Eva could feel the heat radiating off him in waves, adding to her own unbearable temperature. Cheeks ardent, Eva tried stepping back, yanking her arm to freedom. His grip didn't let up.

"It's not fair!" Eva growled. "You're not letting me use bismuto! Of course I wouldn't be able to move fast enough."

"Why? We are both valco."

She found his gaze on her lips. It made her aflutter and dis-tracted. "I am less than you and you know it. It's not fair."

He released her hand and allowed her to step back. Sweat ran down her neck, and Eva couldn't be sure if she was relieved or dis-appointed. She glanced up at the cloudless sky and cursed it, for not even granting them the slightest reprieve of a breeze or cloud.

She tossed her weapon to the ground and crossed her arms. "I'm terrible at this."

"You're just tired."

"And sore," she muttered, remembering the swing he'd given her earlier with the fake sword as he demonstrated a move. It had bruised her side and continued to throb. "*And bad*," she empha-sized in defeat.

Javier picked up the sword for her. "Again, Eva. No one is good at the beginning."

"What if someone takes my sword? Or disarms me? Why don't you teach me something hand-to-hand or close combat."

"Close combat, huh?" He scratched his unshaven cheek, smirk-ing. "Maybe you're better suited to a knife."

It sounded so much easier that Eva beamed. "Yes! A knife."

He burst out laughing. "You're so lazy!"

"Fuck you!"

"Are you sure? I'm kind of sweaty." He tugged at his collar.

Eva's face steamed more than it already was. The suggestion was a thrill. But she wasn't going to back down. "As I said, fuck you. Give me a knife and let's go."

He meandered around the yard until he found a fallen twig. He handed it to her.

"You've got to be joking."

"It is the ideal length," he said. "Now listen, I'm no master, but I have an idea or two about how to use one." He closed the distance between them and grasped her forearm, where he pretend-sliced her. As she flinched, he pointed at the blood vessels on her inner forearm and said, "If you manage to get close, and get a good slice right here, it should be enough to disarm an attacker or make them lose their grip."

She nodded, even if the strength in *his* grip made it hard to focus. How assured he was with her skin.

He repeated the motion to show her. "Watch how I do it. Now you try." He grabbed her hand and taught her the proper grip. "Pretend this is the sharp side. It's what you'll cut with."

He swung for her face. He did it slowly, and Eva already knew she'd never have such an easy opening in a real fight. She dodged the punch and swiped at his forearm with the twig, scraping a pink line on his pale skin.

Javier gasped.

"I'm sorry! I thought you'd move away." Eva grabbed his forearm to run her thumb along the scrape.

He cocked an eyebrow, watching her nurse the scratch. "I was making it easy on you."

Eva quickly let go.

"There's a follow-up move you can do if you don't disarm the attacker." He showed her how to flick her wrist. "You can take advantage of their shock to slice their arm." With his forefinger he made a pretend slice on her forearm, like they'd practiced, and rounded around to swipe at her triceps. Eva flinched from the tickling sensation, and he chuckled. As their gazes met, Eva realized she liked seeing his smile. How he seemed at ease around her.

"You ready?" he asked.

Instead of answering, Eva repeated the motion as best as she could remember. He allowed her the pretend slice on his forearm, and she went for the back of his arm. Suddenly he sidestepped her. In a flash, he whirled behind her, trapping her in a chokehold.

"Javier Armando!" Eva gasped, squirming.

"Using my full name, are you?"

She could breathe, but his grip arrested her body against his.

"This wasn't part of the instruction."

"A real fighter wouldn't let you off the hook so easily. Besides, blame my ego. I can't let you win." His breath caressed the back of her ear, sending shivers through her spine.

Her body reacted traitorously, tensing from the press of his. Eva held her breath, her mind ablaze with fantasies of being desired. She was unable to shake the thought of what it would feel like—a true intimacy. She felt teased, purposely distracted. Was he grabbing her like this because he also craved the feel of her body? Or was this just a game to prove how utterly helpless she was before him?

A little voice in the depths of her mind—*her voice*—laughed at her naïveté. Javier had never given an inkling that her proximity affected him. He wasn't a boy. He was a man able to take what he desired, all appropriate under the stipulations of their marriage. She should just trust his words. They might be on the same side now, but they hadn't yet called a truce in their battle of egos.

Rahmagut mocked her. He reminded her how Javier had little control against the tiniebla he housed, which burned with adoration for the god *she* housed. *"His desires can't ever be true."*

"How kind of you to spare my feelings," Eva hissed to herself.

She fumed, from Javier's games and how easily she fell for them. Instead of tugging on his chokehold to free herself, Eva pressed her fingers together to summon the swelling strength of bismuto. If he was going to cheat, then she could as well.

She elbowed him in the belly, knocking the air out of him. It worked brilliantly to free her.

He gasped for air, his face red. "You're not supposed to use magic!"

"As you said: In a real fight, everything counts." She kicked the fallen twig away. "I'm tired of this. And I must go supply the soldiers with bismuto before the luncheon."

"You'll never learn to defend yourself at this pace."

Eva didn't spare him a glance as she said, "I clearly lack the talent."

"I was right to teach you geomancia the way I did."

Eva ground her teeth. Perhaps he was right.

The Bravo soldiers were resplendent in their freshly pressed uniforms while they waited before the gates of Segolita for the tiniebla raid. The morning sunlight bounced off their golden-threaded epaulettes as they lined up before Eva, who painstakingly titrated bismuto into dozens of rings. Since Tierra'e Sol, she'd taken the task of supplying her father's forces with geomancia solutions, for no one else had her quickness and precision in mixing them. Eva's solutions resulted in their most potent colors: the galios chartreuse, the litios water clear, and the bismutos a most saturated azure.

The distribution of supplies was set up against the wall's outer ring, which provided just enough shade for the table with the geomancia potions, first aid supplies, and armory. Parties employed by the other families also waited for deployment near the gates.

Don Samón's soldiers smiled cheekily and offered Eva grateful nods as Reina, part of the assembly line, plopped adequately sized rings in their expectant hands.

"You've seen what they've done to those people on our ride here," one of the soldiers grumbled as she approached the supply table where Eva worked.

"Chained them and dragged them into the city for a mass inquisition. No one gets a fair trial," her companion added. "They beat them bloody until they confess to some crime they didn't commit. I heard the jails are overflowing. That'll be us soon enough."

"Is there a problem?" Reina said above the murmur.

The grumbling soldiers exchanged glances.

One said, "We can all agree it's better if we're not suspected by Las Orquídeas Blancas. We can fight with our swords just fine."

"How it shows you've never killed a tiniebla before in your life," Reina said, crossing her arms.

"You need to use bismuto to see the tinieblas," Eva piped up gently, as Reina's standoffish attitude would not be reaching any hearts.

The soldiers quieted. Suddenly all eyes fell on Eva. They waited for her words the same way they would wait for those of Don Samón, who hadn't yet arrived to see them off. She stood up. As she glanced at the expectant faces, she saw no malice or reproach in them, just curiosity and, in some, reverence.

"The scouts have confirmed tiniebla sightings in the jungles and morichales," Eva said. "Monseñor Lorenzo will not be punishing you for keeping the people of Segolita safe. The walls are not enough."

She gestured at the fortification behind her. "My father has spoken: We can't wait until they breach the city walls to take action."

"We know this is the only way to see tinieblas, but you speak as if the fanatics are acting rationally," a younger soldier said, glancing nervously at the passersby.

"Don't be craven," Reina barked. "We won't have a repeat of Carao. You will be ready, because I need your help."

"And if anyone tries to doubt you, show them the Bravo sigil you wear proudly," Eva added. "My father's name matters in this city. You will be exempt."

The mood changed. There were nods of agreements, and the bismuto distribution line resumed.

When no one was looking, Reina shot Eva a glance loaded with meaning. Eva nodded, conveying that she wholeheartedly agreed with the plan they'd discussed the day before arriving to Segolita: Geomancia was too useful to forgo while in the city. And despite having Don Samón's full trust and protection to keep using it, they were better off sparing him the complete truth for as long as possible. Eva knew finding out about Rahmagut would break his heart.

"The Orquídeas use geomancia," Reina told Eva after she handed a replenished ring to the last soldier in the queue. "The other families continue to use it as well."

Indeed, the Águila and Silva party leaders were aglow with it. "Hypocrites," Eva whispered.

"*A human's innate nature,*" Rahmagut noted, as if anyone had asked for his opinion.

"All right, time to get a move on." Reina stretched her shoulders cockily and dove into the awaiting crowd.

Eva jumped as a hand clamped on her shoulder. Summoned by her thoughts, her father was standing behind her.

"I was watching from afar," Don Samón said softly as the soldiers separated into groups with Reina leading the first party. "It makes me proud to see it."

Eva pushed off her chair. "Proud of Reina?" she said, testing.

He shrugged, his lip quirking. "Absolutely. And of you."

Wings fluttered in Eva's belly.

Reina saw him from afar, waved, and Don Samón nodded his approval. Then the parties were off.

"Let us head back to the house," Don Samón said. "There is something I must show you."

"I have to bathe and dress for the luncheon."

He nodded. "It will not take long."

Javier was dressed in a smart suit, his hair freshly washed and his jaw shaved, when Eva and Don Samón returned to Casa Bravo.

"Doña Tomasa told me she saw you sparring together in the yard," Don Samón said, pleased.

Eva grumbled, "I am terrible." She avoided Javier's gaze.

"Maybe you can abandon this idea of learning the sword and let me hire someone to keep you safe."

"Then *I* will feel inadequate, for not protecting my wife," Javier said.

Eva forced herself to ignore the sparks in her chest.

"It doesn't hurt to have a few extra hands. And I'd loathe seeing Eva battered and calloused. She is a lady of the Bravo line, after all."

"Not yet," Eva said, pouting. They'd discussed it at length already: the much overdue errand of inscribing Eva's birth and legitimacy with Segolita's keeper of names.

"We shall sort it out today at the cabildo. I promise you shall have your birthright," Don Samón said, herding her down a corridor. He gestured for Javier to follow as well. "But for now, let this demonstrate my commitment to you."

They walked to the study, a well-lit room with towering bookcases and richly engraved dark wood furniture.

"You have big shoes to fill," Don Samón said. "Don't be burdened by the responsibility of training as a fighter. It is not becoming of women of your status, and it is not what the society of Segolita would expect from my daughter."

Eva wanted to roll her eyes. Celeste was trained and capable, and no one batted an eye.

Behind the desk was a nondescript door. Its key and the door were enchanted, Don Samón told them as an aside, unlocking only when wielded by someone with Bravo blood. He handed Eva the key and beamed as the door clicked open for her with ease.

Their candle revealed a spiraling stone staircase leading to an underground cellar. They headed down together. Without proper ventilation, the air was hot and stale. Eva's fingertips trailed dust as she leaned against the wall for support, for the steps were thin and worn.

At the landing, there was a lever enchanted with iridio, the handle pulsing mildly in gold. Don Samón pulled it down, activating light to strip away the darkness.

Three underground floors were filled with multitudes of packed bookcases. Dusty desks and worktables sat in niches lit by candelabra. Curious artifacts like those filling Don Samón's study in Tierra'e Sol were here as well. The Bravo standard, two mirrored laurels on a diagonal partition of navy-and-yellow fabric, let off a sprinkle of dust when Don Samón tapped it as he passed by. Eva rushed to the balcony railing and gasped at what was obviously a vault door on the bottommost floor.

The Void god was pleased and intrigued.

"Our family's treasury: our material wealth and the accumulated knowledge of our ancestors. As my firstborn, it's your right to know of it."

Javier whistled. "This is grander than what we have in Águila Manor."

"Oh?" Don Samón said.

"The gold is in the vaults, but Enrique ties up the excess in the manor. He spends and spends because we've run out of vault space."

Don Samón chuckled. "Well, don't let this vault fool you. It was built through many generations, in secret. Your brother is richer than me by orders of magnitude."

Eva gestured at the descending staircase. "How is that possible? How rich is he?" Eva wasn't sure if she was dizzy from the lack of oxygen or from the opulence exuding from this vault.

Don Samón led them deeper, past the labyrinthine bookcases. "The vault is mostly empty. I spent all the gold during the revolution. What remains of value are the books and findings the family has stored here. Soon, we will be forced to sell off this property and make some difficult decisions about what to toss or transport to Tierra'e Sol."

"But it is your family home," Eva said. "You were born here."

"A home filled with gold amassed from nozariel slave labor—riches siphoned and hoarded by everyone that came before me. It is a fortune I inherited because of whom I was born to, and not because I earned it," Don Samón said. "I felt no qualms in spending every last escudo if such was the price of our freedom. There are more important things in life, Eva."

"I feel like you're lecturing me, but I understand." Eva had been willing to gamble away everything when she fled her home filled with comforts and riches.

He smiled. "Soon enough, when we end tinieblas and put a stop to iridio, this vault will be mostly defunct. It needs magic to function."

Eva's stomach coiled with a pang. She wrinkled her nose to keep the discomfort from showing. "*It doesn't have to come true,*" she thought, hoping it would diminish the aches. Her knuckles turned white as she gripped the balcony railing.

"It is Maria Elena who stops me from selling it. She pretends to be ignorant of the cost of running this household. If we keep this up, you and Ludivina will end up in ruin after I'm gone."

"Good thing Eva married a man set to inherit the Águila fortune," Javier said. Eva and Don Samón burst into laughter at the joke. "She will be so well taken care of."

Laughing, Eva placed a hand on his forearm. Her cheeks warmed. Perhaps her earlier assessment had been unfair, and his desires weren't so different from hers. Their future was so close to being guaranteed, all that remained was securing a separation from his inner demon. As far as Eva and Rahmagut were concerned... They had already accepted a bound fate. Such was the price to pay to wield the magical strength of a god. So far, Eva had no complaints.

24

Shedding Old Blood

The process to take the Bravo name happened faster than Eva expected. In attires worthy of the subsequently planned luncheon with the president and the caudillos, Don Samón, Javier, and Eva took the family carriage for the short, three-block journey to the cabildo. Javier brought the iridio-enhanced marriage papers they'd signed so many sunrises ago.

Eva wore a navy long-sleeved dress with a red fitted bodice embroidered in golden laurels. Epaulettes sat on her shoulders. She glimpsed her reflection in the mirror as she clipped a hibiscus-shaped brooch over her braided updo and smirked. She looked like she was preparing to attend a war meeting, her dress a feminine counterpart to Don Samón's military uniform. She used a crushed mineral powder to coat her antlers with an ivory color, to abate any suspicions, knowing Don Samón meant to show off her antlers as proof of their ties. The Void gem leeched the heat from her hip, safely tucked within an inner pocket.

They took the papers to a stuffy room not unlike Don Alberto's office in Galeno. Segolita's keeper of names certified that their marriage was lawful, made them sign papers in which Eva and Javier took each other's family names, and amended Don Samón's log in his family's book, including Eva as his firstborn progeny.

In her head, Eva turned the names around and around, hiding

a secret smile. She found delight in them, and that they were hers: *Eva Kesaré Bravo de Águila*. She was no longer property of Galeno. She had a place where she belonged.

As they emerged from the office, they found the cabildo's garden bustling with people. Carriages packed the driveway as representatives from the wealthiest families of Venazia and Fedria arrived.

The entrance hall buzzed with conversation. People in their best garments kissed each other's knuckles or cheeks. A server handed Eva a dainty glass of red wine, crowing that it was imported from the Old World.

Eva put on her hat of propriety and walked with her arm entwined in Javier's, following Don Samón's vanguard. She grew hot and blushed at the many who oohed and aahed as Don Samón introduced her. Eva tried learning the names of the hands she shook: Cárdenas, Palacios, Valderrama, Pescador. Her heart fluttered as she recognized the old names of Galeno. Surely someone from the Serranos, an envoy sent by the governor perhaps, would be here.

Her suspicions proved to be true sooner than she preferred.

Doña Antonia waltzed through the front doors of the cabildo, head raised high and arm in arm with Monseñor Lorenzo, archbishop of Galeno, the man who'd sentenced Doña Rosa to death. She spotted Eva through the crowd in an instant. The color drained from her grandmother's cheeks. Immediately, her eyes watered.

Even across the hall, Eva felt the pang of betrayal impacting her. She understood the hurt her grandmother wore behind those eyes—the pain Eva had personally inflicted by running away.

This reunion was inevitable. Eva had expected they would cross paths soon enough, and she had prepared and steeled herself accordingly. As Doña Antonia began crossing the hall, so did Eva, her heart thunderous. Javier followed behind her.

"Bendición," Eva said, a word that automatically supplanted any greeting with her grandmother.

Doña Antonia sized her up, dabbed the corners of her eye, then said, "The Virgin bless you."

Some of the walls between them crumbled as Eva placed a soft kiss on her grandmother's cheek. Doña Antonia gently grabbed Eva's arm, the touch speaking of the heartache she'd endured.

"You're safe," Doña Antonia said. "Parading about with valcos, I have been told."

"You wished such an outcome for me," Eva said stiffly.

Doña Antonia took a deep breath. "I wished for you to marry a prince, not to join the ranks of the monster who defiled my Dulce."

Eva's cheeks and neck burned. Every injustice and ache she'd endured at her grandmother's hand came crashing down again. Her heart twisted. "Don't repeat that lie to me."

"*I'm* the liar? How dare you speak to me that way. Show some respect to your grandmother."

"Your lies ruined my mother's life," Eva hissed.

Javier gently squeezed her elbow. "Eva," he warned in her ear.

A few heads turned in their direction, but Monseñor Lorenzo piped up, "This may not be the best setting to discuss old grievances. Maybe the gardens?"

"I don't wish to go anywhere with her. She may try to trap me against my will again." Eva sneered. "Keep sending mercenaries, because they will all fail."

Doña Antonia's eyes doubled in size. She took a step closer. To Eva's ears only, she rebuked, "I only wish for your safety. Everything I did, I did to protect you."

So, her desire to control every aspect of her progeny's lives hadn't dimmed. It dawned on Eva: The tears and the hurt in her voice, they were all fake. Wouldn't someone remorseful sing a different tune at this moment? But Doña Antonia wielded no regret. "Because you'd rather I be miserable in your clutches than free to become the person I was always meant to be? I'm fine!"

Outraged, Doña Antonia grasped Eva's wrist and dragged her through the archway to the gardens. Eva allowed it only because yanking herself free would create more of a scene.

Under the high noon sun, the heavy lines of Doña Antonia's weariness were all the more apparent. "You speak so harshly about me, but you are not fine. I cry myself to sleep every night thinking of the path you're taking—that will only lead to our suffering. We loved you and raised you to be educated and proper, and now you are trapped with the same valco monsters who took my Dulce's sanity. Don't you see it? They are doing the same to you." She glanced behind them, where Javier was forced to exchange pleasantries with the archbishop.

"I am a valco," Eva reminded her as her heart raced. She tried to keep her voice low, but there were too many things to be said—too many reasons to want to scream. "Your hatred for them is hatred for me."

"No, you're my granddaughter, my blood. The ability to be good is within you. We were *so close* to weeding out those amoral tendencies from you. And now I grow sick, imagining how you're ruining our name and reputation by running away—"

"I am married," Eva said with a straight face. "Javier is my husband. My reputation is fine."

Doña Antonia glared at Javier's antlers. Eva hoped Doña Antonia would grow annoyed at the way Javier was immune to condescension. How he was utterly unfazed by Monseñor Lorenzo's company.

"Monseñor Lorenzo has expressed suspicions to me. About you."

"About me?" Eva croaked. She almost raked at her forearm.

"You've associated yourself with those Águilas. *They* are the reason for the tinieblas. *They* thrive when the country is in chaos. I raised you to be smarter, Eva Kesaré!"

"The caudillo's iridio is the only reason we have *something* to ward off tinieblas!"

Doña Antonia grabbed Eva's wrist, drawing her closer. "Please come back to us. I miss you, and I love you." A bead of sweat traveled down her temple, and her plum lip coloring cracked. Her breath was sour. In her eyes, Eva indeed saw the slightest slivers of love. "I do not want to see you embroiled with those valcos. When a true inquisition is sent their way, I don't want to see you burn with them."

Eva yanked her arm free. This wasn't love. The ache of everything she'd endured in Galeno flared, renewed. How could her grandmother have this power to hurt? And why were they still arguing about the same old story?

"The future is not for valcos, or nozariels," Doña Antonia said. "Look around you. We are building a country for our kind. For good, proper people who follow the Virgin's path. I do not want to lose you to the inevitable."

"*Stop*," Eva insisted as tears gathered in her eyes. She didn't let them fall. She wasn't going to allow her grandmother the satisfaction. "Valcos are not evil. Nozariels are not evil. We are not wrong for not following your way of thinking. The Liberator, *my father*, the man who freed this land so you could have a most luxurious *and safe* life, is not a bad man. The tinieblas are the enemy. They don't care who does or doesn't believe in the Virgin."

"*Well done*," Rahmagut said, startling Eva.

"*Leave me alone*," she snapped inwardly, whirling on her heel to rejoin her husband.

Doña Antonia pursued. "Eva Kesaré de Galeno!"

Eva turned. "My name is Eva Kesaré Bravo de Águila. Recognize those names? They are from valco families. *I* am valco. I don't intend to return to Galeno as the granddaughter you control. If you can't accept this, then I beg you to leave me alone."

She found Javier's arm and linked hers through his as Doña Antonia did the same with the archbishop. Eva let the crowd swallow them while Monseñor Lorenzo whispered in Doña Antonia's ear. She tried not to imagine all the tales of damnation they told when she wasn't around.

As greetings and pleasantries ended, the crowd navigated to the banquet hall. Javier steered Eva near a vestibule, where it was dark, hot, and mostly private. He released her arm, making her face him. "You're upset," he said.

Eva bit her tongue to not let his concern incense her emotions more. "My grandmother has not changed at all."

"Why would she?"

Eva exhaled, lost. "I don't know—I thought my leaving would shake some sense into her. But she still hates my father and she'll never accept us."

He grabbed her hand and squeezed it. "Eva, haven't we proved to you that we are your people now?"

"Yes."

"Then forget about the Serranos. You're better than them. They don't deserve you."

"I just...I always assumed one day we would make up. But..." Now she would have to mourn them.

Javier hesitated, his hand stopping short of grabbing her arm to bring her closer. In a way, Eva was glad for it. The last thing she needed was to cry now.

They couldn't talk more, as the thinning crowd would only highlight their absence. As they headed into the banquet hall, with its glittering chandeliers, vaulted ceilings, and bold scarlet curtains, Eva spotted the imposing antlers of Enrique Águila above the crowd. Javier stiffened beside her.

Eva took in the sight of Enrique as her father automatically navigated through the crowd to greet him. He was dressed in white satin pants and a navy jacket with the bodice and sleeves embroidered in intricate golden laurels. A golden epaulette sat on each of his broad shoulders. His blood-red gaze met with Don Samón's as they approached. He smiled faintly, though there wasn't a sliver of mirth behind that look.

Celeste stood beside her father like another radiant accessory. His heir, who wielded his strength and temperament hidden beneath a likeness inherited from Laurel. She wore a formfitting sleeveless black dress with stuffed shoulder pads, giving her a sharp symmetrical look. An embroidered golden eagle curled from her neck to her waistband. Celeste offered Eva a thin smile, which quickly vanished at the sight of Javier.

"I thought you were too retired to participate in these theatrics," Enrique said, extending a hand to Don Samón.

As the men met, the conversation in the room quieted noticeably. Intrigued by this reunion of the last two notable valco houses, people turned their curious eyes to look.

"It's not an act when so many lives have been lost," Don Samón said. "When people's livelihoods are at stake."

"I heard a hateful rumor of that duskling of yours theorizing I am behind it all. I see you didn't bring her today." Enrique made a point of glancing about the room. "Ah, no. Instead, you brought my disappointment of a brother."

Javier's jaw rippled, but his face showed little of the rage surely simmering beneath. "Nice to see you again as well, Brother."

"Samón, what does it say about you that you adopt the dregs I discard?"

Don Samón shrugged, unfazed. "That I have compassion. A heart."

The young man next to Celeste scoffed, making Eva notice him for the first time. He had olive skin and silky black hair parted down the middle. He was dressed in a navy liqui liqui perfectly tailored to a lean frame. Over his breast he wore a gold badge of red enamel surrounding a golden crocodile.

Don Samón turned to him. "And you are?"

"Francisco Silva, Señor Libertador," he said, extending a hand. "Eldest grandson of His Majesty Don Rodrigo Silva."

Eva froze, seeing him in a different light. Indeed, he looked familiar because he was a Silva. Eva had once chucked wine at his distant cousin, the pig Marcelino Silva.

"A prince of Venazia..." Don Samón muttered, noticing Enrique's vulpine smirk about Francisco's obvious proximity to Celeste.

"Heir to the throne, after my father, may the Virgin bless him with a long life," Francisco said.

"And my soon to be son-in-law," Enrique added casually.

Celeste's smile seemed more diplomatic than genuine. For once, her usual confidence didn't exude from her. She glanced away.

Enrique offered Francisco a rare smile and nod of approval, and the young man beamed.

"You have betrothed Celeste to the royal family?" Don Samón said.

"This is not the place to debate what I decide for my family," Enrique challenged. "If you want to discuss things left unsettled, why don't we talk about the woman from Apartaderos, who I have been kind enough to request without making demands?"

"For you, there is no separation between a request and a demand."

Enrique turned up his nose, saying, "Your week is up. I have waited long enough. If you desire to keep the peace between us, you'd do well to hand her over. For someone who professes his compassion so loudly, you seem unable to comprehend the pain Celeste and I have had to endure ever since that treacherous hag trapped Laurel's soul in this world, without rest."

Eva frowned at the insinuation. Javier had made it sound like the caudillo and Doña Ursulina had worked hand in hand, coconspirators in following Rahmagut's legend. Then again, why should she be surprised of his professed innocence? Celeste standing by his side despite all that had transpired indicated lies skulked somewhere.

The caudillo's gaze flickered to Eva. "Imagine if the same had happened to Dulce Serrano. What would you do?"

The words struck accurately. Eva knew to how take them, however, if only to avoid fueling the tension rising like a gas on the cusp of ignition.

"Where is your compassion now, *Libertador*?"

"Shouldn't you be advocating for the living, instead of the dead?" Javier said.

Enrique's red eyes zeroed in on his younger brother with murderous intent. Eva didn't fail to notice his fingers twitching, refraining from turning into a fist.

"The purpose of today is not to discuss your family, nor your demands," Don Samón said, stoppering any further escalations. "The reason for our meeting is the tinieblas. I don't need you strong-arming me now."

Enrique took his time lifting his glare from Javier, who didn't back down. Out of pride or self-preservation, Eva didn't know. She just knew she liked it.

"Ah yes, the tinieblas that are driven by the returned gods, who walk among us, according to Monseñor Lorenzo," Enrique said, his nonchalance a bait.

Don Samón nodded. "That is a theory."

"And have you looked within your own ranks? I can't help but be intrigued by how your entourage is composed of those who conspired with Ursulina at the tomb you were supposed to guard."

Eva held her breath, her chest wringing.

"I abhor what you imply," Don Samón said. "And you're basing your presumptions on what?"

"Celeste was there," Enrique said as he placed a possessive hand on her shoulder.

Eva had to stop herself from glaring at Celeste, her teeth grinding.

"The more emotion you show, the more you will be suspected," Rahmagut said, as if she didn't already know that.

But she couldn't swallow the words any longer. "If that's your only source, then your information would have gaps." Eva's cheeks heated as she became the center of Enrique's attention. She glanced at her father, giving him the key to squash Enrique's accusations: "She was incapacitated for most of the night."

"Well, there you have it," Don Samón said quickly.

As Enrique appraised her, Eva realized her folly in reminding him of Javier's actions. Perhaps this was what Don Samón had wanted to avoid. But why couldn't Enrique just be grateful that Celeste lived?

Still evaluating Eva, Enrique asked Don Samón, "You trust her?"

"Like you trust your own daughter," Don Samón said without hesitation. "Both have recounted the events of the tomb and given us no further clues. It's obvious that it brings them great discomfort to talk about it. Do you intend to put Celeste through that again, in front of the whole junta?"

Enrique took a deep breath. "I do not."

"Very well. Then let us eat," Don Samón said as he extended a hand toward the slowly populating dining table.

Enrique nodded and followed. Eva watched them, awed at how they could exchange scathing words without clawing each other's eyes out.

Celeste resisted Francisco's guide to the dining table, whispering of how she wished to catch up with her uncle. The moment

Francisco was out of earshot, she told Eva, "How dare you discount what I went through at the tomb."

Eva was stunned. "I'll do it again if you try to accuse us of causing the tinieblas. And you lived and recovered perfectly, as far as I can tell. You didn't even waste a second in finding someone to marry. I thought you and Reina were supposed to have feelings or something?"

Celeste's face hardened. "Don't speak about things you don't know. Besides, this is rich, coming from someone whose marriage happened faster than the blink of an eye. Did you know your husband was vying for my hand before he went for yours? Me—his own niece. Just so he could have access to my inheritance. Truly the actions of a despicable, *sick* man."

Javier was silent, struck. "I was foolish, and ignorant," he said, grabbing Eva's hand. "I didn't know better things were coming my way."

Eva yanked her arm free, incensed he would be so blatant about the way he'd used her. And she loathed being compared to Celeste, something she already did aplenty herself. To hear of Javier's intentions spoken so brazenly only highlighted all the metrics by which Celeste was innately superior.

Likely aware of the same, Celeste smirked. "One day I'm going to be the master of iridio and of the Águila name. Mi papá has this philosophy of hiding away in the mountains, but I don't see why we need to keep pretending we haven't the best army in Venazia, and the gold to back it. There's no reason why I shouldn't be a queen."

"All this for a crown?" Javier mocked.

She gave him an angry look. "You're in no position to judge me. I could out you to the whole junta."

Eva sucked in a breath.

Her reaction pleased Celeste, who went on. "I could tell them there's a tiniebla inside these very walls."

"*Celeste,*" Eva said. She realized her mistake in angering Celeste. Her silence would certainly come at a price.

Celeste ignored Eva, stepping closer to Javier with her eyes like ice. "Your life would be forfeit so fast. Would you like to taste the fear you put me through?"

Guarded, Javier replied, "I already begged for your forgiveness, but you refuse to consider my side." Eva didn't miss the flicker of hurt in his eyes.

Celeste shook her head. "If you weren't who you are, none of it would have happened." She gave Eva a long look, measuring her words in their silence. And Eva could do nothing but swallow the admonishment. Any retort or reply that further angered Celeste would be their undoing.

"So yes, I am doing this for a crown. So that I am not beholden to my father's plots. So that I can be in a position where I can make a real change, like my mother wanted." Celeste's eyes burned with intensity. "I will have the legitimacy of the Silva crown, and the wealth of our family. Pardon, *my* family. You don't belong to it anymore." She turned on her heel and found her assigned seat at the table, her ponytail swaying like a black cascade.

Tremors shook Javier's shoulder. It wasn't until Eva glanced down, seeing him restraining his left wrist with his right hand, that she noticed the spread of his leathery corruption taking over his left hand. His fingernails were inky, as if his blood had curdled black. Flexed, his fingers looked like claws.

"Breathe," Eva whispered, wrapping his corrupted hand within hers. She searched his face and was terrified of the blackened veins creeping up his temples. Her grip did nothing to ease the corruption.

Javier shuddered like he was moments away from pouncing on Celeste.

Eva tugged him to the corner of the room, seeking refuge behind a group of philosophizing people. "Breathe, Javier. I command it."

The words forced him to face her. Streaks of black marred his red irises. He took in bigger lugs of air, his body reacting to her command.

"You cannot lose control here," she whispered heatedly, grasping his face and making him focus on her eyes. "The leaders of

Venazia and Fedria are here. The Pentimiento Church is here. If they smell even a hint of that tiniebla, they will execute you." Her last words trembled.

His throat bobbed. "Brother would love that. He's given up on me."

"And do you need his approval? You said it yourself: I'm your new family, even if you're just using me."

His brows arched. The black streaks in his irises retreated. She didn't have to hold his face to get his attention. She had it fully. Eva shrank under his gaze. How foolish she felt for saying the words—how they revealed her feelings.

"I'm not using you," he said softly.

"You said you got a better thing."

His mouth opened and closed, baffled. "But I did. After everything I've done and all that's happened since Laurel cursed me, you're the best thing that's happened to me."

Eva blinked. Heat crawled to her neck and ears. She searched his eyes and found nothing but sincerity. Her words failed her.

"What did you think I meant?"

"Nothing," Eva said quickly, turning for the dining table.

His hand shot out to grab her wrist, stopping her. Eva's chest hitched as she had to meet his eyes.

"Thank you—for forcing some sense into me," he said.

She nodded, and blazed with emotions. Gratitude, that their paths had collided when they did, hurling her into a life she'd always dreamed of. Joy, for having someone on her side who treasured her this fiercely. And courage, to protect what they had at all costs. Namely, with the swift and thorough eradication of all tinieblas. Not just for his sake, but to divert Enrique's suspicions about Rahmagut, which had already landed on her.

25

An Águila Trade

An immense peace filled the cathedral outside of service hours. Somehow, its stone walls managed to abate the heat, refreshing Maior as she padded toward the circular stone well positioned before the altar. This well was the largest she'd ever seen inside a church, and rightfully so, for the cathedral was the seat of Pentimiento in Fedria. Its shallow waters glimmered from the candles placed along the well's edges, often reflecting the Virgin's face as Her statue loomed behind the altar. Supplicants, like Maior, reverently approached the unlit candles and lit a new one before kneeling against the well for prayer.

With the Virgin's eyes on her, Maior always started by giving thanks, for her health and the roof over her head. Lately, she'd made a habit of praying for Reina's good health and protection as well. Then Maior begged for the mental fortitude to endure one more night trapped in Doña Laurel's memories. She prayed for an epiphany to one day show her how she was meant to free herself. Soon, she would have clarity. Maior had faith in it.

Here, the Virgin was depicted with a gem-studded crown, a pink tunic, and a golden scepter in Her grip. How demure the scepter made Her look, unlike in the stone chapel of Apartaderos, where She appeared fierce with a sword. Incense, as well as the faint note of the well's holy water, filled Maior's nose. She took a deep breath, the familiar scents grounding her and transporting her to her birthplace, where Apartaderos's stone chapel was built around a freshwater well. The Virgin's divinity had first manifested in the water, according to the holy book, and She'd reappeared on the Fedrian shores before the thirsty and starved first settlers. Thus, every place of worship needed to center on water. Maior was glad this was still the case in Segolita.

Her prayers ended, Maior helped Doña Tomasa, Casa Bravo's head matron, stand. The woman was nozariel, but she didn't have her tail.

"Is it as you imagined?" Doña Tomasa whispered as they headed for a side door.

"That and more," Maior said happily.

After Maior had expressed her restless need to fill her time, Doña Tomasa had brought her first to the cathedral, and now they were headed to the cabildo. Casa Bravo was overstaffed, and few tasks needed tending to. Maior couldn't let the days pass her by, idly sitting by the drawing room window with the reading book in her lap, aching for Reina's return. She hadn't grown up accustomed to being served and cared for. She had talents that could be put to use, and a desperation to free herself from Laurel's possession. And Reina and Eva were of no help. As soon as the rising sun had peeked over Casa Bravo and their bellies were filled with arepas, Eva and Javier had departed for the cabildo, apparently with an invitation to access the presidential library, and Reina had left to join more tiniebla raids.

Thankfully, no one used geomancia within the cathedral grounds, so Maior could cross the side gardens without worrying someone would spot the dead presence hovering over her head.

"Monseñor Lorenzo will be delighted to make your acquaintance. Ever since the country was thrown into chaos, he's needed any help he can get."

Maior nodded. She grew giddy from the opportunity to meet such an important figure. Only once had she seen the archbishop of Sadul Fuerte, who was head of the Pentimiento Church south of the mountains. But Monseñor Lorenzo was archbishop of northern

Venazia, based in Galeno, as the immense geographical separation caused by the Páramo made it a necessity for Venazia to have multiple archbishops.

"Does Fedria have only one archbishop?" Maior asked, needing the clarification.

"Yes, Monseñor Sebastian." Doña Tomasa gave her a smile. Her black curls were tightly wrapped in a fuchsia-colored headband that complemented the pastel shade of her dress. "But it is Monseñor Lorenzo who is leading the Orquídeas' efforts."

"Ah," Maior said.

"Monseñor Sebastian leads the Sunday service, if you want to meet him."

"One day, I'm sure…" Maior muttered. She had considered the possibilities of seeking the archbishops' guidance regarding her *problem*. They were closest to the Virgin. Surely, they had the wisdom to light her path. But what if their solution was an exorcism? Or worse, if they delivered the news that only her death would guarantee their separation?

The cobbled path out of the cathedral gardens opened to the large town square, which bustled with crossing carriages, children selling candies, and flocks of pigeons that took to the air like clouds of black and gray. They entered the cabildo through a side door, arriving in a wing where people were hard at work distributing all kinds of supplies. Maior spotted nurses, handymen, and other volunteers. Their black banner flapped from the entrances.

"Las Orquídeas Blancas are funding a great effort. It's been a while since I've seen the parish so unified," Doña Tomasa said with pride.

"All of this is necessary against the tinieblas?" Maior said, avoiding getting in anyone's way.

"Many are injured and destitute when they arrive seeking refuge," a voice said from behind.

Maior turned and met a tall man with shiny black hair wearing a cassock. "For some, this help is all they have," he added.

"Monseñor Lorenzo! We were just heading to the induction." Doña Tomasa introduced Maior and conveyed her intentions of joining the efforts as a nurse.

Monseñor Lorenzo nodded with a gentle smile. He gestured for them to cross another hall and enter a circular theater slowly being populated by other volunteers.

"I consider it the Virgin's will when new, capable hands join our cause."

"It's my pleasure to help," Maior said. "It's what I used to do back home with my order: Las Hermanas de Piedra."

His eyes searched hers as he tried to recall the name. "That rings a bell. Apartaderos?"

Maior beamed and nodded.

"My, you've come a long way!"

She looked away to her espadrilles, blushing to think of Reina as her reason.

"I've received many a correspondence from Las Hermanas de Piedra in my tenure. They are users of geomancia," the archbishop said slowly. He had a tone of suspicion that startled even Doña Tomasa.

But Maior came prepared. Her talents were best used in tandem with galio. "Only for saving lives. Our service was always to the people. I have nothing to hide, Monseñor. I am true in my devotion. You can search me and you'll find nothing but faith and love for the Virgin."

He smiled faintly. "That is the kind of conviction I want to see in our members." He pointed to a seat at the front of the theater, the honorary spot, which Maior obediently took. Doña Tomasa bid goodbye.

The archbishop paced the lecturer's raised stage, pensive. "Now, while you are here, it is imperative that the nursing techniques you follow and promulgate are those permissible under our faith. Just because we can do something doesn't mean we shall. Discipline is one of our main tenants."

Maior nodded, feeling her ears heating from the indirect admonishment.

He addressed the other volunteers, who listened quietly. "We are unified in our drive to restore light into the lives of those displaced by darkness. You have seen the refugees pouring through the city gates. You have seen how hope has left their eyes. Your mission will be to restore this light. From the gofer to the surgeon, each one of you is valuable and necessary."

Monseñor Lorenzo shot a smile to Maior. "I have faith in your ability to do this. It is why the Virgin brought you through those doors—why we crossed paths."

Maior was inspired; her chest fluttered.

"So go out there and use those talents the Virgin gifted you. Serve as Her vessel." Monseñor Lorenzo clapped once and the volunteers rose with smiles and invigorated purpose, Maior among them.

"Señorita Maior, will you accompany me?" he said as the theater quieted.

"Of course, Monseñor."

They headed through another door together, letting the corridor's shadows envelop them. "Doña Tomasa works in Casa Bravo. I take it that is where you stay?" he asked.

Maior's cheeks heated from how he had already appraised her. "Sí, Monseñor."

"Are you new there? What is your role in the Liberator's household?"

"I'm a nurse. But we live in Tierra'e Sol. We answered the president's summons." Maior loathed getting into the details of her complicated ties to the Liberator. Too many questions and answers would inevitably lead to Reina. With anyone else, Maior would love nothing more than to talk about her. But Maior craved staying within the archbishop's good graces.

"I would like to know if the Liberator is true to the effort against tinieblas. Why did you feel the need to come here instead?"

Maior cleared her throat, her heartbeat skipping. She couldn't cast suspicions on Don Samón. "He's serious in his fight. I came only because I have a strong love for the Virgin. Like you said, we all answered a calling that made us cross paths."

He chuckled, satisfied. They entered an office lined with bookcases. A globe sat atop the center desk, morose in a room darkened by shadows.

"Indeed, people like you make me proud to do what I do," Monseñor Lorenzo said. "You were probably too young to remember what these colonies looked like before the revolution, but now Fedria and Venazia are lands of great promise. Of freedom and equality."

Maior nodded as patriotism surged through her veins.

"Their longevity must be protected at all costs, don't you agree?"

"Absolutely."

"Those tinieblas pose an existential threat to our future. They seed discord in people's hearts."

"I saw it with my own eyes when I arrived in this city," Maior said with blazing agreement.

The archbishop yanked the curtains open. Dust surged in the air. Sunlight streamed through the dirty window, angling directly over the globe on the center table, which beamed with color against the desk and the ceiling in a curious simulation of a night sky. Maior watched it with awed, rounded eyes.

Monseñor Lorenzo coughed, clearing the dust from his sinuses. "The tinieblas are seen as a proof of magic, and they make people turn to old beliefs best left forgotten—beliefs the church has worked hard to erase and overcome, for they are barbaric. If only you knew of the tales spoken by the archbishops before me: how the people of this land behaved like animals before we arrived, relying on witchery and sacrifice. But the Virgin is the correct goddess. Her teachings are proper and just, and with them we achieve peace. We cannot have unification if everyone picks and chooses what rules to follow."

Maior was unsure of how to reply. She wasn't surprised to find his rhetoric so outdated and limited, but it also wasn't her place to debate him, not now.

He chuckled. "Don't worry, it is not for you or me to decide what to believe in. Those rules have already been written as holy word by the one and only true goddess. Now, enough candor. I brought you here because you are a nurse and I assume you know the written word." He waved a hand behind him to the door. "The other inductees—well, all I saw were maids and beggars using this job just to secure their supper."

She tried not to let her frown show. Her literacy remained basic. Maior was no different from the other volunteers, but their lack of education didn't make any of them less than.

"We are in the astronomer's office," he explained, oblivious. "I don't have the time to sift through every book on these shelves, so I must delegate this task to you. Collect every star chart and map you can find. Search any letter, manual, or book that talks about eclipses—the solar kind. Take note if anything mentions the recurrence of one, and if it will happen in our lifetimes. Mark the passages with a tab or bookmark, then bring it all to my office on the second floor. It's right next to the servants' staircase; you will not miss it."

Maior gave a quick bow as the archbishop offered one last, doting smile. Then he left her alone to the stars.

Maior agonized in the silence of the office. How was she supposed to admit her literacy was too rudimentary for such a task? How could she backtrack and disappoint him? Chatter passed in the corridors outside, and footsteps. What if she found some other volunteer and delegated the job? Then what would the archbishop think of her?

Sighing deeply, she decided to give it a try. Perhaps the Virgin had set her up because she was ready.

She read slowly through spines and tables of content and indexes. She spotted a dictionary, and it came in handy. Nevertheless, she managed to amass a useful stack of books for the archbishop.

The afternoon was fast ending when Maior picked up the sizable stack. She left the door to the astronomer's office ajar and, with the books hindering her view, asked a passerby for instructions to the servants' staircase. It was right next to the great hall hosting the Orquídeas' operation, beside a foyer leading to the gardens. Following the directions, she made a turn for the stairs, only to crash into a hard chest. Her stack flew in the air before tumbling all over the tiled floor.

"*¡Cónchale!*" she yelled. She collapsed to collect her work, dismayed that her painstakingly arranged tabs had spilled out of place.

"Apologies," the other person said automatically, kneeling to help.

Maior recognized the voice. Her hand froze in midair as her eyes met none other than Javier's.

He, too, hesitated, robbed of words. "Maior? What are you doing here?"

His eyes flickered above her head, as if unable to stop himself from acknowledging her affliction. And it made Maior's face burn. She fumbled to grab the papers and manuals as quickly as she could, fear sending her heart into a mad race. She couldn't manage a reply.

"Please, let me help," he said as he began gathering her stack without waiting for permission.

"It's all right," Maior said shakily. She accepted the books from him with trembling hands.

"Where are you taking those? I can help you."

Fear prickled her spine, taking her voice once again. Perhaps she was no better than a silly, meek girl for cowering before him. For they had supped at the same table and lingered in the same room in the past, united under the Bravo banner. But Maior had always had Reina by her side. And not once had he spoken to her directly since his release, so why start now?

"I'm taking these to the archbishop," she said, standing, her gaze on her shoes.

"His office is upstairs. You cannot see with all those books; you will fall. Let me help."

She was spared from rejecting him when footsteps echoed in the adjacent corridor. Maior held her breath, anticipating relief, when the person turned the corner.

Antlers nearly reaching the ceiling. Golden epaulettes cresting broad shoulders. Eyes that reminded Maior of recently spilled blood.

Her stomach sank as Enrique Águila emerged into the corridor. He paused. Maior took a step back, her chest constricting and her windpipes blocking the air she so desperately needed.

"Enrique," Javier said.

"Javier," Enrique said, then his gaze shamelessly lingered on the image of his dead wife above Maior. "And Maior de Apartaderos."

Heat prickled the corners of Maior's eyes. She took another step back and almost whimpered as her shoulder pressed into the stained-glass window, ending the last of her freedom. How foolish and powerless she felt with the stack of books in her arms and nothing but the wall behind her.

"Such serendipity to find you both here. What brings you to the cabildo?" Enrique asked.

"I could ask you the same thing, but you will say it is none of my concern, so I shall echo your answer," Javier said.

Enrique was amused. He glanced at Maior again. "I have taught you well."

"I don't disgrace my family name," Javier said.

"You say that, and yet you have latched yourself to Samón."

"How is that a disgrace? He is the most beloved valco in this land," Javier said, and Enrique's face hardened as the thinly veiled insult landed right on target.

Enrique took a step forward, as did Javier. Maior glimpsed at the door. She would have to cross by either brother for the servants' stairs or the side door. Her attempts to escape could be so easily foiled.

"Nevertheless, we are family," Enrique said, "and I raised you to believe your place is in Águila Manor."

"Then why do I feel like I've been banished?"

"I needed to deliver the correct punishment for making an attempt on Celeste's life. Where is your apology for that?"

Javier faltered. "I . . . I was not myself. I'm sorry."

"Celeste told me," Enrique said, taking another step such that they were an arm's length apart. Enrique's hand landed on his shoulder. "I'm sure she will forgive you, in due time, once you return home."

Javier frowned in confusion.

"I know of the petulant things she's said to you, but we are family, and what is this if not another family spat that can be resolved with dialogue and forgiveness?"

"You can't mean that."

Maior looked to the stairs again. Was this the distraction she needed to get away?

Enrique's hand fell. His eyes hardened before traveling to Maior once again, arresting her in place as if he could sense her intentions. He watched her shamelessly.

"I raised you to understand all you can gain by having a place in my household," Enrique told his brother. "And I meant to offer it to you once again. But seeing you with Samón yesterday clouded my judgment. It made me say things I don't mean."

"I know your temper well," Javier said.

"Let us return to the Páramo and put this shit-smelling city behind us."

Javier's throat bobbed.

"I care little about the humans and their problems. I merely came here for the woman from Apartaderos," Enrique said, turning to face Maior.

Maior's chest rose and fell as panic seized her. Cold sweat trickled down her neck. She was trapped and suffocated as they toyed with her fate like a mouse caught between two felines.

"I know you want to play games with Samón, acting as if you hold a shred of loyalty for him. But this politicking is unnecessary and exhausting to watch. Let us take her this instant."

Both their gazes hovered above her. They couldn't even acknowledge her as the person she was, only as the vessel of their Benevolent Lady. Suddenly, she found herself back on that moonless night, when a figure had stood against the fluttering curtains of her bedroom window. She remembered the impotence as Javier's spell paralyzed her body but not her mind. Like now, she had been frozen with fear as her body hit the ground, terrorized and unable to gain the agency to fight back or scream. She remembered the hateful, victorious look Javier had given her as he sprinted for her in Rahmagut's tomb, his sword in midair. Even if she ran now, she was utterly powerless against them.

"Return as my brother and lend your sword to protect our household. Samón only pretends to care about her for Reina. But you and I know she can be easily dealt with." Enrique placed his hand on Javier's shoulder again, squeezing. He offered Javier a small smile. "It's time to come home."

This time, Javier's gaze found Maior's eyes for a second that dragged into a lifetime. Her throat closed from the inevitability. This redemption was everything he'd wanted. He had every reason to take it. Tears prickled her eyes. Should she even bother to beg? Would she have the chance to scream?

Then Javier shook Enrique's hand off. "No," he said, facing his older brother.

Enrique's eye twitched. "No?"

Maior let out a breath. She could cry.

"Do you seriously expect me to betray the Liberator and my wife?" Javier snarled. "On your pathetic promises that you'll welcome me back?"

A laugh croaked out of Enrique. He stepped forward, as did Javier. "Yes. I expect you to let go of these trifles turning you into a disappointment."

"I don't care about your opinion anymore."

"Says the spoiled boy who spent his entire life in my shadow, clawing for my approval. For my wealth."

"I am a man!" Javier further reduced the distance and their antlers clattered. "I left the house pursuing my own path, as you repeatedly begged."

"I did not beg you for anything. I commanded it," Enrique growled. "And you did leave, but instead of growing the respect of our name, you attached yourself to the teat of a lesser family. Congratulations on the marriage, by the way." He shoved Javier back several steps with ease. Maior flinched, expecting him to crash into her. "May it be fruitful. Otherwise, what is the point?"

"Fruitful? Like your marriage was?" Javier said with his teeth bared. He recovered, squaring up.

Enrique stomped forward with his fists curled.

Javier's left hand clamped over the hilt of his sword. Unlike Enrique, he was armed.

Enrique's eyes widened. A vulpine smile replaced his frown. "You dare duel me?"

Maior watched the brothers in tense expectation. Her chest was too small for her heartbeats.

A single click from Javier's scabbard answered for him. "I *refuse* to take any more of your shit." He unsheathed the blade with a sharp whistle.

Enrique raised his hands in an arch and slapped them together. The gesture stirred eddies of air, lifting Maior's hair. As he spread his arms apart, a great sword manifested, from the pommel in Enrique's left hand to the blade's tip in his right. A blade-summoning spell like Celeste's. Likely, she'd learned it from him.

Faster than a blink, Javier grabbed Maior by the shoulders and shoved her through the side door. "Get away from here!"

The wind buffeted behind them as Enrique gave his sword a fierce wave, unhindered by his epaulette-bearing jacket.

Outside, their swords clashed. Instead of fleeing the cabildo, Maior circled the building. She had a feeling Javier had been unwise to challenge Enrique. She needed to find Eva.

26

The Amalgamation

The late afternoon was sweltering when Eva burst into the cabildo's topiary gardens. The air was sweet from the honeysuckles climbing the outdoor trellises, a contradiction to the bitter panic coursing through Eva's veins. She found them within the topiaries, the hum of cicadas matching the vibration of the iridio pulsing from the Águila brothers' duel.

For her own safety, Eva had begged Maior to return to Casa Bravo alone.

Eva nearly screamed Javier's name with an order to stop him. But Enrique's brutal swings halted her. Her blood congealed as she realized the slightest lapse in Javier's concentration would only lead to his gory end.

Panicked, Eva grasped for her iridio pendant, which, ever since the Pucho incident, she carried in her dress pocket.

The Void god's presence paced the confines of her mind like a jaguar who'd sniffed first blood. *"What are you going to do with that? You know of this man's strength. Are you going to oppose him?"*

Eva's breaths became uneven as she watched the brothers circling the naturally formed perimeter of their fight.

"You care for Javier."

"He is my husband," she snapped, angry she had to keep repeating this fact at all.

She flinched as Javier's blade clanged against Enrique's, block-ing. It happened like a lightning strike. Were she blinking, she would have missed it. She squeezed her pendant.

"Enrique might kill you for it, if you dare interfere."

If things got out of control, she fully intended to do something.

"What do you care?" she asked the god.

"I like this body. It's strong."

Eva didn't have time to feel flattered. Enrique feigned a blow that Javier parried, but it was bait. He deftly swung in the opposite direction for a slash that nearly gutted Javier. Miraculously, Javier stepped back, his quick footing saving him from the spilling of his innards all over the cobbles. Enrique moved with confidence and the natural strength of his bigger build.

"But I do wonder—what would it be like to be in control of a body like that?"

"You're not in control," Eva thought vehemently. No reply came, but her belly tingled.

Noticing Eva, Enrique said, "Tell your wife to head inside, unless you want her to witness you taking your last pitiful breath."

"I'm not going anywhere!" she snarled.

"Stay out of this," Javier said, mopping the sweat and spit from his mouth. "I don't need your help."

That's a lie, Eva wanted to howl at him. How could he expect her to watch idly?

Enrique's strikes broke Javier's defenses. He moved in, deliv-ering one, two, three brutal swings. Javier blocked each one, but the force sent him closer to the cabildo's brick wall, until he was trapped.

Enrique clicked his tongue and laughed. He wiped the single line of blood Javier had managed to draw on his cheek. In contrast, Javier sucked in one desperate breath after another. Strands of hair had broken free from his ponytail, and deep red lines spread about his gashed tunic.

"Your hatred for me runs so deep that you will kill me?" Javier said, freeing himself and making space between them.

"If you were so concerned about your worthless life, then you should have thought twice before you raised your hand against me!" Enrique growled, charging in a flurry of attacks that were nothing more than a flutter of silver to Eva. "I made you who you are, yet this is how you repay me." Their blades made contact in a shrill of metal, a jarring nail on glass.

"Javier is going to lose."

Eva's heart drilled against her rib cage. *"Shut up!"*

As if to prove Rahmagut right, Enrique found an opening, slicing Javier's chest. Javier gasped, his free hand clamping the deep cut as a torrent of blood showered the cobbles.

"No!" Eva cried, torn between respecting his wishes and the inevitability Rahmagut predicted. Should she run for her father? Or would Enrique be true to his promise while she sought help? Eva had the wild thought of blasting him with iridio, *as well as* the image of him slashing her belly open in retaliation for her nerve.

Enrique's laughter ended as he noticed the inky black creeping along Javier's temples. The corruption inundated Javier's eyes. "I see you're still sick, despite your pathetic plot to backstab me," he said. "Wasn't that the point of ruining my plans?"

"I never intended to let you fulfill Rahmagut's legend." Javier panted as he sheathed his blade, entwining his hands for an incantation. "Ursulina and I—we both loathed you. I don't care for her reasons; all I know is that I never intended to bring that despicable wife of yours back to life." His fingers worked quickly to ignite the golden threads of galio healing, which stopped his bleeding, stitching his wound closed. "Laurel is the reason I'm like this. That is why you loved her—because she was evil just like you." He chuckled darkly. "Me, you, her, we're all rotten on the inside. The only difference is I don't pretend otherwise." His voice was murky, like the grip he had on his sanity had finally snapped. Darkness wormed in and out of his cheeks and clawed hands. His sclera was filled with black. "She played the saint after she ruined me, but she was always a monster. And the night she bled to death—that was the happiest moment of my entire life!"

A deadly ire glowed in Enrique's eyes. In a flash of silver, he speared the air with his blade, aiming it right for Javier's neck.

Eva screamed.

Javier swerved out of the way, barely dodging the blade. The sharp metal slid over his collarbone, slicing skin and revealing bone.

"*You insolent worm,*" the caudillo growled, reducing the distance. "You'll insult her memory for the last time." He grabbed Javier's left wrist with both hands and fractured it like a branch in half.

The sickening crack of bone imprinted onto Eva's skin, as did Javier's shocked, agonized scream.

Enrique then grabbed Javier's other hand and repeated the brutalization, snapping the right wrist. "There—why don't you use your little galio tricks now?"

Javier collapsed to his knees, howling, his face red. Black blood trickled down his nostrils and ears as if the darkness was finding new ways to exude out of him.

Eva froze, realizing the tiniebla was gleefully emerging from the shackles of Javier's humanity.

"Since the moment you were born, you've always been an envious creature, coveting what's mine," Enrique said with unadulterated hatred. His iridio-summoned sword reappeared in his grip. "You were always a problem, terrorizing my home—my marriage—always prowling in the dark. A monster indeed. And like every tiniebla, you deserve nothing but obliteration."

He swung, the sword angled to decapitate the only person who had ever made Eva feel truly seen.

"*Do it,*" Rahmagut said.

Black fire burst from Eva's lungs as she placed herself between the caudillo and his brother. The flames exploded from her chaotically, kindled by the sound of Javier's pain. "Enough!" Eva howled as she materialized a thick litio barrier that blocked Enrique's blow. Thunder reverberated upon contact, sparks flying. The sound dizzied her, as did her rage.

Enrique backed away as the black flames bit at his jacket. The flames spread over the gardens, turbulent, a display of iridio geomancia beyond anything Eva had ever summoned before. She trembled, glancing about in terror at the horrible destruction she caused. The heat and smoke smothered them. But once released, the flames couldn't be reeled back.

Screams echoed in the distance as a plume curled into the air. People opened the cabildo windows to ogle and point, yelling, "Fire!"

Enrique's grip on his blade slackened. "What are you?"

Deep inside her, Rahmagut cackled, his laughter growing louder as the horror in the garden evolved.

She glared at Enrique. "You know my name—you know my father," she snarled, her breaths coming out as scorching plumes.

"No. You are something more," Enrique said as he pointed his summoned sword directly at her. "How convenient that Samón suddenly reacquaints with his daughter the moment Rahmagut is freed from his tomb."

Eva crouched beside Javier, who was hunched over his mangled hands. The broken bones poked against his skin, stretching it in all the wrong angles. The bruising of spoiled blood turned his wrists black. "Get up," she begged. They needed to get away before Enrique got any more ideas of torturing him. Distantly, screams filled the air. There were notes of despair, along with yelled commands to bring buckets of water to the cabildo. Eva forced herself to ignore her anxieties about more people pouring into the gardens and realizing she was the source of the flames.

Javier stood a moment before she commanded it of him. He sucked in a breath, swallowing the pain.

"Look at you: a spoiled, sniveling man, incomplete without the coddling of a woman," Enrique said, like the words were the winning blow.

Eva could hardly hear anything beyond her thundering heart. But she faced him. She had to. "You've already won. Do not pursue us," she said, in her anger opening up her link to Rahmagut. His strength filled her like electricity coursing through her veins.

In Enrique's gaze, she saw he understood she was changed and dangerous. Nevertheless, he said, "There is no victory in a world without Laurel."

Eva's heart skipped a beat. The words sobered her up. In a way, she understood the hollowness. Who would she have become if he had taken Javier today?

"Then look elsewhere," she said. "Javier and I can't give you what you want."

His eyes narrowed as, miraculously, he watched them leave uninterrupted. Eva kept their personal space enclosed in her barrier of litio. It worked twofold: to protect them from Enrique, should he decide to use his blade against them, and by opening a path through the fire. As crowds of people rushed to the cabildo with water extracted from the nearby canal, Eva and Javier managed to escape the chaos. If they were followed or noticed, she didn't have the mind to know.

The brisk walk back to Casa Bravo was short. There were no words exchanged. No consolation for his injury. Every so often, Eva glanced Javier's way, worried for his constitution. But he'd steeled himself. He swallowed the humiliation and pain, forcing the darkness out of his eyes even as it continued to slither in and out of his cheeks.

The discord brewing in the streets of La Parroquia served as a distraction, and Eva managed to shove away Rahmagut's influence. Thankfully, the god retreated quietly.

Javier let out the breath keeping him in one piece as soon as they entered their bedroom. He sat on the bed with trembling shoulders. "I am not well," he said, glancing away.

Eva made for the door, muttering, "I will fetch Maior—"

"*No*," Javier barked with a murky echo that froze her in place. "Don't leave me."

Eva gulped, her heart sinking. She sat beside him as it dawned on her: This vulnerability was for only her to see. He needed her.

Gently, she brushed back the sticky hairs clinging to his temples. His skin scorched beneath her fingertips. There was no color in his cheeks, just the incessant undulation of darkness. Eva found his gaze and held it, detailing the rare beauty of his red irises, which persevered.

"You must find me utterly pathetic and repugnant," he said.

Her heart wrung. "No. I find you foolish, for worrying about that now." She blinked away the moisture in her eyes as she considered he was paying the price for his loyalty—for protecting Maior. "You have a fever," she said softly. "Lie down. My galio can numb the pain for now, but I can't fix your wrists. I'm not good enough. We need to get a proper healer."

He obeyed wordlessly. "Not yet—please."

She soothed him as promised, and he lifted his mangled hands to his chest, curling like a child against the pillow. A foul odor crept to Eva's nose. A sharp, sickly rotting.

"Javier, what's happening?" Eva said, the corners of her eyes prickling again.

"The tiniebla—it's deafening. It laughs at me." His voice was muffled against the sheets. Perspiration exuded from his temples and neck. His tunic clung to his back, sweaty. He started writhing in pain.

"Did I fuck up the galio spell?" Eva said, rubbing his shoulder, hoping he would face her. A pit hollowed in her stomach as she imagined the worst.

Pressed to the pillow, he muttered her name, begging for relief. Then he arched as if his entire body were ablaze.

"Speak to me!" she cried. She wanted to take him in an embrace, hold him and serve as an anchor, but his wrists were in no shape to be touched at all.

"*His time is running out,*" the wicked voice within her answered. "*Soon all we'll have left is a loyal servant.*"

"*Tell me how to help him!*" Eva barked at him.

"*I cannot.*"

Javier howled to the ceiling in utter agony. He bared his teeth, surrendering his eyes to the inky black.

Tears blurred the sight of him. "Please don't leave me," Eva said, brushing the hair from his scorching forehead. Her heart raced frantically; she felt impotent and lost. Was she the fool for heeding his words and not seeking help?

She grabbed his face and pressed her nose against his. The rotten stink of his tiniebla filled her lungs. With gritted teeth, she ordered, "I command you to withdraw! Leave my husband this instant!"

Rahmagut's chuckles echoed through her.

How could his transformation happen so quickly? All this time Eva had thought there would be another day. She had freed Javier from his prison cell. He was surrounded by people. He had no reason to lose his sanity so soon.

Tears stained her cheeks. "You will leave Javier alone!" she commanded, first yanking his antlers, then cupping his jaw to force him to face her. The black veins were stark against his pale cheekbones. A leatherlike texture crept up the left side of his neck.

Instead of answering her, he groaned and curled into a ball in her arms. The tips of his antlers pricked her skin and drew blood. His ache was so sharp he held himself with his broken hands. Eva was immobilized in confusion and helplessness.

He buried his face in her belly. He yelled her name again, muffled against her dress. And Eva brought him closer. She rubbed his arched back and caressed his hair as he writhed and moaned, but her nursing achieved absolutely nothing.

Javier gave one last scream, and an eruption filled the room. Black blood burst out of his tunic and pants, drenching the bed, as a tail suddenly unfurled from his tailbone.

Then he exhaled into silence.

Eva gaped, stunned. He surrendered in her arms. She held him without moving, relieved that his breathing was steadying. Nevertheless, she couldn't believe the new, monstrous appendage.

The length of the tail was covered in coarse black hair. It was long like a nozariel's. Locks of silky starlight-colored hair curled at the tip, wet with the remnants of the black blood staining the bedsheets. As Javier sat up with his eyes clear of the corruption, retreating from Eva's embrace, the tail twitched and coiled, prehensile.

Eva covered her mouth.

Realizing something was amiss, Javier glanced back. Then his eyes doubled in size. *"What the fuck?"* He tried reaching for it, only earning himself sharp pain from his brutalized hands. The tail thrashed as he cursed a second time.

"My command worked," Eva murmured, wiping the sweat from her own sticky bangs. "Let me check your chest." She tugged his tunic.

He glared at her hands like he wanted to stop her. He was shaking.

"Please," Eva said, searching his eyes. "I know this is horrible, but I want to see if at least the turning has stopped for now."

He licked his lips, then nodded.

"How are you feeling?"

"Relieved," he said, downcast.

She lifted the tunic, finding his chest blotched in leathery scutes. The hastily patched cuts on his chest and collarbone were thick, tender lines of red and black blood. Her gaze glided to his lower belly, which was exposed to her. With a blush creeping to her cheeks, she smoothed down the tunic and smiled meekly. "Just a few extra patches," she said, minimizing the damage. "But it's done for now, right? What is the tiniebla saying now?"

"It is silent."

She tucked his sweaty hair behind his ears. Wings fluttered within her. "At least we have one more day."

"You expect me to be happy about this?"

"I am happy I didn't lose you."

He pursed his lips angrily.

"We can't waste the time we have. I must fetch Maior."

She piled the bloody sheets in a corner and helped him change into a clean tunic. Eva considered offering to help with his pants, but he was already bitter and moody about needing the assistance. She left him sitting on the bed, the tail switching behind him like an irrepressible display of his indignation.

27

New Saints and Old Gods

Eva found Maior and Reina in their bedroom. They were in heated debate about Enrique's actions, but they followed Eva to her room without question.

Trailing behind her, Reina said, "People are saying the cabildo caught fire."

Eva shot her a meaningful look, conveying to drop it. As Maior awaited a reply, she muttered, "The fire came from their duel." And it was answer enough.

The moment they stepped into her bedroom, the door closing behind them, Javier barked, "I didn't ask for Reina."

Maior gasped upon seeing Javier. Reina coughed and covered her mouth. Soon, it became clear she was stifling a laugh. "You grew a fucking tail."

"You find this amusing?" Javier said.

In a way, it was a relief to see them bicker.

"I'm sorry, but yes," Reina said. "It is poetic fucking justice, after you made a mockery of mine." To make a point, her own tail whipped behind her.

Javier glowered at Eva, and she knew she deserved the admonishment. But her friends gave Eva a reassurance she realized she'd needed the moment Maior began inspecting Javier's broken wrists. Reina and Maior were her confidantes. No one else understood the intricacies of their plight as intimately. With them, she didn't feel utterly alone.

"I must thank you, though," Reina said with crossed arms, as if she had difficulty mustering the words. "For standing up to your brother."

Javier's brows rose. His animosity evaporated. "Enrique miscalculated my loyalties. I know what I did in the past," he said, regarding Maior. "But I am your ally now."

Reina nodded.

Maior headed for the door, muttering about fetching her galio solutions enhanced with spiderwebs for the mending. Except she nearly crashed into Doña Tomasa on the way out.

"What is all this screaming?" the woman said as she rushed in, bewildered. "I meant to check in: Is the young master in pain—" Her words crumbled in her mouth at the sight of him. She gasped in horror.

Reina acted quickly, dragging her inside and closing the door behind them. "Easy now," Reina warned, lifting her forefinger to her lips. "There's no need to panic."

And it was evidently necessary. Javier was monstrous, resembling more a demon than the person he used to be. He had patches of scutes on his neck, black veins crawling down his temples and cheekbones, pinky fingers dipped in oily shadow, nails like talons, and a newly sprouted tail curling behind him. An amalgamation of human, valco, nozariel, and animal. He embodied what the cautionary stories at contrapunteo duels warned about, if one were to stray too far from the Virgin's purview. The last thing they needed was for Doña Tomasa to spread his tale through La Parroquia, sending the gossip directly to the archbishop's ears.

"No need to panic?" The color drained from the woman's sun-spotted cheeks. "What has happened here?"

Eva couldn't handle explanations. She let Reina give a quick excuse. Javier merely watched with a scowl.

Doña Tomasa crossed herself. "It's clear a devil has latched on to this home."

"There is no devil!" Eva snarled. "Javier was cursed, and he needs a cure." She hated feeling Rahmagut's amusement at the assertion. He always acted like he knew better, but he never offered any guidance whatsoever.

"I can mend the broken wrists," Maior piped up, "but I don't know how to revert his changes." She told Doña Tomasa, "He needs our help."

A silence filled the room. Eva's cheeks scorched. She had begged Javier to trust her, yet her hands were tied when it came to any kind of curse breaking.

"There may be someone who can help you," Doña Tomasa said, gulping. She crossed herself again. "Mi comadre knows a sanadero. He tries to heal, and when he can't, he'll make every effort to make the illness manageable, for the time you have left."

"He's not going to die of this," Eva insisted. But as she glanced about the room and saw their shifting eyes, she realized no one else believed this—not even Javier.

Doña Tomasa nodded. "Good Penitents don't go to Don Juan. He heals when every other prayer has failed."

"Take me to him," Eva said.

"I don't want Don Samón blaming me for turning you to the old gods." Doña Tomasa wrung her hands. "I am baptized and faithful. The family requires it to work here. I could lose everything."

"We won't say a word to anybody if you don't either," Reina said. Her eyes held a threat to secure the woman's silence. For it, Eva was endlessly grateful.

As soon as they came to an agreement, Maior set to work on mending Javier's mangled wrists. Eva could watch it for only so long. It was a gruesome task, as Maior had to use the enhanced galio solution to reposition the bone as close as she could to the natural arrangement. Javier endured it with a gag and a generous glass of aguardiente.

Nausea hit Eva like a stone. She rushed out of the room before Maior finished, not stopping until she reached the outhouse, where she retched out the contents of her stomach.

Doña Tomasa made quick work of gathering the bloodied sheets and burning them in the courtyard. At some point, Don Samón returned with his Céspedes wife and Ludivina, but they were too caught up in the events of the cabildo to notice the dark cloud reigning over the house.

"I got a cart ready," Reina told Eva as she watched the charring of the sheets. Smoke from the cabildo's fire already fogged the air, masking their destruction of evidence. "I know Segolita. I can help you navigate the streets."

Eva faced her with big eyes.

"I'm sorry for mocking Javier. It was in poor taste," Reina said, squeezing Eva's shoulder. The comforting gesture wasn't an invitation, but Eva couldn't help giving in to it. She threw her arms around Reina. She felt so shaken. Once again, Reina and Maior had been there for her.

"It's all right," Reina said, petting Eva's hair. They pulled away. "Maybe it's best if Javier doesn't go—" Reina started, but was interrupted by Don Samón stepping into the yard, calling for her.

He pointed behind him. "A fire broke out in the cabildo. Were you aware?"

Eva's pulse spiked.

"Yes," Reina answered for them.

He must have noticed Eva's weary appearance, or the grime splattering her skirt. Then his gaze found the small pyre behind them and he said, "Is something the matter?"

"Nothing to worry about," Eva lied. Thinking quickly, she added, "Just womanly things."

The answer seemed to discomfort him. He didn't believe them. With thinned lips, he searched her eyes, and Eva's chest pounded as she was unwilling to speak of today's chaos.

"Did you want something?" Reina asked him.

It was the distraction Eva needed, as Don Samón ordered Reina to go with him to the city gates, where a sentry claimed to have spotted tinieblas. Reina had no choice but to leave Eva on her own.

Finally, Maior emerged into the yard, fatigued but hopeful, and announced that Javier's bones were mended and bandaged. Eva and Maior stared, then threw their arms around each other. Maior pressed her face into Eva's chest, tears wetting her bodice. "He saved me from the caudillo, Eva."

"I know." Eva squeezed her back with all her strength, taking a big breath of relief.

At least for now, they were all safe.

The sun set behind the tall townhomes of Segolita as their carriage took them to a barrio called Frente al Río for its proximity to Segolita's river. They passed dilapidated buildings made of clay or stepped bricks, one on top of the other, hugging the rising hills of Segolita. Their carriage left them where the road turned to endless stairs. Debris and greenery burst from the seams of every step and building. Clotheslines zigzagged the slim alleyways between homes. Children and cats scurried up and down the steps. Nozariel mothers sat on porches, some betting on Calamity, others braiding the long, curly hair of their daughters. Distantly, Eva heard the beat of a drum, and the melody of a guitar.

Doña Tomasa led the way, unfazed. But Eva grew self-conscious and wary of the faces gawking at her antlers. She also found it hard to ignore the obvious poverty entrenched within Segolita's own walls when, right next door, La Parroquia overflowed with Fedria's concentration of wealth. She saw bloated children and poorly dressed elderly people forced to beg for coin. People who used rattan or cowhide curtains as the fourth wall of their homes. As they climbed, they passed an alleyway where there was a great commotion. Eva craned her neck and saw an elderly man beating a trespassing iguana with a broomstick, while the neighbors cheered behind him.

They reached a house with a façade of red bricks and potted, wilting ferns surrounding the doorway. Doña Tomasa told them to wait outside, welcomed herself into the shadowed depths of the drawing room, and yelled, "¡Comadre!"

A plump woman emerged from the house, flanked by a tailless child. The woman patted the boy's shoulder and told Eva, "Jaimito will take you to the sanadero."

Jaimito stuck out a palm. Eva understood the ask, so she gave him two escudos. He beamed, pocketed the coins, and beckoned them to follow him up even more steps. With a disapproving look, Doña Tomasa announced her leave back to Casa Bravo.

Soon enough, after climbing what felt like hundreds of steps, they reached the highest point of the hill, where the houses sat with the jungle profusion behind them. Jaimito approached a woman sitting on a porch. She sucked on a chewed-up sugarcane, watching them.

"Don Juan home?" Jaimito asked her.

Instead of answering, the woman leaned to the window and said, "Pa, there's a valco looking for you." Then she pointed to the open doorway behind her as their invitation to proceed.

They passed a drawing room, then entered a courtyard where a rooster and two goats snoozed. A man sat on a rocking chair across the yard, his eyes hidden beneath the shade of his jipijapa hat. He had a bucket of sugarcane beside him, from which he munched.

"A valco in Frente al Río. Now that's something you don't see every day." He tipped his hat back for a better look at Eva, then chuckled. "Which god did I anger to deserve such a visit?"

Eva took a deep breath for courage, then she approached with Maior, who offered him an escudo if he would listen to their tale.

Sluggishly, Don Juan stood up, his knobby knees creaking. His hands were leathery and dehydrated, thick veins protruding from sun-spotted skin. He wore an all-white outfit, including the jipijapa hat and his espadrilles.

He invited them to cross the doorway to his outdoor kitchen, where there was a large table and benches for seating. As Eva passed the threshold, a bat flitted through the door and out toward the sugarcane planting bordering the property. She squealed.

"Watch your step," he said. "Snakes come from the sugarcanes." They settled on the rattan benches and exchanged some introductions. His interest was piqued when Eva admitted she'd inherited her antlers from the Liberator.

He offered them mistela from a batch he'd made for a new mother in the neighborhood. Eva hesitated, remembering the milk snake, but she accepted it to keep him amiable. The drink was sickly sweet and exceedingly more alcoholic than the one she'd shared with Doña Rosa.

Once she could no longer delay it anymore, Eva said, "We need healing. We need to break a curse."

He licked his lips. They had crusty white bits at the corners. "Go to a medic."

"I am a medic. This isn't something I can nurse," Maior said.

He smiled. His canine was yellowed, and he was missing the tooth beside it. "Go to a priest."

"You know what the church thinks of us," Eva said.

Don Juan laughed. "It is cute that you seek to compare yourself to me. Please don't tell me you are this blind to our differences."

Eva lowered her head. "I'm sorry. But being valco doesn't give me an exception. They'll come after me for geomancia all the same."

"Indeed. The days of geomancia are ending. Things are not the same as during the war, when geomancia proved useful to those caudillos seeking fame." Don Juan picked at the flaky calluses on his palms. "At least, this was what I thought, until recently. These days, my dreams are more riotous than ever, and I feel a disturbance in the tide. The Orquídeas try to smother the supernatural, yet it feels as if a boiling kettle is about to blow." He took a sip of his mistela. "There are presences with us at this moment. I see two of you here, but more exist unseen, pretending they are not influencing the persons you have become."

Eva stilled. She could tell Rahmagut awaited Don Juan's bait. The sanadero had his full attention. She glanced at Maior and found her confused.

Don Juan headed to the kitchen counter. "You have entities clinging to your shoulders and feeding off your lives. This is why you have come, yes?"

"How do you know?" Maior said.

"Do you think I live on these hills, in the house my grandmother built, surviving on the measly escudos the desperate bring me, for pleasure? I'm a recluse because I cannot stifle the unseen, and I refuse to mold to the laws down in the valley, where those humans decry magic while mocking me with the wealth they stole from my ancestors. You came to see the sanadero of Frente al Río because you have an ailment no one else will cure. Stop insulting me and speak your truth already."

He returned cradling a large bowl made from a dried gourd, which held a sprinkling of grains, seeds, dirt, and sunflower petals. In his other hand was a cane that he used to hike farther into the sugarcane planting behind the house.

Eva and Maior followed him across an unruly underbrush of yerba buena. It reminded Eva of her days with Doña Rosa, her throat constricting from the memory. She felt guilty. What if she ended up embroiling him in the Orquídeas' inquisition? She couldn't cost another innocent their life.

They stopped by a creek. Faraway laughter came from across the water, people chattering across the sugarcanes.

"We desperately need your healing. My husband needs your healing."

Don Juan pretended to look around. "I don't see no marido."

"He's too weak to travel," Maior said. "We were hoping you would come with us."

"You want me to go into the valley, down all those stairs, so I can see your husband?" He pointed the cane at his swollen ankles. "With these legs?"

"I'll pay whatever you ask. I'll do anything!" Eva said.

"Do you even know what I do?"

"You mix herbs and make galio poultices," Eva said, bold yet desperate. "Your healing works because the magic of galio is real."

"No. The saints are who heal, not I."

Eva frowned.

"I don't have the hubris of believing I create miracles. The saints do." He pointed at the small icons that lay strewn about the creek bed and the surrounding greenery. Sitting atop a large boulder near the creek was a small shrine with a clay Virgin. Instead of holding Her iconic scepter, She cradled a clay marigold, the yellow paint flaking off. This Virgin was surrounded by an offering of wilting flowers and coconut-shell bowls holding rainwater. Eva caught a rustle from the corner of her eye, as if someone was watching them from the bushes, but met only green when she turned to look.

Oblivious, Don Juan went on. "I'll do a prayer and maybe if the saints are feeling amiable to your problems, they might give you what you want."

Eva grew angry. She didn't want a prayer. She wanted someone who had knowledge of arcane geomancia and would answer all her questions. Within her, Rahmagut cackled. But she couldn't even muster the strength to tell him to shut up. She felt so spent. Time was slipping through her fingers, and she was utterly useless at helping Javier.

"This—this might work," Maior added quickly. "It's what Las Hermanas de Piedra taught me back home. Galio and prayer work hand in hand."

Don Juan shrugged. "There is no galio. Only prayer and sacrifice. Surrender to the will of the saints."

"And has it worked?" Eva asked.

Offended, he narrowed his eyes. "It's my family's way of healing. I learned from my father, who learned from his parents before him. I follow my ancestors' path. That is why this creek is my home. Even while the humans had us in chains, this land never stopped being ours. That's why I returned here to continue our traditions the way they've always been done: with prayer. You lay your faith in the saints' hands, and they will do what they must."

"How is your healing different from Pentimiento?" Eva challenged.

"Stupid girl! Don't speak about things you don't understand. The humans forced the image of their saints and their Virgin on us, yes, so we took their names and put them on our gods. They lashed us and withheld our food if we didn't learn their language and practice their prayers. They gave us Segolean names, but we never forgot the ones given to us at birth. Yes, we prayed daily as they expected it of us; we said the things they wanted to hear." He jabbed his chest and said, "But in our hearts, we were worshipping the true spirits of the land. We lay worship to the goddess of the river and to the bringer of the sun. Only the ignorant, the brainwashed, and the conformist think I'm praying to their saints when they see the effigies in my home. Their Virgin and their saints don't have power in this land. Our gods do. I embrace them because they have always been ours." He gestured at the stunted antlers crowning Eva. "Though I shouldn't be surprised to hear such ignorance from a human and a mixed breed."

Hot indignation flushed Eva's cheeks.

"Call it the gods or the saints or the Virgin. It doesn't matter. What matters is the power that's real, so put yourself at their mercy and they might listen."

"*I have no mercy for anybody*," Rahmagut noted.

"In that case, can you make the prayer back in town? Please let me take you to him."

Don Juan chuckled. He beckoned Eva to approach him, where he had crept closer to the crystalline creek. "Here lies an ancient entity," he said, gesturing to the lazy flow of green water. Tadpoles twirled about the bank, hiding within the shade of wildflowers. "It feeds the city. It nourishes our conucos. It grows the sugarcane that entertains our afternoons. So why don't you give it a prayer?"

Eva stared at the water, still discomfited. "But Javier—*my husband*—is in La Parroquia." She shot a helpless glance at Maior. Were they wasting their time?

A sudden rush of water stunned her. Eva gasped, jumping in surprise as bits of dirt and sunflower petals clung to her curls and cheeks. Soaked, she flailed, realizing Don Juan had somehow doused her with river water.

He muttered quick words she couldn't comprehend. The laughter from across the river echoed again. But before she could yell at his insanity, she was thrust into a mind that wasn't her own.

28

River Memories

Night veiled the sky.

A whirlwind of constellations illuminated the view where she stood at the highest point of a crag. The stars were a glittering, magical spectacle from far away, until they rained upon the valley, cutting the air at speeds too fast to comprehend. The earth shook as they made impact, spreading fire and destruction over the village below.

Eva watched it, stunned, despair choking her. She'd had the instinct to rush forth—to pretend she could be a savior. But the truth rooted her to the spot: She stood there, alive and unscathed, unlike those who shared her blood, merely out of luck.

For two sunsets and two sunrises she'd gone scavenging for medicine out of desperation, as her family stayed behind bleeding and wasting away from the illness that raged through the village. Of those who caught it, not a single person had lived.

Leaving was the chance to escape the malady; the hope to find a cure. She'd left with the fear of never seeing her family again. Now the starfall made this fear her reality.

His reality. The thought flitted through his mind with surety and was confirmed by the large masculine hands before him. Veins bulging and calluses protruding. Light brown skin. *His* hands.

He never descended the crag. Rahmagut could see it plainly

from his vantage point. His home at the edge of the village roared in flames. The thatched roof was easy fuel for the fire it fed. Other homes also burned. One great star cratered the area where the village center had stood. He'd arrived moments after the shock wave battered every watching eye. For those who'd survived the impact, the fire did the rest.

There was nothing for him ahead. So Rahmagut turned on his heel and gave his back to the place where he'd been born. The home where he'd married his first love, and where he'd watched the birth of his firstborn. Tears streaked his cheeks, but he knew his family had crossed the threshold to a better realm. Their mortal life had been marked by suffering. Now it was his burden alone to carry their memories.

He traveled aimlessly away from the fire raging behind him, his journey unhindered by a dry season. The days were hot and lonely, but the nights were worse. Drenched in sweat and with his heart racing, he awoke from nightmares of falling stars. They gave him no reprieve as he mourned his family in painful solitude. How was he meant to live so utterly alone?

One night, a large star with a cyan tail appeared in the sky. It surfaced only after sunset, as if shying away from Ches's scornful eye. Filled with hatred over his loss, Rahmagut followed it. Maybe he could prevent another tragedy wherever the star intended to collide.

It took him to the mountains.

He knew of the valco kingdom cradled there. He'd heard the stories from the antlered traders who had once exchanged their purple potatoes for his freshwater pearls. But when he arrived at their elevated lands, begging for community, he was denied. The matriarchs eyed his tail with distrust. The patriarchs narrowed their eyes at his build—so obviously that of a warrior.

The valco gates shut behind him, and the star's tail grew weaker. On its last day, he discovered a cavern pulsing with magic much like the stars that had ended his village had pulsed with light.

His fingertips tingled as he extracted the first glittering rock. His skin hummed as he dove deeper into darkness.

Rahmagut wasn't ignorant of the benefits of the land's minerals. But with this new rock—fire came easily. He used it to give himself the sight of night, and the ability to stare directly into Ches's light without being blinded. Every experiment yielded a new possibility.

The cave was endless in its offerings. The more he dug, the more ore he found. Eventually, he gave it a name befitting its rainbow-glittering surface: iridio.

With the rocks, he returned to the valco kingdom and charmed the leadership with ease. Rahmagut laughed as the valcos became delighted by iridio's power, which was easily seen with their red eyes. In exchange for his ore, they allowed trade and dialogue. Some were greedy and foolish enough to follow him back to its source, intending to steal his prize. But Rahmagut had been bred a warrior, and he had a newly forged iridio-tipped spear. He had no qualms tainting his hands with the red of their blood. He felt no regret when he gutted them. Sometimes, he even drew joy from scalping their antlers. And the iridio made it easier. Everything was easier.

It wasn't long until he earned the reputation of being generous in trade, cunning in diplomacy, and ruthless in battle. Nevertheless, he was nozariel, a strange kind to these lands. The valcos refused him a home in their kingdom, so he decided to make his own.

The mountain provided him the stone to build a thatch-roofed house like the one where he'd been born. This humble home, built right at the entrance of his treasure trove, became his kingdom.

Then one stormy night a winged goddess burst through his front door, freezing and begging for shelter. She was willowy and intelligent, with hair like a waterfall in nighttime and eyes resembling the shadows of dusk. She called herself a yare, as made apparent by her bat-like wings, and hailed from the peninsula where the landmass reached for the sea like a claw. She quickly became Rahmagut's second love, and so he made her his queen.

The humility was fleeting, for the wealth he attained from the iridio reserves was vast and ever growing. Soon he needed more thatch-roofed attachments to house his mountains of gold.

Pilgrims crossed the Llanos and traipsed into the mountains

for a glimpse at this magnanimous man who'd built a fortune from thin air. When an earthquake rocked the valco kingdom, he welcomed survivors under his ever-expanding roofs. Even packs of yares, after hearing of the winged queen, soared over those mountain peaks to ally themselves to Rahmagut's kingdom. Rahmagut had always been a charismatic man. But the confidence iridio gave him entranced all who saw him. Without having to try, he was popular and beloved, and his following multiplied.

It wasn't long before another disaster upended Rahmagut's happiness. Endless storms and unforgiving mudslides raged through the Páramo, flooding his homesteads and those of his followers. Rahmagut swallowed his pride and once again descended into the valley, to beg the valcos for refuge. But upon his arrival, the valco kingdom shut its gates. No amount of iridio or bribery would change their minds. The elders begged for Rahmagut's forgiveness, as the rains had flooded their conucos and everything their terraced farmlands yielded rotted from the damp. With empty stores, they couldn't risk their livelihood by welcoming more hungry transients.

And that was the problem with valcos, descendants of Ches. They were a stubborn war breed, easily swayed by instincts yet suspicious of those not crowned by antlers. Rahmagut had all the iridio, but he was outnumbered.

One night, when the worry of losing his new family to the rains crested his anxieties, he was once again visited by the cyan star, this time in a dream. It gave him a revelation: With the iridio, he could force an eagle to be birthed out of a mountain goat, or a caiman to burst through the birthing belly of a jaguar. He tried it, and what emerged was a bloody, amalgamated, ravenous creature, unnatural and not meant for this world. But it listened to him.

Rahmagut waited until the moon eclipsed the sun, to shroud his actions from Ches's scornful eye, and repeated the atrocity hundreds of times. He created atrophied foxes, misshapen condors, and heart-hungry lions. The creatures didn't belong in this world, as was apparent from their lack of visible form. They were shadows. Thus, he gave them a fitting name: tinieblas.

With them, he stormed the valco kingdom. His followers reveled in the massacre of the valcos, who deserved their downfall for their selfishness. Even his queen rallied the yares, and they swooped down in the night, their bat wings and outstretched claws sparking terror in all those who'd denied them.

When it was over, his followers claimed a home of their choosing. His tinieblas secured a brand-new kingdom. And standing upon the ashes of the destruction he had wrought, Rahmagut stared up at the dawning sun, to make a mockery of the valco deity, and declared himself a god.

To ensure his authority would never again be questioned, he took to wife a woman from each one of the eight major valco houses. Though none could surpass his flying queen, the ninth.

"*I remember.*"

The words snapped her out of the vision. With a gasp, Eva fell to her knees. The sugarcanes and the creek came into focus. Soaked and dizzy, she found herself back in Don Juan's creek bed.

"*I remember,*" Rahmagut repeated. Despite the disorientation, his presence blared. He glowed with excitement from recalling fond, long-lost memories. He replayed them over and over, plucking out instances of great joy, like when he bested the valcos' strongest warriors, or when his new wives submitted to him. Eva's mind fogged from the interference, as if she couldn't separate his memories from the fabric of her reality. She pressed her hands against her temples, squeezing painfully, forcing herself to focus on the creek's gentle flow.

Maior's voice rang above her. Her tone was pitched with exasperation.

"You doubted the truth of the saints," Don Juan said flippantly. "I told you the river had power and you were ready to brand me a fool. I could not stand for that."

"Eva?" Maior knelt by her side. "Are you okay?"

Eva nodded as her mind came out of its addled stupor. If she focused hard enough, she could ignore Rahmagut's glee. She took a deep, grounding breath. Her heart raced as she considered Rah-magut's brutal past, the way he'd created tinieblas and slaughtered valcos. Though Eva was tempted to judge him for it, she'd seen with her own eyes how his actions were forged from suffering and desperation. He was a conqueror through and through. And most importantly, the memories revealed him as mortal.

Like a fire doused by water, Rahmagut's joy soured. He awaited her next thoughts.

"*But you are no longer*," she tactfully told him, assuming there was more to this story.

She accepted Maior's help to her feet. Wiping the water from her face and clothes, she turned to Don Juan. "What did you do to me?" Anger flooded her, for the assault. "I'm soaked!"

"You came here requesting help for your husband, yet you're withholding a very important truth," Don Juan growled. "You hold the essence of an entity within you. A dark, hungry presence. You dare take from my healing and you don't even do me the cour-tesy of admitting it'll benefit a devil!"

Maior's confusion traveled from the sanadero to Eva. She frowned.

"You didn't ask!" Eva said. She couldn't believe his nerve. She wasn't about to announce to a stranger that Rahmagut had made her body his new home. She squinted, forcing herself to be pres-ent in this moment. Meanwhile, Rahmagut coursed the length of his memories, like a saltwater fish back in its natural habitat. His memories threatened to overcome her thoughts. "*Please stop it*," she said, carefully avoiding another insult.

"*There is power in knowledge, niña. In remembering.*"

"I am not a niña."

How she hated the patronizing connotation of that word. How it revealed the way he viewed her: as inferior and inexperienced.

"*You wanted my memories, and now we have them.*"

"What is he talking about, Eva?" Maior asked.

Eva stepped back, hugging herself.

"I knew from the moment I laid eyes on you." Don Juan ges-tured at Eva's entire figure. "You walked into my home with a darkness enshrouding you. A power, though I cannot attest to whether it is the leech, or if you are the one doing the leeching."

Eva's chest wrung at the frown Maior directed at her.

"It is a darkness like a tiniebla's. You hold the god of the Void within you," Don Juan whispered, as if that would stop Rahmagut from hearing the fear and dislike dripping from his words. Don Juan pointed his cane at Eva. "Is this a trick? What are you getting out of this?"

"No!" Eva howled. "I'm not lying about Javier. We are desperate!"

"*You* are the one possessed by Rahmagut?" Maior muttered in disbelief.

"You utter his name as if you don't fear him," Don Juan said with a scoff.

Maior backed up, her hand snaking into her cleavage, reaching for the Virgin charm hanging there. "I do fear him," Maior said in a small voice, her rounded eyes directed at Eva, perhaps fearing Eva herself.

"If you are not lying, then you will speak the truth, woman!" Don Juan told Eva, shaking his cane again. "Why did you fall into a trance when I showered you with Arca's water? Tell your companion what you saw. Tell her how it opened your eyes to the demon who possesses you."

Rahmagut was too pleased with his memories to care about Don Juan's accusations. He idled within Eva like a recently fed lion. She nodded to Maior.

"It's true?" Maior whispered. "You have...him?"

"The god of the Void chose me after the tomb collapsed."

Don Juan sucked in a breath and stepped into the shallows. He splashed water over his shoulders and face, muttering under his breath. He placed it over himself like a baptism, or a protection.

"All this time you've had him?" Maior said.

Eva nodded. And to displace some of that disappointment onto someone else, she added, "Rahmagut went into me, and Ches went into Reina."

Maior's mouth dropped.

The sound of crickets became loud in their silence. The sun dipped below the horizon, elongating the shadows from the sugarcanes flanking the river. A wild dog yapped in the distance. The profusion of leaves shuddered, and once again Eva thought she saw movement. Eyes that came and went, coy and fleeting.

"Why didn't you tell me?" Maior said.

Eva just shrugged. "It's not an easy thing to admit. Reina didn't tell you, and she's your lover." Bringing Reina into this was a cheap move, but Eva wasn't the only one guilty of lies. They'd had their reasons. And Maior's frightened expression only proved they'd been right.

Eva turned to Don Juan, who finally decided to emerge from the water. "It doesn't feel like he's fully returned, though. It feels like there are pieces of him missing, or sealed, or forgotten. What you did to me, it restored his memories."

"It is the work of Arca. I prayed to her, and she cleansed." In their faces was bewilderment, so he added, "Do you know what this river is?"

Eva and Maior shook their heads in unison.

"You can trace it to the morichales and you will find it connects to the great Río'e Marle."

"Río'e Marle?" Eva parroted.

"Yes. Not only does it separate our nations, but it's also the basin that gives life to this land. All that grows from its waters is thanks to her. The river is the embodiment of Arca, and your Virgin."

Maior winced.

"And the tale of Princess Marle?" Eva challenged.

Don Juan aired his linen shirt with disdain. "A story that has entirely erased Arca. Of course humans tell it, all while withholding a very important fact: The jaguar who raised Princess Marle, who allowed her to discover the lengths of the river, was an earthly form of the goddess Arca, granter of purification, nourishing, and new beginnings. It's funny, though, how your priests claim it was the Virgin who appeared on the shores of the Cow Sea, welcoming humans into our land. But this was Arca all along. So many lies just to avoid seeing what's right in front of them. Even your churches have wells carrying her waters. Except they're wrong, because that Segolean Virgin cannot rule over our land. We already have our own gods, our own magic." He gestured to the sugarcanes, and as Eva glanced back, she definitely saw a hand disappear within the leaves.

Don Juan added, "Their Virgin—She never made it across the ocean."

"But your bowl had other things in it," Eva said, "sunflower petals and seeds. There's more to it."

He snorted. "Call it an offering—my sacrifice. Nevertheless, I can't control what or when she chooses to cleanse. She is a goddess, and I am mortal."

Maior hugged herself with a pained look. Eva tried grazing the back of her elbow, but she pulled away.

"Don't look so miserable," Don Juan told her. "You're still praying to a divine being. Why does her identity change your relationship? Are you untrue in your devotion?"

"That's not it!" Maior said, dismayed.

Unbothered, he asked Eva, "And you said Ches was in someone else?"

Eva nodded. Her belly twisted from the admission. It was Rahmagut imparting pain.

"So that explains the dreams…" Don Juan trailed off in thought. "If they inhabit your bodies, then they must have no other choice."

Maior watched Eva as if seeing her in a new light. It was discomforting. "Does that mean…" Maior said slowly. "Does that mean that Eva and Reina are the only things holding them to this world? What if they are killed? What then?"

The words were a knife.

Maior quickly explained herself. "That is Monseñor Lorenzo's goal."

Eva didn't withhold her sneer, nor her anger.

Don Juan laughed at Maior. "Maybe that's true for your possession!"

Maior's neck and cheeks reddened.

"Did you think I could pick up on a god possessing your companion and not notice the woman in you?" He smirked, showing his yellowed canines. "Don't be alarmed—ghosts and gods are different." He pointed at Eva. "Yes, she is a mortal prison to the god of the Void, but should her life expire, he can merely find another host."

Rahmagut chuckled his agreement. It unsettled Eva how he was so sure of himself now, with his returned memories, the power balance tipping. Once she had a moment alone, she planned to interrogate him.

Don Juan padded back into his house. Eva and Maior followed in silence. Eva tried taking Maior's hand, but Maior evaded her, putting a wall between them. More questions than ever remained, but the gesture dried up Eva's sympathy. She decided to focus on the reason why they came at all: Javier and the tiniebla.

Don Juan went from corner to corner, lighting candles to lift the gloom. He had a multitude of shrines and icons he'd arranged about his house.

Maior approached Don Juan as he lit one such candle. "If ghosts are different from gods, can she be removed? The spirit haunting me, I mean. Can the Virgin—*Arca*, can she purify me from my possession?"

Don Juan exhaled his weariness. "Have you tried praying yet?"

Tears glimmered in Maior's eyes.

He grimaced at her reaction.

Eva's heart ached, for all of them. She hugged herself tighter, her gaze avoiding Maior's and Don Juan's and settling on the packed ground. "I will pray, if it's necessary," Eva said.

"Don't lie to yourself." Don Juan waved a hand in the air, dismissive. "I will see this marido of yours, but no goddess or saint will listen to the words of she who is home to the god of the Void."

29

Two Villains

It was a good thing the moon was high, lighting them, when Eva, Maior, and Don Juan arrived at Casa Bravo. It made it easy to avoid any curious glances as they smuggled the elder through the stables and into the backyard without need of a candle. Don Juan had agreed to descend from his hill and be chauffeured to La Parroquia in exchange for a sizable bag of escudos.

Javier was lying restlessly when Eva entered the room. His hair was wet from a recent bath. He rose, and life returned to his eyes at the sight of her. The tail swayed behind him. It was a shock to see it—a reminder of its permanence.

"Come outside," she told him.

He almost grabbed a coat, to conceal the appendage perhaps. But Eva reassured him that everyone was asleep.

Don Juan waited in Maior's company behind the outdoor oven.

The sanadero's face wrinkled even more as his eyes fell on Javier's transformations. He muttered soft prayers under his voice, his distrust for Javier palpable.

"What's the meaning of this?" Javier said, mirroring Don Juan's energy.

Eva ignored him, asking Don Juan instead, "Can you tell what he has?"

Don Juan's lips twisted more. He uncapped the flask with water from his creek. For a moment Eva imagined him chucking it straight at Javier's face. When he didn't, Eva was glad for it.

He instructed Javier to extend his reluctant left hand. Javier winced as Maior gently unraveled his bandages, revealing his hand bruised black. Don Juan dropped a few droplets on Javier's corrupted pinky finger. The skin sizzled and Javier gasped, pulling away.

"Tinieblas cannot cross my creek," Don Juan said with severe eyes. "Living up the hill with the riled tinieblas trying to breach the city, I had to pray for Arca's protection, and this is how she answered." He stepped back, his teeth bared. "The woman holding the god of the Void and her marido, who is a tiniebla."

"*Insolent creature*," Rahmagut scoffed, withdrawing.

Javier glowered like he was considering slicing Don Juan's neck open.

"I don't want to be involved with your lot," Don Juan said.

"Then I will not pay you." Eva hated whispering when all she wanted to do was yell.

Maior gave Eva a stunned look. Don Juan clicked his tongue, as if he'd already appraised her accurately.

Eva clenched her fists to coil her rage. "*Please*. We know what he has, and we need a cure."

"Even if I wanted to help you, this is too advanced."

"Even for you?" Eva croaked. "Even for Arca?"

Don Juan squared up in his short stature. He asked Javier, "Did you have visions when I poured the water? A moment of clarity? Or just pain?"

"You burned me," Javier said.

"Sometimes you have to burn a wound before it can begin to heal," Maior offered meekly.

Don Juan ignored her. "Arca chose to open your eyes," he told Eva. Then he turned to Javier. "And she showed us that you're no different from a tiniebla. If you are doused in my creek waters, instead of cleansing you, it might destroy you."

"Brilliant," Javier said, and he turned like he meant to walk away. Eva understood his pain. She gently grabbed his arm to stop him.

"Is there nothing you can do?" she asked the sanadero.

"You can pray and hope a god answers. There are other ways to break curses, I suppose. Ways that involve iridio's reversing properties. But you have a tiniebla in you and I don't see how this can serve as hope."

"What is it?" Eva said. If iridio could be used as a solution, there was no one else better positioned than her to use it.

"It helps to use the remains of the spirit that has taken possession. Can you get a piece of the tiniebla? Hair? Fingernails? Horns?"

"Can it be any tiniebla?" Eva asked.

"It must be one related to your curse."

Javier groaned. "Then no."

Don Juan shrugged. "Like I said, this method will give you no hope. Unless you can find the bone remains of that tiniebla you house—"

"I was cursed to turn into one, but it wasn't the tiniebla who did it," Javier snarled.

"Who cursed you? Was it a wrathful spirit? A witch? Can you get something from their body?"

Silence enveloped them. Javier's brows quivered, as if undecided on whether to rise or descend.

"No," Eva answered for him. "And what will that do?"

"That is the next-best connection. I know a thing or two about curses. The person who places a curse is the closest one to its lifting. Can you find the person who cursed you? Can you get their hair or blood?"

"She's dead," Javier snapped.

Eva hated acknowledging the presence hovering above Maior. She knew how much even a flickering gaze could sting Maior. As they spent so many hours together, Eva was an expert at ignoring the ghostly Laurel. But she couldn't at this moment. Laurel's image waned and shifted with the light, a face with no life.

With a nonchalant shrug, Don Juan said, "Can you get her dead hair or bones?"

There was no breeze, yet Eva shuddered from a chill. She imagined a sickly picture, of decaying flesh and worms. When had Laurel passed? This was a gap in her knowledge.

Maior crossed herself, looking away. Red blotched her cheeks.

"You're speaking about exhuming a body," Javier said.

"How desperate are you?" Don Juan said.

With gritted teeth, Javier said, "I don't care about respecting that woman's grave. It is simply inaccessible to us."

"Then your hands are tied," Don Juan concluded. "I will take a ride back to my home now—and my escudos. Come find me once you have some of her remains. Otherwise, keep me out of it."

As Don Juan retreated, Eva stared at Maior to get her attention. This was the moment to ask about Laurel—to clarify the solution to her possession. But Maior avoided Eva, instead offering to ready the carriage for Don Juan's return home. The walls between them remained steadfast and unmoving. And how could Eva blurt out a question about Maior's possession to Don Juan? Such an overstepping of boundaries would only salt Maior's wounded feelings. Either way, there was nothing they could do. Eva did know one thing: Enrique's wife had been buried beside his mother, in Águila Manor.

Javier grabbed the back of Eva's arm. She startled, and he frowned at the reaction.

"I'm sorry," she said. The apology was anticlimactic. It rang hollow in her chest, for failing to help him.

She explained her reasoning for bringing Don Juan to Casa Bravo, and told him about Rahmagut's returned memories. She had thought Don Juan could offer some salvation. And she shrank before the indifference with which he listened, as if he'd already resigned himself to his fate.

"I'd like to access the vault," he told her.

"Tonight? Don't you want to rest?"

"I cannot sleep, so I will scour the library."

"*A waste of time,*" Rahmagut said, emerging. "*You didn't know my real history because it has been forcibly rewritten and erased. Did you ever imagine me as the man that I am? No—you saw me as the horned devil of your Penitent tales. All those books will offer no clarity. I guarantee it.*"

Eva was so worn out she couldn't muster the energy to argue. To Javier she said, "You need me to come as well?"

"No. But you must be the one to use its key. A relation of blood. Remember? I am not there yet."

Eva's cheeks warmed as she turned the words in her mind. *He was not there yet.*

After transferring the bag of escudos to Don Juan's expectant grasp, Eva followed Javier into Don Samón's study. In her grip, the golden key unlocked the vault without any effort at all.

Javier descended the shadowy staircase alone. Eva left him to it and prepared a bath for herself.

Moonlight gleamed through the open window as Eva ran a wet cloth down her shoulders, the soap-scented water helping her mop the smoke and sweat from her skin. She lay in the copper tub in solitude, her eyes closing as she yearned for the peace she'd lived in in Tierra'e Sol. Back then, the promise of her newfound powers had given her so much confidence. Now she felt so powerless. She could barely scratch the surface of what was known and possible, and there were no answers.

"*Did you ever curse anyone to become a tiniebla?*" Eva prodded within the depths of her consciousness.

Rahmagut uncoiled, stretching like a cat. It wasn't common for him to surface while she was this exposed. Eva noted he was kind and considerate, for such an infamous god. His amused laughter rolled through her.

"*Why would I turn anyone into one? I had all tinieblas at my fingertips,*" he said.

"*Did you ever break curses?*"

"*The sanadero is right. You will need to unearth her bones.*"

Dismayed, Eva melted into the lukewarm water. She'd put her hair in a high bun, but loose curls dipped down and were wetted.

"*Did you remember how you ended up sealed?*"

"*You saw as much as I.*"

Eva wanted to stomp and whine. "*Why can't you help Javier? You are a god,*" she said, recalling the contradiction of his memories.

Her stomach twisting painfully was her punishment. He retreated, and she received no reply.

Eva slipped on a fresh cotton nightgown. She patted her empty bed, concerned. Javier wasn't all right. She couldn't leave him to suffer alone.

Soon enough, her feet took her to the dimly lit library, where Javier perused one manual after another. He was engrossed in a tome of stained, fragile pages. Eva allowed herself to indulge in his company, for it was a treasure, before whatever existed between them expired from his curse. She blushed. Somehow, without her noticing, she'd begun to truly care.

He saw her approach and smiled faintly. "No luck yet," he said. Maybe it'd been a trick of the light, but Eva thought she saw a glimmer of wetness in his eyes.

The black veins had retreated from his cheekbones and temples, returning the sculpted and pearlescent quality of his skin. His lashes shrouded his gaze as he read. They were starlight wispy, and ethereal. A rarity. He was such a beautiful man, perfect for her in a way she hadn't seen until now. How it burned her that she should lose him to a tiniebla.

"I'm sorry," she whispered when she couldn't take it anymore.

Javier shut the book and inserted it back into its place. He approached her. "You keep apologizing, but you had no hand in this."

Her arms ached to reach forward, as if driven by the curiosity of whether all he needed was an embrace. But an embrace of hers? How could she think herself so special, worthy of making him forget the horrors of his curse?

"Today has been one failure after another," she said. And it'd been long and arduous. How she ached to tuck into bed. Except... every second wasted only escorted Javier closer to his inevitable turning.

She held her breath as he lifted her chin. "Eva, you saved my life."

A steady rhythm traveled from her chest to her ears. The touch sparked a craving. She wanted to lean into it, but she hesitated because of his injured wrist. "Do you really think...he meant to kill you?"

"Enrique wasn't going to forgive me for denying him Maior. And this wasn't the first time we fought about Laurel. When I lived with him, I simply couldn't hide my hatred of her." His teeth bared at the memory. "Today felt like the mask had finally snapped—this illusion that we should be allies just because we're kin." He shook his head. "I knew I had to give it my all. Every instinct told me so. And when I fell—" His voice broke.

Eva couldn't withstand it anymore. She closed whatever distance lingered between them and wrapped her arms around him. He smelled of the same soap she'd used for her bath. A warmth spread through her as he hugged her back.

"I knew my time was done. Enrique has never been someone to show mercy. Besides, I didn't want it. I thought—better this than lose myself to a monster." He laughed bitterly. "Better to serve *some* good than to become a creature with no other desire but to devour hearts."

Eva squeezed the back of his tunic. His death had been a real possibility. Her blood spiked in anger. If her barrier had failed. If her geomancia hadn't measured up to Enrique's strength. But if she had truly lost him, Eva wouldn't have just burned down the cabildo in retaliation. She would have tested her rage against Enrique himself.

Shivers ran through her as Javier's hand traveled down and settled on her lower back, pressing her closer. She was enveloped in his strength. He held her so tightly. She felt his reluctance to let go, as if he were starved for physical touch. The molding of their bodies together—it was so real and perfect. It dizzied her.

They parted as Eva found herself missing the red of his eyes. If Enrique had snuffed that out—if she didn't have Javier as her coconspirator anymore—

Anger took her again. She shoved him away and said, "How could you be happy with leaving me on my own?" She found him speechless, so she let the anger gain power. "I have a god of darkness inside me and you are the only one who understands!" She pounded her chest. "Without you I am alone—unsupported."

"Eva..."

"So don't say you accepted Enrique taking your life! Don't say you are ready to give in to the tiniebla! Fight!"

Ignoring his injured wrists, he yanked her into his arms. He squeezed her as if to appease her, curving his body and resting his chin on her neck.

"You scared me back there. Did you not think about me?" she said, wiggling in his arms, trying and failing to pound her fist on his chest. "I don't want to be alone," she said in a small voice. Where would she find someone who valued her, with her darkness? Already Maior distrusted her. Soon, Don Samón would, too.

Javier freed her, but only to take in the depth of her eyes for a sliver of a moment before he pressed his lips against hers.

Sparks ignited in her chest. She kissed him back, her heart light and fluttery like a feather as she discovered that the feel of his lips was better than anything she'd imagined. His hands cupped her head, trapping her to him. And she grew warm, melting. For once, she wanted to surrender to him.

When his tongue breached her lips, Eva crumbled, reduced to raw sensation and shivers.

She squeezed the back of his tunic again. Her heart was in a race. No distance felt close enough. She took a deep breath and realized he tasted exactly as she had hoped.

Maybe she was pressing herself against him too hard. While their lips clashed, their footing became unstable. He backed up against the niche behind them, pulling her with him. They fell onto a bench.

Eva inhaled deeply as they pulled away.

This close, his eyes were two brilliant red orbs, speckled with brown and hazel, perhaps the lingering traces of his human blood. They rounded with desire, and uncertainty. Javier lightly tugged the lock of hair she'd accidentally wetted in the tub. "You have such pretty curls," he said absentmindedly.

More sparks ignited in her chest. She shuddered as his hand ran down her arm. She could feel the longing for more in his touch.

"I expected you to push me away," he admitted.

Eva swallowed thickly. Maybe he had a point. "Then why didn't you ask, if you weren't sure I was ready?"

"Better to ask for forgiveness than permission."

"So now you're joking about forcing yourself on me."

"Yet you kissed me back."

She raised her hands in the air, exasperated. "That is not the point."

"What is?"

"The point is perhaps I wasn't ready. The point is maybe in this case, it is better to ask than risk doing yet another thing that makes me not trust you." She knew she was a hypocrite, when she'd already violated his trust before. And her body had very obviously reacted with desire, delighted in giving in to this next step. But she was tired of having a relationship tainted by wrongs.

"So you didn't want it?"

Eva dug her hands in her hair. "I know you're not this obtuse."

He massaged his bandaged hands. Had his wrists stopped hurting already? Eva was impressed by Maior's capabilities.

His jaw tightened as if he were gathering the words. As if he couldn't bring himself to give her the honesty she craved.

Right as she was about to give up—right as she was ready to rise and resume their pointless search through the books—Javier tugged her pinky, then took her whole hand.

"I didn't *not* think about you when I was dueling Enrique—and about my future. I mean, how could I not? The stakes were clear. Either I was going to make it, or not. And that affected me. You. Us."

His eyes observed hers with hesitation.

"And I *do* think about you—maybe a little too much," he admitted. "I think about how I sealed my own fate with the way I treated you. About how I caused my own curse with the way I treated everyone else."

He paused and the darkness crept into the edges of his eyes. But he swallowed it away.

Sometimes Eva wondered if this cheapened his words. If he truly held the power to swallow away the tiniebla's darkness, then he was wholly liable for all the horrible things he'd done.

"I think about how I don't have many nights left—or time—how *I don't have fucking time*. I think about all the things I wanted for my future, and how they're nothing but wistful dreams now. With this curse, I'll never be the person I thought I would be. I always wanted to be a father. Did you know that? I never knew mine. I never knew what it was like to be raised by parents who cared—instead I had to grow up with *him*. And I used to think to myself: *When it's my turn, I will do it right. A proper house. A life to be proud of.* Yet here I am, with you."

Eva's brows plummeted. She held her breath.

"But this tiniebla ruined it. I finally found the match I was looking for—I had the beginnings of the life I wanted, a valco bride so perfect for me it was as if I had manifested you into existence . . . and it actually possessed me to hurt you." His gaze flitted to the small mark at the corner of her lip. It would be there forevermore. He took a deep breath. "This tiniebla—every time I attempt to right my path, it takes control and forces my hand until there isn't a drop of trust for me left in anyone—not even you."

Eva didn't try to fill the silence. There was too much to process. Her heart swelled, and in that state, it ached as well.

"And if my days are numbered, which that sanadero pretty much confirmed, I wanted to indulge, just a little bit. I wanted to see what it would feel like. I decided to take what I wanted."

The meaning was as clear as the moonlit sky that night. Eva stared at her hands, away from his gaze, as her chest warmed.

"And I know I could lie and blame it all on the tiniebla and continue with this act, making excuses for my behavior, until my mind is gone. But the truth is I've been a bastard, and I'm sorry. It would be untrue to blame the tiniebla for everything."

She glanced up, surprised, her mouth sagging a little.

"I'm sorry for hitting you. I'm sorry for letting it take over all those times it did. I'm fucking sorry for staining my hands with Celeste's blood. I'm sorry for being cruel to you. For not being truthful of my intentions and tricking you into marrying me. For laughing at your expense and chipping away at your hope for what we were supposed to be."

He sighed and Eva trembled. There was honesty in his words, finally. It was what she'd always wanted.

He let go and dug his fingers in his hair, hunching. His tail curled behind him. "*Fuck*—and I ruined it! I'm a bastard. It's all I've known. It's what I've always been. Until I met you, I didn't know how else to be. The truth is...sometimes the right words could be right there in front of me, but it feels good to say the wrong ones."

After meeting Enrique, Eva could see how Javier became this way. If the Águilas thrived only by kicking those beneath them, then he'd been built precisely as intended.

"And you changed me, did you know that? You made me care about doing the right thing."

A smile tugged at her lips. He flinched when she grazed his shoulder.

"Javier."

His despair was palpable as he met her gaze. The weight of his curse. Everyone's scorn, which was well deserved, if Eva was being honest. The lack of trust that had tainted their first kiss.

Her heart raced before the words rolled out of her. "I accept your apology." She offered a meek smile. "I think Maior and Reina have already forgiven you as well."

He frowned, but nodded.

Her hand crawled to his lap. She wanted this closeness. She wanted to hear him say again and again how she felt good to him. It was just her pride keeping her away.

"And I'm sorry for trying to take control of you," she muttered. "It was a violation of your freedom. I was a villain, too."

His teeth were white and straight in his wicked smile.

In this regard, they were meant for each other. Two villains trapped in a plot of their own design.

"I never needed you to apologize. I deserved it." He leaned closer. His lips were but a breath away. "So, can we do it again?"

Eva was robbed of words.

"This time, right," he said, "with your permission."

The message was clear. She held all the power, exactly how she liked it. So, she bridged the gap between them and gave him her lips. He took them greedily.

Pressed against her, he muttered, "And again?"

She became butter. She was all sensation. She was fire and light. And she wanted it so much.

"Again?" he repeated after their lips parted for air.

She grabbed his jaw and said, "Shut up and yes."

JAVIER ARMANDO ÁGUILA DE BRAVO

30

Toying with Sin

It wasn't hard for Maior to keep a wall up, as Reina didn't return to bed until late that night. The galio tonic kept her awake. She'd taken it with no intention of surrendering to another one of *those* dreams. She couldn't close her eyes without seeing Enrique, the painful longing on his face as he stared at Laurel's ghost. She couldn't let go of the truth forced out of Eva's lips: Reina had chosen to keep her in the dark about Ches. When Reina returned, winded and sweaty from what Maior could only surmise was another arduous raid against tinieblas, Maior merely faked her soft, snoozing breaths, until Reina crept under the sheets and gave in to her weariness with ease.

Then Maior wept quietly to herself.

She didn't try to abate the tears. She let the emotions run through her, for it'd been an exhausting day. In a way, Enrique wasn't the one who frightened her the most anymore. His desires were barbaric but evident. No. Maior's tears welled from the heartache of betrayal, of being wounded by those she loved the most: the Virgin, Eva, and Reina.

All this time, Maior had lived in blissful ignorance, glued to Reina's web of lies. And Maior was the foolish one for it. Since their first encounter, Reina had never hidden her deceptive nature. She had always been up-front that her actions were guided by veiled motivations. Maior was the lovesick idiot for assuming Reina would change for her.

Maior hugged herself, careful to keep her sobs tight and small. She hushed as Reina stirred, but Reina's tiredness was too deep.

Eva also hadn't deemed Maior worthy of her secrets. A sanadero had to force the truth out of her. Did Eva assume Maior would judge her? Did Reina?

Maior choked as she realized they all saw her as some mindless fanatic, so entrenched in the Pentimiento faith that she couldn't be trusted with their secrets. Eva, Maior understood. But Reina? She bit down another sob.

Perhaps they were right. Maior gave daily prayers to the Virgin. She followed the path prescribed in the holy book, forgiving and withholding judgment of others. She volunteered her time and skills as a form of worship. Yet the one thing she wanted the most, her cleansing from Laurel's oppression, the Virgin refused her.

Have you tried praying yet?

Don Juan's words echoed in her mind, and she wept more.

The next morning, Maior didn't have to pretend all was well, nor hide her puffy eyes as Reina woke with the dawn. Reina snaked out of bed, quiet as ever, and disappeared from Casa Bravo as she always did in the mornings. Where she once assumed Reina had gone to train, now Maior was filled with doubt. Where was Reina spending her time? Why did she always return with blisters like sunburns on her arms? How appropriate, for someone hosting the ancient god of the sun.

After helping to knead and shape a generous amount of arepas for the household, Maior returned to her room. She carefully mixed the last of her collected spiderwebs into a new galio tincture. In a clear, crystal vial, she let the silvery threads disappear into solution, imagining them serving as ropes and tethers for mending Javier's bones. Most of the grueling resetting work, she'd done the night before. But she prepared a new vial for good measure.

Javier was alone when she knocked and welcomed herself into his room.

"Eva's gone to the vault," he explained.

Javier ferried a chair to his bedroom desk and offered it to her before sitting on the nearby bed's edge. He wore a loose shirt and casual pants. And for someone who'd grown a tail and had his hands brutalized, he seemed in good spirits.

The shirt allowed easy access to his chest, where Maior checked his cuts. The injuries were sealed, thanks to the galio ointment she'd applied the night before, though crude blue-and-black scabs had taken their place.

"Are you all right?" he asked. "Your eyes—"

Heat crept to Maior's cheeks, and to the corners of her eyes again, but she swallowed it away. "Allergies," she lied.

He watched her in silence while she unwrapped the bandages, as if he didn't buy it. But he said nothing more.

His hands were bruised black, stark against the paleness of his forearm. Maior took each wrist and noticed how he winced as she rotated the joints, testing. Her galio healing expedited his recovery. But it would be a long time before he could move his hands without pain. Perhaps longer before he could handle a quill or needle with dexterous precision.

Part of her ached to apologize. She was at fault for his injuries. If she hadn't frozen up like a mouse before two cats, it wouldn't have happened. Nothing good came to her when she was frightened. As she noticed his tail flicking and coiling as a visible manifestation of his pain, Maior's heart wrung with guilt. How could she ever erase her own contributions to yesterday's events? Javier had paid a steep price for her indecisiveness.

She couldn't idle any longer. She couldn't wait for Reina to deem her worthy of sharing her secrets. She couldn't be so useless to need Javier's and Reina's constant protection. She couldn't await the Virgin's mercy, when it was so obvious She—or *Arca*—was unwilling to give it.

Maior had once escaped Águila Manor with a pair of litio rings. If she hadn't taken the risk, she likely would have ended up with her throat slit by Doña Ursulina's sacrificial knife. The situation would only get worse; more people would get hurt. She had to take matters into her own hands.

"You're quite the adept geomancer," Javier said as Maior tightened a fresh roll of bandage around his left hand. "You might one day surpass me."

Maior snorted playfully. "Perhaps I already have."

He tipped his chin. She knew the agreement was just a lie.

"I wanted to thank you for protecting me against Enrique. I know Reina already thanked you, but it's I who should be grateful."

He looked away to the window. "You're welcome, but I didn't just do it out of loyalty or duty. I hate Enrique."

She smiled. "We have that in common." She fastened a clip on the right-hand bandage. "Do you think he wants to kill me?" She searched his red eyes. They were exactly like his brother's.

Javier hesitated, as if measuring his words. "He wants his wife back."

"And if I die, he'll never have that. Ever. I'm his only chance."

He frowned, studying her. "He loved Laurel more than anything."

Maior stared down at Javier's hands. His fingernails had morphed to soot-colored talons, his turning hastened because of her. "And he hasn't moved on," she muttered to herself.

"I suppose he didn't allow himself any room to mourn her. He always believed he'd get her back." Javier leaned back to stare out the window, where a diligent gardener was trimming the jasmine. "For two years he was completely possessed by the idea, as if he knew her return was...inevitable."

Maior's heart skipped. Dread twisted her belly. Her palms grew clammy and wet as she said, "What if I turn myself in, return to Águila Manor?"

Javier cleared his throat like he'd swallowed something spicy. Color blotched his neck. "You can't be serious."

Maior leaned forward. His uncertainty fueled her. The words were dangerous because the path was plausible. "You heard Don Juan—the only thing that can break your curse is Laurel's remains."

"You're not doing this for me."

Maior smiled. "You're right. I'll also be cleansed of her, with her remains. I confirmed it with Don Juan when I was helping him into the carriage."

Javier winced.

"Laurel cursed you, and she haunts me. Both can be resolved with her bones."

"I get it. That's our solution—"

"Laurel's grave is in Águila Manor, right?"

"Yes."

Maior said, "Then it's impossible for either you or Eva to get anywhere near it. You'll need a miracle to access her."

Javier scowled. She gently pet his bandaged hand. "I'm sorry, but you know I'm right. But if I turn myself in, Enrique will send me back. I'm sure he has access to Gegania by now." Her heart beat feverishly as she said, "He won't keep me here, where the Liberator or Reina can try to negotiate for me—"

"Reina will raise hell. She'll gut me."

Maior smiled sadly. He was right. But Maior wasn't Reina's doll, to be dragged here and there, useful only to warm her bed while she withheld the most shocking truth of all.

"No, because your job will be to convince them to get me back. Once I'm in Águila Manor, Reina will see no other choice but to come for me, right? Meanwhile, I'll be there, *getting Laurel*." Maior's palms became clammy at the mere thought of the sin she was considering. But she was out of options, and Javier was out of time. "I'll be safe because Enrique will probably stay here pretending to care about the tiniebla uprising. He'll head back only once everything blows over, right?"

"You don't fear Enrique?"

"I hate being tied to Laurel more. And...I don't want to explain." Both Eva and Reina already minimized her pain. She saw no reason why Javier would behave differently. Just because her life wasn't in immediate, physical danger, it didn't mean that she didn't suffer, imprisoned in her own mind. Besides, she didn't owe them complete honesty, when they didn't give theirs.

Javier waited, giving her the space to change her mind. How odd it was, to see concern etched across his Águila eyes. And it struck her then: Not once had he acknowledged Laurel's image. This whole time...he'd exhibited incredible restraint.

Maior kneaded her hands. Perhaps he was worthy of trust, but she couldn't stomach opening up about the dreams. She couldn't ruin his morning by admitting she'd seen exactly how he'd been cursed.

"We both know he's obsessed with Laurel," she said. "If he harms me, he won't get her back."

Javier's grimace was unabated. "I nearly lost my life protecting you."

Maior's big eyes trained on his. He was right. But so was she. "And I'm grateful, but it only gives me more reason to do it. I don't want anyone else getting hurt because of me. Enrique is like a bull. No one can get in his way. I know this is insane—"

"It's suicidal."

Maior shook her head. "We don't have to act now. I—I just can't wait forever." The corners of her eyes prickled. The tears weren't through with her.

He nodded, and there was belief in his face. He respected her plan and resolve. The realization cleared those tears from her eyes.

Casa Bravo was quiet in the late morning. A troupial's song filled the courtyards and open corridors. Soft breezes kept the house cool. Everyone was busy and absent, with Eva and Javier hidden in their family vault, Don Samón and Maria Elena politicking about La Parroquia, and again Reina nowhere to be seen.

Maior cloistered herself within the vast residence. The thought of returning to the cabildo to rejoin Las Orquídeas Blancas filled her with anxiety. She was too brittle and vulnerable. If she returned, she could run into Enrique again. She had a plan, sure, but she needed to gather the fortitude to set it in motion.

She helped Doña Tomasa wash and hang laundry up to dry, to keep herself busy. Then, as she returned to her room with a fresh set of sheets, she found Reina sitting on the bed's edge, braiding her recently washed hair.

Reina reached for Maior's wrist, but Maior evaded her. "Did you have a productive morning?" Maior said. A useless question that would receive only a half truth.

Reina flexed her forearm. "I grow stronger."

"Whatever for?"

Reina grabbed Maior anyway and brought her closer. "To slay anyone who would harm you." She looked deeply into Maior's eyes. "Are you still thinking about Enrique? Are you all right?"

Maior avoided Reina's eyes. "He's never going to give me up."

"And neither will I."

Maior peeled herself from the embrace. The words softened Maior's edges. She was enamored by the implication, but they were unable to patch up the hollow in her belly. As long as she didn't have Reina's honesty, she would never be whole.

Maior sat beside her. She reached for Reina's tail, which was always docile in her grasp. Maior liked coiling the curls at the tip. The hair was so soft and shiny.

"The sanadero said some unsettling things, when we visited his house," Maior said, fishing. "He confirmed what the Orquídeas say: The gods of the sun and the Void walk among us. They possess someone, like Laurel possesses me."

She took in Reina's eyes. They were a soft brown, both sour and sweet like tamarind, dilating as they withheld the truth Maior now knew. Maior held her breath, waiting. Here she presented Reina another chance on a silver platter.

But instead of taking it—instead of being true and honest, as Maior so desperately wanted her to—Reina grabbed Maior's hands and said, "Have you heard of the Dancing Devils?"

Maior deflated. "No."

Reina ran her hands along Maior's forearms, squeezing, the desire evident in her massaging fingertips. The effect was completely lost in Maior's disbelief.

"It's a big celebration here in Segolita," Reina said. "The whole city floods with dancing people wearing red outfits." She smiled. "Any red you own will do. It's a big Penitent tradition. At the end of the procession, you end up at one of the churches, where you make a promise to the Virgin. She's supposed to answer your prayer in exchange for the promise."

A brightness sparked in Maior's chest. Her eyebrows rose.

"Can I take you tomorrow?" Reina offered, her gaze finding Maior's lips. "You can speak to the Virgin about Laurel. You can make a promise. I'm sure She will listen to you. Would you like to try that?"

Warm tears pooled in the corners of Maior's eyes. Reina gently gathered them with her thumbs and wiped them away. She kissed Maior's forehead.

Maior gave in. And she knew she was wicked for conceiving such a plan. Unearthing Laurel meant violating every good moral the Virgin had taught her. Of course the Virgin would withhold Her cleansing blessing, if She predicted how easily Maior would give in to darkness.

"I cannot stand the parties," Reina said. "They are...not for me. But I'll go for you."

Maior squeezed Reina, who held her. Maior could feel the fluttering rhythm of Reina's heart. Despite the dishonest undercurrent souring this moment, Maior couldn't ignore how strongly her own heart blazed for her. In Reina's embrace, Maior could forget everything. She could *forgive* anything. Maybe Reina wasn't ready to be honest. Maybe she was working up the courage, and Maior just needed to give her time.

"We can try that," Maior said with words muffled by Reina's shirt. "Don Juan said if the Virgin wills it, then I can be cured of Laurel."

Not just the Virgin, but any deity, in fact.

Maior realized she hadn't an inkling of what Reina's relationship with Ches was like. Did he haunt her dreams, like Laurel haunted Maior's? Was he here now, watching them snake their arms around each other, as their clothes became a burdensome barrier—as Reina unraveled Maior's dress and worshipped her skin?

And what was so wrong with Maior, that every god turned a blind eye?

31

The Dancing Devils

Sweat trickled down Reina's shoulders. The breezes were a reprieve to the blisters on her skin, which felt ready to pop under the merciless morning sun. Reina didn't shy away from the pain. She knew this was the price to pay anytime she skulked away to the jungles, as dawn broke over the horizon, where she stretched her endurance of Duality.

This had become her routine. A ritual: pain, followed by the thrill of strength, which every day became more permanent. Her shoulders and arms were knotted and sharp. Her legs had grown powerful and nimble, even without bismuto's enhancement. Sometimes, she thought back to the miserable thing she'd been when she left Segolita. Seeing how far she'd come brought her great satisfaction.

Swollen with Duality, Reina scoured the jungles for tinieblas. She was excellent at slaying them. Every swing and decapitation was an offering to her god. She was the light, and the tinieblas were the shadows to be vanquished by her hand.

But the number of tinieblas grew every morning. When she'd started these practices, Reina had to hike deep into the morichales to find the first one. Now, a good dozen always prowled near the city walls, beyond the river that snaked into Segolita. The tinieblas seemed endless, their oppression showing in the weary faces of the soldiers posted about the city walls. Every day, there was a new raid. Reina participated during the afternoons and evenings, representing the Liberator's commitment to Segolita's safety. But the battles were a mere bandage on the true problem. At this rate, Reina feared one day she might be forced to reveal her Duality to the soldiers who fought alongside her.

That morning, as Duality blazed through her mind, she asked Ches, "*Why don't you speak to me?*" She was thinking of Eva, who'd asserted that Rahmagut whispered in her ear at all times.

"*Would you have me behave like a mortal, giving orders to cover for my insecurities and inability to act on my own?*" he asked, scornful. "*Would you have me beg you to act as my hand? I do not ask. I merely take, if I wish to.*"

"*But you haven't taken.*" Reina knew she was insolent, but she also trusted him to be reasonable.

"*That is because your mortal plights do not concern me. Now focus on Duality—I command you to hasten your mastery. Once you overcome this step, then you shall be worthy of addressing me.*"

Reina practiced for another hour perhaps, for it was all her body could handle before black dots impeded her vision. Sweaty and tired, Reina returned to Casa Bravo.

The scent of buttery mantecadas gave her pause at the edge of the outdoor kitchen. Amid the bustle of the baker and the maids, her gaze found a certain short, black-haired woman. The source of her happiness, was all Reina could think as she watched Maior's floury hands ferry the tin sheets to the wood-fired oven. A flush of red from the kitchen's heat colored Maior's cheeks, and her cream apron was dusted white in flours and sugars. She was in her element. And Reina was happy to see her happy.

A shuddery breath left Reina as she imagined their future: A warm kitchen, the air spiced from the medley of ingredients bubbling on its central hearth. A dog, maybe, circling their legs in search of scraps. A house sitting amid the mango trees of Tierra'e Sol, with chirping parakeets and scuttling iguanas as their only neighbors. And the inner peace of knowing no caudillo or tiniebla would burst through their doors to take or destroy the humble nothings she and Maior had worked hard to obtain for themselves.

"Reina," Maior said, snapping Reina out of her daydreams. She wore the dark circles of exhaustion under her eyes. Again, she hadn't slept.

Maior patted Reina on the cheek. "What's that look about?"

Reina wiped the smile from her lips. "Nothing."

Maior wrinkled her nose. "Go wash. You smell like a chigüire."

Reina wished she could steal a kiss, but Casa Bravo was filled with women like Doña Tomasa, who already gave Reina mean looks for being nozariel yet enjoying the comforts of staying as a guest. The last thing she wanted was to give them reasons to inconvenience or outright shun Maior.

Maior squeezed Reina's hand before she could walk away. "We'll go to the Dancing Devils after?"

Reina sucked in a discomforted breath, but nodded. She wasn't sure if any promise or prayer would serve as a solution, but Reina was willing to endure the celebration if it brought Maior happiness.

"Just temper your expectations, all right?" Reina said gently.

Maior glared with weary eyes. The animosity threw Reina off guard. Was this from exhaustion, or something else entirely?

"But I'm hopeful something good will come of it," Reina added to appease her.

The words rang hollow as Maior shook her head and returned to the baking.

Reina retreated to her quarter with a tightening in her chest. The future she envisioned felt so real and within grasp. She already had the most important aspect: Maior, who was perfect for Reina in every way, with or without Laurel. She had the house she was building in Tierra'e Sol. The last component was the most crucial and hardest to procure: their peace, achievable only once Reina solved the problem of the tinieblas and eliminated Enrique's threats. Either by exorcising Laurel, or with his death.

Thankfully, Reina's hands knew how to achieve the latter.

After cleaning up and breaking fast with mantecadas, Reina ran into Eva in the drawing room. The woman sat in the shadows, biting her nails as she stared at the merriment beginning to awaken on the streets.

Reina cleared her throat, announcing herself. "How is Javier?"

Eva shrugged. "Nowhere closer to breaking his curse. I don't think the solution is in this city."

Reina searched within herself, yet she couldn't scrape very much compassion for him. "You look tired," she muttered.

"Yes—well, I've been spending all my nights in my father's library looking for a curse breaker."

"Have you found anything on the topic of tinieblas?"

Eva wrinkled her nose with displeasure. "Not exactly. I just keep finding books about conquest. It's weird how the old books are so shameless in logging all the valcos, nozariels, and yares that the Segoleans slaughtered. They're so proud of their genocide."

Reina snorted. "I heard talk of what was discussed about the tinieblas at the junta," she said. "There were no useful ideas. Just bickering between caudillos."

Eva blew at her own bangs, exasperated. "Are we wasting our time?"

On the contrary, Reina was biding hers. Growing stronger until she felt confident enough to murder Enrique in his sleep.

"I heard someone had the brilliant idea about sending a crew of hunters to murder all animals so that no new tinieblas could have the opportunity to spawn," Reina offered with her arms crossed, her tone acid at the idea's stupidity.

Eva grimaced. "How— That's mad."

"A waste of time, honestly," Reina said.

"We should be studying them," Eva said. "We should figure out what they're after, really. If it's just hearts, why unite as hordes? And why Segolita?"

Reina took her in: The gold bands around her fingers encapsulating geomancia solutions, her neck holding an iridio pendant. The blackened antlers and her curls floating about her, as if defying the downward pull of gravity. If Reina closed her eyes, she knew she'd be able to sense Eva without hearing or touching her. Eva's presence would blare even within the metaphysical. Perhaps it was her strength, absorbing the energy in the air like a void, representative of the entity she housed. Reina remembered Ches's words and shuddered.

"Javier has a tiniebla in him," Reina said.

Eva nodded. "And as time passes it gets worse. He's changing too fast."

"Can you ask it what it wants?"

Eva stared at her boots. "The tiniebla is a darkness. It speaks because Javier has intelligence."

"Not because its intelligence is inherent," Reina supplied, understanding.

"Exactly. But I can't ask Javier to let go. I'm afraid of how he changes anytime that happens. I don't think we'd be able to comprehend a pure tiniebla. I don't think it has the sentience to speak."

"It's all instinct."

"But I can control them." Eva paused, and her cheeks reddened at the admission. Reina understood the taboo, and Eva's hesitation, so she offered her an encouraging nod. It emboldened Eva to say, "I can capture one. Or a couple. We can see how they behave in a controlled way. We can see what they're after."

The drawing room was bloated with silence as Eva's eyes searched Reina's. Undoubtedly, Eva was considering the consequences of this sin they were discussing. It made Reina think of Doña Ursulina, and her darkness.

"It could give us some kind of clue . . . but my father would hate to see it."

Reina understood. Don Samón's penchant for patience was proving to be an irritation. While he'd been angered by Enrique's attempt to snatch Maior away, once again he'd advised Reina to wait. He'd put her on standby, tightening her leash with excuses of talking it out. But was he so ignorant of Enrique's true nature? *No*—rather, Reina was doubting whether Don Samón cared. He'd abandoned Eva's mother for the benefit of the many. Why would he prioritize Maior's happiness over his alliance with Enrique? Reina swallowed the thoughts with difficulty, her blood simmering as it did when she'd left him in anger.

"Don Samón doesn't have to know," Reina said, peeking down the corridor to make sure no one could hear their plotting. "I kill tinieblas every day. More keep coming for the city, and that number increases the longer we sit here doing nothing."

The way Eva's throat bobbed was almost endearing. "So you think I should do it? I shouldn't wait for my father's permission?"

Agreement burned in their gazes.

"It's just a matter of where you can hide them," Reina said.

Eva stared at the people crossing the streets, all dressed in red. "There is a place...in this house. The vault. Only family is allowed to go down there. But that makes it perfect, because I can keep them there and no one will see them."

The plan clicked into place sooner than Reina could have predicted. It was so simple she couldn't believe she hadn't considered it before. "The Dancing Devils is today," Reina offered. "They'll be starting within the hour. People will be flocking to the churches. During the procession, most streets will be empty. There will be dancing in the evening. Everyone will be out of the way when you return. And besides, no one should be burning bismuto. This can stay between us."

Eva scratched her forearm rash. Her fingernails came up red as she split the skin.

"If things turn sour, I can just destroy them," Reina said. A pair of tinieblas might have been a concern for past her, but not anymore.

Eva rose to meet Reina eye to eye. "It's for a purpose. The people of Segolita—and Javier's life," she said.

"You don't have to explain it to me. I'm with you completely."

They sorted out the details in a bounce of ideas, before Maior entered the room dressed in a dyed-red shirt and her hair up in two pigtails bound by red ribbons. The carved Virgin Reina had gifted her rested against her bosom, never replaced. Reina beamed. Again, she was struck with the desire to kiss her. This time, she didn't hesitate.

The Dancing Devils was a regional celebration of Segolita, occurring once a year, starting at noon with hours of reverence for the Virgin and culminating in more parties in the evening.

The beat of drums came faintly in the distance as Maior and Reina left La Parroquia for a smaller neighborhood. The intention was to join a procession heading to a church other than the cathedral, and hopefully avoid crossing paths with Enrique. Often, Maior's pinky would brush against Reina's, and she knew Maior did it on purpose. Reina glanced down, met Maior's smiling eyes, and looked away as her belly tingled in delight. Her fingers ached to take Maior's whole hand. No, actually, they ached to make Maior hers once again. How she'd much rather be hidden behind the curtains of their room than be stuck repeating endless prayers to a goddess who often forgot about her existence. But for Maior, she would endure it.

Upon turning a corner, they came across a mass of people in red. Volunteers exited a community center wearing red masks of wide-eyed, sharp-fanged, and black-horned grinning devils.

A pang of nostalgia hit Reina. For a second, she was transported to a similarly sunny and hot day, when she stood under the shade of Doña Florinda's mamoncillo holding her father's hand, waiting for the devils to begin their dance. In her mouth was the sweetness of the melcocha her father had bought her from a street vendor. She'd been happy, in those days. Now most memories of Juan Vicente felt like a fever dream, suppressed beneath her hatred for what the city became for her after his passing.

Reina spotted a melcocha vendor by the street corner, a boy hardly older than ten. She detoured to the him and brightened his smile by paying twice the asking price for a stick of the twirled brown sugarcane sweet. Maior's eyes brightened as her lips sucked on the molasses.

Doing this had become a sport: showing Maior the new foods and customs of Segolita, demonstrating how the capital of the former colony was a mixture of human and nozariel cultures. And through Maior's eyes, Reina saw the city in a new light. She was rediscovering beauty in places where she used to see only pain. Or maybe Maior's light was so incandescent that Reina had no choice but to take in the world with a different lens.

Reina's heart swelled. Finally, she couldn't help herself any longer. She squeezed Maior's shoulders and kissed her on the crown of her head.

Paper flags of goldenrod, cerulean, and scarlet flapped overhead, strung from rope crisscrossing the streets. The decorations were a familiar sight. What wasn't familiar were the black banners with white orchids stitched at their center, erected by the devout acolytes of Las Orquídeas Blancas. As people streamed out of their homes to join the Dancing Devils' throng, they crossed themselves while they passed the black banners.

Reina narrowed her eyes, uncomfortable with how much influence Las Orquídeas Blancas had amassed already.

"They're handing out maracas." Maior pointed to the boys flitting through the crowd giving instruments to anyone wishing to participate. One approached Maior and handed her one, as she was dressed in red.

"You're supposed to shake it in your left hand, to ward off evil," Reina explained. With her hand on the sheathed Nightcleaver, she must have appeared too intimidating to be handed one as well. For this, she couldn't complain.

Two men walked behind her, jeering, and Reina picked up on the words, which made the tips of her ears burn.

"Girl's got a tail."

"Aye. Maybe she ought to be at the front, with one of 'em masks. Give that tail some purpose, for once."

Maior shot the men a mean look. They didn't notice, which was just as well, for Reina wasn't in the mood to get in a fight.

With red cheeks, Maior said, "How could you let them get away with that?"

"I'm tired."

"*Tired?*"

"This whole city hates tails. Humans hate tails. *Nozariels* hate tails." She was the prime example: All it did was give her headaches in moments like these. It wasn't just the tails either. Their nozariel marks were better off staying concealed. "Do you want me to pick a fight with every single person here?"

Maior pointed farther up the procession, where one of the masked dancers had a red tail stitched to his costume. "They have tails."

Reina tucked Maior's hair behind her ear as she said, "Mi amor, that's the point."

They reached the first stop of the procession, sparing Reina from having to explain herself. A house decorated with flapping flags of the nation's tricolor. There stood a holy man dressed in red. The masked dancers pushed forward and knelt before the holy man, who initiated prayers.

To Maior's ear, Reina whispered, "They're supposed to shed the devil parts."

The costumed dancers detached their paper wings. Reina knew they were supposed to represent the yares' wings. The wings, the tails, the horned mask to which some people even attached antlers. The meaning was not lost on her: Pray to the Virgin, welcome Her into your life, and you, too, shall be cleansed of the devilish attributes of your ancestors.

Maior watched the stripping of wings quietly. She hesitated for a moment, her brows bunching with a myriad of thoughts she never voiced. In the end, she joined the prayers anyway. And there was no need to teach her those. The Penitent litanies were the same in the Llanos, in Tierra'e Sol, and in the Páramo.

Reina grew even hotter as the procession continued under the high noon sun, the masked dancers leading the festivities. The musicians slapped the leather tops of their drums in a rhythm the maracas picked up. Throngs of red-dressed revelers surrounded them, twirling and stomping on their espadrilles.

Did Reina have a right to feel betrayed? She understood Maior desperately wanted her Virgin's blessing to rid herself of Laurel's ghost. But Maior still swallowed the tradition without objection, as if its foundation wasn't built entirely on an othering of Reina's kind. This acquiescence . . . it left Reina burning.

The crowd stopped in the next station, where a different holy man said some words, igniting the ripping off of the dancers' tails.

Reina could feel the eyes of the people surrounding her. She could feel their wordless chastisement: How dare she walk around with a tail intact? She crossed her arms, discomfort pouring out of her like the sweat drenching her back.

Was she a fool for enduring this for Maior's sake? Did this mean they were fundamentally incompatible? And what did that say about Reina, if time and time again she latched on to people who deep down believed she was born wrong?

Her hatred for Segolita resurfaced as they approached the town square facing the church at the end of the procession. The crowd had nearly quadrupled in size. Shoulders bumped against hers. Someone shoved Maior, and in her anger, Reina did nothing to tug her to safety.

In front of the church stood the parish priest. He raised his hands to the crowd and gave the final blessing, inviting the dancers to come into the Virgin's light. The dancers shed their devil masks, kneeling and giving one more prayer, finalizing their transformation back to a human appearance.

"You have to make a promise now," Reina told Maior bitterly. Maior's mouth hung open in surprise, so Reina clarified, "To the Virgin's altar. Make a promise that you'll give up something in exchange for Her exorcising Laurel. It has to be a worthy sacrifice."

Reina ground her teeth. Would Maior's promise involve giving Reina up, if such was the price to separate her from Laurel?

Instead of following the stream of revelers going into the church, Maior snaked her hand into Reina's crossed arms. "I don't want to go in," Maior said. She unlatched Reina's arms and entwined her fingers within Reina's grip, meeting Reina's resistance. "My relationship with the Virgin doesn't include praying for changing the way certain people are."

"You pick and choose what to pray for and believe in? Doesn't that invalidate its truth—its authority?"

Maior gestured at the crowd growing within the church. "I just distrust their interpretation. It doesn't have to be the law of the land. They can be wrong." She squeezed Reina's hand in hers, as if to make a point, the sweat on their palms merging, sticky.

"And you believe your way is the right way—not theirs?"

Maior tugged Reina's hand and forced Reina to meet her eyes. "Reina, are you trying to bait me? Do you want me to say that just because I'm a Penitent I find you wrong or repugnant?"

The tips of Reina's ears burned.

"Because that couldn't be further from the truth. I am completely and utterly yours and I don't care that you're nozariel. I *love* your tail and your ears and your nose and all your little quirks, and I just wish you would stop hating yourself over it so much."

"I'm not making myself hate it—*they are*!" She waved a hand at the people behind them, who, in the noise of the celebration, didn't notice their argument.

Maior's eyes doubled in size. She yanked Reina's hand again like she was pulling the ear of a petulant child. "They don't have power over us, or over you. Soon enough we'll go back to Tierra'e Sol and you can forget all about this city. None of it matters."

Maior gave her hand another tug, milder this time, and said, "Look at me."

Reina obeyed. Her heart hammered in her chest as she plunged into the depths of Maior's eyes. In them, she drowned. She took in the hot indignation that swirled in their color, which always reminded Reina of the bottom of a rum barrel. Robust, with the sweet promise of sugarcane.

"We matter, right?"

Reina's heartbeats deafened her ears.

"I matter?" Maior muttered.

Reina wanted to howl that she was her everything. "Of course."

"Then trust me when I say you are perfect the way you are? Except maybe for your stubbornness."

Reina smiled. It was her turn to tug Maior's hand. Stars were born and exploded in her chest as Reina realized how lucky she was to get to hold Maior's hand like this. To get to have her at all. And indeed, Reina had been unfair for keeping her at arm's length, afraid of being judged for the god she housed and worshipped.

Reina had let her insecurities misjudge Maior. She was ashamed of keeping secrets. She was ashamed of not letting Maior in, as she deserved to.

"I trust you completely," Reina said, wishing they were somewhere private so she could take her in a kiss. "And I haven't been honest with you. There is something—"

"Is that the flush of young love?" A voice rang behind them, seizing the moment from Reina.

Reina shook Maior's hand free instinctually, as if they had been caught doing something wrong.

She turned to meet the newcomer. But her surprise wasn't unmerited, as she met the hooded green eyes of Esteban the Cat.

32

Sunfire

Her grandfather grinned, catching her speechless. Maior looked between them in confusion.

"I never imagined you were one to join in on the Dancing Devils. I thought Ursulina was devout to...a different kind of god. Is this Juan Vicente's doing?"

"No. I'm not here to pray," Reina said, blushing. "Are you?"

"I came for you."

Maior's bewilderment was even more apparent in the silence that seized Reina.

"You came for me? How did you find me?"

Esteban shrugged, his gray hair swaying with the merciful breeze passing through the plaza. He wore a white linen shirt, sticking out amid the crowd of red-dressed revelers. A large knife was sheathed on his belt, and another was tucked into his right boot. "I tracked you, from Casa Bravo." At the deepening of Reina's frown, he added, "It wasn't hard to figure it out. You're in the service of the Liberator, as you so eloquently informed me the last time we met." He appraised Maior. "And who is this lovely bird?"

Reina's instinct was to step between them. She felt exposed, and she wondered if she'd been a fool for wandering these streets, when someone could so easily take Maior away.

"My name is Maior de Apartaderos. And you are?"

"De Apartaderos, huh? It's been a long time since I set foot in that stone chapel. Esteban the Cat, pleased to make your acquaintance." He doubled over with a little flourish, drawing a smile from Maior. It disarmed Reina.

"That is not a full name," Maior noted.

"To me, names are not important. Anyone who needs to know me will know who Esteban the Cat is."

"He is Juan Vicente's father," Reina said, aware Maior sought his name to place him within the genealogy of Fedrian or Venazian families. A sudden thought struck her: how the name Maior de Duvianos had such a lovely ring to it. Reina bit the inside of her cheek hard, avoiding Maior's eyes.

"Indeed. This cat is Reina's grandfather."

"You said you didn't want anything to do with me."

"I did say that." He shielded his eyes with a hand and gestured to the palm tree flanking the plaza, inviting them to its shade. "Does it surprise you that I'm not as severe as your grandmother? Not everything I say must be the final word. I am allowed to change my mind."

Reina was robbed of words. Maior beamed, as if reacting in Reina's stead.

"You, on the other hand, seem to be following in Ursulina's footsteps," Esteban said, his shrewd gaze surfing from Reina to Maior. "So is Maior de Apartaderos to you what Feleva was to Ursulina?"

The heat of disagreement returned to Reina's cheeks. "No. We're nothing like them." The answer didn't land well with Maior, so she quickly added, "Maior is my partner, and we're equals."

Esteban's toothy smirk widened, like he'd gotten what he wanted out of her. "I only joke."

"Reina is nothing like Ursulina," Maior said. "I wouldn't be with her if she were."

Reina just stared at her boots. She wanted to believe the words, but she knew darkness lurked within her. Well, now she had the light of her god to right her wrongs...

"No, she isn't," Esteban said. "Ursulina would have never

sought me out in the dregs of the city. She would think it's beneath her, my lifestyle."

"I don't think that at all," Reina said.

"Indeed. Unless you were just desperate to connect with this vagabond." He laughed as she frowned. "Only jokes! Thank you for coming for me, and for giving me the opportunity to make this choice."

He handed her a bundle of correspondence. A stack of rumpled and stained letters, the twirling cursive reminding Reina of a letter she'd received and opened in this very city some years ago. A pang took the air from her. The ache of causing her grandmother's death, which she had buried deep within, resurfaced and burned anew. For a moment, she'd had a family.

"Ursulina's letters," Esteban said. "We exchanged correspondence for years. I wasn't completely ignorant of her exploits. I kept the letters because I feared I would have to answer for one of the many horrible things we did in our youth. Maybe I thought they would prove I wasn't the mastermind. Or maybe I'm just a nostalgic fool." He nodded at the stack. "Take them. They're your inheritance, in a way."

Reina ran her thumb through the worn papers, her heart racing. Her gaze glided over the topmost one:

Esteban,
I debated whether you deserved to hear from me at all...

Reina wanted to run indoors and find a cool shadow in which to lose herself within the letters. They were an insight to her grandmother's past. A peek into the heart Doña Ursulina had guarded so well...

"You wanted to understand the nature of our relationship. How we got to be broken and estranged. Obviously, the letters paint only a partial picture. But I'm here, if you want to ask me directly."

"Why didn't you ever reconnect? Why didn't you ever reach out to her, or to my father?"

Esteban bowed his head. "Ursulina's true love was Feleva, not me. I was an obstacle to that relationship. A reminder of the mistakes we made. Ursulina and I were not fit to be parents. I believe Juan Vicente realized this for himself, when he started his own family and made his own life far from us. I take it he also sought to distance himself from Enrique?"

Reina nodded with a pinched face. Even his name was enough to spark her ire. "I'm glad for that. I lived in his household for only two years and that was more than enough."

He chuckled. "That's exactly how I felt about Feleva, after our relationship imploded." He waved between them. "Reina, you and I, let's start anew. It's what you wanted, no?"

Reina also ached for stability, and Esteban had proved this wasn't his forte. But she nodded.

She could feel the delight radiating off Maior.

"I'll personally chat with the Liberator and see if he has any interest in hiring this old man. If I'm too old for the sword, then maybe I can be of service with the cuatro—"

A scream sundered Esteban's words. More followed, howls and wails compounding from a panic. Reina turned in the direction of the church, where a crowd was amassing outside its stone façade. She summoned the sight of bismuto, thinking tinieblas must have snuck into the city somehow. She thought of Eva and their plan, but Casa Bravo was far from here.

She shoved the letters back into Esteban's hands and pushed through the crowd, past the yelling men and panicking abuelas, picking up their howls of "Open the door! Make way!"

Black smoke curled behind the church, the smell of combustion burrowing itself up Reina's nostrils. It had different notes: incense, wood, fabric. The church was burning from the inside out.

Bloodcurdling screams raised Reina's flesh in goose bumps. She shoved to the entrance and found that its studded door was designed to open inwardly. But the panicked people attempting to push out blocked it, trapping them inside.

She backed away and nearly collided into Maior, who said, "The church is on fire?"

Reina's heart hammered in her chest. She felt a weakness, warning her that a refill of iridio would be needed soon. But the thought was pushed out of her mind as she realized that the immense crowd of revelers who'd gone inside to make their promises had no way of fleeing. In their panic, the crowd had trapped itself within.

"The door's jammed," Esteban muttered behind them. "They're going to cook to death."

Reina ran to the back of the church, where surely there had to be another door. She found the exit jammed shut in the same manner, with an immovable mass of panicked bodies blocking it from the inside.

"Move back!" Reina howled through the door. "Make way!" She rammed the door to no avail. She shot more enhancing bismuto through her muscles, kicking it with all her strength. The door didn't even shudder.

To her left, the window's stained glass exploded. The smell of burning intensified. And the horrified screams.

Reina couldn't handle it anymore. She wasn't thinking. She just needed to act.

She opened her chest to the sun-roaring energy of Duality. Ches awoke within her. He wore her body like a suit, stretching, his power blistering her skin from within. Reina forced her eyes to exist in this moment. She squinted, ignoring the flashing images of the lives lived before and after hers.

"*Save them,*" Ches commanded in agreement.

Reina leapt through one of the windows. The fire lapped her skin, reaching for her clothes. Inside, the church was aglow. Flames consumed the effigy in its center, burning through bouquets of carnations and birds-of-paradise. Bodies littered the farthest edges of the large crowds panicking at both of the blocked doors.

Black smoke stung her eyes and clogged her breathing. Reina crouched beside the closest person and discovered they had merely fainted from the smoke. She hauled the unconscious body over her shoulder, sprinted to the window, and tossed them on the grass. She repeated this extraction three times before she accepted the futility of it.

Maior stood there, among the crowd of helpless spectators, watching Reina. Reina read Maior's lips saying, "There's no time."

The church groaned behind her as the wooden beams support-ing the roof began to give.

Reina couldn't breathe. The people inside were going to burn alive. Every single one of them.

"Let us take down the wall."

Ches was right: If there was no exit, they had to create one themselves.

Reina braced herself before tackling the wall. The stone caved under her brutish mauling. With Duality, her bones were stronger than tempered metal; her skin armored like marble. She rammed herself against the wall where it was fracturing, crashing it open.

Heat from the fire met her head-on, compounded with the scream of supplicants. A miasma welcomed her. The smell of burn-ing flesh slapped Reina across the face as a man screamed from the top of his lungs. He was the first to be consumed by the fire's ire.

With cracked nails, Reina dug the remaining stone out of her way. She kicked and shoved, the stone blistering to the touch. A plume of black smoke whirled out of the new opening, along with the first panicked reveler who noticed the new exit. Someone from the outside witnesses ran to her side. A burly man with the heroic instinct to assist. But it quickly became clear that his attempts amounted to nothing, when Reina was already bursting with the strength of a god.

"Stay back!" she roared as the panicked crowd rerouted in her direction. The words came out with her god's might. She was a snarling jaguar guarding the opening, forcing them into a single file to avoid the crush that had trapped them within in the first place.

Those who could still walk rushed through the wall breach. Some helped the unconscious bodies of the unfortunate who had succumbed to the heat or smoke. Red fabric burned to their skin, their faces soot-stained, the revelers streamed out one by one. Some ran to the arms of family members; others collapsed on the grasses far from the church.

Palpitations shook Reina's chest, the adrenaline wearing down. Finally, she backed away and beheld the cavity's crumbling enormity.

A carving along the church's belly. Reina sucked in one quivery breath after another. She stared at her hands, her abused fingers blistering and bubbling. She couldn't catch her breath. Not from the panic, but in awe, at the enormity of the power she wielded. At the boundless possibilities of Duality and Ches's trust in her.

She was aglow in radiance. Sunlight seeped from her pores. Cones of light extended from her fingertips. A halo enveloped her and made her Duality obvious to the panicked people surrounding the church. There was awe in their eyes, until the sight of her tail seeded them with doubt and fear. Reina found Maior's eyes within the crowd.

In a thunder of flames and brimstone the church's roof collapsed. The remains of the building were seized by the greedy fire. Instead of thinning, the crowd thickened around the perimeter of the smoking destruction, with Reina at the center.

It dawned on her, how she must look. The destruction of their holy grounds with her nozariel body showered in gold before the church's fiery remains. If anything, their stares of terror and wonder were justified.

An elderly woman approached; her ash-stained clothes marking her as one of the survivors. "An angel!" she wailed before throwing herself at Reina's feet. More elderly survivors followed her lead, approaching to worship her. Nevertheless, within the crowd stood one of the carriers of the black banners, and his face was twisted with suspicion. It took him only a moment before he instigated a different tune: "No—a witch! An agent of that pagan demon!"

The crowd vibrated with confusion and disagreement. There were people alight with gratitude, and those who grimaced at the heresy of her glowing body. Behind her, the flames roared in opposition to the arriving firefighters, who chucked buckets of water in an attempt to stop it from spreading farther. The sounds and the chaos—it was dizzying.

Reina exhaled as her knees gave out. The blisters on her skin popped and spilled, staining her clothes with blood. Her cheeks stung from Duality. Her gums quivered, igniting the nerves in her molars.

"*Let go*," Ches commanded. He knew she was at her limit.

The realization lifted her heart to the sky. Her god cared.

Herding the praying grandmothers aside, Maior reached Reina's side and cradled her.

Reina smiled, comforted. There was no one else she would rather have at this moment, as her body gave out from overusing Ches's power.

She was in love.

In the protection of Maior's arms, Reina let go. She burrowed her face into Maior's chest. Maior held her tight while Reina's muscles were taken by spasms. Reina counted the seconds before she could regain the strength to speak and ask for the soothing numbing of galio. She just needed enough healing so she could walk back to the residence and lick her self-inflicted wounds in privacy.

Then a terrible pain seized her. A familiar ache. The smashing of boulders against her chest. She recognized it for what it was: the iridio deficiency making itself known, warning her she was walking an assured path to her end. Reina gritted her teeth and writhed in Maior's arms.

"What's happening?" Maior squeaked.

"*Fuck!*" Reina hugged herself, fighting to contain the agony. "Iridio. It ran out faster than I expected."

Maior's eyes doubled in size. "What? Reina!"

She deserved her chastisement. Her iridio had burned through her without her noticing precisely because of Duality. She groaned.

"What's the matter with her?" Esteban said as he rushed closer.

"She needs iridio—I don't have any." Maior's voice shook with panic. "It's all back in the house."

Reina's screams gave fuel to the people who already wanted to accuse her of plotting against the Virgin and the saints. She couldn't see them, but she could feel them closing in around her, puzzled and fearful of the odd sight. The world was a dizzying haze of pain, but the danger of the situation wasn't lost on Reina. She couldn't let herself perish here. She had to be stronger than this.

Reina opened herself up to Ches's Duality again. She hissed, solar flames corroding her. It was pain on pain on pain, so much she could forget she had a heartache at all. Or maybe with Ches's sunlight, she didn't need the iridio to live. Indeed, with Duality, the devilish, whispering voices were silent.

She pushed herself off Maior, once again aglow. Ches's reproach clutched her throat and warned her: "*You're useless to me as a corpse.*"

"I need to get back to the house," Reina groaned.

Esteban surprised her by lifting her in his arms. Feverishly, Reina smiled and uttered a thanks, glimpsing Esteban as gold-radiant from his use of bismuto.

No one disrupted them on the walk back to Casa Bravo, but they were followed. Reina wasn't so far gone not to notice the gofers who would later charge an escudo or two for the where-abouts of the woman who had mitigated the tragedy at the church.

Surprisingly, the house was empty as Esteban deposited her in her room, where the iridio was stored inside a cool drawer. He waited outside the door while Maior titrated a generous amount into Reina's heart. And Reina sighed with relief, releasing the Duality.

Her joints were swollen. Her skin was bleeding and blistered. Her mouth was parched, and her lips cracked. Reina was nauseated and had an ache in her side. Maybe there was internal damage.

Maior wiped the sweat from Reina's forehead. "Why do you insist on risking your life?"

"Would you have preferred they died?"

The silence between them was a vicious, uncomfortable thing. Normally, Reina craved it. But today she found herself pining for Maior's validation. Then Esteban knocked, shattering the moment. He entered the room and sat on the bed's edge.

"Good. You live," he said.

"I probably wouldn't have made it if it weren't for you," Reina admitted a bit sleepily.

He nodded. "Anything you need, just say the word."

Reina saw the truth in his eyes. He wanted the same as her: Redemption, perhaps. A shot at family.

"All right. How will I find you?"

He shrugged. "I'll find you. And if not, I'm known in these

parts. Esteban the Cat is the name." He placed the stack of letters on the side table, then left with a wink.

Once he was gone, Reina reached for Maior, seeking a kiss, and instead met severe eyes.

"I'm not happy about this," Maior said.

Reina leaned back, weary. "What else would you have me do? You saw how many people were in there."

"I don't know." Maior's tone was a lash. It was the opposite of what Reina deserved. "But I would have chosen you over them." Maior's eyes glistened with the dawn of tears. "How little do you think of me? Just because I have faith in the Virgin doesn't mean I want to trade you for—for some helpless cause—for people who were ready to turn on you!"

Reina stiffened. She was in no mood to explain how little her life mattered in this city. The people's mixed reactions did all the talking. "I couldn't let it happen. I had to act."

Maior waved at the door and said, "Back there you said we were equals, yet this is the first time I see you doing that—exerting yourself that way. This is the first time I see you not supplying yourself with iridio like you're supposed to."

Maior was right, and thus no reply was adequate. Reina chose silence.

"And I have given you so much patience and *so many chances*, yet you refused to be honest with me—you refuse to tell me the most important truth about you: that you are the one who is host to Ches."

The heat of shame crept into Reina.

"That is why you come to me every morning with blisters and burns," Maior barked. "Even Eva trusted me enough to tell me about herself. And yet, you—*you*—" Maior glanced about the room, as if grappling for the right words. "You who are supposed to be my lover. The only person with whom I've shared myself *entirely*. You can't even trust me enough to tell me this?"

Seconds passed as Maior waited for an answer. Reina's chest throbbed with a new ache.

"I . . . I planned to tell you."

"*When?*" Maior howled.

The hot sting of tears clawed at the corners of Reina's eyes. Her heart fluttered in fear. By Ches, what had she done?

"Today—Esteban interrupted me—"

"How convenient. And why did it take you so long to trust me, Reina?" Maior's tears broke loose. Her cheeks glimmered with the sadness Reina herself had painted there. "Why didn't you tell me sooner, before I had to watch you nearly kill yourself at that church today?"

Reina ached to wipe Maior's tears. How she wanted to kiss them away, beg for forgiveness. She couldn't bear being the source of them. "I—I wasn't sure—you don't believe in Ches."

Maior's eyebrows shot up. "I was almost sacrificed to Rahma-gut's legend. Why wouldn't I believe in Ches?"

"Penitents think he's a false god."

"And I'm a good little Penitent, right? I was going to turn you in to Las Orquídeas Blancas once I found out?"

Reina groaned. "That's not why."

"Enlighten me!" Maior cheeks were an angry red color.

Reina glanced away, feeling every bit a fool for cowering in this moment. She could slay tinieblas and scorch her body with Duality, but receiving Maior's anger was much worse. "Did you forget that I'm completely alone?" Reina said, and Maior's cheeks flushed redder. "You're all I have. And I'm terrified of losing you." It was such a simple truth. Yet it took so much courage to say it.

Maior backed down.

"I didn't tell you immediately because I didn't know how far we would go. I was distrusting and broken after Celeste and Doña Ursulina twisted a knife in my heart. It's made it hard for me to give my full trust to anyone." Reina swallowed away whatever tears threatened to get in the way of her confession. "But you've earned my trust. You're nothing like the people who've hurt me in past. Actually: You're the person who matters to me most. And yes, I continued to hesitate because being host to Ches, it means I have a burden to bear. It means that I couldn't just ignore all those people today, and that I must push my body, to make it worthy of his power. I hesitated—like a fool, I know—but I wanted to make sure you weren't going to change your mind about me before I dumped another reason why I'm an oddity on you."

A broken laugh burst from Maior. "Change my mind? You fool." She drew closer. The walls between them crumbled. "Do you think I'd be in this horrible city if changing my mind was a possibility?" She tried to squeeze Reina's cheeks, but her skin was too raw, and Reina winced. With a sad look, Maior pulled away. "I'm not angry because you host a god. I'm angry because we're supposed to be a team, and you're not treating me as an equal."

Reina endured the pain of her blisters to grab Maior's hands. She craved touching her. She never wanted to let go. "I'm so sorry for keeping you in the dark."

"If you must use his power—if you must injure yourself—"

"It's only temporary! Every time it gets easier to handle. One day I'll be able to use it without any pain at all." Reina reached deep within her. She tried seeking Ches's affirmation, but he remained silent.

"Either way, let me support you," Maior said. "Stop assuming that the goddess I pray to will impact the way I feel about you. The Virgin—Ches—they can coexist. We are not enemies."

Reina cupped Maior's cheek. Her heart fluttered as Maior leaned into the gesture. "You're blasphemous," Reina joked.

Maior giggled. "No. I just want to be happy."

33

Caged Tinieblas

Eva fully expected Javier to want to remain hidden in Casa Bravo when she approached him with the idea of capturing a tiniebla. She was prepared to trek into the jungle alone, for Reina had lit a fire in her. But despite his new appendage and the pain in his bandaged wrists, Javier armed himself. He put on an indigo liqui liqui concealing as much of his neck as possible and silken gloves.

Don Samón saw them in passing, and he winced, as if he had just remembered the tail he'd seen during breakfast the day before.

Eva greeted her father, a bit nervous he would read the plan etched across her face.

Don Samón scratched his beard and told Javier, "You know, there's an illusion spell you can use. Valco spies used it during the war to hide their antlers from human eyes."

"It's a nozariel tail. They can just assume I am mixed," Javier said indifferently.

Don Samón beamed. "A human, nozariel, valco. That used to be my dream."

Javier scoffed and headed for the door.

Eva followed him like a bright-eyed puppy. "And the people who already know you?" she said, a bit cheekily.

"It is none of their concern."

Eva tried to temper her smile, even as her hand ached to take his. How she craved the adoration he showed her when they were alone. "I'm proud of you, for not letting it get to you," she said as they crossed the cobbled roads to the city gates.

"I don't have the luxury of feeling sorry for myself. We've already wasted enough time."

Segolita's jungle swallowed them, sparing them from the punishing noon sun. Javier walked in silence, his blade hacking away at the overgrowth blocking their path while Eva followed in his shadow. Lizards scuttled out of view. Crimson-plumed macaws squawked as they took off in opposite directions. Their boots sank in quicksand.

The journey was torturous but short. They found the first dozen tinieblas at the foot of an outcrop. Eva seized them before the creatures could stampede in their direction, her chest concaving from the Void's spell malaise.

"How many can you handle?" Javier asked, his blade raised should her control ever wane or waver.

Her pendant's iridio solution sloshed in abundance, yet she could still sense its depletion.

"Slay all but three," she said.

In an instant, it was done.

Eva's heart hammered as they took the same path back to the city. The tinieblas walked beside her, bipedal, one with the body of a donkey, another with the green and black scales of a tegu lizard, and the third muscular and brown furred, resembling a large monkey. Eva specifically chose to keep the least repugnant trio. They were amalgamated from limbs and pieces belonging to different animals. The ones with the sickly hairless faces of people—those she gladly let Javier slay.

The tinieblas proceeded in the direction Eva willed, but their eyes were trained on her, twisted and ravenous, suffocating her. They turned the air putrid, the welts and cuts from their lack of self-preservation festering. Eva bridled them with a clutched fist. Yet doubt filled her. Doña Ursulina had controlled a dozen tinieblas back in the tomb. She had used them to transport the damas for their sacrifice. Was Eva just as wicked?

"*You're only evil if you use them for evil*," the Void god reassured.

In that case, how could they look so grotesque? If they weren't but a product of wrongness? Of course Rahmagut would see them differently. They were his creations.

She forced herself to ignore the way their contracted pupils followed her with razor-sharp focus.

Rahmagut's amusement was undeterred.

Javier asked Eva to linger back as they neared the city gates. She obeyed begrudgingly, as her pendant's iridio solution was fast depleting. With his fingers aglow in his gold geomancia, Javier snuck behind the half dozen guards, who idled as the crowds had thinned after the Dancing Devils' procession. The glimmering threads of Javier's galio twirled in the air before worming into the unsuspecting guards' ears.

"That should dispel any bismuto they might be using," he muttered as he escorted her into the city.

His company reassured her. He made her feel completely safe. Eva nodded as they entered with the tinieblas, unimpeded.

Just as Reina had predicted, the cobbled streets were empty. A charred breeze welcomed them, likely from the burning of an effigy or some other Penitent symbol. Eva was surprised by the cleverness of their plan—and her good luck.

The colonial façades of La Parroquia were devoid of activity as they entered the neighborhood. With her depleting iridio solution (and against Javier's wishes), Eva made the decision to head for Casa Bravo's front entrance, rather than reroute toward the back stables for the sake of secrecy.

They turned a corner, and immediately it proved to be a mistake. Enrique Águila, Monseñor Lorenzo, and a posse of golden-armored Águila soldiers stood before the marbled doorway of Casa Bravo.

Eva would have done a turnabout. She would have turned on her heel and willed the tinieblas back around the corner from whence they'd come, before anyone took notice. But the sight gave her pause: Facing the caudillo was none other than Maior. In all her shortness, Maior stood with arms crossed over her chest, facing Enrique.

"*Eva*," Javier warned her.

In Eva's stunned hesitation, Enrique's gaze found her. His eyes narrowed, then widened as he saw Eva and her tinieblas. "*You*," he said across the street. He chuckled, pleased by her presentation.

Maior used the opportunity to scurry inside. Enrique noticed, but he let it go. Eva understood. He needn't pursue Maior at all, when Eva was giving him all the ammunition he could use in his game against her father.

"It's not what it looks like!" Eva said, her belly quivering as Enrique marched in her direction. He was followed by his men in golden armor, and by the archbishop.

The Águila soldiers glowed with the use of geomancia. As they unsheathed their blades and pointed them at the tinieblas, Eva realized that indeed her fears were coming true. They were all burning bismuto, aside perhaps from the archbishop and Enrique, who didn't need it. They all saw her for what she was: A master and wielder of tinieblas. A bearer of darkness.

Javier stepped between them.

Enrique's teeth bared in a smirk at the sight of Javier's newly sprouted appendage. "You don't fail to sink lower every time I see you."

"What are you doing here?" Javier said.

"We came to arrest the hosts of Ches and Rahmagut," Enrique said.

"With what proof do you make those claims?" Javier said, watching the expectant Águila soldiers, his fingers draping over the hilt of his sheathed sword.

"The church of La Santísima Diosa was desecrated—it was burned to the ground by that demon-spirit Ches, through the body of his apostate agent," Monseñor Lorenzo said. "Witnesses confirm the apostate is a nozariel woman hiding in this residence."

"And *you* gave me all the proof I needed to investigate further, at the cabildo," Enrique told Eva, smug. "As I told you and the junta, Monseñor Lorenzo, it makes perfect sense that Samón would collect and keep both gods under his purview. He guarded that tomb, biding his time until his irrelevancy was apparent. Now he alone intends to hold and use the power of the gods of the sun and the Void."

Monseñor Lorenzo scoffed. "They are no gods."

Eva's control over the tinieblas shuddered, tugged by said god.

Enrique continued. "Samón has lost his good sense and his mind. He is no longer looking out for the interests of our sister nations. You ask me what proof I have? You are standing proof of it. Look at you: Javier, the tinieblas, and the master who leashes them all. Now, come peacefully, and this may yet be resolved without bloodshed—"

"I would be very careful with how I proceed, if I were you." Don Samón's low voice came as he emerged from the house. Maior followed courageously.

Eva could finally breathe. With her father around, Enrique would have no choice but to bridle his aggression.

"No—I can arrest them now and be justified for it," Enrique said. "So you admit it? That all along you knew about the gods?"

"I said no such thing," Don Samón said, approaching, his disgust over the tinieblas obvious, and his hurt.

"Eva Kesaré, explain yourself," he said, taking her in, noticing the morichal's grime coating the hem of her skirt and boots. Her knuckles were drained of blood as she constricted the tinieblas in place; they stood motionless, eyes fixed to their master.

She'd acted without his counsel. She'd kept secrets. Her heart raced. This wasn't how she'd wanted him to find out. Maybe she couldn't justify Rahmagut, but she had a reason for the tinieblas. "I grew tired of waiting for someone to do something about the tinieblas—"

"So you brought them into the city yourself?" Enrique interrupted like the bastard he was. He smiled.

"No! I thought if we're ever going to figure out a way to banish them—to break Javier's curse—we need to learn how they behave, what they want, and what they're made of."

"How convenient—do you hear her speak? Do you hear Rahmagut's excuses through her lips?" Enrique said. "Why would the god of the Void not understand the nature of his own creatures?"

"You brought tinieblas within the city walls?" Monseñor Lorenzo barked. "Are you this selfish, to taint a whole city with your sin?"

Eva's fist twitched. How she wished she could release her hold and unleash one on him. She faced her father and said, "No one is speaking for me, I swear it! I just couldn't sit idly anymore. People are suffering while *they* waste their time doing inquisitions." She brazenly pointed her chin at Monseñor Lorenzo.

Don Samón considered his options in excruciating silence. And Enrique waited with his vulpine satisfaction.

Eva sucked in a breath as she felt the last of her iridio depleting. The moment her potion ran out, the Void spell would shatter, and she'd lose control.

"Where were you taking them?" Don Samón asked Eva.

"Enough wasted time!" Monseñor Lorenzo said. "I understand your penchant for believing such blasphemy, Liberator, as fathers cannot help but love and believe their children. But there are no excuses. The girl pretends she wants to end tinieblas, yet she's bringing them into a city made safe by our efforts?" He turned to Enrique, his face red with conviction. "We have finally found both hosts. The problem of tinieblas will be solved once we put these demon holders to their deaths. The spirits will be vanquished, and the Virgin's balance will be restored." He straightened with his nose raised, as he had once stood to denounce Doña Rosa's "crimes." Eva couldn't wipe the memory of that night, or her hatred for this man. "Arrest her and the nozariel woman, for the arson and destruction she caused on one of our holy sanctuaries."

"What?" Maior cried. "She saved your people! She didn't cause anything!"

"She cannot be innocent if she holds that *Ches*. Now, make way so we may collect her," Monseñor Lorenzo said, snapping his fingers at the men in Águila armor. Though no one moved—they listened only to their caudillo. And it became abundantly clear why someone with so much hatred for valcos and nozariels would ally himself with Enrique Águila. Monseñor Lorenzo needed the manpower.

Don Samón approached Enrique. The air was charged as both valcos stood in opposition. "Since when are you the church's dog?"

Enrique's bared canines glinted under the sun.

"Do you think I don't see right through your gambits?" Don Samón said. "What *real* proof do you have about the gods?"

"If you see right through my stratagem, then you know exactly how to end this," Enrique said. He needn't glance at Maior. The intentions were an unspoken, charged undercurrent.

The color emptied from Monseñor Lorenzo's face. "A church has burned to the ground!"

Don Samón ignored him. "I know Reina would never endanger the lives of anyone. If there was a fire, there must be another explanation. I am adamant in this. I will not stand here and tolerate accusations clearly born out of an abuse of power and a befuddling of the truth."

"My iridio is running out. The spell will break," Eva interrupted in a weak voice. She hated admitting it. But all this would be for nothing if she lost control and the tinieblas were slayed. Enrique had already outed her—what more did she have to lose? "Please, let us see how they behave, in a controlled way. If you care about the fight against tinieblas, let's see this through. Then you can do whatever you want with me."

Enrique's laughter echoed in the empty street. "The girl hammers her own casket."

Don Samón's eyes were shiny with a torrent of betrayal. He watched Eva like he was seeing her for the first time as she truly was: a creature of darkness, and the holder of Rahmagut.

"Very well, I shall allow it," Enrique finally said. He offered the archbishop an insolent sideways glance. "Let's see what testing these tinieblas will yield. It may be beneficial to us, Padre."

"That doesn't discount the act of blasphemy performed by that nozariel! A sacred space went up in flames! I trust what my acolytes witnessed. That woman must be arrested!"

Both valco commanders ignored Monseñor Lorenzo's blubbering

as Don Samón guided Eva through the many open corridors of Casa Bravo to the stables. Her father had no words; his disappointment was loud in his silence.

In the stables, several large hound cages sat abandoned. Relief flooded Eva, as the cages could fit one tiniebla each. She commanded the demons to trap themselves within, listening for the click of their locks. Then she let go.

The tinieblas awoke from their stupor with a startling ferocity. They rammed against the bars, denting the metal, enraged. Growling and snarling, their eyes following Eva as she backed away against a wall.

Monseñor Lorenzo also retreated to a corner with a clutched rosary as he saw the cages rattling.

"*They won't look away*," Eva told the entity she housed. "*Can you tell what they want?*"

"*Tinieblas have no thoughts. They are soulless*," Rahmagut noted uselessly.

"*But they want something.*" Not only did they seem ravenous and united for a single cause, but they were also spawning more than ever, uncontrollably, overwhelming the living. "*You are the creator of tinieblas. They exist because of you.*"

Rahmagut's anger rose up in her throat. An indignation at not having the answer she desired; scorn that his impotence hampered his divinity.

"Tell your daughter to let go of her control," Enrique said.

"I am not controlling them," she said.

"But they only have eyes for you," Javier muttered with the same uncertainty she felt.

Eva paced the stables, walking behind Javier, then Don Samón, clearly stepping away from the tinieblas' line of vision. Nevertheless, their eyes followed her every move. A chill crawled up her back. The sounds in the stables emptied as everyone held their collective breath. As they witnessed the tinieblas hungering for a single person in the room.

Enrique said, "Open the cages. Let us see who they choose to go after."

"No. That is madness. I will not allow it," Don Samón said.

In the silence, it became obvious that even the archbishop had abandoned his prayers. The slightest glow of gold surrounded his body. For a moment, Eva wondered if this was the strength of his rosary, until she realized he'd resorted to using bismuto himself. *Hypocrite*, she thought.

"What is your plan, Eva?" Don Samón said.

Eva opened her mouth, and no word came out.

The archbishop was outraged. "Libertador! Is this not proof enough? You house that entity within your own walls. Are you so blinded—so unfazed?" Monseñor Lorenzo's mouth twisted. He gave Eva a nasty look. "It is obvious that the tinieblas crave you. I know you, Eva Kesaré *de Galeno*. You were a cohort of that witch I had to eliminate to save Galeno from damnation." He raised his brows. "It was not something I took pleasure in. A task I had to see to the end, for the betterment of all."

The words left unsaid were abundantly clear: His mistake had been to let her go.

"You are the host of that Void demon—that is why the tinieblas are coming after you," Monseñor Lorenzo concluded. He turned to Enrique and Don Samón. "Retrace every attack and every uprising. You will find this young woman in the direction of the tinieblas' march."

"*No*," Eva thought, grasping for Rahmagut's reassurance, but he offered none.

Perhaps her silence was incriminating enough.

A hollow opened in Eva's heart as the archbishop's words cleared any doubt or excuse Don Samón could have had in her favor. He looked at her like she was a stranger. His eyes quivered with distrust. He was believing the truth she'd withheld since the moment she'd emerged from the tomb as Rahmagut's hand.

The archbishop turned his ire to Don Samón. "I see I have no ally in you—that is why your kind cannot be trusted. Enrique, command their arrests at once!"

The Águila soldiers waited.

"You insult my kind, yet you believe you can order me around like your servant," Enrique said. He never wavered, as if whatever truth was unveiled didn't impact the means to his ends. "Samón, will you really see your daughter burn, god of the Void or not?"

The tiniebla snarls were all that disrupted the quiet, until her father said, "No."

"What are you willing to exchange for her safety?" Enrique said.

Monseñor Lorenzo's righteous indignation radiated in waves. He glared at Enrique, whose shifting loyalties said everything about his true intentions. The caudillo of Sadul Fuerte didn't care about the deaths left in the wake of the tinieblas' march. In fact, the trade of iridio used in this fight fattened his coffers. Chaos was the tune he knew best. He didn't care about the Virgin, nor about Monseñor Lorenzo's mission.

"The other caudillos shall be hearing about this," the archbishop snarled, storming out of the stables. Immediately, Don Samón followed, begging for understanding—always playing the diplomat.

As much as Eva wanted to savor the archbishop's retreat, she couldn't look away from the tinieblas. They watched her without blinking, intently, ignoring everyone else in the room.

"*What if it's the Void gem they want?*" There had to be a reason beyond her hosting Rahmagut.

Rahmagut took his time to say, "*I would know, if I had my memories.*"

Eva plucked the Void gem from her pocket.

"*Be careful,*" Rahmagut growled as she lifted the black gem between her fingers and held it up in the dim light. The gem leeched the heat from her touch. It also emptied her confidence, as if it were a never-ending sink of magic. It glittered like an agglomeration of stars in the vastness of a black sky. Eva raised it higher, hoping the tinieblas would shift their attention to her stretched hand.

"Of course my leech of a brother would attach himself to such a power," Enrique said. He marched at Eva, mesmerized by the black gem. He tried grabbing her by the wrist, but Javier forced himself between them, spitting a string of insults.

In the scuffle, the gem slipped out of her grip, flying in the air.

A sharp, icy fear prickled Eva's skin in goose bumps. Within her, Rahmagut screamed, "*No!*"

The Void gem clattered to the ground and rolled within reach of the first cage.

Rahmagut seized control of her body, throwing Eva after the gem before a tiniebla could snag it. Her hands clamped over it, shielding it, and a tiniebla's talons shredded her cheek instead. But Eva hardly registered the pain. She was in a daze, controlled by Rahmagut, struck by the gem's rapid suction underneath her palm.

Rahmagut's panic blared in her chest—his fear from the ruptured power. Eva realized the fall had fissured the gem's surface. And as she gazed into the fissure, as she got lost within the blackness of its depths, her eyes opened to his truth.

34

The Calamity

For days, the sorrow prevented Rahmagut from breathing. Rain clattered against his roof and shook his house, and it felt deserved. Once again, he found himself mourning the death of his progeny.

All the riches and power his iridio afforded him—all the stability and stature of conquering the valco kingdom—did nothing to save his child's life.

There was another plague. The sickness was consuming his beloved winged queen. Rahmagut knew she was a strong woman with the fortitude to overcome it. And yet he held doubt.

What if again, one by one, everyone he loved was taken away from him? What would be the point of wielding iridio if he could succumb to this hidden enemy that rocked their bodies and made their temples burn, boiling them to death? Everything he'd worked for—it felt permeable, easily toppled.

He couldn't have it. He *would not* have it.

His new magic surely held the power of longevity.

Rahmagut knew the stories of Ches, of Arca, and of all the immortal entities who gave their light, sun, and water to the mortals, who were the ones to die. Those gods shaped the land with their power, living through countless generations. Why couldn't he also join their ranks? Why not his wives? To his prayers and questions, Ches remained quiet.

Perhaps Rahmagut didn't deserve a reply after his repeated insults. But what a fragile ego that god of the sun had. Scorned, Rahmagut sought a solution for himself.

He toiled for days in the caves holding his glittering iridio trove. He concentrated its power, compacting as much iridio as could fit his fist. Then suddenly the mountain shook as, with a great implosion, a gem was formed in his palm. It had the constitution of a diamond, but instead of being hot to the touch, it leeched his heat and happiness upon contact. Wide-eyed, Rahmagut stared at the glimmering black surface and was convinced that such a concentration of iridio was enough to achieve his ascension. A life leech, it would cure him of his mortality. He tested it on his queen, mother of his deceased winged son, and saw how it obliterated the illness ravaging her body. It was proof enough.

He took his nine wives and traveled the length of the continent, testing bites of power from his new gemstone. Everywhere he went, it wilted the flowers it touched. It grounded the macaws slicing the mauve skies of the Llanos. Its proximity filled his youngest wife with melancholia, and with ideas of her being not a willing lover, but a captive. Finally, on an island populated by nothing more than iguanas and sparse palm trees, Rahmagut mastered the usage of his heat-sucking gem.

His wives built him a bonfire and fed him toasted coconuts and a liquor fermented from sea grapes. He kissed them all on the mouth and grew hard as he watched them kiss each other. They reveled in their upcoming ascension, toasting to the longevity of godhood. Then he lifted the Void gem up to the star-studded sky and cracked its surface, opening its pressurized center. Within its core was the world-shattering energy to strip them of their mortality. He knew, from the moment he discovered the iridio buried in those mountains, that he was meant to become a god.

In swirls of blue and purple, the Void gem expanded in his hand. It swelled to become a circle of light-sucking black. In the air, it grew disproportionally, bending light and matter as if it were the center of the world. Air whizzed past him. Trees were lifted and absorbed within. Seagulls cawed, plucked from flight by the gem's pull. The white-soft sand beneath Rahmagut's sandals lifted like a swirl of stars to be absorbed into his gem's hungry nucleus.

Rahmagut laughed as he felt the power of his ingenuity. But the joy crumbled on his lips as, in the chaos, the fake niceties dissolved from his wives' demeanors. Instead of laughing with him, his winged queen howled in pain, her wings breaking and ripping from her back, her black mane scalped from her skull. Horror poured from the others as their clothes and skin shredded, disintegrating on the quick trip to the gem's black center.

That was when Rahmagut realized the control had never been in his hands. When it became clear he couldn't force the gem to stop its suction. When he realized there was no end to the insatiable pull of this hole he'd opened. It wasn't driven by desire or primal motivation. It wasn't alive. It was a rift in the physical world.

In his greed for immortality, he'd broken life for everyone else.

It happened in a mere split second, but Rahmagut watched every moment unfold, an imprinting on his memory that never should have been forgotten: Despite his large build, the void lifted him into the air. He was sucked into the threshold, and just as his heart sank, expecting obliteration, a bright light appeared in the corner of his eye.

Like the dazzling rise of dawn, a figure came into his field of vision. A man with valco antlers. Ches materialized before him, unveiling the night with his arrival just as the black hole began rending the land later to be renamed Fedria.

He'd never forget Ches's look of insurmountable scorn as he seized the fabric of reality, which the black hole had torn, and pulled it back together with every ounce of his divine strength. Ches's very essence bulged in concentrated effort. He stopped the black hole's unraveling, howling as he stitched the rift shut. Maybe he hadn't meant to, but because of their proximity both he and Rahmagut were trapped, the physical framework shutting behind them.

Rahmagut knew he wouldn't survive such a place, absent of physical matter. He used a spell of binding in a pinch, one he'd designed, and affixed himself to Ches.

On the beach, where life and the world carried on, the Void

gem sank into the sand, dormant, not to be found again until many years later.

Thus, in a darkness so vast there was no beginning or end, nor any hint of light, Rahmagut survived like a parasite, attached to a sun god too drained to do anything but slumber. He discovered that, on his own, he couldn't unseal the Void to return; and without his strength, Ches couldn't either. But bound to Ches's divinity, Rahmagut learned the ability to influence the mortal world. From the Void, he could stir the spawning of tinieblas. He could plant mortals with dreams, sowing the myth of his conquest while reframing himself as a god. He whispered instructions to all who worshipped him, ordering them to build him a tomb with the Void gem, for safekeeping. He demanded sacrifices from his followers, for which he could grant boons when a cyan iridio rock traversed the sky every forty-two years. Bound together, every offering made to Rahmagut refilled Ches's divine well.

In the dark realm, Rahmagut bided his return. And he plotted. He had hundreds of years to ruminate on why he had been able to control the gem in the mountains but not on the coast. He concluded that it was due to the abundance of iridio in his trove. Rahmagut was sure that if he tried again, taking the Void gem to where the iridio source sat nestled beneath the mountains, he would be successful in controlling it.

Finally, when the final sacrifice refilled Ches's power such that he could break out of the Void, Rahmagut emerged with him. He was mortal, and Ches was his only source of divinity. So Rahmagut took a piece of Ches, his pupils, sparing himself from a guaranteed destruction once they tore apart. With them, he would have *some* godly strength until he could complete his ascension.

Returned, Rahmagut set his plan into motion, roaring a command to all his tinieblas: "*Find me and take me to the mountains.*" He was a specter without a body, so he took the nearest one most attuned to iridio, the quarter valco whose power radiated like a star's. But he never anticipated her consciousness overriding his, burying his memories and befuddling the next steps to guarantee his full return.

Ches chose the half-breed nozariel, his most ardent worshipper. But without his pupils, he hadn't the vision to anticipate Rahmagut's next step.

The truth impacted Eva like a punch. She was dizzied by the images. Tears blurred her vision as someone yanked her by the shoulders. They called her name. A voice she recognized. She couldn't pinpoint why, but it brought her great comfort.

The voice soothed her shaking body, stopping the clattering of her teeth and the foaming of her mouth. A throb made her head feel like bursting. Eva managed to open her eyes and found herself in Javier's arms. He cradled her. He begged her to snap out of it. In her grip, the Void gem leeched the heat from her hand, turning her fingers into icicles. The fissuring on the gem's surface strengthened its innate behavior. The nature of a mass-sucking void.

Javier searched her eyes. The worry creasing his face eased. She was back to herself, but she ached, for her foolishness. Again, she'd toyed with magic so dark and strong, beyond her comprehension. Eva wanted to chuck the gem across the room, to get as far away from it as possible. But Rahmagut's will overrode hers. This was his gem, his power. He'd created it. And he needed it to solidify his divinity.

For he was a god. So what if he had once walked as a mortal? He had slumbered alongside the creator of the sun. And he was back. In a meek female body, but one with the potential to realize the goals quickly falling into place, now that he remembered how he got here in the first place:

First, to secure a male body to better suit his appearance and desires.

Second, to snare the host of the only god capable of stopping him.

And third, in a place so abundant with iridio, where he'd be able to control the Void gem, to destroy said god from existence. Surely, Ches sought to obliterate Rahmagut in return.

Eva had to wrangle her thoughts away from Rahmagut. She had to fight to regain cognitive control. As she came to, she heard another voice saying to Javier, "Remember what we discussed." Eva turned in his embrace to see it was Maior speaking. She didn't understand what they were doing. What had they discussed? And most importantly, how long had Eva lost consciousness?

"Yes—I remember," Javier muttered.

Maior gave Eva's arm a squeeze. She kissed Eva on the forehead. "Tell Reina that I know we're supposed to tell each other everything—but there's no time anymore. I must go now."

Eva seized Maior by the collar. "What?"

Maior peeled Eva's fingers away. She shushed her. "Don't worry, you're in good hands. Your husband is a master of galio." Then she walked away.

Eva took in a deep breath. Javier helped her sit up on the hay-packed floor. She realized they were still at the stables, the caged tinieblas still tackling their enclosures, desperate to fulfill their command. Eva glanced at the door just in time to see the swish of Maior's skirts as she exited the stables, trailing Enrique's departing shadow. The Águila soldiers followed.

Eva tried speaking but was stopped by a sharp pain on her lip. Fresh blood tainted her hand when she tapped her cheek.

"I'm sorry I couldn't close the wound. I used up all my galio to stop your convulsion," Javier explained.

She was weak, but she accepted his help to get up to her feet. Blood trickled down to her collar, staining her dress. The tiniebla had indeed managed to slice her face open.

Distantly, from the adjacent courtyard, came Don Samón's words: "Where are you going?" There was a pause, followed by Don Samón's "Answer me!"

Eva didn't hear a reply. Rather, her father returned to the stables, flustered, his ears and neck blotched red from the fast-toppling chaos. His eyes widened as he saw her wound. He rushed to her, then hesitated. Perhaps he was remembering why they were in this mess to begin with.

"Eva—your face," Don Samón said.

"I just need to mix some more galio solution and I can take care of it," Javier said.

Don Samón's voice trembled as he said, "I knew there was something you were keeping from me. Both you and Reina are embroiled in the same lies! When were you planning to tell me about Rahmagut?"

Shame filled Eva's belly like putrid, stagnant oil.

"Did I never earn your trust?" Don Samón said. "I gave you so many opportunities to tell me—all those times we told each other we would start anew—did that mean nothing to you?"

"Father—"

"Las Orquídeas Blancas want your death! I cannot protect you if I'm kept in the dark."

"Eva is injured. She just convulsed. Maybe it's best if you discuss this later," Javier said, his tone indicating the suggestion was nonnegotiable.

"Did you know?" Don Samón asked him.

"I am her husband."

Don Samón watched them with pursed lips. Then he swept out of the stables. As he left, Eva's tears broke through.

She wanted to sob. She wanted to bury herself so deep in a tunnel where Rahmagut wouldn't be able to use her body for his evil deeds. But with her shredded cheek, even crying was too painful.

Don Samón's hurt was etched in her memory. Eva would never forget the way his light had dimmed as he realized she was little more than a stranger. As her withheld truths and stupidity declawed every effort he'd made to protect them against Enrique's aggression. Eva wasn't a good daughter. She was a liar, selfish in her pursuits. Perhaps Rahmagut had been the cunning one to choose her.

Laughter echoed in her ears.

Javier took her in his arms protectively. He held her without touching her wounded cheek.

Eva said, "I'm sorry—"

"Stop apologizing."

She clung to him, his embrace steadying her. "Where is Maior going? What did you discuss?"

He was silent. His red gaze flickered behind her, making sure they were alone. Then he looked deeply into her eyes. Eva grew anxious. She couldn't shake the feeling that once again they had set off a chain of awful, unavoidable events, starting with the caprice of the god inhabiting her.

Finally, Javier whispered, "She's going to exhume Laurel's bones, in Águila Manor."

35

Valco Stratagems

Reina awoke to a dark sky, dusk casting long shadows over her bedroom. She was sore from her neck to her toes. Maior had healed her skin before she slumbered, so at least she didn't have to contend with the burns. But her muscles and joints protested as Reina rolled off the bed. She would have slept for another hour, but hunger and dehydration forced her to action.

Casa Bravo was quiet as the evening descended. Reina passed the drawing room and saw Maria Elena praying the rosary with her comadre. She continued to the kitchen, where one of the cooks offered her a lukewarm bowl of black beans and rice. When she asked about Maior's whereabouts, the cook answered with a shrug. Reina ate while pacing the house seeking Eva, remembering the last-minute plan they had concocted before the Dancing Devils' fire had ruined her day.

Reina heard agitated voices coming from Don Samón's study.

"How many caudillos are turning to the archbishop?" Don Samón's voice trailed out from the slightly ajar door.

"Monseñor Lorenzo is enraged at Enrique's betrayal, and his petitioning has been so passionate he's succeeded in turning many against you," said another voice. Reina recognized it as Don Rigoberto's. "There are those who are quick to accept a solution to the tinieblas, a few who fear acting in a way that would antagonize

Enrique—as they don't know where he stands after he disappeared without a word—and some who still believe in your honor."

Reina allowed herself into the room, finding Eva and Javier there as well. All wore grave expressions. Perhaps she was out of line entering uninvited, but too much had occurred that day for her to assume the agitation in their voices didn't involve either her or Eva.

Don Samón stood behind the dark oak desk, leaning on his fists. "Reina? Where have you been?"

Reina took stock of the room, how Javier's clothes had an almost imperceptible splattering of blood. How Eva was wearing a freshly laundered gown and a bandage wrapped around her head, concealing her left cheek. A line of red seeped through the bandaging.

"I . . ." Reina's answer trailed off uncertainly. "I'm sorry, I was injured today—"

"I was informed of what happened at La Santísima Diosa," Don Samón said.

Reina shuddered. She held her breath. Which version had he heard, exactly? And how much was she supposed to divulge now?

"The caudillos want answers about the church, and about what you are," Don Rigoberto said. He shifted on his feet, and while normally Reina expected the disdain with which he'd treated her since Carao, he also seemed . . . fearful. "Las Orquídeas Blancas have been informed of what you did. The archbishop says you are possessed and must be tried for the destruction of the church."

Dread pummeled Reina. She forced herself to take a breath and keep from overreacting in front of the Liberator and his hostile comrade, even as anger bubbled through her. How could she be blamed for something she only helped ease? How could the humans focus only on the otherworldly nature of her strength, rather than on the miracle it had granted them? Those lives were spared because of her.

Reina set her empty bowl on a nearby table and gave the Liberator her back. "Are you going to demand I explain myself?" she growled. "If Las Orquídeas Blancas have brought you these accusations, and you believe them, then—"

"I did not say I believed any of it," Don Samón said, cutting her off.

Reina turned and glared at all of them. She took in Eva as her heart thrummed a new tune in her chest. Eva stared at the ground, her lashes shrouding her eyes. What was wrong with her? Javier had a pained look as well, which only fed Reina's apprehension. That was when it dawned on her.

"Where's Maior?"

Don Samón gestured at the seat across from him at the desk. "You better sit down."

"No," she retorted in a lower octave. "Where is Maior?" She didn't move, for she didn't need appeasement. She just needed her answer.

Don Samón sighed deeply. "Maior has gone with Enrique."

"*What?*" Reina's voice broke. The betrayal was like a punch to the stomach. It knocked the air out of her. It drained the blood from her face. Reina felt small and stupid for trusting that Maior would be safe from Enrique in Casa Bravo. In a white-knuckled grip, she clutched the leather back of the chair across from the Liberator. "You let him take her?"

"He didn't take her, as you imagine," Javier said.

Reina whirled to face him, her fists constricting.

He quickly added, "She went with him of her own accord."

"That's a lie!" She marched at him and stopped only a breath away. "Maior despises Enrique almost as much as I do. She understands what it means to be returned to him." The panic shook her shoulders. It renewed her heartache. The idea of Maior in Enrique's hands made her want to puke. It made her want to run out of the house to rip the city from its cobbles to its rafters. She wanted terror to bubble in their blood, just like it bubbled in hers.

Javier said, "None of this would have happened if you'd been there at all—"

She yanked him by the collar and raised a fist.

"Reina!" Don Samón shouted.

Don Rigoberto chuckled under his breath, as if her actions were reaffirming his opinion of her.

"It was Maior's idea!" Javier said, diffusing her fist's trajectory.

"Why?" Reina said softly.

Javier shoved her off. He backed away to face them all. He sized Don Rigoberto up, then said, "Does he need to be here for this?"

Don Rigoberto scowled. "You insolent boy."

"I am not a boy, and we received your message loud and clear. So why don't you run along to the president and tell him the Liberator will thank him once he grows the backbone to stand up against the church," Javier said, his tail slapping the air behind him, agitated. "I know the archbishop is a fearmonger, so it's no surprise to me that he's fixated on Eva and Reina. But asking for their heads is nothing more than a knee-jerk reaction born out of his hatred for our kind. He has no proof that killing the hosts will solve the tinieblas, *nor* that it will vanquish the gods."

Reina ground her teeth, her chest constricting over her wildly beating heart. So they all knew...

Don Samón's frown deepened. "Rigoberto, please forgive my son-in-law, who clearly forgot all his manners this evening." Javier crossed his arms bitterly. "And please give us a moment of privacy. Maria Elena is in the drawing room. I'm sure she'll be happy to keep you company."

Don Rigoberto slammed the study door behind him.

Reina faced Javier with unappeased anger. He'd done this for her, but she refused his solidarity. "Explain," she growled.

He took a deep breath, brushing his loose hairs back. "Maior talked to me about getting Laurel's remains. Yes, it sounds vile, but the sanadero himself said this was the way to cleanse us: Maior, who has Laurel's ghost, and me, because she was the one who cursed me."

Bile rose in Reina's throat. How could she be hearing about this now, after it was already done?

"But Laurel is in Águila Manor, a place hostile to all of us!" Eva said. "How could you endorse this?"

"I didn't like it," Javier emphasized. "But Maior was adamant, and desperate. And it's better than sitting here waiting for someone to miraculously hand me a way to break my curse. I don't know why she wouldn't tell you. Frankly, that's not my concern."

Reina shoved him. Javier stepped back, shaken but not abated.

"You said I could trust you from now on!" Reina snarled. She could feel the tears pooling in the corners of her eyes. A panic wound in her chest.

"It wasn't my place to stop her," Javier said swiftly. "I had to get Eva away from the tiniebla."

To Eva, he said, "You went into a trance, and nothing I did would snap you out of it. I emptied my galio solution on spells for you and it didn't do a blood-damned thing. You calmed when you calmed and I had no hand in it, to be honest.

"Next thing I knew, Maior was offering herself up to Enrique, because it was *so obvious* that Enrique only involved himself with the archbishop as leverage." Javier swiped the perspiration from his temples, then he faced Don Samón. "He baited the archbishop into arresting Eva and Reina just so you would be forced to trade Maior for Eva—it's what he always wanted."

Don Samón scowled. "Enrique despises me this much?"

"My brother has no love for anyone, besides himself and his dead wife," Javier said. "And he has always been envious of your popularity with the humans—how it gives you the political influence he lacks. He knows your achievements and kindness are the only things stopping humans from publicly shunning and revolting against all valcos."

Don Samón nodded. "You cannot have influence out of fear alone."

Javier wasted no time in telling Reina, "Maior traded her safety for your freedom. Why don't you focus your energies on that instead?"

"Because I'm too busy focusing on not bashing your face in," she replied.

Reina considered the archbishop's animosity and Enrique's machinations, but instead of understanding what drove Maior to make such a reckless decision, she just felt empty. Reina could not care less about the archbishop's threats, or the fear he sowed in people's minds. She wasn't meek. She could run from the church and the caudillos, and take her freedom, by force if necessary. She felt no obligations to respect the Penitent beliefs designed to minimize her existence and erase Ches.

But Maior in Enrique's hands—that made her choke up.

She wanted to shove Javier again, to let out her anger, but he squared up. The next move would make them come to blows. It was written all over his face. But it didn't stop her from yelling at him. "Anything can happen to Maior in his clutches. Enrique is twisted, and selfish. *He could rape her!*"

Don Samón rounded his desk, approaching her. He grabbed Reina's shoulder, squeezing painfully, the strength in his hand stopping her.

Reina's eyes burned as she was reminded of Doña Laurel, and how the task of resurrecting her had consumed everyone in Águila Manor—how Enrique had forced Reina and Javier to do horrible things for it. Of course Enrique wouldn't so easily relinquish this objective, after Doña Ursulina beguiled him with ideas that it was possible. Of course he would cling to the slimmest of hopes, which Maior afforded him. Enrique was capable of anything.

"I couldn't stop her, Reina," Javier said. "Maior wanted this so badly she came to *me*, out of all people."

"She thought you'd be amenable to unearthing Doña Laurel's bones because you're a bastard without honor," Reina snarled. "You always hated Doña Laurel. She knew you wouldn't hesitate."

She met Javier's glare. His silence was her victory. She'd cut down to the quick, and there was no refuting this truth. "What did she want from you, exactly?"

"The reassurance that we would fetch her from Águila Manor. That's it. She expects Enrique to send her directly to the manor by way of Gegania, to avoid the chance of losing her again to you or to Don Samón, which gives her the opportunity to access Laurel's remains. She couldn't tell you or Eva because she knew you wouldn't agree."

Reina's heart shattered again. She backed away, completely disarmed and fissured. Just a few hours ago Maior had begged Reina to treat her like an equal. They were supposed to never hide things from each other anymore. They'd agreed, and Reina had thought she'd finally found the happiness she'd always longed for. Yet...her fears for Maior's safety didn't blind her to the truth left unsaid: how Maior had exhausted all other avenues and alternatives. This plan of exhuming a body, with *Javier*, screamed of desperation. And Reina was responsible for it. Maior had asked for help, repeatedly, but Reina had been too wrapped up in her own problems to listen.

Silence swallowed the room, like the darkness from the settling evening. A deep weariness seized Reina. "Do you believe in this plan?" she asked him, wary.

His throat bobbed. The lack of reply was answer enough.

Reina backed farther away. "We have to get Maior back," she said softly. The words were for her commander. Her last plea. "You told me to be patient with Enrique. But your waiting game—it made things worse, and it took away the person I love."

Her heart skipped a beat. The words rushed out of her, but the person who needed to hear them wasn't even in the room.

Don Samón's face was severe and unyielding. "You will have me wage war against the only other valco with any kind of power in this land that used to belong to us? A land that every day grows more hostile to our kind? You ask me to contest the person who hoards all the iridio needed for our fight against tinieblas?"

"Yes?"

"You will have me stand by your side, when you couldn't even be truthful about Ches, to *me*, your commander who believed in you? After I was repeatedly lied to?"

It was her turn to be robbed of words.

Don Samón's gaze traveled from Reina to Eva. "Your lack of honesty has blindsided and declawed me. Both of you! I knew you were keeping me in the dark about this, but I gave you the chance to tell me—*ample time*!" He pointed at both, enraged. "And this is how the truth comes out? How can I act when I don't have all the information? And how can I trust you've told me everything I *need* to know to act? Did you distrust my honor and commitment to you this much?"

"Father..." Eva muttered. "I wasn't ready."

"The world will not wait for you to be ready!" he roared at her. "Suddenly I'm realizing I have enemies everywhere, and a daughter who schemes behind my back."

Eva looked down, picking at her cuticles. She drew blood.

"The archbishop wants you both dead," he noted.

Ice filled Reina's veins. "I have no desire to separate from Ches."

Don Samón gave her a look of bewilderment.

"I never did. That's why I didn't tell you. He has no physical body anymore, so he needs mine. And I give it gladly."

Don Samón glanced at Eva, asking, "And you?" Indeed, Reina also wondered.

Eva's lips trembled as if she couldn't muster the right words. Or was that her inability to answer at all? Finally, she said meekly, "The gods will endure whether we live or not."

"The archbishop will not touch you," Javier said, bringing Eva into his arms.

Reina ground her teeth. How nice that they could be safe, together. Once again, she was faced with the reminder that everyone else's happiness came before hers.

She took a deep breath, gathering her thoughts. She was a different person now. She didn't need her grandmother's validation to survive, nor Enrique's. She didn't need Don Samón's approval to act as her heart dictated. She had the power to shape her own future, and the strength of a god.

"I'm disappointed in both of you," Don Samón said frigidly. "But that doesn't change my commitment to you." To Eva he said, "You are my daughter." And to Reina, "And you have been loyal to us. So let this demonstrate my loyalty to you—we will go for Maior. But in return, I would like this to be the end of your lies."

Reina's jaw tightened. A glimmer of hope sparked in her chest. She nodded.

"It is not safe for us to stay in Segolita. Pursuing Enrique might be the best next move. I will talk to him." He paused, his gaze boring into each one of them. "But I warn you: With Maior surrendering herself to him, I have lost all leverage. We'll have to hope he's amenable to my begging." He crossed his arms and gave them his back. "But if what Don Rigoberto said is true, about the archbishop poisoning the minds of the other caudillos—and if indeed the gods are tied to you permanently—then I'm afraid I will have no choice but to reestablish my alliance with Enrique."

Reina's hope was squashed beneath his words. "After he plotted to have your daughter killed?"

"It was but a stratagem that weakened us. His intentions are obvious to me now with his disappearance from Segolita. But if we're not a united force, and Las Orquídeas Blancas raise arms against us, then my daughter *will* be killed."

Reina could hear no more. She didn't care about the Orquídeas' fears of Ches. All she cared about was Maior. And she had no stomach to imagine a universe where she was once again under Enrique's yoke. No, this time, he'd gone too far.

She was exhausted by Don Samón's patience and politicking. The Liberator had spoken about loyalty, but it was precisely Reina's loyalty that had driven her to partake in evil deeds, delivering her to this moment where she was so dangerously close to losing the love of her life. Now Reina intended to act on her own.

"I don't need Enrique's protection, or yours," she said, striding toward the door. "If an alliance with Enrique is the price to pay, then I don't want it."

She slammed the door shut behind her.

Part 3

36

Catatumbo

Leaving Segolita wasn't difficult, when there was so little Eva had packed to begin with. She had a short and restless sleep, shattered when Javier brought Don Samón's orders that they meant to embark before the break of dawn. Under the light of the moon, the staff readied their chests and arsenals for departure.

Maria Elena watched the commotion from the drawing room, a lonesome candle in one hand. Eva was surprised the woman was up so early to see them off. As Eva shuffled to Don Samón's carriage, she overheard them arguing about Ludivina's custody. Maria Elena enjoyed her freedom in the city, Don Samón reminded her, and she never had an instinct for motherhood. It wouldn't harm Ludivina to stay with her mother, Maria Elena insisted, pointing out that a ten-year-old had no business going with him to parley with a man as dangerous as Enrique. Maria Elena won the debate, which Eva thought was the correct turn of events. Ludivina gave her father tearful kisses on the cheek before squeezing Eva and bidding her goodbye.

The caravan took off before sunrise would make their departure obvious. Eva craned her neck here and there, looking for signs of Reina, not seeing her until they were crossing the city gates. Reina rode in the very back, in the company of an older soldier and a man whose face was hidden beneath a jipijapa hat.

The caudillo encampment bordering Segolita's walls was sparser than usual without the Águila host. Nothing but mud and trash remained. Don Samón ordered their march east, after a sentry returned with news that Enrique had mobilized in the direction of Lake Catatumbo.

Long stretches of silence filled their carriage while the rising sun painted the horizon in gold. Herons cut through the clear skies, reflecting over the wetlands like shadowed smears. Still wounded, Don Samón spared few words. Javier also refrained from speaking. There were times when Eva nearly mustered the courage to confess about the Void gem. Except her lips betrayed her. Eva's mouth remained clamped shut as Rahmagut's dark influence swirled within her, stronger than ever.

"Catatumbo is a lake charged with magic," Don Samón explained to Eva as the convoy stopped by a creek for a brief rest. Two chigüires watched them from the banks, frozen, as if pretending they could camouflage within the muddy waters by waiting perfectly still. Her father drank from his flask, wiping high noon perspiration from his brows. "But I don't get why Enrique would head there, unless it has to do with Maior."

Eva chewed the bitter information, but she could supply no differing opinion. Perhaps Enrique's direction had something to do with Gegania. But if Enrique had access to the house's tunnels, he and his men could have easily returned to the Páramo by now. It didn't make sense.

Their journey ended as the setting sun left the sky in reds and oranges. Ahead, the horizon was a black line of shadows, helmed by storm clouds. But as Eva glimpsed the tents with Águila banners flapping in the furious wind, she was reassured that her father had led them in the right direction.

"Catatumbo means house of lightning," Don Samón said as he tugged the curtains for a better look outside. "In the old language that was spoken in these parts, before the Segoleans."

Before Eva could even open her mouth to ask why, she saw the first riotous vein light the sky. Lightning flashed within those rolling clouds. Five other bolts followed in close succession, and thunder. Wind buffeted the carriage. Eva could feel the charge in the air. The bite on her skin and the ever-present hum of geomancia, likely coming from beneath the lake's surface. It was a tug on her chest. Not only was the lake a beautiful sight, reflecting the gamut of blue bolts as they lit the sky, but she could feel its power, the slight whispers in the air; the electric charge stinging her forearms, hinting at an unknown entity existing beyond what their eyes could see.

"*There's a god in those clouds,*" Rahmagut said. "*A wielder of light and energy. He gave fire to humankind, and afterward, since he was no longer needed, he was forgotten. The lightning is how he attempts to remind mortals of his existence.*" He chuckled. "*One desperate attempt after another.*"

"*Does he have a name?*"

"*Names give power.*"

"*And you wish to be the only god who remains,*" Eva said, knowing him all too well.

With the flashes of Catatumbo's light, the carriages finished the journey to the encampment's fringes, where they were blocked by Águila soldiers. Don Samón emerged from their carriage. Lightning revealed his antlers, and the soldiers cowered.

"I only wish to parley with Enrique," he said. "If I wanted to battle you, I wouldn't have approached so noticeably."

The nearest soldier with the most badges on his jacket nodded, approving his entry.

Don Samón gave Javier orders to oversee setting up their camp on the perimeter. Eva followed her father, accompanying him to the encampment's center, where Enrique's tent stood like a makeshift castle upon a small hill. From its door, it had a view of the surrounding tents to the west, with a view of the lake to the east.

The soldier posted outside the tent announced their arrival, allowing them in. Inside, thick beeswax candles washed the space in a welcoming warmth that never touched Enrique's eyes. He stood behind a large table at the center, his hand ferrying a goblet to his lips. He appeared unfazed to see them.

Eva had braced herself to find Maior in shackles upon entering.

She held her breath, expecting the worst as she took in the make-shift separations within the tent, the hanging leather walls that created fur-covered opulent areas for the caudillo to sleep, eat, and bathe in. Thankfully, the space was empty, except for Enrique, and Celeste, who was storming for the exit.

Celeste paused, just as stunned as Eva.

Don Samón offered Celeste a quick greeting before crossing the tent for Enrique's table.

"Where is Maior?" Eva said, grabbing Celeste by the wrist before she could leave.

Celeste glowered at the spot where their hands touched. "That is forward of you."

"I just want Maior back, please."

"If you're here, that means Reina is, too?"

Eva shrugged.

Celeste exhaled loudly. She didn't wield the smug look in her eyes from the last time Eva saw her. Her black hair was frizzy, and her face was blotched with pink.

Celeste pulled her wrist free. "You should leave. There'll be no changing Father's mind about Maior. I already tried."

"Where have you taken her?" Eva asked.

Celeste cast a look of hatred behind her, to her father, who was already in a heated argument with Don Samón. "I suppose I no longer care if you know this or not," she muttered, blowing at her bangs. "Maior is not here. Father sent her back to the manor immediately."

Eva ground her teeth. Maior's plan was unfolding exactly as she had hoped. But instead of relief, all Eva could muster was apprehension. "Then why are you here?"

"We had Gegania connected to the silver mines west of Segolita. Until those imbecile miners blew up the geomancia mineral vein. The connection caved after Maior left, cutting us off. We reestablished a connection there, but it was too unstable for the whole army to go through, especially with those silver miners meddling with the veins."

"So you came here to create a new connection?" Eva supplied.

Celeste pursed her lips. "All kinds of metals are plentiful here. The connection will be robust. It'll take a day or two."

"Your father doesn't care about the tinieblas, does he? Did he ever care about protecting Segolita?" Eva knew she was a hypocrite for asking such questions, when the darkness attracting the tinieblas resided within her. At least she had the reassurance that the city would experience some peace and quiet now that she'd left.

Celeste grimaced. Wind buffeted the tent walls, disrupting a silence that underscored Celeste's discomfort.

"Do *you* care?" Eva prodded.

"I do! I want to have a solution for the people. It is we, the ones with wealth and resources, who can do anything about it," Celeste said. "But I'm a jaguar without fangs. I go where my father orders me to."

Heated, Eva said, "Are you really so resigned to your luxuries? Didn't you say, last I saw you, that you wanted to be a queen for the people? But you continue to do your father's bidding—"

Her words shattered as, across the tent, Don Samón roared to Enrique, "You need me! Without my backing the other caudillos will never accept you. They're not ignorant of your tyrannical actions. They're beginning to believe the rumors, about the murders and the babes sacrificed. You paint valcos in a bad light."

Deadly ice coated Enrique's façade as he said, "I don't need their acceptance when my iridio is the only thing keeping them safe at night. See how easily that archbishop scurried back into his cockroach nest once he saw I had no interest in being used?"

"Rather, he realized *you* were using *him*," Don Samón said.

"That is how the world works. We all have something to gain from one another." Enrique circled his table, slowly diminishing the distance between himself and Don Samón. "I could have continued to back him. I could have supported his efforts to eliminate Rahmagut through your daughter."

Pain speared Eva's belly. She gripped it, keeping a straight face. Rahmagut was playing games with her. He hurt her because he could.

Enrique went on. "In fact, you should be thanking me for

backing off. You should consider that as my act of friendship to you. But perhaps I'm the foolish one, for allowing you to keep such power."

"You're not allowing me anything," Don Samón snarled. "And you will stay away from my daughter."

Enrique scoffed.

"You're making a mistake. You won't last, with such hubris. It's obvious Laurel took your sanity with her to the grave." Don Samón whirled for the door, commanding Eva to follow him as he passed her.

"What about Maior?" Eva whispered, trailing behind him.

"She caused this. Perhaps you ought to respect her decision," he growled in a low voice.

Eva glanced back as they left the tent. Shudders rippled through her at the disdain in Enrique's eyes, at the twisting of his upper lip. He saw them as a nuisance, as ants. And despite the dejection in their retreat, Eva felt a wild sort of elation. Rahmagut's presence infected her with his joy. For what? Eva had no idea. But it was another confirmation that she was walking directly into a path of his design.

37

The Monster Inside

Don Samón's attendants set up camp for the night on the eastern edge of the Águila encampment. Eva and Javier's tent was a short walk away from the muddy banks of Lake Catatumbo. The young soldier who patrolled the area told them no tinieblas had emerged from the water itself—that it was just rumors. His words took Eva back to the night when the tinieblas had stormed the beachfront of Isla Madre. She shuddered. All this time, she had been their target.

"*I can control tinieblas,*" she told the god while the attendants prepared her temporary bed. "*I will never let them take me away.*"

"*And I can control you.*"

Eva pretended to ignore him, even as a shiver ran through her. He couldn't do that. She still had a grip on her consciousness.

Once the servants exited, Javier lit candles and placed them on every steady surface, making the space seem homey. Eva could almost ignore the transient nature of the tent, if not for the storming winds slapping the walls. The constant grumble of thunder.

He offered her an uncertain smile as he shook himself free from his vest. "You should let me look at your face. I got more geomancia solutions before we left. Maybe there is something to be done about the scar."

Finally, in the privacy of the tent, she let out a much-needed exhale.

"Eva?"

She didn't answer right away. She was worn out, unable to shake off the heaviness weighing her ever since her collapse at the stables. There was so much to confess. She had no idea where to start, but she had to say something. She had to speak about Rahmagut's plans while she still could.

Eva knew this would paint her as a fool, for both underestimating Rahmagut's possession and disagreeing with Don Samón when he suggested there was darkness in iridio and Void magic.

Javier must have noticed the way she hugged herself with uncertainty. He moved closer. His hands were warm as they took hers. Eva's chest fluttered with a song. She was surprised at the intensity of his attention. Ever since his duel with Enrique, Javier had been different. *Tender* was not a word she'd ever imagined using to describe him, and yet...

Eva allowed herself to drown in his eyes. They reminded her of the night when they first met in person. Back then, his niceties had all been a farce. Now they had time and history together. He was the person she trusted most, despite how little his trust meant to everyone else.

But Eva wasn't foolish enough to disregard the added complications of his tiniebla. Did he have true agency over his affections? Would she be able to rely on him against Rahmagut? What if his attraction had been forged from the tiniebla's devotion toward the god he hosted?

It would make sense.

Rahmagut laughed, like her fears were his entertainment. As if he were watching the petty drama of a stupid girl. Perhaps he was.

"Can you tell what your tiniebla desires?" Eva asked.

"If I let it take over, it might speak about what it wants," Javier said. "It'll use my intelligence and my body to act like a person, like it did back in Tierra'e Sol." His eyes darkened, his tail switching. "But you can't ask me to let it take over. I lose myself more and more every time."

"No, I wasn't," she said quickly. She moved away and settled on the bed with her back to him. She was so weary and scared. For the first time, Rahmagut felt like a true oppression. She was never his jailer.

"Eva?" Javier approached. "What's the matter?"

Her fear gripped her. It pained her to admit the truth, for it felt like losing. It wounded her pride, how wrong she'd been about thinking she could coexist with a god.

Like a ringmaster supervising her performance, whip in hand, Rahmagut was pleased.

Javier sat beside her and squeezed her arm.

Eva thought she'd feel emboldened by the proximity. Rather, it only highlighted her lack of courage and adequacy. How all this time she'd been lying to herself, claiming she was strong enough to withstand the possession. How she was arrogant enough to think she could use Rahmagut's strength to break Javier's curse.

"Is it something I did?" Then, after a beat, Javier added darkly, "You agree with Reina, that I'm a bastard for not dissuading Maior?"

That stirred a chuckle in her. "I'm not happy about you two plotting and you letting her act so recklessly, if you're wondering."

"You told me to make amends with the people I have wronged."

She faced him. "That's your definition of making amends?"

"Maior is a grown woman. She's free to make her own choices. She wanted to take matters into her own hands." His eyes searched hers. She could see his uncertainty, and his desire to please her.

"Fine," she muttered. "But I still believe it was the wrong thing to do. I'm convinced of that now, especially after seeing how Enrique treats my father. Will we have a peaceful resolution? Can we even get Maior back?"

"Enrique may own all the iridio, but he cannot overcome our combined strength," Javier said. "Have you forgotten that you house a god? And so does Reina."

His knuckles trailed the edge of her jaw, gracing her stray curls. The sensation made her shiver again, this time irresistibly, in a good way. But she couldn't melt into it. She couldn't react exactly as he wanted her to until she got to the bottom of her doubt. Until she got her answer: Did he like her for her, or was he being influenced by his tiniebla's obsession?

She averted her gaze.

"You're keeping something from me." Somehow, he'd drawn closer. "How can I help if you refuse to trust me? It's supposed to be *us* against *them*."

Eva thought she could hear his insecurities.

"Of course, you hold all the power."

"I am talking to my husband," she thought, aching to shout the words over and over until Rahmagut left her alone.

Eva gripped Javier's hand, giving it a squeeze. "I trust you—it's just not easy to say." Her tremors returned. All day she'd been clutching the truth she'd glimpsed. The way Rahmagut had taken Ches's divinity, and how he now planned to eliminate him completely. She feared for Reina, and for their friendship, which already felt shattered. She feared for her own life.

"I know what the tinieblas want." She waited for a question or an objection. All she received was his stunned silence. "Javier... when I was in that trance, I saw Rahmagut's past." She let it pour out. "All this time, I have coexisted with him in ignorance, because he didn't have his memories. It was like he was just a power in me. Something I could use. But now that he has his memories, it's different. He's stronger."

Rahmagut's laughter distracted her. It raised the hairs along her arms.

"I know his past now. I saw it first when the sanadero dumped his cleansing water over me. Then I took another look into his life when I fractured the Void gem in the stables."

"The gem Enrique wanted to take?"

She nodded, fishing within the tightness of her bodice for the black gemstone she always kept on her body. Rahmagut didn't say anything, but she could feel his irritation for revealing their secret. She held it in the dim candlelight. The fissured line was charged. It stole her heat rapidly. And now that Eva knew of its power, she made a point of avoiding skin contact with that fracture.

When Javier reached to grab the gem in curiosity, Rahmagut jerked her hand away. Javier frowned at the reaction, but Eva didn't have the heart to admit her lack of control. She sucked in a breath.

"Calamity tells Rahmagut's story," she explained. "Ever since the stables, I haven't been able to get it out of my mind: Arbiters say Calamity is a game that tells Ches and Rahmagut's ancient war, and all this time I thought those were just stories. Just some fiction to embellish a gambling game. But it's all true."

Eva recounted the memories she'd witnessed. From Rahmagut leaving his ancestral homeland to conquering the valco kingdom to nearly destroying the world with the indomitable power of the Void gem he'd forged.

"This gem... Rahmagut wanted to use it to ascend, but it backfired. And it still has the power to make everything implode," she whispered as she held it over her lap with trembling fingertips. She couldn't set it aside. Rahmagut didn't have to warn her, but she knew he wasn't going to let her part with the gem.

She was grateful for Javier's patience as she added, "Ches had to intervene. That's why the gods were sealed in Tierra'e Sol."

"Careful, niña."

She squeezed her eyes shut to ignore him. "We unsealed his spirit at the tomb, but he's not fully returned. He'll always need a body. He needs *me*. He can't return to his full power, not without being in a place of concentrated iridio, such that he has enough strength to control the gem."

"You're not wrong."

"Enough," she thought.

"A place of concentrated iridio?" Javier asked. "Like the Páramo Mountains?"

"That's where he needs to be to control the Void gem. That's where he wants to seal Ches away forever," Eva said.

"But there are gaps to your understanding."

"Leave me alone." Eva pressed her palm to her temple, as if that would do anything to silence him.

"Spilling my truth to your useless husband won't change anything. You forget he is also my tiniebla."

"Stop."

"What you see is only what I want you to see. You are my tool and my puppet."

"Shut up!" she shouted, startling Javier. She clamped her hands over her mouth.

Javier's stunned eyes searched her. His mouth opened, but he closed it. He read her, and it spared her from having to speak of her awful reality: Whether she liked it or not, she shared a body with an ancient entity, who didn't care about the well-being of his host.

"He's speaking to you now?"

Eva licked her lips. "He always does. Now more than ever."

Javier opened his arms, and Eva melted into them. He held her tightly as the shivers ran through her. How could she have been so ignorant all this time? How could she have accepted her possession? Rahmagut was an illness. A rot.

Her stomach roiled with pain. She twisted in Javier's arms, moaning. This was her punishment. She understood it well.

So she knew she needed to speak the truth, before Rahmagut silenced her entirely.

"When we destroyed the tomb, Rahmagut claimed my body, and Ches chose Reina's." Eva whimpered as the pain ran through her belly viciously, twisting and constricting her innards. "We know this." She squeezed her eyes shut and cocooned her frame within Javier's. "But he also sent out a call—a command—to every tiniebla."

She had to focus on this moment, on the warmth of Javier's hand grasping her shoulder, to ignore Rahmagut scraping the boundaries of her consciousness. He wanted to stop her. If she didn't focus on her words, she might even lose control of her own lips. Eva pressed her forehead against Javier's chest as much as her antlers allowed, feeling the quickening pounding of his heart, noting how she liked the rhythm of it. His embrace grounded her. It reminded her that they had signed a binding magical contract. Despite the darkness, the possessions, the tinieblas, and the deaths, they at least had each other.

"He commanded the tinieblas to come after me," she said, forcing the words out.

At that, Javier distanced himself. "Why didn't you say something sooner?"

"I—I had no idea until yesterday. Rahmagut's memories were buried beneath the weight of my consciousness when he took my body. I swear I asked him, and he said he didn't remember—or he lied."

Again, Rahmagut's laughter echoed in her mind, louder this time.

"He can't take my body, not yet." Once, she might have thought not ever, but now she couldn't be sure. "So he's having the tinieblas take me to the mountains. To the fallen star, where most of the unspent iridio still exists. He needs that much to control the power of the Void gem, so that it doesn't implode again. The gem is that strong."

Quick like lightning, Javier grabbed Eva's wrist, lifting the Void gem before his eyes.

Eva squirmed to pull away, not because she felt uncomfortable, but because Rahmagut yanked her arm this way and that, threatened by Javier's scrutiny.

"A world-rending gemstone?" Javier said. His cheeks drained of color. The black stain of his corruption crept along the edges of his eyes.

"If this breaks—if it's unleashed somehow—it could end the world. I saw it in Rahmagut's memories. When he used it to ascend, he lost control and created this massive force that sucked everything into the Void. Ches had to intervene. But when he sealed it, Ches accidentally trapped himself with Rahmagut, who clung to him. Then when they emerged, at the tomb, Rahmagut took Ches's pupils—to have a piece of his divinity."

Her belly burned. She groaned and writhed.

Javier frowned, his grip constricting her blood flow. "Why do you carry it?"

"Javier, you're hurting me," she whimpered.

He was immediately sobered by her words. The darkness retreated and he let her go.

Eva felt like a little girl, desperately wanting to cry. "I didn't know how dangerous it was—just like I didn't know his plans—*ah*!" A fire-like flaring spread through her groin and up her stomach. It encroached on her chest, and for a moment Eva imagined Rahmagut trying to compress her lungs. She imagined him swelling her throat to suffocate the life out of her.

Javier helped her lie down on the bed. "What's happening?"

"*He's* hurting me."

"Where?"

She squirmed, but his eyes flicked to her belly as she twisted and gripped it with one hand.

Javier rubbed his hands together. The soft glow of his golden geomancia gilded his skin, contrasting the monstrosity of his hands—his claws.

She trembled while Javier loosened her bodice's fastenings. His eyes were trained on hers as he slowly lifted her chemise, revealing the skin underneath. He gave her a second, to voice a protest, before he pressed his golden-glowing palm against her diaphragm.

The relief of his galio was instant. Like a dousing of water. A weighted warmth. It smothered Rahmagut's laughter, and his antagonism. Eva took a breath and nearly whimpered in relief when Javier's healing hand drowned out Rahmagut completely.

She sighed happily. The god was subdued, for now.

As she glanced up, she found Javier's gaze heavy with more than just concern for her well-being. He let out a small breath, as if all this time he'd been holding it.

"Does that help?" he said so gently her chest fluttered.

Eva nodded as his massaging inched upward. Underneath the chemise, his hand lingered between her breasts, as if he wanted to feel her heart.

Without Rahmagut's influence, she managed to lower the Void gem to the bedside bench. She could breathe freely without its constant drain. Javier had given her this.

She closed her eyes and arched her back, pushing against Javier's hand. It was an invitation for him to lean forward. They lay side by side with his hand still pressed next to her heart.

"You said I could trust you," she said softly. There was no need for loud words between them.

"And I meant it. I want you to."

Behind him, his tail switched from side to side like an expectant cat's. Eva wondered if he was aware of it at all.

"Then I need you to answer me truthfully," she said.

He nodded, inching closer. His lashes shrouded his eyes as he took in the fullness of her lips. His desire for them was obvious.

"Tinieblas are attracted to me because of Rahmagut's command."

He studied her smattering of sun spots, then her eyes.

"They're ordered to take me to the Páramo."

He nodded.

"Does that mean you're attracted to me because of the tiniebla?"

His teeth shone beneath his smile. He coughed, then laughed.

She almost smacked him across the chest, but she didn't want to disrupt this balance, this perfect molding of their bodies. "It's not funny!"

He grew serious. "I thought you were beautiful when I first saw you. I wasn't lying when I said it—before Rahmagut possessed you."

Eva swallowed thickly. Could his hand pressed against her chest feel her heart skipping a beat?

"I felt truly clever for tricking you into marrying me."

This time, she did smack him.

"But it's not just because you have a famous father, or blood that was born to wield iridio. Now I know you have a quality I can't describe, a way of being open to the world. So many people live their lives afraid of the unknown, but not you." He glanced away as if he were too shy to say the words. "You have more courage than you give yourself credit for. And a sense of self-preservation that's borderline capricious."

Eva was stunned, to be so thoroughly appraised.

"I just know I like it." He smirked. "And it's forever mine."

She reached for the ribbon holding his low ponytail and freed his silky locks from its hold. How she loved their thin softness. "You *just* like it?"

He shifted his weight, so she could feel the press of the bulge between his legs.

Heat flushed her cheeks. There was a long pause as their eyes met. His uncertainty was clear in his face.

His hand moved from her heart, gently gliding over her skin to cup her breast. His thumb brushed her nipple as he gave her a soft, expectant squeeze.

Eva held her breath with a racing heart, her core clenching.

"No, I don't *just* like you," he said. "But I don't want to sound like an idiot, demanding things from you just because I'm your husband. And you don't have to play a role for me. You don't have to do anything you don't want to. But..." He squeezed her breast again, like he was indulging. "I'd like to have you—to make you mine—before it is too late."

Flutters filled her belly. Eva fought with herself to contain her shuddering. She reveled in his honesty, in the words she'd wanted from him for so long. "When would it be too late?"

The question had the opposite effect she desired, as he frowned.

She brushed his starlight hair behind his ear and whispered, "I want you, too." She wanted to feel like a woman in his arms. She wanted to see what it would feel like to be so close to him, freed of barriers, until the separation between their skin was nothing but a mere change in pigmentation. With her cheeks ablaze, she said, "I'm ready for it."

His eyes drowned in hers, hesitant, as if he were giving her the space to second-guess or renege. He kissed her gingerly at first, testing with his thumb rolling her nipple. When Eva whimpered, his lips devoured hers.

Eva trembled. She was floating. She was drunk on his scent and on the obvious intoxication he had from her. She kissed him back roughly, vibrating from this never-ending fight for dominance that had marked their relationship from the beginning.

Freed from his reservations, Javier tugged her chemise off and grasped her sides, his clawed hands gentle as they kneaded her breasts. "You're so beautiful," he said, his gaze roving over her skin, smiling when he met her eyes.

Eva burned. "No—*you are*," she said, meaning it.

He kissed her neck and her collarbone until his mouth found a feast in her nipples. Eva arched into him, breathless, aflame from the need in his nips. She moaned, surrendering to his touch as a fire sprouted from her core. His attention made her throb. How she wanted him closer, bared, inside her.

She had to force them apart to undo his shirt. In the dimming candlelight, her fingertips traveled from his neck to his chest, discovering territory she'd never touched before. They trailed along the leathery blotches of his corruption and feathered the scutes dotting his sides. She caressed his lower belly, reaching for his pants. He, too, quivered, his muscles tensing while he battled to keep himself in one piece before her.

He dug his teeth into his lower lip. "Are you sure? Even when I'm like this?"

In a way, it felt strange to imagine him without his tail and the manifestations of his turning. She was wretched for thinking it, but she liked the way he looked, weathered and complicated, exactly as he truly was.

"Am I supposed to reject you because of it?" Upon his hesitation, she kissed him again, guiding his hand to her center, where he could feel how thoroughly ready she was. "I want you to have me. Make me yours," she whispered against his lips.

He stripped the rest of her clothes, and she helped him shed the last of his. Almost reverently, he spread her open for him. He paused right at her moist entrance, the head pressing and imposing, beaded with his own slick. Eva trembled in anticipation, finding his eyes cloudy. He waited, frozen. When she nodded, he entered her slowly.

Eva squeezed her eyes shut as she got accustomed to his size. Her heart pounded from feeling him in such an intimate way, how he stretched her, filling her all the way. She was so vulnerable and exposed beneath him, flushed.

He pulled her up so she could sit on him, his shoulders tensing and his hands gripping her from behind, his claws digging into her skin. He buried his nose in the crook of her neck, taking heavy gulps as if her skin were his source of air, as if without her he would drown. "You're delicious," he hummed, making her toes curl. He was quivery, and frail, so she squeezed her arms around him, becoming the glue holding him together.

"Really?" she murmured, greedy for the validation.

"Better than anything I could have imagined." He moved again and sighed.

"You imagined me?" she asked, smiling, her belly swirling with stars.

He looked into her eyes. "How could I not? When it was just me in that prison—those times you got so close it was a tease, only to leave me by myself," he said with an impish grin.

Her toes curled again as she pictured it. He'd desired her for so long. "I won't leave you anymore," she whispered before kissing him.

He moved her with clumsy desperation, until he found his rhythm. He said her name as if it tasted like honey in his mouth. He gasped it between breaths, tickling her neck, repeating it as she rolled her body closer to his. Eva's hands roved his back, finding his skin vibrating beneath her fingertips. And she arched into him, delighted, feeling him throb and shudder as he thrust with every muscle, aching for deliverance.

Delicious pleasure coiled in her belly. She grabbed his face and forced his lips onto hers, tongues clashing just as she crashed into him, each thrust bringing them closer to the sun. She had wings and was ready to jump off the cliff, where an ocean of storming sensation awaited for her plunge—

Suddenly he stopped. He squeezed her outer thighs, forcing her to cease each rolling movement. "No—wait—stop," he said in a single breath.

Eva blinked, dazed, already craving his movement inside her. "What's wrong?"

"I can't," he said, pulling her off him. He threw himself beside her on the bed, his gaze on everything but her.

A coldness took over her. She was left throbbing in his absence. Eva hugged herself, concealing her breasts and feeling foolish, used.

After a while, he said, "I can't put a monster in you."

An incredulous cough burst out of her. She paused in disbelief, awaiting the joke. Then it dawned on her that he was completely serious. How in his frowning eyes there was a battle between the satisfaction of their coupling and the fear of its consequences.

So she tested him. She curled up beside him and was welcomed into his arms.

"You know what I'm becoming. I can't risk it. I can't hurt you—"

Eva squeezed his cheeks and forced him to face her. "You are not a monster. It's your actions that define you, not your curse."

"It's on my skin. It will be in my seed."

She didn't know what to say. Thunder rolled outside. The tent walls shook and wavered. Eva let the moments trickle by, for there was nothing she could say to abate this fear. It made it painfully obvious how far they were beyond their depths.

"Back when I used to live with Enrique, I used to wish for a monster to rip out of Laurel," Javier said. "I used to wish for her to birth a tiniebla, after she cursed me to become one."

Eva held her breath as she listened.

"It was rotten, I know. In the end, she died giving birth, just as I had wished it. The same could happen to you. It'll be my punishment." He turned to her, aching to appease her. "And yes, I regret the way I acted—the things I said. You say I'm defined by my actions. Well, there you go: I've been a monster all my life. This turning, it's appropriate, for the person I was. Sure, I can make a last-ditch attempt with Laurel's bones, but..."

"It will only make you into one," she finished for him.

He winced but nodded. "I don't want to be that person anymore. But what's done is done."

Eva grabbed the sheets and covered them. She pressed herself by his side. "I'm sorry."

"What? It's not your fault."

"I wasted your time with my empty confidence. I led you on, thinking I could find a cure."

He shook his head and leaned closer, gently brushing back her bangs. His gaze surfed her cheeks and her lips, her wayward curls. He took her in so deeply, it made the flutters in her belly surface anew. "Eva, you held me and comforted me when I was sprouting a tail."

She held her breath.

"I was a disgusting mess, and you stuck by me." He paused, as if at a loss for words. "I realized that day—you're the only person who cares about me. Without you, I am alone. There's nothing you need to apologize for, ever."

She could barely breathe. He turned to the ceiling again. "The sanadero said my time to revert this is almost through. I'll never go back to the person I was. I'll always be . . . this thing."

Eva ran her hand over his belly, tracing the patches of his turning. His stomach quivered underneath her touch. "Maybe that's okay."

He faced her with wounded eyes. Every inch of him begged for a different outcome. She could see it in the lines of his eyes, in the downward turning of his lips.

She placed soft, feathery kisses along the blotchy scutes of his neck. Skin to skin, she said, "This is only physical. I'm not going to reject you if you keep changing." Her hand found his heart. "What matters is who you are on the inside."

She knew she sounded like a romantic. But she ached to be the column he leaned on. She wanted their bedroom to be a place where honesty was their chosen language. Yes, they lived surrounded by a constant state of discord, but at least they had this: a marriage where there was trust.

If he maintained his sanity and his agency, the outward appearance was the least of her concerns. Even when he'd sprouted the tail and claws, she still saw him as she did on that first day of their meeting: beautiful, otherworldly, and unattainable. Well, now she had him.

"And I like the way you've changed," she said. "The way you look at me—the way I can trust that you'll protect me at all costs. I feel like I have someone on my side, unconditionally. I feel spoiled." She giggled.

He kissed her deeply, his tongue breaching her lips.

As she took a breath, she said, "Don't give up yet. Something might surprise us in the future. But if this is what you must become, nothing about us changes. I still feel really lucky."

He gave her a smile. It was a rare one. His face opened in a way that occurred only for her.

"Now, don't be mean and deny me," she said with a playful pout. She grabbed his tail and ran her fingers along its length, pleased when he shivered from her touch. "I want all of you, monster or not."

He rolled over her and pressed a palm against her navel, pensive. Eva trembled. Was he imagining her belly growing, every day swelling with a part of him? His throat bobbed and she offered him a small smile.

Finally, he sheathed himself in her slowly, angling his hip to reach deeper than ever before. Eva arched her hips to meet his, her legs tangling with his as he stretched and filled her again.

"Like this?" he asked, grinding into her, ravenous but confident.

Pleasure wound in Eva. *"Yes."*

He met her gaze and held it, his eyes vibrant. "Thank you, for being my wife. For giving me this. I know I don't deserve you."

"The person you are now does. Being with you makes me happy," she said as she caressed his cheekbone.

He grabbed her wrist, burying his face in her palm and placing tender kisses where her skin was soft. He moaned into her hand. "After everything that's happened, I—I never imagined it would be possible to feel this good. I don't want this moment to end."

"Slow down?" she offered, even as she grew greedier of his thrusts. She brought him closer and took his lips, giddy at how docile he was in her arms.

He dug deeper into her, his smile roguish, as if he were too addicted to her to do so.

"There will be other times," she muttered, arching into him, finding a new angle where each delicious stroke pulled her closer to the edge. She couldn't get enough of him.

He fluffed away her curls and kissed her forehead. "Eva...I'm so close—I want you to be sure."

She thought of the amapola he never shared. It had wounded her then, but now she understood he wanted her to have full agency over the decisions they made. Just like now.

She pushed back his sweaty hair, drinking in the sight of him, how his pupils were enlarged in this trance.

Whatever happened, she knew she wouldn't be alone.

"I want you to," she whispered in his ear.

He groaned into her neck, burrowing his face in her hair. And she squealed, gasping as he filled her up so completely. They were in tune. She felt him crest, and the ocean parted for her as well, lapping over her, the waves of pleasure thrashing every nerve as she reached her own release.

Javier held her when it was done, not that he was steady himself. She curled into his arms, contentedly closing her eyes. They nestled comfortably on the bedding as Javier kissed her cheek and her eyelid and her sweaty temple. He gently pushed back her coiled bangs and murmured, "That was incredible. Thank you, my fallen star."

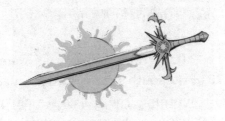

38

Settling Scores

Reina's worn leather gloves slid over her bandaged hands. She ignored the friction's sting as she finished arming herself. She stared at herself in the dirty standing mirror of her tent. Her bangs had grown to the point that she could easily tie the hair into her long braid. The bags under her eyes were more pronounced than ever. And her eyes were puffy from last night's crying, when she'd let it all out.

She couldn't get Maior out of her thoughts. A piece of her had been ripped out against her will. Lately, her breaths came short and chaotic anytime she was reminded of Maior's flight.

The Liberator's promises had failed her, and Reina had enough of trusting him. It was clear now that he viewed the needs of the many above the needs of himself, or of her. He was a man who had once abandoned his daughter to the Serranos, all for the good of a nation. How could she have allowed him to convince her that he'd ever ensure Maior's safety? Maior was just one person. His relationship to Enrique and the longevity of valco bloodlines mattered more. It always had.

Eva, as Rahmagut's host, couldn't be relied on. And Javier had never been worthy of anyone's trust. How desperate had Maior been, to think his assurances amounted to anything?

Reina would have to solve this matter on her own.

She'd bathed after returning from the swampy morichales bordering the lake to the south, where she'd practiced Duality with the rising sun. This morning, she'd been strong enough to share her mind with Ches without the temple-splitting headache it usually gave her. Only her extremities had blistered from his power. Normally it fell on Maior to patch her up. Reina moved away from the mirror, breathless from the reminder. She pressed a fist against the raggedness of her chest, fighting the ache. The hurt molded into a rage. So she folded it, tied it with a neat bow, then tucked it away for later.

A rustling at the flaps of her tent announced Esteban's entrance. He brought a plate of topocho and pork roasted on the firepit, and a clay jug sloshing with guarapo. Pucho de Las Garras entered behind him. The three sat by her rudimentary table and broke fast together.

Esteban and Pucho had traveled with her upon her request. As soon as Reina had left Don Samón's study, she'd snuck out to look for Esteban. She'd easily found her grandfather in the Old Quarter, perhaps because he wanted to be found, and she'd asked him to come with her, needing the backup. He wanted to be part of her life? This was his chance to prove it, she'd told him, expecting him to decline. To her surprise, not only had Esteban agreed, but when she'd met him by the city gates, she saw Pucho tagging along as well.

Seeing the confusion etched on Reina's face, Pucho had said, "Do you really think I'm going to let this old man pick a fight with Enrique by himself? That valco's got Esteban's build, and knees that are twenty years younger. Not to mention the valco blood. You are outmatched without me."

Esteban had smacked Pucho on the shoulder. "He's got a debt to repay," he clarified with a smirk.

"What's surprising is that he'd call on his debt *for you*," Pucho told Reina, his pointy nozariel canines glinting in the torchlight as they passed the gates.

Esteban nodded proudly. "I still have one more fight left in me, and I'm suddenly finding myself enamored with the idea of having a granddaughter. Who would have guessed that I would grow this soft in my old age?"

Reina laughed with them. Esteban and Pucho bantered throughout the ride and kept her too occupied to ruminate on Maior. Their jokes and stories distracted Reina from imagining the horrible things Enrique could be doing to Maior—the reason for why he would want her so badly. For that, she was grateful.

Pucho made himself scarce anytime the caravan stopped for water and breaks, as a Bravo soldier was bound to recognize him. When they'd finally reached Catatumbo, it had been at night, which allowed him to slink into Reina's tent unnoticed.

"So what kind of name is Pucho?" Reina now asked with topocho in her mouth. "Never heard it before," she said, sipping on her lukewarm guarapo.

Pucho scratched his scruffy jaw. "Where I'm from, it means the last bit—the spare one."

"Ah—so not your true name."

"A term of endearment. You see, my parents, they had seven of us, but I was the last by twelve years. That oven had been out of work for a while." He chuckled to himself. "I was a surprise no one was expecting. And my dad, he was a joker—it's where I got it from—and he started calling me El Pucho, for being the last one. And it stuck. Everyone in my village called me that. But then came the rains." He sighed. "It rained for days and days and there was a mudslide that took out most of the village, my whole family included."

Reina covered her mouth in pity. Esteban patted his shoulder.

"There was an old couple in Las Garras that survived the mudslide, but their home was gone. So they packed what they could and took pity on me and brought me along with them to Segolita. I was shaken—terrified. I didn't speak for a while. When we got there, the couple took me to an orphanage, but when the nun asked for my real name, they didn't know it. And I wasn't speaking, not yet. So they told her what they knew, 'El Pucho de Las Garras,' and the rest is history."

Reina offered him an understanding smile. "It's a good name."

He laughed. Between mouthfuls of his topocho, and like it was his turn to interrogate, Pucho asked, "And where'd you get such a shiny sword? Did you use it against me when we fought? How come I never noticed it?"

"It was nighttime," Reina said. "You do know I'm host to Ches, right?" She glanced to her grandfather, wondering if he'd conveyed the news.

Pucho laughed. "I suppose now I do. A good half of the riffraff in the Old Quarter can describe you with pretty good accuracy, from how much people have been talking about you. Rumors of your deeds at La Santísima Diosa have spread all over the city. It lit a fire in every nozariel I've talked to."

Reina blushed. "Really?"

"They all want a hero, like the Liberator, but of their own kind," Esteban supplied.

Reina exhaled weakly. "I'm not a hero. I only did what I had to do."

"Then why did Ches give you such a fancy blade?" Esteban said.

"Why did he choose your body?" Pucho added.

Before Reina could say the truth of how it had happened, craving the self-flagellation, Esteban lifted a hand, stopping her excuses. "You risk your life for strangers, yet you decline the accolades. That is the stuff heroes are made of."

Reina's cheeks heated even more.

Pucho slugged the last of his drink with gusto. "Whatever you want to call yourself doesn't matter. All they care about is that this is a true sign of Ches. We all grew up with stories and traditions of worshipping him—but some of us tricked ourselves into believing they were just old tales to be forgotten. Myths."

Esteban raised his hand at this, agreeing.

Pucho went on. "But you, glowing with Ches's sunlight? You give proof of the unknown and the unseen, beyond geomancia. It validates all those who still cling to the traditions of their ancestors. Besides, proof of his existence suggests a different picture from what the priests want us to believe. It gives a hope that *we*—" He gestured between him and Reina. "We aren't wrong for merely existing."

Reina took a deep swallow, her chest constricting with emotion. She knew exactly what he meant. Indeed, she gave physical form to a forgotten god. She wielded his power, making it real. And she deserved to use this strength to guarantee her happiness. All the pain she endured for Duality—she deserved some recompense.

Esteban beamed, crossing his arms in amazement. "Now you have me wishing I'd known you sooner."

Reina bit down on her smile. She looked away to her grimy boots. "Me, too."

Pucho leaned forward and said, "Now, let's hunker down and discuss our very unheroic plans. Who are we kidnapping? And when?"

The plan was simple: While Reina and Esteban joined the tiniebla-hunting parties dispatching to the south of Lake Catatumbo, as commanded by Don Samón, Pucho would search the Águila encampment for Maior, using his anonymity as cover. If necessary, he would wait until Enrique also partook in a raid—or left for the privy, Pucho offered with a snicker—to sneak into Enrique's tent to look for her. Depending on where Maior was being kept, together they would rescue her and take her as far as their blades would allow them.

Reina and Esteban left at noon. But with the overabundance of tinieblas marching for the lake, they didn't make it back to the encampment until the sun was close to setting.

Reina ran to her tent, aglow with hope for good news, Esteban trailing behind her. She entered and found Pucho splayed over her bedroll like an overfed feline.

"She's not here," Pucho said with a shrug. "Trust me, I looked everywhere, even in Enrique's tent."

His nonchalance infuriated her. Anger and panic swirled in her belly. She had already gone too long without knowing Maior's whereabouts. She'd wasted her day killing tinieblas for this? And why was she the only one who gave a fuck about Maior?

"But you know who's here? The caudillo's daughter, *and* her royal betrothed," Pucho said, raising his eyebrows suggestively. "I say we take them—force a trade with Enrique."

Reina groaned. She had no intention of attempting such a move, but if Celeste was here, then at least she could get some answers. Fuming, she stormed out of her tent, leaving Pucho and Esteban in confusion.

She snuck along the labyrinthine paths made by Águila tents, too fast and heated for any soldier to stop her. Not that her presence was questioned. It was clear Enrique was merely on standby. But waiting for what?

Finally, Reina caught sight of a silky black ponytail swaying with the wind. She recognized the laurel-embroidered jacket with the padded shoulders and trailed Celeste to a tent on the rising hill. Celeste was accompanied by a skinny man their age. Reina followed them into the tent without invitation.

"Reina!" Celeste gasped as she entered.

"I heard of your betrothal," Reina said dryly.

The young man, an heir of the royal Silvas, shot some expletives her way. Too bad Reina was impervious to anything but Celeste's gaze.

"You wouldn't understand it," Celeste said. "And either way, I don't owe you anything."

Francisco Silva tried stepping between Reina and Celeste, so Reina squared off. "I care very little about your rank," she told him. "And I *will* hurt you if you get in my way. Do not test me."

He shot a nervous glance at the fist curled at her side.

Celeste placed a hand on his shoulder. "It's okay, Francisco. I know her. We just need to talk."

The gentleness and patience Celeste afforded him boiled Reina's blood. Where had this compassion been when she and Maior had needed it?

"Give us the tent, please."

Francisco glared at Reina as he exited. She could tell he was holding an insult on the tip of his tongue. Part of her wished he would just say it; she ached to hurt something.

"I thought you weren't keen on playing cousin, last time I saw you," Reina said. "But don't you owe me an explanation as to why you're able to move on so fast?"

Celeste's lips twisted. Reina knew that look. She had seen it on Javier and Enrique before. The signature Águila disdain.

"I'd have to have been heartbroken in order to move on, don't you think?" Celeste said.

Reina stepped closer. "So I was right? Everything you said in Tierra'e Sol was another manipulation? All that begging for me to come with you?"

Celeste stepped up to the challenge. They were but a breath away, fists curled and foreheads itching to clash.

"You made your choice," Celeste said. "Isn't that why you're here? Because you're beside yourself with worry for that woman? I'm not the one who's going around lugging their entire emotional baggage from one person to another. Do you even know how to be alone?"

Reina shoved her. "That's rich coming from you, someone who has everything in the world yet is the loneliest person I've ever known."

Celeste regained her footing and clocked Reina on the lip so fast she couldn't dodge it. Reina crashed into a table behind her. She recovered and served Celeste a punch in the gut.

"Just because I made you my everything once doesn't mean you get to use it against me for the rest of my life," Reina said as she watched Celeste double over. Reina wiped the blood from her split lip.

"I am not lonely!" Celeste heaved. She tried kicking Reina's shin, to get her on the floor, but Reina moved out of reach.

"Then why did you use me as nothing more than a follower?" With the clarity of hindsight, the one-sidedness of their friendship was crystal clear to Reina. It made it more painful, to think back on every moment and strip it of the meaning she'd assigned it. "You treated me like I was beneath you."

"Why else do you think my mother wanted you in the house?" Celeste tackled Reina, her antlers pricking Reina's chest.

Pain blazed through Reina as she crashed into the table a second time, impacting her spine.

"Just like Ursulina served Father, you were supposed to serve me!"

The words stung more than any punch could have. Reina shoved her back. They rolled to the ground after Celeste made a grab for Reina's braid, bringing her down.

Tears crowded Reina's eyes as she climbed onto Celeste and wrapped both hands around her neck. Celeste kicked and tried prying her grip open, but Reina was the stronger one.

"I loved you," Reina growled. "And now you can't stand that I love someone else. Now you punish me for it."

Reina's heart pounded as she watched Celeste's cheeks turn purple, as her eyes bulged with panic. But she couldn't sit there and choke the life out of Celeste. She didn't have it in her. Reina felt so empty as she stared into Celeste's eyes. Celeste wasn't the true source of her ire.

Reina shoved off, freeing her. She backed away and gave a wide clearance, should Celeste try to go at her again. "Where's Maior? She saved your life. Have some compassion. You can't seriously agree with whatever your father has planned for her. You're better than this!"

Celeste massaged her neck. Hoarsely, she said, "She's not here. You know she's not. Father's not going to let her slip away—not again."

The answer knocked the air out of Reina. "Why do you have to be so vile to me?" she said softly. Part of her wished Celeste wouldn't hear her—that she never had to know the answer.

Still on the ground, Celeste glared. "We made you. You are who you are because of us. You had no right to abandon me."

And now that Reina knew Celeste's true nature, she wouldn't hesitate in doing it again.

Reina bolted out of the tent in a fury. She couldn't swallow her anger any longer. The world blurred around her. She passed tents and soldiers oblivious to her hurt. Because no one ever bothered to look, or to care. Reina had coursed through this life alone, and only Maior had paused and considered her as someone with feelings and needs. As an equal worthy of honest love and compassion.

Reina pressed a fist to her mouth, to stop herself from sobbing aloud. Panic welled in her diaphragm as she imagined Maior in Enrique's dungeon. He'd taken her by way of Gegania already.

Reina embraced her rage.

She opened her chest up to Ches's power, welcoming the explosion of light. His sunlight veined her body. Her breathing quickened. The burning of his sunlight stung her skin, a throb building in her sinuses, but she held on. She had the constitution to wield it. She'd trained for this, and her eyes were clear. With the clarity of her hatred, Reina existed in this moment as a wielder of Ches's strength. She curled her fists before her. With Duality, she was aglow.

"*Do not act recklessly,*" Ches commanded.

"*I won't.*"

"*If you perish, you'll have wasted my efforts.*"

"*Then help me,*" she thought insolently.

Enrique's tent was at the top of the hill, where he ruled over the encampment like the tyrant he was. She didn't have to go far in search of him. As she crossed the meeting grounds, she caught sight of his massive antlers reflecting bonfire light. With his soldiers, Enrique lifted a goblet to the sky. A bottle of anise sat open on the bench beside him.

The celebratory setting made her see red. Of course he had reason to feast. He didn't care about the tinieblas. To him, people's suffering was only a tool to achieve his goals.

Her blade swished out of its scabbard. It lengthened her reach, and she pointed it directly at him. The soldiers who noticed her had the instinct to step between them. But the glow of Duality rightfully spooked them, and they stepped aside.

"Where did you take Maior?" Reina growled.

Enrique downed the last of his drink. He wiped his mouth and faced her as dusk shrouded the encampment.

"Would you look at that: Ursulina's brat." He smiled. "Like a proper pest, always managing to come back."

"Where is she?" Reina said, never slowing her stride.

He appraised her blade, his gaze gliding over the thin sharpness of its construction. Reina hoped he could tell it was forged by an immortal. She hoped he understood its danger in her grip.

"Lower your weapon, duskling."

"You took her to the Páramo through Gegania, didn't you?" Reina said as they circled each other, leaving a wide berth between them. Onlookers gathered at the edges, molding a circular arena around them.

"Your questions bore me. Enough with the crying spectacle. Why are her whereabouts any of your concern? Maior de Aparta-deros gave herself willingly to me. She *chose* to come with me. So I took her, and I will not be giving her back."

"You bastard!" she howled, charging with the speed of Duality.

Enrique quickly slapped his hands together, materializing his red-glowing sword as he pulled them apart.

A thunder reverberated in the encampment as their blades clashed. His shoulders bulged as he parried, but Reina had expected it. She maneuvered back, fluid like the wind, letting the air between them take the brunt of his strength.

"I'm going to take your head," she said with her heart racing to a mad tune. "And after I'm done with you, I going to burn your miserable manor to the ground."

"You will burn my family home?" They circled the arena, trad-ing places. Enrique summoned a litio barrier that coated his entire body in a red glow. "Didn't you beg, borrow, and steal to live there? Didn't you grovel at my feet for the honor of serving me?"

Quick footed, she swiveled back to slice his side. He stepped away, parrying with a strike so close it severed a loose curl by her temple. They traded places again.

He laughed. "I find it amusing: You, your father, and your grandmother—nothing called you to my territory, to my wealth, yet you couldn't help yourselves. Leeches, all of you. Always com-ing back for more."

"Reina!" a familiar voice called from behind her.

Esteban pushed to the front line of spectators. Reina cursed, as she couldn't spot Pucho in his company or anywhere within the crowd. She couldn't bear Esteban intervening alone. She'd asked for their help, sure, but not so they could lose their lives.

His presence distracted Enrique, whose face darkened with recognition. "What are you doing here?"

Did he know the truth about Juan Vicente? Did Esteban and Enrique have a history? It didn't matter anymore. She didn't care if Enrique died in utter ignorance, or if he had known their truth all along. They might share blood, but he was not her family.

"Stay out of this!" Reina yelled at Esteban.

To prove she didn't need Esteban's help, she lunged again at Enrique, who leapt into the air as quickly as the lightning striking Catatumbo behind him. She missed him completely. He twisted in the air, kicking her so hard on the back that she crashed to the ground and ate dirt. The taste of iron bloomed in her mouth. The impact skinned her elbows, leaving a streak of blood on the ground. Nightcleaver flew out of her reach.

Enrique went for it, unaware the blade responded only to her. Reina scrambled to her feet and managed to snatch the blade. She swung back, slicing low for his shins, taking advantage of his proximity. Her strike was blocked by his litio barrier, barely managing a superficial cut.

"Enough! Both of you!" Esteban howled.

"Keep your words to yourself, old man, or I'll sever your tongue after I'm done with the duskling," Enrique said, never once lifting his gaze from Reina.

With a scowl, Esteban dove back into the crowd, disappearing into the night.

"You're going to learn why I command this army. Not because of my name, or because of the iridio. It's because I am undefeated in battle. And you will pay for this lesson with your life." Enrique flicked his fingers in an elaborate motion. A scute-like black plating materialized over his antlers, his elbows and knees, and the epaulette-bearing military jacket. "I always knew I'd have to end you with my own hands one day," he said in a dangerous, amused tone. "Ursulina groomed you—I knew you wouldn't be so easily discarded. But what you fail to realize is that I delight in crushing even the most resilient of cockroaches."

Reina's pulse rang in her ears. Her fingers trembled with adrenaline. Her hatred for him swelled.

"What's the woman from Apartaderos to you? Your life is mostly worthless, but it's clearly a waste to see it squandered like this. You're making a fool of your commander."

"This has nothing to do with the Liberator," she said. "I don't need his permission to take your life."

He chuckled. The men around them egged him on to finish her off. They fabricated ideas that she was stalling. That she was an easy pick.

Reina shoved the strength of Duality to her extremities. She opened her heart and her mind and let go of the last ounce of restraint. Beneath her clothes, her skin bubbled. She was a blazing beacon against the night.

Cries of "Witch! Demon!" were thrown around in the watching crowd, but they backed away nonetheless, afraid.

As Ches watched, Reina reminded him of Enrique's tyranny. He never cared when his iridio lured monsters into the homes of innocents. He inflated its price, denying people the reagent needed to repel tinieblas. He had forced Maior into surrendering herself, all so he could resume his romance with a dead woman. His death at her hands was justified.

Reina charged, her blade firmly gripped in both hands. Their swords clashed. They met with thunder. Sparks lit the air from the impact. The sky flashed blue and purple as lightning struck the lake. They pulled back for a sliver of an instance and struck again. A right swing and left parry. Enrique stepped back with each swing. She gained ground.

She gazed into his blood-red eyes as their blades locked against each other. She was shorter, and slimmer, but she was stronger. Perspiration trickled down his temples. His jaw trembled from the exertion. She hoped his confidence would soon become fear.

"So this is the strength of that god?" Enrique said through gritted teeth.

He didn't deserve any explanations, or mercy. All he'd earned was her ire, after all the slurs, the tricks, and the insults. After forcing her to be an instrument that harmed innocents. She ground her teeth as she pushed against him with all the strength Ches could provide. Her muscles tore as she shoved him back.

"Reina!" a voice thundered from the crowd. The soldiers parted as the Liberator emerged with worried eyes.

Reina ignored him. She leapt into the air, seizing the distraction he had caused for Enrique. Her grip burned in her hands as she swung for his neck with every last ounce of strength in her body. She could already imagine it, the burst of blood as she decapitated the caudillo of Sadul Fuerte with one clean slash.

Except Enrique lowered himself, and she struck his armored antler instead.

Nightcleaver became stuck. It happened in the blink of an eye. An instant when she dangled from his antler, her heart plummeting. But there was no reprieve.

Enrique rounded on her. With a sickening crash, his fist punched her temple, fissuring it, making it cave. The pain was a dizzying explosion. Blood squirted from her eye. Her conviction made her hang on, and it was a mistake. As the last thing she saw was his vein-bulged fist pummeling her a second time.

She flew into the air without her blade. It was a mercy when the world went black.

39

The Caudillo and the Liberator

Eva found Don Rigoberto in her father's tent as she walked in without invitation or announcement. Don Rigoberto flinched from the intrusion. His military jacket was wrinkled, his hair was windswept, and his face was blotched the ruddy color of exhaustion.

"Don Rigoberto?" she muttered, surprised to see him again. Her belly coiled. Lately, anytime he made an appearance, it was always to deliver disquieting news.

"Doña Eva," he said, tipping his chin. "It's good to see you again. You look radiant."

"What are you doing here?"

His throat bobbed. "I bring tidings from Segolita." He didn't seem to mind her presence, or perhaps there was no time to. "I rode as fast as I could, to make it here before Las Orquídeas Blancas. I'm afraid a score of soldiers marches this way, helmed by Monseñor Lorenzo. They mean to apprehend you and Reina, for the crime of hosting the ancient gods of the sun and the Void."

Eva exhaled weakly. Don Samón groaned. He circled his table and placed a hand on Don Rigoberto's shoulder, his smile tight and thin. "Thank you for this great effort, Don Rigoberto. I will never forget your loyalty."

Don Rigoberto straightened proudly. "I remember a time when your presence in the cabildo ushered in great prosperity for the city. The last thing I want is to see our hard work dismantled by religious fanatism and misinformation. You must not bend to them. They do not have the president's leave."

"When did your tune change?" Eva asked. She couldn't remember the last time he regarded news of the gods with much esteem.

"Never," he said stiffly. "But I also know Reina didn't destroy La Santísima Diosa. Witnesses tell a different story from what the archbishop is using as justification. If el Libertador stands with you, then it must be for a reason. There is no value in loyalty and honor if they can be so easily toppled."

Don Samón nodded. "And I'm in your debt."

"Impossible. You saved me more times than I care to tally."

Don Samón turned to Eva and said, "And what did you want to tell me, Eva?"

Eva nearly flinched as disappointment weighed his eyes. Was he having regrets of giving her his name? Chaos had circled their lives ever since he took her in. She understood if he did. At this point, she was nothing but a bringer of misery.

She wrung her hands as she approached. Her chest thrummed uncomfortably. Equal parts anxiety and Rahmagut wanting to bully her into silence.

"It's about the tinieblas."

The pounding in her chest threatened to deafen her. She found it hard to breathe. Still, Eva squeezed her eyes closed and fought to shut off Rahmagut's influence.

"Would you like Don Rigoberto to step outside?" Don Samón said softly.

And it fractured her even more, to hear in his tenor how he still trusted her. She was the luckiest person for having him as a father. Even in the face of challenge, his patience and commitment were undaunted.

But before the truth could pour out of her, an older man with the constitution of a warrior burst into the tent. Don Rigoberto and Don Samón looked surprised, but they all seemed to know each other.

"Esteban? Why are you here?" Don Samón said.

The man was in his sixth decade, but he'd lived a violent life. It was obvious by the scars on his face and by the large hand clamped over his sheathed knife. "I came with your caravan. I just didn't bother to make my presence known."

"Why?"

"Because I didn't do it for you. I came for my granddaughter, Reina. Who at this present moment is dueling Enrique *to the death*!"

A million horrible images flashed through Eva's mind. But she was deafened by Rahmagut's antagonistic cackles, once again reminding her she was nothing but a lapa heading straight for the hunter's trap.

They rushed out of the tent, joining a flock of people heading in the same direction, murmurs of a fight igniting the crowd with fervor. Halfway through the march into the Águila encampment, Javier joined them. His proximity eased Eva's anxieties. He took her hand and brought her closer.

The air over the crowd's center sparked with leftover geomancia in a riotous rhythm not unlike the lightning of Lake Catatumbo. Something like thunder rang through the encampment, a sound Eva was well accustomed to by now: the clash of geomancia-enhanced blades. At the vanguard, Don Samón cut through the throng, making way for Eva and Javier, who followed behind. "Reina!" he yelled.

Eva pushed through to stand beside him. She gasped as she saw Reina in midair, aglow as sunlight lapped every inch of her body. Enrique's gaze flitted to Don Samón, distracted. Everything happened too quickly, but Eva was painfully aware, as Rahmagut cringed within her, that Rahmagut feared for Enrique's fate.

Why? was all Eva could think.

With fury in her eyes, Reina swung for the caudillo's head. But she missed completely.

Eva screamed as Enrique's large fist crashed into Reina's skull with a crack—as he pummeled her a second time, sending her flying into the air. The light of life left Reina's eyes. Eva's heart constricted as Reina's unconscious body hit the ground with a thud. And Rahmagut's delight blared within her, poisoning her horror. It made Eva want to double over and retch.

Don Samón flew in between Reina and Enrique, who'd raised his massive sword for a finishing blow. "Stop!" he roared.

Eva freed herself from Javier's grip and threw herself beside Reina. Her hands trembled as she lifted Reina into her lap. Blood streamed from Reina's right eye. Splintered bone jutted out of her cheek. Crying her name, Eva lowered her ear to Reina's nostril, feeling for her breathing. There was but the slightest trickle of air.

"Step aside, Samón," Enrique said. He tried grabbing for the blade lodged in his antler, to pull it out, only to discover nothing there.

Ches's golden blade materialized on the ground beside Reina.

"You're clearly victorious. Leave the woman be," Don Samón said with ice and ire in his voice.

Enrique glanced at the bleeding Reina. He scoffed. "Look at her. A sack of blood. What life is left for the creature? She knew the consequences of dueling me."

A hand squeezed Eva's shoulder. She jumped, only to realize Javier had knelt beside her.

"*Heal her!*" she shouted at him.

Fear and uncertainty flashed through his face in equal parts. He summoned galio to his fingers. They quivered as he attempted to rearrange bone structure. Eva's heart thrummed dissonantly. She prayed that Enrique hadn't caused irreparable damage. Then she summoned her own galio and tried her best to mimic whatever Javier was doing.

"Move aside, Samón." Enrique's voice thundered. "Tell your minions to back off. I will finish her off. It's what she wanted when she decided to duel me."

"I will not allow that."

"Blood will be spilled tonight!" Enrique roared, circling the arena, inching closer to Don Samón, who matched his rhythm.

Lightning speared the rolling clouds above them. It revealed the bloodthirst in Enrique's eyes, and the severity of Don Samón's.

Eva noticed the intent curiosity within the crowd, as everyone watched the caudillo and the Liberator. Two valcos driven to the climax of their lifelong rivalry, one that always teetered on the line between affinity and enmity.

Blood erupted from Reina's mouth and nose as she returned to consciousness. Still, Javier's healing hands kneaded her temples and throat, drenched in her blood. Reina squirmed and coughed from the pain. To be conscious in this state, it looked beyond agonizing.

"Then duel *me*," Don Samón said, unsheathing his saber. With it, he kept the caudillo at a distance. "If you must duel someone, duel me."

"You'd do this for her? Why?"

"Because you never should have taken her bait to begin with. You are a battle-hardened commander. You should have known better."

"Precisely. This is her punishment."

"I mean that Reina is in my retinue. Her actions are my actions. Your aggression toward her is an insult to me, and I demand reparations in the form of a duel."

Enrique smirked, surprised but pleased.

A hush of anticipation blanketed the encampment, broken only by Reina's bloody gurgles. Eva felt exposed. She clutched her iridio pendant tightly while Javier did his work.

Thunder shook the lake's encampment, until Eva realized the sounds weren't just Catatumbo's lightning, but storming footsteps. Discord erupted beyond the crowd, and the commanding voice of a man yelled, "Make way! Move out of my way!"

The onlookers parted as new soldiers joined the fray, helmed by a man in a black cassock. Monseñor Lorenzo and his Orquídeas had arrived.

The archbishop paused, stunned at the sight of the valcos with their raised swords. At the bloody display of Reina being patched together. "Is this the execution I have been asking for?" he asked.

Enrique shot him an insolent look. He bared his teeth. "Aye. I will deliver you the nozariel, if you stay out of this."

"How pathetic is your honor that you place your trust in him again?" Don Samón told Monseñor Lorenzo.

The archbishop's lips quivered. He pointed at Eva and Reina and ordered his followers, "Arrest the heathens."

"If you value your lives, you will not heed that command!" Don Samón howled at the watching crowd.

Whistles cut the air as both Águila and Bravo soldiers unsheathed their swords in reaction to the antagonistic Orquídeas. Then a quiet overtook the campgrounds, the air charged in painful anticipation as they all understood: A single wrong move would be enough to trigger chaos.

"Let us prevent a massacre," Don Samón told Enrique, lifting the point of his saber so it glinted with the firelight. "Instead of relying on the swords of our subordinates, I challenge you to a valco duel to settle this once and for all."

Enrique cocked an eyebrow, but he was listening.

"If I win, you will abandon your fight against Reina, and you will return Maior de Apartaderos. Afterward, you will not request her in any exchange or negotiation. The matter of the woman from Apartaderos will be officially settled."

"And if you lose?" Enrique said, curling every syllable dramatically under his tongue.

"Name your prize."

Without hesitating Enrique said, "I will have proved my strength is superior to yours, and you will use your influence and title of Liberator for my benefit. The human will be mine to keep. The nozariel will be mine to slay. You will hand over your progeny to the church, who will exorcise her of the Void demon causing this tiniebla uprising."

Eva couldn't stop her shoulders from shaking.

"No," Don Samón said.

"No? And what makes you think you get a choice?" Enrique said, tilting his head in Monseñor Lorenzo's direction.

Eva looked to the archbishop, only to find his glare already trained on her. She scowled back. How she despised his beady eyes and the sanctimonious lifting of his nose. He prowled the fringes of the arena like a vulture, too weak to interrupt the actual predators at the center.

"Keep my daughter out of this."

Enrique shrugged. "How precious, the way you initiate this duel with terms favorable only to you. But that's not how things work. I will not shield you from the Orquídeas."

"*Enrique*," Don Samón growled.

"Archbishop, do you agree to the terms?" Enrique said.

Monseñor Lorenzo scowled. "As long as we slay the fake gods."

"Then you leave me no choice but to defeat you," Don Samón told Enrique, giving his free wrist a flick. With fingers in the formation of enhancing bismuto, he gave his arm a wide arch, imbuing his body and saber with his geomancia's golden glow. "Come," he said.

Enrique lunged with his massive sword, which flashed red as it sliced horizontally. Samón leapt in the air, flipped overhead, and landed at the other side of the arena.

As Enrique straightened up, his gaze settled on Reina, as if he were considering violating the terms of the duel. It'd be an easy pick, in Reina's weakened state. So Eva pressed her hands together and immediately manifested a thick litio barrier around them. The glass glimmered with at least a hand's length in thickness.

Samón marched at Enrique, who met his sword halfway.

"I wonder if you would support the duskling if you learned of the things she did before she joined your ranks," Enrique goaded.

Their swords met with a shrill that reverberated across the camp. Eva's heart thrummed in agonizing anticipation. Samón wielded his saber in a single-handed grip, his left hand tucked behind his back. He shared Enrique's height, but there was a difference in builds. Not from lack of trying, Eva knew, but because Enrique had inherited a bigger frame.

"The things she did to remain fed and sheltered in your household, you mean? The things you forced everyone to do?" Samón growled as he shoved off Enrique's blade. "The kidnapped babes and the virgins taken from their homes?"

Enrique whirled to feign a strike. As Samón blocked, Enrique swiped at the ground, kicking the Liberator off balance. Eva screamed as Enrique drove his sword right for her father's heart.

Samón swerved out of the way, twisting in the air to jump back to his feet. He lashed the air with his engraved saber, shooting iridio-fueled lightning directly at Enrique's chest. The electricity impacted Enrique right in the heart, shattering his summoned scute-like armor. The plates disintegrated.

"Do you really think I'm ignorant of your exploits?" Samón barked.

Enrique laughed. "But you allowed them."

They charged at each other so fast Eva barely registered one swipe before they were parrying with another. Sparks burst from every collision. Around them, the clouds thundered. The air was charged, not just from Catatumbo's lightning, but with the geomancia exuding from their enmity. Every soldier watched, mesmerized by the duel. Save for the dueling valcos, an eeriness settled over the grounds. It reminded Eva of the calm before tinieblas attacked.

"I must do something," Eva told Javier, who pulled Reina's hair back to stop her from flailing as he massaged the bloody side of her face. Reina looked delirious with pain, but at least she was alive and his healing was working.

"It's a valco duel. You will destroy your father's honor if you intervene," he said.

She was stunned. Was that what she'd done with his duel?

Enrique swung ferociously, forcing Samón to step back with every strike. They circled the arena as the spectating soldiers pushed against each other, nervously avoiding the swords' wayward slashes.

Imbued with electrifying bismuto not unlike the lightning overhead, Samón's blade crackled the air. "I allowed you to act freely out of respect for the alliance we forged during the war—for our friendship," he told Enrique. There was hurt in his voice. "Why do I have to remind you? We are the last of our kind."

"You say we are the last of our kind, yet you abandoned Dulce to her fate," Enrique growled as he swung down. Samón leapt back, and the ground beneath caved from the impact. "You left her to rot with those humans while she carried a valco inside her."

"For the sake of our victory over Segol."

Enrique spit between them. "The humans don't care about you."

A silence filled the arena. Eva had to agree.

"But you and I, we operate differently," Enrique went on. "I did not treat Laurel like you treated Dulce. I do not bend for humans. And I will not relinquish my wife," he said, sweat rolling down his temples, his spittle finding the air.

He thrust his sword at the Liberator's middle. Faster than Eva could blink, Samón lifted his saber to block the impact, sidestepping the sword. Their blades clattered like shattering glass. Uncontrolled, the bismuto in Samón's saber exploded. Energy was released with a boom, air buffeting all around them. Flames licked Enrique's and Samón's wielding hands. They were hurled back in opposite directions, as were their blades.

They scrambled to their feet. Enrique sprinted for Samón before he could retrieve his saber. Enrique punched him across the face. Dizzied, Samón stepped back. He shook the pain away, only barely dodging a second punch. Samón rammed his forehead against Enrique's, where their antlers clattered, caught.

Enrique blinked, disoriented, as Samón pummeled him in the gut over and over, his knuckles growing bloody. Finally, he knocked the wind out of Enrique. Eva's heart soared as Enrique sagged. Then he was shoved to the ground.

A lull took over the arena as Enrique could barely lift himself up to his knees. He was dazed, without air. His body stopped glowing with his geomancia's red.

Samón stood before him, hurrying to catch his breath. Sweat slicked his hair. Blood trickled from his split lip and hands. The skin around his forearm was raw, as the explosion had eaten away at his sleeves, fusing the fabric to his flesh.

The campgrounds hushed.

There was a darkness in Enrique's eyes as he muttered, "This isn't over."

"Opponents would shake hands, in the valco duels of old," Don Samón said, swaying. He gave Enrique his hand.

Enrique's lip twitched. He took it and lifted himself to his feet.

The tightness clutching Eva's heart eased. She could breathe. Her father was victorious. They could get Maior back.

Don Samón faced the watching crowd and said, "Now sheathe your weapons and refuse any more bloodshed. Our duel determined tonight's outcome, and I have won."

"I said: *This isn't over!*" Enrique yelled, pressing his hands together. With a crazed howl he summoned his massive sword.

Don Samón turned just as Enrique's sword materialized in his grip. He didn't need to fetch his blade. He could simply summon it again.

Someone called Enrique within the crowd—Celeste, as she withdrew after watching the duel.

The caudillo flashed forward, and he drove his enormous sword through Don Samón's stomach.

Blood sprayed out of his back as the blade impaled him all the way. Mouth agape, Don Samón collapsed into Enrique's arms. Enrique let him fall to his knees.

A scream became lodged in Eva's throat as Enrique stepped on the sword's pommel, pressing his boot down and tearing her father's innards even more. Enrique used the sword as leverage to keep Don Samón pinned before him. Then he grabbed Don Samón's antlers with both hands.

Blood gurgled out of Don Samón's mouth. He glanced up, meeting Enrique's manic eyes. Red streamed out of his lips as he begged for honor—for mercy.

"Valcos are dead," Enrique growled. "There is no one to enforce this fantasy of yours—this valco duel of old." The veins on his hands protruded as he gripped Don Samón's antlers. "You betrayed your own kind when you chose to stand by the nozariel. Your honor does not matter if you are dead."

Enrique's jacket splintered and burst as he yanked the antlers in opposite directions. He howled, using all his strength. A sickening ripping and cracking filled the silence of the camp. Enrique ripped Don Samón's antlers from his skull, tearing the scalp and pulling his hair apart.

There was a last gurgle of pain, before the light left the Liberator forever.

40

Up in Flames

Enrique's sword disintegrated, leaving a gaping hole in Don Samón's belly. He tossed the body to the ground unceremoniously and threw the antlers still attached to flesh and sinew before the archbishop. Blood seeped into the dirt beneath Don Samón's corpse, forming a black, sickly sludge.

A wail of despair burst out of Eva. Her litio barrier melted. She shoved Reina off her lap and ran to the mangled remains of her father. Tremors shook her as she took in the emptiness of his eyes. As she saw the pain forevermore etched across his agape mouth.

Tears and a rush of heat flooded her face. She knelt by his side, unable to see anything but a blur of red. She squeezed him, his big frame still searing from adrenaline but brutalized. She buried her face in his neck, quivering with sobs. His blood bathed her.

Enrique addressed Don Samón's allies within the crowd. Someone shouted at the caudillo—Don Rigoberto perhaps. Eva couldn't make out the voices in her despair.

Her body trembled as she considered the future stolen from her. For a moment, Eva had tasted the life she'd always ached for. She'd found the place of belonging where she could be herself. She'd experienced the unconditional love of a parent. She'd had a father who dreamed of nothing but simple moments together. She'd had his love, which he'd never hidden.

It had all ended tonight. Enrique had ripped it from their hands.

The world narrowed around her to this singular pain. A deep hollow opened in Eva's chest. She couldn't open her eyes. She could barely breathe. Face marred with tears, Eva howled.

Her cry triggered pandemonium.

Swords whistled and clashed in the air. Yells descended all around her. Bravo, Águila, and the archbishop's soldiers warred each other, loyalties scorned, their honor tainted. Enrique's kill was first blood, and the massacre Don Samón had tried to prevent happened anyway.

Eva lowered her father's body to the slurry beneath him. She ignored Javier's calls.

Purple lightning veined the sky as Eva rose. The clouds thundered. She wished she could bring down the sky's punishment on Enrique and all his sycophants.

Despite the chaos, no one dared approach the center, where she and Enrique stood before his kill.

"You violated the terms of your duel," Eva said. She couldn't keep herself steady. She was dizzy with rage.

He scowled. The disdain for the life he'd taken was crystal clear in his eyes.

"Your father was a fool. His pleas for honor were going to get him killed one way or another. Better it happened at my hands. I gifted him a warrior's death."

Eva loosened her restraint over Rahmagut. Her extremities burned and itched as his strength coursed through her veins. She knew what she needed to sacrifice to wield his divine power. She knew that every inch of allowance she granted him was a part of her she wouldn't get back. And Rahmagut flooded her gladly. He prowled the edges of her vision. His satisfaction sweetened her tongue.

Lightning materialized in her hands. It crackled rabidly, stripping every shadow from the arena. It fizzed the blood in her hands and clothes. It lit Enrique's face in shades of neon. For a split moment, Eva saw his fear.

Monseñor Lorenzo emerged from the fighting, flustered and

surrounded by a handful of his Orquídeas. He howled at Eva, "There it is! Undeniable proof of her communion with the god of the Void."

Both Enrique and Eva watched him with hatred.

"You won your valco duel—now it's time to hand over those witches!" Monseñor Lorenzo said. Spittle flew in the air as he ordered, "Submit them to their exorcism. Bring her to me! On her knees!"

His soldiers poured around Eva. Enrique used the distraction to disappear into the fighting crowd.

Eva's heart thrummed a mad tune. But she wasn't afraid. With a lash of her hand, she electrocuted the first fool who crossed her. Javier stood at her back with his sword drawn. He blocked and parried, keeping a handful of soldiers at bay.

Esteban entered the fray, accompanied by a nozariel Eva immediately recognized: the mercenary who'd attempted to kidnap her in Hato de los Lobos. Side by side, both men fended off any who made a go at the incapacitated Reina.

A sword was brandished in Eva's direction. It meant to cut her from shoulder to belly. Rahmagut took over and sidestepped the blade for her. He shoved the base of her palm up the man's nose, shattering bone. The soldier flew back, crashing into the men rushing behind him.

The air tasted charged. Eva knew what to do; whether that was from her own instincts or Rahmagut's, it didn't matter. She lifted her hands to the sky and tugged the bolts veining the clouds over Lake Catatumbo. The lightning came to her, and she rerouted it to the fanatical soldiers who came after her.

Tears and rage flooded her face as the bodies amassed at her feet. She was monstrous. She was an indomitable beast. And it felt good.

Deep in her belly, she hungered for revenge. She was a hollow creature without the future she'd wished for so hard it hurt.

She searched for Enrique within the chaos, but he was gone, swallowed by the tumult and the piling bodies felled by the warring factions. Only the obsessed Monseñor Lorenzo remained.

Eva approached him. He watched her with his self-righteous satisfaction. He called her a pagan; a liar; a whore who slept with Rahmagut and who tainted all that was right and good. He lifted his rosary in the air, as if it could slow her down, and yelled at his soldiers to grab her once and for all.

The hunger in Eva's blood wasn't appeased, even as she smote one man after another. Blue and black veins bulged in her hands. She could feel the hug of Rahmagut's corruption. Was this what Javier felt, when he surrendered to the whims of his tiniebla? Eva understood why he let go so often. It felt euphoric.

Eva zeroed in on Monseñor Lorenzo, memorizing his black eyes and pale face, the perspiration sticking his hair to his temples.

In trembling hands, he lifted his rosary even higher. "From the moment I saw you, I knew you were wrong."

Eva didn't have words for him, so she waited to hear his piece. She wanted to bask in the power she held at her fingertips and take her time. It amused her, letting him believe he could dictate the night's outcome.

"I warned Doña Antonia. I told her you were the sort to open up your soul to the devil. And I was right! Look at you, demon! I will see you face the Virgin's judgment. I will see you burn!"

Eva's lip twitched. "Like you burned Doña Rosa?"

"The curandera? Precisely. Like I burned her."

Eva was flooded with the sorrow and shame she'd lived with for her inaction. She'd done nothing but run when the archbishop stormed the Contadors' residence with his false accusations. Doña Rosa never communed with Rahmagut; Eva did.

"You look at me as if I took pleasure in her death, but that couldn't be further from the truth. *No.* Such an act was necessary, and it was a waste," he said, watching Eva beneath his lifted nose. "She was a beautiful woman, surprisingly witty for her pedigree, and I offered to acquit her. I truly did try." He scowled at the memory. "But she denied me. She chose her loyalties to that demon Rahmagut instead, rejecting the salvation I so willingly offered her! *She* drove herself to her own ruination, because I would rather see her burn than allow her devotions to that demon—"

"You're a monster!" Eva howled, understanding. As if forced by her disgust, the sky thundered. "She was more innocent than you'll ever be!"

"One cannot be spoiled by darkness when working on behalf of the Virgin."

Rahmagut hated the archbishop nearly as much as she did. It was obvious as his emotions transmuted with her rage into something else. An entity that was equal parts Eva, equal parts Rahmagut.

She lifted a hand, gripping the air with gnarled fingers, her nails turning black. Ropes of iridio shot from her hands, seizing Monseñor Lorenzo, constricting his arms and torso. Instead of her gold signature, the iridio geomancia was black.

Monseñor Lorenzo spluttered, confused. Eva curled her hand to herself, yanking him forward. She tossed him to the ground. His mouth filled with dirt as his rosary flew in the air and clattered at her feet. Eva stepped on it, to prove how useless it was against her.

She smirked down at him. Her veins hummed with a hatred Rahmagut indulged. He egged her on. He goaded and reminded her: first the archbishop, for Doña Rosa, then Enrique, for her father.

As Monseñor Lorenzo stood up, Eva summoned the indomitable power of iridio from her pendant. With Rahmagut's strength within her, she needed only a few droplets to gather flames in her palms.

The archbishop gaped. "What are you doing?"

"You condemned an innocent woman to her death for your own satisfaction—for a Virgin who never crossed the ocean." Rahmagut begged to be given control, and thus Eva allowed him to seize her lips so he could add, "A false goddess, deified by the killers and rapists who invaded this land. You used her name to excuse my erasure. You painted me as your devil. You ruined countless lives in the name of a narrative you were never around to write for yourself."

Eva enjoyed the eloquence. It brought true fear to the archbishop's eyes. She took back control and added, "So I will cleanse you, just like you 'cleansed' Doña Rosa."

The flames poured out of her palms, shooting the wavering

archbishop directly in the chest. He yelled, first from the shock, then from the all-consuming heat. The fire multiplied, fed by his overabundant robes.

A shrill scream broke through the night as Monseñor Lorenzo's skin was eaten by the flames. The stench of charred flesh swelled around him. Eva didn't care to cover her nose. She didn't care to look away from the dazzling flames as they fed on the fuel his body so readily gave.

The archbishop surrendered to his knees before collapsing onto the ground. He rolled in a desperate, final attempt to snuff out the fire. But Eva had fashioned her flames from iridio. They were going to burn until there was nothing left but ashes.

Tears blurred her vision. A deep sorrow embraced her as she realized Doña Rosa's last moments had been just like this. Agonizing and never-ending pain. When oblivion was the only respite.

Behind her, Javier watched her, frozen in abject terror, silent and expectant. The throngs of soldiers waited as well. What kind of monster was she, to take a life in such a brutal way?

Eva shook. She thought burning him to death would bring her absolution. She'd reasoned it was justice, for what Doña Rosa had endured. The archbishop had driven her to enact his own ruin. It had been an act of self-preservation. A display of her strength.

Yet Eva couldn't shake the regret as she watched the flames die over his ashes. It was funny. All her life Eva had tried to flee her true nature. But she still managed to circle back to this path, where she became the thing written on the lines of her fate. A monster, as everyone in Galeno had called her behind closed doors.

But if this had been her natural progression, why was shame clutching her throat and stopping her from breathing?

She was exhausted and forlorn. She was tired of fighting. So she closed her eyes and lifted her mouth to the sky, exhaling.

When she breathed in, it was Rahmagut who rose from the depths of her consciousness.

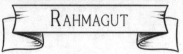

RAHMAGUT

41

A God for the Godless

Rahmagut appraised the battleground, the corpses, and the soldiers who remained standing. He extended Eva's hands, flexed the fingers, and watched them respond. It was his turn to have control. He didn't have to negotiate or battle her for it. Rather, Eva had curled deep within her mind. A coward, retreating after condemning the holy man to his fiery death.

Rahmagut had killed many in his lifetime. He knew it wasn't productive to dwell. One day she would learn this as well—or not. It didn't matter to him.

He smiled at the vermin who watched him, frozen in uncertainty. He could see the demoralization in their faces. They were confused by the deaths in their leadership. There was no one with the morale to oppose him—or rather, what they thought was Eva Kesaré.

Her body was convenient that way. But Rahmagut wasn't satisfied. He had plans to get something better.

A horn sounded in the distance. A beating of drums followed. Far beyond the crowd, someone yelled, "Tinieblas!" and more chaos broke loose.

There was a scramble as soldiers realigned their priorities. Without Monseñor Lorenzo's direction, Las Orquídeas Blancas scattered, some taking up arms against the incoming tinieblas.

Rahmagut watched them with a smirk. His creations, which he'd held back from the fray while the valcos dueled, now marched in right on time.

They served as the distraction he needed.

He turned to the presence behind him, which he'd never shaken off or forgotten. For how could he? Rahmagut could taste the changes in the air. He could scent the undercurrents of magic from those ascended. And no power was stronger than that of the god of the sun.

A faint light radiated from Reina. Within her, Ches's presence was meek only because Reina was incapacitated. But Rahmagut knew how far Ches's power stretched. If there was anyone to fear in this campground, it was him. He couldn't let her regain consciousness.

He ran at her, to snatch her, but was flung in the opposite direction as someone yanked him by the arm. He regained his footing and whirled, enraged.

It was Javier, who stepped in front of Reina, his eyes bright with fear. "You're not Eva," he muttered, and there was pain in his voice. Then he told his companions, "That's not Eva anymore!"

The nozariel and the elderly human pointed their weapons at Rahmagut, hesitant.

"How do you know?" the gray-haired human said. Samón had called him Esteban.

Color drained from Javier's face. "Look at her eyes—*her pupils!*"

So the piece of Ches he'd stolen had become apparent. Rahmagut smirked. It made sense that such a divine quality would not be suppressed.

"And the tiniebla in me is rejoicing for his god," Javier added, his voice soft and wounded.

The raw disappointment awoke Eva from her self-banishment.

"Eva, are you there? Answer me!" Javier said.

Indeed, Eva fought for control. She regretted relinquishing it. But Rahmagut was steadfast and victorious. He took a hearty breath. "Enough with the sentimentalities," he told Javier. "You wish to be with your wife? Submit to me." He raised a hand, gesturing for the tiniebla housed within Javier's body. "Bring me the woman," Rahmagut commanded.

Black veins trailed over Javier's cheekbones and temples. He twitched and twisted. He ground his teeth, battling against the darkness. His tail thrashed and his claws curled.

But a voice from within Rahmagut abated the command. "*No!*" Eva cried, blocking Rahmagut's strings.

"We cannot stay here," Esteban told Javier. He gestured for Pucho to pick up Reina's body.

"You will hand her over," Rahmagut growled. He shot a flaming ball in their direction, but the nozariel man was quick on his feet. Rahmagut sprinted at them. If he couldn't shoot them down, then he could pummel them to death. Except Javier intercepted him. And faced with Javier, Eva screamed in an attempt to break through. The sound was deafening, addling Rahmagut.

The interference bought Reina's allies enough time to retreat. Javier, battling his inner demon, was the last one to disappear into the night.

In the end, Rahmagut won control.

"*But I let them get away,*" Eva sniped.

Rahmagut ignored her. Sarcasm was the only power she had left. Ches's incapacitated host slipping from his grasp was but a small setback, which would be corrected in due time.

He crossed the camp to the battlefront, where Águila soldiers had formed a phalanx as their last resort against getting overrun by tinieblas. To the inexperienced eye, the situation looked dire. But Rahmagut knew it was only a matter of time before a competent geomancer incinerated them with a stockpile of iridio. Surely, the caudillo of Sadul Fuerte had such firepower in his arsenal.

Rahmagut needed the tinieblas alive, for now. They were his army. Their strength was his strength.

He hurried to the hilltop where Enrique Águila watched the battle from afar. The caudillo's shoulders were slumped. Exhaustion weighed his breath. Fighting the Liberator had taken a toll on his body, even if he pretended it didn't.

The thought sent a jab of pain through his chest—Eva's pain. Rahmagut swallowed it down. He'd have to endure it for only so long. Soon enough, he'd have the body he desired, and he wouldn't have to deal with the woman's mourning.

Enrique noticed Rahmagut's approach.

"You know I am not Samón's brat any longer," Rahmagut said.

Enrique's jaw moved with tension. He squinted, and Rahmagut didn't miss the fleeting surprise. The shock of seeing the additional pupils in Eva's eyes. "The god of the Void."

"It wasn't long ago that you wished to beg me for favors."

Enrique scowled. "Why would el dios del Vacío take such a pitiful woman?"

Rahmagut would have been incensed by the insolence, but he was patient. He had spent days hiding behind Eva's façade. He could handle the almost-jabs. Soon enough Enrique's payment would come due.

"Don't underestimate the Bravo line. Their affinity for iridio is stronger than that of your blood."

"I already proved myself stronger than Samón," Enrique growled with his eyes aglow.

"By stabbing him in the back."

"Predators do not mourn the food in their belly."

"Well said, and who am I to object?"

Enrique shifted on his feet, wary. Did he not know how to place the woman before him? Rahmagut enjoyed the thought of the discomfort he inspired. He understood. Most mortals would be confused, if not terrified.

"*Why are you playing games with him?*" Eva muttered from the darkness where she resided.

"*Have you never seen a cat play with a mouse? His is the body I want,*" Rahmagut told her. It didn't hurt to admit it, finally.

He had to stop himself from visibly smiling. His objectives were so close he could almost taste them. Initially, he hadn't been sure which half valco would be most convenient. Samón's bloodline had been made for the use of iridio, as evident by Eva's prowess. But Enrique's physique was obviously superior. For an instant, Rahmagut had considered Javier. It was a weakness of thought that lasted a mere second. Of course, no human had ever been in the running. And as Rahmagut had been born nozariel, he understood the limitations of their breed, especially in this land changed by human invaders. If he truly had his pick, he would have chosen a yare... His chest coiled at the memory of his winged queen.

"So why have you come to me?" Enrique finally said.

It was the question Rahmagut had been waiting for.

He approached fearlessly, for he knew no other demeanor would convince the caudillo. They stood side by side while taking in the ravaged battlegrounds.

"This god is in need of a favor. You are the only one who will understand. After all, your wealth and reputation exist because of a favor I once granted the great Feleva Águila." There was nothing great about the woman, but he needed to embellish the tale to satisfy Enrique's vanity. Rahmagut waited with a smirk. As Enrique's curiosity was piqued, it became clear he had no idea he sat on wealth gifted by Rahmagut himself. Of course, Feleva Águila had fed everyone lies.

"The iridio," Rahmagut said softly. "After I departed this world, its location and power became lost—a mystery. Until I unveiled it to your mother, in return for the sacrifice she made forty-two years ago."

Enrique gave him a scowl.

"Your mother led you to believe that she discovered it by accident, but that couldn't be further from the truth."

"You will not besmirch my mother's name."

"But I am not," Rahmagut said. "I merely intend for this information to reassure you of my generosity, in case you need convincing. You are the master of iridio because I granted it to her."

The sky thundered.

Rahmagut lifted a hand to the riotous clouds, fingers flexed. He made a big show of the gesture, as unnecessary as it was. Then he threw his hand down as he commanded the tinieblas to stand, unmoving, in place. The effect of his hold over the shadowed creatures was obvious. Enrique's brows rippled while he watched the tinieblas frozen in time. The closest ones were easily slaughtered and banished by Enrique's soldiers. Rahmagut swatted at the air, as if shooing away a particularly pesky bug, and the tinieblas began retreating from the banks of Lake Catatumbo.

"They are my demons. They do as I bid," Rahmagut said, moistening his lips. "Your scorched archbishop was not incorrect: They rise on my command."

Enrique's broad shoulders tensed with the instinct to strike Rahmagut down. Was that the last vestige of his honor? Rahmagut found the charade cute.

The moment passed as Enrique's brows ascended. "What is this favor you seek?"

"*He will not fall for you,*" the little bitch within him said. He took a deep breath to shove her presence out of his consciousness. It was his time to be in control.

In truth, he could achieve all he needed with Eva's own two hands, as feeble as they were. But why lift a finger when others could move the pieces on his behalf? And besides, Rahmagut enjoyed keeping a close eye on his mark. One way or another, he was going to have Enrique's body as his own. A valco with the name, wealth, and capabilities to suit his return.

"I am a returned deity. Ursulina guaranteed my reemergence when she spilled the blood of my brides and summoned the power of the Void. But it also brought back my greatest threat—"

"Ches," Enrique said, cutting him off. "You shared a tomb with the god of the sun."

Hot ire blazed through Rahmagut. His underarms itched. Enrique's eagerness to prove he knew of Rahmagut's enemy irked him, like he was trying to rub it in. Rahmagut took a deep breath. One day, he was going to smite any and all who dared to use that name against him. He wasn't going to forget this.

Lightning thundered overhead in his anger.

Enrique backed off.

"I intend to destroy him," Rahmagut said.

"You want to get rid of Reina before he can become a real threat?" Enrique said.

Rahmagut tensed. He allowed Enrique's assumptions. "The nozariel who hosts him slipped away from my grasp. I need her brought to the iridio mines."

"And why would I do your bidding?"

Rahmagut paced the hill where they stood. He let the iridio in his pendant pulse through Eva's body, crackling over her skin, showering her in black radiance. His geomancia colors didn't conform to the hues mortals could see. It manifested as black. He supposed it accounted for all the people felled by his hands.

The Void gem weighed Eva's pocket. One day, he would be ready to use it.

"Back there, you proved your might to every soldier in this camp," Rahmagut said. "And you earned their fear as well. Soon, Samón's allies will take the tale of his martyrdom to every city and every caudillo. It will earn you the scorn of both the president and the Penitents. And what do humans do when they're afraid?" Rahmagut wanted to make sure the scenario was fully painted in Enrique's mind. "They band together—they use it as an excuse to strengthen their ranks." In this, Samón had been right. "It will be your undoing. You gave them an excuse to fear and plot against the last valco bloodline of this land."

Enrique's jaw tightened while he considered Rahmagut, but he waited.

"They will come for you. Just as the archbishop came for Eva."

"And you're here to be my salvation?" Enrique said. The insolent wretch.

Rahmagut chuckled. "Don't you know my legends? I never offer such things, unless there is something for me to claim in return."

"And what is that?"

Rahmagut's upper lip quirked. Words nearly rolled out of his mouth—the admittance of wanting Enrique's body. *Eva* almost made him confess. Rahmagut ground his teeth to keep his mouth shut as Eva's influence fought and clawed to break through.

"*Silence!*" he howled within himself. "*I am in control now!*"

Rahmagut slammed her into the deep confines of their shared mind. Then he locked the door and threw away the key.

Returning to the present, Rahmagut told Enrique, "You are a godless man, I know. But you will believe in a god once I pluck Laurel's soul from the other side of death's door and bring her back to your hands."

Enrique froze. It was his turn to radiate anger.

Rahmagut let him simmer for a moment or two. "It is why you attempted to summon my favor, is it not? You know it's not beyond my capabilities."

Rahmagut inhaled deeply, reminding himself of his power. He had the Void gem in his possession. He had accomplished what no mortal had dared.

He had half a mind to smite Enrique. But if he did, what body would be adequate enough to house him? He had to keep the valco man intact. It was his best option for his return. It would truly make Rahmagut untestable. But he couldn't take him just yet. Confronting Ches, in Reina, would be all the easier if he retained Eva's countenance. Enrique had done nothing but earn everyone's ire. The humans and their fears, Rahmagut could later handle. With his tinieblas and his divinity, his ascension was all but guaranteed. But Ches was the one and true threat.

Rahmagut opened his arms as eddies of air enveloped him. They elevated him above the ground. He was lifted to Enrique's eye level and beyond.

"With my favor and alliance, you can have the strength of tinieblas at your fingertips—a whole army of them. If I will it—and believe me when I say I reward my disciples—you can have the return of your wife."

Mesmerized by the display of power, Enrique lowered himself to one knee. He tilted his head and antlers down. *Never show a predator your neck*, Rahmagut thought vaguely, but perhaps this was the point. Perhaps this was Enrique's capitulation.

Rahmagut cupped the crown of Enrique's head. Enrique flinched as a spark shocked them both.

"I am not a god you pray to. I am a god you act for. Help me collect the nozariel housing Ches. Bring her to the fallen iridio star."

Enrique glanced up, his blood-red eyes illuminated by Catatumbo's perpetual lightning. They glowed with his pain.

Rahmagut could read people. It was how he'd cemented his legacy after discovering the fallen star. He recognized Enrique's hunger and hurt. Enrique was as desperate to abate his heartache as all the other mortals Rahmagut had had to cross paths with to get to this point.

"*That's the thing about mortals,*" he thought, feeling charitable enough to impart the lesson to Eva. "*They always want something. They always hunger for more.*"

"Fuck you *for working with that monster,*" she snarled.

"I don't have to collect Reina," Enrique said, enthralled by Rahmagut's all-consuming energy. "She will come to us. She will come for Maior de Apartaderos. She will march directly into our arms."

42

The Returned Lady

Maior's skin hummed when she first emerged from the sodden tunnel to Gegania and the cold of the mountains embraced her.

The acidic smells of the earth. The faint mountain light filtering through fogged windows. The Páramo air was a crisp refreshment on her tongue. She returned to her homeland as if she'd never stepped out of her past. As if she were back within the humid stone walls of her chapel, humming an aguinaldo for the Virgin while wiping the pews with a wet cloth.

Her breath caught with melancholy. She was home, but at what cost?

A smile came to her naturally, and it convinced the guard who escorted her through Gegania's corridors into believing she was delighted to return to Águila Manor. She walked willingly, at their pace, proving they could sheath the swords they had pressed against her lower back. She was docile and amenable. She walked with every ounce of feminine grace she could muster. With her rosy cheeks and her pout, they were disarmed.

Maior was successful because the caudillo of Sadul Fuerte thought so little of her. He truly believed she was so meek and worthless that she would surrender her life just because she couldn't stand Laurel's dreams at night. Come to think of it, maybe this was how he thought of most people, based on the stories Reina had told of her time at Águila Manor.

There had been some truths to her sentiment. Laurel's influence tired and oppressed her. It was as if she meant to burst out of Maior's mind, to seize Maior's body for herself. Laurel might be just a shade, but based on everything she had witnessed, Maior was loath to underestimate her. Thus, she was justified in her willingness to do anything to end it, even this sin she was planning.

This frustration had seeped into her words while Enrique himself had escorted her to the mines, where he had his connection to Gegania. With her lashes shrouding her eyes, Maior had softly admitted how she felt imprisoned. How she was fighting the inevitable. But if he could agree to Reina's and Eva's safety, then Maior would gladly serve as Laurel's vessel.

Enrique bought the act. He took pity, instructing his soldiers to escort her to Águila Manor. All the while his gaze lingered a little too long over Maior's freckled cleavage.

A gilded carriage awaited her at the foot of Gegania's conuco, on a path surrounded by small frailejones and a medley of buttercups. Her armored escort surrounded her as she boarded the carriage. One soldier rode ahead on a horse. One sat across from her inside the carriage. And two more followed the caravan on horseback. Enrique spared no expense in securing her escort.

"We got orders to tidy a guest room for your use," the head matron said as Maior climbed out of the carriage on the muddy grounds flanking the large stone manor.

Maior let her surprise fuel her demure smile. So she wasn't going to be trapped in the underground room. Afterward, while a maid bathed her and brushed her hair, Maior was able to extract the truth out of her gossip. This was a reward, for turning herself in. "You've pleased the caudillo," the maid said with a giggle and a blush. "He's a generous man. He'll shower you in comforts and luxury. He wants you to be rewarded." And it sickened Maior, how his staff pretended to be ignorant of his villainy.

Águila Manor was a cold, forlorn place. While a guard tailed her, preventing Maior from initiating her plan, she had much time on her hands. In the moments of quiet loneliness, her heart twisted and ached for Reina's company. For Reina's friendship and her smiles. The tender devotion she gave Maior. Her steadfast embraces, where Maior felt safest. Maior hoped she could have her again one day. She accepted the hurt, reassuring herself that this temporary separation would be worth it, if it could guarantee Reina's safety. She also ached as she thought about how Eva must have taken the news—if Eva felt betrayed by Maior acting on her own.

She ate alone her first day back, and every meal afterward for some time. She had the long dining table, with its unlit candelabra and wilting centerpieces, all to herself. There, on golden cutlery and gilded porcelain dishes, she was served grilled trout, or smoked cheese floating in a cup of hot chocolate, or hearty hen stews. An overabundance of meals she couldn't finish by herself, which were thrown to the dogs afterward, wasted.

"I heard tinieblas are pouring into Segolita," a criada noted while she tucked the sheets around Maior's bed one morning. "The people from Segolita must have angered the Virgin. Otherwise—I don't understand why else the tinieblas only go there."

Standing before the gossamer curtains of her room, Maior nodded mutely. Indeed, security in Águila Manor was sparse. As far as she was concerned, the guards roaming the grounds were on duty just to keep her there. It was an oddity, the criada noted.

Three days crawled past. Maior tried keeping herself busy by offering to help in the kitchens. Of course, this caused an outrage, and she was promptly kicked out. With the guard in tow, Maior entered Laurel's bedroom. She cataloged the vast collection of rich gowns Laurel used to own. Then she opened every seibó and drawer, curious about their contents. Within them, she found the trinkets from her dreams: a solid-gold hairbrush of thick bristles, the sapphire necklace inherited from Laurel's mother, and the sharp ornamental knife the caudillo had gifted his wife. Maior brought all three to her room, testing the guard, but he never stopped her. Had he convinced himself Laurel's possession was influencing her actions?

Later, she perused the library, but the books were dense, and dull, and written in curling calligraphy that didn't help her attempts to learn how to read. Without Reina's help, her reading practice was painful.

Again, heartache stopped Maior from breathing. *Reina*. Maior gulped and closed her eyes. These days, it was best not to think of her. She couldn't let it distract her.

Of course Reina was probably blowing this out of proportion. Of course Maior would have to beg for Reina's forgiveness once this was over. Reina lacked Maior's patience, and this was okay. It was how she'd freed herself from Águila Manor the first time. Well, now the Águilas didn't have the witch Ursulina to place Maior in a perpetual sleep. Now Enrique was dressing her in Laurel's clothes and ordering the servants to treat her like the lady of the house. Yes, he had a guard watch her every move, but every hour and every day her jailer grew more comfortable with her perceived complacency. It would be only a matter of time before they gave her freedom.

With the guard at her tail, Maior didn't dare enter Enrique's study or exhume Laurel. He followed her everywhere, except when it was time to bathe and sleep. For her virtue could not be tarnished, the criada who brushed her hair with Laurel's golden brush reminded her. After all, Maior had been brought here for the caudillo and nothing else. Then, as if her words were of no consequence, the criada added, "The Benevolent Lady used to only ever use this brush. The bristles are from a rucio horse's tail, made especially for her, because her hair was so thick and wavy, just like yours."

Later Maior entered the Virgin's chapel, built on Águila grounds for the devout Laurel's convenience. There, Maior's jailer assumed her piety came from Laurel's manifestation. Thus, when he talked with the other guards posted about the grounds, he sold the belief that Maior was Doña Laurel returned. In a new body, shorter and stouter, sure, but it was the same old soul.

Maior didn't even have to sell the lie, not when they craved believing it this much.

On the sunny afternoon of her fourth day, while wrapped in a wool ruana, Maior took a stroll through the burial grounds housing Feleva's and Laurel's remains. A marble angel marked Laurel's grave. At the angel's feet was a vase bursting with freshly picked flowers.

How deep would she have to dig to reach her body? Maior crossed herself as she toyed with the thought. A chill ran through her. She was wretched for thinking it. One day her soul would be punished for such a crime. Yet she would be equally cursed if she remained in this state forever. Every path led to a fiery hell.

A rumbling sound filled the air from a distance, as if thundering clouds were rolling down the mountains. Only the sky was a bright blue, cloudless. It didn't take long for the commotion to pour out of the fir groves. A cavalry bearing the golden eagle standard, followed by carriages heavy with supplies. At the center of the procession came Enrique's gilded carriage.

Maior stood by the chapel's doorway, its elevation giving it a view of the roads leading up to the manor. With a fluttery heart, she watched Enrique and Celeste dismount. Then her mouth dropped as a third figure emerged from the carriage. *"Eva?"*

There was no time to agonize. Her guard told her to get back inside, to greet her new master. Shoulders quivering, Maior descended the mossy paths and lost herself in the hubbub of the arriving host.

She was ordered to wait in the dining hall, in her usual spot underneath the wrought iron chandelier. Enrique entered the dining hall and spotted her, as if she were a beacon guiding his gaze. Maior wrung her hands underneath the table as he approached. She'd been confident about her plan when she had arrived at an empty manor, but the overabundance of soldiers complicated everything.

"You're still here. Good," he said.

If he could smell her fear—well, that would only work to her advantage.

"I had a generous welcome," she said softly.

He told her escort, "Thank you for your service, but it will not be needed any longer. Report to your unit captain for a new assignment."

The man nodded and left.

"Thank you," Maior said, "for the trust."

He gave her a long look. His red gaze trailed up above her crown. "It's the least I can give you, for what you've offered," he said.

The details of her offer remained unspoken between them, exactly as Maior preferred it.

Celeste entered the dining hall, stopping near the doorway at the sight of Maior. Her face twisted with a scowl. "You actually brought her back here? So, what, you plan to make her the lady of the house? You have no shame, do you?"

A flicker of hurt flashed through Enrique's eyes, but he steeled himself. "I don't have to explain myself to you."

Without a regard for Maior's presence, Celeste said, "My mother is dead! Learn to mourn her and overcome your loss. Father, what are you doing?"

"I don't do this just for Laurel."

"Could have fooled me."

"You live under my roof and enjoy the comforts of my wealth, so I beg you to watch your tongue. Learn to weather what you perceive as injustices and accept my decisions. We are valcos. Do you think your grandmother built her legacy and ours by following the laws of humans and bending to their conventions?"

Hurt broke Celeste's scowl. She looked resigned. "If this is what you call legacy, then I don't want to be a part of it." She left without waiting for another word.

Enrique glanced at Maior, as if gauging her read of their vulnerabilities. In the silence that followed, he didn't appear as the indomitable commander he presented to everyone, but rather as a morally defeated man, standing over a reputation that quaked beneath his feet. Maior understood Celeste's pain. But she presented a compassionate countenance, saying nothing, as she knew Enrique expected of her.

His white-and-gold cape surfed the air as he departed, leaving Maior to her own devices. She remained at the dining table, quiet, as people trailed in and out of the adjacent halls, until the descending sun brought dusk to the manor. With the arriving nighttime came a hush that lulled the property, as soldiers retreated to the barracks or disbanded to go home. Thankfully, the caudillo and his daughter didn't return to the dining hall. In the silence of the manor, Maior had the courage to search for Eva.

She found her in the backyard, gazing up at the starry sky, almost in a daze. Maior stepped out, calling her name several times, but was ignored.

"You're here," Maior said in a wispy breath of relief. She ached to throw her arms around Eva, to embrace her. "But how? What has happened?"

Eva didn't spare Maior a glance, or an answer. She whirled on her heels and headed down a cold corridor Maior recognized immediately. Once, what almost felt like a lifetime ago, Reina had dragged Maior past these same walls.

"Where are you going?" Maior said in Eva's trail.

"A powerful geomancer used to live in this manor," Eva said coldly. "She should have what I need."

"Doña Ursulina," Maior muttered. Her spine prickled with leftover fear. She clenched her molars, but Maior forced herself to ignore the reaction. Eva was her best friend, and Doña Ursulina was dead. There was no reason why she should fear this place again.

Eva yanked the rotting-wood door of the underground dungeon. Without an ounce of hesitation, Eva stormed down the stairs. She shot fireballs at the wall sconces, lighting the path as she went. Following, Maior breathed through her mouth to avoid the scent of decay.

She knew which door belonged to Doña Ursulina's laboratory, her body recoiling as she arrived at the landing. "What are you doing?" Maior asked behind Eva, following her steps.

"I have been watching the moon every night since my return," Eva said as she shot even more fire wisps to the sconces lighting the room.

The light revealed a space frozen in time, untouched since perhaps the last time Doña Ursulina used it. The table at the center was covered in stacks of books, neatly assorted, as if she had made quick work of organizing her sources before departing Águila Manor for the last time. Sitting on the table was the monstrous object from Maior's dreams: the clay-coated deer skull flute.

Eva opened the star maps. She shifted through the thin papers, one by one, completely consumed and ignoring Maior.

The words sparked a memory in her. "This reminds me... Monseñor Lorenzo had me look through star maps. He was also tracking the moon."

Eva barked a laugh. "The archbishop?"

Finally, Maior seized Eva's wrist. "Those are Ursulina's things— Eva, you need to be careful—"

Eva wrenched herself free. Maior backed away, shocked at the darkness in Eva's eyes, the oddity of them. Eva followed her steps, diminishing the distance and shoving Maior with such force that the back of Maior's head clattered against the wall.

Face cloaked in shadow, Eva sneered, "You are familiar."

Maior held her breath.

"Though I shouldn't expect anything less from you," Eva said as she looked deeply into Maior's eyes, "my youngest wife. Always the insolent one."

Eva's name lodged in Maior's mouth. In that moment, Maior noticed the age weighing Eva's face. The predatorial curl of her smile. The extra pupil in each eye. She swallowed Eva's name down. Instead, she gasped, "*Rahmagut*."

43

A Willing Copy

Eva's smirk widened. "It took you long enough. You call your-self a follower of the Virgin and can't even recognize when the demon in your books is staring you in the eyes."

Maior couldn't breathe or speak. She couldn't look away from Eva's demon eyes. Her hands ached to reach under her dress for the necklace of the Virgin she wore at all times—the treasure Reina had gifted her. But it would probably be futile.

Palpitations filled her chest, and her palms grew clammy.

The reality of the situation became clear, and painfully so: Eva had joined the Águilas because she no longer had any agency over her body. She had lost the battle.

What did this mean for Maior? Where was Javier? And Reina? Who would come for her? Was she once again completely on her own?

One horrible thought after another crossed her mind. But the worst was the circumstances she'd designed—that she'd put herself in Enrique's arms.

"Deep breaths," the god of the Void commanded with amusement.

"You've taken Eva. Where is she?"

"Trapped. Begging to be let out. Begging me not to gut you this very instant." His gaze trailed above Maior. He licked the corners of his lips. It reminded her of a viper. "But don't panic. Gutting you would be disadvantageous. Enrique needs to believe he can get his wife back. You plan to play games with him, don't you?"

He stepped back, giving space for Maior's courage to return. She could breathe normally again.

"Play games? How can you say that?" she muttered, even if the god was completely correct. Part of her knew it wasn't smart to toy with a deity. But she couldn't give breath to her intentions so easily. And if he was true, like the Virgin was true, then surely he could see right through her.

"Am I supposed to believe you abandoned your lover for Enrique for no reason at all?" Rahmagut said. "Do you intend to insult my intelligence?"

No. But the unspoken meaning wasn't lost to Maior. *His intelligence. His assumptions.* He wasn't omniscient. He wasn't a god at all.

The firelight surrounding them flickered this way and that, disturbed. Shadows formed and elongated along Eva's features. Rahmagut watched her dangerously. He was testing her.

Maior gulped. She pressed herself against the cold stone wall behind her, hugging herself. She wished the Virgin would give her a sign or return some warmth. But Águila Manor was a godless territory. Though, she supposed, it was now Rahmagut's domain.

"No—I don't mean to insult you," she lied in a whisper. Her instincts urged her to do anything to appease Rahmagut's inevitable wrath. But she couldn't betray the Virgin.

Thankfully, Rahmagut wasn't interested in humiliating her. He returned to the table. His movements reminded Maior of a snake, as he ran a hand along the fragile paper cataloging Doña Ursulina's findings. "You may play games with Enrique," he said. "You may keep his fantasy alive, if you wish. But enough with the machinations." He shot her a look of disdain. "You're a pawn in a game you don't understand. Your little move of coming here caused the Liberator's death."

The air caught in Maior's throat. "What?"

Rahmagut laughed. He lifted some dust from the table with his forefinger, inspecting it. "It was...messy, to say the least. Reina—oh, brokenhearted Reina. She dueled Enrique and lost." A giggle bubbled out of him. "She retained her life only through sheer luck."

The news was a punch to the gut. Maior gripped her sides hard, her belly plummeting to the depths of hell. "Is she all right?" She realized the futility of her question. Why should he care about Reina?

He didn't answer. He just watched her, Eva's teeth glinting in the firelight beneath a curled lip. "Samón stepped in to save her, and he lost his life. A toppling of dominoes that ended up playing to my advantage, but only out of luck, and sooner than I had anticipated. So enough with the reckless plays. You shall act when I bid you to."

Like icy mountain water, dread showered Maior. What had she caused? And how could Reina act so recklessly? Maior had assumed Reina would have an overreaction to her leaving, sure—but not one as foolish as dueling the caudillo. No, *Maior* had been the foolish one, for not heeding Reina's threats when she gave them. Fighting Enrique had been on Reina's mind since they lived in Tierra'e Sol. Why hadn't Maior foreseen this?

Maior wanted to collapse to her knees and weep. She should have listened.

"Where is Reina now?" Apprehension suffocated her.

Rahmagut's lip twitched in poorly masked irritation. "Enrique brutalized her. He bashed her skull in. I heard the crack."

"*No.*" She clamped a hand over her mouth.

Chuckling, Rahmagut added, "Then he did the same to Samón. It was mesmerizing, the way he ripped his antlers from his skull. I enjoyed seeing what Enrique could do with his bare hands."

Maior sobbed.

"But enough with the questions. This is not an interrogation, nor do I owe you answers. You serve a singular purpose, and that is to do your job of teasing Enrique with the promise of his dead wife. Nothing about that has changed since the moment her soul was affixed to your body."

Maior's stomach roiled with nausea.

"Soon enough, when it is time—" He paused and faced the star map splayed over the table. His finger lazily trailed over to the illustration of a moon completely eclipsing the sun behind it. "I will make sure you know what role you are meant to play next."

Maior didn't linger for another word. She whirled out with tears clouding her eyes.

She climbed the steps desperately, not stopping until she reached the courtyard, where she could take a deep lug of fresh mountain air. None of it was enough. None of it could satiate the anxiety clawing up her lungs.

Reina.

Maior shivered. She'd ruined the small happiness of their love, all for Laurel's bones. Everything indicated that she'd made a terrible mistake. But she had felt so trapped, facing two equally terrible paths. The short reprieve and freedom Maior thought she had bought for Reina by turning herself in was nothing but a fiction. Maybe if there had been a moment to talk things over, it would have turned out differently. Another sob choked her throat.

"Maior?" a voice like incense said behind her.

Maior turned around, flinching, her eyes still flooded with tears.

The meek starlight illuminated Celeste, who paused at the sight of Maior breaking down. Her eyes flickered above Maior's head for the briefest of seconds, but she masked her indiscretion well.

The women stood in silence. Maior was too exhausted to pretend to be embarrassed about her heartbreak. She waited for the insult that surely would come her way, for humoring Enrique's desires. For being everyone's inferior replacement.

Celeste's fist curled ever so slightly, her eyes searching Maior's. She opened her mouth, and closed it, giving up. Then she approached with open arms.

Maior was too fractured to reject the gesture. They diminished the distance between them. Celeste draped Maior in a hug, resting her chin on Maior's crown as Maior shuddered and wept.

Above Maior's sniffles, Celeste said, "I'm sorry."

"I just wanted them to leave Reina alone. I didn't want her to get hurt." And how spectacularly that had blown up in her face.

Celeste squeezed her and whispered, "Reina's a fighter. She will be all right."

Maior wished she had Celeste's confidence.

"Maior de Apartaderos?" a severe voice said from the doorway.

They parted, and the head matron briefly faltered when she noticed Celeste, who waited with her authoritative mien.

Maior wiped the moisture from the corners of her eyes as Celeste asked the head matron, "Well?"

The woman cleared her throat with discomfort. "It's the caudillo. He requests that Maior accompany him for supper." She ran her hands along her stained apron as if it brought her great displeasure to convey the message. "He instructed me to say it's an invitation, not a command."

Celeste scoffed. "You can tell mi papá that—"

"It's all right. Don't trouble yourself over me," Maior interrupted quickly. She steeled her heart. She allowed icicles to crust around it.

Don Samón was dead. Eva had surrendered to Rahmagut. And Reina was on the brink of death.

What was done was done. It would be pointless to dwell on the things she could have done differently. And most importantly, god of the Void or not, Rahmagut was wrong. Maior wasn't a doll to be paraded around for his benefit. She had a mission in her mind and faith in her heart. She couldn't abandon the plan that had brought her back to these cold mountain lands. Otherwise, the price she had paid would truly be for naught.

"I must carry on, for Reina."

Celeste watched her as if she were seeing her in a new light.

Maior offered Celeste a smile, grateful for the contact that helped ground her. Celeste was like her father in some ways, but she also was her own person. Someone with good in her, otherwise Reina would have never fallen in love with her. But it was useless to pretend they could be friends now. There was no universe in which Maior's plans and Celeste would ever be in alignment. She hoped one day Celeste would forgive her.

Maior brushed back her black hair, puffing the ends so it would

have a bounce. She squeezed her cheeks, flooding them with red-
ness. She puckered her lips. Finally, she threw her shoulders back
and said, "Take me to him."

She followed the head matron through the shadowed corridors
and up the stone steps to the third floor. Her heart hammered as
the head matron knocked on his bedroom door and a "Come in"
was given in reply.

With those judgmental pursed lips, the head matron motioned
for Maior to allow herself in.

Maior entered a room shrouded in darkness, save for the cande-
labrum placed at the center of Enrique's personal dining table. He
sat facing a plate of steaming grilled trout. Across him, where surely
the empty chair was meant for Maior, was a tea tray accompanied
by almojábanas and guava bocadillos. How Maior missed almojábanas from the Páramo. But in this setting, her stomach roiled with
nausea.

Enrique had shed the armor in which he had arrived. He wore
a simple cotton shirt and casual pants now. His hair was damp, and
his left arm was bound to a splint. He welcomed her to take a seat
across from him.

Her heart was riotous as she crossed the fur-covered floor to join
him. She wrung her hands and slid into the plush brocade chair.

"I didn't expect you to accept my invitation," he said, lifting the
steaming tea up to his lips.

Maior tried to steady her breath. She knew he could hear every
discomfort and reaction in her body. Perhaps it could work to her
advantage. He'd suspect her otherwise.

She looked down at the food to avoid his violently red eyes.
"What is it that you expect, then?"

He forked his trout awkwardly. It was clear he found no comfort
or mastery in the use of his right hand. He chewed and swallowed
his first bite before saying, "I expect you to beg to be exempt from
the plans I have for you. I expect to be unimpressed."

Hatred curled in her belly. She was weighed by it, like a block of
black tar that threatened to corrupt her faith. "The plans to bring
back Doña Laurel?"

"I have not managed my grief well. It was Ursulina, who did such a good job convincing me it is possible. You are all that keeps Laurel tied to this world."

"Are you afraid to let her go?" she said, prodding. She had to get the obvious out of the way. How much time did she have? What were the extents of his plans? And why request her company, if he saw her as nothing more than a vessel to his dead wife's soul? Why not command it of her?

Once she had the courage to look up, she was surprised by his wounded gaze. He was watching his wife. Then his eyes flicked down, as if he'd been caught staring inappropriately.

Seeing his obvious desire chilled her heart even more. Maior was glad for her indifference, which gave her an upper hand. She was impervious to the natural advantage he thought he wielded as an attractive, wealthy man. Any other woman would have cowered. Any other would have used this moment to daydream of a different outcome, where it was her and not the returned Laurel who satisfied his needs and became lady of his opulent household. Perhaps this was why he had invited her to his quarters. Perhaps his heart was corrupted with doubt.

"You represent possibilities," he said after a while. "You keep her. You stop her from being gone."

Enrique was a selfish, godless man, if he truly believed there was no eternal salvation awaiting his wife. Laurel had had love for the Virgin. This was obvious from every dream Maior witnessed. She would have wanted to move on. But in front of Maior was a man so self-absorbed he kept his wife rooted in an earthly prison, on the premise of a what-if.

Maior made a show of appraising his left arm hanging from the sling, to change the subject. He was left-handed. He'd likely gained his injury as he snuffed the life out of the Liberator.

I heard the crack. Rahmagut's words reverberated within her.

A hatred so sharp took hold of Maior. It gripped her arms and compressed her chest. Maior didn't have a mind to move or breathe. She held Enrique's gaze with unmoving eyes, and it was a miracle she could keep her calm.

She thought of the Virgin. Surely, She was giving Maior the strength to swallow the enmity threatening to consume her at this very moment.

Like so many other people in her life, Enrique clearly underestimated her. It was obvious as he met her eyes, unbothered by what she might know of how he came to be injured, because he believed she was powerless. And perhaps...he was right. But Maior didn't come to this room for the purpose of raising a white flag.

"You're wounded," she said in the demure voice he expected of her.

"Do not concern yourself with my injuries. I heal quickly. It is not the first, nor will it be the last."

"I used to be a nurse, back in Apartaderos," she said.

His silence was a sign he had no interest in the life she used to live.

Slowly, Maior pushed her chair back and unfurled to her feet. "I have some galio on me, if you will allow me to look at it." She lifted her hands so he could see her rings.

When he didn't immediately reject her, she walked behind him. A heady silence enveloped them. Maior treaded gradually. She let every second drag. Every moment was another proof of his doubts. Why was he allowing this dance, if not because loneliness had already crushed his heart?

Maior grabbed the chair beside him and moved close to remove the sling holding his arm. The white fabric crumpled to the ground. He winced, and she offered him a meek apology. Still, his eyes were trained on her as she nudged back the collar of his shirt to reveal his pale skin. He wore new bruises and old scars.

She found she was quite adept at mesmerizing him while her hands massaged the pulled ligaments back into place. Just like with his staff, it was easy to disarm him because he *wanted* to believe. As she met his eyes, closer now than ever, she saw how desperately he longed for this intimacy. He had let Ursulina's dark magic muddle his good sense. He was poisoned by promises of having Laurel in a cheap look-alike.

For this was exactly how Maior felt. As the staff dressed her in blue gowns and styled her hair with Laurel's brush. As Enrique invited her into the privacy of his bedroom. She was a just-good-enough replacement. And it made Maior sick. It made her insides roil and storm. Here was a man who had ruined lives and sullied his hands in the name of nothing. For he was godless—that much was certain. Still, he dared to close his eyes and sigh in relief at her ministrations. He took no issue with the lives he ended and the repugnant prospect of using her to satisfy his pleasures. All Maior wanted was to hurl.

She swallowed her displeasure down and finished restoring his arm to its natural position. Her fingers were slow and gentle as she arranged his shirt back into place.

Enrique opened his eyes and watched her expectantly. It was clear: He desired more of her.

She stopped breathing. Fear gripped her. She paused and reconsidered the danger she was placing herself in. Then she remembered Reina's brutalization. Reina had almost died for Maior's sake. To protect her honor and safety.

Maior had no honor that needed saving, for she had her faith. She had always lived a life alone, in the shadows of her stone chapel in Apartaderos. She had learned to fend for herself out of necessity. She had freed herself from Doña Ursulina's dungeon on her own. Having Reina had been a delightful reprieve, but as Enrique had no intentions of giving them peace, Maior also had no choice but to take matters into her own hands. With patience, she was going to get what she wanted: a separation from Laurel and the freedom to love Reina without fear of being wrenched apart. Reina's incapacitation and Eva's possession had forced a wedge in her original plans, sure, but Maior survived because she was flexible yet steadfast.

As she stepped away, her foot caught on the white cloth pooled on the floor. Maior glanced down at it. One day, she knew, he expected the same to happen to her clothes.

"Is that better?" she said, watching his disappointment as she returned to the other side of the table.

He nodded. "I should feel lucky to have such an adept healer within my ranks."

Maior looked down with a smile. Her heart grew fearful as she considered the power he had handed her on a silver platter. It was a double-edged sword, but she would be a fool not to use it to her advantage. And it would serve her, as she now had the responsibility of getting herself out of this bind. With no one coming to save her, Maior had to prepare for the worst.

44

The Man-Eating Caiman

Even the overcast sky was too bright for Reina as she came to. Finding herself in one piece was a surprise. She opened her eyes; her vision was blurred and distant. She rolled over on the bed, shielding her eyes as sleep abandoned her. She was warm, wrapped in soft, cozy fabrics, but her skull split with a sharp ache.

More pain stabbed her temple as light poured in from the nearby window. Reina moaned, digging her forehead against the mattress beneath her. She heard footsteps approaching.

A clawlike grip twisted her to face the ceiling. Then a cool palm pressed against her aching temple. Instantly, Reina was showered in relief.

She was seasoned enough in geomancia to recognize the soothing effects of galio. It sparked hope in her heart. If she opened her eyes, would she see Maior gazing down at her, a blush on her rosy cheeks dotted with new Tierra'e Sol freckles? Reina's heart warmed from the image.

Instead, she met a long face framed by silky whitish hair. Beneath the opening of the collar was a patch of scutes. Reina blinked and realized she was staring into Javier's eyes.

"What's your name?" he asked her, and she gave it automatically—the complete version. "Who am I?" he asked as follow-up.

"Javier."

"Where are we?"

The question prompted her to sit up. Black dots flooded her vision. She glimpsed rows of beds populated by other ailing and moaning people. They were in an infirmary of sorts.

Reina wavered from the exertion. Javier pressed her shoulder back down against the bed. She writhed under his grip, uncomfortable with his closeness. This lack of space between them generally only led them to blows.

"I don't know," she moaned. "I can't tell. Where are we? Is Maior here?"

Her heart did a silly little flip. Maybe Maior's departure and Reina's fight had all been a horrible dream. Maybe Maior was going to walk in through those infirmary doors at any moment now, to chastise Javier's rough handling and take over Reina's care. Everything that had happened leading up to Reina's splitting headache...maybe it was nothing but a nightmare. She desperately needed it to be so.

Javier's brows fell. He looked away. Reina hated knowing him so well she could surmise the words left unsaid.

"She's still gone, isn't she?" Reina said. She had a tightness in her chest. She wished she could cover herself up in the sheets so Javier wouldn't have to see the heartache streaking her face.

He moved away from the bed and gave her his back. "Lunch is ready. I numbed your injuries. Come eat if you can manage it."

She grasped his wrist before he could leave.

"I can't remember how we got here," she said. The honesty didn't come easy. But the ignorance felt worse.

In his pause, she noticed the bags under his eyes. The oiliness of his scalp. The unshaved fuzz on his jaw. It filled her with dread.

"You challenged my brother to a duel," he said. "And you were nearly killed."

He opened his lips as if there was more to be said. An addendum to what had happened. Reina pieced together the rest on her own. "You saved my life?"

He shrugged and left her to the silence.

Her armor and clothes were piled beside the rudimentary bed where she'd slept. Her skin was smooth, as if someone had endured the painstaking task of cleaning her up. She had dueled the caudillo. She should be covered in blood and grime. She hoped it hadn't been Javier.

The bahareque walls of the infirmary were made of mud and bamboo, and the floor was just packed dirt. The caw of a parrot drifted in through the open windows, which allowed in a natural overcast light. A breeze carried the scent of approaching rain and the heat of the morichales. She was surrounded by beds filled with recovering civilians and moaning soldiers, some wearing Bravo armor. Children who sniffled from their own wounds or by the bedside of a parent. A bloody stink weighed the air.

Reina dressed. A curtain of cow leather hanging from the doorway separated the infirmary from a kitchen. Beyond the curtain, the kitchen area bustled with the sounds of a spitting fire, boiling stews, and many hushed conversations. Reina parted the curtain and stepped into the large hall.

Dried pork rinds and bags of ripe plantains and onions hung from the ceiling near the kitchen. An impressive brick oven took the entirety of one wall. Countrywomen donning stained aprons labored over many dishes. Naked bahareque walls colored the space in brown, and the smell of boiling plantain leaves suffused the air. The room had several flour-dusted tables, workstations for a communal kitchen or a bakery, where Javier, Esteban, and Pucho sat. Reina nearly tripped on a basket of avocados as she approached. Esteban saw her and rose to greet her.

"Who changed me?" was the first thing Reina asked.

"Reina—come eat. We heated a bollo for you," Esteban said, gesturing to a flimsy rattan bench marking her spot at the table.

"Who changed me?" Reina repeated, glaring at Javier, who ignored her in lieu of his food.

"That would be Doña Marisol," her grandfather said mildly, gesturing to the stout elderly woman sitting near the end of the table. One side of her gray hair was tucked behind a pointed ear.

Reina sat with a clenched jaw.

Between spoonfuls of his meal, Javier said, "That's the part that bothers you? You just ought to be grateful to still be alive."

"I wouldn't want your grimy claws on me either," Pucho noted impishly as he slugged his drink.

Javier glowered.

Reina scratched her temple, feeling an itch where the caudillo had struck her. She screwed her eyes shut, scouring the depths of her memory for a recollection of what had happened after she challenged Enrique. Her fingers curled into fists as she remembered the brain-splitting pain of his punch. Yet somehow, she was still in one piece.

Ches's influence was dormant within her. Reina lifted a hand to her heart, prodding for that connection of Duality. She couldn't feel him at all.

Esteban placed a hand on her shoulder, grounding her. "Reina? Do you remember anything?"

Her chest constricted again. Maybe it was her fear, or her pride, but Reina refused to admit that no, she didn't. She pretended her spoon was keeping her busy. But she had a lump in her throat. Every swallow was torturously forced.

Javier clanked his bowl against the table and glared at her. "You don't remember antagonizing Enrique?"

The people surrounding them paused their conversations and their eating to stare.

A heat crept into Reina's cheeks from the shame. She loathed being accountable to him, but even Esteban and Pucho awaited her words. "I picked a fight—but—but I don't remember the outcome."

"Oh yes, because you obviously were victorious," Javier said, gesturing to the house where they ate, populated by weathered and injured people, a place they wouldn't be finding themselves in had she been the victor. "Don Samón is dead!" he yelled at her.

The news hit her with as much force as Enrique's fist. Reina froze, taken in silence, as the glossiness in Javier's eyes confirmed he wasn't lying. She glanced at her grandfather, who merely stared at the empty bowl before him, gaze lost to his thoughts. Pucho had no more jokes.

A hush blanketed the hall. But there was no color to further drain from anyone's face. Everyone already knew.

From a far corner, someone sobbed. Another woman threw her arms around the closest person to her, visibly expressing the hopelessness that gripped every one of them.

Javier shoved off his bench. "Of course you don't fucking remember anything! You'd be dead if it weren't for me, and for Don Samón, who had to stop Enrique from bashing your brains to mush!"

"What happened?" Reina asked pathetically.

"Enrique killed him."

"The caudillo killed Don Samón?" Reina repeated, to let it sink in, just as her heart was sinking into the depths of the Void. Once again, she tried to scratch for Ches's thoughts, but found him absent. Where was the connection she knew she could always tap into?

"He died to save you! Traded his life for yours!" Javier snapped.

Reina stopped herself from breathing. The consequences of her rashness settled over her skin like acid. Consequences that Don Samón had predicted with startling accuracy. He'd warned her against giving in to her emotions. And now he was dead.

She hugged herself. It wasn't enough to ease the chills.

Where are you? she thought. She received nothing but silence. She glanced about the kitchen, realizing she hadn't considered Eva's whereabouts. "Where is Eva?"

Breathing heavily, Javier glared at Reina with such a raw mixture of hurt and hatred. "Rahmagut took hold of her. She's gone."

"Sit down, lad," Esteban barked. "I've said this before: As long as there is life, the road is not ended. She is not gone."

"Because you know how to get the god of the Void to let go of her body?" Javier snarled, the blackened veins of his temples bulging. He turned away from them.

It was Esteban who had the patience to relay to Reina the events following her defeat. The devilish whispers of her heart were stirred awake as Esteban narrated the chaos of the encampment. Panic filled her at the recounting of her reckless use of Duality resulting in Don Samón's duel and death. In the subsequent bloody show-down of Águila soldiers versus anyone loyal to the Liberator. In Eva losing herself. The burning of the archbishop and the smiting of his followers. And finally, the way Rahmagut had attempted to snag Reina. For what? They could only assume the worst.

Esteban told her how they had managed a narrow escape along-side the Bravo soldiers still left standing. He recounted how they used the shroud of night to cross the Llanos with her limp body slumped over Pucho's shoulder. Like specters in the night, they arrived at this finca fortified by a militia of its residents. Tinie-blas had passed through these lands more than once, hence the wounded survivors sleeping in the infirmary room. The neigh-boring village, home to all the people here, had been decimated. And what once had been the home of an affluent family was now repurposed as the last fortification these people had against the tinieblas. Doña Marisol was the kind matriarch who offered them a roof while Javier coaxed life back into Reina with the remains of his galio solution.

"Why did you save me?" Reina asked Javier, unable to stop her-self. It was an ungrateful question, but it came from the same well of animosity that poisoned their relationship—the one coloring the way they saw each other from the very first day they met. Reina wondered whether she would have done the same. Probably, for Eva's sake.

No. That was a lie.

She would do the same because she no longer wanted Javier dead.

Javier glared. "Because you dying does absolutely nothing to get Eva back. Because I prefer you owing me than being dead." As she opened her mouth to protest, he added, "Because one day I will be calling on you to repay that debt by helping me against Enrique."

Her hands twitched. Fear speared through her. She had already failed. Losing their commander had been her only reward.

"You called me a fool for dueling him," Reina said.

"That is the only adequate word for you," Javier said.

"But didn't you do it once already?" She cocked an eyebrow at his tail and added, "To disastrous results? Why would you attempt it again?"

Javier stood up again, like he wanted to fight her. "I have no choice. Apparently, Enrique also took Eva—*Rahmagut.*"

Reina tried to make sense of the information but couldn't. Enrique had much to gain from Rahmagut, sure, but what did Rahmagut want with him? An even heavier weight of lead dropped to her belly as Reina considered their alliance. Enrique and Rahmagut, together, was a disquieting thought.

"Enrique took her, but I'm not abandoning her. I will free her from my brother, and from that god," Javier said between gritted teeth.

Now you know how I feel, Reina almost said, but she swallowed her words.

"And how do you plan to accomplish such a feat?" Esteban asked.

"Don Juan, the sanadero," Javier said. "Don Juan is in Segolita. I'll drag him to the Páramo myself. I will make him cleanse Eva. He can do it." He nodded, as if forcing himself to believe such a fantasy.

Pucho laughed.

"You will kidnap an innocent person? What makes you think he'll want to cooperate after you force him from his home?" Esteban said.

"You'll be surprised what people will do when you threaten their lives."

Esteban shook his head. "Then you're no different from that brother of yours. You are Feleva's children, indeed."

The silence was loud with Javier's outrage. Once, such a statement would have landed as a compliment. But, somehow, while Reina hadn't been looking, Javier had changed.

"Mother didn't raise me. You would know this, if you hadn't left her."

"Don't speak about things you don't know," Esteban said, meeting Javier's glare in earnest.

Javier turned to Reina with depleted patience. "I lost the inheritance owed to me. I am losing my fight against this tiniebla. But I will not lose my wife," he said. "Even if there's no other outcome for me but to become this beast"—he pounded his chest—"I will free Eva with my last fucking breath. You either help me, or you don't." Then he stormed out of the house.

Reina refused to breathe in the silence he left behind. She understood every ounce of hurt in his voice. And she wanted the same, desperately. She ached for those days when their group was whole, when she could dream about a life with Maior because Maior was right there beside her.

But this defeat shattered every length of her carapace. She was raw and naked and weak.

Again, she begged and prodded for Ches, and his absence only fed her heartache. What if he, too, had forsaken her?

Tears gathered in her eyes.

Reina couldn't eat. She couldn't move. She sat on the bench as her shoulders shook from the shame. As her mind fabricated images of Don Samón's death.

How could she have been so foolish? Don Samón had warned her more than once. He'd begged her to stand down, and her hubris had single-handedly initiated their downfall.

"Javier is right, Reina," Esteban said.

"I already failed against the caudillo, and you saw what I caused. How can I justify doing it again?"

"Yes, well, if it were easy, we'd *all* be hosts to gods, and we'd *all* wield shiny golden swords," Pucho drawled.

Her stomach coiled painfully. *Did* she have Ches anymore?

"We retreated to lick our wounds, but you must retaliate," Esteban said sternly. With his chin, he gestured at the Bravo soldiers who watched their conversation from the fringes. Reina realized they'd been watching like flies on the wall, standing by. "Don Samón brought you into his inner circle because he believed in you, as I believe in you," her grandfather said. "The Liberator died for you. The honorable thing is to fight and avenge his death. I understand—I also quake at the thought of Enrique Águila allied with the god of the Void, but *you* have the god of the sun. Look around you, Reina. We are all in need of a beacon."

A sob burst out of her. She dug her hands into her scalp, digging, seeking to split her skin in the hope it would distract her from her heartache. The lump in her throat grew. Her lungs constricted and she couldn't breathe—not that she deserved to. Maybe Esteban was right, but it didn't abate the ache of her actions ruining everything she cared for in a single stroke. How could she trust her own judgment anymore? And what if she was without Ches? She would be nothing but a defeated woman, with their hopes on her shoulders.

Before her lack of reply could disquiet Esteban and Pucho, footsteps thrummed into the hall. Reina saw Don Rigoberto entering, followed by more soldiers.

"You've awoken," he said with a spark to his eye.

Reina nodded stiffly.

He took a seat across from her. "We've cleared the tinieblas from the vicinity. There weren't many. It seems they aren't marching for us anymore."

"Javier told us the tinieblas were coming after Eva. Their god had commanded them to take her to the mountains, where the rest of the iridio lies," Esteban said.

Before Reina could make sense of the information, Don Rigoberto said, "I suppose that is comforting, in a way. It'll be news the president will appreciate. Reina, I would like to apologize for doubting your suspicions of Enrique Águila—Don Samón told me you tried to counsel him, back in Carao. Enrique is a godless man, and we must make efforts to eliminate him. I have sent letters to Segolita detailing everything I witnessed in Catatumbo."

Don Rigoberto wiped his face, as if hiding the wetness in his eyes, the wound of losing a close friend. His throat bobbed. "The news of Don Samón's death will be a blow to morale, but it will also stir a hunger for revenge and justice. I expect there may be some in the cabildo who will beg us not to take up arms against Enrique, for he's still master of iridio—"

"Cravens," Pucho spat.

Don Rigoberto nodded. "Yes, and I will not agree with their caution. Enrique has allied himself to Rahmagut, you say? Then the tinieblas will be at his whims. That is a threat I cannot ignore." His gaze weighed on Reina. His unspoken expectation was clear. "Everyone who witnessed Don Samón's brutal killing is ready to act." He rose, waving a hand at all the watching eyes. "But if we are to have a chance against Rahmagut, we will need a god on our side."

Reina forwent breathing. All eyes fell on her. She had their undivided attention, except from the one she needed the most.

"I need a moment alone," she said before rushing out of the house.

Outside, heat mirages blurred a small pasture fencing in a donkey and some pigs. Armed soldiers were posted along the hastily crafted gates to the driveway. Reina could see their wavering hope in their posture. The tinieblas and the news of the Liberator had worn everyone down to threads.

Her feet aimlessly took her into the morichales surrounding Doña Marisol's conuco. Reina stepped into the sun as the clouds parted, letting the afternoon sunlight bite her skin, hoping it would bring her closer to her god. For she couldn't feel him. Had Ches left for another body after she'd nearly died? Perhaps she *had* died, and Javier's mastery of galio had somehow plucked her back into the world of the living. Reina trembled. How could she deliver this news to Don Rigoberto and her grandfather? To everyone who expected her to lead now that the Liberator was dead?

She leaned against a palm tree, and the heartache returned, choking her.

Don Samón was gone. And she hadn't even been conscious to witness his fall. She hadn't even been there to gather his remains.

The Liberator, *gone*. Another sob spilled out.

He had been the first person to see the true worth in her— the one who had noticed her capabilities under the light. Her commander and protector, who had coached her and guided her through the beginning of what was supposed to be her new life.

How he had honored her by bringing her under his wing.

"And you would be dishonoring his memory by doing nothing," a voice said behind her.

Reina startled, whirling to see a man crowned in valco antlers. Sunlight gilded him in gold.

She exhaled, relieved and elated. She was so happy she could throw herself at his feet.

"Don't," Ches said.

The tears she'd been holding back quenched her cheeks. She covered her face in her hands to hide the ugly crying. When the sadness passed her, she saw Ches waiting. He ordered her to stroll with him under the morichal's canopy.

A breeze rose around them. It smelled sweet, of fruit and flowers and rebirth. The path was cracked beneath their feet, parched.

"I thought you had left me."

"I have explained the rules. Only in death will I empty your body."

Reina chewed on her inner cheeks as she considered his words. He could force her to drive a blade through her belly, or to walk into the depths of Río'e Marle until her lungs flooded with water. He could leave her whenever he wanted. Yet he never violated her consent. Her chest palpitated, bursting with love for him. His presence was a balm, completely muting the devilish whispers of iridio from her heart.

"But I'm no longer confident you deserve me," he added.

She almost asked why, but she agreed. "Because I used your power selfishly."

In silence came his agreement.

Wind rustled the palms overhead. It enveloped her, refreshing her sunburned cheekbones and neck. His patience gave her courage to admit it. "I used your strength for myself," she added. "I trained for Duality only with the purpose of settling my score with Enrique." In a shamed whisper, her admittance poured out of her: "I used you, and I caused this mess."

Duality had intoxicated her with hubris. She'd used it recklessly before she'd been ready, ignorant of her shortcomings. Reina was ashamed. The consequences were a costly death and a pang to the nation, but she had to live with them.

They paused at the bank of a brown river. A huddle of capybaras heard Reina's footsteps and scurried into the woods. Peeking over the water's serene surface were the beady eyes of a large man-eating caiman, who watched her.

"Had your life ended, you would have wasted my time," Ches said without compassion. "Don't you see it yet? I don't have a material body. Fully unleashed, my power is too strong for any mortal body to wield. Duality must be trained and nurtured. Without you or someone trained to handle it, I'll be forced to inhabit and destroy one mortal host after another, if I ever wish to tap into my true strength—and you have allowed Rahmagut to get to the point where I *will need* to use my true strength."

Reina's heart raced. She shrunk before him.

"I told you I didn't have much of a choice in who I used as host when I emerged from the tomb, but your own mind has already illustrated that this constraint was not final or permanent: At any moment, I could have taken your life and forced you to deliver me to a better subject."

Reina burned. The words were harsh, but her mind spun and arrived at the truth. "Does that mean...you *do* choose me?" she said in a small voice.

His eyes glimmered with the sunlight filtering through the leaves. For such a stoic façade, Reina thought she saw his emotions shift from admonishment to agreement. She deserved the reprimand he meant to give her, but perhaps he wasn't planning to discard her after all.

He said, "You have an aptitude for picking yourself up. Only few can endure the physical and mental toil of sharing a body with me. The emotional burden, of never again being alone—of having me in your moments of both extreme sadness and pleasure. With you, I have arrived at the mortal with the constitution, tenacity, and faith for Duality to be successful. These are qualifications I do not take for granted."

Her eyes grew teary. They blurred his image. *He found value in her.* She was worthy enough for him, a glove sized precisely for his divine hand.

"Qualifications I need now more than ever, as Rahmagut

bolsters his tinieblas to antagonize me," Ches said. "They are his army. They seed sorrow and despair in the hearts of mortals, undermining my existence and that of every other divine entity. For we are gods, and without worship, we have no power."

Reina thought of the people back in the finca. How their cheeks were hollowed, and their eyes were bloodshot from the constant presence of tears. How long before they stopped offering their food to Ches? Or before the Penitents stopped their litanies to the Virgin? She recalled the spark in Don Rigoberto's and Esteban's eyes, how they looked to her for salvation.

"Please give me another chance," Reina begged. She was done pretending to be coy. She longed for Ches's ever-present company within her. She wanted the reassurance of his power, which she was meant to use to restore the balance Rahmagut had tipped in favor of darkness.

Those sunlight eyes met hers.

This time, Reina did fall to her knees. She pressed her forehead against the riverbank, right by Ches's feet. "I will serve as your hand. I will rid this world of tinieblas, just as you intended me to."

Her heart twisted as the true implications of her words sank in. This path would put her at odds with Eva. This road meant ignoring how much she ached to be reunited with Maior. But Reina now knew she couldn't act selfishly. It had been her downfall from the beginning. From the misguided pursuit of kidnapping the damas to please her grandmother, to using Duality to challenge Enrique over a broken heart. Rahmagut was the true antagonist—

"Watch out!" a familiar voice suddenly yelled behind her.

They yanked her by the shoulder and tossed her back into the undergrowth. She crashed into the bark of a palm tree. Shrubs and needles pricked her cheeks.

Something large splashed the riverbank. A great guttural bellow disrupted the peace of the morichal.

Reina crawled to her feet, shocked, and saw Javier kicking the maw of the large caiman away. She scanned the riverbank and the path she'd just walked. There was no sign of Ches.

"Do you have a death wish?" Javier hollered at her, giving the reptile's nostril another kick so that it would retreat underwater. His boots sank in the mud. He swiped the perspiration off his temples. "I didn't just save you from Enrique's clutches just so you could become lunch to a caimán cebao!"

Reina watched him huff with impatience. Once again, Javier had saved her life.

He was her friend.

"*A realization I gave you,*" Ches noted within her, smug.

Reina blinked.

Within her. He was *within* her. He was giving her another chance.

And indeed, Ches had known Javier would be there for her, proving she wasn't alone. She'd failed once, believing she had to act on her own, presuming no one cared about her pain after Maior's departure, but she had been wrong.

Happiness welled in Reina. She opened her heart to Duality, letting the sunlight rush through her, gilding her. She was aglow in love for Ches, and with his power. There was no pain as her fingertips pulsed and her veins hummed. She existed with him in perfect harmony, smiling.

Javier watched her, stunned.

"Let's defeat Rahmagut—together," Reina said. She dusted bits of dry leaves and muddy grime off herself. "We can no longer waste our energies bickering and fighting each other—whatever happened between us in the past stays that way, in the past."

She had Javier's full attention. He nodded. "It's what I've wanted."

Reina extended her radiant fingertips, showing how the light came so easily and painlessly.

"You wield his power completely?" he asked. "The strength of a god?"

"Yes, and I must use it to restore balance. The death and despair brought by tinieblas—they're Rahmagut's doing. And we were wrong to ignore his return. We were wrong to have Eva shoulder the weight of carrying him and reeling him in all on her own. Las Orquídeas Blancas were right about Rahmagut. We must go for Eva. We must save her from him."

Javier winced. "What do you mean they were right? You can't mean that she must be killed."

"No." She smiled, hoping it eased his anxieties.

"So? Can Ches speak to you? Has he told you how you both might separate? Would it work the same for Eva and Rahmagut?"

The harsh truth was on the tip of Reina's tongue, until she decided to soften her delivery, for his sake. "Ches can abandon me whenever he wants, through my death."

Red colored Javier's neck.

"Which means: If Rahmagut took control of Eva's body, and she's alive, then he must need her somehow," Reina supplied. Perhaps it would be a reassurance.

"Her life is in danger," he said, his voice quivering.

Reina nodded.

Javier paced the riverbank, pensive. The man-eating caiman watched his steps from beneath the surface. "Back in Casa Bravo, when Eva brought Don Juan, he said that if a god wills it, they can cleanse a possession," Javier said.

Reina waited, her jaw tight.

"But I'm not implying mine," he said quickly. "I know my curse is too advanced. I'm talking about Eva and Rahmagut. If Ches's divine power is at your disposal, then can't you separate them?"

Ches's confirmation was like an embrace of warm water. Like stepping under sunrays on a chilly Páramo morning. "Yes," Reina said solemnly.

The hope in Javier's eyes was so bright.

"I can cleanse her, perhaps, but that doesn't solve the problem of Rahmagut. He can still inhabit another body, and he must be annihilated." Those last words, Reina wasn't sure if they were entirely her own.

Javier nodded, pacing again. The water rippled as the caiman matched his movements, back and forth, hypnotized in hunger.

"Eva—Rahmagut—they have this thing called a Void gem," Javier said. "It's like...a concentration of iridio. Eva said Rahmagut can only properly control it in the Páramo. He wanted to take you to the mountains because there he can use it to destroy Ches."

The back of Reina's neck prickled painfully. "Are you suggesting I take it from her? This gem?"

Javier chewed on lip. "It's risky. Eva feared its power. She told me it was the reason why the gods were sealed during the Calamity. It almost destroyed the world."

"And he could fracture the world again? Or worse, be successful?" Reina whispered.

Javier nodded.

"Then I see no other option," Reina said. "You're right: I must take this gem from him. I must use his own weapon against him."

She gulped. Whatever doubts wanted to crawl out of her were quickly thwarted by Ches. Reina didn't know how to begin annihilating a god. But Ches had given her a second chance. She could not squander it.

"It falls on me to destroy Rahmagut," Reina said.

She extended a hand for Javier to take. His gaze lowered to it.

"We will avenge Don Samón's death, in due time. I will repay my debt to you by helping you save Eva. But first, we must end the threat of tinieblas. And to do that, we must vanquish Rahmagut forever."

Finally, she wielded the conviction Don Rigoberto, Esteban, and Pucho had demanded of her. She was ready to head back inside and lead their march. Confronting Enrique and Rahmagut was a risky gamble, but ignoring their alliance would be a worse choice.

Javier's handshake was hot and firm. Reina could feel his belief in her. He was going to follow her to the ends of the earth, if it meant Eva's salvation. In a way, it warmed her heart.

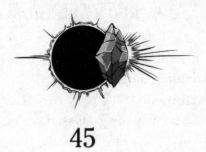

45

The Summoning

High above the underground laboratory, the evening sky thundered. Veins of lightning split the sky. A riotous display of crimson and violet colors, the kinds that would make the ignorant stare up and fear the return of the devil.

Their devil *had* returned, Rahmagut supposed. His name had been slandered for generations, since the very first Segol settlers set foot on this land and saw people worshipping the clay-sculpted image that represented his legendary rise to power. No other mortal had ever come close to what he had accomplished. Yet his achievements and his image were tarnished by the fanatical and the ignorant. It enraged him. Rahmagut felt scorned.

He had no sympathy if the tinieblas he summoned tore through fincas and the homes of humble campesinos to reach him. He couldn't care about the hearts that would surely be ripped out and devoured as his tinieblas crossed the Páramo upon his command. All those who slandered him: Today would be their reckoning. He hoped they begged their Virgin for mercy. He hoped they died realizing their prayers would go unanswered.

Doña Ursulina had a conjuring table encrusted with reactive pieces of iridio. She had the diaries and recollections of accomplished geomancers in her bookcases. She had a large book with detailed diagrams of the stars' alignments and the rotation of the sun and the moon over the sky. She had condor feathers and rabbit skulls and the dried skin of a tigra mariposa as reagents. Her underground laboratory proved to be a great boon. Rahmagut didn't have to waste his time collecting ingredients. All he had to do was reach into the depths of his power and, with all the reagents, call the tinieblas to him. As they traveled from all reaches of the land, he waited for them to accumulate for five days and nights.

On the sixth day, which he'd awaited according to what was recorded in the star maps, he met his Void creatures on the Águila grounds. A lone scout returned from the mountains after spotting the amalgamated demons and sprinted out of the fir grove with panic in his eyes. He meant to alert the rest of the Águila guards. It was bothersome.

Rahmagut did nothing as one of the tinieblas pounced on the panicked man and tore open his neck before clawing a hole through his heart. The alarm died with his last breath.

"*You're vile*," Eva reminded him, as she often did. Per usual, he ignored her.

He couldn't shut her up. He had tried. Rahmagut had total control of her body, but Eva poisoned his hold. She retained a piece of herself in the depths of his consciousness and spoke to him in moments when he least needed her to. Calling him vile, a liar, or a monster. Names that had been directed at him in the past and had no effect on him anymore. She gave him intense heartburn after he'd gloated about Enrique bringing Samón's antlers as a trophy to hang over his study. Palpitations and cold sweats that made Rahmagut wonder if she was willing to drive her own body to death in her rancor. Eventually, though, she withdrew.

Her meek ways of exerting the last shreds of her thoughts didn't bother him. Eva was aware of what lay ahead, for he'd made no efforts to conceal it from her: Once Ches was no more, Rahmagut was going to end her life and seize control of Enrique's body.

For now, he kept her, as her outward appearance was but another advantage against Ches's nozariel host during the inevitable confrontation. He smirked, imagining how easy it was going to be to obliterate an opponent too preoccupied with keeping Eva's body intact.

Soft footsteps joined Rahmagut in the yard. Maior approached. Her body had a soft lavender glow of bismuto about her. She sucked in a breath and crossed herself.

Rahmagut's words materialized as a cloud of condensation as he said, "Don't fear them, unless you mean to get in my way."

Maior trembled as more tinieblas emerged from the woods. Creatures with six or eight limbs, talons the size of dueling knives, and third eyes that sprouted from faces resembling condors and jaguars and mountain goats. Horns jutted out of their heads. Their bodies were armored with caiman scutes, just as their maws were lined by hundreds of blood-soiled teeth. The army of tinieblas encroached on the manor grounds. They filled the air with their snarls and hoots. Standing at their center, Rahmagut felt invincible.

Ches's pupils gave Rahmagut the immortality to persevere forever. Should his vessel perish, he could simply find and inhabit another. In a way, this gave him the longevity of godhood. And with the tinieblas and Enrique's gold, he'd have the indomitable power of a conqueror again. As far as Rahmagut was concerned, he already exhibited all the markings of a deity. But his ascension wouldn't be permanent if Ches could strip it all whenever he willed it. For as long as Ches was present in the land, Rahmagut would have no rest.

"How could I even stop you?" Maior reproached softly. "What do you plan to do with them?"

"They're a display of my power. Your *husband* fears the retaliation of the caudillos who witnessed how he brutalized the Liberator. I promised him my protection."

Her cheeks flushed red with indignation. "He's not my husband," she growled, then glanced up behind her to the second-story study window overlooking the yard. Standing behind fluttering curtains, Enrique supervised the agglomeration of tinieblas over his grounds.

"I plan to use them to end Reina's life," Rahmagut said, amused.

Maior's pursed lips quivered.

Rahmagut laughed. "Oh, all right. Do as we discussed, and I shall spare her." The lie came easy. But if by now she didn't understand how their possessions worked, then she didn't deserve to understand the truth.

His gaze traveled to the skyline beyond the mountains, where the dawning sun peeled layers of darkness from the night. Any other day, Rahmagut would have waited in the valley where Águila Manor sat over the iridio reserves for Ches and his host to arrive. Any other day, he might have even considered a nighttime ambush, using Maior as bait. But today Rahmagut didn't need to cower from the sun. On the sixth day of his summoning, as documented by Doña Ursulina's star map and confirmed by the witch's spells of iridio, the sun was going to disappear.

"Reassure Enrique I'm not abandoning him," Rahmagut ordered Maior. "Tell him this business does not concern him." After all, Rahmagut couldn't risk damaging his future vessel by getting him involved. "I shall be back before the day's end."

Without a moment to waste, Rahmagut entered his throng of tinieblas. They made room for their master, engulfing him in the center of their snarls and putrefaction. Reminiscing of other times when he'd led legions into battle, Rahmagut began his climb up the trails of the mountain to meet the sun.

46

The Five Peaks

The days of travel passed in the blink of an eye, unremarkable against the anxiety of confronting Rahmagut and the fear for Maior's well-being, one landscape blurring into the next. It smelled of death before Reina could even glimpse the cross sitting atop Apartaderos's stone chapel. Black smoke curled on the horizon. The sight filled Reina with urgency. At the vanguard, she waved for her army to hurry, Don Rigoberto and Esteban hollering commands. Javier rode beside her. Their mounts were worn from the hike up the Páramo, yet they had no option but to press them farther and faster. Nightcleaver pulsed in her grip. If a fight awaited her, Reina was ready for it.

She dismounted as they reached the fog blanketing the village's perimeter. The smell of black smoke stung her nose. Swords clanked and whistled in the distance. The air was filled with screams of exhaustion, despair, and, insidiously, the growls of tinieblas. The houses bordering the village were in disarray: flowerpots upturned on patios; windows shattered; produce strewn on the ground, stomped to mush. Reina imagined coming across the town center and seeing it littered with corpses.

Finally, she arrived at the inn, across from the statue of the three revolutionary women. A tiniebla broke out of the fog like a terror but was immediately sundered in half by a machete. It disintegrated, revealing the person who had slain it: a man dressed in rudimentary leather, a bloodstained ruana, and boots with badly worn heels.

Another tiniebla entered the square. It snapped at the poorly armored man, who fell from the shock. Reina lunged to the rescue, slicing the tiniebla across the belly with practiced ease. She gave the man a hand up as the attacking tiniebla was banished.

A small party of similarly apprehensive and exhausted fighters emerged from the fog, meeting Reina's host with their swords raised. "State your purpose!" the man said.

Javier stepped forward, letting his antlers arrest their attention. "We are returning home," he lied.

The men's shoulders slackened. They lowered their weapons, their bodies glowing from the meek spell of bismuto allowing them to see the tinieblas prowling their village. They were just a militia of townsfolk who had no choice but to raise up machetes and pitch-forks against the shadowed invaders.

"Returning home? I don't remember offering you an invita-tion," someone said from the fog. Murmurs broke out within the crowd as it parted, allowing Celeste to step through.

She was dressed in armor splotched with dried blood. Hers or someone else's, it was hard to tell. Her tall boots thundered against the cobbles in the heady silence as she reduced the distance between them. Strands of her silky black bangs clung to her temples, sweaty. Her scythe pulsed with her signature red iridio.

Reina steeled herself as those Páramo-sky eyes found her.

Celeste sucked in a breath, and her cheeks paled, as if she were seeing a ghost. Indeed, their last interaction had been in Lake Catatumbo. Had Celeste been there, when Enrique nearly killed her?

"*Reina*," she said softly.

Seeing Celeste was like tearing the scabs off Reina's barely heal-ing heart. She wasn't sure who owed the first apology, but Reina's pride wouldn't let her bend to Celeste ever again. And maybe that was a good thing.

As if sensing animosity between them, the militia also took

wide stances. They prepared to follow Celeste's command. She was the daughter of their caudillo, after all.

"We march against the tinieblas," Reina said.

"I see. Not because you're still chasing after Maior?"

"Look around you! Apartaderos is on the verge of falling, and you're still clinging to that?" Reina growled, annoyed.

Celeste was stunned as the Bravo soldiers emerged from the fog behind Reina and Javier. Esteban, Pucho, and Don Rigoberto surrounded Reina. Celeste moved her scythe as if she intended to stand against them.

"You brought an army," Celeste said.

"These men were loyal to the Liberator. Now they are loyal to his firstborn," Don Rigoberto said stiffly. "Don Samón made Doña Eva Kesaré Bravo de Águila his heir."

Celeste stiffened.

Weary, Reina said, "Celeste, we're not here to fight you. We came—"

A high-pitched scream robbed the words from her mouth. It came from the direction of the stone chapel—Maior's former home—to the east. Snarls announced the arrival of even more tinieblas to the south. Celeste barked a command and the militia scattered in both directions.

"Protect Apartaderos," Reina commanded the Bravos.

Celeste ran toward the screams, and Reina followed. "This would be a lot easier if Apartaderos had absolutely any kind of fortification," Celeste said as she cleaved the fog with her scythe.

"No need if we're supposed to be at peace," Reina said bitterly. That was when it dawned on her: Celeste had been at this for hours, if not days.

"Does this look like peace to you?" Celeste growled.

Reina flanked Celeste as four winged tinieblas swooped down on them, screeching, their talons curled with the intention of gutting them.

She opened her chest up to slip into Duality. Her skin glowed with Ches's sunlight moments before one of the tinieblas—an amalgamation of a condor and a bear—struck. She blocked the first strike with Nightcleaver, then ducked as a second tiniebla slashed for her throat. With a lightning-fast arc, Celeste sliced the condor-like tiniebla from behind.

Celeste huffed and said, "You're not the only one who cares about the people of this territory. These lands are my birthright."

One of the winged tinieblas rounded behind Celeste, talons outstretched once again. Celeste saw the threat reflected in Reina's eyes. Reading Reina's intentions, Celeste swerved out of the way to allow for Reina to leap forward. Reina slashed vertically, in mid-air, rending the tiniebla in two. She ended the other two winged creatures circling in the air as well. As she landed, a tiniebla on four legs broke out of the fog, roaring, its claws swiping for Reina. Celeste intervened automatically, stepping between them to block and parry. Then she severed the tiniebla's head.

They fell into a familiar pace, as if no time or hurt feelings had passed at all. As if they were back in the yard of Águila Manor, training under the tutelage of their sword master.

Exhaling in relief, Reina said, "How many have you killed?"

Celeste doubled over to catch her breath. "I've stopped keeping track."

Reina wiped the sweaty loose hair from her forehead as she took in the village. Houses were damaged. Wounded people limped toward the inn, which was guarded by the weary militia. The last standing haven. Thankfully, Reina's army was swift and effective in ending the remaining tinieblas. But they couldn't stay here. Protecting Apartaderos was a mere patch on the problem. Reina needed to get to the source of the illness.

Celeste stepped closer, taking in the soft glow of sunlight emitting from Reina's skin. "You have the god of the sun, and Eva the god of the Void."

"We share this space," Reina said, and her voice came out deep and ancient, layered with Ches's.

Reina could see Celeste was battling with herself, unsure of how to react. Nevertheless, the walls between them began to crumble. They had said truly awful things to one another. But instead of driving them apart, their fight felt like it had been a catharsis.

"Rahmagut—he's back home," Celeste said. "He's the one who's summoned all these tinieblas. He's creating an army for himself, and Father's letting him run amok." Celeste's eyes grew glossy, like it pained her. "He's sitting at home, playing house with Maior, while people are dying." Her voice broke as she gestured at the dilapidation of Apartaderos.

Reina had to remind herself that Celeste wasn't meaning to hurt her. She had to take a deep breath and ignore the panic it sparked in her veins. Ches helped ground her.

"What does Enrique want with Rahmagut?" Reina asked as footsteps approached her. Javier, Esteban, and Pucho returned to her side.

"Father knows he acted like a coward and a tyrant when he killed the Liberator. He knows the other families lost all respect for him."

"They never had any respect," Javier spat. "It was always fear."

Celeste's brows ascended. "Well, now the truth is out and our house is vulnerable, so he's letting Rahmagut, in Eva, do whatever he pleases in exchange for an army of tinieblas."

Something like thunder rumbled in the distance. The sounds of a terrible march, coupled by the snarling of Rahmagut's creatures, traveled up to the village. The fog was too close to the ground, impeding the view, so Reina led the way out of Apartaderos to a nearby small hill with a better vantage of the frailejón-dotted mountains. She glimpsed those trails she'd trekked time and time again. The horde of tinieblas was like a blanket of shadows. Thousands of them. They stomped the greenery and ravaged any shepherd, hiker, or unsuspecting traveler, leaving bloody death in their wake. The sight made Reina's veins run cold.

"I cannot stay here," Reina said. "They're coming for me. I am the one Rahmagut wants."

Celeste's grip clamped around Reina's wrist.

"The farther away I am—the longer I avoid it—the more people will suffer. The tinieblas are for me. They always were."

"You're mad! There are thousands of them, and your army is not enough!"

"If Rahmagut falls, the tinieblas fall as well," Ches said through Reina's voice. His resurgence shocked Celeste, but not Reina. She still held on to Duality. She shared her body in harmony with him.

Celeste searched Reina's eyes as if she were appraising her for the first time. Maybe she was finally noticing all the ways Reina had changed.

Ches went on. "Rahmagut believes he is in rank with me. I shall descend on him and prove this couldn't be further from the truth."

Suddenly, Celeste threw her arms around Reina. It took her by surprise. In their closeness, she could feel the unsteady fear shaking Celeste's frame. Reina indulged in hugging her back, for the memory of their friendship.

"I'm so happy I get to do this again," Celeste said with her voice muffled by Reina's jacket. "Rahmagut acts as if your death is so assured. I thought I would have to mourn you."

Reina squeezed her and pulled away. "Do you stand with the caudillo?"

Celeste's eyes glimmered in anger. She shook her head. "After seeing the way he acted in Lake Catatumbo, I realized he has changed for the worse. I'm ashamed to call myself his daughter. He stands with the god of the Void, and I do not."

"This is inspiring and everything, but how are we going to reach Eva with all those tinieblas?" Javier said. "And we cannot harm her."

Ches, in Reina, took several steps forward, arresting their attention. He said, "Back when this land was young, when I took my time in flattening the Llanos and filling the seas, I came to be followed by five eagles." He lifted Nightcleaver to the sky, extending Reina's reach the same way he was often depicted in the icons and statues.

"The legend of the five eagles," Pucho muttered.

Reina smiled at him. A screech ripped through the stillness of the village. The clouds parted, gracing the tip of Reina's blade with a gleam of sunlight.

"They're real?" Esteban whispered in awe.

Ches shot him a coy look. "You see me standing before you, and you wonder if the powers that shaped this world are real?"

An eagle swooped down from those parted clouds, then another. They flew together in a dance, circling each other in the air. The third, fourth, and fifth followed in close succession. They were larger than the condors normally roaming the Páramo. Larger than the most obscene and monstrous tiniebla. They chirped and screeched in a language of their own, their wingspans casting large shadows over Apartaderos. The soldiers and the militia poured out of the inn and houses to gawk and point in wonder like ants before giants.

The first eagle descended before Reina. A gust buffeted her face as it landed, smelling of crisp mountain air. The rest followed suit.

"Eagles like our namesake," Celeste said, awestruck.

"As you know, their sacrifice was never realized: Mortals couldn't use their peaks to reach me, for the closer the land is to me, the more dangerous it becomes. But they still ache to be of service, so they shall aid us in demonstrating what true divinity looks like. Rahmagut produces half-formed monsters; I give life to giants."

Reina approached the closest one, which leaned forward as Reina curved her palm over its beak. She met a resistance like steel. Its talons were sharp and long like swords. It was the largest animal she'd ever seen. Could it even be called an animal? A *primordial creature* was the more appropriate label. And it watched her back, its yellow eyes glimmering with understanding. It didn't need words or sounds to communicate. Through Ches she could sense its obedience.

"Does that mean the glaciers are no more?" Javier asked.

"The glaciers will persevere for as long as the eagles live," Ches said. He turned to the group who watched Reina curiously, awaiting instructions. "I shall descend the mountain astride my eagles. If you wish to support me against Rahmagut, then you may descend astride or on foot."

Esteban stretched his arms in the air. His back popped audibly. "You know what? I might go on foot, indeed."

"Grandfather," Reina said, "someone will have to lead the soldiers."

"*Grandfather?*" Celeste blurted out.

They ignored her. "I need good fighters to assist Don Rigoberto on foot," Reina told Pucho and Esteban.

"It'll give us time to flush out whatever tinieblas try to attack Apartaderos," Pucho said with excitement. He rolled his shoulders smugly. "We'll clear a path to you."

Esteban nodded. "I think I remember these trails. I grow old but the land doesn't."

"Celeste, did you bring any stores of bismuto? Can you resupply my soldiers?" Reina asked.

"Yes. But after this is over, you have some explaining to do," Celeste told Reina with a pointed finger. "So make sure you come home." She smiled. "It's where you and I belong."

Reina considered it. She matched Celeste's smile, though not as earnestly. "It is decided, then," she said, letting Ches guide her toward the eagle, noting the confidence with which he climbed on its back. The eagle never once faltered. It was obvious this wasn't the first time.

She waited for Celeste and Javier to do the same. They mounted the eagles flanking Reina, while two more riderless eagles followed.

"Celeste, focus on the tinieblas," Reina commanded as the eagle beneath her huffed and shuddered, adjusting to the new weight, its wings opening to take flight. "Javier, you seize Eva—gently, like you wanted to."

Celeste snickered.

"Very funny," Javier said as the eagle beneath him unfurled violently.

With a gust that shook every shrub and frailejón dotting the wilderness, the eagles took flight.

"And I'll handle Rahmagut," Reina and Ches said.

CHES

47

Mistress of Tinieblas

I shall spare her life.

Maior wasn't a fool to buy Rahmagut's words.

Even though Rahmagut ascended the mountain with his tinieblas, some of his demons stayed behind. They prowled the Águila corridors with their mandibles leaking rotting saliva. They skulked past open doors with their talons scraping the flagstones. Even the crosses nailed over doorways did nothing to abate them. Outside, they lurked on the grounds as well. The human staff couldn't see them without bismuto, but the air was infected with their oppression. There was a weight in the atmosphere. A stifling of thought and conversation as people could sense something was amiss.

Once she headed back inside, Maior paused by a window and watched the creatures with wringing hands. Rahmagut's tinieblas had turned Águila Manor into an impregnable fortress.

Every doubt crept around Maior, constricting her freedom to breathe. If Rahmagut intercepted Reina in the mountains, if he took her life—Maior hiccuped a broken breath—then her plans would be pointless. This was not how she had envisioned anything playing out.

For a week, Maior had bid her time as tinieblas slowly crept onto the property, restricting her movements and her access to the burial grounds behind the Virgin's chapel. All the while she'd considered the best moment to act, memorizing Enrique's routine and that of every servant loyal to him. She knew she'd have only one opportunity, and she couldn't botch it. But as she watched the tiniebla army disappear into the mountain trails, Maior realized the time had arrived. Today she would stain her hands with sin.

She broke her fast in the dining hall. As usual, Maior sat in Laurel's spot beside Enrique, who took his chair at the head of the table soon after. In silence, they were given freshly baked bread to be dipped into a bowl of pisca. Celeste never joined them.

Once she was full, Maior muttered the message Rahmagut had asked her to convey: He meant to return—the tinieblas patrolling the grounds were proof of it. Enrique's reply was an unbothered nod.

"I asked the servants to move your belongings to my chamber," the caudillo said as he dabbed the corners of his lips with a napkin.

The news froze her for an instant.

He sipped on his coffee, indifferent to her reaction. "The dresses that fit you and anything else you have been wearing lately. Tell the criadas to help you move anything you feel attached to. You may take whatever you like."

Somehow, she managed to meet his gaze and feign a small smile.

"Laurel almost never used her bed," he said by way of explaining. "You must know this, from your dreams."

Indeed, every night Enrique and Laurel shared the same bed. Every night, they fucked.

Her heart skipped a beat as she recognized that he had arranged this in preparation for Rahmagut's victory over Ches. Soon, the moment would come for him to make his decision: Would he choose to free Laurel by slitting Maior's throat? Or would he keep pretending she was his wife returned?

A horrible voice in the back of Maior's head whispered how, indeed, Enrique surely sought to sample what he posed to gain by keeping her. She felt the urge to retch.

"Unless you are not ready?"

It was a farce. Maior knew she had no power to reject him. Could he hear the panic in her heart at this moment? Could he sense the spike of blood rushing through her, as she imagined the night ahead? She let out a little exhale to compose herself. "I'm just surprised it's happening so soon," she said, and her words were true.

Slowly, he rose and walked behind her. His big hand fell on her shoulder. Maybe it was his attempt at reassuring her, but the heat radiating off his hand repulsed her. His proximity raised goose bumps along her skin. Maior bit the insides of her cheeks, hard, to stop herself from crying aloud.

"I will accept your decision, whatever it is," he said softly. "Come to my bedchamber once you're ready. If not tonight, there will always be tomorrow."

He walked away, and his patience sickened her. The way he bided his time. The plans he had for her. Maior rushed out of the dining hall and puked her breakfast all over the yard. A tiniebla watched her without compassion.

Maior cleared her tears and headed back inside. The emptying of her meal filled her with adrenaline, or perhaps it was courage, after Enrique's proposal. Maior lacked any hesitation as she made a detour to the rotting-wood door of the underground.

A single candle pocketed her in meek yellow light as she descended the slick stone steps. Ursulina's door groaned angrily when Maior pushed it open, her heart pounding with courage. Were it not for the steadfast flame, she'd be blanketed by the dark.

She padded to one of the oak cases, looking for the deer skull flute. There was a large fissure on the clay, with a visible line of some adhesive where the caudillo had patched it together. Maior's chest thrummed. With this flute she could command a tiniebla or two to exhume Laurel for her. She wouldn't have to get her hands dirty. She could command them to guard her while she escaped through the mountains. Such a simple solution, and it all hinged on one factor . . .

With shaking hands Maior brought the mouth opening to her lips. She blew and a coarse puff came out. Not the high-pitched whistle of her dream. Maior tried again and her heart further sank at the sound. Then again. The result was the same.

A sob escaped her lips.

So the instrument hadn't been properly fixed. But what of its magic? She couldn't give up so easily. She bundled it in some linen she found nearby and hurried out of the underground.

There was a great hubbub as she crossed one courtyard. The head matron was flushed in the face as she observed the arrival of an ailing young man. Another maid helped him up. Stunned, Maior saw that the young man was drenched in blood from his ruana to his espadrilles. He cried and writhed in agony. Maior recognized it for what it was.

"Don't concern yourself with it, mi señora," a maid told her as she passed by Maior.

Maior winced, loathing the moniker.

She followed them to the infirmary, where the young man was unceremoniously dropped on an empty bed. She placed the flute on a bedside table, rolled up her sleeves, and ordered the servants to make way. "His heart has a tiniebla's rot," Maior said, slicing open his ruana and shirt for a look at his chest. She chewed on her cheeks from the pang of nostalgia—the memory of Reina and Juan Pablo.

"He was attacked by a tiniebla?" the maid said, and Maior nearly choked on a laugh from the absurd panic in the girl's voice. How could they not have an inkling of what their caudillo was doing to their land?

The young man groaned.

"How can you know such a thing?" the head matron asked her. Unlike the rest of the staff, she didn't waste her time with titles and monikers. She didn't pretend Maior was Laurel returned.

"Don't you use bismuto in this manor?" Maior snapped. She waved at the fogged window in the corner. "Look for yourself! Enrique welcomed Rahmagut into this home. How can you continue to follow that man?"

Whatever discomfort twisted the head matron's face was interrupted by the young man's sharp cry. He clawed at his exposed chest, desperately drawing pink lines over his heart.

The door to the infirmary slowly creaked open. A snarling amalgamated monster peeked into the room with hungry, white-fogged eyes. Saliva poured out of its maw. Its talons twitched, as if restraining the urge to have a go at them—to tear each of their hearts out. What stopped it? Had Rahmagut ordered them to hold back? Then what of this young man?

The maid and the head matron glanced at the door as well. They couldn't see the monster watching them from the doorway. Nevertheless, Maior didn't miss their shivering, as if they were shaking off a sudden chill.

This young man and the soldier from earlier—they were just the first victims. Soon, more lives would be lost to this madness.

She focused on kneading the young man's chest with the soothing effects of a galio spell. At first, he kicked and begged for help, until Maior deftly guided him into a heavy sleep. Her fingertips traced his breast, right over his heart. She could imagine it beneath the layers of skin, muscle, and ribs, all this protection becoming moot against the tiniebla's rot. She even knew exactly what it took to end the heart's misery. A sharp blade tilted in a horizontal direction, to slide between the true ribs, with enough force to reach the heart.

His chest muscles constricted visibly as the tiniebla's corruption developed and spread. His veins turned black beneath his brown skin. Just as it had when Juan Pablo was taken. Maior's lashes fluttered with unshed tears. This sleep would be this young man's last, probably. For all of Maior's talents and knowledge of the body, she knew she didn't have it in her to help him. And she couldn't muster the resolution to take his life.

She felt all the more grateful for the miracle that was Reina's life.

"What is happening?" the head matron asked Maior.

"Go back to your quarters. Lock the doors if you must. Offer a prayer to the Virgin, because darkness is coming," Maior muttered, wiping away her tears.

She grabbed the flute and headed for the door, where the tiniebla watched them. In close proximity, the sickly sweetness of rot traveled up her nostrils. Maior had to breathe through her mouth to ease the nausea. She approached it against all instinct.

A hunger filled the tiniebla's eyes as it glanced down at Maior's shorter frame. Its heavy breathing filled the silence. Suddenly the head matron grabbed the back of Maior's arm as if to stop her.

"There's something there," the head matron said.

Indeed.

Maior guided the women through the doorway, her heart drilling against her ribs as they drew dangerously close to the tiniebla's reach. Rahmagut must have prohibited the tinieblas from harming her and the staff. There was no other explanation.

She ordered the servants to pray in their quarters and waited until they disappeared around the corner. With a pounding chest and sweat-slicked palms, Maior unwrapped the deer skull flute and pressed the opening to her lips, blowing a coarse tune. The sound was wrong.

"Come with me," she commanded the tiniebla.

The tiniebla didn't even twitch. Maior tested walking away, to see if it would follow her, but the creature just watched her from afar, violence and hunger in its eyes.

Maior rushed out to the yard and abandoned the broken flute on a bench. She couldn't help the tears that streamed down her cheeks.

There was no time to cry over her foiled plans. If anything, she was the fool for assuming Enrique had succeeded in repairing the flute. She would have to dirty her own hands.

Maior headed into one of the larders, where she had stored her materials little by little. Sitting on a rickety bench was a cloth concealing a shovel, a hammer and a lever, and a small vial of bismuto for good measure. With the bundle in hand, she crossed the muddy yard and entered the chapel flanking the burial grounds. She deposited her bundle in the chapel's storage room.

Before leaving, she knelt before the Virgin's well and prayed until her mouth grew dry. Maior begged for forgiveness in tears. She begged for her Virgin's understanding, for she knew she was rushing headfirst into a path of damnation.

Later, the manor's third story was quiet and empty as Maior trekked down its cold corridors with Enrique's chamber as her destination. She carried a few possessions up, following the caudillo's invitation, for she had to pretend all was well. She had to carry on with this game they were playing, for her sake and his.

Maior entered the room holding her breath, her heart at her throat. She was entering his demesne, a place where she lacked any sort of advantage. A place where no one would come to her rescue should she scream for help. She exhaled in relief when she found the room empty.

The curtains were drawn, blocking out the day's overcast light. Enrique's room smelled of the mountains, of the fir scent that clung to his hair and clothes. The space was tidy. Every item and furniture stood exactly as Maior remembered it, save for a familiar chest that had been recently brought up. Laurel's.

Maior stacked her items atop the chest. She walked over to his massive four-poster bed, where the pillows were placed near the middle, allowing a wide berth for his antlers. The left was Laurel's side. It would also be hers, if the courage to follow through with her plans escaped her. If she surrendered to Enrique. She could have this comfortable peace in misery, she supposed. The Liberator was dead, Eva belonged to Rahmagut, and Reina was defeated. Whatever punishment came her way, Maior deserved it.

"Mi señora," a voice said as Maior stepped out of Enrique's room. She jumped, but it was just the criada who tended to her room. "What are you doing up here? I have been looking for you." She was a coy thing, with cheeks that blushed at inconsequential things far too often for Maior's taste.

Maior made sure the criada saw her holding the sapphire necklace and the golden brush. "I was leaving a few of my things in his room."

"Oh, yes!" There it was, that annoying blush. "Don Enrique told me about today." She trailed Maior as they rerouted to Laurel's room. "I shall bathe you and dress you in the softest gown we have. I want this to be perfect for you."

Maior didn't let her see her grimace. "I want to wear her necklace, to remind him of her," she said.

The criada giggled. "Of course! And it's all yours now. Oh— this makes me so hopeful. I miss seeing Don Enrique happy."

Laurel's bedroom windows faced the mountains. A copper bathtub had been placed by the windows, beside the soft-fluttering gossamer curtains. The water steamed with the sweet scents of honey and rose, and was foggy from a milky substance the criada had poured into it right before Maior climbed in.

When it was time to come out of the water, the criada dressed her in a light blue gown with lace covering the cleavage. The fabric was soft and easily loosened by the satin cords interlacing across her back. The skirt was a sheer satin, single layered and embroidered with gold and blue designs. They sat across from Laurel's vanity mirror while the criada brushed Maior's hair over and over meticulously, as if to train her hair into adopting Laurel's natural waves.

Maior placed the sapphire atop her cleavage, in the spot where she'd normally have her treasured Virgin. She stared at herself in the mirror and found a stranger with rosy cheeks and rouge lips.

The criada squeezed her shoulders from behind.

"Do I really look just like her?"

It suddenly occurred to Maior that she had no solid recollection of what Laurel looked like. She hadn't bothered to inspect herself in a mirror while using bismuto. The idea was too painful to attempt. In her dreams, she always took Laurel's point of view. Laurel existed in Maior's thoughts blurred around the edges. Less as a memory and more as a concept that brought her anguish. But she had to look just like Laurel. Otherwise, how could they all so easily convince themselves she was the Benevolent Lady returned?

"I think you shouldn't worry about that," the criada said. "I think this will simply be a new chapter for Don Enrique's life."

Maior's stomach twisted.

"So go and make him happy. This household could use some joy. We all need this to work."

That was when Maior noticed it: the sky going dark. They turned to the window, watching in silence as the afternoon sun disappeared. As darkness poured over the land and into the room.

Maior knew this was her punishment. The Virgin had forsaken her, just as She had forsaken this house. Rahmagut never meant to spare Reina. And no one was coming for Maior. What awaited her now was a nightmare she'd crafted for herself.

48

Where the Star Fell

Lost within herself, Eva was bound with nothing but the consolation of remembering her life. She wallowed in the memories,
enduring the bad moments for a taste of the good. She withstood
the sorrow of finding the milk snake latched to her sister's breast, if
only to see the pride in Don Samón's eyes as he introduced her to
his friends. She watched the disappointment in her grandmother's
eyes time and time again and lost her breath from the sadness of
bidding Néstor goodbye, only to experience the sweet rapture of
being skin to skin in Javier's arms. Like an addict, she let the memories take her, for within them, she could forget her reality.

In this fugue of remembrance, she could avoid witnessing
Rahmagut loosing his tinieblas on the innocents who lived in the
Páramo. It veiled her vision anytime Rahmagut entered Enrique's
study, where her father's antlers had been mounted on the wall like
a hunter's prize. It let her forget all those instances when she clawed
and fought to take control, only to discover how painfully powerless she was against a god.

Thus, Eva hid within the darkness of his mind. She ignored the
window to the world that were her eyes. She numbed herself to the
never-ending desire to say "Stop!" after failing so many times.

Rahmagut ascended the Páramo surrounded by his tinieblas'
stink of death. He passed the pine grove bordering Águila Manor.

He stepped over humidity-slicked ferns and mora-bearing bushes. He dodged the marcescent frailejones that dominated the higher altitudes. All were new sights and smells to Eva, but she blocked out the experience, for it brought her too much pain. For Rahmagut, this hike was nothing but a meditative countdown to the moment when he used *Eva's body* to kill Reina.

They stopped upon reaching a rocky outcrop. A cave-in covered the entrance to a tunnel. Rahmagut beheld the boulders and told her, *"Here used to be my home. I built it atop the iridio."*

In the darkness, Eva gave him her back. She refused to acknowledge the sight.

"Your dearest friend Reina shall meet us here," he said, his amusement manifesting like a breeze. It was a light thing, tickling her forearms in the darkness of his conscience.

"I can give you control. Maybe you can speak a few words."

All he wanted was to use her as bait. Eva would spit at his feet if she could.

"Don't you at least want to say goodbye?" Rahmagut mocked. *"To change bodies, I'll have to slit your throat and bleed you dry."*

Eva retreated to the darkest moments of her memories. She found the more they hurt, the more she could ignore Rahmagut's present tyranny.

She thought of her father. He would think her a coward for withdrawing, and a fool for allowing Rahmagut to bewitch her with promises of power. All along, Don Samón had been right. Eva had thought herself so powerful after a few tastes of iridio. She had imagined herself so capable, sharing her body with a demon god. Now all she looked forward to was this promised end. At least in death, she wouldn't be so ashamed.

An explosion yanked her back to the present. Besides her sadness, Eva could feel the physical changes in her body. Her heart raced with Rahmagut's elation. Reina had arrived as he had so carefully plotted.

"I'm glad you made it," Rahmagut said above the growling and snarling of his tinieblas. "Spared me from dragging you here by the hair."

Curious, Eva peeked through the windows of her eyes. She saw Reina astride a titan of an eagle, silent in her admonishment. Gold gilded Reina's skin—she was blinding like the sun. Four other equally enormous creatures circled the air around her, occasionally swooping down to pick off a tiniebla or two. Eva was surprised to see Javier and Celeste mounted on the eagles.

"Why don't you come down and fight me like a man?" Rahmagut hollered, using Eva's hands to shoot a fireball in the air. The eagle ducked a split second before impact. "Are you a god, or are you a coward?"

Despite her sorrow, Eva wasn't oblivious to the truth. Reina, Javier, and Celeste circled in the air with caution because they'd come for her. Her heart gave a little jolt. How she loathed Rahmagut using her as bait. If she was going to die, the least she could do was help take him down.

With a wave, Rahmagut commanded the horde of tinieblas forward. The horde stomped the hill in a manic fervor. They used the frailejones as leverage to launch into the air, swiping for blood. They climbed atop one another, jumping for the eagles. Tinieblas with bat wings and other plumed wings soared into the air, clawing at Reina.

As his impatience grew, Rahmagut made a fist in the air and summoned a fireball like a flaming sun. Eva clenched her soul, winding tightly to grab some control. The exertion was like a painful twisting of her spine and innards, but she weathered it, screaming. It deviated Rahmagut's hurling hand. He missed Reina completely, striking Celeste's eagle square on the chest instead.

"*Stay out of this—where you belong!*" Rahmagut howled, shoving Eva deep within the darkness, putting a lid on the last of her influence.

Reina and Javier rushed to the hill where Celeste hit the ground with such force she cratered the mountain. Their grounding proved to be a mistake, as the tinieblas rerouted like a carnivorous flock. They stormed up the hill, snarling, one by one their bodies fading to nothing against Javier's and Reina's swordplay.

From their shared cognizance, Eva knew the iridio beneath them was plentiful enough that Rahmagut could control his Void gem even as he approached them. He withdrew the gem from the confines of her bodice and held it in the air. All he needed now was to snare Reina in place...

Suddenly a thrumming sound filled the air—marching footsteps, arising from the east. Bismuto-burning Bravo men stormed up the mountain, carving a path to assist Reina and Javier. They were led by Esteban and Pucho, who maneuvered through the battlefield with practiced ease. Eva even recognized Don Rigoberto among them. They cleared one tiniebla after another, ferociously, their wits and experience with the sword making up for the tinieblas outnumbering them.

With enough time, there would be no more tinieblas to slay. Rahmagut would be alone in Eva's meek body. It was his folly, Eva noted, letting them get so good against tinieblas.

"*Enough!*" Rahmagut told her.

"*You made them tiniebla-slaying experts.*"

"*Let this be your final warning: If you don't stay silent, I will rip the antlers from Javier's head, like Enrique did to Samón. I will use your own hands. I'll make sure he's alive to watch it happen.*"

True fear stunned Eva, until she realized there was no need for such a threat unless her diversion was having a strong enough impact. He needed her to be silent. Thus, she screamed at the top of her lungs into his mind.

It addled him like he had once addled her. Rahmagut gripped her curls and pounded her temples. "Silence!" he howled.

The next thing Eva knew, she was flung to the ground. The back of her head clattered against something hard and ragged. Black spots flooded their vision. When Rahmagut finally opened Eva's eyes, they saw it was Javier pinning her down.

Reina and the eagles rushed to support Javier, keeping the tinieblas at bay.

"Snap out of it, Eva," Javier said between gritted teeth. He'd pinned the hand holding the Void gem to the ground, where Reina could easily pry it out of Rahmagut's grip.

"Your Eva is gone!" Rahmagut snarled. "She thought she could wrestle me for control, but she was overconfident, and a failure."

Eva pressed herself close to the windows of her eyes, hungry to take Javier in. She cataloged every fleck of color in his eyes, every line and blemish on his cheeks. She lifted a hand and pressed it to the image of him, aching to have the strength to come through and break herself from Rahmagut's hold. But she was trapped. Rahmagut was right.

"Eva!" Javier pleaded.

Reina approached cautiously for the gem.

"No!" Rahmagut barked as Reina knelt beside them, her eyes zeroed in on the imploding star he held in Eva's hand.

It wasn't meant to be pried away from him! Rage blazed through Rahmagut. It nearly scorched Eva, so she pulled back, withdrawing to the cooler depths of their shared consciousness.

"Remember what you told me: He's not a real god—even if he's won now. I know you can break free," Javier said with pleading eyes. It was an expression Eva never imagined possible in him. The real fear of losing her. The tenderness he wore only for her. "You're the strongest caster I've ever met. *You can fight.* I've always believed in you, my fallen star."

In the darkness of Rahmagut's mind, Eva wanted to scream. She wanted to punch and thrash against his control until her inner body bled, battered. But Rahmagut bound her, steadfast and malicious. His grip was too strong. Eva wept.

"Fool!" Rahmagut hollered. Eva's free fist punched Javier in the face. Lightning-quick pain shot through her elbow from the impact. "You are my servant," Rahmagut growled, and he reached into the Void, taking hold of the tiniebla housed within Javier. "So serve *me!*"

Javier pulled away mechanically, his will battling the tiniebla's for control. But soon enough, his eyes flooded with inky black. His veins bulged. Before Reina could notice the switch in him, he pounced on her.

Rahmagut rose to his feet as Tiniebla Javier yanked Nightcleaver from Reina's grip and tossed it out of her reach. He pinned her to the ground, pummeling her stomach over and over.

"Snap out of it!" Reina told Javier, wrestling him. "Don't let it take you, damn it. Fight it!"

Rahmagut's laughter tuned out Eva's screams, and her fear as she watched Javier and Reina duel. Reina obviously had the upper hand, as her fist crashed against Javier's face and his fingernails raked blood from Reina's cheeks.

"*She will end him for me*," Rahmagut purred to the darkness. "*I told you: You will watch him die. She's an expert in slaying tinieblas, indeed.*"

Rahmagut delighted in the sight of Reina kneeing Javier in the groin and punching him with her fist radiant in sunlight. Rahmagut made sure Eva witnessed every moment of it. And Eva screamed with rage, for there was no appeasing the tiniebla possessing Javier. She banged her fists against Rahmagut's darkness. It felt futile. She was muted and ousted, banished and meek. And she had failed everyone.

The tiniebla always got up, even as Reina dislocated Javier's left shoulder and slashed red rivulets on his chest. In Javier's body, the tiniebla knew no pain.

He would be worn down to blood and bone if they kept this up.

Suddenly Celeste appeared. Her shoulders and arms were covered in bloody blisters. Her military jacket was charred at the edges. She lunged at Javier, wrenching him from Reina and pinning him down with her body weight. Her efforts didn't amount to much. If Javier and Celeste were ever equally matched, the tiniebla changed the paradigm by utilizing every ounce of strength, lacking any instinct for self-preservation.

Reina hesitated in leaving Celeste to handle Javier on her own.

Rahmagut used the split-second distraction to sprint down the hill, ever closer to the entrance of his former home. Closer to the mass of iridio stored beneath the mountain. He stalled, smirking, his fist around the gem growing cold from the Void gem's heat leech.

Reina's footsteps thundered in pursuit. She tackled him before he could climb up the path toward the cave—just as Rahmagut hoped she would. The impact sent both Eva and Reina plummeting to the other side of the path, down a scree. Rocks scraped Eva's cheeks and shrubs prickled her hands and shoulders. Blood gushed in her mouth as she bit her tongue. They ended up by the bank of a small creek of crystalline water. Rahmagut opened Eva's eyes to the sight of wildflowers. A butterfly fluttered away from the interruption.

As Rahmagut got up, Eva saw they'd arrived at an open grassland cratered with lakes of all shapes and sizes. Creeks branched between them, as part of a river that fed them with runoff from the higher peaks. Frailejones dotted the land, skirted by the short yellow grasses that cushioned Eva's fall.

"*The point of impact,*" Rahmagut told Eva. "*This is where the fallen star crashed millions of years ago, bringing iridio into this world.*" He scanned the landscape, taking great satisfaction in its familiarity. How he was at home. "*The iridio—that is the real deity. And I was the one who harnessed it.*"

Rahmagut's delight curled around Eva like a sickly-sweet plume of smoke.

Reina approached them. She lifted the sword tip to Eva's face. It glinted with a ray of sunlight from the fragmented clouds, dazzling them for the briefest second. Her eyes were aglow with wrath, and they were ancient. Eva realized she faced the god of the sun.

"What's so fucking funny?" Reina growled, lowering her weapon.

"If you kill her, I will just take Celeste. You will have to slay everyone you hold dear," Rahmagut said, injecting much amusement into his voice. "This will be the test: Is your god a tyrant? Will he sacrifice everyone you love in his vendetta against me? Because he has no other recourse against my cunning."

Reina's fist crashed into Eva's cheek. Pain blazed through Eva in the clattering of teeth. A metallic taste spread in her mouth.

Rahmagut staggered back. He laughed deeply, wiping the blood from his chin. "Here I thought you were motivated to save your friend." He swayed, once again placing himself within reach of Reina's fist. "But...you don't seem to care about her well-being? Should we fight and destroy her body in the process?"

He pounced on Reina, his footing quick and sure. Reina ducked away from the punch but took Eva's other fist to the belly. Reina shoved her off and Eva landed on her back.

"*Enough!*" Eva howled with tears running down her face. Rahmagut didn't listen. He just laughed.

Her hatred for him grew. It multiplied like the merciless tinieblas he had amassed in the Páramo. Everyone had been right about him.

"Your tinieblas will soon fall. You have nothing left," Reina said.

Rahmagut chuckled, because he knew exactly what came next. He lifted his gaze to the sky, finding the moon as it finally began its predetermined journey in front of the sun. The reason why he chose to meet Ches in broad daylight—because he wouldn't need the shroud of night.

As the moon traveled over the sun, the shadows around them adopted the eclipse's form. They crawled beneath frailejones and skuttled through the grasses, mirroring the joining of the sun and the moon. Stunned, Reina turned to the heavens. She noticed the beginnings of the eclipse and her face paled. She knew it only meant the end.

The grasses flattened with footsteps behind them. Rahmagut whirled toward the intruder, then realized it was Javier emerging from the hill. Worry lanced through Eva, for Celeste's absence was telling. Was this to be a repeat of the suffering they lived through at the tomb?

Driven by Rahmagut's command, Javier charged at Reina, further brutalizing his body against her. Their fight was a distraction while the moon crept over the sun.

Eva pounded the edges of Rahmagut's darkness as Rahmagut lifted the Void gem up into the air. She screamed and howled and rammed her shoulders against the suffocating darkness of his will. Her uproar made small dents in his concentration, but it wasn't enough. She was never enough.

He levitated the Void gem, sending it floating up above his outstretched palms. The fracture Eva had caused on the Void gem widened. It split. A miasma broke out of its center, and a wild, indomitable pull began sucking the air in. Dirt and grass lifted. Flower petals were plucked out. Bugs shot up from their burrows.

Rahmagut's concentration was a tight band around the gem.

His summoned iridio seeped out from under the earth. It manifested as a curling plume in Rahmagut's signature black. The iridio wrapped around Eva's outstretched hands and over the bursting Void gem, reeling it in to Rahmagut, forcing him to be its tether to the earth.

And this moment, right as the Void gem was fully opened and awaiting Rahmagut's direction, was when the veil of Rahmagut's control felt thinnest. Eva was no longer bound. She could step forward in the darkness, ever closer to the windows that were her eyes. She knew: If she willed it hard enough, she'd be able to retake control of her body. She would be back, but she wouldn't know how to control the Void gem. She would end it all—destroy Rahmagut for the price of breaking the fabric of reality, as he'd once done before his sealing. Only this time, the moon was eclipsing Ches's power. They would have no one to save them.

The moon continued its trajectory, and Reina gripped her shirt. She fell to her knees, sucking big gulps of air. Her eyes bulged and her cheeks reddened.

Reina yanked her shirt open and reached into her pocket. She uncapped a small vial filled with a black liquid—her refill of iridio. But Javier snatched it out of her hands. They wrestled for it, Reina's face purple from exertion, until Javier slammed the vial against a rock, shattering it. The precious substance was lost to the soil.

Rahmagut chuckled as he levitated the gem above them. The Void gem took in heated air and regurgitated iridio like black fire. It roared with a force unlike any Eva had ever seen before. It grew bigger, resembling an iridio-spitting star, of black-and-purple corrupted miasma. Panic seized Eva. If she didn't do something, Ches would be gone.

Reina noticed Rahmagut's approach and tried crawling away.

"Didn't you say I had nothing left? Look at yourself," Rahmagut said, then nodded a wordless command to his awaiting tiniebla.

Javier pinned Reina to the grass before she could put much distance between her and Rahmagut's Void gem.

Darkness shrouded the vast hills and mountains of the Páramo as the moon reached the moment of totality. The world became awash in shades of black. Without sunlight, the cold strangled the mountain. A silence hushed the lakes, save for the Void gem's roaring. Behind the moon, the sun formed a ring in the sky. It was a beautiful sight, were it not for the promise of his assured destruction.

Reina's face warped in fear. Her eyes hollowed as she saw the eclipse and the inevitability of Rahmagut's plan as clearly as Eva did.

Eva knew what the world would be like if Rahmagut was left alone, unchecked, without Ches as a deterrent to his ambition. She had already witnessed the killing and the darkness. She'd seen his utter disregard for mortal life. And it was an irony, because Rahmagut had been born a mortal. He hadn't emerged with the dawning of the world, like Ches and the other deities. He merely shoved his presence into their ranks, drunk on iridio, at the cost of everything.

Eva couldn't let him win. Despite the devastating consequences, she had to take the power away, if only for a moment, until the moon made way for Ches's rays. Even if she perished in the process, this was the price to pay for her arrogance, to correct her mistake.

With a vicious wave of her hands, Eva pounded against Rahmagut's control, shattering his hold over her body. He had spent all his concentration on the Void gem. He had not imagined her bold enough to act in this moment, which risked their annihilation.

Eva took over. She slipped into her body, all nerves and pain.

Immediately, the iridio commanded by Rahmagut skulked back beneath the earth. The Void gem quivered on the verge of eruption. Time slowed to a crawl. Eva could already imagine it: the Void gem's outburst indiscriminately sucking everything into oblivion.

Rahmagut roared at her. He insulted her intelligence and begged her to let go, or else they would all be obliterated.

Instead of bending, Eva summoned the iridio beneath the earth back to her hands. It trailed up as glimmering bands of gold—*her* signature color. It mantled her hands and circled the Void gem. The satin-like bands wrapped the imploding star over and over, muting its roaring. Eva ground her molars and commanded the iridio beneath the mountain with all her might until the bands succeeded in controlling the star.

She reeled it in for mere seconds.

But the Void gem would not be so easily controlled.

49

River Purity

Without Ches's sunlight or iridio, Reina's chest caved. Her heart raced in desperation, depleting the last of the fuel keeping her alive.

Suddenly, Rahmagut went quiet. Reina squirmed underneath Javier's grip for a look and saw a different face controlling the Void gem. Bands of gold wound around the Void gem, binding it.

Gold was Eva's geomancia hue. *Eva was back.*

Despite the tremendous heartache, Reina punched Javier's jaw so hard she thought she heard it dislocate. He flew far, and Reina scrambled to her feet. Her nerves and ligaments were ablaze. The pain was reminiscent of what she'd endured against her grandmother in the tomb, when she was willing to sacrifice it all. Except today the stakes were worse.

Reina glimpsed Eva's eyes. No longer were they dotted by two pupils each. They glimmered with magic and fear. There were no words to be said, yet Reina understood. Eva was seconds away from losing control. She needed help.

Crazed to obey Rahmagut's command, Javier lunged at Reina. She evaded him, and as she snatched her fallen Nightcleaver, a wild idea dawned on her.

What was this eclipse, if not the absence of sunlight shrouding the land in darkness?

With fire burning her lungs, Reina sprinted up the hill—as far as she could get before Javier pounced. She mustered every ounce of faith and strength in her body and lanced Nightcleaver into the sky, directly at the eclipse.

All sounds emptied from the mountain. The blade swiveled in the air dozens of times, dull without the sun's light.

Reina watched it spin with a thrumming heart. Javier tackled her to the ground, her mouth filling with dirt. He whispered foul things into her ear, reminded her of all the terrible things his god planned to do to her. Still, she never peeled her gaze from the blade's edge and the ferocity with which it spun. Reina's belief in the tales of her ancestors, and of her god, was reaffirmed when in the last flip Nightcleaver sliced the moon's shroud in half, making way for sunlight to pour over the world as it always meant to.

The moment it did, Ches's presence flooded her body.

"I am back."

Radiant sunlight burst through her every pore. With the returned strength, she flung Javier off her. The creature regained its footing, but he watched her from a distance with apprehension, realizing she wasn't meek and dying anymore.

Reina ran down the hill and grabbed Eva from behind by the shoulders. They lifted their hands in the air, like a prayer to the heavens, reeling in the black star. "Hold on. I got you," Reina whispered to Eva's ear, imparting some of Ches's radiance and giving Eva the strength and guidance to reverse the Void gem's opening.

Slowly and carefully, together they shrunk the star. Their control was precise, honed from Ches's previous experience and their unified hatred of Rahmagut.

The gem returned to its original size of a walnut. Reina took it from Eva's hands. It was a wonder, how something so delicate and precious had the power to rend the world. Eva exhaled in relief and smiled upon being unburdened of it.

"Take her to the river," Ches commanded Reina.

Reina extended a hand. "Come with me," she told Eva gently.

Eva squeezed her temples with both hands and screwed her eyes shut, as if she were weathering a migraine. Indeed, Rahmagut was a blight. But despite her internal riot, Eva took Reina's hand.

With a steady grip, Reina led her to the river source of the creeks and lakes. Reina's heart felt whole and ready to burst. She had so much love for her friend, who'd ultimately saved them all. Eva was enduring Rahmagut so they could have this moment.

Tiniebla Javier followed them from the fringes like a hunting wolf.

They arrived at the mountain river. The water was emerald in color, housing a myriad of fish and mollusks along its banks. When Reina crouched and tickled the surface, she found it icy. Maybe it would be dangerous afterward. Maybe they would have to deal with the possibility of freezing to death. But Ches's intention was clear.

In touching the water, Reina understood its cleansing properties. The power of the river had always been there, just like the sun's. They'd just gotten so used to it, taking it for granted. Reina thought of the Penitent tales. How the Virgin had risen from the mouth of the river to meet Her disciples. What was the Virgin in that tale, if not the river's power itself?

"Arca." Ches placed the name on Reina's lips, addressing the river water.

Renamed for a new belief system, but still the same.

Reina met Eva's eyes. "Do you trust me?" she asked.

Eva nodded.

Reina guided Eva into the icy water. They walked in waist-deep, steeling their bodies against the current, dodging moss-covered boulders and stepping on the steady ones. Javier lurked by the riverbank, watching, but understanding his strength was a drop in the ocean of Reina's Duality.

"First, we must take back what Rahmagut stole," Ches told them. Then, just for Eva, he said, "When you go underwater, do not close your eyes. Even if it stings. Even if he fights. Focus on me. You will know when it is done."

Reina helped Eva down into the water, bringing Eva to her knees. There were tears in Eva's eyes right before Reina pressed down on Eva's collar, taking her beneath the glimmering surface.

Blurred around the edges, Eva stared up at Reina in a mixture of fear and hope. Then the real battle began.

Eva—or Rahmagut—squirmed under Reina's hold, violently clawing to get out. She splashed water, soaking Reina. She flapped and kicked as air gurgled out of her. Rahmagut was strong beneath Reina's grip, doing everything he could to free himself from his assured expulsion.

With one hand trapping Eva underwater, Ches lifted Reina's other hand above Eva's face. He curled her fingers in a tugging motion, pulling and pulling until two black orbs blobbed out of Eva's agape eyes. Plucked, the two pupils spun and levitated in the air before Ches pressed them into his own eyes—Reina's.

Suddenly the world took on a different, incandescent color. Everything vibrated around the edges, as if the matter making up the world was in a transient state of flux, multiple probabilities presenting themselves to Reina's eyes. A past, present, and future. She noticed another hand in the water, draping over Reina's to help keep Rahmagut from resurfacing. Reina glanced up and saw it belonged to a nozariel woman with river-water hair. She had rainbows in her eyes, and her skin was slick and moist, as if she was made from the river itself. Surrounding them were other spectators as well, a dozen ghostly eyes who watched them from the bushes and from behind the frailejones, spirits unseen by mortal eyes. Reina understood what had been returned to Ches: his sight.

"He is not divine anymore. We can remove him now," Ches said.

It was two gods against a false one.

Eva thrashed beneath the water, first enraged, then fearful. Her screeches gurgled and echoed. And Reina's heart clenched from Eva's despair. What was she doing, if not suffocating the life out of her friend?

"*For how long?*" she asked Ches.

"*Lay your trust on me, or else I will take over. We cannot spare another mistake.*"

Arca offered Reina a sad smile.

Reina was tempted to close her eyes, to avoid imprinting the horrible image of Eva's drowning on her mind. But she steeled herself, thinking of Nightcleaver; of the five peaks turned to eagles; of Arca's appearance. All ancient tales from Ches's mythos proving to be true. She had no reason to doubt him.

Eva's last bubbling gurgles broke the surface, then her body went limp. A blackness like ink exuded from Eva's skin, hair, and clothes. It surrounded them, smelling of oil and decomposition.

Rahmagut.

Without the pupils' divinity, his spirit couldn't linger, so he dissipated into his afterlife.

"Give me the reins," Ches told Reina, and she obliged, letting go of Duality's equal control.

The clouds parted for them. Late afternoon sunlight poured out of the skies, gilding Reina and empowering Ches.

Arca watched with rainbow eyes as, in the cradle of his palm, Ches lifted the Void gem into the air. Under the sunlight, the stone glimmered as if a whole new universe was condensed in that small, walnut-sized gem. In a fist, Ches squeezed it with all his strength. Arca's hands cupped around Reina's fist, steadying it. Her touch soothed the corrosive feel of the gem's resistance against Ches's grip. It spared Reina from the pain of having the gem's void-sucking edges dig into her skin.

With a howl, Ches shattered the gem into dust.

A loud shock wave boomed from Reina's fist. It clattered her teeth and split the river waters. The frailejones' marcescent leaves shuddered to the ground. The watching spirits were flung back against the wildflowers, jipijapa hats flying in the air. Faraway birds took flight, spooked, as the mountain shook with the implosion.

A hush enveloped them when it was all over. The Void gem and Rahmagut were no more.

50

Darkness, Banished

It is done," Ches muttered, then surrendered control back to Reina.

Arca nodded. She also retreated into her waters, merging with their purity.

Someone pulled Reina by the shoulder, shattering her stupor. Javier. Despite his monstrous countenance, Reina could see intelligence and recognition in the crimson of his eyes. He was back. Reina relinquished Eva, and he dragged her lifeless body to the bank. That was when it dawned on Reina—the enormous consequences of the act she'd committed.

In that moment, Reina had trusted the process. She'd trusted her god, for he was the good against Rahmagut's evil. But also...Ches had always been honest about their fates: Eva's death at her hands.

Reina's chest wrung viciously. Adrenaline and panic ravaged her until Reina couldn't manage a proper breath. She waddled out of the water maladroitly, terrified of her own culpability as Javier desperately pumped his palms against Eva's chest, his black claws aglow with the gold of his galio.

Reina's mouth opened, but no words could ever be adequate. She understood Javier's despair. Her throat constricted with guilt. She'd done this. This was the outcome. Why hadn't she realized it sooner? She'd prevented Eva from taking air. Ches had warned her that his and Rahmagut's hold could be severed only through death. What else was supposed to happen?

She collapsed to her knees. There was a sheen in Javier's eyes. As Reina lifted a hand to the corner of her eye, she realized she was on the verge of tears as well. She dug her fingers into her scalp, distraught. She'd caused the Liberator's death. She couldn't have caused Eva's as well—

Suddenly water gurgled out of Eva's throat. It was a great burst, then Eva gave a desperate gasp. The life returned to her as she spluttered. Air refilled her lungs.

Eva's eyes were glossy and confused as she stared about, taking in Javier's and Reina's shock.

"Eva!" they said at the same time.

Javier threw himself on her. He took her in his arms and squeezed. And it was a joy to see, because it meant some normalcy could be restored. They were a step closer to happiness.

After Javier pulled away, Reina cupped Eva's cheeks and took in the brightness of her eyes. How glad Reina was to see her alive.

With a smoky wheeze, Eva told them, "Rahmagut is gone. I am me again."

A laugh of relief exploded from Reina. She nodded, and the tears she'd been holding back poured down her cheeks. "He's gone, and you're alive." She wiped Eva's bangs from her forehead, and Eva smiled at the tender gesture.

What a joy! To be victorious and to have her friend in one piece.

Reina kissed her on the cheek and squeezed her so hard Eva whimpered.

With their waning adrenaline, their injuries flared. As Reina pulled away from the embrace, she glimpsed Javier massaging his shoulder. His jaw was purpling, but as he tapped it with his galio-gilded claw, the swelling receded. His tunic was stained red, but he didn't seem to be actively bleeding.

Realization dawned on Reina. She rose and turned to him. "You're back to yourself," she noted.

Javier frowned with shame.

"Where's the tiniebla?"

"I don't feel it anymore," Javier said. "It's gone." Still, his tail continued to swish behind him. Scutes plated his neck. There were new feathers on his left wrist, sprouting beneath his sleeve. Perhaps his amalgamated visage was permanent.

Eva accepted Javier's help in getting up. She closed her eyes as Javier showered her with his healing.

"Does that mean annihilating Rahmagut ended the tinieblas?" Reina said with her chest feather-light. She searched his eyes. If the tiniebla continued to lurk, she hoped it would betray its presence.

"Are you holding it back?" Eva said.

"No. It's not there."

"Like Rahmagut," Reina whispered. Reenergized, she sprinted up the hill, looking for Celeste, the eagles, her host, and the tinieblas, where the battle should be raging on if vanquishing Rahmagut had achieved nothing.

She was met by an empty field dotted with worn Bravo soldiers, including a bloody Esteban and Pucho, who were helping up Celeste. The eagles were in various states of injury, their wings broken, tattered, and bleeding. One heaved slowly, curled on the ground and incapacitated, its feathers mottled from Rahmagut's fireball. There were no tinieblas.

Reina grinned.

"*Rahmagut conceived tinieblas and kept them alive with the darkness he siphoned from the Void, an ability he gained from my divinity,*" Ches said, resurfacing just for the affirmation. His presence within her retreated before Reina could think to counter with more questions.

Celeste spotted her and limped in her direction. As Celeste finished her trek up the hill, they hugged. It was a steadying embrace. Reina could feel the love of her friendship. They let go as her people approached. The Bravo soldiers raised their fists in the air and hooted. Esteban's eyes glowed with pride. Pucho's and Don Rigoberto's with awe and admiration.

They were together again. Rahmagut was gone. Eva was alive. But there was one last thing Reina needed to do before she was truly whole.

51

A New Benevolent Lady

Maior's flickering candle gave her courage as she crossed the empty corridor to Enrique's bedchamber. Dusk was rapidly falling, bringing long, haunting shadows that followed her. Sometime while Maior had bathed, the tinieblas had emptied out of the grounds, but the apprehension they inspired had not. The manor was so quiet even a mouse couldn't scurry unnoticed. The servants lingered in corridors and in the kitchen, fearful after seeing the sun leaving the sky. Maior had played her part that afternoon, as the criada watched her like a hawk. She'd have no freedom until nighttime, when she would have the shroud of darkness to deal with Laurel's remains.

She closed his door behind her, trapping herself within. The room was empty, without Enrique's oppressive energy. Gingerly, as she called herself a fool, she approached his four-poster bed and sat under the curtain's shadow. Her hand ran the length of the covers, tracing the rich yet soft texture of the sheets, noting the exquisite threading, feeling the firmness of the pillow on Laurel's side. It reassured her.

There was so much opulence right beneath her fingertips. She could get used to the luxuries, if she truly tried.

She would have so much influence as the returned Laurel, and the love of every servant in Águila Manor. She would have the most powerful man in Venazia at her fingertips. A valco who'd communed and aligned himself with the god of the Void. He had a mountain of iridio, vaults filled with gold, and an army of seasoned soldiers. Enrique could give her a rich life; all she needed to do was ask.

A life plentiful with things she didn't need. For Maior had only one true need: the freedom and agency taken from her since the night Javier had plucked her from Apartaderos.

If she surrendered to him, she would have freedom in this gilded cage.

Eventually, the door opened, shattering her solace. Maior stiffened with her back to the doorway. She could hear Enrique pausing at the threshold, noting his solitude wasn't so lonely after all.

"So you came," he said, sweeping in and letting the heavy door close behind him.

Maior turned slowly, holding her breath. He was windswept and red-cheeked from the Páramo's cold. Maior imagined he'd gone riding to the woods, and her neck heated. The criada had told her of the old valco superstition that a ride in the mountains aided with the miracle of conception. Feleva did this for her sons. Enrique did it for Laurel...and he was doing it again.

"I didn't want to be rude," she said. "It's just a lot to get used to."

He winced as he lifted his arm to take his jacket off. Maior saw it for what it was: an opening. She approached him, saying, "Your shoulder hasn't healed."

"I complimented your abilities, yet all you did was numb the pain."

Maior allowed a small smile. "I thought valcos were supposed to heal quicker. I didn't think I needed to do the heavy lifting."

His gaze traveled to her crown. Was he seeking reassurance that his deceased wife was still there? Then it landed on her cleavage, where Laurel's sapphire sat above her breasts.

"You're wearing Laurel's jewel."

Maior hoped he judged her as vain and materialistic. "You told me to take whatever I was fond of—"

"I don't care. I can afford a thousand more sapphires."

With a small voice, she sweetened her lie. "I don't know why, but I feel drawn to it."

"Her influence?"

Maior looked away demurely. She hoped her rosy cheeks sold the lie.

"Let me look at the injury again." She helped unbutton his shirt. He had to sit, for he was much taller than her. "Lucky for you, I always carry galio with me."

"Good girl."

She met his blood-red gaze, unable to breathe. Once again, every doubt squeezed her—begged her to run. But she needed the freedom this game afforded her. She needed him to believe it was safe for her to roam freely, resuming Laurel's life, without the watchful eye of a guard, or the head matron. His desperation to have Laurel back was the greatest power she had.

Her fingers trembled as she removed the bandage, revealing a shoulder flexed. Heat radiated off his skin as she pressed her fingers up to his collarbone. His veins shuddered beneath her touch. Was it discomfort? Or anticipation? It would be easier if she could read him, but there was no tether between them.

She let out a breath, and it sounded like a sigh.

He had no surprise, just amusement. "There's no need to feel overwhelmed. I am unarmed."

Maior faked a smile. "That doesn't change the truth: I stand before the most powerful man in Venazia."

Her stomach twisted. She needed to end this foolish game. She ought to be running away, not tucking herself directly into the wolf's maw.

He glared at the darkness of dusk beyond the window. "That I am," he said. "I proved it in open combat. I showed it to all those sycophants who have been bootlicking Samón since the war ended."

His tone angered her. She ground her molars to keep it together.

"I ended his life," he added.

She steeled herself for this test. He was gauging her loyalty. Did she stand with the Liberator, or would she truly play the role of his wife returned?

"How?" Keeping him talking prolonged the inevitable.

"I impaled him through the middle and ripped the antlers from his head."

Hatred for his lack of remorse filled her. The way he talked of the Liberator. Instead of making her want to flee, his words enraged her to see her plan to the end.

Her hands, small against his shoulders, nudged back the shirt so that it would pool behind him on the bed. His chest was bared for her, all muscles and battle scars. As his gaze searched hers, she could tell he delighted in the attention. He wanted her to be impressed.

"I thought Don Samón was your ally from the war and you were friends," she said, because he would suspect her otherwise. "Why did he deserve to be killed that way? You didn't need to prove anything."

Meticulously, she folded his shirt and placed it atop the chest of drawers next to the bed.

"The fool tried to save Reina's life."

Maior had already heard the tale from Rahmagut. Yet the words were a knife all the same.

She forced herself to ignore her thrumming heart. She swallowed down the image and focused on the present. Her fingers glowed lavender as she massaged the length of his bicep up to his shoulder and down his collarbone. Ligaments realigned themselves underneath her touch. The muscle was repaired. Enrique closed his eyes and leaned into it.

She gave his arm one long massage, tracing down to the wrist, pausing to knead his hand. As he relaxed, she tugged off his geomancia rings. All six were solid gold and dented from rough wear. She slipped them off one by one. As he opened his eyes again, she squeezed the knuckles, imparting some of that soothing galio relief to his joints. Finally, she circled back to the chest of drawers and plopped the rings atop his shirt.

"Reina tried to duel me," he said. "She acted as if you were a prize to be bartered in a swordfight."

Another audible breath escaped Maior's lips. The pain was too sharp to conceal. In shame, she turned away.

The bed creaked as he stood. His hand traced the back of her arm, as if he were capable of imparting comfort. Instead she was repulsed.

"She didn't respect your decision to come to me," he said. "For that, she paid dearly. Though not as much as she would have if I'd been allowed to get my way. That's why I took Samón's life. I needed to demonstrate my words have weight. This is a brutal world, and I needed to reassert my authority."

Shivers ran through Maior as his hands continued tracing the length of her exposed shoulders. His fingers traveled south and stopped at the weak knot the criada had used to tie her dress in place.

"You, on the other hand, made the right choice, for it is the winners who rewrite history. You chose a victor."

Despite her best efforts, Maior couldn't keep herself from trembling. Her heart hammered painfully against her ribs. She'd never had any choice. She'd been cursed and bound by Doña Ursulina's plotting.

"You're afraid," he said. "But you shouldn't be."

With the last ounce of courage she wielded, Maior turned around. She was heads shorter than him, fragile against his twisted intentions.

"Let me prove it to you." He gently lifted her chin so their eyes would meet. The contact sent a chill through her. "What do you want? Tell me and it shall be yours."

She winced. Against her better judgment, she said, "Why? Why do you care about what I want?"

His jaw moved.

"I am no one," she whispered.

He stepped back, as if hesitant to speak the truth. Silence weighed the space between them. "The aristocracy of Sadul Fuerte attended Laurel's funeral. They witnessed her burial."

More chills swept through Maior as she read between the lines. No matter how much she spun it in her head, she arrived at the same conclusion: He couldn't have Laurel back, god of the Void or not. He'd realized this, and Maior was a fool for not seeing it sooner. It would raise too many questions. It would further taint

the animosity he'd earned after taking the Liberator's life. Rahmagut's army of tinieblas wouldn't matter if all the caudillo of Sadul
Fuerte inspired in the campesinos was repulsion.

He saw her understanding. "Publicly, I cannot be married to
Laurel again."

It made perfect sense, why he'd instructed his staff to treat her
like the lady of the house. A new Benevolent Lady.

Heat flooded her sinuses—the beginning of tears. Her panic
began to take hold. She almost glanced at the door.

"All of them—they all have a reason to fear me—as they should.
But not you," he said softly. And she despised his fake tenderness.
She loathed these attempts to mold something positive between
them. He was the reason her life had been upended. She would
never forget he was the source of Reina's pain.

"And what do *you* want?" she whispered.

His eyes traveled to her crown. They lost themselves in the
image of Laurel.

He was a pitiful, empty man, unwilling to let go.

"I want a son."

Maior sucked in a breath.

"I have a legacy to pass on, and a daughter who won't speak to
me. I am nothing but my name, which Mother forged from iridio and blood. I've accepted that I've lost the love of my life, but
amends can be made. I am no longer overshadowed by Samón's
fame. I have proved I am not to be defied. With Rahmagut's allegiance, I am not beholden to an alliance with the other caudillos.
They've all been reminded of my strength."

Maior swallowed thickly. She realized the time to flee had
passed.

He traced her jaw. "I want you to play this role, as it was intended
from the very beginning. As the lady of this house, you shall have
anything you want."

She couldn't breathe, her heart racing. She gave him her back,
tilting her head, knowing the power it had to entice him closer.
"Anything I want?" How she wanted her freedom more than anything else.

"Yes. Laurel's death. Ursulina's and Javier's betrayals. Celeste's hatred. Let us make this pain worth something." He ran his hand from her neck to her shoulder blade and stopped again on the knot holding her dress together. "Give me an heir, and I shall give you everything."

There was no real exchange in his offer. She was but a rabbit willingly stepping into a trap. She was cornered in this room, between him and the bed.

"So ask and it shall be yours," he added, tugging the knot and releasing the cord's hold on her gown, on her dignity.

He grabbed her by the waist. She bent over. She had to do it. Maybe one day the Virgin would forgive her. Maybe one day, she would forgive herself.

As he tugged the soft fabric farther down, unveiling her back and undressing her, Maior reached for the cold steel underneath Laurel's pillow. She took it with both hands, turned around, and thrust it horizontally between his true ribs, right into his heart.

The world stopped as his eyes doubled in size. The knife with the ornamental handle—his gift to Laurel—was cold in her grip, but her hands were showered with the warmth of his blood. She shoved it farther in, then yanked it to the side, damaging as much tissue as possible.

"What I want is freedom," she said between gritted teeth. "From you and from your wretched wife."

His hands shot out for her wrists and squeezed them hard, capable of snapping them in two. "You—" Blood poured out of his mouth.

"You took me from my home. You tried to kill the woman I love. You treated me as an object, and not the person I am."

With a struggle, Maior yanked the knife out, unleashing red rivulets that soaked his pants and her fallen dress. The knife clattered to the ground between their feet.

"I would never lie with you. I don't like men. And most importantly, I loathe you—you narcissistic, pitiful *monster*—"

Enrique howled. He grabbed her by the neck and tossed her back on the bed, squeezing her trachea as the hatred of betrayal burned in his eyes. He trapped her with his body, his hand attempting to break her neck.

She wanted to laugh. She had a thousand things to say, but she couldn't even breathe. Black dots blurred her vision, and tears. She didn't even bother to kick or fight. If her life was going to end in his grip, she at least had the reassurance that she was taking him with her to the depths of hell. May the Virgin forgive her.

He gurgled. His eyes rolled back, and his grip loosened. Maior found an opening to claw his fingers apart. The air returned to her lungs.

She shoved the heavy body aside with the last of her strength. She was soaked in his blood.

With a wildly beating heart, Maior sat up. She shook uncontrollably. She lifted a hand to her neck and winced at the damage he'd caused in the last seconds of his life. Her galio healing came automatically, easing some of it for now.

Nevertheless, the adrenaline of victory enraptured her. Her plan had worked.

She slid off the bed, her hands leaving red prints on the sheets. She covered herself up in the blood-sopped dress and left bloody footprints as she descended to the first floor. Soon enough, a servant or two would come across the gore. There was no point in trying to cover it up. Even as she was weak and choked with emotion—as the full gravity of the sin she'd committed fell over her shoulders—she had to keep going.

As she emerged in the back corridor of the manor, she found the yard door already wide open. A lit wall sconce illuminated the space, revealing the figure standing in the doorway. Broad shoulders and a thrashing tail with a tip of soft black curls.

"Maior?"

Maior let out a gasp as Reina closed the distance between them in one breath.

The shock of seeing Reina alive, unscathed, breathing, holding her, knocked the air out of Maior. Her knees buckled, and she collapsed into Reina's arms.

This was a dream. It had to be the reason why the knife had

impaled the right spot, unimpeded by her fear or his ribs. It had to be the only explanation.

"*You're bleeding*," Reina whispered. In a panic, she inspected Maior's body, grimacing at the blood-soaked lace.

Maior half laughed, half cried, exhausted and delirious. "It's not my blood," she repeated over and over like a litany, her bloody hands squeezing Reina's cheeks, delighted that Reina was solid and alive beneath her touch. Reina wasn't a dream. She was real.

"Whose is it?"

More figures appeared behind Reina, boots and armors clanking against the flagstones. More antlered people flanked her. Chiefly Eva, whose eyes became illuminated by the lit sconces and no longer held the weight of an ancient darkness behind them.

Maior's voice was weak as she said, "Enrique's. I killed him. I killed Enrique."

Reina cupped Maior's cheek, and Maior leaned into it, craving more.

Tears blurred Maior's vision. Like a torrent, they were unleashed. She was a killer, but she'd done it for them. "You don't have to worry about Enrique."

Reina exhaled in awe. Maior melted into her arms. She clung to her as if Reina were the last raft in the vast cruelty of a never-ending ocean. Maior squeezed her. She buried her nose in Reina's neck and took a gulp of her scent. Reina was windswept and sweaty, the musk of the mountain saturating her braid. Yet she smelled exactly as Maior remembered her. And somehow, she was here.

Somehow, they had found each other again.

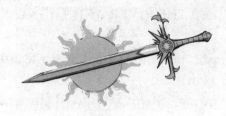

52

A Manor to Build a Home In

The morning arrived with black clouds. They parked over Águila Manor and produced a torrent of rain that spilled over the flagstones. Reina watched from the back patio's shade as the wind buffeted the hanging orchids. She extended a bruised hand to feel the icy shower. It made her remember those days when she used to take solace in the mountain downpours. When she used them as an excuse to stay huddled and hidden, a reprieve from tasks that placed bitter flavors in her mouth. Reina took in a big whiff of the crisp air and realized she didn't feel that weight anymore. She could stand in the manor's protection and feel like she was whole and free.

Javier emerged from the weeping trees, soaked and mud splattered. He hurried under the manor's shade, joining her.

"Is something the matter?" Reina asked.

"Couldn't sleep—I went for a hike."

He didn't retreat inside, but rather paused in silence beside her. Reina grew uncomfortable. She could tell there was something in his mind.

"I haven't thanked you for all you've done," he said. "For helping me with Eva."

"You don't have to. It was my duty."

"Yes, I do." His eyes were severe, darkened with leftover fright.

It felt intimate, seeing him without the armor of animosity he'd always worn before her. "She's all I have. All my changes and defeats—they don't matter, if I have her. And I would have lost her forever if it weren't for you. I want you to know that I'm in your debt."

Reina's heart jolted. She didn't hide her smile. "You love her?"

He gave her no answer, which was just as well. The affirmation wasn't for her ears anyway.

"I don't care about debts," she said. "All I care about is that you're on my side. That I can trust you." Her smile widened, reciprocated by his smirk of agreement.

"Anything you need, I'll be here," he said, heading for the doorway. "Now I must bathe, and eat. I shall tend to Maior's wound when she wakes up."

Guilt constricted Reina's chest. "I conferred with Ches," she said before he could disappear into the manor's darkness. He flinched, pausing with his back to her. Reina almost draped a hand on his shoulder. "I'm sorry, I did try, but he says your changes cannot be undone. You are not haunted or spelled or poisoned, to be cleansed. You are changed."

"A permanent transmutation," he muttered. Reina thought she could hear the wound in his voice.

"Not that my opinion matters, but...you look weathered, in a good way."

He chuckled and left.

Reina also headed inside, seeking to break fast. She caught sight of Celeste and followed her to the front porch, where Celeste doled out orders to a courier and his driver.

"We're sending for the priest," Celeste explained, watching the carriage leaving the manor's winding driveway.

"You will give him a Pentimiento burial?" Reina asked. She found it odd for a man without faith.

"I know he would have wanted to rest beside mi mamá. Besides,

I need to establish my legitimacy in Sadul Fuerte, and it helps to have the clergy on my side."

Reina faced her, searching Celeste's eyes for any sign of pain. If there was any, Celeste hid it well. "The heir of Feleva Águila," Reina said. "He wanted that for you."

Celeste extended her hand, which Reina tugged before grasping Celeste's smaller frame into a side embrace.

"I already mourned him. I mourned him before he even died. He did horrible things."

Reina more than agreed, but it was a wasted exercise to list all the reasons why Enrique deserved his demise. What she knew as fact, however, was that no god nor goddess would be welcoming him into a heavenly afterlife.

"I feel as if it's *my* duty to atone for it."

"If you will inherit the family, then yes." Like an afterthought, Reina added, "Javier can help you."

Celeste pressed her lips into a bitter line. "You freed Eva from Rahmagut and destroyed him," she said. "He is gone?"

Reina nodded.

"And what about Ches? Both gods of the sun and the Void returned at the same time. But Ches remains?"

Reina ground her teeth at the insinuation that Rahmagut was equivalent. "I will be his vessel until the end of my days."

It was the greatest duty she could fulfill.

"What happens afterward?" Celeste wondered.

"When I'm on my deathbed, I'll find someone else to take the helm." Reina shrugged. She hoped she had time to find and train someone capable and devout like her. A believer of his divinity. Someone adept at withstanding Duality. A nozariel, hopefully.

As usual, Ches was silent, observant. He had already lived thousands of lives. He didn't need to interfere with hers.

Celeste tittered. "Reina, pillar to the cult of Ches."

Reina tried not to smile, even if she did like the sound of such a title.

"I think breakfast is being served," Celeste said. "Join me?"

Reina followed her inside.

Leading the way, Celeste said, "I'll be arranging a carriage for Eva and Javier as well. Eva expressed her wish to travel to Segolita. She means to arrange for her father's funeral."

Reina's gut twisted from the news. She wasn't ready to say goodbye. She would have considered going with them, but she loathed that city.

"I'm surprised Javier's open to enduring Segolita, with his changes," Reina said.

"Part of me believes he deserves it," Celeste said.

"No. Otherwise you and I ought to be worse off," Reina said as they entered the vast dining hall.

They were quiet in the wake of Reina's words, pretending to be distracted by the scurrying maids arranging porcelain plates and serving a basket of arepas. But it was the truth. Reina, too, had done monstrous things. They had hurt innocents, and each other. Javier's transformation was not a deserved heavenly punishment. It was merely his turn of the tide.

Pucho beamed as they approached. His mouth was too full to greet them. Esteban raised his cup of coffee in the air, muttering a good morning. He sat at the head of the table like a warmhearted, jovial human version of Enrique. Reina was disturbed by their likeness.

"What about you, Reina? Will you stay?" Celeste asked. "I can put you down in the records...We could legitimize our ties—"

"Celeste, that's not necessary. I don't want your family money— all these things—"

"But the iridio," Celeste said, pausing before sitting down. "You need it to live."

Reina cupped the raggedness on her chest. It was an inconvenience, but it was part of who she was.

Pucho and Esteban looked from Reina to Celeste, curious yet entertained.

Celeste's eyes grew glossy.

Reina could tell Celeste was moments away from begging. She took a seat across Celeste and said, "We're cousins. I'm not going anywhere. I just don't need the pomp and show of the gentry. I don't need to participate in Sadul Fuerte politics."

Pucho cocked an eyebrow theatrically for Esteban, who nodded knowingly.

Oblivious, Celeste said, "Let me handle that. Father raised me to be the Águila heir that I am."

Reina gave some space for the maid to pour her coffee. It was an odd thing, to sit at this table and be the one being served.

"Let me be the caudilla I was groomed to be, and you can be my left-hand woman, how Ursulina was to my father." A frown overtook Reina. At once, Celeste understood her mistake. "But not like that—you can be my left-hand woman because I need you as *my* pillar. I'm not going to be someone that will use my power over you—"

"You have no power over me."

Blushing, Celeste glanced between Pucho and Esteban, as if finally realizing the folly of approaching this conversation before them. It made Reina wonder: Was this another manipulation?

"Exactly," Celeste said. "You'll be here because you love me, and I love you, and we're family."

Reina nearly scoffed. Despite all that had happened, Celeste's belief in herself remained unscathed. Reina took a sip of her coffee, the strong flavor easing her. "Will you punish Maior for what happened last night?"

"No. I understand her circumstances. My father was long gone." Celeste's voice broke. "I gave the command and only my approved version of events will be recounted in Sadul Fuerte. Maior will not be mentioned."

"Will you punish her for loving me?" Reina didn't care if Pucho and Esteban witnessed this. She intended to stand with Maior. She would profess her love and devotion from the top of the mountains, if necessary.

Celeste's face reddened. She glanced down at her empty plate, her lips pursing. Then she took a deep breath and met Reina's gaze with a straight-backed, magnanimous mien. "I acted childishly—selfishly." She spared a glance for the unwilling spectators. But her honesty was undiminished: "I was jealous and afraid of being alone, but you deserve to be happy." She smiled. "You deserve to be with the person you choose. I only beg that you consider our bond. I have no one else anymore."

"What about your princely betrothed?"

Celeste rolled her eyes. "A political necessity."

Reina gave the smile she knew Celeste wanted. "Thank you for being honest. I suppose I don't mind staying. Perhaps we can keep Gegania connected to Tierra'e Sol, if Eva and Javier decide to live there. I know Maior will want that."

Celeste's eyes glimmered, wide. "I will see it done. You are home. Welcome."

Joy flooded Reina. Finally, they were aligned. She stole a look at her grandfather and Pucho and knew she was fortunate. The journey had been arduous, but she'd found a family she could trust.

Esteban leaned back, satisfied. "You remind me of Feleva, before the ambition took her."

Celeste's blush returned. "The more I hear of her, the more disappointed I become."

He shrugged. "Listen to Reina and you won't turn out like her."

It was Reina's turn to blush.

"You both have a dark legacy to undo," Esteban added.

Reina smirked. "Maybe you can guide us."

"Bad idea. He'll turn you into an alcoholic," Pucho said, snorting into his drink. Celeste laughed. Reina let the mirth fill her up.

Guided by a servant, Don Rigoberto joined the table with a much improved mood. "Buen provecho," he told them, gesturing for them to continue with their meal.

"I was told you will be riding with Eva to Segolita," Celeste said.

He grabbed an arepa and juggled it as if it burned his fingertips. "The president will want to know about Ches and Rahmagut." Reina shifted uncomfortably on her seat, but he surprised her by saying, "I will spare no details in recounting the miracle you granted us. You liberated us from tinieblas. That alone deserves a celebration."

Reina warmed. She opened her mouth, but Pucho cut her off. "Don't underestimate your own people. When the truth is told, there will be those who listen."

"No one will deny our combined voices," Don Rigoberto added in that pompous way of his.

"To Ches, and Reina," Esteban said, lifting his drink.

All followed.

Reina embraced the heat flooding her cheeks. She beamed. "Thank you," she said. "But I don't act alone anymore. We did it together."

53

Águila Bravo

The air in Javier's bedroom was weighed by dust. A cobweb was interlaced above the doorway. It was small, and new perhaps, but nevertheless a testament to the fact that the bedroom had been left untouched and abandoned since Javier had departed the manor.

Eva returned cautiously to his domain, a place that had been part of his previous life. She had fallen asleep in his arms but woke up to the sheets cold beside her, so she went for breakfast alone. She'd managed to snag the last of the cold arepas—which surprised her, for they were made of wheat—and had eaten in Don Rigoberto's company.

She was content. She was safe. She was free from Rahmagut at last. But she missed Javier.

The room had a four-poster bed with the curtains drawn. Furniture of sturdy dark wood filled the space. Thick drapes shielded the view of a rainy yard, parted only for a single line of light. A painting hung from the wall near the entrance, depicting a confident woman with white locks and thick antlers holding a bald, pink-cheeked infant. Sitting beside her was another white-haired youth. Even in the painting Eva could recognize the young man's dead-blood stare. She paused. Feleva and her sons, painted during a time when the country had been at war and Feleva sat at the height of her power amassed from Rahmagut's gifted iridio.

Would Javier have grown up to be just like Enrique, had Feleva been the one to raise him? Eva was glad such hadn't been the outcome.

It was a curiosity that this portrait was hidden here, though, in the shadows. In fact, save for this bedroom, the whole manor seemed devoid of Javier's influence. Had he ever called Águila Manor home? Or had he lived like Eva, a stranger amid his own blood?

Silent in her espadrilles, Eva approached the bed where Javier sat on the edge, his back to the door. His hair was damp, but he was dressed in freshly laundered clothes.

Black feathers grew from the length of his left forearm. As Eva neared him, she caught him plucking one such feather.

She rushed to him and grabbed his claw to stop him. "Javier," she said, chastising.

He wasn't surprised to be caught. He looked exhausted, disappointed.

"I am a monster," he said, though this time Eva caught the undercurrent of acceptance in his tone.

She sat beside him, observing the black scutes covering his neck up to the jawline like a plated suit. His black feathers started at his left wrist and ended at his elbow, resembling an asymmetrical sleeve. They were silky soft and raven-black shiny, developed during his loss of control at the lakes. The tiniebla's darkness had been ended, but its physical amalgamation remained.

Still, his face was free from the tiniebla's turning, unblemished save for the bruising on his jaw. His crimson valco eyes shone, adoring yet unchanged.

She leaned into him, craving the closeness. "Well, I find you incredibly irresistible," she said, tugging his collar. "In fact, I want to know what else has changed."

Laughter burst out of him. Eva noticed his canines were pointier than usual.

He propped himself up on his elbows, allowing her to untie the string of his collar, loosening the shirt. Eva paused, deciding this shedding of clothes was better saved for later.

"You're going to deny me?" he said. "I missed you."

Her cheeks blazed. "I missed you, too. But I have questions, and I don't want to get distracted. Where did you go last night?"

He bit his lip. "I couldn't sleep. I went hiking, and when I came back it was morning already. Soon I must go tend to Maior's wounds. Enrique crushed her windpipe."

Eva winced. She shoved the image out of her thoughts—how they'd found Maior soaked in Enrique's blood, and the horrific circumstances placing Maior in that situation. Though it was comforting to see Javier caring for Maior. Not even in her wildest dreams had Eva imagined this convergence where Reina, Javier, Maior, and Celeste were so unified. They had become her people.

"Is the tiniebla gone?" Eva asked.

"Yes—I'm sure of it now. But I'm stuck like this."

"Then your turning has stopped. This is as far as it'll go."

He paused, searching her face as if curious about her feelings on the matter. His self-consciousness was heavy, and unnecessary. Hadn't she proved already how she treasured him, regardless of feather, scute, or animal appendage? Unless he was accurately predicting the way humans shunned all those who didn't look and behave exactly as expected. In that regard, Eva was as powerless as him.

She lowered herself onto the bed, tugging him beside her.

"You can't be ashamed of who you've become, Javier," Eva said. "I can't do this on my own."

His gaze lingered on her lips a second too long. "Do what?"

"I must honor my father's memory. I have to return to Segolita to organize his memorial and take the helm of the family. Don Rigoberto has already hinted that this is his expectation. Those Bravo men who fought for me demand it. And it's what I wanted, right? When I took my father's name so flippantly? I can't hide away just because it's hard and we're comfortable in this room with some peace, finally."

Her eyes welled. Part of her wished she could wipe her father's last moments from her memory. Part of her knew such a request was a disrespect. He had given his life for Reina and Maior—for

Eva. He had given every ounce of himself for the country. It was only right that Eva followed in his footsteps.

Slowly, and as if knowing she needed it, Javier gathered her in his arms. She pressed her forehead to his chest, swallowing down her sobs. She didn't want to cry anymore.

"You want to take your monster to Segolita?" he muttered.

Eva pinched his stomach. Still, she liked the possessive claim he assigned to his words.

"You can't mean to abandon me now," she said, her words muffled by his shirt. "I know it's hard, but we have to do it. We are the last of our kind. You have a great name behind you, and so do I."

He squeezed her harder. "The Penitents will try to come after me. They'll call me a devil."

She pulled away. "No. We will find a way to make it work. But I refuse to hide away. You and Celeste now lead the richest family in all the land. We are Águila Bravo. Rahmagut's death ended the tinieblas, but not the use of iridio. Our parents freed these nations. Now we must be the ones to shape them."

Eva understood her duties, now more than ever. She'd made a terrible mistake ignorantly hosting Rahmagut, allowing him to use the power innate to her blood for his gain. She should have prioritized severing herself from him. She should have focused on becoming a worthy daughter to someone who had liberated a nation. Now, with this second shot at life Reina had granted her, Eva couldn't be selfish with her position. She had to honor Don Samón's work of shepherding a united people. She had to be plentiful like her father wanted, for the survival of their dying species.

"We must lead our kind forward," she added.

Javier stiffened. They held their breath.

After a while his lips softened into a smile, his eyes brightening. "You will give me little valcos?"

She brushed back a lock of starlight, remembering his wish for the future. Her belly warmed as she imagined it. "As many as we can handle."

The rains ended and the sun came out. Sunlight poured through the curtain aperture, catching his left eye. At that moment, Eva was reminded of their travels through El Carmín, how she'd noted his eyes were brilliant garnets, the most beautiful she had ever seen. She had hated him then. Now Eva loathed to imagine a world where he wasn't hers, all claws and feathers and tail.

He was all hers.

There was no tiniebla anymore, nor a god simmering beneath her surface to entice him to love her. They were bared as they were, true in their affections. Eva reminded herself to breathe.

"Abrázame," he said.

She obeyed like a little girl, pressing close to him. She cherished every prickle and rustle of his new skin. She breathed deeply. Here was her home. She delighted in the hardness between them, a desire that burned only for her.

He took her lips, parting for an instant to mutter, "So what are we waiting for?"

She giggled, gleeful for the path ahead, and gave in.

No longer were they bound by the rules of their families, or by the ties of magic. Eva hadn't just been cleansed by Arca's water. Now her future was also clear for her to seize. Finally, she could have what she'd always wanted: A life of her own design. A future with people who treasured her as she was. A destiny she could personally calligraph, with iridio of course.

54

Warm Waters

Reina came into Laurel's bedroom and found Maior still fast asleep. She was buried beneath the soft blankets, lips graced by the angled sunrays coming through the window. Dust particles floated around her, a fall of snow against her soft cheeks. With the rains ended, the sun was bright. Reina liked to think the skies had gifted her this. So she could find Maior gilded in sunlight, safe.

Maior had bathed the blood off. When Reina had helped her, she was glad to find not a single cut on her body, though her neck was developing a deep bruise. The mark of Maior's courage.

Maybe it was her staring that made Maior stir. She yawned, rubbing the sleep from her eyes.

"Good morning," Reina said.

She had to fight against herself not to climb into the bed. She wanted to give Maior space, however much she needed. In the end, she didn't have to wait for long. Maior lifted the wool covers as an invitation for Reina to crawl in. Reina's heart grew weak as she took in Maior's eyes.

"You came for me," Maior said with a small smile. Her voice was meek, her vocal cords damaged by Enrique's last-ditch effort to end a life. "I'm sorry for keeping you in the dark."

Reina's breathing constricted when she thought about it. "I nearly lost my mind—"

Maior cupped Reina's cheek. "I'm sorry, but I had to do something. I'm tired of being a prisoner to Laurel."

By now Reina understood, yet it didn't take away the torture of those nights without her.

"I exorcised Rahmagut from Eva. The Virgin helped me," Reina said with a cheeky smirk.

Maior raised her brows.

"You're right. She's real, like Ches is. He calls Her Arca, but I think you shouldn't change the name you use for Her. I don't think it matters."

"The Virgin helped you?"

Reina's hand mimicked the flow of water. "The river purifies because Her power flows through it. She emerged when I needed to end Rahmagut, and She helped me. Arca listens to Ches, and his will and mine are aligned." Reina's cheeks grew warm at the assertion. But there was no sensation of Ches's disagreement. "She will listen to me. We can do this for you. You don't have to feel like you need to act alone anymore."

Maior glanced away. Under the rays of sunlight, Reina could marvel at the soft peach fuzz lining Maior's cheeks.

"I don't have to exhume Laurel's bones?"

Reina grinned. "You can be cleansed, and Doña Laurel can have her rest. I want to do it for you, when you're ready."

Maior sat up. "I am done waiting."

Wind buffeted their faces as the eagle landed in the yard hours later. Wrapped in a ruana, Maior accepted Reina's help to mount the giant. Reina was pleased to see Javier's promise had been true, with the bruise around Maior's neck now faded.

Attuned to her thoughts, the eagle took flight. It soared over the firs and the grasses and the frailejones, Maior gasping and oohing at the sights. Reina couldn't shed her smirk of satisfaction. She could command such a creature to fly them over the mountain trails, which would otherwise have taken her hours or days to traverse on foot. Reina chose the eagle with the most recuperated constitution after the battle. The others rested somewhere in the crests, healing in peace.

Deep in the mountains, her eagle descended near waters that pooled over several terraced elevations. The air warmed as they circled the lagoons. Reina commanded the eagle to land on the topmost terrace, the largest of all, beside a jade-green glimmering pool with a stunning view of the hills.

There, the sky was a never-ending blue. The sun shone overhead, saturating the wildflowers surrounding the spring. The eagle gave its feathers a great ruffling, lifting dust into the air, then padded beneath the shade of a nearby outcrop to wait.

Reina knelt by the water, testing its warmth. The destination had been a surprise. Maior watched her with curiosity from a distance.

"I found these springs when I used to live in Águila Manor," Reina explained. "I didn't want you to be cold."

Maior's brows bunched up in understanding. She smiled.

Reina helped Maior unwrap her ruana, then the rest of her clothes, save for her undergarments. Reina followed in kind.

"Are you ready?" she asked, extending a hand as she waited by the pool's edge. Its emanating steam was a seduction against the cold mountain air.

Maior shivered, perhaps from the chill, or from her anticipation. The cold flight had painted her cheeks a deep shade of rose. She accepted Reina's hand.

They lowered themselves slowly, stepping on steady boulders. Reina's eyes were trained on Maior's for reassurance. At the pool's center, where the water reached their chests, Reina opened herself up to Duality.

Sunlight coated her wet skin. She could slip into Duality without the display, but she wanted Maior to see it. The pool's depths glimmered with her gold. Cones of light emanated from her fingertips. She spread sunrays over Maior's cheeks as her thumb dug into Maior's lower lip. Reina forced herself to ignore her longing for it.

"Do you trust me?" Reina asked, and Maior nodded.

Reina gently pressed Maior underwater. Obedient, Maior

sucked in a breath and submerged all the way. Reina's other hand lifted over the water's surface, guided by Ches. He tugged with ease, for they had Arca's agreement, and Laurel gave no resistance. Reina plucked Laurel's shade. It melted into the pool, disappearing forever. The whole process took a breath, two at most.

Maior emerged with a big gulp. Her sheer undergown clung to her curves, transparent from the water. Her face and neck were flushed, but her eyes were vibrant.

"Is it done?" Reina said, aching for the validation. She wanted the verbal confirmation showing how she could so easily tap into Duality and grant Maior a miracle. "How do you feel?"

"Feather-light. Free."

Reina released Duality and Ches slumbered. She grasped Maior's hands and squeezed hard.

"Unafraid," Maior added, wading closer, her lower lip tender red as she bit down on it.

Reina beamed. "Seeing you happy . . . it makes my world."

Maior's eyes glimmered.

"I'm sorry for never properly listening to you and understanding how much Doña Laurel bothered you," Reina admitted. "My inability to see things the way you did—I know it hurt you, and I never want to do that again. Doña Laurel showed me kindness in my darkest moments. I couldn't believe she could hurt anyone . . . or haunt you."

Maior nodded, patient.

A sadness crept into Reina. "Without you, I lost my mind. I made a horrible mistake. I forced Don Samón to fight—"

"*Enrique* did that," Maior growled. "Do not blame yourself for his death."

Reina nodded. She sat on a submerged boulder, nestling into a nook within the lagoon. Maior approached, welcoming Reina into her bosom, where Reina allowed her tears to be shed. There were few, but they were necessary.

Reina squeezed Maior so hard, grateful. "I still regret it. All because I thought I was better off doing things on my own. I regret bringing you heartache. That's not the lover I want to be." She pulled away, losing herself in Maior's eyes. "I don't want to hide anything from you ever again." She tucked a lock of hair behind Maior's ear. "I want to involve you in my plans. I want you in my future."

Maior's eyes grew wide.

"Those days ... I lost my senses because without you—nothing mattered. What would be the point of fighting if I lost the person I loved?"

Maior turned red. Suddenly Reina realized the weight of her words. She had said them so often already, but never to the person it mattered to most.

Maior stepped back. "You love me?"

Reina's heart raced. There was no reason to hide it. If saying it filled her with happiness. If Maior's lips tasted like sugarcane and in her arms was where Reina felt at home.

"I do," Reina said. She wanted to repeat it again and again. "I love you." Her heart flipped and fluttered, like a hopeful baby bird taking its first flight.

Maior threw herself on her. She squeezed Reina's cheeks and said, "I love you, too!" before crashing their lips together. Between clumsy kisses, she said, "I did it for you." *Kiss.* "I did it for us." *Kiss.* "I did it for the freedom to have this." *A very long kiss.* "I did it because I love you, and because I don't want to be afraid, or need anyone's permission to feel what I feel and live like I want to live."

Reina squeezed her back. This was also her dream. And now it was realized.

There was no more weight on Reina's shoulders. No fear of who might tear them apart. There was just desire, and happiness. From Maior's attention, Reina fed. She was full on life, on love. Finally, while the mountain hummed sleepily with the sound of birds, and Maior's eager hands unraveled Reina's bindings, Reina accepted she had everything she'd ever wanted, and more.

Geomancia

Known Branches of Geomancia

Litio: Branch for spells of protection. Litio is extracted from petalites and spodumenes. Rings of litio are worn on the index finger. Proper solutions of litio are clear in color. Litio can block the healing of galio spells by creating a barrier around the body.

Galio: Branch for spells of healing. Rings of galio are worn on the middle finger. Proper solutions of galio are chartreuse in color. Galio can inhibit the alchemical changes in the body that come from bismuto enhancement.

Bismuto: Branch for spells of physical enhancement. Rings of bismuto are worn on the ring finger. Proper solutions of bismuto are azure in color. Bismuto can shatter the barriers cast by litio spells.

Iridio: Branch in active development. Iridio is extracted from a meteor in the Páramo Mountains. Solutions of iridio can be worn anywhere on the body. Proper solutions of iridio are black in color.

Visual Manifestation of Geomancia

- Red for the assertive conductors
- Blue for the analytical thinkers
- Purple for the supportive caretakers
- Gold for the persuasive promoters

Glossary of Terms

aguinaldo—verses sung to the melody of four-string guitars and maracas, typical of the Páramo region.

almojábanas—a cheese bread.

amapola—a fruit endemic to coastal Fedria, spherical in shape, with thin green skin and the stem area flaring upward like a red flower. The insides are a fleshy red. It is believed those who share the same amapola are forever bound by the bands of fate.

araguaney—a deciduous tree that blooms yellow flowers.

arbiter—the game master of Calamity.

Arca—goddess of the river, granter of purification, nourishing, and new beginnings.

cachicamo—an armadillo.

Calamity—a gambling card game retelling the disasters Ches's and Rahmagut's strife brought upon the land: an earthquake, a flood, a plague, a horde, a day of shrouded sun, a star fall, and a legion of valcos.

campesino(a)—rural folk.

caporal—head rancher in the hato, highest ranking overseer of all jobs relating to the raising of cattle.

caudillo—a military commander and protector of lands.

Ches—believed to be the god of the sun by the indigenous societies of Venazia and Fedria.

chigüire—a capybara.

conchudo—hard-shelled.

contrapunteo—a subgenre of joropo, in which two or more singers improvise a verse duel to the melody of a four-string guitar and maracas.

conuco—a small farm, garden, or planting area.

cuatro—a four-string guitar.

escudo—a gold coin, currency of the Viceroyalty of Venazia and adapted in Venazia and Fedria.

Fedria—a sovereign republic east of Río'e Marle, first established in 344 KD upon the declaration of independence. Segolita is its capital city.

frailejón—a tree endemic to the Páramo, with marcescent succulent leaves.

guarapo—a sweet, tea-like drink made from fermented fruit and sweetened with sugarcane.

hato—a farm with the specialization of raising cattle.

Las Hermanas de Piedra—a Penitent order of nurses and nuns founded in Apartaderos, who strive for convergence between Pentimiento teachings and geomancia.

junta—a meeting between politicians to determine government policy or to reach agreements between feuding entities.

liqui liqui—a ceremonial outfit of a high-collared and long-sleeved shirt and straight pants, worn for revels and special occasions.

llanero—a rancher and landowner from the Llanos.

the Llanos—an area of tropical grasslands and savannas.

mal de ojo—an illness characterized by weakness, fever, and loose bowels, imparted by envious eyes, most notably on babes.

melcocha—a hard candy made from sugarcane.

mistela—an alcoholic drink mixed with fermented fruits or fruit juices, gifted to new mothers and served while meeting newborns.

mora—a fruit endemic to the Páramo range, similar to a blackberry but sweeter and juicier.

morrocoy—a tortoise.

nozariel—an intelligent bipedal species native to the Llanos and the Cow Sea coast. They are similar to humans in appearance, distinguishable by their pointed ears, sharp canines, prehensile tails, and scutes on skin—predominantly on the nose bridge, shoulders, elbows, and knees.

pan de bono—a cheese bread made from yucca flour.

Penitent—one who practices Pentimiento.

Pentimiento—the monotheistic religion of the humans of Segol.

pernil—slow-roasted marinated pork.

Princess Marle—a nozariel princess said to have been raised by a jaguar. She discovered the length of Río'e Marle astride the jaguar who'd reared her.

quesillo—a cheesecake-like dessert.

Rahmagut—a nozariel conqueror who ascended to godliness. He is believed to be master of the Void by the indigenous societies of Venazia and Fedria.

Sadul—a legendary valco warrior after which Sadul Fuerte is named.

Segol—the human empire across the ocean.

seibó—a cabinet used to store heirlooms, silverware, Grandmother's china, and other valuable trinkets.

tigra mariposa—a speckled viper endemic to the Llanos.

tiniebla—chimera-like creatures spawned by Rahmagut's attempts to create life. They are typically born from animals, corrupted and amalgamated, without a heart.

tonada—a folk song that takes inspiration from the day-to-day of rural campesinos, with lyrics about farming, herding, harvesting, fishing, humble living, broken hearts, etc.

topocho—boiled unripe plantain.

el Vacío—the Void, Rahmagut's domain.

valco—an intelligent bipedal species native to the Páramo range. They are similar to humans in appearance, distinguishable by their antlers, the absence of hair melanin, and red-pigmented irises. They are of dense bone structure and muscle.

Venazia—sovereign stratocracy west of Río'e Marle, first established in 344 KD upon the declaration of independence. Puerto Carcosa is its capital city.

the Virgin—the goddess of Pentimiento.

yare—an intelligent bipedal species native to Las Garras. They are similar to humans in appearance, distinguishable by horns and lizard-like wings. Known as man-eaters, they were eradicated by Segol shortly after the humans' arrival.

Acknowledgments

The River and the Star exists thanks to Naomi Davis, Daphne Tonge, and Caitlin Lomas. Thank you for giving this duology your fierce support and an amazing launch. Thank you for believing in my story and for amplifying my voice.

My ability to fit all the twists and turns within the scope of this vast story is thanks to Hassan Sefidrou, who helped me make sure my unhinged ideas made sense in this book, and who was my pillar during all the difficult times.

Cat Aquino and Alyea Canada are the true MVPs behind this operation. Thank you for your editorial guidance, and for being wonderful people to work with. I'm so incredibly lucky *The River and the Star* landed in your hands.

Special thanks to Rachel Fikes, Lisa Slinkard, Maria José Morillo Flores, and all the early readers for their very valuable feedback.

Thank you to the teams at Orbit US, Daphne Press, Ne/oN Libri, Faeris, and 12Point Audio for publishing such beautiful and high-quality books and for allowing me to reach readers far and wide. Thank you to Natalia Castellanos and Lucy Walker-Evans for lending their talent to bring my characters to life.

Thank you to BookEnds Literary and Sophie Sheumaker for staying on top of administrative affairs.

Thank you to my patrons for their enthusiasm, for sticking around, and for sharing my work with their communities.

Thank you to H. M. Long, Essa Hansen, Kritika H. Rao, Sunyi Dean, Aparna Verma, Chelsea Conradt, Mariely Lares, Ehigbor Okosun, Melissa Caruso, Bethany Jacobs, Alexander Darwin,

Adrian M. Gibson, Tlotlo Tsamaase, Tzeyi Koay, M. J. Kuhn, and Sue Lynn Tan for teaching me much about publishing, allowing me to see the industry with an objective eye, and keeping me afloat with their friendship and community.

Thank you to all the authors, booksellers, publicists, marketers, and readers who uplifted my work when *The Sun and the Void* was published.

Meet the Author

Jaxon Gluck

GABRIELA ROMERO LACRUZ is a multidisciplinary artist and the author of the #1 *Sunday Times* bestselling novel *The Sun and the Void*. She graduated with a BS in chemical engineering from the University of Houston and, after a stint in oil and gas, launched the Moonborn, a clothing, accessories, and stationery brand featuring her own illustrations. She writes dark and twisty fantasy stories set in places that remind her of her homeland, so in her mind, she's never too far from the beaches and mountains of Venezuela. She also illustrates books for children and adults.

Find out more about Gabriela Romero Lacruz and other Orbit authors by registering for the free monthly newsletter at orbitbooks.net.

Follow us:

/orbitbooksUS

/orbitbooks

/orbitbooks

Join our mailing list
to receive alerts on our
latest releases and deals.

orbitbooks.net

Enter our monthly
giveaway for the chance
to win some epic prizes.

orbitloot.com